I0723692

IN PAIN AND BLOOD

SPELLSTER AND THE HOUND - BOOK 1 -

ALDREA ALIEN

Thardrandian Publications

ISBN: 978-1991157119
First Edition: January 2018
Second Edition: July 2023

10 9 8 7 6 5 4 3 2 1

Dedicated to my
critique partners, my editor
and beta readers.

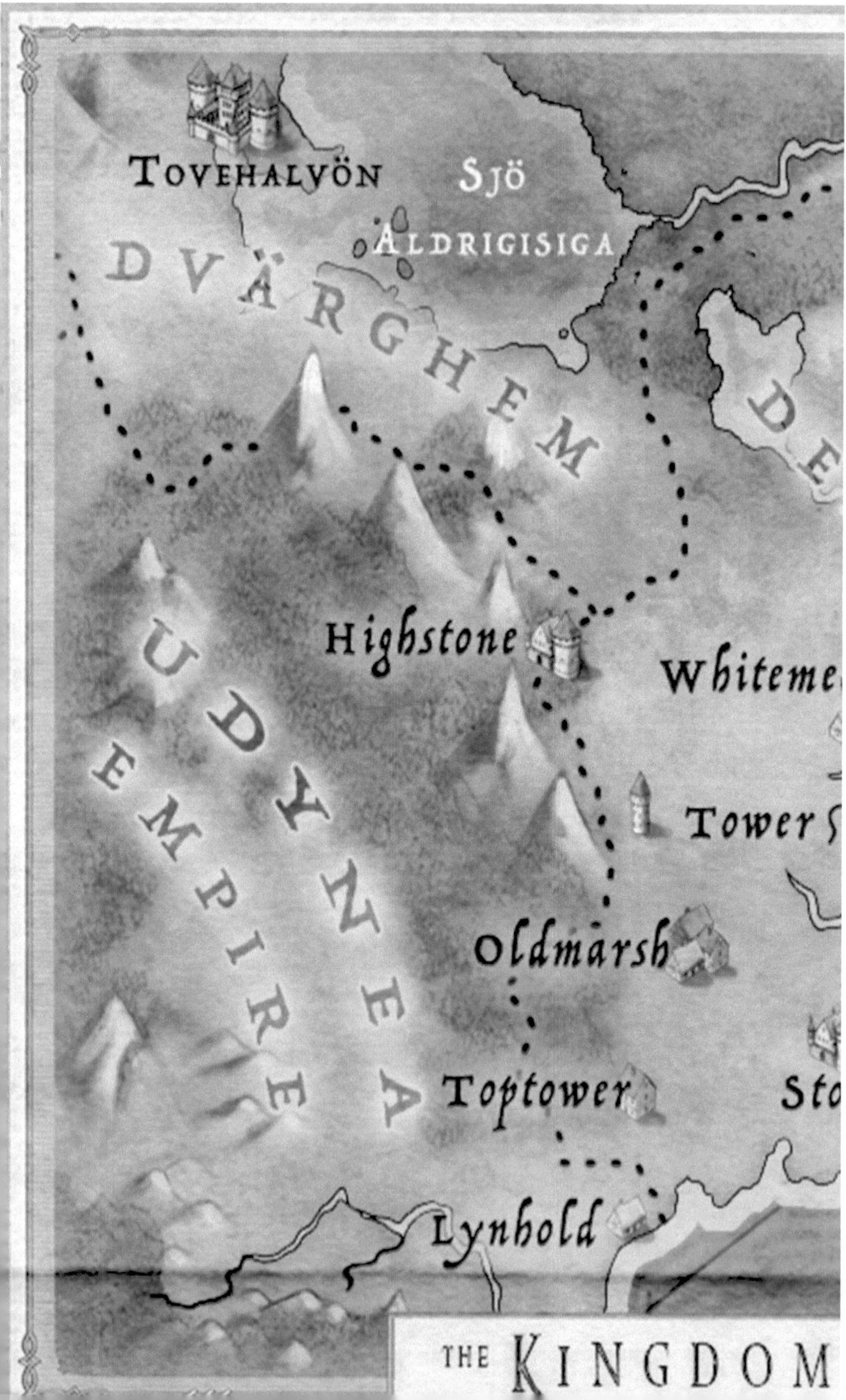

TOVEHALVÖN
SJÖ ALDRIGISIGA
DVÄRGHEM
UDYNEA EMPIRE
DE
Highstone
Whiteme
Tower
Oldmarsh
Toptower
Sto
Lynhold
THE KINGDOM

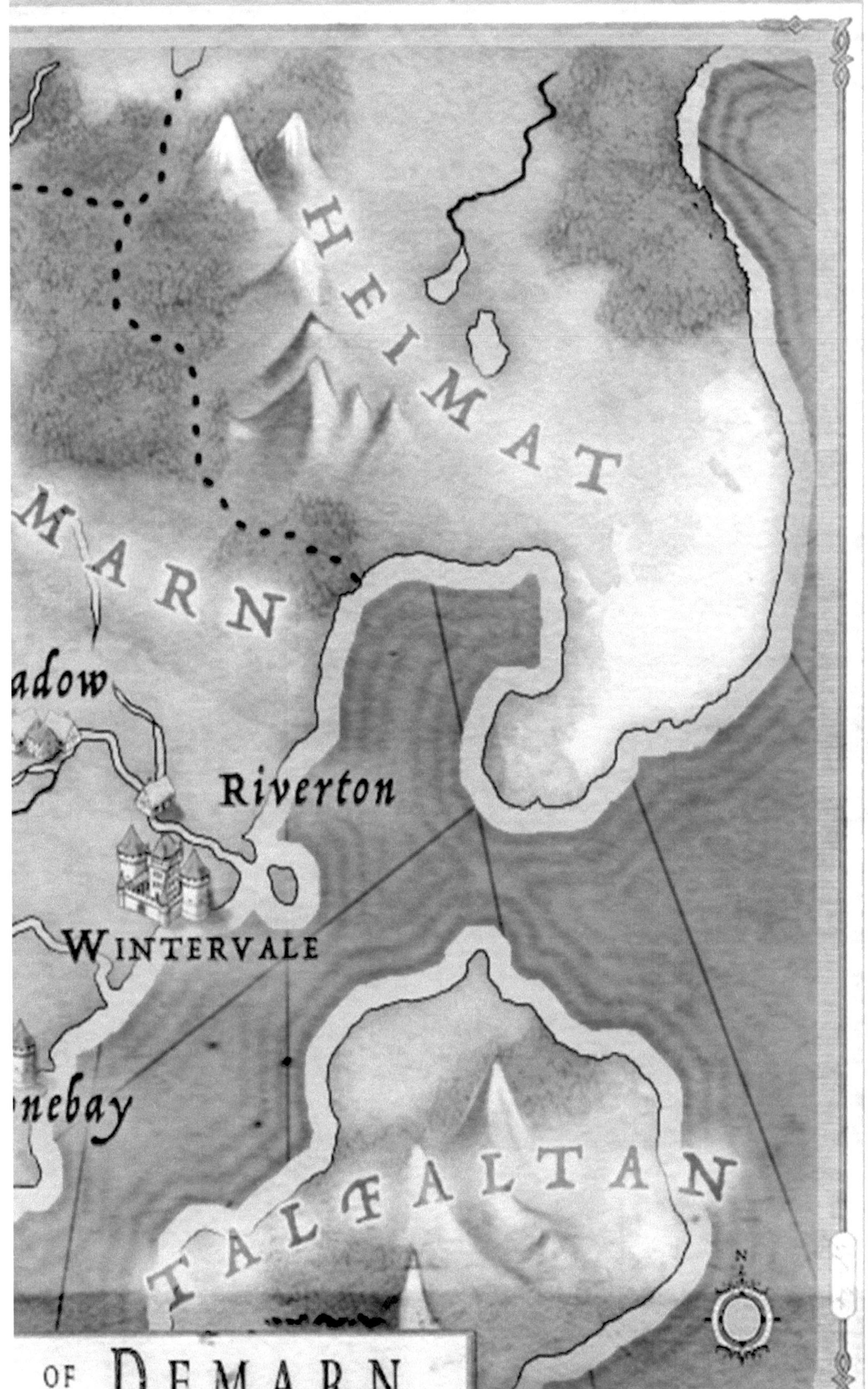

HEIMAT
MARN
adow
Riverton
WINTERVALE
nebay
TALFALTAN
OF DEMARN
N

PROLOGUE

Tracker strained to hear anything unusual over the rhythmic beat of his horse's gait. He leant forward in his saddle as they trotted down the road as if the adjustment in his seating would help. Nothing stood in his way but empty road, the dirt compacted by centuries of use and baking under the noonday sun. A troubling sight after the throng of fleeing travellers he'd passed a few hours ago.

He searched the trees crowding either side of the road, on the lookout for any threats lurking in the shadows. That proved just as fruitless as he had expected. Above the trees ahead, just visible through the canopy of lush green, a thin coil of smoke reached for the clouds.

He'd felt the blast long before he saw smoke. A sudden intense flare of power that halted as abruptly as it began. The classic sign of a spellster reacting on instinct, putting their all into one attack.

That sensation had also been prior to encountering those fleeing from the source. Those travellers had spoken tales of fire and unfettered magic. He had hoped they had seen wrong, that fear and imagination had exaggerated their memories. But whilst farmers and merchants were more skittish than the average mercenary troupe when it came to the unexpected, they were seldom wrong about the damage a spellster wrought.

A breeze ruffled through the trees, it toyed with the leaves, grasses and his many dangling earrings with equal ease. A slightly stronger puff cooled his brow, refreshing if not for the hint of wood smoke and charred flesh.

Frowning, he drew his horse to a halt. That aroma alone wasn't a cause for concern. There could be any number of reasons behind it. A travelling party's campfire. A farmhouse's hearth. A robbing gone wrong.

In this case, he knew the cause had to be magic.

His horse jogged sideways in the middle of the road. Tracker growled under his breath at the animal. Lullaby was no less a stranger to death than himself, but the wind continued to spread the smell, growing stronger with every gust.

Tracker cupped a hand to his face, hoping to block out most of the smell, and peered through the gap the road cut through the canopy trees. The thin plume of black smoke he had followed seemed to have vanished. It had been barely perceptive even to his elven sight.

He gave a tentative sniff, trying to gauge how close the site of such smoke was. The wind carried notes of charred wood and a familiar oiliness he tried not to think about.

His hand had been the one to set precious cargo—a young girl of only ten—on a wagon heading on a weeks-long journey to Dvärghem. The merchants had accepted his coin, had sworn that their guards were enough security to ward off bandits.

But if the girl had felt threatened enough to reveal herself as a spellster, to attack with all her might, then the merchants were clearly wrong.

He kneed his horse forward. The animal baulked at the instruction, clearly sensing his rider's own hesitation in heading towards the scent.

Tracker could've turned away. He didn't want to investigate, to witness the destruction he dreaded was behind what he sensed. It might not have been his first death caused by magic, but he had witnessed his fill of it in the past month.

However, his training as a King's Hound compelled him to do his duty. To ensure the dangerous spellster, the *child*, was secured or dead.

It didn't help that he knew the truth, could feel in the air that the source behind such magic was long gone. Dead or fleeing beyond the range of his senses. A part of him remained optimistic on it being the latter. Clinging to that hope was the only way he could move closer.

He hadn't given the spellster any orders, but the shroud of blame cloaked him regardless. If he hadn't put her on that wagon, then any destruction she had wrought, any casualties, would never have happened.

They marched hesitantly closer. The road rose, taking the easy path around the rubble of what he guessed was an ancient outpost. Dozens of such places dotted the kingdom, relics of a time when spellsters once ruled.

His gaze lingered on the slabs of stone. Could bandits have sheltered there? Had they snuck up on the merchants, seeing the wagon as easy prey?

Cresting the rise, he drew his horse to a halt.

The remains of a covered wagon stood in the middle of the road, the arches that once supported canvas laid bare like charred ribs. The unfortunate beasts tasked with hauling the wagon had suffered the same fate.

People lay scattered about the wagon. Armed and not. It was hard to determine whether the weapons were wielded by friend or foe. Perhaps both.

A part of him had hoped it to be an illusion, a skill the girl had been so good at that the tower overseers had wanted to send a child into war. She couldn't fool him, nor any other of the King's Hounds, but it didn't stop the wistful longing. He had promised to keep her safe, to do what her guardian had risked imprisonment for.

But the fact that he—a King's Hound, immune to magic—saw the aftermath of the chaos, only meant it was real.

And he had put her here.

He hung his head. *I am sorry.* He should've tried harder, thought of a better way to get her beyond Demarn's borders to lands where her magic, her ability to craft illusions, wouldn't see her thrown into a war as the overseers in the spellster tower had planned.

The breeze continued to shiver through the trees. It kicked up ash and dust, sending the gritty powder every which way. Along with the stench of charred flesh. Be it cattle or humanoid, it all smelt the same.

His horse snorted. The animal's senses were stronger and the foulness in the air choked Tracker's throat.

They circled the wagon until the wind was at their backs. It didn't matter what angle he took in the disaster, the level of destruction was all the same. The lingering taste of magic permeated the stench. He scanned the site, looking for any sign that the spellster responsible somehow still lived.

The scorching on the ground suggested the source had burnt hot and fast, snuffing itself just as quickly as it had begun, taking allies alongside enemies. There was a definite ring shape to the blast, radiating from within the wagon. A child's fear response. Or perhaps an act done in anger to the violence they witnessed to kind people.

It would've been quick. The wagon's interior would've succumbed in a blink. The cattle seared in a single breath. People thrown off their feet by the blast and cooked where they lay.

It should never have gotten that far.

Dismounting, Tracker crept closer. He didn't expect anything to erupt from the site's charred bones, but approaching in any other manner felt wrong.

The bodies on the outer circle bore mismatched armour and weapons that, even negating the fresh layer of soot coating them, had seen better days. He nudged one with his boot. The leather padding their shoulder gave with a dry crackle. *Definitely bandits.* At least they couldn't hurt anyone further.

Tracker ground his teeth. His fingers flexed, balling and opening. He irrationally wished for one of the bastards to still be alive, if only to become an outlet to enact the rage bubbling inside him.

He didn't come across scenes like this very often, few were brave or foolish enough to take on a spellster, but when he did, the irrationality of it all had him wanting to add to the violence. To beat sense into those who had instigated this outcome, who had driven a quiet spellster, a *child*, to the point where *this* happened.

As one of the King's Hounds, charged with hunting spellsters, he was meant to encourage the rumours of their dangers amongst the populace. It left people wary of harbouring those with even a suspicion of magic.

And *this*?

It hadn't been her fault, but that wouldn't matter. Who would care to hear the truth? Not his mistress, nor the kingdom.

Rumours of this attack would spread, the blame placed on her shoulders. *Just another dangerous spellster*. Another precautionary tale added to the pile, painting this little girl as a monster, even though she hadn't been looking to destroy lives.

Closer to the wagon, the bodies became less identifiable. He could speculate that the ones bearing swords were once guards, but the driver or the other passengers could've easily taken up arms against an attack. The only figure he could be certain of was the small frame of charred bones sitting in what remained of the wagon.

Her hand still clung to the throwing knife he had gifted her, the same one she had plucked from the air during his pursuit. In the scant few days they had travelled together, she begged him to teach her how to use the blade. He had remained unrelenting until the last, teaching her a few moves that would help in close combat.

Had she been preparing herself to fight? To *die*?

Wrapping her remains in his cloak, he hauled her from the wagon. It would take hours for him to bury all these people on his own, time he couldn't spare. He was meant to burn spellster remains to ash, but he couldn't bring himself to do that either.

The ground was hard, baked by the summer heat. Still, he beat at the earth, chopping it up with a bandit's sword, before his search amongst their weapons brought up a metal buckler. He used the small shield as a shovel, piling the dirt high on either side. The hole didn't have to be big—the girl had been a typical elven child, short and slight—but he needed the hole to be deep to keep the wildlife from digging her up.

He had tried to do the right thing, even abandoning the code every King's Hound was raised to follow. The girl had left the tower unleashed, that should've meant her death. But she'd been so young and following at her guardian's heels, just as she likely had done since she could walk.

The tower still held her guardian. The overseers had sent him after the child, unaware that he already knew what his prey was, had met her and her guardian whilst they fled the tower. He had helped stage the girl's death. Although, with her illusions, his part had been small.

He should've done more. Should've escorted her to the border himself.

It would've been risky. All it would've taken was for another hound to come upon them, to pull enough threads together. Tracker would've been routed. Branded a bad dog. Punished to the point of begging for death.

All for trying to keep a child away from the battlefront.

With the hole completed, Tracker tossed the buckler to one side and reached for the girl. He gently lowered her in, pausing only to tuck his cloak securely around her as though she only slept. He laid the knife atop the bundle. It would do her no good now, but she deserved to enter the afterlife with something.

He scooped the dirt back into the hole, muttering a soft prayer as he worked. The temple songs of his youth often spoke of the gods looking kindly upon those who died in battle. He hoped it was true. She might not have fought off these bandits with steel and muscle, but she definitely had a warrior's heart.

He liked to think his daughter would've been the same.

With the girl buried, Tracker got to his feet. He dusted the dirt from his hands and returned to his horse. The threat he'd been sent to contain had nullified itself. There was nothing to be done here beyond giving the rest of these people a respectful burial. The King's Hound stationed at Oldmarsh could see to that. Whisper did little else beyond sit in his cosy outpost and relay messages to elsewhere in the kingdom, having him oversee a few city guards would at least get the man off his backside.

Mounting his horse, Tracker took one last look at the site, hoping with all his heart that it would somehow vanish like a winter mist and reveal the girl to be safe.

When the site refused to bend to his prayers, he turned his back on it and resumed his journey back the way he had come. It was going to take him over a week to get back on the right road, and a few more days of hard riding to return to his original task. He should've been in Toptower by now. He had passed the border city in his travels almost a month ago, had spent just as long trying to reach it, the multiple diversions along the way only pulling him further from the village.

If this diversion led him to finding the trail cold once he arrived?

The mistress wouldn't be pleased. The messages to deal with such threats were rarely to any specific hound, but to the first to scour the village reports.

It had just been him and rumours always came second to an identifiable threat. What else could he have done but answer them? Allow one spellster to steal village children at treat them as though they were her personal larder? Let another wander free whilst drawing more innocent people into her web?

If it led to this rumoured spellster slipping through his grasp, he would simply have to bear the punishment. He wasn't a stranger to that.

It might even be the final blow that saw him travelling down the winding river of the afterlife. The gods had to know he was getting too old for this life. Those amongst the King's Hounds rarely made old bones and he had suffered through three decades. Even if it meant the sweet, soul-destroying embrace of Aerona the Executioner, he was prepared to face her.

To face death.

CHAPTER 1

Dylan strode through the lower levels of the tower. The evening bell that sent the majority of its residents scurrying to their quarters had chimed some time ago, leaving the hallways empty save for a few servants and the occasional straggler. He passed them all in silence, giving a brief nod to the former and overtly ignoring the latter. The servants replied in kind, his fellow spellsters seemed even more intent on paying no heed to his presence.

If this were any other time of the day, he would've dared to ask if they'd seen the petite elf he searched for. But evening seemed specially crafted for secrets. Acknowledgement of another meant placing your fate in their hands for good or ill, and the guardians—for all their encouragement of spellsters living a proper life—had rather different views on what was considered as right.

Where are you, Ness? He had already searched her quarters and the library. Maybe, given the late hour, she was off having some fun of her own. *Like I should be having right now.* He shook his head. So the woman he had attempted to woo wasn't interested in some meaningless fun... with him, anyway. Being bitter over it wasn't going to change her mind or anything else.

A shape moved in the dark, the faint outline of a person, their head turning to watch him. *Another guardian.* He had passed several in his travels. Whether they were the deliciously dark hulks in leather armour or the softer figures in grey uniforms bearing the king's emblem, he couldn't remember a time when there hadn't been guardians about, watching their every move, forever protecting them from the outside.

He rounded a corner and spied a familiar figure scurrying down the hall like the world was about to end. Nestria, his long-time friend and occasional lover.

"Ness!"

The pause in her steps was the only acknowledgement he got. Dylan hitched up the skirts of his robe and hastened to catch up with her. She seemed especially lively tonight. The utter disarray of her usually immaculate bun of brown hair didn't help. *What has she been up to?* Especially when it left her in such a state.

"I've been looking all over for you, my delectable dear." Dylan flashed his most charming smile, the one she always liked, and gently brushed back one of the frizzy wisps curling about her long, pointed ears. "You know, I was thinking that—"

"Turned you down, did she?" His friend grinned up at him, her hurried pace turning leisurely as they veered into the hallways leading to the tower's duelling arena. They'd been playing this game for well over a decade now, spending time in each other's company when other options weren't viable, so it hardly surprised him to have her jump straight to the point.

He hung his head, shaking it slightly to let dark tangles of hair fall across his face, and peered at her through the strands. "Apparently, she's not into tall men." He grimaced. "Or humans, for that matter."

The wrinkles collecting at the corners of Nestria's large eyes deepened. Without a pause in her step, she tipped onto her toes and patted his cheek. "Poor baby. I *did* try to warn you."

Dylan shrugged. He'd already assumed her reaction was a possibility before propositioning her. But what harm was there in asking? "The worst she could've done was refuse." Loudly. Whilst telling him what a monster he was for even thinking that way about her.

Nestria wrinkled her nose, the tip twitching like a rabbit's. "She's done far worse than that."

He didn't doubt it. "So…" He leant into her, nudging her shoulder with his elbow. "I'm pretty certain there's a vacant storeroom nearby. How about you and me go do a little snuggling? I'll do that ice trick you like so much."

Her nose twitched again, this time deliberately. "As much as I love being your fallback option, I've got plans."

"Oh?" They'd come to a halt at last, having passed several closed doors to stop at the massive entrance that opened out into the duelling arena. He looked about the hallway. No one else was waiting. "Who with?"

"Mary's—"

"Ness!" Dylan gasped. "*Mary?* Well, well." He grinned and barrelled on. "I knew *she* was a client of your own gorgeous gender, but I'd no idea *you* were as well. Why if I had—"

"By the gods!" She punctuated each word with a slap of his arm. "Stop storing your mind in your smallclothes for once." The already delicate pink hue of her cheeks grew steadily pinker as she spoke, whether from anger, embarrassment or a mixture of both, he wasn't sure. "And, if you ever want to get into mine again, you'll hold your tongue before insinuating I'm indecisive, even as a jest."

He bowed his head apologetically.

"Mary's guardian—" She held up a finger as he went to open his mouth, the gleam of impending death in her eyes warning him back into silence. "—has convinced the overseers to grant us full sanction to use the duelling arena for her experiment." Those big brown eyes widened further, brimming with childlike glee.

Mary, he mused, rubbing his chin. The woman was one of the few alchemists within the tower, not at all strong in the usual magical feats attributed to the typical spellster. What was she working on? "Is this so she can test her theory about the dog metal?" That had been the rumour, he was sure of it. Something big, too.

He absently toyed with the tuft of hair growing beneath his bottom lip. If he could just remember what that theory was.

"Dog metal?" Nestria echoed, her lips flattening in a failed effort to contain her amusement. "You've spent far too much time listening to Sulin. But yes, because of that. She swears the shield is stable, but hurling magic at a piece of *infitialis*—" She slowly spoke each syllable of the metal's name as if he'd never heard of the stuff. "—this size could be dangerous."

He knew that. Sharing a room for over a decade with one of the most adept alchemists in the tower had left him with a far better idea of the metal they worked with than most spellsters. Sulin often spoke of how the *infitialis* ore had to be coaxed into a stable state via weeks of careful manipulation.

But he'd never heard of anyone crafting an entire shield from it before.

"So Mary's using you as the ammunition." Stood to reason that a test of how much damage the metal could handle would be best achieved by getting one of the strongest spellsters to blast it. *No half measures.* Brave that, considering he'd heard of even worked metal exploding for no apparent reason. Maybe he had misjudged Mary when he'd labelled her as a bit on the meek side for his tastes.

Dylan peered over Nestria's head—not a difficult thing when the elf barely came to his shoulder—as she opened one of the twin doors. Try as he might, he couldn't spot the other woman within the arena's confinement. "Has she got someone to play target?"

Nestria shook her head. "She's fixing it to one of the practice blocks right now. The overseers won't allow another living being to participate until they've seen the first tests." She grinned at him, barring the doorway with one arm. Those brown eyes sparkled a warning of mischief if he dared attempt passage. "That also includes no unsanctioned spectators."

"Well, then." He bowed low, flashing another smile. He hadn't any desire to get on the wrong side of the overseers' attention. People who did that tended to vanish. "I shall leave you and your darling cohort to your work. Don't blow up anything you're not meant to."

"Oh, Dylan?" she called as he turned to leave. "If you're so terribly desperate for company, you could always try the woman who's recently returned from the front lines."

"Very funny." He glared at her over his shoulder, the seriousness on her face turning the rest of him. *There's actually a leashed spellster in the tower?* "Why's she here?" Only the leashed ever stepped foot outside of the tower confines and when they did, it was to serve the king's army. They didn't return. *Not unless it's to compare against prospective recruits.* And yet, his guardian hadn't given any indication of casualties on the front line that would necessitate new spellsters.

"There was a new call for fresh spellsters just last week. All the adept fighters are competing for the honour to join the king's army tomorrow." Nestria leant her head on the door edge and frowned. "Didn't your guardian tell you? *Again?*"

No, she did not. But then his guardian spent a lot of time dissuading him from the very thought of ever leaving the tower. "Ah, you know Tricia. Everything outside is hell-bent on killing me." He made a display of wrinkling his nose. "Still, I think I'll give visiting a leashed spellster a pass. Call me crazy, but I do enjoy a little magical reciprocation and I'd rather not have to speak with whoever has control over her power to get it."

"You debauched monster," Nestria teased.

"Guilty. Utterly so." He waved his hands at her in a shooing motion. "Go. *Before* Mary yells at you." He cupped a hand around his mouth and whispered loudly, "I hear she can be quite the sharp-tongued one."

She giggled into her balled hand. "Off with you, then, or I'll be sure to blame you for making me late."

He clutched at his chest, feigning injury. "You wound me, good lady."

The giggling increased in volume, muffled only by her heavy, cream-coloured sleeves. "Mary'll do much more if you're the reason we have to reschedule."

"Does that mean you'd then be free?" Dylan winked at her less-than-serious glare. "Try not to vaporise too much of the arena, my dear." The tower had a number of smaller training arenas, but nothing else that could handle a pair of strong spellsters fighting in earnest.

She waved him away, grinning, before vanishing behind the thick door.

Whistling to himself, he strolled back along the hallway. Nestria wasn't the most confident spellster when it came to combat techniques, preferring to go on the defensive even when her guardian gave her full sanction to attack. Still, she'd have fun. What spellster wouldn't enjoy a night of unleashing their full abilities upon a harmless object?

He frowned as he ascended the stairway leading to the senior quarters. *Well, maybe not* that *harmless.* The last he heard of Mary's theory was through Sulin. The man hadn't been convinced that what she planned was entirely safe. *But if the overseers have sanctioned it...* They wouldn't let any spellster do something dangerous.

She's strong. Dylan knew that through experience, being one of the few Nestria actively chose to spar with. Although he'd yet to meet a willing opponent that could match him the last time he'd stepped into a duelling arena, she came close. *Would* if she'd put just a little more effort into her teachings. Still, if something went wrong, if the metal *did* explode, Nestria was fully capable of shielding herself.

A pity he hadn't known about it sooner. He was a bit rusty with some of the stronger attacks, preferring to spend his free time researching the texts of the lost dwarven culture, but he could've given the overseers a proper display of battle tactics. Maybe it would've been enough to convince them to let him compete.

Was it too late to join? There was much about his magic that made him eligible. He'd a fair grasp of battle spells. Perhaps not as fresh as those who trained daily, but there was also his flair for healing, which should be helpful on the front line and an instant mark in his favour.

He flexed his fingers, trying not to let them clench. Why hadn't Tricia told him? Yes, it would mean being fitted with one of those collars and having his magical abilities suppressed until ordered to use them. But it was his only chance of having a life beyond the tower and its walls. He could actually walk through the forests and fields he'd only ever seen out the tower windows.

For that chance, he would suffer being leashed.

"It's rather late for you to be up," a familiar voice said, pulling him out of his musing.

His head snapped up. Tricia, his personal guardian, stood at the top of the stairs. He took in the crossed arms, accompanied by the measured tapping of her foot, and swallowed. "Mother," he murmured, giving her a small bow.

She wasn't his actual parent, despite having raised him from birth. No spellster was allowed to have direct responsibility for their own child. He doubted his parents even knew which of the countless spellster children was theirs any more than he knew which couple had been responsible for his creation.

By the quirk in Tricia's pursed lips, humouring him was not on her agenda. "*You* should be in bed, young man."

Dylan scrunched his shoulders, trying to look as small as possible as he climbed the remaining steps between them. "I was talking to Ness."

His guardian harrumphed. "I swear, that girl is nothing but trouble for you."

He smiled to himself. If his childhood friend's ramblings were anything to go by, Nestria's guardian often said the same thing of him.

Having joined Tricia on the landing, he resumed trudging through the hallway to his quarters. As he expected, his guardian followed, silently ensuring he made it there. Perfect. "Did you know Mary's trying out her theory on the *infitialis* metal?"

"Yes." Her lips twisted sourly. The deep brown scar marring the plumpness of her left cheek darkened further. "Her guardian is far too lenient with her, but the overseers have decided."

They walked for a while, the hallways solely theirs. Unlike the lower quarters where the children and servants slept, guardian presence here, especially at night, was limited to those who'd had a hand in raising the spellsters sleeping here, all on the basis that they'd done a proper job in instilling the right rules into their charges.

He rubbed the back of his neck, trying to think of a suitable way to broach the subject of the impending competition. "I heard there's a leashed spellster in residence."

Tricia gave a noncommittal mumble. Such a response was unsurprising. Any time someone mentioned life beyond the tower walls, especially the decades-long war they had with the Udynean Empire or the people they sent to fight on the border, she seemed to prefer ignoring the issue.

"Ness says they're looking for recruits and I... was thinking of competing?"

She came to an abrupt halt and stared up at him, completely horrified. "You want to *leave* the tower? Have you heard nothing I've told you over the years?" Tricia threw up her hands. "It's a dangerous world out there. This tower is your home and you want to just... *leave?*"

"No, I..." No spellster could ever just leave. They needed to be leashed first and that took overseer permission. Trying otherwise meant spending a lifetime being hunted by the king's hounds. "I want to join the king's army."

"Child, you don't know what you're asking." Her calloused and wrinkled hands cupped his face. "You know why we keep your kind here."

He rolled his eyes. It was a long time since he had been a child. The better part of nineteen years, in fact. Whilst most of the other guardians stopped keeping a tight rein on their charges long before they neared their third decade, Tricia seemed intent on mothering him into his old age. "Of course I know," he mumbled. "It's to keep us safe. But I—"

She pinched his cheek. "Precisely. Now let's get you to bed." Turning him, she sent him walking down the hallway with a pat on the backside.

"But I'm *good*," he pressed. "You know I am. Let me enter, let me *fight*, and I'll show the overseers how much of an asset I could be to the army's ranks." He was certain her reluctance in having him leave had been the reason behind why they hadn't let him compete the last time they came looking for spellsters to beef up their numbers. If he let her do it again, he'd never get the chance.

At his back, his guardian scoffed. "A little thing like you?"

Little? He towered over her, over most people. It had been that way ever since he'd hit adolescence. Once, that distinct trait had led him to believe one of the few towering guardians could've been responsible for his birth. A theory he'd abandoned several years ago after stumbling upon the man in question with another man.

"Just look at you," Tricia went on. She squeezed his biceps, almost nonexistent compared to the toned and muscular arms of the guardians. "How long do you think you'd last out in the world?" She snorted. "A day at the most, I would think."

True, he lacked a good deal in some quarters, like physical strength, but his magic was always there to take up the slack. *That* was what the overseers would judge him by. "But—"

"That's enough," she snapped, grasping his arm and whirling him around to face her. "After everything I've taught you, how can you still wish to leave? You will swear to me that you won't pursue this any further, is that understood?"

He sighed. "Yes, Mother." If he could just get *one* overseer to consider him, then he wouldn't need his guardian's backing.

Tricia stroked his cheek. "It's for your own good, dear. Your kind really should stay where they belong."

Locked away. It made sense when he was younger. There was so much that could go wrong whilst they learnt to control their power. But he knew what he was doing. He wasn't a danger to anyone who didn't deserve a bolt up the arse.

"Honestly, I don't know what's gotten into you. You've put so much effort into deciphering the ancient dwarven texts and the overseers are immensely impressed with your latest find. How can you want to throw all that away to...?" She harrumphed again and shook her head. "Why?"

Dylan hung his head. Nothing he said, no matter the reasoning, would be enough to sway her. "I'm sorry, Mother."

They completed the rest of their journey to his quarters in silence, bar the occasional mutter or huff from his guardian. They spoke their goodbyes, the words hollow and clinging to the familiarity of tradition.

He opened the door, almost colliding into his roommate who stood on the other side. Sulin stared, his eyes wide and mouth open, his hand still poised for the handle that'd just swung past his fingers. The usual richly dark shade of his skin had gained the ashen tinge of shock. Dylan was fairly certain it was Tricia's presence and not his that was having an adverse effect on his friend.

Even though she wasn't his friend's guardian, Tricia wasted no time in turning her sharp eyes towards Sulin. "And just where did you think you were going, young man?"

"I was..." Those dark brown eyes flicked to Dylan's face. Whatever the man saw in that second, the faint twitch of those angular brows spoke of him swiftly changing his mind. "Just on my way to inform you of how Dylan had not yet returned to his quarters." There was a squeak to his voice, giving a harsh edge to the man's usual undulating tone. "But I see that you have found him, so I no longer have a reason to leave this room." His gaze returned to Dylan as he spoke those last few words. The amenable smile turned glassy, silently threatening a dozen painful deaths.

Grimacing an apology and nodding as his guardian said farewell once more, Dylan slipped into the room. Sulin might not deliver on his threats of violence, but he'd certainly mete out one hell of a tongue lashing.

Behind him, Sulin shut the door. Leaning back on the heavy wood, his roommate groaned long and loud. "How could you do this to me?" His voice returned to its smooth, rolling accent. The elf originated from Stonebay, a city on the east coast and, although Sulin had lived here for twenty-odd years, his accent hadn't left and had a habit of thickening whenever he was irritated, growing faster with each breath. "I had finally gotten Tillie to agree to give me a chance. *Finally*. Do you understand that? Do you have any idea how hard it is to win her favour? *Do you?*"

Dylan opened his mouth to reply.

"Excruciatingly so!" Sulin marched across the room, pacing the gap between their beds and gesturing wildly. "*All* you had to do was stay out of trouble for one night. *One.*"

Sighing, Dylan settled on the not-so-forgiving mattress of his bed. Yes, he knew how difficult it was to garner a second of Launtil's time, even on a wholly non-physical level as she was often more interested in plants than people.

"I also had plans," Dylan grumbled. They'd been tentative ones that might've had the potential for more. "But apparently, I'm a horrid slime of a creature for even insinuating that she'd want to sleep with the likes of me." The rather shrill notes still echoed in his ears. He was surprised his friend hadn't heard the woman berating him.

Not that it was the first time he had been insulted in such a way. He didn't care if a prospective partner was human or elven, but not every elven woman was as amenable to laying with those outside their species as others. And he'd been angling for a kiss at most, always did with a new partner. Not that he would've turned down more, but he wasn't one for pushing that option. More suggesting.

"You *are* horrid." Sulin plonked next to him on the bed. Although the elf was far shorter than him, the man's heavier build easily lifted Dylan's half of the mattress. "Do you even listen to yourself when you flirt?"

Laughter bubbled in his chest. He wasn't the worst in the tower. There was Mark, whose idea of flirting tended to involve a lot of bragging about his prowess. Dylan knew he wasn't all that bad at what he did, or at least the tower held those who were worse, but he also wasn't the sort to blurt out how many he'd lain with or how loudly they screamed his name. Not when actions spoke far better. "At least I'm not wagging body parts in their face and hoping they get it like you do."

Sulin stuck his tongue out at him, although it had been a long time since Dylan had considered the split organ as a single unit, at least a decade now, ever since the accident that had the poor alchemist abed for days and in pain for weeks. It didn't help that his friend was partial to independently wiggling the tips. Like he was now. The way they twisted in his mouth, writhing against each other like two wet serpents, was disturbing in a hypnotic sort of fashion and just that little bit arousing.

By the gods, what does it even feel like to kiss that? Dylan shook his head, letting the thought sink back into whatever depths it'd come from. "You're disgusting." He shoved Sulin's shoulder. "Put those away already."

The tongues retracted and Dylan swallowed. The sight of those pink tips gradually sliding between his friend's dark lips was no less stirring than the rest of their performance. Unsettling and powerful all at once.

"Tomorrow, you are helping me explain, yes? You owe me that much."

Dylan rolled his eyes. "Fine." He bit the corner of his lip, thinking over Nestria's words about the leashed spellster and the competition for a place in the king's army. Then there was Mary and her experimental shield. "Do you happen to know where Ness is right now?"

Sulin frowned. The action, coupled with the square cut of his tightly-curled hair and sharply angled ears, always made him seem far too serious. "This is a trick question, right? You want me to say she's with someone when she is actually fast asleep or some other equally boring thing."

He filled his roommate in on the elf's whereabouts and what he suspected Mary had planned for the night. Through it all, he stared unwaveringly at the elf's face. Saw the horror swiftly growing in those ever-widening eyes.

His friend jumped to his feet. "They are doing *what?*" He paced back and forth, muttering and tugging at his earlobe. "No, no, no. This is bad. The damn dog metal's not stable enough to handle what she plans." He swung around. "We have to get down there."

"But—" He wanted to leave their quarters? After Tricia had escorted Dylan here? "If I leave, I'll be in direct violation of my guardian's orders." He'd no desire to spend the next month re-cataloguing the main library. Not whilst others fought for the right to join the king's army.

Sulin grasped Dylan's robe, nearly lifting him off his feet. The fabric creaked in his grip. "And if we don't, Ness will die."

CHAPTER 2

They raced through the hallways, trailing cries in their wake. First, it was merely the startled yelps of the occasional servant as they ran through the upper levels and descended the stairs. Then, as they reached the bottom level and neared the duelling arena, they barrelled into the command to halt from the guardians patrolling the area.

Sulin slowed, half heeding the calls.

Dylan let his friend fall behind. If there was anything life-threatening going on in the arena, Sulin's magic was nowhere near strong enough to shield him from it, let alone able to protect anyone else.

They would be punished for this, being out of their quarters at night, doubly so for disobeying direct orders. At least a week's worth of denying them any meals. They might even get solitary confinement. Yet, if his defiance of their cries saved Nestria and Mary, he'd weather whatever sentence they gave him. *Please, don't let me be too late.*

He turned down the long corridor leading to the arena. The charge of lightning—an attack they both favoured—permeated the air. He slowed, scanning the hallway for any sign of guardian presence. Surely, if something was wrong, then there would be people trying to right it.

The stench of scorched air grew stronger as he neared the doors.

Dylan focused and a small film of purple shimmered to life around him. Bracing himself, he flung open the doors.

Nestria stood in the middle of the arena, the unconscious form of Mary at her feet. Lightning flashed around them, forking as they smashed into the wide, shimmering barrier encircling them.

The attack came from the alchemist's experimental *infitialis* shield. It sparked and crackled, each flare pulsing through the room until it connected with something.

He ran for the pair, the barrier around him thrumming with each hit. He dared to glance up. The big shield that protected spectators, which currently consisted of just the overseers, appeared to be holding up better than their personal barriers.

"Dylan!" Nestria screamed as he neared. "What are you doing?" Lightning stabbed her shield with a dreadful crackling sizzle. She winced, then squared her shoulders. "Get out of here! I can handle this."

No, you can't. His dear friend held her ground. For now. She wouldn't for much longer. Not against this barrage. They needed to leave the arena's confines, let the shield that encompassed the area contain the blast once the metal finally shattered. And it *would*. If there was one thing the *infitialis* metal did well, it was exploding.

He pulled the elf's slight form tight against him and focused on widening his shield, pushing the narrow oval out until it matched Nestria's range. The effort caused a dull ache in the base of his skull. Manageable, for now.

Lightning crackled around them.

What if one of us fails? No, he couldn't think of failure. Combined, their power should be enough to block out any force. Dylan bent to the alchemist's inert form and slung her arm over his shoulder. "We have to get out of here."

Nestria nodded, flinching as another bolt struck. Only when she moved to help him did he notice how she favoured one side, and the multitude of scorch marks adorning both women's robes. His friend might be fast enough defending herself in sparring, but nothing was faster than lightning.

With them supporting Mary on either side, they hobbled towards the entrance. The doors seemed a lot farther away than they'd been a moment ago. Still, they struggled onwards, fighting to keep the unconscious woman from dragging—a feat that would've been a lot easier had they both been stronger and of similar height.

At their backs, the crackling grew louder, more erratic. He dared a hasty look over Nestria's head to where Mary had lashed the shield to the old targeting blocks. The metal disc was fracturing. Each crack poured more power behind the lightning. Blue and purple branches of it flashed around them, glancing off their shields.

A particularly heavy blow smacked right across the barriers. Dylan flinched. His gaze fastened onto their exit. The closed, scorched doors seemed to be getting no closer. They had to make it out in time. He wasn't certain if their shields would hold up against the final blast.

A bolt landed a direct hit to their flank.

Nestria cried out. Her shield wavered. Flickering pulses of purple light danced around them as she fought to keep the barrier up. A second blow slapped off it and her defence fell.

Whiteness lanced across Dylan's vision. The suddenness of taking the blast's whole force was like a punch to the jaw. He staggered, blind for several steps. The unconscious woman all but slipped from his hands.

Shaking his head, he put all his effort into maintaining the shield. Like claws squeezing his skull, the dull ache pinched his brain. No matter how he tried, he couldn't stretch the shield to encompass them all and continue to maintain its strength. Pushing any harder only made his head feel as though it were trapped in a vice.

Instead, he turned to face the cracking disc of metal and focused on picturing a wall. It formed between them and the unstable experiment, far stronger than his previous attempts. The lightning smashed against this new barrier, fracturing along the surface. But the wall held.

"What are you doing?" Nestria screamed. She hunkered behind him, dragging the still unresponsive Mary down with her. A thin glow surrounded her, flickering and failing as she sought to shield them.

He crouched next to the women and wrapped his arms around Nestria's slim shoulders. "Trust me." If he could press the fracturing, twisting and glowing mass that was the metal disc up against the arena's shield and hold it there, then perhaps he could limit the damage the experiment did when it exploded.

His shield edged closer. Forks of lightning climbed the surface, the tips curled and cracked at the top. He kept going. The outward face of his shield brushed the curve of *infitialis*. Dylan held his breath. The main property of the metal was its ability to negate magic. If his barrier dropped now…

His heart skipped a beat as the gossamer shield bulged, sending a visible shudder shimmering across the surface.

He flinched, his eyes unable to stay open. They were going to die. The barrier would fall and they'd be electrocuted well before being blown up was a problem.

After a few seconds had passed without incident, he dared to peek.

The shield held. It shuddered with each bolt spewing from the metal disc, but the barrier remained very much intact. He just had to keep it that way.

Slowly, he pushed the shield closer to the arena's edge. The target block grated along the dusty ground. Each jump and tilt sent a bigger flare from the disc's core. Thunder, originally a low rumble, boomed around the domed space.

At last, there was no more room for the block to go. Dylan altered his focus, moulding his flat barrier to sit seamlessly against the arena's shield. What remained of the alchemist's experiment twisted further, warping under the pressure of being hemmed on all sides.

He gritted his teeth and concentrated on keeping the wall in place. If he let his shield drop, even for a heartbeat, they'd be dead before the next pulse. "Ness!" he groaned, flailing his hand behind him in search of the woman.

Warm, familiar fingers wrapped around his wrist. They were coated in something slick. He didn't dare look away from the barrier to find out what.

"Can you…" He puffed, trying to find the air to speak. Words should not be this hard. "…carry Mary… on your own?"

"She's too heavy."

"Then…" The room blurred. Warm dampness flooded his eyes. He blinked it away. *I have to focus.* He might be able to hold on long enough, but if not… "Leave us."

Nestria tightened her grip on his arm. "Dylan…"

He dared the briefest of glances at her face, felt his barrier wavering and snapped his attention back. Behind his shield, the alchemist's experiment glowed with an intense blue light. "Go." There was no point in letting her die alongside him if he failed to contain the blast.

If she gave an answer, he didn't hear it.

The pause between each pulse of lightning grew closer, hitting his barrier with a rapid staccato rhythm. He hunched down as far as he could, drawn between covering his eyes from the glare and knowing he had to keep watching. Any second now and the metal would—

The world went white and fuzzy.

A muffled boom echoed through the arena. His shield bulged under the pressure. He pushed back, trying to control a barrier he could no longer see even as he felt it ripping apart. The strain seared through him, tugging his very existence in all directions. The room spun. Already, he was sweating from every pore. Any moment now and his brain was going to leak out his ears. *Can't stop.* It only had to hold for a little longer…

His shield shattered, unleashing the full force behind the blast. Stunned by the sudden absence of pressure, Dylan blindly threw himself to the ground. Bodies huddled against him. He flung his arms around Nestria and Mary, pulling them close, shielding them in the only way left to him.

Only when the blast's last echoes had finished circling the arena did he dare to lift his head. *We're alive.* The thought came sluggishly and a little on the tentative side. *Were* they alive? The compacted dirt under his chin certainly felt like that of the arena floor, but who was to say the afterlife didn't start out this way?

He rolled off the women to sprawl on the ground. Everything had a purple glare to it. His chin stung like he had scraped it to the bone.

Already, he felt the familiar tug of his power working on fixing the injury.

The smoky aroma of burnt linen filled his nose. Summoning what energy he could, Dylan patted himself down. There were a few singed spots on the skirts of his robe. He was whole, seemingly in no danger and most definitely alive.

The arena's main entrance opened, the customary bang of the doors muffled and tame compared to the previous blast that had assaulted his ears. Dylan rolled his head to the side and blurrily watched the blazing outline of two figures running across the room. One of them wore the flapping robes of a spellster and was most likely Sulin, the other…

Dylan blinked, his vision slowly restoring, and took in the woman wearing the dark grey leather tunic of the guardians. *Tricia?* He sat up, his body strongly objecting to the sudden movement. How had she gotten here so soon? Had she been one of the voices calling for them to stop? *I'm in so much trouble.*

Sulin blew past them with barely a glance in their direction, making straight for the twisted pieces of the shield. Dylan idly followed the alchemist's actions with a sort of distant fascination. The pieces slowly lifted as Sulin manipulated the meagre talent he possessed to examine the smoking remains without direct contact.

"Dylan?" Tricia collapsed beside him. "What did you think were you doing, child?" She grabbed his head, turning it this way and that, examining him for injuries until she was satisfied there weren't any. "You could've been killed," she whispered, drawing him into a tight hug.

He squirmed. Such a display of concern only made it worse. What punishment was she concocting? Would she have him escorted around the tower like some of the other spellsters? For how long? He shrank from his guardian's grasp. "I'm all right, Mother."

Tricia sat back, a rare proud smile curving her lips. "You *are.*" She fussed with his hair, tucking several dark strands behind his ears. "My brave boy."

Embarrassment gently warmed his cheeks. He had been stupid, not brave. His gaze slid back to where Sulin was crouched over the remains of the *infitialis* shield. The elf was shaking his head and muttering to himself, but there seemed to be a distinct lack of concern on the alchemist's face. That meant the danger was over. From the shield, at least.

Beside them, Nestria groaned. She sat up, her movements oddly stiff.

He crawled across the space between them. "Ness?" Had that final blast struck her as hard as it had done him? "Are you all right?"

She rubbed at her head. "Just a bump. I've had worse falling out of bed."

His gaze slid to Nestria's robe. A large, dark red patch had formed on her left sleeve. Higher still, the pale fabric was a charred mess. "Bit more than a bump."

Those big brown eyes lowered to where he held her arm. She gasped as he gently removed the blood-soaked sleeve. Blood ran down her arm, trickling from raw peeling skin. Dylan tracked the burnt flesh up her arm until it culminated in a hideous charred and weeping wound near her shoulder. More of the rawness above suggested further injury beneath her robe.

"First bolt must've struck before I got a shield up. Funny, I don't even remember it." Nestria fingered her forearm, hissing only when she made contact with the blistering skin of her wrist. "It barely hurts."

Keeping his grip light, he focused on healing her by teasing out the body's natural ability to mend itself and encouraging it to quicken. The blood stopped flowing. The peeled skin flaked away and the rawness of the flesh underneath faded, leaving behind a strangely delicate branch-like pattern of pink scars. Even these had begun to fade into a silver-purple by the time his power halted.

Nestria beamed up at him. "Thanks."

He shrugged. It wasn't the first time he had healed her, it likely wouldn't be the last.

"We must get this poor girl to the infirmary," Tricia said, drawing his attention back to the unconscious alchemist lying beside him. Despite her singed robes, she didn't appear to have suffered any serious injuries. Just a few scrapes she had likely gotten when she fell. "Sulin. Help me carry her." She beckoned the man away from the pieces of *infitialis*.

Sulin obeyed, eyeing the remains with every step.

His guardian huffed. "If it was going to explode again, it would've done so by now."

Dylan stood, staggering slightly as his legs objected to taking his weight. "If he wants to examine the shield further, I can help with Mary."

Tricia snorted. "Don't be ridiculous, child. You haven't the strength at the best of times." She bent to hoist Mary off the ground, waiting for the alchemist to secure the woman's other side. "Nestria, be a dear and tell the healers on duty that they've a patient."

"Yes, Madam Guardian." Nestria curtsied and, hitching up her skirts, raced out of the arena whilst the others slowly made their way to the door.

Dylan trailed after them. He could've gone back to his quarters.

Unlike Mary and Nestria, his healer training had left him with the innate ability to mend any injuries without him having to think on it. All he truly needed was time to recuperate, but the healer in him wouldn't allow him to leave Mary's side until she was in the care of those who were better at such magic than he.

Noises followed in their wake as they neared the infirmary. Soft, almost nonexistent, even to ears listening for the sounds; the careful opening of doors and hushed conversation. Those closest to the duelling arena would've heard the shield explode and would be curious to know what had caused it. Then again, when he considered how rumour flowed through the tower's heart like water rushing downstream, they likely already knew of Mary's experiment.

Come tomorrow morning, everyone would know the woman had failed. Mary would be punished. The overseers were very particular when it came to wasting even a shard of *infitialis*. Her guardian would likely share a measure of that punishment as well.

Thanks to Nestria, the healers on duty were waiting at the door by the time they arrived. They hustled Mary to a bed, leaving the rest of them to aimlessly linger near the entrance.

"She'll be all right, won't she?" Nestria asked the healers.

"Of course she will," Dylan answered before any of them could. Those few who chose to practise their craft in the infirmary were the best healers the tower had. He had once thought of joining them—had even trained enough to gain an apprenticeship with one of the few masters—until the call of the army started in his blood. "She'll be wide awake by morning and ready to improve her work in no time."

"Gods," Sulin groaned. "I hope not. That woman's experiments are always costing us a hefty chunk of dog metal."

Dylan frowned. It was one thing to lose a fragment here and there during a young alchemist's training, but a piece as big as the shield? "It can't be salvaged?"

The alchemist shook his head. "Not after a blast like that. Reusing it will only risk having whatever it is used for blow up again. Can you imagine if someone crafted a collar from it?"

Dylan had never seen one of the collars they used up close, although he did know they were made only by the best alchemists. Nor had he ever heard of one exploding, but if the metal was unstable... "Be rather like wrapping a viper around one's neck," he murmured half to himself.

"Which is why I plan to insist the metal is disposed of," Tricia said. "I also think it's time you three were back in your quarters. The healers don't need you lot wandering about like abandoned chicks. Come on." She flapped her hands at them as if they were children. "Off to bed with you."

They turned to obey only to find the overseers standing in the infirmary's doorway. Not a one appeared the slightest bit harmed. They looked even less amused. Behind them stood Mary's guardian. Even with much of her face lost in the shadows, the woman's focus on her unconscious charge was palpable.

"Am I correct that this is your charge, Guardian?" one of the men asked Tricia, indicating Dylan.

His guardian stiffened at the address. "Yes, sir."

"We witnessed quite the display this evening," said one of the women. "It would seem your evaluation of his strength is incorrect. One must wonder if you've been paying your charge the proper amount of attention due to him. His years do not grant him full absolution from your watch."

Tricia bowed. "Yes, madam. I am aware he has displayed a somewhat unusual burst of— That is to say, I have of course been keeping a close eye on his talents. I'm certain you recall how he is most useful in translating the ancient dwarven texts. The hedgewitches are—"

"Enough," snapped a second man. "However pleasing his skill may be to these so-called *dwarven* scholars, it does not supersede compliance with the king's will. If it is discovered you have been deliberately concealing his potential..." His threat trickled off.

Dylan swallowed. He hadn't ever witnessed a guardian being reprimanded, but he had heard rumours. Whispers of spellsters being assigned new guardians with no sign of what had become of the former.

Again, Tricia bowed. No doubt, she had a better grasp on what punishments the overseers could dispense. "Understood, sir."

The woman beside the man cleared her throat. "You will inform your charge that, in light of recent events, he will compete alongside the other candidates for the honour of joining the army. You are to make it clear he is expected to be in the arena. Refusal will grant him a month's solitary."

Dylan's jaw dropped open. Excitement and panic balled themselves into one thick knot in his throat. Compete? *Him?* They were actually going to let him compete in the next brawl?

That was in two days' time. He might have bested Mary's experiment, but he hadn't actually practised against another spellster in years. Would a sparring session with Nestria be enough? She would've recovered from the blast, but she also might be reluctant to test his full might after what she had witnessed. Henrie, then? His friend wasn't a good offensive partner, but his shields were strong.

Tricia's final bow was fawningly low. "Of course, madam. I will ensure he is there."

"See that you do," another overseer said, the sole elven one of the group.

As one, the overseers turned and left.

Mary's guardian dove through the doorway the instant she had a chance. She hastened to her charge's side, demanding answers from the healers before they could give a proper diagnosis.

Tricia sank to the floor the moment the overseers were out of sight. "What have you done, child?" she whispered. "Did it not occur to you that the overseers were watching your every move?"

Dylan wet his lips. He hadn't given a passing thought as to how the overseers would see this, but he was now allowed to compete, to have a chance to prove he was good enough to fight in the army. Just like he wanted. "I—"

"Have I not told you enough times that the outside world isn't safe? Why… why would you do this to me? Was I not good to you?"

Guilt gnawed at his gut. He had heard of guardians who were harsh with their charges, sometimes brutally so. But whilst she could be strict at times, Tricia had never laid a hand on him. "Mother…"

His guardian slowly got to her feet. Seemingly composed once more, she busied herself with dusting off her tunic before facing him. Her features were devoid of all expression. "My sweet boy." The endearment was just as hollow. "Don't win. If you value your life, you will fail the brawl. Have them think this was a fluke and let another be leashed."

Fail? His pride wouldn't allow that. "You've always taught me to be the best I can be. If I'm competing, then I *will* win."

One side of Tricia's mouth lifted. "Yes." There was pride on her face, but it was small and overshadowed by a haunting sadness. "Then you will die." She reached up to cup his cheek, her fingertips rough against his skin. "This is not the ending I raised you for."

He frowned. What better end could she possibly imagine for him? To be sent into battle, to assist in the war, was an honour.

One he would gladly accept.

CHAPTER 3

Dawn couldn't come fast enough. Dylan woke several times during the night. Each moment had him thinking the sun couldn't be too far below the horizon and, after waiting for what felt like eternity, was proven wrong. After the fifth such turn, he gave up on the very idea of sleep, opting to sneak down to the baths and make use of the tubs whilst almost everyone else remained in their beds.

No one stopped him as he slunk through the tower corridors. There was no one *to* stop him. Apparently, even the guardians sought their beds after a while. A fact he wished he had known sooner. A lot of trouble could be made when it was certain that no one watched.

It was a strange experience, entering the bathing chamber without a horde of others at his side. Illuminated only by the single torch he dared to ignite, the ruddy light failed to reach the corners of the room. It made the already cavernous space seem even bigger, but it was more than enough to see by.

He stripped and knelt next to a tub—little more than a wooden half-barrel—to dip his hand into the frigid water. Heat, the prelude to a fireball, radiated from his palm. There were other ways to heat the water, and he was careful to use the more accepted methods when around impressionable children, but this was the quickest.

Only once steam rose from the tub did he withdraw his hand. He liked to bathe when the water was almost too hot to touch and... Well, whenever would he get another chance to cleanse himself like this if he won the competition?

Never. That was the whole point of being leashed. The collar would strip him of the ability to use his power unsanctioned. Those in the army would hardly let him be so frivolous with his magic.

Still kneeling, Dylan set about washing his hair. He bent over the barrel to lather the black locks and rinse them out with a carefully maintained funnel of water, ensuring every drop fell back into the barrel it had come from rather than the cold stone floor.

He stepped in the tub, the water lapping about his knees—it'd been several decades since the last time he could actually sit in these things without his legs scrunched up. The mute coldness of the room nipped at his extremities. He hastily scrubbed at his skin with cloth and soap, warding off the chill by subtly heating the air around him.

The chamber was usually full of sound. The yelling and splashing of boys trying to see who could make the biggest wave out of the meagre water the half-barrels contained, whilst the older ones, often himself included, yelled just as loudly for them to hurry up so they could also bathe. Alone, the gentle trickle of water running down his body and back into the tub seemed almost intrusive.

It didn't take him long to be clean and dry, his hair helped along by the careful application of a little magical heat applied to the locks. He snuffed the torch and crept back up to his quarters to begin his usual grooming routine.

Dylan cracked open the door to find Sulin awake and partially dressed.

The alchemist swung about, hopping on one foot, the other leg half in a boot. "Dylan? I... I thought they had called you to practice. Is that where you have been this early in the morning?" The elf flopped onto his bed and finished hauling his boot on. "Or did you creep out to make it a late one?"

Wrinkling his nose, Dylan picked up his razor, a gift from his guardian several decades back, and deftly began stropping the blade. It wouldn't do to attend the training arena looking scraggy. "Sneak out after being caught twice last night? Hardly." His gaze slid to the room's tiny window. The sky was still dark, but he could see a hint of light on the horizon. "I couldn't sleep, so I made use of what'll be the last time I bathe here."

Sulin frowned as he bent to pull on his other boot. "You are that certain of winning?"

Dylan sat before his dresser and, after igniting the single candle with a click of his fingers, vigorously worked his shaving soap into a lather. "The overseers wouldn't let me in if they didn't believe I've a decent chance." There were several spellsters who could claim a similar level of power and combat talent as he. How many of them had made it through the bouts? He wished he knew.

"I suppose that is true."

"Besides," Dylan mumbled as he slathered foam on his face, "the person I *have* to at least break even with at the end is the leashed one." How hard could that be when she would have to seek sanction to fight in the first place? *Very.* Especially if she had been any good at keeping the Udynean forces back.

They both fell silent as he started to shave, him due to necessity and Sulin due to finishing his own morning routine. Usually, Dylan would do multiple passes with the razor, ensuring that the parts he shaved were smooth. But his hand kept shaking and his breath would not stay even. One pass would have to suffice for today, lest he did something foolish like accidentally cutting his jugular.

Still, there was one piece his pride wouldn't let be with a quick onceover. Dylan drew the candle closer, intent on the little tuft of hair beneath his bottom lip. *Was* it even? He stared at the mirror, his eyes watering at the strain of keeping them focused. It certainly looked that way.

"I cannot understand why you do not just shave that thing off. Or grow a decent beard like other humans."

Satisfied with his trimming, he lowered the razor and let his eyes adjust to take in Sulin's grinning reflection. The elf didn't share this particular daily routine. He didn't need to, considering elves couldn't grow beards. They had hair everywhere else, albeit finer than their human counterparts, just not on their lower faces.

It was a trait Dylan didn't envy. He didn't look his age now, shaving only served to make him look younger. As for growing a beard... he had tried in his mid-twenties and gave up after seeing the scrappy thing that'd attached itself to his face. The little patch was all that remained, all he could reliably cultivate.

With his hands steadying, Dylan returned to ridding himself of the last few pesky hairs that'd surfaced overnight. Tiny black saplings poking out of a hillside that was a rather neutral colour. To call it a lighter shade of beige was being generous. It wasn't the warm peachy tone of Nestria's skin, and held not a single evidence of freckling like Mary's bespeckled face. Although, he supposed spending more than a few moments in the garden could change the latter.

A lot of things about his face were neutral, from his soft jaw to his wide mouth, even the colour of his hooded eyes—so dark a brown, that they verged on black—screamed normal. Only his nose, a rather bold affair, deviated from the norm.

"You know, you will not be allowed to preen like that in the army."

Dylan twisted atop the stool and glared at Sulin over his shoulder. "What would you know about what they do in the army?" he muttered as he patted the remaining flecks of foam from his face. His stomach made vague mumblings of breakfast. He tried to ignore it. The dining hall wouldn't be ready to serve them for another half-hour or so.

"I talk to the guardians from time to time. *And* the last two leashed spellsters they brought in." Sulin frowned. "You should *not* compete. It is not an honour to have part of yourself accessible only at their say-so."

The stool screeched as he stood. "It's my only way out of here." He'd spent years of just existing, craving to see the land up close, to walk the streets he had only read about. He couldn't back out now just because his friend thought it was a bad idea. "Besides, the overseers practically gave me an order." To fight. To protect those who couldn't. It wasn't a call he could blithely walk away from.

"What about your guardian's words? Have you given them any thought?"

He had. They'd kept him awake for the other half of the night. Dylan shook his head. "They're just words." Not the ending she wanted for him? All she wanted was for him to stay. She had lied to the overseers to keep him here for years. Who could say if last night's words had been any different? What wouldn't she do to ensure he remained within these walls?

They made their way through the corridors, following the gentle flow of the other early risers heading towards the dining hall. Several of the women muttered amongst themselves as they passed by, glancing over at them only to look back and chatter on.

Dylan frowned. There could be only one thing he knew that would set them gossiping about him and that had to be the way the elven woman, Kaprina, turned down his advances last night. *Great*. Now if he won, everyone was going to think the overseers chose him purely to get him out of the tower. That had to be the worst way to leave.

He could've asked Sulin to edge closer and discover the truth, the man's hearing was far superior and might even have already heard enough whilst walking alongside Dylan, but he wasn't prepared to face the ribbing his friend would dish out at the request.

Nestria stood at the entrance to the dining hall, along with another petite elven woman. The second woman's skin was heavily tanned and freckled, her hair a sun-bleached brown and, sitting proudly upon her face, were a set of those strange wire frames. Launtil, the woman his roommate had attempted to see before they made their dash to the duelling arena.

"Tillie!" Sulin hastened to the woman's side, losing an inch of his height as his shoulders drooped. So small was the woman that even Nestria's relatively average elven stature looked tall. The alchemist, being taller than both by a half-foot, towered over her. "I hope you will forgive me for last night, you see—"

Smiling, Launtil held up her hand to stall the rest of his explanation. "Nestria told me everything." The woman had been born in the Udynea Empire—and into slavery, as was common with most of the elves there. Despite living here for a decade or so, she still carried a slight hint of their accent. It always brought a sort of niggling in the back of Dylan's mind to check if the woman harboured an apricot stone in her mouth.

Sulin flinched. "Ness... *told* you?" His gaze flicked to the other elven woman. "Really?"

"Oh my, yes." Launtil pushed the wire frames further up her nose. Dylan had heard they were a gift from her former owner. In the lenses, her eyes grew bigger. "The entire tower's gossiping on how Mary almost blew up the arena last night and destroyed a huge chunk of *infitialis* in the process. They say she's been given a week's confinement for it."

Dylan gnawed on his bottom lip. Solitary confinement wasn't commonly longer than a day or two. He knew the now-useless piece of *infitialis* was large, and of how the metal was difficult to mine, but he didn't think it worth more than a half-week of solitary. What had the overseers seen in the woman that made them think a longer sentence was necessary?

"What, specifically, does all that have to do with me?" Sulin asked.

"Well, you're the one who warned our dear hero here—" Dylan blinked as Launtil turned her warm smile his way. "—how unstable her experiment was. I dare say that if you hadn't convinced him to return, they'd both be very much dead."

Hero? Was *that* what the women they had passed been gossiping about? He wasn't a hero. He'd simply heard that it could've killed his friend and acted. "Tillie, I really—"

"And Ness tells me the overseers insisted *you* take part in tomorrow's brawl," Launtil continued, turning her full attention towards him. "That's going to stir up quite the hornet's nest. I'd watch out for Sophie if I were you. Poor dear actually might've had a chance this time around. She's going to completely lose her mind when she finds out."

Dylan shrugged. He had crossed paths with Sophie before, although it'd been some years. If she was still as bad at fighting as he had witnessed the last time he ventured near the outside duelling arenas, then she wouldn't be much of an obstacle.

"I would not be too sure about that," Sulin said. "Fredrick stands an equally good chance."

"Fred?" Launtil made a vain attempt to smother her tiny giggle with a hand. "That silly boy only won the bouts so he could show off to his man. He won't actually try to win."

Dylan quietly tucked that piece of knowledge away. He hadn't fought Fredrick before, although he'd heard a great deal about the man's technique of having people drop unconscious at a touch. Still, it would be interesting facing a new opponent.

Launtil gasped. "Oh, but listen to me blathering when you've so little time! This could be your last day in the tower, you shouldn't be wasting it with gossip." The woman's slender fingers wrapped about Dylan's wrist. If he wasn't so used to the touch, the eerie length of elven digits would've been unsettling. Fortunately, this came with a smile. "I hope you get what you want." She turned to Sulin, her smile growing warmer. "See you at the usual table?"

"Sure," Sulin mumbled. Those dark eyes remained locked on her as she joined the throng entering the dining hall, a little sigh escaping his lips when the woman slipped out of sight.

Nestria bumped her hip into their friend's. "All right, lover boy, you can thank me later. I'll take my payment in one of those sparkly brews you concoct."

"I have no knowledge as to what you speak of," Sulin replied in an overloud voice as a pair of guardians strode by. "Alchemists are forbidden to go near strong alcohol, much less make it." He drew her closer, whispering, "Give me a week and I will see what I can do."

"Just remember." She gently pinched his side. "Even if it falls flat between you two, you still owe me."

The alchemist bent to kiss her cheek. "You are a treasure, Ness."

Nestria giggled and lightly slapped his shoulder. "Oh, go on! Quick, before someone else tries out their charms on her."

Smiling and shaking his head, Sulin disappeared through the doorway.

Dylan stood just out of sight of the people already in the dining hall. "Are they really talking about last night?"

"Of course they are. Mary was talking up a storm at dinner yesterday, babbling on about how much she'd done to perfect her shield and how the overseers were going to be so impressed." Nestria crossed her arms and cocked a perfectly arched brow at him. "I'm surprised you didn't notice."

He remembered mumblings. "I was rather occupied."

"I'll bet. Too busy wondering whether you could tumble Kaprina, right?" She grinned. "The answer to which is apparently a very empathetic *no.*"

Dylan winced. He'd shared that the woman had turned him down, but not everything. "Heard the whole story already, huh?"

"You mean the half-dozen rumours of why she turned you down flat? Or the din she made in doing so? Don't beat yourself up over it. She does that to all the human men who ask. Fancies herself as some prize only an elven dick can unlock." She rolled her eyes far enough back that only the whites showed.

He grimaced. "You've got to admit, she does have quite the range. Especially in the high notes." A part of him was certain there was a sliver of magic involved in her screams as they'd vibrated down the hall.

Again, Nestria laughed. "Come on, *hero.*" She circled behind him and shoved him towards the dining hall entrance. "Let's get you fed and into a practice arena. I know it's just a day, but you've got to get *some* training into you if you're going to beat the competition and you can't do it on an empty stomach."

There were several dining halls around the tower; one for the guardians, one for the young and those who tended to them, and then there was this one, which held every spellster past their teens. The dining hall reserved for them was the biggest and, no matter how early he got here, was always packed.

Dylan meandered through the crowd with Nestria at his side. Finding the end of the serving line took some shuffling, and a little negotiating, but they at last managed to get a portion of today's breakfast; bread and cheese, neither one the least bit mouldy, and watery ale.

Gathering their meal, they made a beeline for their usual spot near the far wall, a place they'd staked out as their own during their first years dining here. The wallward tables all sat a little higher than those in the middle, allowing them to see more of the room. They were the least draughty, too.

Someone was already seated there by the time they made it, always was, but the rather attractive elven man who occupied the spot wasn't usually alone. Nor his plate so strangely full.

Nestria plonked herself on the bench, sidling up to the man whilst Dylan took a seat opposite them. "Hey, half of a double H!" She beamed up at him, although 'up' required her to scrunch down until her chin touched the table. "Where's Harriet?"

Henrie glanced up, the perfect bow of his lips stretched into a grim smile. There was a haunted look in those big brown eyes. A bone-deep sadness Dylan had witnessed take other couples.

All at once, he knew. "They discovered you two, didn't they?" The guardians didn't take kindly to spellsters fooling around and came down harshly on those they caught.

The man laughed. It wasn't the light, tinkly sound Dylan had come to associate from the elf, but rather a soft, almost gasping, noise. Henrie nodded. "Not quite. But it was so close. We thought it better if we spent a few days apart. My guardian... He's been so supportive of... Well—" He waved his hand, indicating himself. "You know."

They did, although the memories Dylan had of a time when Henrie hadn't been himself were rather dim. He nodded for the man to continue.

"Sometimes, I forget why he's really there. I never thought that he would try to separate Harry and me, but last night, when they almost caught us..." The words faded. He clapped a long-fingered hand over his mouth as if fearing they'd escape.

"Oh, Hen." Nestria threw her arms around the man's slender

shoulders.

"What's the harm in it? It's not like I can get her pregnant."

I don't think that's the point. If it ever had been, there were rather permanent ways to ensure that everyone with the ability couldn't sire children. "You need a message taken to her or anything?"

Henrie shook his head. "It's just for a week or so. Another couple will catch the guardians' attention soon enough and we'll be safe again." He frowned. "Hopefully."

But never as safe as they had been beforehand. The risks only increased with every near miss. "Just... be careful. I'd hate to think you two wound up like Ben and Jenny." The latter had once been a friend of his, but the man had changed since his closeness to Jenny was discovered by the guardians.

The word was that Ben tolerated only a select few near his lover. That suggested being outed by another spellster, possibly even a rival for Jenny's affections as Ben had been devoted to her since their childhood.

Now they were both barred from the person they most wanted to connect with. Ben had his every action with a woman, any woman, scrutinised as though he would turn rabid at a blink. It was the same for Jenny, just with men. Such was the fate of any couple the guardians found together.

Dylan had nothing with which to compare, had never felt that deeply about someone, but it seemed that love could easily gnaw the light out of a person's soul. He didn't want to witness another pair of friends turn dark.

Henrie steepled his fingers. "That won't happen to us. Harry's smarter than either of them." He tilted his head. Those brown eyes narrowed with a disturbing intensity. "What's this I hear about you competing? You can't actually *want* to join the army."

"I do. If we manage to push Udynea back, then maybe we can convince the guardians to grant more freedoms." He pointed to where a group of silver-haired men and women sat. "Some of them are in their ninth decade and they've never been out of this tower."

"But we're safe here," Nestria said.

"I know." They'd all grown up with the same tale. The people beyond the tower walls didn't want spellsters in their midst, they were frightened of what magic could do. He didn't blame them, not when they'd an all-too-real example of unleashed power bearing down on them from the western border.

"So why would you ever want to leave?"

It wasn't the first time she had asked. Some days, he would pose the same question to himself. He always came back with the same answer. "The easiest way to protect a book is to seal it behind glass, but keeping it safe and unobtainable also denies its true purpose." The guardians stuffed their heads with knowledge of the outside world, the history of not only this kingdom, but all the others. What good was it if they were never allowed to set foot beyond the tower gates? He leant over the table, his gaze unwavering from the elf's face. "I'm sick of doing nothing more than just existing."

Henrie cupped his hands, pressing them to his lips. He stared at Dylan for a long time, before finally speaking. "Your talents—"

"—are wasted here," Dylan finished.

Henrie smirked. "That's what I was going to say. If the overseers think you're strong enough to compete, then win this thing."

Nestria glared at their friend over her mug of ale. She slammed the drink down, sloshing it everywhere. "But then he'll be leashed, his magic usable only at the sanction of others." She turned her glare on him. "Is that what you want?"

"You mean it's not that way now?" True, for the most part, he could use his gift whenever he wished, but he rarely did outside of sparring and the occasional intimate moment. For most other times, it wasn't worth the risk of being caught.

She opened her mouth to speak, then shut it as her gaze shifted over his shoulder.

A tiny figure collided into his back. Strong fingers grabbed his robe, tugging it. "There he is," a familiar voice said. "The hero of the day."

"Jenny." He twisted on the bench, careful to ensure his hands remained steepled on the table before him so that anyone could see he wasn't initiating any contact with the woman clinging to his side. "Heard about that, have we?" He scanned the crowd. Somewhere in that throng was Ben, getting his small reprieve from having his guardian constantly looking over his shoulder. The pair would only be able to mingle briefly, even in public places. Dylan had no intentions of getting between Jenny and her overprotective lover.

The woman smiled. Her lips had barely parted to speak before her eyes, so eerily similar to his in both shape and colour, darted to one side.

"Oh my, yes," said a less-than-welcome voice at his back. "And rumour tells of how the overseers are letting you into the brawl, despite having already chosen the top twenty from the bouts."

He risked a glance from the crowd to the rather severe-looking woman planting herself at Jenny's side. "Sophie, how nice to see you again."

The woman's already narrow lips grew thinner. Her face, especially the large blue eyes, had a sort of etherealness to it that suggested elven ancestry somewhere in her blood even if those flushed pink ears lacked the points. "You better not think that, just because they let you skip the bouts, you're going to win. I've entered the last five contests and—"

"Yet, you're still here," Henrie interjected. He had rounded the table and now stood at Dylan's shoulder. The man leant an arm on the table. "How embarrassing it must be for you to know the overseers haven't sent their best and most powerful spellsters to stop the war."

Sophie sneered at the man, then poked Dylan's chest. "Don't stand in my way. I am leaving this godsforsaken tower."

He gave her his widest, most charming, smile. Even if she didn't win, if the overseers truly thought she was of as much worth as she believed, they would've sent her ages ago. "Well, the brawl will decide that, won't it?"

"That it will." Squaring her fine-boned jaw, Sophie marched off, all but dragging poor Jenny with her.

Dylan leant back to watch them leave and froze. There was a small, slightly soft and globular, weight on his right shoulder. "Hen? Could you get your chest off me?"

The man chuckled long and low. "I could." The elf put more of his weight on Dylan's shoulder. "But I don't think I will right now. I could do with a bit of relief; my back's killing me."

Dylan tipped his head to the side. He didn't like reminding Henrie of his differences, but if the man's monthly issue was troubling him... "You know, you're free to ask me for help if it's too much some months," he whispered. "I do it for Ness all the time." He'd been tending to Nestria's monthly pains since his first successful attempt in suppressing the pangs that had her blacking out.

Of course, neither friend would have that sort of assistance if he managed to come through the brawl as the victor tomorrow.

A twinge of guilt hit him at the memory of Nestria lying on the floor in agony. Maybe he *should* fail.

He mentally waved the thought away. There were plenty of strong healers here to help her through those times. Just as they'd done before he had mastered the ability. She'd be fine without him. Wouldn't she?

Henrie grunted and gave Dylan a playful shove, breaking his musing. "I'm a big boy. I can handle a little pain."

Dylan pursed his lips. Most men didn't experience this particular type of pain. He had learnt from Nestria how bad it could get, but he couldn't imagine having to deal with it as a man. "If you're sure."

"Don't give me that look. Just get on with stuffing your gob already." He reached over the table and grabbed a slice of bread from his previously untouched plate. "*I* am going to place a few wagers on how fast you can take Sophie out, because you know she's already planning on taking you first."

Nestria gave a muffled squeal. She leant across the table, knocking over the remainder of her drink. Her hand waved, holding up two fingers, whilst she visibly fought to swallow a mouthful of bread and cheese.

Finally, she was able to speak. "Put me down for two minutes. I've got a bottle of Sulin's powerful stuff coming my way."

"Are you sure you want to risk it?" Dylan asked. "Two minutes is a rather optimistic goal." He hadn't seen Sophie in a fight since they'd sparred in the same sessions some fifteen years ago. It could take far longer than a few minutes to suss out an opening in her attacks.

His old friend grinned, the candlelight playing along her teeth and making her rather blunt and altogether human-like canines seem longer and more... elven. She winked at him. "Hen's right. If it's truly what you want, then just remember: Soph always fights with fire."

CHAPTER 4

Between bites of bread and cheese, Dylan went over the strengths and weaknesses of the brawl competitors he'd seen sparring in the training grounds. All of them would know by now that he was competing, but he didn't know everyone. There were hundreds of spellsters living here, impossible to know everyone's tactics and, unlike his opponents, he hadn't the time to get himself acquainted with those he squared off against tomorrow.

Whilst it might take time to figure out how to best Sophie, he had seen her fight before. Her fire manipulation was strong, but she'd little else going for her. Fredrick would be a pain if allowed to close and use his knack of putting people to sleep, but if Launtil's information was correct, then he had little to worry about there.

William would be a strong contender, if only for his speed. The man was capable of blasting fire from the front and nipping around to attack an opponent's flank before they had the chance to react.

Henrie returned before either Dylan or Nestria could completely finish their breakfast. He settled on the chair next to Dylan, straddling the seat to cross his arms on the backrest.

Dylan washed down his last mouthful with a generous gulp of ale. He fought to suppress a shudder at the taste. They really were getting ridiculous with how much they diluted it. "What's gotten you looking so smug?" he asked of his returning friend.

Grinning, Henrie shuffled closer. "I now know who all twenty of your opponents are," he whispered into Dylan's ear.

Nestria made a small noise on the other side of the table. This close to them, her elven hearing picked up every word. "That was fast. What did you promise them for that information?"

Henrie flapped a hand, no doubt batting away the heavy insinuation coating Nestria's question. "Unlike some people." He nudged Dylan, even as he continued to smirk at their friend. "I *store* the spirits Sulin crafts rather than piss it all away." He mimed glugging down a bottle.

Nestria wrinkled her nose. "I do *not*—"

"You!" a voice bellowed, their ire echoing around the dining hall. Conversations stilled in the face of it as people, Dylan and Henrie included, turned towards the source.

William marched across the room, the shaking point of his finger leading the charge, singling out a man Dylan had only ever seen in passing. "You dare show your face after what you did? Outing me? Outing Cari?" William was tall, more so than Dylan, and with a great deal more muscle sitting on his frame. He towered over the other man, even though they were both humans. "What gave you the right?"

Dylan leant closer to his friends, whispering even then to avoid catching William's attention. "Do either of you know him?" He surreptitiously indicated the man currently babbling his answer to William.

Nestria shook her head. He had expected as much, given that they typically spent their days working within similar social circles.

Henrie nodded. "That's Elgan. I see him around the greenhouses now and then. He doesn't say much, though. Think he might be from outside."

Whatever answer Elgan gave William, it was enough to give William's already reddened face a hint of purple.

William grabbed the man, hauling him to his feet. "Where I chose to stick it was *my* business." As well as being taller than Dylan, William had an enviously long, black beard that curled slightly at the end, almost as though it wanted to stab the other man in the throat. "If you don't like the fact I lay with other genders, then you should've refused me, not gone running to my guardian to out me."

"Will," Sophie said. She stood at the man's back, the shimmer of her shield flickering in and out of existence. "That's enough." Behind her, stood Jenny who didn't look ready to handle the fight that looked to be brewing.

Dylan slowly got to his feet, only to be hauled back into his seat by Henrie.

"Don't," his friend hissed.

"Save it for the brawl," Sophie continued.

"*Why?*" William shook the man in his grasp. "This mewling sack of shit isn't strong enough to be competing. If I can't beat his arse in the arena, I'll settle for breaking some bones right here."

"It won't matter what he did if you win. None of it will."

Dylan bit his lip. No one said it, but he was certain everyone was thinking the same thing. Even if William won tomorrow, Cari would still be under the close watch of her guardian. *Forever.* All because of this man's... jealousy? His disgust? Dylan knew very well what the majority of the tower thought about those who switched from sleeping with one gender to another.

"*I'm* the sack of shit?" Elgan growled. He fought to tear himself free of William's hold, unable to break the other man's grasp. "At least I'm not some indecisive bastard with standards lower than a worm. I'm sorry about getting Cari caught up in this but, honestly, she's no better."

"Have neither of you heard?" Jenny enquired. When her question was met with silence from both men, she continued, "Cari was found dead this morning."

Stillness fell over the crowd. It wasn't unheard of for spellsters to take their own lives, but they were usually adults brought in by the King's Hounds. The same people who tried to escape the safety being in the tower afforded spellsters. Cari had been tower born, like Dylan and the majority of his close friends.

"*Dead?*" Elgan echoed. Smoke drifted off his robes, emanating from William's hands. If he didn't free himself soon, then the man holding him might just burn Elgan where he stood.

Jenny bowed her head. "The guardians believe it to be self-inflicted."

Snarling like a cornered dog, William threw the man to the floor. "Her blood is on your hands, tattler." Spit flew out of his mouth. Flecks of it dribbled down his beard. He landed a blow on the man, the shake of the blast gusting through the dining hall.

Elgan remained unharmed, largely thanks to his shield.

This only further angered William. He pummelled the magical barrier, his expression growing more monstrous with every blow.

His opponent made no attempt to fight back. Dylan could only assume the man was no match for William's strength. But huddling into a ball, relying solely on his shield, wouldn't keep him from William's wrath forever. A marbled effect, like oil spreading across a puddle, already crazed the surface. The shield flickered in and out of existence, reappearing smaller every time.

Dylan got to his feet, shrugging off Henrie's attempt to keep him in place. Elgan deserved some manner of punishment for being the catalyst that drove Cari to take her life, but he wasn't about to let William beat the man to death.

Others closed around the pair before Dylan had taken more than a few steps. They dragged William back. He fought them, too, necessitating that he was thrown into a shield of another's making and carted him out of the room. It didn't stop him. He clawed and blasted at the sphere encapsulating him, his efforts only serving to fill the inside with smoke and sparks.

Dylan settled back into his seat. He stared at the door, expecting William to come rushing back in to finish what he had started.

Yelling came from the corridor just outside the entrance. He strained to pick out the actual words to no avail. It was definitely William's voice, but muffled far more than it should've been, especially with the dining hall doors still standing open. Perhaps whoever had contained him continued to do so until William's guardians, or the overseers, could arrive.

They would put him in isolation for this. Confined to an *infitialis* cell, he woud be temporarily stripped of his magic, made safe until his guardian had helped him work through his grief and anger. He definitely wasn't in any state to be allowed into the brawl.

One less to fight. That thought wasn't a relief. It had come with a terrible price. "Cari," he whispered into the sudden hush that followed William's expulsion from the room. Being elven, his friends would easily hear the man as though he still stood before them.

"I know," Henrie said, patting Dylan's back. "I can't believe she's gone."

Dylan grunted an agreement. He hadn't known her very well, despite them sharing similar tasks in the library. Most of what he recalled were little things, like her fondness for dwarven folklore or her eerie ability to pinpoint the exact tome someone required. He couldn't imagine what thoughts had driven her to such a decision.

"Well, *I* can't believe Will was indecisive," Nestria said. She lifted her mug, tipping it back to drain the contents.

"What does *that* matter?" Henrie challenged.

"It proves he's even more of an idiot than I gave him credit for," she muttered into her drink, her voice amplified by the empty mug. "Indecisives are too greedy for their own good. They get all the trouble they deserve."

"That's a bit harsh," Dylan said. Of the spellsters who bounced from being intimate from one gender to another, Dylan had never witnessed any of them be the actual cause of any grievances they were blamed for. Why anyone would risk being labelled as such always puzzled him.

Indecisive might, as many people claimed, run the risk of increasing their chances of being caught, but he didn't think it would be more than the rest of them if others didn't intervene. What Elgan had done to William was common.

When it came to the other sexualities, being outed was often brought upon them by bad luck. Occasionally, another was to blame, like what had happened with Ben and Jenny. With indecisives, it was always another spellster who outed them to the guardians. In some instances, they weren't even intimately involved.

But where someone like Ben was monitored largely around women, his every move judged and speculated upon as though the man had no self-control, an indecisive would have the same treatment for all genders no matter their personal feelings. They wouldn't have a moment's peace unless alone or asleep. Each attempt at socialisation would be prodded and poked, pulled apart to find some deeper meaning that wasn't there. William would be shunned, spoken of in hushed tones as though they spoke of a monster. Another example of why indecisives weren't to be trusted.

Dylan couldn't imagine a worst fate to live through.

"*Harry* is indecisive," Henrie pointed out, drawing Dylan back into the heated conversation his friends had been having. They'd both heard Nestria rant on about indecisives before. She always spoke as though they had personally wronged her.

Nestria slammed her empty mug onto the table. "No, she's not. She settled down. Chose a side." She wrinkled her nose at the arguing as it continued outside of the dining hall. "They'd all be better off if they did the same."

The muscle in Henrie's jaw visibly twitched. "I don't appreciate the intonation there," he growled, baring his teeth. His canines weren't the longest Dylan had ever seen on an elf, but they outmatched Nestria's by a half. "Especially when Harry isn't here to defend herself."

Scoffing, Nestria rolled her eyes. "All I'm saying is Harry was on a slippery slope towards being outed before—"

"By who?" Dylan interjected. "*You?* I thought you two were friends." Who could they trust to keep each other's secrets if not those they held dear? Any one of them had the power to send another of their friends into the chasm of solitary or the stifling reality of being forever under their guardian's eye.

"Doesn't matter, does it?" she replied, a little too sweetly for Dylan's liking. "She decided she liked men more."

"She doesn't just like men more," Henrie hissed. "She likes *me* over everyone."

"Which is precisely what I just said."

"No, it isn't."

Dylan leant back in his chair, shutting out his friends as they continued to bicker in low tones. No matter how Henrie tried, there would be no convincing Nestria she was wrong. Especially not about indecisives.

He'd only ever spoken to one apart from Harriet. Most were skittish when it came to the topic, afraid of spouting incriminating words to the wrong people to speak more than a few of truth.

Harriet had tried to explain it once, but he hadn't understood how she had known with such certainty. Couldn't understand how anyone knew. He grasped the concept on a base level. If a person found one gender attractive, then why not two? Or four? Or all five? But it was one thing to recognise when multiple genders were aesthetically pleasing—even Nestria acknowledged that wasn't a peculiar thing to note—but to have that recognition lead to physical attraction and desire for more than one?

He knew picking a side, as Nestria called it, wasn't simple, no matter what she claimed. If one gender could be ignored, then why not another? Or all? He had been propositioned in the not-so-distant past by admittedly handsome men. Accepting their advances over that of women would've been the easier route, negating the avoidance of patrolling guardians whilst hopping from one section of the tower to another.

Some nights, it was even tempting.

Would he like it? He didn't know. He'd never tried, had never considered one night as worth the risk of being labelled as indecisive and spending the rest of his life being trailed everywhere by his guardian.

What he *did* know was that, indecisive or not, those who were outed grew bitter and reckless. Sometimes, dangerous enough to simply disappear. He wouldn't wish that sort of punishment on people he disliked, never mind those he considered as friends. It wouldn't cross Henrie's mind, either. Or Sulin's. Both men had clashes with their own small-minded adversaries.

But Nestria?

Once, he would've asserted her as being not the type to out anyone. But he was getting less certain about that, too.

A chorus of screams erupted from out in the hall, jolting Dylan from his musing. His friends had both stood, facing down each other over the table, but their attention was now drawn to the dining hall's entrance.

More people poured through the doorway. Dylan all but fell over his chair in his haste to join the throng. He sidled between a pair of men who were slower to follow. People pressed against each other until they were almost one block.

At his back, he caught Henrie and Nestria's exasperated cries for him to stay put, amongst other things. Dylan ignored them. He didn't need his friends telling him how the guardians would arrive soon to snuff out any commotion, they always popped up when trouble arose. They might already be there wading through the same swarm of people. Or even have made it to the source.

He finally passed under the door's archway. The crowd out in the corridor held the same number of people, but now they were able to spread out. Being taller than the majority of those around him, Dylan spied the culprit.

Sure enough, William was still the centre of everyone's attention.

Still just as mad, although he didn't look as though he was laying into anyone. It was difficult to tell, with the man only visible from his shoulders and up, but William paced in a circle like a caged rat. He waved his fist at someone out of Dylan's view. Insults came thick and fast, almost blurring into one long word. And—

Dylan's heart stuttered for a bit at the flash of purple in the man's hand. Was William clutching a piece of *infitialis*? He had to be mistaken. The metal was only allowed outside of the laboratories in a worked state and, in any case, a spellster of William's strength wouldn't be allowed near raw ore. Even alchemists weren't allowed access to more than a few specks of the metal until they'd proved a mastery over the instability.

But outside of a collar, worked *infitialis* meant an alchemist's dagger.

Surely, the man wasn't out of his mind enough to snatch one from an alchemist. Spellster or otherwise, everyone knew such weapons were dangerous. Dylan knew from Sulin that the alchemist daggers came with a particularly nasty edge. Not a soul within the tower would be foolish enough to do anything stupid with them.

Dylan squinted at the scene. The space around the man was abnormally large for a simple fight, even one including magic. He elbowed his way through the crowd, halting as he breached the inner ring.

William stood in the middle of the space. In his hands, the blade of a dagger gleamed in the candlelight. As much as Dylan had hoped to be wrong, the colour was an unmistakable shade of purple.

A man lay sprawled on the floor nearby, conscious but clearly shaken. Had the dagger belonged to *this* alchemist? Dylan edged closer, kneeling to lay a hand on the man's shoulder. A quick delve with his magic brought up only a few scrapes and a bruised hip, no doubt gotten in the fall. No cuts. "You're all right."

The alchemist nodded. "I am, but he…" He gestured to William.

William continued to wave the dagger about, slashing the air before anyone who looked like they might come closer.

Dylan's gaze was drawn to a shielded group on the other side of the space. They appeared to protect a second reclining figure, their combined efforts enough of a deterrent for William, even in his agitated state.

Was it Elgan? Too many people crowded around the figure to be certain. An older woman Dylan recognised as one of the healers knelt over them. Had he been struck down by magic or the dagger? If it was the latter, then surely no amount of magic would keep them from death.

"He's gone mad," the alchemist continued. "Barrelled straight into me." He stiffened. "Is that my...?" Frantic, the man patted himself down. "That's *my* dagger!" He grabbed Dylan's shoulders, turning him. "You've got to get it back. The blade... it'll—"

"I know." He'd heard the rumours about *infitialis* daggers before. Where the collars were harmless, if reputedly unpleasant, blades made from the metal needed only to break the skin to kill.

And, with the way William lashed out, the man was definitely going to hurt someone.

Before Dylan could stand and face the man, another figure emerged from the crowd. *Harriet?* His friend hadn't been in the dining hall earlier. Had someone fetched her? But she was no match for William's strength. Did they think her capable of talking him down?

Harriet squared up to William, commanding his attention with a subtle thrum of magic through the air. She stepped closer, her gaze dropping to the dagger for a moment. "Will, please. Stop. You'll get through this, I swear, but you need to—"

"Really?" William scoffed. "It's all so easy for you to say. Isn't it, *settler*?" He practically spat the last word, his bitterness coating every sliding syllable.

"Will!" an unfamiliar voice, deep and authoritative, boomed down the corridor.

The crowd parted to allow a guardian entry.

The man fearlessly strode towards William, his expression stern. "Put the dagger down, son."

"Papa," William murmured, his voice choked with tears. "I want you to know, I don't blame you. This isn't—" His lips trembled into a watery smile. "I can't..." He pressed the dagger blade to his throat.

"Will, no!" The man's guardian rushed for him. As did Harriet and a handful of others quick enough to break from their shock.

A blast rippled from William, expanding like a popped bubble.

Dylan flung up a shield, shaping it to let the force sail over him with little strain to himself. All around, people were buffeted about, tumbling across the floor like balls of hair.

By the time anyone could regain their footing, William had collapsed.

Dylan raced to William's side, reaching the man before the healer could collect herself. Dropping to his knees, he laid a hand on William's throat, trying to slow the flow of blood pumping out. The slice was deep. No chance of the blade having missed an artery.

He unleashed his magic, focusing all his attention on sealing the wound. His power slipped through the man's body, effortlessly working to draw out the energy it needed to focus on the repair.

William wasn't a sickly man. He wouldn't be capable of fighting in the brawl tomorrow, but he would live.

Yet, there was no waning in the flow of blood. The cut failed to shrink and seal.

Dylan floundered for a moment. He'd never tried to heal someone this badly injured. How long did it take for a person to bleed out? He pushed a little of his own power into the mending. William's body latched onto it like a starving kitten. Dylan let it take what was needed. He had plenty to spare.

"It's useless," someone declared.

He glanced up to find the healer standing over them.

"His wound is fatal." She laid a hand on Dylan's shoulder. "You must know that no one has ever healed an *infitialis* cut."

He did. But William also wasn't yet dead. "Then I'll be the first," he growled through clenched teeth, his focus on keeping the man alive wavering slightly. Did she really expect him to stand by whilst William died? What healer wouldn't fight to keep a person from death despite the odds?

The man's body continued to siphon Dylan's power, demanding more with no hint of the gash closing. Never had he encountered a pull like this. The insistent call tugged at his core, clawed at his heart, squeezed his lungs.

Dylan knelt hunched over William, his head spinning. He fought the pull to no avail. Like a twig caught in a maelstrom, the call whisked him along and dragged him under. He struggled to breathe as much as the man he attempted to heal. His chest ached, his heart threatening to burst through his ribs.

If he just put a little more of himself into it, then maybe…

The world grew small and dark. A mumble of voices tumbled through his ears, distant and close, loud and ghostly.

A little more…

His heart stuttered in his chest, echoed by William's fluttering pulse. Was it working? Maybe. He felt something creeping alongside his magic. Sluggish. Warm.

A tiny bit more…

Someone hauled him back from the man. They dragged him across the tiles like he was a delinquent.

Dylan flailed. At first, he fought the person taking him away then, as his mind cleared, he fended off all of William's unconscious attempts to reconnect with Dylan's magic.

The call followed, leaving Dylan clambering backwards until he collapsed into a pair of familiar arms.

"Easy now," Tricia murmured, stroking his hair as though he was still a child. "Have you severed the connection?"

Dylan nodded. Physically laying a hand on an injured person made healing easier, but it wasn't necessary. Once started, the patient could continue using a healer's power to finish mending what they hadn't the strength to. In all his years of healer training, he hadn't encountered a patient with such a vicious need. It had been like feeding a parasite.

But the attempts had suddenly ceased.

His gaze slid to William, dread clogging his throat.

The man lay still. Blood pooled around him, soaking into the gaps between the tiles. William's guardian knelt over the body, his face buried in the robe.

"I couldn't stop it," Dylan whispered. "I—" Was he really *that* out of practice? *No.* Healing Nestria had been easy. "I wasn't... strong enough." Had his guardian been right about his abilities all this time? If he wasn't unable to stop one man from dying, what good was he to the army? They had to need more than weapons.

"You never would be," Tricia replied. "The daggers are designed to leave a wound no magic could heal."

He slowly became aware of the crowd and their silence. Something else pulled their attention away from the death. It had them shuffling about like chickens in a coop.

"All right," a stern voice boomed down the corridor. "There's no point in lingering."

Dylan twisted in his guardian's grasp to spy the overseers marching through the crowd. People hastened to get out of the way, to not fall too long under their eye.

The woman spearheading the group briskly clapped her hands. "You heard. All this fuss only reiterates what we have always told you about dallying with people. You all have your tasks. Get to them."

The alchemist whose dagger William stole slunk closer. He collected his dagger, holding the handle as if expecting the weapon to savage him. Blood dripped off the curved blade as he carried it off. No doubt to the lab. Maybe even to destroy the weapon.

"*You,*" said the sole elven member of the overseers, singling out Dylan with the beckoning crook of her finger. "You must head for the training arenas. This changes nothing about tomorrow."

Dylan found himself woodenly obeying before her words sunk in. Of course the overseers wouldn't delay the brawl because a spellster had taken their life. This wasn't the first time, although, he had only ever heard rumours and suspicions.

But the woman was wrong. William was meant to compete. To win. At least, that was the belief of every person Henrie had spoken to. If the man had been good enough, he could've been the one to turn the war back on the Udynean Empire.

They might've completely lost that chance now.

Tricia clung to his sleeve as he went to leave, rooting him in place. "You can't expect him to compete tomorrow," she challenged. "After what he saw—"

The overseer wrinkled her nose. Those dark green eyes regarded his guardian with disdain. "Those who gain the honour of fighting for our king will witness worse. Or has your comfortable life here made you forget what the Udyneans are capable of?"

"No," Dylan mumbled, despite the question not being aimed at him. He didn't know of any Demarner who wasn't aware of the atrocities the Udynea Empire inflicted upon their western border.

Tricia bowed her head. "Of course I haven't forgotten. But he cannot train. He's exhausted from trying to heal." She gestured to William's body being carried away as if the overseers hadn't noticed what had been at the centre of the chaos.

Dylan frowned. She often assumed that of him, but he was rarely taken to such levels of weariness. The drain on his magic had disorientated him, but he felt no wearier than when he had awoken.

One of the human women scoffed. "Then this is a valuable lesson in not trying to heal such wounds. I'm sure he has learnt not to repeat such mistakes. Just as I am certain he realises how foolish this all was and how William could've avoided his fate."

Choking down the anger bubbling in his throat, Dylan fought to keep his expression neutral. Was she blaming William for his own death? It wasn't his fault. Nestria would disagree, but Dylan would hear no talks of blame falling upon the man.

Another was responsible for today. *Elgan.* Outing was a nasty act. None of them deserved it. It might not always end in a death, but it wasn't uncommon. And this one had taken two lives.

He searched the crowd for Elgan, expecting to find the man slinking off to wreak havoc in someone else's life. There was no chance of him escaping tonight without learning a severe lesson. Not if Dylan had any say in the matter.

His gaze landed on the group that had been shielding someone earlier. With the threat gone, they had dropped their guard.

Elgan knelt in the middle, a hand pressed to his shoulder. Blood soaked his sleeve. Had he been struck? But the healer would've seen to him. Whatever injury William inflected would have—

The dagger. William's wound had been immediately fatal not because of the blade, but the placement. If the *infitialis* blade had broken skin, then it was only a matter of time before Elgan bled out.

Three lives taken. Dylan had never heard of an outed spellster being successful in retaliating against the one who alerted the guardians, but that was the reality Elgan now faced. His death would be slow. It could take hours or days. He might even last a week. But the wound would take him.

And all over what? Because William preferred more than men? Why did it matter so much to people? Dylan didn't care if the women who chose to sleep with him also dallied with others, regardless of what gender those others were. So few were exclusive, everyone shared the same risk.

Grumbling to himself, Dylan stalked down the corridor, aiming for the training arenas. He hadn't even reached his thirtieth year and yet, the older he got, the more disgusted he became over the tower's squabbles and politics. How the elders accepted this was beyond him. There had to be some way to keep it from happening. He couldn't see how, but he would find it.

Was winning the war against the Udynea Empire the key? If spellsters weren't feared and beset upon by normal citizens, then they would be allowed to leave the tower as they chose. They could have communities. Maybe even families. An existence out from under the overseers' sight and influence.

It would take time. It was entirely possible he would never see the outcome. But if he could help be the catalyst, then he would give it his all. To change the future for everyone, to keep deaths like this from happening.

For Ceri. For William.

CHAPTER 5

Dylan leant against the tower's outer wall, his gaze wandering the central structure as he caught his breath. His opponents were only harmless globes of light, but he'd been training for hours, trying to keep his mind away from any thoughts of the brawl or William.

No matter what he did, he couldn't shake the image. The sensation of William dying.

"You want to call it a day?" Nestria asked. She had arrived late afternoon to help him sharpen his reflexes, taking over from another who had looked far too young to be training as hard as Dylan. A lot of the spellsters using the arenas looked to be more in their teenage years. Or maybe he was getting old.

"Not yet," he replied. If he won the brawl, he would be stopping dozens of needless deaths. He had to prove he was worthy of the placement. Had to make it count. Had to be sure he was ready. "Go again."

Before Nestria could summon anything, the bell rang for the evening meal. The announcement also served as a reminder to everyone that being outside was no longer allowed for the day.

Dylan's stomach gurgled in anticipation of a meal. When had he last eaten? He couldn't recall anything beyond breakfast. His focus had already been divided by training and the events of the morning.

That would explain the slight sway in his steps. Skipping meals wasn't ideal at the best of times. If he had known the overseers planned to send him to train, he would've requested something heartier from the cooks. Magic demanded a lot of energy, especially when in heavy use.

Coaxing the elements to obey him was easy. He could pull water and heat from the air—providing the conditions had enough of either—to create ice or make fire. Both were easy magic, things he had learnt as a child. Anything greater required him to put his own energy into it.

Something as intricate as healing would only take from the source of power when the patient had nothing to spare.

Like William.

Closing his eyes, he rubbed at his temples with a thumb and forefinger. That man's face would haunt his dreams for a long time, he just knew it. Longer still if he couldn't make it to the end of the brawl. *It shouldn't have happened.* He wished with all his heart that it hadn't.

Nothing could change that it had.

"Don't look so glum," Nestria said. She gave his back a solid couple of pats, gasping when it was enough to throw him off balance. "Maybe you should ask the cooks for extra tonight?"

"Won't need to," he mumbled. The overseers would ensure all brawl participants were sound enough for tomorrow. He would still need to conserve what he could for the final fight against the leashed one. *If I get that far.*

He shook his head, trying to free the negative thoughts. His balance swayed, forcing him to lean on a nearby tree or fall on his face. *Stupid.* He should've eaten something else hours ago. Should've realised that everything he had eaten during breakfast would've been used during his failed healing attempt. And his training would've taken more.

He couldn't fail due to something as simple as the lack of self-management he currently suffered from.

Nestria followed at his side as they headed for the tower's side entrance. Whilst the central structure held hundreds of rooms, this was the only other way in beyond the main entrance and a few of the lower windows. Once, in the distant past, even that little doorway hadn't existed. "Do you really think you're ready for tomorrow?" she asked, pressing one side of her face against his arm.

"Yes," Dylan grunted as they entered the tower. He had to be.

Others also funnelled through the entrance and down the corridors. Most of them chatted amongst themselves, either about the day's work or sharing idle gossip that was of no interest to Dylan. A few glanced his way and muttered amongst themselves in tones that he couldn't hear, but made Nestria's pale face grow increasingly dark.

Ahead, the crowd parted around a single figure.

Being taller than the majority of those around him, Dylan made out the face long before his friend. *Tricia?* He hesitated, not sure why his guardian was clearly waiting for him at the end of the corridor. Unlike some guardians, Tricia rarely sought him most days. He had his tasks in the library, knew what to do and made little fuss about doing them.

His guardian spotted him and marched through the shifting crowd to halt before them. "A word?" She sent Nestria ahead with the twitch of her head before Dylan could answer. "Come with me." Instead of taking the same path as the others, his guardian continued back the way Dylan had come.

He trailed behind her, questions bubbling and bouncing about his mind. Was this to do with the brawl? He'd never spoken much with those who had been in one, did the overseers insist on participants sleeping in different quarters the night before? Perhaps the participants also dined separately. Giving them a substantial meal away from jealous eyes made sense.

Although, being tasked with escorting him to this room didn't explain Tricia's behaviour. It wasn't blatantly obvious, but the way she walked down the halls lacked any of her usual authority. She paused at each corner they took, peeking around it a fraction of a moment before passing.

If he didn't know better, he would say she skulked like a spellster trying to avoid getting caught after a night in another's bed.

"I've been training all day," he reminded her, as if his gurgling stomach couldn't be heard on the other side of the continent. "I need to eat."

"Here." She unslung a bundle from her hip to shove into his hands. Warmth emanated from within the cloth.

Peeling back the layers revealed a couple of scones brimming with chunks of bacon. She must've swiped them from the kitchens before coming here.

He devoured both to the last crumb. It wasn't enough, but it kept his stomach occupied. Scones also meant the cooks had prepared stew.

"Better?" Tricia barely waited for him to nod before continuing, "We have to move quickly, now. Won't be long before they notice your absence." She hauled open the door and waved him through.

Dylan lingered in the doorway. Beyond, the garden stared back. He had walked the lines of fruit trees and medicinal bushes. Had helped Harriet in potting the more fragile plants that resided in the glasshouses.

It all looked strange in the dusk. Twisted. Foreboding.

"Hurry," his guardian hissed.

"Where are you taking me?" It wasn't like her to shirk the rules. She had heard the bell. She would know he wasn't allowed outside the central tower until daybreak.

Tricia mimed for him to remain silent.

He trailed behind her as she strode down the path leading to the training arenas. At first, he considered the possibility she had gained an exemption for him to practice further despite the lateness, but she didn't pause.

Instead, she led him to the old shed that jutted from the outer wall. Once, the space within the wall itself had been enough to house all the gardening equipment. Now, a completely different structure, made of wood and glass sat closer to the new garden beds.

Was she trying to get him thrown into isolation? He'd been put into one of the cells for venturing into the outer courtyard that separated the tower from the rest of the world. It had only been once during his teenage years and he hadn't intended to leave the confines of the outer wall.

He simply hadn't known the guards would spot him making the attempt.

Dylan wasn't about to do anything that might send him back into those cells. Losing contact with his magic had felt worse than facing death.

A collar would also strip him of his magic. But whilst the sheets of *infitialis* lining the cell walls were one step up from raw metal, the collars were worked. There was something in them—or was it the process of attachment to a person? Wasn't that what Sulin would yammer about?—that enabled the leashed to use magic at the order of those commanding them.

He didn't like the idea, but if it got him to where he wanted to be, then it would be worth the sacrifice.

Tricia halted beneath the lean-to recently tacked onto the front of the shed. With her dark attire, she blended into the shadows. She rattled the handle briefly, before shoving the door open. "Hurry now," she whispered, darting into the shed.

Dylan followed, still not sure what his guardian planned. "What are we doing here?" The shed held nothing of any interest to anyone beyond gardeners and herbalists. He had a smattering of knowledge on toxic plants from his healer training, but little else.

"Shut the door," Tricia hissed.

He obeyed, the act throwing the room into darkness. He brought a globe of light to life, balancing the orb on his palm. Evidence of disuse was all around. Broken tools sat against the wall where people had left them, no doubt to repair, and never returned. Crates, barrels and sacks were piled everywhere with no particular order, many of them covered in dust.

Whilst he knew the old shed had become superfluous, he hadn't realised they'd completely abandoned the place.

"Are you going to tell me why we're here?" He didn't want to disobey his guardian, but maybe the overseers would understand if he did so because of her suspicious behaviour.

"In due time, child." She motioned him to be still with the distracted flap of a hand. "First, I must find out if something is true.

Just keep your light high."

Not knowing what else to do, he settled on a pile of musty sacks—grain from the way it gave beneath him—and watched his guardian pace the room. She'd an odd interest in the far wall, alternating between pressing against the stonework and fussing with items scattered on the floor.

One section of the wall was shielded by crates and barrels, all stacked to the ceiling. Tricia squeezed through a gap between them, disappearing from sight. Muffled mutterings and grunts emanated from the other side.

A slightly clearer exclamation preceded Tricia's demand, "Bring your light."

He squeezed himself through the same gap, ducking after clipping his head on the bottom of a crate. The mass wobbled, threatening to come crashing down. He gave the crate a curious poke to a similar effect. It was almost as though the entire stack was empty. But that couldn't be right. Yet, what could they possibly contain to make them so light?

"Quickly, now!" his guardian snapped.

Dylan pressed on, trying to avoid being buried beneath the crates. It was deeper than his original assessment, almost forming a winding tunnel between the wooden crates and the stone wall in places. The further in he went, the less headroom he had. Eventually, he was forced to either crawl or walk practically doubled over.

Passing the last of the crates, he came to a halt in what appeared to be the far corner of the room. Dylan got to his feet and took in the space. There was nothing here beyond the stone walls, but the space the crates left definitely seemed deliberate. But why would anyone section off a back corner so thoroughly?

"Come closer," Tricia said. She knelt beside the wall, her arm elbow-deep in a hole in the stonework.

"What are you doing?" And why was she rummaging in what looked like a mouse hole?

"Patience."

A rusty click reverberated through the wall and a section of it swung inwards, revealing trimmed grassland stretching all the way to a hulking line of impossibly tall shadows. *Beyond the walls*. He'd seen pieces from the tower windows, distant and hazy like a painting.

He stuck his hand through the opening. A breeze stirred along the low grass, it curled about his ankles and disturbed the dust. *Not an illusion*. His guardian had opened some sort of secret entrance.

How had she known this was here? And for how long?

"Let's go."

He faced Tricia, surprised to find her shouldering a sizable pack.

"Go? You mean—?" He backed away from the doorway. "I can't leave." Only leashed spellsters left the tower. "It's not safe. The King's Hounds…" They would hunt him. Kill him. Maybe even use his blood for whatever unspeakable practices they did.

"I know it's sudden, but we don't have time for me to explain right now."

"No, please, do go on," a voice said from somewhere in the shadows.

Dylan turned to spy a figure stepping out of the gloom. *The elven overseer*. Had she been in the shed the whole time? Or had she snuck in whilst his guardian fussed with the hidden door?

"I have all the time in the world to hear what you have to say," the woman continued.

"Overseer, I—" Tricia fell silent as the overseer held up her hand.

The woman gave a piercing whistle, the sound answered by others both on the other side of the shed door and outside the wall.

People swarmed in through the shed's normal entrance. They smashed the crates blocking the path with wild swings of their swords. Splinters and chunks of wood flew everywhere.

Dylan flung up an arc of a shield, protecting both himself and his guardian from the debris. The figures halted before the shimmering curve of the barrier, half of them looking to the overseer for direction whilst the rest merely stared at him.

The figures were garbed in leather armour. Many continued to brandish their swords as if the blade were of use against his shield. They had to be part of the guard unit that protected the main gate.

Only when he heard Tricia's protesting grunt did Dylan realise another group had come through the secret door. A pair of guards shoved Tricia to the ground, keeping her there with the heel of their hands pressed to the back of her shoulders.

Another couple grabbed Dylan's arms, holding him firmly in place and clearly confused when he didn't try to fight them.

"Drop your shield," the overseer commanded him, her gaze unwavering from his guardian.

Dylan obeyed, the shimmering arc dissipating at a thought.

"You always were a deceptive one," the overseer continued to Tricia. "But it would appear my original misgivings were correct. Although, I must commend you for raising your charge to obey the law, even when freedom is dangled before him. It is good to see that one of you has some semblance of sense."

Tricia muttered something. The words were too muffled for Dylan to make out, but his name had definitely been amongst them.

However, the overseer's elven hearing would've picked up everything. "If you think him that unruly, then perhaps it's time for a firmer hand." She considered him with an edge that set his skin to tingling. Her eyes gleamed in the globe's light like a cat's.

Dylan swallowed, fighting the urge to bring his shield back up.

"Escort the guardian to the dungeon," the woman commanded the guards. "And have the spellster put in isolation."

"No!" Tricia fought the guards restraining her. "Please, not that. He's done nothing wrong. This was my decision. He didn't know about the door."

"And now he does."

His guardian hung her head.

Dylan mimicked the act. He had heard whispers—the shadows of rumours—of spellsters managing to escape. Never how. And none ever returned. The overseers wouldn't allow him to spread word of this place to anyone.

"If you don't win," the overseer said. "Then, you'll be placed back into isolation. Understood?"

He nodded. He comprehended what she meant entirely. Isolation was a punitive measure, not a life sentence. Losing the brawl might see him returned to the cells, but he wouldn't be there for long.

His gaze drifted to the grassland. He could free himself from the guards. Maybe even escape long enough to lose them, if he was lucky. But they would only send the King's Hounds after him. He'd become another mark on the list of those who had mysteriously disappeared.

"Dylan," his guardian grunted as they hauled to her feet. No longer pinned down by the guards, she tugged the hem of her tunic straight. "I know I said not to win, but—"

"I'll make you proud." He had to.

That same sad pride curled her lips. She gave a stern bob of her head. "I know you will, my sweet boy." Turning to the guards flanking her, she gave them a curt nod and marched out the shed's normal door as if she hadn't just been apprehended.

The guards holding Dylan soon followed. He didn't struggle, but they kept their grip firm nevertheless.

Outside, the shadow of the tower shrouded the grounds. It wouldn't have stopped any elven eyes, but there appeared to be no one else around. Not even one of the hundreds of servants that lived in the tower's outer wall and kept the tower running.

Inside was no different. Everywhere they went, the corridors were deserted. Strange, even for the time of day. Had they sent word ahead? Somehow gotten the guardians to clear the path of every single spellster? Why? The isolation cells weren't a secret.

Were the overseers afraid he might reveal what he knew? What good would shouting about a secret entrance do him? Anyone who heard would think he raved nonsense. Everyone knew the tower complex had one entrance. It was an undisputed fact.

The steps leading to the isolation cells were smaller than Dylan remembered from his last excursion down here. Each one was only wide enough for half of his foot, necessitating that he sidle down them or risk losing his balance and break his neck.

A door stood at the bottom of the stairs, the only thing between them and the cells. It might as well not have been there. The thrum of *infitialis* hit his senses long before he stepped inside.

Simple torchlight illuminated the room and its several dozen cells. Each light source was spaced out to light up four cell entrances. The doors looked so ordinary. Simple iron and wood with no openings beyond a little flap at the base. Only a spellster's senses would pick up the rarer metal that lined each cell.

The moans of other spellsters reached his ears. Some of it was little more than crying. Others swore—begged—they'd behave, if only the guards would let them out. One, the sound coming from somewhere at the far end, sounded like the raspy trail of a person who had screamed themselves hoarse and still wasn't ready to give in.

Dylan took a deep breath. *Ignore it.* There was nothing he could do. Not for them. Not for himself. They all had to get through their time here on their own.

The guards spoke with those assigned to watch over the cells. One of them hauled open a door. The torchlight fell upon the interior. Little shared the space, just a bucket and a sack of straw. "In you go."

Dylan shuffled closer to the cell entrance, stalling having his magic severed for as long as he could. Already, the closeness to the metal had a numbness soaking into his bones like a winter mist. *It's only for the night.* Most of the spellsters sent down here had to suffer far longer than that.

The guard gave him a shove and he stumbled into the cell, halting a few steps in.

The door slammed shut at his back, throwing him into utter darkness.

He rubbed at his arms, trying to stave off a chill that had nothing to do with the cell's temperature. The spark running through his blood that he had always associated with his magic was snuffed. Suppressed. Not as shocking as his first time down here, but no less absolute.

The metallic swing of a flap preceded a beam of light from the bottom of the door. A tray slid through the gap, the array of food upon it far more than the last simple meal he'd been given during his time here. It looked to be more of the scones Tricia had given him alongside a bowl of stew, as well as a smaller dish containing nuts and dried fruit.

He fell upon the meal, shoving a scone into his mouth before the flap had a chance to fully shut. Thrown back into darkness by the second mouthful, he consumed the rest via touch and smell.

With stomach full, he felt along the walls until he found a corner to settle in. *I can do this.* It was one night. He had weathered more in the past. Then he just had to fight twenty people, including the leashed one. All of whom would've been well-rested and properly fed. *I can't lose.*

He wished the little voice telling him so sounded surer.

CHAPTER 6

Even at its darkest, the hallway leading to the duelling arena had never seemed this ominous. Dylan marched along its dismal barren length, hemmed in by nineteen others like they were guards leading him to the slaughter, his stomach bubbling with more than what mere nerves could account for.

This could very well be the last day he would be able to choose when he used magic. Leashing took place immediately after the brawls and the victor was taken from the tower the next morning.

Before now, he would've considered the thought with jubilation. Was this not what he had wanted since childhood? To show how his power made him an asset to the kingdom rather than a liability?

And yet, the thought of losing his friends, the men and women as dear to him as any sibling could be, struck him cold. Losing might mean his death, but winning would mean never seeing them again. Not even for the chance to say goodbye.

He closed his eyes and took a deep breath. This was not the time for second thoughts. Winning would also make him a part of the defence standing between his friends and the brutish might of the Udynean Empire. He would make that count.

Dylan peered at the surrounding competition, trying to recognise faces and determine their weaknesses. To his left marched Sophie, reputedly one to prefer fire as a weapon over other, cleaner, attacks. She'd tied back her pale yellow hair, making her naturally cold face even more hostile, but it was definitely her.

The person ahead of her with a frizzy mop of dirty-blond hair had a memorable air about him. Dylan couldn't make out a face, but it had to be Fredrick. The man was more swift than strong, able to counter quicker than most, but if he truly was less-than-serious about the brawl, then he would go down before the last of them.

Some of the others seemed familiar, in a distant sort of way. A few eyed him in turn. He hunched his shoulders, trying to shrink his height and look less threatening. Although he had the advantage of them not witnessing his technique whilst in the bouts, the same reason wasn't in his favour. He could very well wind up having to make a split-second decision that could cost him.

Sophie must've caught him looking as her head snapped to him. "Did we get enough rest?" she asked, her grin bordering on manic.

He smiled back. "I got plenty." They wouldn't know where he had truly been. No one would. The best rumours would've given them was his unexplained disappearance. Given the suddenness of his integration into the brawl, most enquiries would've been brushed off as him getting special treatment.

Nor would they be aware of what would happen to him if he didn't win. Even Dylan wasn't entirely certain. The army always needed spellsters to bolster their ranks and counter those amongst the enemy's troops.

If he failed now, would the overseers keep him for the next time? What if there wasn't a next time? What if the army pushed Udynea back and spellsters weren't needed? Would they truly confine him to the isolation cells for the rest of his life?

Don't think about it. He had to keep his focus on now, on the brawl and whatever strategies he could recall from his talks with Henrie and Nestria. Whatever happened later would depend on where he stood at the end of the brawl.

They stepped through the archway. No one had tried to mend the arena since the night of the *infitialis* explosion. Strange how he couldn't recall the scorch marks and tiny hollows littering the floor. His gaze swung to the targeting blocks. One still stood where he had pushed it against the arena's shield, its face cracked and charred.

Dylan frowned. The uneven footing would add another degree of difficulty for some. Even with Mary's miscalculation damaging the arena, the overseers had no choice but to use it or postpone the brawl. The tower might have a number of smaller training grounds, but this was the only one surrounded in the old shield, the only one capable of absorbing the magic from a group of strong spellsters fighting in earnest.

The doors swung shut as the last of them entered. As one, the group ventured into the centre of the arena. All around them, amongst the narrow rows of seating, both spellster and servant alike jockeyed for a prime position to watch them battle each other for the chance to defend the border from Udynea.

Already, the overseers stood on their podium, waiting with that same unbending calmness they always showed the world. Like statues.

Dylan searched the throng. His friends sat somewhere in that mass of spectators. His gaze skimmed the lower row, where several adolescents sat alongside their guardians. Not as many as when he'd once sat there. Only those in their mid-teens who displayed the strength and discipline worthy of eventually trying for this honour were allowed to watch at such a young age. A few bore the awed expression that spoke of seeing this place for the first time.

There were his friends, standing on the third row up. Nestria and Henrie waved like mad, whilst Sulin and Launtil struggled to stay in place. None of them looked confused about his absence. Had they been given some lie to keep them placated?

Dylan held up his hand to let them know their antics had been spotted.

Nestria jumped up and down. She increased her mad waving and pointed at her other hand.

He peered at her, just making out how his oldest friend held up two fingers.

Smothering a smile, he gave a vigorous nod. *Two minutes, got it.* He hadn't forgotten Nestria's plan to bet on how long Sophie lasted here. Even if he wound up being bested, the least he could do was ensure she kept Sulin's promised bottle of not-yet-brewed alcohol.

His focus returned to the overseers. *Why are they taking so long?* He had witnessed plenty of brawls since Tricia had first escorted him to his seat fifteen years ago, one of the overseers should've given the signal to spread out by now.

The doors reopened to admit two other women and silence fell across the arena. One of them was clothed in a dark green robe similar to those he had seen on past leashed spellsters, whilst the other woman was covered from the neck down in a black attire very different to the guardians. They had to be the leashed one and her—

"A hound?" one of the men, a brown-haired human with the most amazing green eyes Dylan had ever seen, muttered to his comrades as the mysterious pair marched to the other end of the arena. "I thought they weren't allowed to come here?"

Dylan gave the darkly-clad woman a fresh look. She held herself with a grace he hadn't seen amongst the guardians or the armed guards protecting the tower gates. It was possible she was one of the King's Hounds. He didn't see any reason to be jittery about it. True, the hounds were trained to hunt down rogue spellsters and bring them to the tower, but they already stood in its heart.

"Maybe she's just dressed as one?" a woman suggested to the man.

"Are you mad?" Sophie snapped. She turned on the woman, the tail of her long hair lashing the air. "Do you know of anyone who dared to mock the hounds by wearing their armour? Of course not, because they're all dead." She sneered at the woman. "That there is the real thing."

"I've heard they drink the blood of every spellster they capture," said one of the other dark-haired men. "That's why they're so good at finding the runaways."

Dylan rolled his eyes. His healing tutors once explained how magic couldn't possibly be absorbed through such absurd means. He couldn't believe those rumours still circulated the tower.

Green-eyes nudged the rumour-spreading man into silence. He jerked his chin towards the podium. Both the hound and the leashed woman had halted at the podium's base. The hound appeared interested in them, her head tilted to one side. Was she evaluating them? Already?

And wasn't it dangerous for them to be *within* the shield at this stage? Were the overseers not wary of stray magic hitting the hound? Or did everyone expect the leashed one to shield them from anything remotely dangerous?

The arena fell silent as one of the overseers raised a brass funnel to her lips. "I'm sure none of you need to be reminded of the rules," she said.

A murmur of agreement rippled through the group. Although Dylan had never competed in the bouts, let alone the final brawl, he'd made a point of memorising the rules.

Non-lethal attacks only. No point in letting the victor wipe out what could potentially become a comrade after the next brawl. Of course, *lethal* had a rather wide definition what with the tower's master healers scattered near the edge of the arena, prepared to attend to the fallen. It didn't necessarily negate the chance of being burnt, electrocuted or even suffering asphyxiation.

His gaze dropped from the overseer to the two women at the other end of the arena. The pair stood in the same pose, eyes forward, hands clasped before them as if they were priestesses listening to the bimonthly choral chants.

Last one standing faces the leashed one. It was more a formality by then, but the final test was necessitated in the off chance that the victor got there by luck. It had never happened in the whole time he'd watched the brawls, but the tower operated under the assumption that there was a first time for everything. After all, no one had attempted crafting a shield from *infitialis* before Mary. And no one was likely to be given sanction to try again.

"Take your places," the overseer ordered.

Their group swiftly disbanded, spreading out in precise steps. Each contestant's space would've been assigned by the overseers during the bouts. Dylan scanned their progress, seeking a place where he could insert himself. *There.* Right between Sophie and Green-eyes. *Perfect.* Was it two minutes Nestria had asked of him? He might just be able to do that after all.

Sophie glared at him as he took up position. She drew her hand across her throat in a swift cutting gesture.

Dylan gritted his teeth. He knew the woman had a reputation for being cold, but did she not think of William's fate? Hadn't she seen the man fall? If not, she surely would've heard.

Focus. If Nestria was right about the woman, then her attacks should be easy to shrug off. Shielding against fire was one of the first spells they taught them, which made her choice of attack all the more ridiculous. Small wonder Sophie had failed in the brawl so many times.

Instead of allowing the woman to goad him, he busied himself with rolling up the sleeves of his robe. The others wore the garments their guardians would've gifted them at the beginning of the bouts; brown robes made from a less flammable fabric and cut in a style more suited to battle with closefitting sleeves. No one appeared to have the forethought to dress him in a similar garb, most likely because of his late addition. It was of little consequence. He would've eagerly fought in his smallclothes for this opportunity.

Feeling watched, he glanced back at the podium, his attention drawn to the hound and how they stared right at him. He shrugged his shoulders. *You're imagining things.* Yes, he stood out. Yes, she had likely been told about his guardian's attempt to run with him. All that meant nothing if he couldn't survive to face off against the leashed one.

"Begin!"

Unfettered magic burst to life, crackling through the arena. Blasts of lightning and fire singed the air, testing defences. Dylan surrounded himself with a heavy shield and tucked its focus into the back of his mind.

Heat blazed across his right flank. *Sophie.*

She stood there, outlined in flames. A child's trick that might intimidate the average magic-fearing soldier on the field, but otherwise unimpressive. Smoke poured from the flames, dark and thick. That was slightly more striking. He hadn't ever been able to get magic-fuelled fire to smoke quite so densely.

Sneering, she threw another fireball at him. It struck his shield and sputtered.

Dylan frowned upon seeing the fury on her face. Although they'd never fought each other, the woman couldn't be foolish enough to believe she'd enough raw strength to break his shield. He had rather expected more from her by now; no one got into the brawl without knowing more than basic battle tactics.

Again, she attacked. This time, he flinched. His shield stopped all but air from passing through and Sophie was busily heating the surrounding air to an intolerable temperature. She was trying to steam him out of his shell rather like a mussel. *Clever*. He could use such a technique to his advantage.

Dylan waited for her to fling another blast before switching the focus of his shield to encapsulate her. Two semicircles shimmered in the air on either side of the woman and, before she could register the danger, he slammed them together with Sophie in the middle.

Inside the bubble, his opponent raged. She threw small balls of fire all around her, trying to break the shield. When that didn't work, the woman resorted to hitting the sphere with fist and foot.

Dylan waited. The balance between making the shield dense enough to hold against her barrage whilst remaining that little bit porous to let her breathe required much of his focus, but it would limit the damage the woman made. Providing she was smart enough to extinguish the flames outlining her body before the bubble filled with smoke.

He eyed the already dark air surrounding the woman. Hopefully, the realisation would come soon, he had no desire to suffocate her.

Sudden, close movement on his left had him whipping his head around in time to spy an object flying his way. Another shield, thin and crude, materialised in front of him, its appearance more instinct than command. It trapped the projectile mere inches from his chest.

Dylan stared at the shimmering tip of the conjured spear, his heart hammering. *So much for non-lethal weapons*. He turned aside and let the spear continue its now harmless passage to the ground.

His gaze swung in the direction it had come from. *Green-eyes*.

Dylan shook his head, bitterly chastising himself. He should've predicted someone would attempt to take advantage of his lack of focus whilst he dealt with another. *Sloppy*. If he was going to win this, he had to be careful.

He thrust his hand towards the man. Lightning shot from his fingers, strong enough to stun without killing. It was a fine distinction. One that his opponents should all know by now.

Green-eyes tried to shield himself. He wasn't fast enough. The lightning hit and the man fell, jerking on the ground. His senses would likely be scrambled for a few days, but the healers would ensure no lasting damage.

Satisfied his attacker wouldn't get back up, Dylan turned back to finish dealing with Sophie.

The shield he'd placed around the woman still held and was full of black smoke. All he could make out of Sophie were her hands weakly hammering against the bottom curve of the ball.

Dylan banished the barrier trapping her. The smoke dissipated, revealing Sophie's gasping form. He sent a blast of air in her direction, shoving her against the arena's shield where the healers could easily focus their talents and help clear her lungs of the smoke.

He turned to survey the others, using this brief pause to take in weaknesses. For the most part, they were attacking one-on-one. That was how every other brawl he'd ever watched always started. Grudges could come to a head during the choosing bouts and this was the perfect opportunity to hit hard at a foe without lasting damage.

His gaze slid over those left standing. Some would come for him. Who? He wasn't yet sure.

Dylan absently reformed his shield whilst evaluating those closer. Five possibilities. Far too many combinations to account for in so short a time. *This is going to get messy*. But that was the point. Those fighting in a proper battle didn't attack in orderly one-on-one bouts. Brawls were meant to test how they'd handle such a scenario.

Frowning, he adjusted the strength of his shield, favouring no point over another. It left him with a mediocre defence and demanded a portion of his concentration, but with the uncertainty of who would strike and where from, he needed something that would shift on instinct.

As one, the others straightened. Shields shimmered as they eyed each other, waiting for someone else to strike first, for a weakness to present itself. Dylan joined them, conserving his strength.

Then slowly, one by one, their heads all turned towards him.

Shit. Of course they would turn on him, he was the late addition. If Sophie's feelings on his inclusion were an indication of how the others felt, then they saw him as the special one whom the overseers decided didn't need to fight in the bouts to prove himself. That joining so late hadn't been his idea was a moot point.

He took in his opponents' positions. One on either flank, three spread out along the fore. As long as they remained where they stood, he'd the strength to repel an attack. "*Well?*" he roared. "Come on, then!"

An explosion of fire, ice and lightning filled the air.

He hardened his shield and waited out the assault. Ice melted in the heat of another's fireball, which likewise fizzled out. Steam billowed between him and his attackers. Only the lightning touched his shield, yet the combined charge of dissipating magic turned what should've been a heavy jolt into a measly tickle.

Dylan grinned as the steam evaporated. "Is that the best you've got?"

Shards of ice exploded across his shield in answer.

The woman on his left shrieked and fell. Out the corner of Dylan's eye, he saw red staining the ground. A quick glance revealed several of the shards had hit her straight on.

He took a step towards her, obeying the urge to check if she was still alive, before common sense rooted him in place.

But there was blood. There shouldn't be blood. *It's a non-lethal attack.* At least, providing any major blood vessels weren't hit. The healers wouldn't be able to reach this far into the arena. She could bleed to death before the brawl was over.

Dylan sent a pulse through the air, knocking the four left in range off their feet, and ran for the woman. The shards were melting, tipping over and diluting the blood pooling on the dirt.

The image of William flashed through his mind, flogging him to run faster. He couldn't let her share the same fate.

Widening his shield to accommodate them both, Dylan knelt and grasped her shoulder. He might not be considered a master at healing, but he could give her a chance to reach someone who was.

The shards had punctured a lung. There wasn't much he could do about the blood already clotting within. He focused, coaxing the body's natural healing ability to speed up. It responded, sluggishly. *Come on.* Dylan poured more magic into the act, forcing her body to mend itself. Still, the desired reaction was slow.

Was he too late?

No. He refused to believe that, to let her go without a fight. Not when he had the strength to spare.

Dylan pushed his magic a little bit harder. His chest tightened, his own power fighting against his wishes. His heart felt ready to rip through his ribs. It shouldn't have been this difficult. The shards hadn't hit any major arteries. She should've been able to survive a few—

A wheezy gasp shattered his thoughts.

Relief washed through him, weakening his limbs. She was alive. Her body was still in need of proper healing, but now she was stable enough for him to send her to them. "I'm sorry about this." He gently slipped a cushion of air beneath her and pushed her across the ground, halting her body before she hit the arena shield.

Dylan watched as the healers huddled around her. She would live, no question. If the best of them truly could bring the recently dead back to life, then she would be no great challenge.

Light danced on the edge of his vision. He turned his head to the sight of another falling.

Sighing, Dylan wobbled to his feet. They'd actually gone back to fighting whilst he healed the woman. Would it be too much to hope they managed to strike down the man responsible for her injuries? *They're meant to stick to the—*

The victor turned, fire roaring from her fingers. Dylan strengthened the flank of his shield.

Too late.

Flames flashed through his weakened barrier, licking at his forearm. A scream tore through his throat. The smoky, sickly-sweet stench of cooking flesh filled his nose just as completely as the searing pain eclipsed his mind. He doubled over, cradling his arm. Already, his magic was working to mend the charred skin, but it was slow and draining. *Get up!* He had to retaliate, knock them out before more joined in.

Another blast. Mercifully, his shield still held. The seemingly inadequate protection wobbled at first, regaining its strength as he turned his full attention to keeping his attackers at bay. Three remained of their little group. They spread out, slowly as if trying to hide their attempt at flanking him.

His gaze slid over two of them to settle on the third. The man responsible for the ice blast.

Snarling, Dylan unleashed a barrage of lightning at the trio. The bolts arced across the arena, crackling against shields, seeking out the weak points. They fell, their limbs flopping about like fish. He had probably hit them with too many volts. He didn't care. Non-lethal attacks were apparently off the table.

A dull sting still encompassed his arm, grounding him. His gaze drifted to where another pair fought amongst themselves. A dark-haired woman and Fredrick, the latter of whom seemed to be having some difficulty getting through the other's shield. A quick look around the arena revealed them to be all that was left of the brawl.

Dylan watched them dance around each other like two squabbling sparrows, using the break to catch his breath. If he was going to last in the final fight, he would need all the strength he had left.

When would the leashed one join the attack? They were meant to wait until the end, but some had barrelled into the fray halfway through brawls.

He glanced at the base of the podium. Like statues, the hound and the leashed one remained in place. And it appeared that Dylan's presence continued to garner the hound's attention. Their head shifted as he circled his last two opponents, following his movements like a cat tracking a spider.

He couldn't be imagining it.

Trying to block out the watched sensation, he turned his focus to the pair still battling each other. He could take out Fredrick easily enough whilst the man was distracted, but then he could very well be leaving himself open to the woman's attack if he wasn't careful. Whereas, if Launtil had been correct about the man's intentions to remain in the tower, Fredrick would concede without too much of a toll on Dylan's reserves.

He sent a bolt of lightning at the woman's flank, strong enough to draw her attention and no more.

She responded with a fireball. It was a small and sputtering thing, dying before it had a chance to connect with his shield. The woman needed to take a little more from her defence before she would have any chance of hurting either of them.

Dylan flung his own fireball through the air, arcing it to hit on the far side of her shield. She flinched from the heat, but no more. Could she read his desire to conserve his strength? How much had she seen of his battle with the others? This fight could draw out longer than he desired if she chose to wait them out.

"What's the matter, Trins?" Fredrick yelled. "Scared he might actually be stronger than you?"

Dylan reassessed their opponent, scarcely believing this severe-looking person was Trinsuti. It had been years since he'd seen the bubbly woman who had once frequented the tower's grand library. However, with her dark hair secured in a high bun, the barely pointed ears were in clear sight. Smaller than the average elf's and usually lost amongst the curls that encircled her head like a halo.

"You can't hide forever," Fredrick continued, slowly drawing closer to the woman. "Come out and play!"

Trinsuti's gaze flicked between them. A sneer played on her lips. She stepped back, keeping a definite distance between her and the man. "Actually, I'd rather watch you two fight it out. You like getting nice and close to your opponents, don't you, Fred? Tall, pale and scrawny *is* your type, right?"

Frowning, Dylan turned towards the man.

Fredrick spread his hands wide, palms up, his shoulders hunching in question. He hadn't made a single attempt to attack Dylan, not even a hint.

Still, he eyed the man as Fredrick crept closer to Trinsuti. The steadily growing heat of a fireball encompassed Dylan's hand, ready to unleash the second he saw anything that could be construed as aggression towards him. What sort of attack did Fredrick use that required the man to get close to his target, anyway?

The shimmer of the woman's shield caught his eye. She was adjusting its strength. Sloppily.

Dylan didn't dare to wait and see what Trinsuti planned. He hurled the fireball, realising only as the heat slipped from his fingers that Fredrick was in the direct path. *He'll have a shield up.* Only a complete idiot didn't maintain even a weak barrier during the brawl.

Fredrick twisted, ducking out of the way as Dylan's fireball soared past him, and flung his own burst of flames at the woman. Dylan's hit first, the thrum of the woman's shield failing rumbled across the arena, leaving her defenceless for Fredrick's attack.

Trinsuti screamed as the man's fire hit. She staggered back, battering at the flames that'd caught on her robe hem. They dissipated swiftly, leaving her seemingly unscathed. The fresh shimmer of a newly-formed shield sprang up around her.

Not quickly enough.

Dylan wasn't certain how Fredrick made it to the woman's side in such a short amount of time, but he had managed to sneak behind her before the shield appeared. The man did naught but touch her head and Trinsuti collapsed.

With one blast of air, Dylan sent the woman skittering towards the arena edge. Now, there was but one last opponent to take care of before he needed to face the leashed one. Just one person standing between him and being able to leave the tower, and her isolation cells, far behind.

He faced Fredrick, not certain whether or not he should believe Launtil.

The man smirked. His relaxed stance suggested a lack of willingness to attack first, but that could easily be a ploy. "So, I see you're finally joining the rest of us in competing."

Dylan spread his hand, allowing the lightning to crackle between his fingers. Bolts danced across his skin, raising the hairs along his arms. "A little elf tells me you're not looking to leave the tower."

"My guardian makes me compete every year. Jace made a bet that I'd reach the brawl and..." His explanation faded as he shrugged.

You had to prove him right. So that was what Launtil had meant by the man showing off. "On your left." He swiped a tendril of lightning across the gap between them, deliberately aiming for where the man wouldn't be.

Sure enough, Fredrick dove out of the way. He tumbled across the arena and bounced back onto his feet.

Dylan took a moment to appreciate the graceful ease in which the man moved. Whilst they were of a similar height, Dylan had never been that elegant in his adolescence and the sedentary life of a linguist and historian had only made it worse. "How do you want to do this?"

The man's gaze darted to Dylan's arm. The skin had fully healed, but the sleeve remained in tatters. "I've never been fond of electrocution. Leaves a metallic taste in the back of the mouth, you know?"

"That's a shame." He preferred lightning for its quickness and efficiency. Unlike fire, which was laughably easy to manipulate, learning to master a single bolt took patience and months of training. But, with the right amount of control, that very same bolt could deliver pleasure just as well as deadly pain.

Those brown eyes flicked back up to Dylan's face. "Take me out another way. Please."

He tipped his head in acquiescence and let the bolts dancing up his hand fade. He would have to hit the man hard for anything to be believable, but there were a multitude of ways to make that work. "Come at me."

Fredrick halted in his circling. Those light brown brows lowered, suspicion etching itself onto his face. He ran at Dylan, the barely perceivable outline of a sword forming in his hand.

Dylan sent a blast of wind at the man.

His opponent hit the arena shield with a sick crunch.

Dylan winced and watched, his heart pounding ever harder with each second, as several of the master healers rushed to the man's aid. All around him, the arena echoed with the spectator's bloodlust, but he didn't dare take his eyes off the unconscious man.

It was only when Fredrick sat up, seemingly dazed but none the worse for wear, did Dylan realise he'd been holding his breath.

"Winner," the overseer boomed. "Face your final test."

Dylan turned towards the podium, the realisation of the fervour behind the crowd's excitement slowly sinking in.

He had made it. Survived. Right through to the end. The last one standing amongst the overseer's chosen. No returning to the isolation cells. All that he needed to do was…

Fight the leashed one.

She still stood at the podium base beside the hound, her attention on the hound as they spoke with her. No doubt, they were giving the woman sanction to attack him. Bowing her head, she strode into the centre of the arena.

The sick pounding in his chest increased. He eyed his opponent, taking in her every move in some vain attempt to determine a weakness from the very way she breathed. Uncertainty burrowed through his stomach the closer she got. How could he best someone who had faced the Udynea Empire's soldiers and lived? Surely, she would've picked up techniques he had never seen.

Dylan shook his hands, flexing his fingers. His breath came raggedly, drying his mouth. Being defeated by her only mattered if he fell too soon. Survive long enough and he would leave the tower no matter what.

They circled each other, the shimmer of their shields trembling with each step. Pride demanded he make the first strike. Tactics and encroaching exhaustion suggested he wait, conserve his strength and see what tricks she possessed.

"Attack already!" cried someone in the crowd.

A fireball, as round as he was tall, streaked towards him.

Dylan swung out of the way, flinching from the crackling heat of its passage. The gasping shock of the crowd echoed through the arena. Clearly, the woman had forgotten the non-lethal stance in these fights.

If that's the way you want to play it. This was the time to show everyone precisely what he was capable of. He unleashed a single bolt of lightning, putting all his strength behind the blast.

The woman held out her hand and he watched, stunned, as the bolt's passage slowed. Even as he severed the blast from his power, the lightning twisted in the air, curving back on itself. She flung up her other hand and, with a flick of her wrist, sent his own magic towards him.

Dylan strengthened his shield, gritting his teeth as the lightning struck. Minuscule tendrils broke through the cracks forming in the barrier. They fired around him, nipping at his body and bringing him to his knees. Swearing softly through his teeth, he shook himself. His magic might start repairing the damage even as the lightning hit, but it didn't keep it from stinging. *Well, that's new.*

Fireballs struck the ground around him. Dylan swiftly strengthened his shield, hoping to ride out the barrage. He could surrender now and still be considered worthy, but a small part of him refused to fall that easily. He could win, so long as he could make this quick. *Like the other night.*

But this wasn't like the exploding *infitialis*, he couldn't rely on her destroying herself, but he sensed the limit to his magic creeping up on him. He hadn't fought this long in years. If he faltered now, before she was down for good, it was at all possible he might not be capable of shielding her next attack.

He sank to his knees and focused on the earth beneath his opponent's feet. It had been years since he dared attempt this manoeuvre. Tricia had banned him from training for a month the first time he showed it to her, but his guardian could hardly punish him now. From the moment he was declared the winner, he no longer had a guardian.

With one hand pressed hard against the compacted dirt, he set off the first in a long chain of pulses through the ground. The vibrations started slow, building on top of each other with every burst until the ground around him undulated.

The woman staggered back, her arms waving in a desperate attempt to keep her balance. It was the sign he'd been waiting for.

Dylan sent another pulse her way, this time through the air.

His opponent hit the dirt. Another swipe sent her tumbling across the ground and slamming into the arena shield. There he held her, contained as he'd done to Sophie. Only this time, he ensured the shield was hard enough to let nothing through. All he had to do was hold it long enough for her to pass out and he would win.

To his surprise, she got to her feet, albeit slowly. Her head swung this way and that, taking in what he had done. The faintest shimmer of her own shield formed inside his and, opening her arms wide, she pushed back.

The unexpected internal pressure slapped him across the face. The shield cracked. Dylan clutched at his head. If she pushed much harder, his skull might very well follow suit. Nevertheless, he tightened his hold, restricting what little space he'd given her.

She floundered, her mouth opening and closing like a small bird trying to swallow a wood roach. The woman pounded on the shield just as Sophie had done, using everything she had to break it, but each thump grew weaker.

"The winner is declared fit for war," a voice boomed through the arena. "Spellster, release your opponent."

Dylan glanced up. Their fight had taken him right across the arena to the foot of the podium. The overseers stood on the edge, all eyes trained on him and the leashed one. How long had they watched him slowly suffocate the woman?

"I said, release!"

Bowing his head, he did as commanded, although the shield was slow to dissipate. The sudden cessation of magic snapped through his body. His legs folded, dumping him unceremoniously to the ground. He knelt there, entirely uncaring to the cheers of those watching. Every bone in his body seemed to be made of lodestone.

The woman fell to the ground, unconscious but most certainly alive.

Movement nearby drew his attention.

Dylan lifted his head cautiously. Whatever it was, he couldn't pose any threat to it. He was rather done for now. Would be incapable of anything beyond a few child's tricks until tomorrow and only after a decent night's rest.

The hound was at the leashed one's side. She knelt, checking for vitals despite the steady rise and fall of the woman's chest. The hound glanced up from her charge. There was a predatory look in her eyes, one that could almost be mistaken for curiosity. "Congratulations on joining the army ranks, spellster."

Dylan frowned. Perhaps it was Sulin's doubts or his guardian's past insistence that he remain within the tower, or even the rolling tone of the woman's voice, but the hound's words sounded rather like she was in on a cruel joke that he had somehow become the butt of.

CHAPTER 7

In all his life, Dylan had never dared to venture into the wing where the alchemists worked. Those who hadn't been trained to bend the *infitialis* metal to their will were forbidden and just listening to Sulin made the very act seem like certain death.

Now, he stood in one of their many chambers, waiting for someone to come and leash him.

His stomach churned at the thought. He closed his eyes, trying to calm his mind. It didn't work. *I chose this.* He could've fallen at any time during the brawl. True, he wasn't entirely certain what would've happened to him afterwards. Death seemed the likeliest outcome, but it was still a choice he could've made. But this?

All at once, it somehow seemed the worst option.

To never use your own magic unless someone lets you, Sulin's voice echoed through his mind. Old words of what the collar meant for the leashed.

Dylan balled his hands, surprised to find they were shaking. This wouldn't be like the isolation cells. He would be out in the world, free of these walls, walking the land.

Just without his magic.

How bad could it really be? Other people lived perfectly normal lives without such power. He could, too. It wasn't as though he relied on it for every act.

He tried to distract himself by searching the room, but the area was no larger than the isolation cell he had stepped out of this morning, wide enough to pace a few strides either way. It held little of interest. Not even a pallet to sleep upon.

He had expected something different, bigger and overflowing with all manner of interesting objects and tubes. The hound had escorted him past a few such rooms containing massive frames supporting an assortment of glass pipes. Other places seemed bare beyond a solid wooden table and a sooty metal screen. The latter was no doubt where they tested their *infitialis* creations.

So why was this room empty?

His gaze slid to the walls. They weren't sheathed in the purple metal like the isolation cells. Nor did they bear a single sign of magic having been wrought upon them at any stage. No telltale melting or scouring of the stone. Not a testing room, then. And, despite its resemblance, it was entirely the wrong place for a cell.

The door opened to admit a human woman. She looked him over, her eyes—so big and as dark as a shadow—seemed to swell with pity. "So you're the winner, then."

He straightened. "Didn't you watch the brawl?" He had always been under the impression that it was expected of every spellster.

A faint sneer touched her lips. "I've no interest in such things. It's disgusting how they keep us locked in here, trotting us out only when it serves their purpose." Her bitterness suggested that she was perhaps one of those born beyond the tower walls. After so many centuries of segregation, spellsters born amongst the common folk were unlikely to have more than a limited amount of magical talent. And they often became alchemists.

"Are you here to leash me?"

It was a curious thing, how *infitialis* worked. Back in the days, when the old empire of Domian was more than ruins and bits of lore, they figured out that encircling a spellster's body with a ring of the metal, however crudely, would effectively nullify their magic.

Centuries of refinement had given them the collars multiple kingdoms now used to control which spellsters used their power and how. He was about to become one of them. Permanently.

He still wasn't sure if such knowledge was a blessing or a curse.

She sighed. "Unfortunately, yes." As if to prove her word, the alchemist withdrew a short length of strangely fluid-moving metal from her belt pouch. It jingled in her hand, the purple sheen reflecting the torchlight and staining her pale hands.

Dylan swallowed the sudden uneasy lump in his throat. That piece of metal looked insignificant to the cell walls, yet its effect was far more powerful. From afar, it looked to be a solid piece. Sulin had once told him the collars were wrought into a series of small links, similar to the guardians' chain mail. Although it would only encompass his neck, it was enough.

A question flashed through the dread creeping across his mind. "This won't hurt, will it?" Ever since the first time he'd been thrown into an isolation cell, he had assumed leashing felt no different, but he hadn't ever spoken to a leashed one beyond a few words. He certainly hadn't given any thought towards asking what it was like to be leashed.

Now, he rather wished he had.

"Hurt?" the woman mused as she stepped closer. "Perhaps, but not in the way you believe."

He flinched as she wrapped the collar around his neck, expecting the same coldness as the cell walls. It wasn't. If anything, the metal exuded a slight warmth. But that familiar chill burrowed into him, somewhere deep within his being.

He'd only ever experienced a numbing from within the darkness of the isolation cells. The world seemed dimmer. Sounds were no longer as sharp. Oddly enough, his throat hurt. As did his knees. And there was this awful noise in his ears, a distortion of screams.

It took him a moment to realise that sound was him. He had fallen to the floor, screaming. He had expected the numbness in his core, but not the dull pain vibrating down to his bones. Not the way it throbbed through his skull.

Certainly not the panicked finality of it all.

His fingers curled behind the collar. He wrenched and twisted and clawed at the links to no avail. There was no seam to be had. No simple weakness to exploit. He was trapped. Made safe for those beyond the tower.

Why had he been so eager to win?

Dylan stretched a hand across the dusty stones. Even knowing he couldn't, he still tried to bring the smallest fork of lightning to life between his fingers.

The collar crackled, sparks singed his skin.

He flinched, a thin squeak slipping through his lips. What was this? Everyone knew the collar was meant to make him incapable of accessing his magic without sanction. Nobody said anything about it punishing him for an attempt.

He tried again. Maybe if he pushed through the pain, he could…

Nothing.

Tears rolled down his face, blurring the world further. "I can't," he whimpered. Beyond the cells, he had always been able to, from the first time he could conjure at will rather than on instinct, he had always been capable of this one little trick. *Never again.* Not without sanction. A part of him was locked away for the rest of his life. Its control someone else's to command.

"Yes," someone answered. A woman, but with a softer voice than the alchemist's. "That's right."

Dylan sat up, rubbing his temples. It felt like his skull was trapped in a vice despite all evidence to the contrary. Was that due to the collar or some lingering after-effect of the brawl? Slowly turning his head, he searched for the source of the sound.

The leashed one stood in the doorway. It was just them. How long had he been screaming for the alchemist to leave?

Only now, with the leashed one so close, did he note a distinct lack of spark to her eyes. Why hadn't he noticed sooner? He would've wondered, would've heeded his guardian's warning.

"We all try to rid ourselves of it at first," the woman continued, her words devoid of passion. She spoke as if reciting text or, perhaps, to also remind herself. "We all scream when we can't. We all cry. But we endure. Our king demands that we do."

Because they need us. That was why they subjected spellsters to this nightmare. *To keep Udynea at bay.* All the vibrancy of life gone in a heartbeat. He was never going to get that back. *To shield those we hold dear to us.* His thoughts drifted to Tricia, to Sulin and Nestria. Of Henrie and Harriet. Even Launtil. Friends and more. *Family.* People he would never see again.

None of them would've been capable of surviving the brawl never mind a true fight. So it had to be him.

Dylan clambered to his feet, starkly refusing to heed the wobbling in his legs. *They need me.* He understood that now. He had first pushed entering the brawl in the hope of seeing a world that had mostly been words on a page. Then he had fought to save himself.

But it wasn't about any of that. Not anymore.

He would leave for the army camp come the morning. There, he would help push the enemy back across the border. All for those he held dear. For them, he would suffer living this dim and muffled world.

~ ~ ~

Morning came and, with it, the order to move out. Dylan's stomach fluttered as he followed the hound and the other leashed spellster through the lower corridors. He hadn't set foot outside the tower in his whole life and now...

I'm never coming back. The thought skittered through his mind, tangling with the knots of pain like a water bird caught in a fishing net.

His head hadn't stopped hurting since the leashing. An unseen band squeezed his temples and burrowed deep between his eyes in an unrelenting cycle. He had spent much of the night with his forehead pressed to the rough stone wall beside his cot, trying to alleviate the pain to no avail.

Perhaps the headaches would've subsided if he had been allowed one last night in a familiar room, surrounded by those he held dear. But even with him leashed, the overseers wouldn't risk him speaking about the secret entrance.

At least he'd been given a bed. Not one he could call *his* but rather one slated for the tower's rare visitors.

If he needed any more proof that he was no longer a part of this place, that had been it.

He clung a little tighter to the small pouch hanging from his belt. It held all the precious few personal effects he was allowed to take with him. The dark green, army-issued robes like those the woman wore would come once he reached the main encampment, which sat several weeks away—the better part of three if on foot. He really should've spent more of his time outside, instead of studying dwarven texts and chasing women.

I'll be getting that time now. All he had ever dared to dream and likely more. The very thought of leaving everything frightened him more than he had ever considered. Never had he believed a part of him would long to stay in the tower with its dreary, repetitive life.

His hand strayed to the collar. He wriggled a finger beneath the links, idly searching for the join that wasn't there. He had spent hours doing the same thing last night, foolish and arrogant enough to believe that, after centuries of spellsters being leashed this way, *he* would be the one to find a loophole. Whatever the alchemists did to *infitialis*, its effects were absolute.

All his magic, every last scrap of power he could ever bring to bear, was hidden behind a simple meshwork of metal.

They left the last of the corridors through the main entrance, stepping into the courtyard, the area still shadowed at this time of day. From here, a spellster had a choice of going left to the gardens or, rarely, venturing towards a self-contained building that housed the tower's laundry. Others could pass through the massive gates leading to a smaller courtyard separating the outside world from the tower complex.

More people lingered in the main courtyard than usual.

Dylan hesitated atop the stairs leading into the courtyard. He had heard of the crowds that congregated in the wake of past leashed ones. He'd never been part of one, though. It seemed rather morbid, watching as a friend was led out of the tower to never return. Like a funeral procession giving the dead their final farewells.

Dylan hunched his shoulders. He didn't want to be remembered like this.

Still, his gaze slid over the crowd, heeding the perverse desire to know if his friends stood amongst them, fearing it wasn't true and dreading that it was.

His gaze settled on a familiar face. Not of his friends, but of Sophie. She glared at him, her lips flattened into a thin line. All along the front row on his right were those he had competed against. Fredrick, Trinsuti, the man with green eyes that had tried to skewer him. Even the woman he had risked losing the brawl to heal.

They bowed as he passed.

He inclined his head in acknowledgement before returning his search to the crowd closer to the gateway. Maybe his friends had opted to stay away from the courtyard, to pretend he wasn't leaving forever. That was what he would've done.

But no, there was Nestria, standing at the edge of the crowd on his left with his roommate at her side. He raised his hand and wriggled his fingers slightly to let her know he had noticed her presence.

She turned from him to cling to Sulin and bury her face into his robes. The man absently patted her back, his gaze unwavering from Dylan's procession.

His vision blurred. Dylan dried his eyes under the pretence of adjusting his hair. He couldn't remember a time when the Nestria hadn't been in his life. Yes, he had known that winning the brawl would mean leaving everyone he knew behind, but with his guardian always blocking his chances, years had passed since it felt like a feasible goal. *Not until yesterday.*

And now…

After all that time of trying to leave, he found he wasn't yet ready to say goodbye. There was so much he needed to do, so many things he had left unsaid.

"Spellster."

He pulled his attention from his friends to the hound. The woman glared at him, her tan face taut with displeasure. He had stopped somewhere along the way whilst they continued, putting some distance between him and the women he followed.

Grimacing apologetically, Dylan hastened back to the hound's side. If he was to spend the journey to the army camp in her company, he would rather do so without antagonising her.

Hurried movement through the crowd on his right drew Dylan's eye. He spied Henrie pushing through the throng, Harriet trailing close behind, and slowed.

The elf reached the edge of the crowd and stopped, halting so abruptly that Harriet almost collided into him. Dylan had known the man almost as long as Nestria. He still remembered the hours they used to spend at night talking through a hole in the wall. That'd been several decades ago. He couldn't recall what they had spoken about in those first few nights, but the terrible weeping that originally drew him to the little crack joining the main boy's quarters to Henrie's little room had fast vanished.

Henrie didn't turn away once he realised he'd been spotted. He met Dylan's stare, smiled and bowed his head in farewell. At his side, Harriet pressed close enough to her lover for their arms to touch without raising suspicion. Her chin shook. If Dylan had been closer, he didn't doubt he would've seen the tears brimming in her big eyes.

Anyone would think he was going off to die.

A wry smile twisted his lips. He wasn't dead. Nor did he have any plans on dying any time in the near future. He was going to prove what an asset he was to the kingdom. Make every action count. If he tried hard enough, then maybe they wouldn't need to leash another.

He reached the hound's side and the gates to the outer courtyard creaked open. He'd never seen them in such a state, had barely paid them any mind throughout his twenty-nine years.

His gut quivered as he watched the gap widen. His guardian's words, old warnings given in his adolescence, ghosted about his mind. *Leave here and the hounds will hunt you.* Although some foolhardy spellsters had tried to see the outer gates, he hadn't dared to venture near the small courtyard after his sole botched attempt. Back then, leaving had seemed like a death sentence.

And now?

He absently felt his way along the collar, the metal unnervingly warm against his skin. It would protect him from the hounds, no doubts there. They weren't interested in leashed spellsters destined for the army. Without his magic, he was little threat to anyone. Less than that, really. He was no threat at all.

As much as he hated to admit it, his guardian was right. Without the aid of others, he wouldn't live long beyond these walls.

Ahead of him, the two women slipped through the gates. Dylan went to follow when something small brushed against his back. He whirled around to find Launtil standing there.

She smiled at him, her head tipped back in what had to be an uncomfortable angle. It might have been the teeth—the pronounced canines evidence of a near-pure elven bloodline—or the savage glint in her big, brown eyes, but there was something feral lurking in the expression. "You give no quarter to those enslaving bastards, you hear me?"

Dylan inclined his head. If he was to believe anyone's word about what those in the Udynea Empire did to elves and the poor, it was hers. The life she had lived before the fates carried her here was exactly why the crown sent leashed spellsters to the border, to stop Demarn from becoming another slave resource of elven and human alike. "I'll do everything I can." What that would be, he wasn't sure, but his answer seemed to please her.

He hurried to catch up with the hound before she could call him again. His gaze alighted on the outer gates and his legs suddenly couldn't move. Dread and giddiness washed over him in equal measure.

The gates stood open. A rare sight even for those who saw the courtyard on a regular basis. They were usually barred and watched over by a dozen guards. Or so he had heard.

Those selfsame people now stood to one side, waiting for them to depart. Standing near the entrance were four horses, two of which were harnessed to an already laden wagon.

Dylan eyed the saddled animals, his stomach sinking slightly. "You're not expecting me to ride one of them, are you?" he asked the hound. He had seen pictures of them in books and read tales of valiant knights riding into battle atop great warhorses, but that was the extent of his experience with them.

Laughing, the woman shook her head and grinned up at him. The top of her head barely reached his chin, which put her around the same height as his guardian, just with paler skin and more muscle. "Of course not. You will travel in the wagon alongside our gear. We will be heading south, for the most part, just our little group..."

The longer she spoke, the easier it was to pick up the nuances that came with her accent. Beneath the similar smooth and rolling coastal tone of his old roommate was something else. He wanted to ask if she had been born outside of Demarn, but he doubted she would answer such an intimate query.

"...until we reach Toptower, anyway," she continued. "That is where we will meet up with the rather non-magical troops and go on to the main camp." The smile she gave him had a slight malicious tilt to it. "Horseback all the way, yes?"

He took a deep breath, fighting to keep his expression neutral. Travelling on the seat of a cart didn't sound quite so bad, but riding a horse? The very idea made his stomach do all sorts of interesting flips.

However well he believed his thoughts hidden, they must've been evident in his expression, for the hound patted his back. "Do not worry so. I will ensure there is a nice, quiet nag waiting to take you the rest of the way."

"Really?" Everything he had ever heard about hounds hadn't given him any cause to believe they were at all thoughtful. Even the guardians tended to paint them as cruel and calculating beings who couldn't be trusted. "Thank you."

Grunting, she shrugged. "Do not mistake this for being soft. I am tasked with fetching a spellster. Getting you to the camp in one piece is my priority. It just simply would not be prudent to let one of the king's elite weapons become damaged before they can be used."

Weapon? He was more than that and he would prove it once they reached the army camp. His magic would be used for more than the death of an enemy. He would heal those who should've died so they could return to their families, even if he couldn't.

"Wait!"

Dylan turned at the cry, scarcely believing his ears. *Tricia?* Had the overseers allowed her the leniency of a farewell?

His guardian raced across the courtyard, tailed by a pair of guards. She wasn't meant to be here, only the guards and the hound's retinue.

"Guardian," the hound said. She intersected Tricia before the older woman could reach Dylan, stopping his guardian with a firm hand on her shoulder. "I understand that your people often form attachments to your charges, but there are certain stipulations of your creed that require you to leave at once, yes?"

There was. Winning the brawl, being leashed, all of it meant his life was no longer her concern. He truly belonged to the king now, part of his army. Any ties he once had were to be severed.

"Just let me say goodbye." Even as Tricia pleaded with the hound, her gaze remained locked on him. "I'll never see him again. Please, give me this one thing."

The hound hesitated. She glanced at him, then at the guards trotting up, before bowing her head. "Be quick."

Tricia was moving before the hound could finish talking. She flung her arms around him, all but crushing him. "My boy…"

"A-are you crying?" he managed between breaths.

Her wavering little laugh shook them. "Don't you worry about me." She stepped back, smiling even though two glistening trails of moisture ran down her face. "You just stay strong, you hear? Promise me you'll stay strong."

He frowned. Uncertainty bubbled away in his gut. What did she know about the conditions he was going into? Why hadn't he asked her earlier? Why hadn't she offered to prepare him for what he might face in the world beyond the borders she had laid?

Dylan wrapped his arms around her shoulders and squeezed. "I promise." It was too late for regrets.

"And don't—"

"That is enough, guardian." The hound was at his side again, those slate-grey eyes colder now.

Tricia's smile wavered. It was a minuscule thing, the slight tick of her cheek that set the dark scar to twitching. She opened her mouth, clearly wanting to say more, then closed it without a word.

Dylan steeled himself. One of them would have to say it before he left and if she wasn't going to… "Goodbye, Mother."

Her eyes closed. The wry smile that often accompanied him speaking the word twitched her lips. She nodded and, although she spoke too softly for him to hear, her lips formed two very distinct words. "My son."

"We have a lot of ground to cover before nightfall," the hound said, gently turning him towards the wagon. "It is past time that we left."

His stomach quivered, clenching with an inexplicable urge to expel his breakfast. A strong desire to pull free of the hound's grasp and fling himself at his guardian's feet welled within. *You wanted this*, he sharply reminded himself. From the first time he had shown an aptitude for combat, he had wanted nothing more than to fight for the kingdom.

So why did leaving feel so... hollow?

His shuffling feet halted him beside the wagon. He placed a foot on the step, preparing to hoist himself into the seat next to the driver when a phlegm-rattling cough drew his gaze up to the man holding the reins.

The driver shook his head and, glaring down his bulbous pink nose, jerked a thumb at the tray behind him.

Dylan took in the laden array of sacks and barrels crammed in with various instruments of cookery and the like. "Surely, you don't expect me to travel the whole way like cargo."

The man sneered and jerked his thumb again. "Get in the back, spellster." The gravelly voice practically growled the title.

Dropping to the flagstones, Dylan made his way to the back of the wagon. After picking through their supplies, he squeezed himself between the sacks up front. It wasn't too bad. The wagon walls were high enough to provide shelter from the wind and, if it rained, he was in easy reach of the tenting canvas.

The wagon swayed as the driver urged the horses on. A shadow fell over them. Barely moving, he rolled his eyes up to spy the arch of the tower gateway slipping by. Dylan peered over the edge of the cart. All around him lay hills covered in grass and forests.

He was outside the tower complex.

It was that simple. No walls. No more endless days of study. His magic might have been bound, but he was free.

He slid a little lower in his seat, a sliver of uncertainty settling into his heart. The world seemed far bigger than what he'd seen from the tower windows. Not a single wall no matter where he looked, just the world stretching before him. Nothing to mark a boundary. He could walk for days without a thing to stop him.

Strange, how a thought that had once carried a promise of freedom now seemed rather final.

CHAPTER 8

If Tracker had any choice in the matter, he'd never set foot into any settlement sitting on the ever-dwindling border shared with the Udynea Empire, especially not Toptower. But enter he must. The mayor had called for one of the King's Hounds and he had been assigned the task. It didn't matter that it had taken him far longer to get here than originally planned.

At least it was far from the capital and the messages coming in by anything other than a rider were reportedly sporadic. If he was lucky, his prey had chosen to leave and he could spend a few weeks being blissfully unaware of anything beyond the mundane troubles of normal citizens.

Few shared the road with him. There was the odd wagon and a group of scruffy young men that had the appearance of travelling for some time. No others on horseback. Late afternoon was typically a time for farmers to be coming in from their fields.

Tracker eyed the town's high walls as his horse continued its swaying plod ever closer to the gate. Toptower encompassed one of the land's many hills, the settlement having built up around an old sentry tower. The structure that gave the town its name still jutted high above the walls, too far from any single gate to protect the surrounding area. Maybe in the distant past.

Not that any natural defence would be much of a barrier to a spellster attack. Demarn's untamed forests and valleys were littered with the toppled ruins of such encounters. No matter how strong a fortress' foundation was built, it took only one decent blast of magic by a skilled spellster to bring down any wall.

If their army ever fell to Udynea's might, this town would be next.

Tracker shaded his eyes and peered westward. A road trailed off from the town into the forest. If he squinted, he could make out the grey smoke drifting up from the army campfires. The encampment had stood between Demarn and the enemy for centuries. But it also used to be a lot further from Toptower.

There was little else surrounding the town. Fields of young wheat and oat flanked him, the green stalks swaying in the breeze. Much of the food grown here would go to keep the army fed.

It also left few places for a rogue spellster to hide. He doubted they lurked in the city. Fetcher, a fellow hound tasked with escorting new recruits from the spellster tower, often visited the city. That their mistress hadn't sent her to dig into the rumours meant Fetcher was currently occupied with her usual task. *Pity*. He enjoyed her company. Unlike many of his acquaintances, their connection wasn't based on sex—as far as he was aware, Fetcher despised the act.

What he had with the woman was the closest thing he had gotten to a true friendship since losing Wynne and Zinnala to their betrayer. The fact Fetcher carried more than a sliver of compassion for the very spellsters she escorted also helped. In a job that demanded they harden themselves, she had somehow maintained her childhood softness.

In anyone else, the mistress would've demanded that part be eradicated.

The snort of cattle jolted Tracker from his musing. His horse had sidled onto the side of the road to let a laden cart wheel on by, heading away from the town's northern gates. The guards seated on either side suggested their barrelled cargo held more than the local beer. They eyed him with overall disdain, almost begging for trouble.

Tracker ignored their passage, guiding his horse back onto surer footing once the cart had passed. His ears caught the beginning of a slur before the word was muffled. He ignored that, too. He'd heard plenty over the years, most of them uninspired.

The forming of this one likely had to do with the points of his ears, the subdued tone coming from someone recognising his status as a King's Hound. The presence of a lowly elf having an elite status often confused the simple-minded.

He continued onwards to the northern gate. Guards stood on either side, stopping to talk with everyone coming in and out. Those on foot were questioned to establish their business, whilst the merchant carts had their wares thoroughly checked.

Tracker watched it all with idle curiosity. What had made the town's guard captain twitchy enough to order such inspections?

One guard made to stop him, their advance intercepted by another in their ranks. The second whispered into the first's ear, then they both saluted him.

He bowed his head in response. His black leather armour would've been recognisable as attire worn only by the King's Hounds. Those who knew of them rarely got in their way.

He would need to gather reports from all four gates, although he didn't think the southern one would have anything of interest. Most travellers came and went from the east or the north. Anyone with enough brains would use that crowd as cover to venture both in and out of the city. He also doubted the western gate held the information he sought as those heading west were likely heading for the army encampment. Not a place an unleashed spellster would go near.

Inside the town walls, the streets bustled. People hurried along, eager to be done with their tasks before dusk. Merchants called for prospective buyers or made deals with those they already had. Children ran up and down the streets, ducking into alleyways or scurrying through thicker crowds. Some played, others ran errands, one definitely swiped a woman's coin pouch.

He wove through it all, the presence of his warhorse doing much towards clearing a path for him. Lullaby was a solid animal, meticulously trained by Tracker over the years. His hooves had caved plenty of heads and, whilst he showed no such aggression now, he was quick to act on a whistled command. Those few who stood their ground did so only under duress.

After a few enquiries, his travels halted outside of an inn.

The place didn't look like much, a single-story building cringing amongst the larger establishments surrounding it, including an establishment that definitely housed a certain type of entertainment. The brothel also likely contributed to the crowd milling around. Some even staggered from the building directly to the inn.

Tracker had bunked down in far worse places. As long as he'd a place to sleep free of livestock, no matter how small, he was content.

The stables were as uninspiring as the inn and little more than a line of shadowy stalls sheltered by a thatched roof. Tracker sniffed the air as he dismounted. The aroma of fresh manure wafted on the breeze, but that was to be expected. What he couldn't smell was decay. No musty hay or rotting straw. No lingering dampness. That spoke a great deal towards the care given.

A stable hand appeared from one of the stalls, carrying a shovel and bucket laden with manure. They had their back to Tracker, their attention miles away.

Tracker cleared his throat.

The figure turned, revealing a boyish, freckled face. Ice-blue eyes widened and his mouth dropped open for a split second before the young man composed himself. "Sir hound!" He hastened to stash his tools and wipe down his hands. "My apologies. How may I be of assistance?"

"My horse," Tracker replied as if it wasn't obvious. "Be careful with him. No quick movements. *Or* whistling." The animal hadn't ever responded to another's casual tune, but it paid to be cautious.

Nodding, the stable hand carefully smoothed down his mop of

dirty-blonde hair before taking the reins with something akin to reverence. "Hello, beauty," he cooed as if Lullaby wasn't clearly bred for battle. "I've a cosy stall just waiting for you. Let's get you fed and rubbed down, shall we?" The young man continued his chatter as he led Lullaby away, swiftly leaving Tracker alone in the courtyard.

Satisfied his horse was in good hands, Tracker strode into the inn.

The common room was a lot smaller than he expected. Tables crowded the space, leaving a maze of little pathways to navigate through. A fireplace lit the far end of the room, smoky candles illuminated the rest. How humans saw in this dimness was beyond him.

Many of the seats he sidled past were occupied, the patrons either deep in their drinks or dozing over empty tankards. The majority were human, with a cluster of elves in the far corner.

The bartender openly sneered at his approach. That dark, venomous gaze travelled down Tracker, clearly marking the scimitar and daggers hanging at his hip. It wasn't unheard of for elves to be armed so heavily, especially this close to the army encampment, but most carried common arming swords.

"How may I help you?" He pointedly gave Tracker another look-over before grating out, "*Sir?*"

Tracker smiled back. Clearly, the man hadn't encountered Fetcher or he would recognise one of the King's Hounds. "I require a bed. For tonight, at least." His search to uncover a spellster, or even the source of the rumour, would undoubtedly take longer than a single day, but his bunking prospects could change after meeting with the guard captain tomorrow. "I also have a horse in your stables." He threw a silver coin onto the counter. "That should more than cover it."

The bartender watched the coin bounce, waiting until it had stopped on its own before picking up the coin and testing it. His greying brows rose upon discovering the money was real.

Tracker threw a copper onto the counter. "Where can one find a decent brothel in this hellhole?" His enquiry wasn't solely of the carnal nature. Whilst a little casual sex would be welcomed to wind down for the evening, especially after spending days in the saddle, visiting any brothel always wound up being for more than pleasure.

He had learnt in his youth that, beyond taverns and inns, brothels held a wealth of information. But where subtle enquiries to a drunken patron yielded varied results, he could practically guarantee any prostitute worth their coin had information on their clients that they really shouldn't.

The bartender pocketed both coins. "Across the street."

Tracker had seen the sign, *The Soldier's Fancy*. He didn't doubt the brothel employed a prostitute who was exactly what he preferred, maybe even a selection of them. But he had also seen the calibre of clients the bouncer admitted, some of whom still graced the inn's common room. "I meant a *clean* establishment."

The man sneered. "No clean brothel's going to service an elf, no matter how much you pretty yourself up."

"I happen to speak their language." Tracker slid another silver coin across the counter. "And yours, too, yes?"

This coin barely left Tracker's possession before the bartender snatched it up. "You'll want *The Creaming Tart*, then. It's in the western quarter, halfway down Baker's Row."

Tipping his head in acknowledgement, Tracker turned from the man and aimed for the exit. "I'll be back for my key," he shot over his shoulder. The stable hand would bring in his effects and probably rummage through them in the process. Not that there was much. Beyond his tent and the meagre remains of supplies, he'd little else of interest to another. Travelling light was expected of the King's Hounds.

Out of the inn, Tracker sauntered through the town, keeping the tower on his left as he headed westward. Like the spokes of a wheel, the main streets radiated from the tower. Those intersecting them curved like the inner designs of a spider's web. It put his travelling in a series of arcs and arrow-straight paths.

The streets grew still as the daylight finally faded. The way remained illuminated thanks to a duo of gangly guards tasked with igniting the selection of lanterns and torches dotted about the town. The latter sputtered in the breeze winding between the buildings.

Through it all, Tracker sensed no magic, not even the ghost of a spellster's presence. It was possible they operated outside the town's walls. That would certainly explain the guards' actions.

After a while, there was very little in the way of people, too. Did Toptower have a curfew? He didn't recall Fetcher ever mentioning one.

Although, it *had* been a number of years since he'd seen her. Perhaps the curfew was new, put in place as a response to the mysterious vanishings. But he also hadn't seen much in the way of patrols or even guards, beyond those at the gate.

Just another thing to add to the list of enquiries he would make come the morning. For now, he wanted to forget all about spellsters and his duty. Hopefully, this brothel had someone capable of the task.

Eventually, he reached the western quarter and, after some wandering, a street bearing the sign of Baker's Row. The street itself was empty of civilians, the street level of every building he walked by clearly closed for the day. Despite the street's name, very few looked to be bakeries.

In the levels above, signs of life drifted out into the world, be it the flicker of candlelight or the chatter of families slipping through open windows. The aroma of multiple meals also wafted on the wind, the smell both a mixture of clashing savoury dishes, yet enticing enough to have his stomach growl.

He had almost reached the end of the street when he spied a distinctive sign illuminated by a nearby lantern. Brothels weren't illegal in Demarn—it had surprised him the first time a Tirglasian sailor told him how such businesses weren't looked upon so kindly elsewhere—but the lengths some artists went to suggest what truly went on behind the doors was often a comedic delight in itself.

The Creaming Tart was no exception. The sign's image was definitely the dessert in question, albeit, the shape and design also had a vague resemblance to female genitalia. He supposed the... artistically painted fluid running from the centre was also no doubt meant to be a certain dairy product.

His gaze slid to the windows. Only a few were illuminated. If this had been *The Gilded Lily*, almost all of them would be lit up. No one but him seemed to be outside the place or even near enough to be making their way here.

Maybe the town *did* have a curfew.

His gaze dropped to the alcove before the brothel's entrance. A veritable mountain of a woman stood guard. Such a sight was more familiar, if less friendly than he was used to.

The bouncer sneered as he approached. "No entry without payment," she declared, squaring her broad shoulders as if expecting a fight.

"Naturally." Even in his visits to *The Gilded Lily*, where they knew he had the funds, he readily paid. Tracker retrieved a gold coin from his money pouch and flipped it towards the woman. Admittedly, the amount was a touch excessive, but much of his current funds had been donated to him by a group of bandits he had encountered on the way south.

The woman glanced at the coin, her brows lifting and her attention darting back to him. "Don't often see mercenaries travelling alone."

"I am no mercenary." He understood how she could mistake him for one. Whilst his armour was distinct and people who had dealt with the King's Hounds before would recognise it, they didn't make a habit of announcing themselves as such.

"No," she agreed, pocketing the coin. "You don't look the warrior type." Her eyes narrowed as she whispered, "Assassin?"

Of a sort. Whilst his orders came from a member of the royal family, his targets weren't exactly the political kind. Fixing her with a disinterested stare, Tracker murmured, "That is classified." Hopefully, it was enough to have her drop the conversation.

Nodding slowly, the bouncer fell back into silence, only the twitch of her brow let slip her curiosity. With a jerk of her head, she gestured for him to enter as she returned to her task of keeping watch. Over what, Tracker wasn't certain of. It seemed that he might be the brothel's final patron for the night.

Tracker stepped through the main entrance only to be greeted by a dimly lit foyer. Much of the area was dark wood, the dull surfaces only adding to the gloom. A single flight of stairs led upwards and to the right, arching over a closed door.

The design gave him the overall impression of the sectioned living quarters found in the poorer areas of a city. Perhaps this part of Toptower had once been considered just that, with an economic shift being responsible for its current, more upmarket, standing.

But that didn't explain why the foyer was silent and devoid of anything he would remotely classify as welcoming. Very different to the other brothels he had visited. Most, like *The Gilded Lily*, filled their common room with music and dancing that was designed to be heard from the foyer. From there, they entertained prospective clients until a worker, or more, was chosen and they vanished upstairs for additional fun.

Perhaps the owner of this business had moved all of that up a level. There was a clear pathway up the stairs. Although, he heard no such merriment above either.

The sign and bouncer reassured him that he was in the correct kind of establishment, but it certainly wasn't the high-end sort he was used to. What of the barkeeper's suggestion that this was at least clean? Hard to tell without seeing the workers or their clients. That the foyer wasn't rundown gave him some hope.

It couldn't be a scam, could it? All this seemed a little too elaborate and a lot of work for a few coins here and there.

He turned back to the door. If he couldn't pay for sex here, then he would find someone eager for a good time elsewhere. It meant the loss of a gold coin, but that was of no consequence.

The hurried tap of feet reached him as he grabbed the door handle.

"Good sir," someone called from atop the stairs, pulling his attention back to a woman descending the stairs. "My apologies for the delay. I was several stories up." She froze halfway down, her warm smile icing over as he turned. Her gaze darted from clearly observing his ears to the sword at his hip.

Then she must've considered he wouldn't have made it through the door without a proper display of wealth, for her expression defrosted and she resumed trotting down the stairs. "I take it you have heard about my fine array of women? I assure you, they're all eager to service a discerning customer."

Tracker's brows rose. He'd never been in a brothel that explicitly suggested a gender upon entering. Every place he'd been to hosted a wide variety of genders. Did *The Creaming Tart* not follow that trend? "Your establishment is *just* women?" Whilst he considered himself a man with very little boundaries when it came to sexual preference, he did have a slight lean towards those with a penis. That didn't mean sex with them was always satisfactory. The problem being that most came with a one-and-done attitude that many brothel workers lacked. They were also typically harder to impregnate, something all of the King's Hounds were meant to avoid. "No other genders at all?"

Scoffing, the brothel mistress circled to stand between him and the door. "Men are too emotional to be part of my house. I've several women with dangling equipment if that's your desire. What do you prefer? Tall? Short? A figure with some plump? We've a vast variety." She ushered him up the stairs much like a parent with a wayward child. That wasn't normal, but he could see her getting desperate if business was slow. Of the two brothels he'd seen within the town, this was certainly the less lively.

Reaching the top of the stairs, the place started looking more like the usual establishments he visited. The area beyond the landing carried on to his left, down a narrow hall ending in another set of stairs. Doors dotted the passageway, all of them closed. If he didn't know any better, he would assume all the women were busy with clients, but he would've heard evidence of such acts. In his experience, even the quietest of beings gained a voice once within a brothel's walls.

"Ladies!" the mistress called, clapping her hands. The action threw Tracker back into a memory of his early childhood, of being summoned by the minders who raised would-be hounds.

The doors all opened and a group of women dutifully trotted out to stand along the room's far wall. The brothel mistress hadn't lied about the diversity in their height or size. There was a pair of elves, the duo pressing themselves hard against the wall, but the rest were all human.

The mistress looked over the group, seemingly displeased. "There are a few more, if none of these take your fancy. I'll go get them." She stalked off down the hall.

Ignoring the jab, Tracker made a show of mulling over his selection. Most of the women displayed an odd meekness. Every prostitute he'd ever met carried a certain pride in themselves.

These women all look like they dreaded being picked.

His gaze landed on the two statuesque types leaning into the corner. Both women had to be nearing six foot, maybe taller. The dark-haired one was quite svelte and clearly comfortable in a gown that showed a great deal of tanned thigh and frilly undergarments. The other woman—a russet-haired, bronze beauty like himself—was almost the first's opposite, having a soft curviness about her that was always nice to snuggle with afterwards.

The dark-haired one sneered at him. "I don't do elves," she said before he could make any sort of decision. "Their little pricks are too much of a disappointment."

Tracker grinned. *That* was the confidence he expected to find in those working here. "I am quite certain that mine is the same size as yours, my dear woman." As frilly as the woman's clothes were, the bulge within her undergarments was unmistakable. One of those with the dangling equipment the mistress had alluded to. "I could be wrong, of course. It is nothing that cannot be addressed with a little measuring contest, yes? I am game to whip it out right here if you are."

"We like the taller types, then?" the mistress said, returning from down the hall, preceded by a handful of other women.

"Indeed." He would freely admit such a weakness. The act of having to climb up his chosen bed partner was exhilarating in its own right.

A familiar sensation tugged at his senses, drawing his attention to the gaggle of women the mistress had ushered in. A couple of them were obviously pregnant. One was close to due.

It was her that his senses drew him to. More specifically, the spellster child she carried.

A weary sigh slipped out his lips. Even when he wanted to forget for the briefest of moments, the universe reminded him of his duties.

"You." He singled out the woman, grabbing her arm before anyone objected. Being an elf, his fingers were longer than a human's, but the digits wrapped around her pale, almost ghostly, wrist as if he had grabbed a child. "I will have this one." He needed to speak with her, to learn if she knew the father was a spellster and where they might've gone.

He could very well be done with this town before the night was over.

CHAPTER 9

Tracker followed the pregnant woman into a room. Most brothels arranged for their prostitutes to have their own rooms to work in. It allowed for personalisation, especially for those trained in the more extreme arts. By the end of his time in *The Gilded Lily*, his own accommodations had been quite elaborate with ropes and swings hanging from the ceiling, and rings dotted all around his bed.

He took in the room's lack of anything beyond a bed and a chest, unease bubbling through his veins. He hadn't expected this room to be as lush, but it should've held other items. This room had more in common with a prison cell.

Settling himself on the edge of the bed, Tracker tried not to think of all the other things that could currently be sharing the obviously dirty linen. "What is your name, my dear woman?" He struggled to keep his voice calm. His body vibrated with the desire to chase down something. Anything.

Fiddling with the ties to her gown, she glanced over to the door. "You may call me Lucky."

"Because I am about to get lucky, yes?" Scoffing, he shook his head. How he hated the insistence of some brothels changing their prostitutes' names. When he chose sex, he wanted it to be with the actual person, not a concept.

The woman parted her gown to reveal her as being naked beyond a pair of tattered undergarments that barely clung to her form. "What is your desire?" The unobstructed view also exposed just how exceedingly thin her limbs and neck were. Almost skeletal.

Was the mistress starving her? He had heard rumours—horrified whispers spoken in the dark—of brothels using such abuse to force a miscarriage. Never before had he witnessed irrefutable evidence.

"Please, my dear woman, you can stop." Tracker held up a hand to halt her from further disrobing. "There truly is no need for you to continue. I still intend to pay for your time, but am uninterested in having sex with you." Even without her skittishness, the very notion had vanished from his mind the instant he felt the unborn child's magic. Seeing how undernourished the woman was only amplified his indifference to the act.

The woman swiftly closed her gown, confusion scrunching her face.

"Your real name?" he gently prodded. "If I may?"

"It's Crystal."

Tracker bowed his head in acknowledgement. He should've guessed, what with the pale, crystalline violet shade of her eyes. "Well, Crystal, do you know who I am? Or rather, what?"

"Apart from a very well-armed elf?" She smiled. "We get mercenaries and soldiers coming through all the time, good sir."

"And the King's Hounds. You have heard of them, yes?"

The woman's eyes widened. One hand cradled her abdomen. "Is it—?"

"Yes, the child you carry possesses magic." How much, he couldn't be sure. It was difficult to tell with adults and, in his experience with children, they had growth spurts in more than the physical sense.

"I knew it," she whispered. "A part of me has always known."

"The one who impregnated you? They were also a spellster. They have long since vanished, yes?" In a town that had at least one hound passing through every few months, it would be foolish for an unleashed spellster to linger. But his mission here could be as simple as that.

Crystal nodded. "He left six months ago, before even *I* knew for certain that..." She caressed her belly, a sad smile curving her lips. "He wasn't meant to be gone this long. A few weeks. A month, at most. I had to come here just to make enough to keep a roof over my head."

"I am sorry to hear that." Either the spellster had fled the prospect of parenthood or, far more likely, a hound had encountered him. "I am also sorry to inform you that one of the King's Hounds will come for your child." Given that Tracker knew precisely who to look for, the hound mistress might even send him. "They will be raised in the tower." Where they'd never set foot outside the walls again.

Such was the fate of every spellster child born in Demarn. The kings of old had considered incarceration kinder than the alternative.

The woman caressed her belly with both hands as if the bony digits were enough to shield the unborn child from the truth. "You can't take them." As defiant as the words tried to be, her chin still wobbled. "They're still inside me, still growing."

"But you are close to giving birth." That was the only way he could have sensed it. Any other time before the final month, he could've bumped straight into her and felt nothing. "I am afraid I must report your condition to the pack." He hated doing it, but he'd seen the outcome of children left in the care of those who couldn't teach them.

The scent of blackened wood doused by the rain. The crunch of charcoal beneath his boots. The charred mass of a family huddled in what had once been a bed, their arms wrapped around the small frame they tried to comfort.

Tracker blinked away the memory. He'd been too late, just like with the last one.

He couldn't let it happen again.

"There has to be another way." Crystal settled next to him on the bed, one leg tucked beneath her in a clear preparation to spring back. "I'll do whatever's needed, I just—" The woman bowed her head. "I've lost so much, sacrificed even more. I don't know what I'd do if I lost them, too."

A different face overlaid hers in his mind's eye. A young human, barely fifteen. *Wynne.* Lover to him, Zinnala and Hunk. Mother to their daughter. Dead because of their decision to take the safe route and linger rather than flee.

He didn't need to ask himself what she would've done if faced with a mother desperate to keep their child. She would've stuck to the creed, just as she'd done with her own child, wavering only when faced with Zinnala's fears.

Forgive me, my loves. The two women often sang his praises whenever he defeated his opponents during training, Wynne in particular crowing about him being the perfect hound. A claim that always earned Hunk's ire.

He wasn't. Otherwise, the hound mistress wouldn't have tried so hard to break him, to extinguish all thought beyond the cold facts of his tasks.

No proper King's Hound would ever consider aiding a parent in keeping their spellster child.

Sighing, Tracker rummaged amongst his coins, fishing out a single blackened disc of metal bearing the royal insignia. "Take this to the local merchant guild." He wasn't meant to hand over the sigils to another, but he had since given up on that ruling long ago. "They will give you enough gold for you to make the journey to Dvärghem."

Bewilderment furrowed her brow. "Why would I travel to the dwarf's land?"

"They can ensure your child is not taken from you." When it came to spellster children, he typically dealt with orphans. Only the young could be dwarf-claimed but, given that the mother would arrive still pregnant or with a newborn in tow, this would be an unusual case. The hedgewitches would still accept her, no less so than anyone else seeking refuge. "Keeping the child *is* what you want, yes?"

"Yes," she echoed. "But..." Shaking her head, the woman returned the sigil. "If my mistress found out I had this, she'd take it for herself."

"I understand." He'd heard of such mistresses. He hadn't the displeasure of working under one as, even during his unwilling service at *The Gilded Lily* in his late teens, any extra money the patrons gave had always been his. Still, there were ways around them. "Would she also stop you from leaving?"

The woman picked at the hem of her robe and shook her head vehemently.

He leant back on the bed, fixing her with a cool stare. He'd been to plenty of brothels in his lifetime. He knew the mannerisms that made up those who willingly chose this profession. Her very demeanour suggested her position here wasn't a choice she had made. If the mistress truly was keeping her here against her will, then this woman would not be the only one.

Sure enough, her gaze dropped. Her head bobbed in a barely perceptible nod.

Tracker closed his eyes. He dug his fingers into the bedding and breathed deep. Anything to keep himself still. If he moved now, someone was going to die. Slowly and painfully. "Then, it seems I must resort to taking you," he managed to say with little of his ire slipping out.

Her head snapped up, fear and shock widening her eyes. "Sir Hound? I don't under—"

"Gather your things." He stood, dusting off his hands. His fingers itched for his throwing knives. Just one knick of a blade and the mistress would fall. It wouldn't even be murder, more of a mercy-killing. "You are leaving with me. Now." She could bunk with him for the evening and he would see her on the way to Dvärghem come the morning.

Going north from here would take her directly past the spellster tower, but hounds didn't linger there for long and few had the ability to sense magic in those yet to be born. Even he hadn't known until they stood in the same room. She could walk straight past another hound with them being none the wiser.

If she continued her way north at Whitemeadow, there were only villages where hounds rode through on a random patrol. She'd a decent chance of making it.

The woman had very little to her name. No personal effects and one set of threadbare clothes that couldn't quite stretch over her belly.

A sigh slipped out Tracker's nose at the sight. He would have to furnish her with something decent if she was to reach the dwarven border alive, especially given that summer was almost done with the world. He would also need to do so alone if he didn't want the extra attention.

Not many would think twice of someone escorting a prostitute into an inn room, but through a marketplace was certain a different issue. Crystal would need to remain confined to his inn room whilst he did so. He didn't like the idea, but purchasing clothes obviously not for someone of his build or height would draw less interest than having an obviously pregnant woman trailing behind a King's Hound.

With nothing else suitable to fully cover her, Tracker draped the woman's slim shoulders in the blanket.

He eased the door open, relieved that the brothel mistress was at least not the sort who locked her patrons in. Ushering Crystal out into the empty corridor, he led the way towards the stairs.

His senses twitched at every groan and creak of the floorboards underfoot. He doubted the building housed any actual danger to himself, but being caught risked dragging others into a fight. He had already failed at protecting so many others, he didn't want more innocent blood on his hands.

All around them, the rooms carried an edgy stillness. The women within knew precisely what he was attempting and, whilst they clearly weren't going to stop them, they also wouldn't help. How many were in the same bind? Didn't they realise that escaping as a horde would have a far more favourable outcome? Or had they all been terrified into obedience?

Tracker silently cursed himself for not recognising the unease earlier. The very idea of people being snatched up and forced into this profession was more in line with some cautionary folklore of old than reality. That very notion of implausibility was likely the reason why this brothel kept running unchallenged.

The creak of another's footsteps coming from the room to his left caught his attention. He halted, hoping with all his heart that was just another prostitute and not who he thought.

The sounds died down, along with the rapid tempo of his heart. Maybe he *would* get Crystal out of here with little trouble.

"Good sir," the brothel mistress called after them. "Is something the matter? If she isn't to your satisfaction, I can get another whore."

Tracker straightened, his hand casually coming to rest on the hilt of his scimitar. Subterfuge clearly wasn't at play tonight. A more direct stance would have to do. "Under the authority of the king, this woman is now the responsibility of the King's Hounds." He turned to fix the mistress with a hard stare and gently swept Crystal behind him. "We are leaving this establishment."

The mistress tilted her head like a confused pigeon. She strolled down the hall like a cat on the prowl. "I thought the King's Hounds hunted spellsters? She has no magic, I would know."

"She does not," he agreed, although he wasn't entirely certain if a spellster pregnancy could mask the mother's magic. He'd never met an expecting spellster. "But the child does."

The mistress sauntered by them as if they were of no consequence, coming to a halt at the top of the stairs. "But there's nothing to stop you waiting until it's born, correct? From what I've heard, spellster children are taken from their parents all the time."

He fought to keep his expression neutral. "Are you saying she cannot leave?" The beginning hiss of a snarl escaped on the words.

"It is a matter of business. She owes me a great deal. I took her in after her lover flew the coop, kept her fed and clothed. None of that was free." She laughed. "Why, if I did that for every waif who comes my way, I'd be destitute myself."

His fingers tightened around his scimitar's hilt. Drawing the blade and letting the edge taste blood was tempting. The kingdom certainly wouldn't miss the woman.

But there were laws, certain procedures, he was to follow. The creed was very clear on involving himself in a town's legalities. It wasn't a done thing. Doing so drew attention, alerted spellsters hidden amongst innocent civilians.

In this instance, it would complicate getting Crystal and her unborn child away from here.

Tracker carefully detached his grasp from the hilt. "If you are forcing her to work, to take on clients when she is an unwilling party, that is not business, that is torture." He turned to the surrounding rooms. Other prostitutes milled about in them. Some remained unseen, others peeked through gaps in their doors. None of them appeared willing to make themselves known, but they also refused to tear themselves away from the drama.

How many worked here against their will? Did the local authorities know how this woman ran her so-called business? He doubted it.

Tomorrow, he would return with the city guard to shut down this place and see the mistress thrown in jail. But first, he had to ensure Crystal's safety and that meant getting her as far from this brothel as he could tonight.

He bowed his head. "If you will excuse us?" Not waiting for an answer—and knowing it wouldn't be the one he was after—he guided Crystal past the woman and down the stairs, ensuring he was between them at all times.

"You think you can just walk out with my investment?" she snarled. "Guards!"

The scramble of several pairs of feet reached Tracker's ears a moment before the door below the stairs burst open. Three men piled through the opening. They overflowed the space, each one wielding a different blunt weapon. By the way the trio twisted their expressions and postured, they were more used to intimidating their opponents than actually fighting.

Tracker had brought down bigger targets than them.

Keeping one hand on Crystal's hip to ensure she remained tucked behind him, he sought out his throwing knives with the other. Many of their blades bore traces of various poisons, some potent enough to drop a strong spellster. For these three, it would only take a scratch. "I will give you all one chance to lay down your weapons," he declared to the men.

The trio didn't even pause. They charged at him, their weapons at the ready.

And fell before their second step, each one with a knife embedded in the face.

Tracker turned back to the brothel mistress, his fingers twitching to give her a similar fate. She would fall with just as much ease. But he was already interfering with so much and what good would a jail sentence do for those she had abused?

The creed be damned. This wouldn't be the first time he had ignored it.

He flung a knife at the mistress, cursing under his breath as she ducked behind the stair railing. Even her gasp as the blade sailed by suggested she had also missed being nicked.

"Izzy!" the woman screamed, still stumbling down the stairs and keeping out of Tracker's sight. "For gods' sake, you better not be slacking!"

"Who is Izzy?" he asked of Crystal, gaining an answer only in the woman's brief glance towards the front door. "The bouncer?"

Crystal nodded.

Tracker had actually forgotten about the bouncer. He had assumed the woman would appear alongside the brothel mistress' previous call for aid if she was still within earshot.

The door Tracker had been inching towards slammed open. The bouncer filled the space, one hand curled around a baton that looked heavy enough to break bones. She froze halfway through the door, her head jerking left to right as she took in the chaos confined in such a small space.

"It is Izzy, yes?" Tracker slipped another knife from its sheath, ready to use it the instant she came at him. "I do not wish to fight you." He had witnessed too many pointless deaths just in these past few months. If he could convince her to stay out of this conflict, he'd consider it a triumph. "And I am willing to believe you knew nothing about your employer's true nature. Or of why these women never seem to leave."

Doubt flickered across Izzy's face at his final words. Her gaze slid from him to the dead men. "Where did they come from?" she demanded of him as if he knew. "And what do you think you're doing with that prostitute?"

Relieved that she was at least willing to talk, Tracker sheathed his throwing knife. If he could reason with her, then it was another on his side and someone who could alert the guards without him becoming entangled. "To answer your last question first, I am aiding this dear woman in her desire to escape this place."

"Escape?" Izzy echoed. She glanced from him to Crystal, then to the brothel mistress, clearly no less puzzled.

"Fool!" the mistress snapped. "Ignore him and do your job."

"You must have noticed something is not right here, yes?" Tracker persisted. "That, no matter the time of day, the only people to exit are those you permit in? But the women here, they must visit family, friends or even spend time wandering the markets."

Izzy's brows lowered, as did the tension in her body. "I figured they went out a back way, that it happened on the day shifts I wasn't working."

Crystal stepped forward, one hand reaching back to rest on Tracker's chest, insurance that he was within reach. "There isn't another way out, Iz. We don't leave. Ever. She threatens to drag us back or see us thrown in jail."

"May the gods damn you," the mistress snarled. "Don't I pay you to deal with cur like this?" she demanded of Izzy, shoving her as if the other woman wasn't twice her size.

Izzy barely budged. "You pay me to keep out those with no money and to deal with clients who get rough. I'm not the warder of some sick jail."

"You'd believe a runaway and an elf?" Scoffing, the brothel mistress snatched the baton from Izzy's lax grasp. "You're fired. I'll deal with this matter myself." She lunged for Crystal, the baton raised.

Tracker drew Crystal out of range, putting himself between the pair.

He needn't have bothered. The brothel mistress had barely taken a step, her progress halted by Izzy's firm grasp on her upraised arm.

"So, it's true," the bouncer growled.

The mistress flailed in Izzy's grasp, swatting ineffectively at the lightly armoured chest and arms, kicking out like a child throwing a tantrum. "Let me go, you little—"

Her tirade stopped as Izzy thwacked her over the back of the head with the baton. She collapsed unceremoniously to the floor.

With the brothel's mistress unconscious and no one else to take charge, Izzy strode out into the evening air to alert the town's guard.

Tracker lingered in the foyer, keeping one eye on the mistress, even though he doubted she would wake for some time. He also checked on Crystal, who seemed no worse the wear beyond her nerves being frayed. That would likely change once they reached somewhere she deemed as safe. The way an individual's mind managed to compartmentalise things never failed to amaze him.

"We can leave," he gently reminded her, gesturing to the front door Izzy had left open on her way out. If they hurried, they could be several blocks away before the city guard got near the place. Only the mistress and the bouncer would even know of them being here.

Crystal shook her head. "I can't. Not yet. The guards. They'll want to talk to me, won't they?"

It was a possibility. Despite the law being the same throughout Demarn, those governing each settlement had different methods when it came to dealing with crime. "Of course, your words would carry a great deal of leverage, but I am certain the guards will find enough evidence without it." A single testimonial would be enough to have this place shut down and the brothel mistress jailed.

He tilted his head, listening to the whisper of footsteps from above. The other women would've heard the commotion, it was only a matter of time before one or two grew bold enough to discover the cause. How many of them were here unwillingly? Crystal couldn't be the only one. As much as he wanted it to be otherwise, people like the brothel's mistress didn't generally stop at a single victim.

"Even so, I…" She pulled the blanket tighter around her. "I want to make sure she can't do this to anyone else."

Tracker bowed his head. "As you desire." He could forcibly take her from this place, and she likely knew that, but if she needed to see the guards take away the very person who had caused her so much misery, then he wasn't going to deny her that closure.

Whatever Izzy told the city guards, they were quicker to respond than Tracker expected. Although, the way the trio burst through the door with their weapons drawn seemed unnecessary. What sort of resistance were they expecting?

The woman leading the charge halted upon seeing Tracker. "Sir Hound." Bowing her head, she smoothly sheathed her sword. "That the one responsible?" She indicated the brothel's mistress with the tip of her chin.

Tracker nodded. "I am uncertain how many women she has here or who was kept against their will, but it was at least one." He guided

Crystal before him. "This one, to be precise."

The guard looked over the woman, her brows lowering. "One's too many."

That was definitely something they agreed upon.

"Ma'am," the guard continued to Crystal. "I have questions, if I may? We can speak here or somewhere else. The guardhouse, if you'd feel safer there."

Crystal cast only a hesitant glance his way before stating, "Here is fine." Drawing herself upright, she ventured into the far corner with the guard.

Tracker stood patiently near the bottom of the stairs, keeping an eye on the door and the landing above them, whilst the pair conversed. He caught scraps of their conversation—with his hearing, it was difficult not to—but tried to be considerate of her privacy and ignore what he could.

"I don't understand it," muttered the only man amongst the trio of guards to the third in their group. The pair had already ensured the mistress was shackled, in the off chance she suddenly awoke, and now examined the downed men. "This place has been around since before my grandpa. It had a good reputation. Why throw all that away?"

The other guard shrugged as she crouched over the second dead body. "I would say that's a question for the captain to ask." She frowned at the mistress' prone form. "If the wench ever comes to again. That bouncer wasn't kidding about knocking her out. Given her a decent egg on the back of her head." She straightened, wiping her hand on the back of the dead man's shirt. "We definitely won't be getting any answers from this lot."

Tracker grimaced. He should've attempted to neutralise them rather than outright kill. His only thought had been in getting Crystal to safety without alerting the city guard. *So much for that.* At least no one asked what he was doing here. They probably assumed it was for the same reason anyone visited a brothel.

The second guard jerked his head up to stare at the stairway. "Looks like we're being watched."

Tracker followed the man's gaze.

Sure enough, a gaggle of wide-eyed women stood in a clump on the landing. They hadn't been there long. None of them looked ready to bolt for the door. Maybe the full reality of their situation had yet to sink in. How long had they been under the mistress' hold? Months? Years? They would definitely need time readjusting to their newfound freedom.

"I think I recognise some of them," the third guard murmured to the other. "Isn't the redhead one of the women supposedly taken by a spellster?”

Her fellow guard halted, alarm freezing his face. He whirled to face Tracker. “Is there a spellster here?”

Tracker shook his head, carefully keeping his attention off Crystal, who still spoke with the first guard. “I would say no unleashed spellster has entered the city for some months. You thought otherwise, yes?”

“You hear rumours all the time,” the man replied as if that statement was enough of an answer.

“And you listened to those rumours, yes?” Any whisper about spellsters often carried a nasty habit of being believed by everyone who heard. People liked having someone to blame and spellsters made the perfect target. It didn’t always mean truth lingered in the whispers. “You sent for a King’s Hound without searching places like this?” Brothels weren’t always the first place a missing person was found at, but they did grant a certain amount of secrecy if people wanted to disappear. He knew of one worker, an elven man called Matz, who had originally escaped the Heimatian guards trailing him from their homeland by jumping from one brothel to the other. “What of the surrounding farms?”

The two guards looked at each other, then shrugged.

Tracker balled his hands to quash the rising anger stirring in his soul. He had come to Toptower because the hound mistress had assigned him the task. He was already later than expected. It had meant letting others escort a terrified spellster child to the dwarven border because being elsewhere when he had a prior duty would’ve alerted his fellow hounds.

That child had died. She would still be alive if he’d been at her side to keep her calm. They could’ve even avoided an attack altogether.

And the guards here hadn’t even bothered to check the logical places before calling for aid?

Taking a deep breath, he softly reminded himself that he wouldn’t have been in the places he had if not for their incompetence. The two spellsters who had destroyed lives would still be out there. And the one whose life he had failed to save might’ve actually lived.

Furthermore, no amount of violence would bring anyone back from the dead. Moving forward and ensuring no other innocents met the same fate was the only way. “I will speak of this with your superiors in the morning. Right now, there are people who require your aid. I would suggest starting with a sweep of the building to flush out the others involved.” They might not have shown themselves, but there had to be others. Three thugs might’ve been enough to keep a group of cowed people in line, but not to run this place.

Although, they also could've been scared off by the guards' arrival. Maybe they had also been in too much of a rush to cover their trail. No one had yet been good enough to hide themselves from him. Being able to find the untraceable was the reason the hound mistress had designated him as a tracker.

Another guard strode through the doorway, spearheading a second group. She paused at the foot of the stairs, staring up it with mild curiosity before turning on her heel and casting an unimpressed eye across the brothel mistress' unconscious form. "She's still here? No matter," she continued before either guard could answer. "Have the fifth unit escort her to our inner cells, we'll see what the mayor thinks of all this in the morning. Although, I doubt they'll be pleased."

The other guards saluted. "At once, commander."

The commander paid them no mind beyond a curt nod, her attention falling upon the three dead men. "Who's responsible for this? The mayor will have a fit if they find out we—"

"*I* did it," Tracker announced.

The woman's brows rose. "Sir Hound? Forgive me, I was not informed of your arrival." She fixed a stern look on the remaining guards. "I trust your execution of these thugs was necessary?"

"Very."

"See that is noted in the report, captain," she ordered the dark-haired woman standing by the door. "I want this whole building cleared out, bottom to top. Everything you find, see that it's catalogued. Every woman you talk to, I want names, townships."

"Already underway, ma'am," the captain replied, signalling the new guards to begin. The address surprised Tracker. No matter the gender, 'sir' had always been considered the respectful address amongst the city guards.

"*And,*" the commander continued with barely a nod of acknowledgement to the captain. "I want to know who else that bitch was working with."

Tracker nodded to himself. Finally, some competence.

"You. Um, miss?" the commander's voice softened as she approached Crystal. "You are one of the victims? I'm afraid we'll need to escort you to—"

"And this is where I step in," Tracker said, inserting himself between the two women. He could already see that he wasn't going to get Crystal out of the town without revealing the true nature of her unborn child.

The commander halted, her brow furrowed in confusion. "What reason would a King's Hound need for a...?" Her eyes widened as realisation lit her face. "She's a—" The woman stepped closer, cupping her mouth as she whispered, "—spellster?"

A single guard froze in trotting up the stairs. The slight point to his ears suggested elven heritage and a possibility of having the same enhanced hearing. He glanced their way, jumping upon meeting Tracker's gaze and continued on.

That could become quite the problem, especially if the man gossiped with his fellow guards.

"She is not," Tracker admitted. "But her child is and, given the current circumstances, I think it best if she is removed from this place immediately, yes?"

The commander nodded thoughtfully. "Where are you bunked?"

Tracker opened his mouth to respond and realised he hadn't paid much attention to the name of the inn. "Just across from *The Soldier's Fancy.*"

The commander nodded. "I know the place. Bit of an armpit. I'll have a few of my people relocate your effects to a more suitable place. In the meantime..." She clapped her hand across Tracker's shoulders, drawing him further from the exit. "You and I have a lot to discuss."

CHAPTER 10

Four days. That was the last time Dylan had seen any sign of a building, of civilisation, which had been in the form of a town the hound called Toptower. They had left the place behind almost as soon as they'd arrived. The cart, too, much to his chagrin.

Dylan wriggled atop the saddle, his backside in danger of going numb, and silently cursed whoever first thought travelling aboard these hairy creatures was a good idea. He longed for the chance to walk under his own power. Even the cart would've been preferable. Although, he remembered little of travelling in it, especially near the beginning of their journey. Pain and nausea, mostly.

The leashed woman, who he had learnt was called Ava, rode at his side seemingly without thought. Like the hound, who rode ahead of them, she looked at ease atop her placid mount.

Dylan wished the same could be said of him, but try as he might, comfort was not a goal easily maintained perched as he was upon the beast's swaying back. The lack of proper, army-issued attire probably didn't help as it forced Dylan to ride side-saddle, whilst the women were able to sit astride their mounts.

He eyed Ava's dark green robes, not for the first time. Each leashed spellster wore the same thing regardless of their gender. They seemed no less forgiving in the leg region than his normal robes. Yet, Ava also wore dark trousers, allowing her to hike up the skirts without baring her entire leg to the elements.

Now he had spent time outside the duelling arena with her, he recalled Ava's presence in the tower. In a vague sense. They'd little in the way of interaction before she went on to win her brawl five years ago, the only thing he clearly remembered of the woman. The face he recalled from the past was different, too. Not as dark or heavily freckled. She still had the sort of doe-eyed features that would've seen her lost in a crowd of elves, even if she did lack the ears.

She had spoken little throughout their journey, falling into complete silence whenever he enquired about the army encampment. Even the hound refused to speak a great deal of the place.

Dylan didn't understand it. Surely, preparing him for his new life was an ideal usage of their time travelling. Even a few pointers here and there at night would've helped, but he got nothing.

He contented himself with the knowledge that, very soon, all this trekking along the rough roads leading to the army camp would be over. The hound insisted the main encampment was almost upon them and he fancied that his ears picked up distant sounds of people, growing stronger with each passing hour.

The hound came to an abrupt halt in the middle of the road, throwing up her hand to indicate they do the same.

Dylan hauled on the reins, but the nag refused to obey until it stood flush with the hound's heavier mount.

The woman frowned, her eyes still trained on the bushes to their left.

He focused on the same spot, straining both sight and hearing to sense what she had picked up, to no avail. He spied little through the bushes beyond more wild undergrowth and the only sounds greater than the breeze was that of their breathing. "What is it?"

She pressed a finger to her lips.

They remained silent for a while longer. Then, as his horse grew restless, he caught the subtle crunch of something walking through the brush.

A scout? Seemed like the most logical answer. People would tend to a perimeter if they were as close to the camp as the hound believed.

But did it mean the people out there were on the same side?

Dylan gnawed on his bottom lip, trying to pinpoint the sound's origins as well as keep an ear out for any orders of attack from the hound. Without his magic, he was weak at best and defenceless at worse. As it stood, the woman was the superior of their trio and the only one able to give the signal to use his magic. He couldn't even summon a shield to keep them safe without her say-so.

If his magic was needed, then the hound would give him sanction to use it. Providing she didn't die from an arrow beforehand.

An elven man, garbed in mottled shades of green and brown, appeared through the bushes, his bow trained on them. "Who goes?" he demanded, his question posed at them as a group.

Behind Dylan, he caught fleeting glimpses of other people emerging from the undergrowth.

"I am Fetcher of the King's Hounds," the hound replied. "I return from the spellster tower with the borrowed spellster and a fresh leashed one." She leant over in her saddle, pressing close enough to Dylan to whisper, "Show them your collar."

Out the corner of his eye, he spied Ava already displaying her collar to the man.

Dylan followed suit, pulling down the edge of his robe and tipping his head back to display the chain mail encircling his neck. A strange knot tangled his gut and flushed his cheeks. He would never consider himself prudish, but revealing the *infitialis* collar to this stranger had an oddly intrusive quality.

Nevertheless, the display seemed to satisfy the man. He lowered his bow and indicated for them to pass with the silent twitch of his head.

Fetcher urged her horse onwards, letting the others fall in behind. Dylan allowed his horse to resume its swaying plod. He ran his finger along the collar, absentmindedly trying to find a hole in the links big enough to fit his nail. Sadly, like fine, tightly-woven linen, there wasn't any give in the meshwork.

On his left, Ava rolled her eyes. In their weeks of travel, he had also learnt she was his junior by two years, but that hadn't stopped her from acting as if she were far older. He recalled her sharp manner far more readily than her face, which led him to the possibility that she'd been one of the generous many who'd rejected his advances. "Do stop that," she snapped. "The camp will think you have fleas or worse."

"It itches." Everywhere itched, now that he turned his attention to it. His skin had gone red after the first day's travel and had shown no sign of fading until the hound granted him sanction to use his magic on their fifth day from the tower.

His innate healing had worked to restore his skin to its original ivory shade almost as soon as the woman finished speaking the order. It had hurt, even with her permission. He still wasn't sure why the collar burned. Originally, Dylan thought the sparks that had seared his skin upon first trying to use unsanctioned magic was a warning measure, but now...

It rather reminded him of the alchemist's unstable shield.

His gaze swung back to Ava. He hadn't asked, but he'd the distinct impression that her collar wasn't as temperamental. Would it also go the same way as the *infitialis* shield? *No.* The collars weren't some experiment. Their usage went back thousands of years, to before elves arrived on the continent.

The hound glanced over her shoulder at them before drawing her horse level with his. "Itching or not, scratching it won't do you any good." She reached out and slapped his hand away. "What use are you to the army if you die of infection, hmm?"

Glowering at the woman, Dylan shook his hand before entangling his fingers in the horse's mane.

"And do not give me that look." She huffed. "Honestly, some of you spellsters are worse than children."

He sucked at his teeth, resisting the altogether juvenile urge to poke his tongue out. Instead, he turned his attention to the road. Unlike the last three days, where the well-trodden path had meandered something fierce, this piece ran arrow-straight and, from the feel of it, was starting to climb.

Dylan leant forward, trying to maintain his balance on the nag's wide back. They rode in silence for a while. There was a strange haze in the distance, like dust being kicked up by the wind. The steadily growing sounds of life he had once fancied hearing were now definite.

"Fetcher?" he finally enquired of the hound. "Is that a family name or a title?" Family names weren't common in the tower, most of the spellsters who had one were also those born elsewhere in the kingdom. Many alluded to the work their families had done for generations. For a few, their name was as simple as the settlement where they'd been brought into the world.

For spellsters like himself, they hadn't even that. All his life, he'd simply been *Dylan*.

The hound's back became rod-stiff. "Never mind about my name," she snapped. "Just remember to stay at my side once we enter the camp."

He gave a noncommittal grunt. It didn't matter that he was leashed and about as useful as a paper shield without sanction, he still wasn't to be given an ounce of trust. Not even to walk unescorted amongst the very people he was to fight alongside. *Do they really fear us so much?* He frowned down at the horse's mane, recalling the wariness with which the people in the villages treated both Ava and himself, as though they expected them to become some terrible demons.

It was all Udynea's doing. If the empire hadn't come blasting at their borders all those centuries ago, the ordinary people of Demarn wouldn't be so ready to oust every spellster. Then everyone in the tower could be leading normal lives, love without fear of losing those they held dear and those who fell pregnant wouldn't have to suffer their babies being taken from them at birth.

"We are here," Fetcher said, breaking him out of his musing.

Dylan lifted his head. He'd been so lost in himself that he hadn't noticed their upward climb lessening or that the sounds of people were now near-deafening after days of hushed wilderness; the clash of soldiers training intermingled with the shouts of people trying to be heard over the din.

The road had opened out to a field that seethed with people like a busy anthill.

His nag carried on following the hound's horse as he stared. Some of the people halted in their duties as their little trio passed, jostling and jeering at each other. A few—amongst both men and women—whistled and called out lewd invitations. At first, he thought the calls were directed at the two women who were known to the soldiers, but as he became accustomed to the cacophony and the cries grew clearer, it was painfully obvious they were meant for him.

Dylan tipped his nose to the sky, trying to block out the suggestions that threatened to set his ears ablaze. They were testing him, he was certain of it. He'd seen those sorts of expressions before, when young men and women started training against their more seasoned peers in the tower. *Fresh meat.*

If they thought he could be intimidated by mere words, they were sorely mistaken.

Instead, he turned his ear to the hum of countless voices that almost sounded like a day in the tower, the noise overlaid by the less familiar clank of metal. Everywhere he looked, people seemed to be going somewhere or doing something.

They reached a group of unsaddled horses confined in a pen of rope. Fetcher whistled as they halted and a woman, flanked by two men, appeared from a nearby tent. The woman took up the reins of the dark brown horse as the hound dismounted. One of the men, a gangly fellow who couldn't have been much older than eighteen, grabbed the reins of Dylan's nag whilst the other man saw to the remaining horse.

Dylan slithered to the ground. His legs wobbled as they took his weight, but mercifully held. He straightened and slowly followed the hound to where she waited by the tent the trio had emerged from. His thighs ached terribly and his neck...

He balled his hands, refusing to heed the call to touch the collar.

"Thank you for your assistance, spellster," Fetcher said to Ava as the woman scurried to their side. "I hereby absolve you of my command, effective immediately. You may return to your superiors."

"Yes, Sir Hound." Giving a brief bow, Ava shuffled off with her head down and her hands clasped before her.

The hound turned her attention back to him. "Come."

He trotted after Fetcher as fast as his still aching legs would allow. His thighs grew better with each step, eventually letting him walk alongside her. They strode past tents arranged in neat lines. Although the wedge-shaped structures were uniform in size, quite a number had the stained and ragged look of age.

Was that where he'd end up, sleeping beneath one of those battered canvas shelters? A far cry from the sturdy beds he'd spent his whole life in. But that was why these people were here, to ensure those who couldn't fight had a chance to sleep on within their homes, content in the knowledge that they were safe.

More people congregated around the tents, eyeing their passage in silence. A few ignored them completely. After the previous calling, he thought the quiet would ease his bubbling stomach. Yet, the knot forming there only grew tighter.

"Where do I go from here?" he asked the hound. No one in the tower had been at all specific in what happened once the winner of the brawl was leashed and at the camp, only that they served as counters to the enemy spellsters who were at the beck and call of the Udynea Empire.

Fetcher slowed. "I was instructed to find the lieutenant upon our arrival. He will assign you to a troop. But we should be swift." Those last words seemed to be for herself as she picked up the pace. "And try to keep your mouth shut except for when he speaks to you, he has quite the temper."

The woman had barely taken another step before someone called her name. She halted, her head swinging in the caller's direction.

A man clothed in naught but a beige undershirt and trousers appeared through the crowd and hastened to their side. "Good to see you're back."

Fetcher jerked her chin at the man's waist. "You seem to be undone."

Grinning sheepishly, the man fumbled with the belt holding his trousers. "Damn thing. Trust *you* to spot that." His gaze swung towards Dylan, eyeing him in the same manner the guardians did when a young spellster was brought in from the outside. Hopeful, but wary. "Did they send a strong one this time?"

The hound peered at Dylan for some time before shrugging. "Who can say? If he keeps his wits about him in the thick of it, then he might be good enough in a fight. He is a bit high maintenance, though."

The man grunted. "They usually are to begin with. Bloody tower coddles them like babes. A few days at the front will sort that out."

"Where is your lieutenant? The one charged with the spellster's care?"

"Infirmary." The man jerked a thumb in the general direction. "Overseeing the wounded."

"That—" Fetcher frowned, clearly troubled. "That is not standard procedure. What happened?"

The man shrugged. "All I know—all anybody knows, really—is that the enemy took out a scouting party. The front line sent the live ones here to get fixed up. Fat chance it'll do them. Those bastards don't hold back for no reason. I'd put a year's pay on them hiding something."

"I do not take sucker's bets." Fetcher lightly slapped his stomach with the back of her hand. "Go finish getting dressed. You know how finicky he gets over his men being out of uniform. I will catch up with you later."

The hound changed direction just as swiftly as the man raced back to his tent. She marched off to a group of large tents on their right.

Dylan silently trailed her, well aware of how intently they were being watched.

The infirmary was little more than a bigger tent. He had thought that, after centuries of being camped in the same place, someone would've made permanent structures for places like this. But he supposed wood burnt just as easily as canvas with more risks, whereas hauling enough stone out here was impractical.

Several soldiers lay groaning on the ground just outside the tent. People busied themselves about them, not seeming to do much but make the injured comfortable.

Dylan glanced at the tent and back. Were these people waiting for someone to take care of them? He gnawed on his bottom lip. Perhaps Fetcher would grant him sanction to heal them.

A man stood nearby, watching the commotion. He turned at their approach. "Ah, Sir Hound. Right on time. It's in the usual place." The man nodded at another tent. Like the infirmary, the flap remained lowered. Unlike the other tent, no one ventured from it.

Fetcher frowned. Those slate-grey eyes darted from the man to the tent and back. "Lieutenant, sir?" she briskly replied and tipped her head in Dylan's direction. "The new spellster?"

The man's cheerful features grew stone-like. "Of course." Those dark eyes, harder than the flint they mimicked, ran over him. "I'll take over your charge from here."

Dylan's collar tingled at the lieutenant's words. He fingered the metal links. Had the man's voice activated some latent magic embedded in the collar's making? Whilst he wasn't certain how it worked—Sulin had once tried to explain, giving up after Dylan had dozed off for the fourth time—he knew the collars would only let him use magic if the given sanction was made by those who had authority over a leashed spellster.

"Very good, sir," the hound said. Giving the lieutenant the briefest of bows, she set off for the tent the man had previously indicated.

Dylan watched her leave, his gaze slowly sliding to linger on the injured soldiers. One of them was clearly bleeding from his gut. Another had an arrow shaft sticking out of her chest. Had they been in the spellster tower, they would be mended by now.

"The bastards hit harder every time," the lieutenant muttered, seemingly to himself. "Always in secret. What are you hiding?" The man faced Dylan. "I hope you're worth it, spellster. We lost a lot of good people to those unleashed bastards when Fetch took one of our own to collect you."

Dylan's focus remained unwavering on the group. Whilst the people tending to them gave blankets and drink, no one saw to the man's bleeding bandage or the woman's arrow wound. "Shouldn't a physician be looking after them?" That was what non-spellster healers were called, wasn't it? Were they in such short supply that people risked dying? Why didn't the crown demand healers serve as well?

"It's already been done." The man spat onto the ground. "Can't do much about a gut full of steel except wait for the Seven Sisters to claim you."

There was *one* other thing, although the man was probably unaware of the alternative. How many of the spellsters here had learnt to use their ability for more than taking lives? Dylan was willing to bet that the number was very low. "I can help them."

The lieutenant gave a sceptical grunt. "Leave them be, spellster. They're in enough pain now. The Sisters are merciful to those who die through battle."

He knew that. Did the man think those in the tower didn't attend the same ceremonies? That they weren't brought up with the same scripture as everyone else? But his way of healing didn't hurt. It shouldn't, providing a would-be healer knew what they were doing. Perhaps one of the others had tried in the past without having the proper knowledge. *Nevertheless...*

Dylan tried to push out. Healing required touch to be accurate, but if he could just slip a tendril of power towards them and give those dying soldiers a greater chance at life—

Sparks fired from the collar, biting into his skin. He gritted his teeth, trying that little bit more, giving up only when the smell of burnt flesh invaded his nostrils. He felt around the collar, seeking to wriggle a finger beneath the metal. His skin stung at the faintest brush of cool air. If he could just find the seam...

"What do you think you're doing, spellster?" the lieutenant demanded, pushing his face close enough that Dylan could make out the man's individual pores. "Trying to remove our collar, are we? Not on my watch."

Dylan quickly lowered his hand. "Please. I can save them." He indicated the soldiers with a jerk of his chin. "Just give me sanction and I—"

"*You?*" the man snarled. His weather-beaten face grew darker with every heartbeat. "I don't know what they taught you in that tower of yours, but let me put you straight. You are a weapon, a tool, a *thing*." He spat the word with more venom than a snake. "Nothing but a sword with a big mouth.”

“Your men are dying.” They didn’t have to. If he could just make the lieutenant see that.

“Yes, and when they pass, they’ll face the Seven Sisters without your magic tainting their honour. I won’t risk their afterlife just because you fancy yourself as being better than our physicians.”

Dylan matched the man glare for glare. “I *am* better.” And healing a man from near death didn’t taint anything. Nowhere in the Divine Scripture did it say that the Seven Sisters guarding the passage of the Eternal River vilified the use of magic, at least no more than they did of any other tool. “I could have those people up and fighting by this time tomorrow.”

The man spat off a few curses before waggling his finger under Dylan’s nose. “You are here for one purpose, and that is to blow a hole in the enemy ranks when you are told. You do not use a sword to heal dying men.”

“But—”

The back of a hand connected with his face. Dylan collapsed, his face smacking into the ground.

Shock dulled his senses. Half-aware of his movements, he wobbled onto his elbows. His shaking fingers, almost moving of their own accord, tentatively worked along his jaw. Half his face was numb, but it seemed to be in one piece. Liquid pooled in his mouth. He spat it out. Red stained the dirt.

Dylan stared at the glob. It had been a long time since he’d seen his own blood.

Out the corner of his eye, he spied Fetcher reappearing from the tent. She gave him a cursory glance, before marching off on whatever errand the crown demanded of her.

The lieutenant stood over him, rubbing his knuckles. “You just don’t take ‘no’ for an answer, do you? This isn’t your precious tower. We don’t coddle your kind here.”

Feeling rushed back to his cheek, the flesh stinging both inside and out. Tears pricked his eyes. He rubbed the grit from them and glared up at the man. “You’d rather let those men die?”

“No, I’d prefer a hundred men like them to bastards like you. But the most I can grant is a comfortable death.” He straightened and commanded a woman clutching a small wooden board over to his side with the twitch of his head. “See that this troublemaker is sent to the front line, immediately.”

“Yes, sir!” The woman bobbed, writing furiously on the board, and scurried off.

“You like to argue with your superiors, precious? We’ll see how long that lasts after facing down some real terrors. Those monsters from Udynea won't show you mercy like I do. Now get up and get yourself cleaned. You want to help people live? You can start by doing what you're bred for."

Dylan waited until the lieutenant had turned his attention back to the injured before daring to touch his cheek again. No blood, not even a graze, just incredible heat. Dylan fumbled in his belt pouch for his shaving mirror. The surface revealed a massive red welt marking his skin.

By the time Dylan had staggered to his feet, the man Fetcher had previously spoken with appeared. He also held a board. Dylan eyed the paper clipped to it. What had the woman written? There was no question it was about him, but what?

"Well, now," the man said. "Fetch certainly wasn't lying about you being high maintenance, was she? Haven't even had the chance to get you measured for your uniform and the lieutenant's sending you into the thick of it. He must've really taken a disliking to you."

Dylan bit his tongue. He hadn't thought of it that way. His first official day in the army and, already, he'd managed to turn someone against him. *Wonderful.* And for what? His gaze swung back to the injured. One of them was now covered in a blanket. *I could've saved them.* His worth was more than that of a sword.

Wasn't it?

They left the infirmary, the layout of the tents thinning and growing increasingly more like sheets draped over poles as they neared the edge of the camp.

"You'll be staying here for the next few nights," the man said, indicating a large tent with a distracted flap of his hand. He rifled through the pages clipped to the board. "There'll be a small group leaving for the front line then. That'll give us time to see you adequately dressed. At least we won't have to make room for another bed. You can have Lilly's."

"Won't she object?"

"She won't be doing anything. She was with the lot you saw outside the infirmary. Took the brunt of their attack."

Dylan frowned. He didn't recall seeing anyone in the army-issued dark green robes amongst the wounded and they wouldn't bring a corpse back to camp. "I don't..." What of the other tent Fetcher had entered? A wounded and leashed spellster would likely require special attention, perhaps something only a hound could do. "Is she—?"

"Dead? Oh, very much so." His head lifted and, for a moment, Dylan swore there was pity on his face. "Just..." He sighed. "Try to keep your head down tomorrow. Remember your place and there'll be no trouble."

Grunting, he slipped into the tent only to halt in the entrance. The tent flap slapped his back, jolting him, but he moved no further.

Blankets lay across the majority of the space, save for a thin strip along the outer edges. Ten distinct spots in all, big enough to perhaps hold two people each although he doubted they would cram twenty bodies into a single tent.

Soft mumbling drew his gaze. One of the spots by the pole was already twice full, the all but unseen occupants huddled beneath the blankets practically sleeping on top of each other. Five other people milled near the far end of the tent. They eyed him with all the wariness of a cornered kitten as he ventured deeper into the space.

Movement on his left caught his eye. An elven woman he vaguely recalled as being of insurmountable will and power, quietly rocked in the corner near the entrance.

His gaze slid back to the others. They seemed unconcerned with their companion's actions. In fact, the more he looked at them, the more he saw the same expression as Ava. It was a sort of hollowness embedded in the eyes, like a light had been snuffed.

Dylan fingered his collar. The metal band didn't *have* to be around his neck. His head, his waist... the *infitialis* worked the same regardless. But a coronet could slip free and a belt was ungainly. Collars didn't fall off so easily.

They need us. The kingdom feared them, that was what his guardian had taught him. The crown put them in leashes of unstable metal because of a need to control what they feared.

Did he look like these people, too? The blatant lack of will? Was the nagging pressure he felt behind his eyes meant to be there? Did it bore into his ability to perceive pain until all feeling vanished?

No, that was impossible. Sulin had never mentioned *infitialis* affecting the mind like that. The only ability it possessed was the suppression and negation of magic. Whatever had happened to these people, the collar wasn't to blame.

That thought didn't make him feel any better.

CHAPTER 11

Grumbling to himself, Tracker exited the farmhouse and headed to his horse. *Still no spellster.* He had been here for almost a fortnight. Had scoured every inch of the city, roamed the surrounding farmland and even delved into the nearby forest. All to no avail.

He could've left within the first few days, chalked the rumours up to the brothel mistress and her unsavoury dealings, or even of ordinary civilians using the notion of a rogue spellster to save face about the true reason their partner or adult child had left.

With each passing day, it seemed far more likely that these women were vanishing with army deserters rather than being picked off by some shadowy spellster he couldn't trace. It wouldn't be the first time.

But Tracker had nowhere pressing to be and Commander Rhiannon's offer of whipping her guards into action had far better prospects than aimlessly patrolling the lower roads and the villages along them.

Ever since he'd brought the unsavoury dealings at *The Creaming Tart* to light, the commander had taken an interest in Tracker's opinion. That also meant he found himself invited to weigh in on township matters that, as a hound, he should've avoided.

It didn't hurt that she was also pleasant company, both in and out of bed. When she wasn't barking commands, she'd a honeyed voice that suggested a childhood closer to the northern border than being locally born. Why she had chosen to make her living here was beyond him. Her voice also gained a hoarse note every now and then, especially when he had her balls deep in his mouth.

His horse waited by the farm's gate, the reins held by the guard captain assigned to assist him by the commander. Tracker was unsure of why she had insisted. If a spellster was the actual cause of any disturbance, the captain would've only become another target and someone Tracker would need to protect.

"Well?" the man asked once Tracker settled into the saddle.

"Nothing more than some light-footed thieves." The likelihood of an unleashed spellster having walked Toptower's streets was minimal and growing less with every incident he investigated. The only definite presence had been Crystal's man and that was months ago.

By the sigh whistling out his nose, the captain sounded disappointed. A strange commonality Tracker found amongst guards. It was as though they *wanted* to encounter a spellster.

He knew why. Those who were considered that much of a threat as to alert city guards were also desperate enough to kill to keep their freedom. No matter their training, the average warrior hadn't the means to de-escalate that sort of situation.

Captain Owain frowned. "The commander won't be happy to hear that."

"Do not concern yourself there." Commander Rhiannon put on a great blustery show, but he could tell she was secretly pleased each time he returned empty-handed. Thieves were troublesome, but an easy threat to handle. "Trust me, she will be relieved to find Toptower is safe." From rogue spellsters, at least. There was always the looming uncertainty of the army standing against the next Udynean charge.

Tracker's assurances seemed to have little effect on the captain's expression. "This was the last possible hidey-hole. That means you'll be leaving, right?"

Tracker wordlessly eyed the captain. They weren't close, not by normal standards, but he did consider the man a friend. "You would miss me so easily, my dear captain?" he teased.

Owain scoffed. "I'll be as happy to see the back of you as the next man. Not like that," he swiftly added as Tracker stifled a laugh. The captain's face grew steadily pinker as he prattled away. "I'll be back to being the king of drinking games with you gone. Never knew an elf who could match me flask for flask and stay upright."

"I've had practice." During his darker days, it was the only way to silence the voices of those he had failed.

"But everyone knows hounds aren't ones to stick around," the captain continued in a clear attempt to veer away from an uncomfortable topic. "That one who brings the leashed spellsters through for the army? She rarely stays a single night in Toptower. You've likely been here longer than she has over the past decade."

Tracker wouldn't be surprised if that were true. Fetcher preferred to keep to herself.

"Plus..." A fresh surge of colour flooded Owain's face. "The commander has been less gruff on the troops since the two of you started, you know... knocking boots."

Grinning, Tracker turned his attention to the surrounding fields to give the man time to compose himself. "I have that effect on a lot of people." He had noticed a softening in Commander Rhiannon's demeanour over the past week, but he couldn't take all the credit. A lot of her ire came from the ineptitude of those under her command. That someone could open up a brothel using kidnapped victims as prostitutes right under her nose had led to an almighty shakeup through the guard ranks. The resulting dust had only begun to settle, but she seemed pleased with the sudden efficiency.

The captain grunted. "How about people like the mayor? I've never seen them so quick to dispense justice like they did with that brothel."

"I had no influence there." The mayor had done more than imprison the brothel mistress, they had sentenced her to death. Her corpse currently hung in the gallows. It had for a week and would continue to do so until decay severed her head from her neck. The women she'd abducted were back with their families or heading there, as quite a number had come from out of town.

He had sent Crystal on without him a few days ago. A lone pregnant woman joining a merchant caravan drew less attention than one travelling with a King's Hound.

A part of him felt guilty. What the woman did now was precisely what he had attempted with a young spellster only for her to end up in flames. But an unborn baby couldn't manifest magic and newborn spellsters could produce little more than a brief shield to keep themselves from further harm. Even then, only after being injured. Pricking their foot with a needle was how they tested them for that very reason.

The rest of their journey was filled with long patches of silence, broken only by the captain's sudden need for conversation. Tracker didn't understand the man's want to fill the air with unnecessary words, but he humoured Owain all the same.

Eventually, they reached the eastern gate. Other travellers stood nearby, waiting for their turn to be granted entry. Most were on foot and were waved through with little fuss. Every cart continued to be thoroughly examined despite the mystery of the missing people being solved. The mayor insisted on keeping a close eye on those entering their town.

Tracker pitied the animals the most. In the midday heat, there wasn't much in the way of shadows to remain cool and many of the cattle and horses showed signs of heavy sweating.

If he had as much influence as Owain claimed, maybe he could suggest some sort of shelter to the mayor.

They rode through the gates, their passage gaining salutes from the guards stationed there. He hadn't learnt all their names—even with there not being any practical reason for him to, he had still picked up a few—but he did recognise a couple of familiar faces.

One of them, a ruddy-faced woman with a bulbous nose, stepped forward. She barely got her lips parted before the captain waved her back to her post. There would be speculation amongst them, talks of whether Tracker had encountered a spellster or not. A fair degree of betting, too.

It made him wonder about the guards in the other towns and cities he'd been summoned to. Had they also made bets on whether he found a spellster? Most of those encounters had been confirmed sightings well before he entered a settlement. What odds did they wager then? How long it would take him?

Whether or not he died?

He wouldn't be the first hound to fall to a spellster. Being immune to direct magic didn't mean immunity to all forms of it. It was rare for a cornered spellster to figure it out, but not impossible. Hounds were trained to hit hard and fast for that very reason.

Inside the town, they parted ways. Owain headed for the guardhouse to inform the commander of their findings, or rather the lack thereof. Tracker turned his horse down a different route, aiming to see if the messenger pigeons had brought in anything new since yesterday.

For most settlements, the pigeons were housed in a central spot. That should've meant the great tower that gave the town its name. The town's main messenger birds did indeed use that as their beacon, but for those containing messages for the King's Hounds, they were found in the northeastern turret on the outer wall. He supposed the hound mistress didn't want their missives getting caught up in army matters.

Leaving his horse at the foot of the stairs, he trotted up to the ramparts, then further up via the turret's spiralling steps.

He had seen many a coop in his lifetime, the biggest being the vast expanse of enclosures in the capital, where the majority of missives to the King's Hounds originated from. But this room was small for the town's size.

The woman who looked after both pigeons and messages stood sideways to the door, her attention fixated on the bird in her hand. No matter how dishevelled her appearance was, she kept a meticulous record of each missive and bird that came her way.

He cleared his throat, just loud enough to make her aware of his presence without startling her or the pigeons.

She lifted her head. As usual, her straw-yellow hair had all the grace of a dishevelled nest. "Sir Hound!" She carefully placed the pigeon into its cage. "I must say, you've excellent timing. This one just flew in." She held out a small tube, the ends still sealed with wax. "Along with a few others I've yet to finish recording."

"You tend to the pigeons," he suggested. "I will look over what they brought." He would need to regardless of who first read them.

Settling at her desk, he started with the tube she had given him, cracking the seal on one end. The slip of paper within was shorter than most messages, containing two words clearly scribbled in haste.

Come home.

Orders he had seen aplenty, his whole life ran on obeying them to some degree, be it passing the message on to closer hounds or dealing with the threat himself. Never had he seen a written command.

Home. It had to mean Wintervale.

The very thought of the place brought back the memory of blood. It coated his tongue, the metallic notes clogging his nostrils and filling his lungs. It hadn't even been his own that was spilt, but that of others suffering where the fault had been his.

The lanterns illuminating the room no longer seemed sufficient to keep the darkness at bay. His head spun and he thanked the simple fact he was already seated.

Clapping a hand over his mouth, Tracker forced himself to swallow the saliva pooling within. He concentrated on breathing until the tension in his body faded, along with the memory of a time when he was young and naive enough to long for a life beyond the death and darkness this one had dealt.

He leant over the table, waiting until the hectic pulse of his heart had stopped thundering in his head. It had been a long time since the thought of that seaside city had such an effect on him. But then, he rarely wasted his time thinking about the place of his nightmares. He hadn't trod its streets for over a decade, not since being granted the status of a King's Hound.

He glanced over his shoulder, seeking to find if the pigeon keeper had noticed, only to discover she had left the room. *Good.* The last thing he needed were rumours of him being unwell.

Knowing he was alone, he returned to the message. It wasn't specifically addressed to him, as was common with most missives. Those in command of the messenger pigeons couldn't even be certain any hound would immediately receive this. Their records would show him being here last week, when he sent a report citing no unleashed spellsters in the vicinity. They would've assumed he had moved on. Everyone knew he wasn't the type to linger.

Maybe this was a sign to leave the town before one of his own arrived. It would take a day or two to tie up a few loose ends, but he had lingered too long as it was.

First eliminating all traces of this order was prudent. He could bullshit his way through not receiving any such command. Pigeons got lost all the time. Hawks. People. The weather.

Checking that the pigeon keeper was still nowhere within immediate sight, he swiftly disposed of the message with a touch of the end to the lit lantern. The paper turned to ash in a flash of flame.

There was only the matter of the tube the message had come in. The design stamped on the side was clearly of the royal insignia—the same one that adorned his sigil coins. Being metal, a simple flame wouldn't easily see it destroyed. What would?

He rolled the tube between his thumb and forefinger. It was a small thing. Letting it fall somewhere on the road would undoubtedly see it trampled by oblivious travellers. And if someone discovered it? Then it was plausible to believe it had slipped off the pigeon.

Unable to come up with any other suitable plan, he pocketed the tube before the pigeon keeper ducked back into the room. There was the matter of her records showing a bird arriving from Wintervale. But that wouldn't reveal what the message said and the issue would only matter should those at Wintervale check. An unlikely scenario.

Besides, if by some divine undertaking, his mistress discovered what he had done, he already knew the consequences. Disobedient hounds were too unpredictable, putting them down was the only option.

Tracker feared neither torture nor death. There was nothing they could do to him, nothing further they could strip him of, if he disobeyed.

With the message now destroyed, he dealt with the rest of the missives in the usual manner, noting down where they'd come from and what they requested. All of them were due to be sent on to other settlements where hounds closer to the target could handle them.

After the third, he noticed a pattern appearing in that every single one of them appeared to be headed for the eastern shore. He had ridden from that direction a month or so ago, the journey quiet bar a couple of incidents. How could so many spellsters have escaped the tower since then?

Tracker shook his head and sealed the final tube. He made quick work of fastening the messages to the correct pigeons before releasing the birds out the window. Whatever was happening, it was for others in the pack to figure out.

Back out on the streets, he returned to Lullaby's saddle and steered his horse through the crowd towards the inn Commander Rhiannon had insisted he swap his original lodgings for.

The Blade and Blanket resided just a block from the town's central tower. It was a clean establishment, on par with many of the more expensive inns Tracker had spent the night at. Taller than most, too, with the top level reserved for the owner, Carwyn, and the man's extensive family.

The stables were no less immaculate, the place overseen by Carwyn's daughter-in-law and five hands that, judging by their healthy complexions and neat attire, were looked after just as well as family. It was a refreshing change from the places he usually bunked at.

Leaving Lullaby in their care, he ventured into the inn's main building. It was too early in the afternoon to seek his bed, but he could enjoy a nice long soak in their bathhouse before gathering the little he had in preparation of leaving in the morning.

A homey, well-lit tavern encompassed the building's ground level. And whilst Carwyn could often be found running the bar, his gaggle of grandchildren aided in keeping the place going smoothly. Three of them were responsible for the hearty meals the place was famed for. A few of the younger ones flitted from one table to the other, collecting and delivering orders alongside the employed waiters, whereas their parents oversaw the employees.

Like every tavern he had ever entered, there wasn't a lack of patrons. At this time of day, many were involved in their meals or drinks, a group closer to the unlit fireplace played dice, their sporadic cheering drowning out most other sounds. Tracker briefly considered joining them for a game, reconsidering when he spied the red crest of crossed swords adorning one man's breast. *Mercenaries.* The town was full of them passing through. These days, many were headed to join the army. A lot of them grew jittery at the presence of a hound.

Typically, a King's Hound lingering in a town they weren't stationed at meant a spellster was definitely nearby. They were trained as children to hunt alone, but that didn't mean the prospect of outside assistance. City guards and mercenaries were usually the types used to take up the slack, the latter being the more preferred option. Tracker had seen this group around the town in the last few days. They had to know that, if he required their expertise, he would've called on them by now.

He skimmed over the rest of the patrons, finding little out of the ordinary amongst them. His gaze settled on the man currently tending to the bar. The inn owner's adopted son, Emyr. No one had told Tracker, but it was obvious. Emyr was elven, whereas both of his fathers were human. Despite them not being related by blood, or even of the same species, he still carried a vague resemblance to Carwyn.

Of either parent, Tracker saw no sign. Odd, especially for Carwyn. The man enjoyed being in the thick of the tavern's atmosphere. A lot of folks came here for the same reason, as well as to hear Carwyn's tales. Tracker had heard a few during the slower night. The old man had the soul of a storyteller.

Tracker was halfway to the bar when Carwyn emerged backwards through the door leading to the storage room. His arm was wrapped around the back of a trio of chairs, the feet of the lower one dragging along the floorboards. The man was a veteran sergeant of the army with plenty of scars and stories to show for it, the most notable being the arm he had lost in a spellster attack thirty years ago. Along with his first husband.

The latter pain was one Tracker understood all too well. Although, he hadn't the courage to do as Carwyn had done and put his heart back out there. An inn owner finding love in a second husband was one thing, a King's Hound was forbidden to become that emotionally invested. He had already faced those consequences once. He had no desire to repeat the bloodshed.

"Let me get that for you, Poppa," said one of the girls. Setting aside her tray of empty mugs, she scurried to her grandfather's side from clear across the other side of the room.

Carwyn merely smiled back and waved her away with the stump of his other arm. "I've got it, sweetling. The day I can't carry a few chairs from one room to the other is the day your papa can put me out to pasture." He glanced Tracker's way, his grin getting a little wider as recognition lit up his face. "Sir Hound! Returned so soon? The usual is it?" Before Tracker could answer, the man turned to Emyr. "My boy, a mead for the hound! On the house."

Grimacing, Tracker held up a hand. "That is not necessary, my dear man." He appreciated the gesture, but he rarely lacked the funds, the crown made sure of it. "The drink is welcomed, but I would prefer to pay."

Emyr accepted the offer with a shrug and filled up a tankard before returning to cleaning the counter.

Settling on a stool, Tracker slid over a few coins and took a deep swallow of his drink.

"Come across any spellsters out there?" Carwyn asked, returning to his task of setting out the chairs he had brought in around a long table that hadn't been there this morning.

The tavern stuttered into silence. People swivelled in their seats or craned their necks to eye Tracker.

"None at all," he revealed. "I would even go so far as to declare the town magic free."

The tension hanging in the air flowed away as though he had freed the bung on a barrel.

Carwyn frowned, clearly not as placated as his patrons. "What about that baker's son? The one whose mother owns the shop off Miner's Way?" he added, as if that information helped Tracker narrow down anything. "I hear he disappeared under mysterious circumstances."

The man's son chuckled. "There's nothing mysterious going on there, Papa. He was found in the Windyhill mill with a broken arm and three bruised ribs."

Tracker knew of the place. It was one of the first spots Commander Rhiannon had him check out. Situated close to the forest edge, it was the town's farthest farmstead. They'd several large millhouses that spent their time grinding much of the flour destined for the army. Plenty of places for someone to hide—and his search had uncovered a few petty criminals—but no spellsters.

"Windyhill?" Carwyn repeated, his grey brows lifting. "What was he doing all the way out there?" By the twinkle in the old man's eyes, he already had a fairly good idea.

"I guess you could ask the miller's son," Emyr replied. "Spoke with his father in the market just the other day. Says his son dislocated his shoulder around the same time, in the same storeroom."

Carwyn grunted. "Boys are doing it wrong, then."

Tracker snorted into his tankard. He recalled the havoc his youth had gotten him into quite well. Broken bones and all. The storerooms in Windyhill had a lot of high places where a fall would be lucky to not kill.

Content his mystery was solved, Carwyn finished up with his task, then shuffled off into the kitchen, no doubt to oversee whatever was being prepared for a customer searching for a hearty meal.

Tracker took a swig of his drink and sighed. "I will miss this."

Frowning, Emyr looked up from drying off a mug. "The mead? I know it's good, but it's not pine-worthy."

He smiled. He had meant the homeliness. The glimpse into what having a loving family was like. It wasn't something he got to see a lot of, mostly because his job often involved breaking them apart.

He would definitely miss the companionship. The King's Hounds trained together as children, but they weren't meant to work as a unit, there weren't enough of them to. The city guards, for all their talk, knew only of spellsters through tales and abstract warnings. Few here had seen one in action, let alone fought them.

More patrons poured in as the afternoon faded into evening, many of them looking to be locals. The raucous from the dicing mercenaries grew louder. Most of them looked drunk enough to keel over if they stood. A few were already dozing up against the wall or face down on the table.

A minstrel joined the crowd and, after a few beers, started playing a dreary tune that Tracker recognised, but the lyrics were vastly different. The song he knew was a warning of a young woman falling for a spellster and suffering for it when the King's Hounds used her as bait.

He couldn't even be offended as he knew far too many hounds who had done just that. *Any means to get the desired outcome.* That was what their mistress taught them.

The slap of a palm hitting bare skin drew his attention.

One of the waiters serving the group of mercenaries was busily prising himself free from the advances of what appeared to be a very drunk man. He was succeeding, but his efforts left him open to being pawed at and partially undressed before he was out of the mercenary's grasp.

"Come on beautiful," the mercenary whined, his words slurring. "We were just starting to have fun."

The waiter marched off, his face red as he scrambled to straighten his clothes. His lips moved, mutters that were garbled even to Tracker's ears, but if any retort came to the man's mind, he was too flustered to speak it.

"Hey!" Emyr snarled. He ducked behind the bar, popping back up with a sizable leather-wrapped club. "That's enough of that."

"Allow me," Tracker offered, setting down his drink. It was rare for him to spend a night at a tavern without some sort of scuffle happening. That it had taken this long was a miracle in itself.

Still, despite how he complained, he enjoyed a good brawl. He had grown lax during his extended stay in the town, beating up a drunk mercenary who misplaced his manners would be an adequate warm-up. He had certainly brought down bigger men.

"You got something to say, pretty boy?"

Giving the man a wide grin, Tracker swivelled on the stool. "Such flattery. My dear man, if you were after someone to fumble under the sheets with, there are better ways to get laid. All of this unwanted molesting of a hardworking waiter is so barbaric. But I suppose savagery is all some of you sellswords know, yes?"

At the man's back, his fellow mercenaries jeered and hollered. Several whistled whilst making obscene gestures. One suggested a method in which the man could not-so-gently take Tracker.

The mercenary's already ruddy complexion grew redder. "I've seen you about town." He jumped to his feet, swaying as he took a step towards Tracker. "You're the one always schmoozing with the city guard. Their commander, right?" He looked to his companions, seeking confirmation, before turning back to Tracker. "You think she'll protect you from me?"

Tracker took in the unsteadiness. Smirking, he leant back on the counter. This certainly wouldn't be a protracted encounter. "Protect? I doubt you could lay a single hand on me."

More jeering followed his declaration, the noise brought to an abrupt silence by one within their group. A tall dark-haired woman with shoulders almost as broad as Tracker's scimitar was long. "Come on," she said, clapping a hand on the man's shoulders. "We should leave."

"Piss off," the man growled, shaking off the woman. "I'll do more than lay a hand on you. I'm going to break you in half." He ran at Tracker, his arms outstretched.

Tracker waited until the man was almost upon him, then ducked to one side and let momentum carry the mercenary into the counter's unforgiving bulk. The man had barely time to right himself before Tracker dealt several blows of his own, finishing with slamming the man's face into the counter and knocking him out.

The mercenary slid gracelessly to the floor, still breathing.

"You were saying?" he enquired of the unconscious man.

"I think it's time you all headed out," Emyr declared, making his point very clear by slapping his club on the counter.

"A grand idea," agreed one of the mercenaries, the same tall dark-haired woman. She strode over to where the unconscious man lay. "I am so sorry about him. I hope this pays for the damages." She tossed several gold coins Emyr's way, then closed one meaty fist on the collar of her companion's shirt. "Come on, you bastards," she called to the others. "Help me carry this sorry lump of flesh back to camp. He can nurse his head whilst on watch."

Like she had opened a sluice gate, the rest of the group got to their feet. They gathered themselves and their more inebriated companions. A pair of them collected their unconscious friend and, dragging the man with them, scuttled out the door.

Shaking his head, Tracker turned back to the bar and the remainder of his drink. He was definitely going to need that soak once he was done here.

"I see we still like getting into trouble."

Tracker turned at the familiar voice. "Fetch!" He raced across the room, his arms spread wide in an open invitation of an embrace.

She suffered the affection with her usual exaggerated grimacing as he squeezed them together. Her responding hug was no less fond. Or tight. The leather of their near-identical armour creaked against each other.

Feeling her grip loosen, Tracker stepped out of the woman's immediate range to give her the distance she preferred. "How has life been treating you, my dear Fetcher?" With one sweep of his arm, he gestured for his fellow hound to seat herself at the bar.

She obliged him, her lips twitching into a crooked smile, and claimed one of the stools. "Life has been no different from the last time we met, still escorting spellsters to their death."

Tracker returned to his own seat and the remainder of his drink. "I hope our mistress does not catch you speaking so disapprovingly of your task."

"And *I* would be less prone to grousing if the people I brought to the army were more suited to their task and less like coddled children." Sneering, she settled at the bar and ordered herself a drink. "Take the fresh one I just delivered to the army." She tugged at her gloves. "He could not even travel under the sun for more than a day without getting heatsick. He will be useless now the army has control of him."

"Sounds pathetic." Tracker plonked himself on the stool next to her, draping himself half on the counter. "Why would they pick such a man?"

"Because he is strong." She took a few deep swallows of her drink, surfacing with a satisfied exhale. "Unleashed and properly trained, he could rival an army on his own."

Tracker grunted. He never understood the crown's insistence on sending their strongest to fight. Raw power was nothing without knowledge and the Udyneans assuredly sent their most cunning. "So, what is your task in this fair town?"

"I'm only stopping in this shithole because my horse threw a shoe."

"Tragic." He leant his chin on his upraised fist. "It truly must vex you beyond words."

She sniggered into her mug, almost spilling the contents down herself. "But what are *you* doing here?"

"There is, supposedly, a rogue spellster nearby. One who is making off with young women."

"Supposedly? Meaning you have yet to catch them in the act? *Slacker.*" She grinned, taking the edge off the old taunt. Of all the King's Hounds he still had contact with, she was the only one he allowed to call him such names.

Still, it stung a little this time. Perhaps because he hadn't been able to find any definite clues of there ever being a spellster. "*Meaning*, I doubt such a person exists."

"Then why stay?"

He shrugged. "The guard commander is cute." He'd a weakness for soft lips and dark eyes. She had both.

Fetcher chuckled. "One of these days, Track, your dick is going to get you into trouble."

"Beyond the kind that leaves people dead, yes? I have already walked that road." And suffered for it. He still wore their names on his skin.

The humour fell from her face. Embarrassment stained her

suntanned cheeks, creeping all the way to the upper curves of her ears. "My apologies. I... forgot."

"Yes? Well, fear not. I have no intentions of repeating history." What need did he have for romantic entanglements when sex was a free commodity? Or, at least, easily bought?

The tavern door swung open, admitting a young woman. "Your horse is ready, Mistress Fetcher ma'am."

Nodding, Fetcher stood. "I best be off."

"Where do you plan on heading from here?"

"East, I think. See what messages have been left at Kory's Rest."

"Few, I should hope." He'd been there not long ago. Most of the missives had been the type to send elsewhere. He'd dealt with the one actual threat. It was what had made him late getting here and on a course that had seen that spellster girl killed in a bandit attack.

He took a longer swallow of mead. Maybe if he drank enough, he would forget.

"What of you? Your task here is done, yes?"

He nodded. "I have a few loose ends to wrap up, but I do not plan to linger beyond tomorrow." Heading north seemed like as good a plan as any. He could travel all the way to the eastern corner of the kingdom and see how the fortress city of Highstone faired. He hadn't been there in a long time. It was the one other place where the kingdom bordered Udynea, as well as Dvärghem. Yet, it saw little in the way of attacks.

"Do not go drinking too much, then." Fetcher gave him a hearty slap on the back. "And take care. Try not to do anything foolish."

"You know me, my dearest Fetcher, I would never break the hound code." A few had tried to bribe him into doing so, finding him unwavering in the face of both money and sex. Little was worth the risk. Not even something as foolish as love.

CHAPTER 12

Dylan trudged through the forest, aware of how much the skirt of his robe swept through the undergrowth. Dew from the grass and leaves soaked the fabric, leaving it clinging to his bare legs. The army-issued attire was a little more form-fitting than what he'd travelled in. It was also meant to be paired with trousers, but he had worn them for all of an hour before the sensation of cloth encasing his legs became unbearable.

The peep and screech of little fantailed birds dogged his every step. It didn't matter where he went—be it out here or in the slipshod encampment that marked the front line—the russet-breasted creatures were always there, seemingly popping out of the very bark. Their presence was a welcome one, a reminder of the tower gardens during summer.

He didn't wander the forest alone, travelling close on the heels of the fair-haired captain in charge of granting him sanction to use his power, should the need arise. It hadn't so far, but their mission was to seek out the enemy, to discover what plan they had cooked up and, hopefully, sabotage it before anyone was aware. Dylan was this party's reassurance should they stumble upon any enemy spellsters.

The captain abruptly halted, indicating Dylan to do the same with the silent lifting of a fist. The man motioned to their left with a jerk of his head.

Something moved amongst the undergrowth. Too swift and sure-footed to hear more than the odd rustle, but the shadows suggested something not normally found wandering the forest.

One of theirs or one of ours? Dylan flexed his fingers, prepared to let loose with a blast of lightning the second sanction was given. After weeks of being able to reach his power only at the behest of a hound, and briefly at that, he longed for a reason to use it beyond healing himself, to have his full power sing through his veins. Even if it meant killing.

A woman emerged from the bushes, elven and quite slight in her dark leather armour. She dashed to the captain's side, saluted and fell into stride with the man as they continued through the forest.

Dylan sighed. *Another false alarm.* After hearing the soldiers talk back in the main camp, he had expected to come across some sort of Udynean resistance by now. Were they even going in the right direction?

As far as he could determine via flashes of sunlight through the treetops, they were still on a westward heading, they were bound to come across Udyneans at some point. The closer they got to the border, the surer everyone seemed that they would unearth some sort of sordid nest of... *them.*

Spellster. His skin crawled at the way the soldiers back at camp spoke the word. It felt dirty. More slur than description. None of them seemed to see anything wrong in how it left their mouths. Or that he *was* one of them.

But he was also leashed. *Tamed.* In their minds, a collar of purple metal made all the difference.

Their own scouts and archers spread out around them somewhere amongst the bushes and the trees. Dylan couldn't see their passage most of the time. When he did, it was in flashes of shadow. An unnerving sight if he hadn't known they were on the same side.

Somewhere out there, the Udynean troops also roamed, waiting for the opportunity to strike.

Except he hadn't seen a hint of them since being stationed here. The full might of the enemy had remained silent for weeks prior to his arrival. It made the soldiers jittery.

From the scraps of conversation Dylan had pieced together, the last time the Udynea Empire halted their assault, they'd attacked several days after with a force strong enough to slaughter a good deal of the army. An act that was, by and large, unprecedented.

That was why this scouting party roamed the forest, to attack before the Udyneans could make another attempt and wipe out the rest of their defences.

"Report," the captain said. "Have you found any sign of these bastards?"

"Only ruins, sir," the woman replied with a shake of her head. She jerked a thumb in the direction she had come from. There was something in her voice—the careful way she spoke each word, drawing out the vowels—that reminded him of Launtil. Could she be another ex-Udynean slave converted to their cause? There were far more of them amongst the soldiers than he had expected. "Could be dwarven."

Dylan's head lifted at that. Ruins suggested something a little more substantial than the arboreal huts the ancient dwarves usually built. Whilst their treetop homes did little to the environment, the choice also left current dwarves with very few remains to study.

The captain cursed under his breath. "Just what we need in the middle of a battlefield."

"Sir? Your orders?" She shuffled from one foot to the other, glancing over her shoulder every so often. "Aren't we meant to mark ruins for the dwarves?"

The man sighed. "Suppose we better go take notes, measure things out, the usual twaddle. Don't want a war with Dvärghem on top of fighting off these magical pissants."

Dylan cleared his throat. "You *are* aware Dvärghem is a peaceful country?" He had dealt only with the odd hedgewitch, who carried daggers to protect themselves from predators and those unaware of their status, but he knew the one thing the dwarves didn't have was an army. On the whole, their country preferred words over weapons.

Sneering, the captain turned his head to examine Dylan out of the corner of his eye. "Well now, precious, aren't you just full of information? Bring in the other scouts." This order was directed at the woman. "And get me whoever can accurately map this ruin."

The woman snapped a salute. "I believe Jasilla's qualified in that field, sir."

The captain grunted, waiting until the woman had vanished back into the undergrowth before muttering, "Great, another bloody elf to deal with. Don't know what the sergeant's thinking sending them all on scouting missions. Why don't the sodding pointy-eared bastards just shuffle off back home?"

Dylan idly scratched at where the bottom edge of his collar dug into his skin. "A lot of them probably would, if that was actually a viable option." He'd heard from several elven spellsters who'd been born beyond the tower that their presence wasn't always an accepted one. He hadn't truly believed it until seeing how disparagingly the human soldiers treated the elven folk fighting alongside them.

He doubted the captain even knew where elves originated from. Every history record Dylan had ever read only spoke of the first elves arriving almost two thousand years ago, a millennium or so after humans had done the same thing.

But where humans had sought to claim the land, with some realms turning to genocide to rid that land of the indigenous dwarven population, the first elves had come seeking only refuge. Their fleet of ships was recorded as being small in number—some claimed five, others three—but each vessel had been of a size to carry thousands. After so long, the continent's entire elven population had to be in the hundreds of thousands now, if not several million.

"The question is," Dylan continued, "are you going to gift them the ships and supplies necessary to do so? For *all* of them?"

The man sneered, the expression warping his thin moustache. "You're awfully mouthy for a leashed spellster. Wish the lieutenant would've let me bring the *cute* black-haired one instead. *She* knows how to stay silent." His lips further twisted into a grin that left Dylan with a flesh-shuddering urge to bathe. "And doesn't mind when her mouth's full."

Dylan frowned. He had seen one black-haired woman amongst the other spellsters on the front line and she was a timid thing, the sort that made it hard to picture as being a source of destruction, as was so often the case when it came to the skilled ones.

Perhaps it was the captain's sleazy smile, but surely, the man wasn't implying that—

"Ha! Look at the shock on your face. Yes, pretty boy, I mean when she's sucking me off." His grin widened, showing a full row of perfect teeth, and he thrust his groin out for emphasis. Dylan really could've done without it. "What's she going to do? Sure as hell can't turn her magic on me."

"That's a misuse of your ranking and abuse of those under your command." Not to mention a dozen other illegal acts if he was forcing her to do the deed. "I could have you reported on those charges alone." Although, if the lieutenant's feelings about spellsters was common, anyone higher up the chain of command probably didn't care what the captain did to their weapon as long as he left her capable of doing her job.

"Already been done, sunshine. Why do you think you're the one they sent?" Chuckling, the man clapped an arm around Dylan's shoulders. "Aw, are we feeling a teensy bit left out? Longing to wrap your lips around a nice fat dick?"

Dylan shrank from the man's touch, instinctively seeking his magic. *Just one bolt.* That was all he needed to take this sick bastard down. He rather doubted the captain would be missed.

His collar crackled. Tiny sparks bit into his neck. He clenched his teeth, focusing on how tantalisingly close his power dangled. He could almost feel it in his grasp. Maybe if he was able to push that little bit more...

He strained until specks of light danced across his vision. Still, the collar held. It burned against his skin, but it held.

"I don't do other men." The captain released him, oblivious as to how close he had come to death, and continued walking. "But don't worry, that pretty face will attract the right sort of attention soon enough. You'll be on your knees and servicing your own little group in no time."

Dylan swallowed the bile sliding up his tongue. He had no interest in men, whether it was doing or being done by. His gaze slid to the captain's dagger sitting temptingly in its sheath. His fingers twitched. Could he…?

No. Even if, by some miracle, he relieved the captain of the weapon, he wouldn't be fast enough to stab the man, much less fatally.

"Hitch up your skirts, princess, we're on the move." With a grin that had Dylan wanting to deck him, the man took off in the direction the scout had indicated.

Dylan's thoughts slid to the razor still tucked nice and safe in his belt pouch. The edge was sharp enough to cut a man's throat. *Maybe in his sleep.* But not yet. He'd wait a few days first, let them think all this marching through the undergrowth had cowed him.

He would not wind up looking like those hollow creatures he had left back at the main encampment.

They forged a path through the forest, pushing aside scrappy bushes and ducking low branches. Dylan begrudgingly lifted the ends of his robe as the hems started to snag on the undergrowth. Twigs scratched at his boots, several snapping up to lash his bare knees.

Just as he was beginning to regret turning down the offer of trousers, they broke into a clearing.

Dylan halted at the tree line, his breath all but stolen at the sight. For the past ten years, he had dedicated his life to translating the records others gave of places like this. Old hints of when the dwarves once roamed over vast tracks of land. He had longed to see a dwarven ruin, however briefly.

To stumble upon this was something of a miracle. True, it was naught but a few stone walls sitting in the dead centre of the clearing, however…

He took a few steps towards the ruin. No contesting the structure was old, but was it truly dwarven? The hedgewitches always said the ancient dwarves lived in the trees—they still did in Dvärghem—and didn't build much out of stone unless natural caves were involved.

Each of the ruins walls was built of great slabs as tall as the average man's waist. Their lines were arrow-straight, distinguishable from each other only due to the thin suggestion of grime between the blocks. If the ruin once had a roof, it was long gone, if he were to judge by the sunlight streaming through the archway. He knew of no human buildings that were so meticulously designed.

So why was it in the middle of nowhere?

The rest of the scouting party appeared in ones and twos. They eyed the ruin, twitchy but curious. None seemed interested in venturing closer.

He glanced at the captain. The man appeared to pay him no mind, being heavily engrossed in debriefing the scouts. Dylan shuffled a few steps towards the ruin. Still, his activity went unnoticed. Perhaps he could get close enough to determine just who had built it.

By the time he had crossed half the distance between the captain and the closest stone wall, Dylan had forsaken all attempts at subtlety. Nevertheless, he would have a quick check over his shoulder every few steps to ensure the captain was nearby. Even if the man wasn't bothered if Dylan wandered a little ways, staying within earshot would be prudent lest the call to attack came.

Finally, the eastern wall of the structure loomed over him. Carvings adorned the slabs closer to the archway, worn by centuries of exposure to the elements. They did indeed look to be dwarven runes. "By the gods," he breathed. He laid a hand on the closest rune, his fingers settling into the double-pronged design. Never had he believed he would get a chance to see these ancient places for himself. Especially not such a rarity.

This had to be a temple. The markings could've once suggested the worship of... something. There were scratches and etching over the runes. Newer. A possible defacing from young Demarn tribes or even other dwarves. What lay beneath could've been a tree, or a valley, or even a depiction of a fork in a river that no longer flowed through these woods.

Dylan sighed and dropped his hand. The runes could've suggested far too many things. The structure being a place of worship was the only certainty he had. Dwarves revered nature, paying equal homage to the land as they did to the animals they hunted. This particular temple could've been dedicated to anything.

What he needed was a compilation of finds in the area. Sadly, the only one he would trust was back in the tower. An actual hedgewitch would've been better, but if there was one within the camp grounds, then he had heard no word of them.

Another scout emerged from the undergrowth, yet another elven woman. The captain spoke briefly with her and the elf strode up to the blocks. She halted beside Dylan to run a finger over the carvings, her lips mumbling slightly.

So, this was the scout who kept track of the dwarven finds. She was a tiny thing, even for an elf, the top of her head barely making the middle of his chest. What did that other woman say her name was?

"Jasilla, isn't it?" Dylan said, ducking his torso so as not to loom over her. "If you want some help, I can—"

"N-no, thank you." She stared up at him, her large eyes—as black as her short-cropped hair—widening further. "Th-that's quite unnecessary." She put a few carefully-measured strides between them as she spoke, her accent the same as the other scout. Her hand raised in a silent warning for him to stay back. "I can manage without your assistance. This doesn't require blowing anything up. Just, uh… go wait by your handler, if you would."

Handler? That was a Udynean term used for those who looked after the slaves. The captain was his warden. Did she not know the difference?

"Off you go, now," Jasilla continued.

Dylan frowned. She hadn't really just spoken to him like he was some child, had she? "I think you've misunderstood my intentions." He hadn't mentioned magic, hadn't managed to mention anything, when it came down to it. "I've done extensive research on ancient dwarven ruins. I've translated hundreds of texts into their language for the hedgewitches. I'm quite capable of aiding in the cataloguing of—"

"Just let me do my job, so we can leave." Her hand flapped as if she aimed to shoo a bird from its perch. "Quickly, if you please. That's a good boy."

Dylan jerked back. Never in his life had he been so flippantly dismissed. Not by his guardian or the teachers, not even by those who had turned down his offer of intimacy.

Uncertain what action she would take if he further pressed the issue, he aimlessly wandered along the wall, eventually finding himself crossing the clearing to stand at the captain's side.

The man seemed uninterested in Dylan's return, opting to glare at the clearing as if it had personally offended him. "I don't like this," he muttered to the scout who had first alerted them of the ruin. "There's something about this clearing that just isn't right. It's too exposed." He pointed near the ruin walls. "Just look at those stumps. This place has been cleared. And none too recently, judging by the discolouration."

Dylan tracked the sweep of the man's arm. He had assumed the area was naturally devoid of anything taller than a foot, but the remains of spindly trees and bushes pockmarked the grass.

Several questions crawled through his mind, prickling his skin. If this place had been cleared, then where was the debris? And who had done the job? *Please, be dwarves.* Even as the thought surfaced, he knew it couldn't have been them. They left ruins as they were found.

"Have our scouts found this place before?" the captain asked the scout.

The woman shook her head. "It's all new territory, sir. I don't think a Demarner's set foot in these parts for decades without tripping over the Udynea Empire."

"And there's been no sign of the bastards?"

Her lips twisted with distaste. "Not even a wisp, sir."

Grunting, the captain rubbed at his chin. He eyed the ruin as if expecting it to burst forth with demons at any second. "Alliance with Dvärghem be damned," he growled. "Take a few of the sharper eyes and keep watch. I'm pulling the rest back to the rendezvous point. Meet us there when the elf's done."

The scout saluted and, towing an elven man in her wake, rushed towards the ruins. The woman's hand came up. Her fingers flashed in a signal of some sort, but the other scouts were all nearby and Jasilla had her back to them, still examining the carvings.

At Dylan's side, another scout's eyes widened. He pulled forth his bow and nocked an arrow. "Sir?" The man nodded at the trio just as Jasilla turned to face the two scouts joining her. "We need to leave, now."

The captain gave the man a curt nod. "Scatter!" he roared. "Spell—" An arrow sliced through the warden's throat before he could spit out the order. The captain fell, gurgling and clutching at his neck. Blood gushed from the wound, staining the grass and soil.

Fire exploded across the clearing.

Heat engulfed them. Dylan threw up a hand, seeking to form a shield. His collar sparked and held.

Around him, screams filled the air. He tried to determine their sources. Was there anyone who could give him sanction to use his magic? He needed only a few words. Who had been next in command? There had to be someone.

More cries came. None sounded like the one he needed. He tried anyway. *I'm allowed.* Surely, he could grant himself sanction if there was no one else. He could protect them, protect himself. Everyone.

Dylan staggered back as another blast hit, blindly feeling for the collar.

"Get down!"

A hard body slammed into him, bearing them to the ground. More arrows sprouted around them like deadly weeds. He turned his head, ready to thank the woman.

Dead eyes stared back. Blood trickled out of a hole punched in her forehead. The tip of an arrow poked through the bone. Bits of brain clung to the shaft.

Bile slid up his throat at the sight. He tried to swallow it, coughing everything back up as he failed. Liquid, thick and acidic, poured out his mouth. The bitter scent clogged his nose and coated his tongue. Smoke choked the air. Flames and heat assaulted him from all around. Screams stuffed his ears.

Dylan dared to lift his head, his stomach already quaking at what it might see. He still lived, thanks to the scout. That wouldn't be true for much longer if he couldn't find a place to lay low. He needed time to think. Just long enough to figure out a way of fighting back.

Ahead of him stood the ruins, devoid of the three scouts that had vacated so hastily. The stones were untouched by the attacks. Even in the midst of battle, Udynea didn't dare antagonise the dwarves by violating their relics. He hoped that would continue to remain true.

Clambering to his feet, he ran for the archway.

Fire and arrows followed in his wake. They caught on his robe, tearing and singeing the hem. Barbs tore at his shins, flames seared his skin. He didn't dare slow to deal with them.

He flung himself through the archway, hitting the ground shoulder first. Rolling along the pebbled yard within, he barely waited for inertia to stop before scrambling to flatten his back against the inner wall.

Only when he was certain that nobody followed did he bat away the licks of fire clinging to his robe and haul out an arrow shaft that had pierced the fabric.

What was he meant to do? *Defend. Attack.* Obviously. That was the whole point of him being here. But how? He was leashed with no one to give him sanction.

His fingers brushed the collar. There had to be a way. Cowering behind a wall whilst everyone died around him was not an option.

Dylan forced his fingers beneath the collar's links. The metal hummed. He sank to his knees, peering through the archway whilst still fumbling to find where the two ends of the collar joined. *Come on.*

An inhuman shriek drew his gaze. Moving fire. A figure engulfed in flames. They staggered across the clearing, flailing and screeching.

Panic sealed his throat. Shaking, he crushed the metal in his grasp. *Come on!* He tried to push out, to douse the flames before they consumed the figure. He could save them. He just needed his magic.

His collar sparked. The links moulded beneath his fingers like hot, searing clay. His throat burned. Tears blurred the world. The all-too-close scent of charring flesh filled his nose. Liquid pooled in his mouth. He clenched his teeth, pushing down whatever was left in his stomach. *Come. On!*

The figure fell, no longer batting at the flames.

Dylan watched, breathless and still, not even daring to blink lest he missed some sign of movement.

None.

No... He was too late. *No!* He couldn't be. He was meant to be stopping this. It was his duty to protect these people.

But how could he with this stupid piece of metal hindering him? He might as well be lighting the fires himself for all the use he was.

The screams of the dying wadded his ears, echoes of the inhuman shriek.

He pawed at the collar, desperately fighting to dispel the barrier between him and his magic. The metal grew hotter. He had to win free of it. They would all die without him to fight back, to save them. There had to be a way. There just *had* to be.

Power touched him. Slowly. A pinhole in a dam. He pushed harder, widening the breach with sheer force.

Great white arcs flew off the metal. Each jolt was another serrated needle digging into his flesh. Pain wracked his body. It emptied his stomach and crushed his lungs. He had to get the damn thing off before it killed him.

The metal in his hands was twig-thin now. And molten.

A shield. Screaming breathlessly, he gave the collar one final wrench and pushed with everything he had left. Just a little more and—

Sudden light, blinding and blue, filled his vision.

Then there was only darkness.

CHAPTER 13

Tracker gave his horse's back one final swipe with his hand, checking that the animal's sleek black hair was dirt-free before flipping his saddle blanket over it. They'd only a half day left before the light faded, more if he pushed Lullaby, but he wasn't about to risk sores or sprains for an extra hour of travel.

The stallion had been his constant companion for years now. He had bought Lullaby as a yearling, trained each quirk, moulded the animal into a warhorse fit to carry royalty. They'd gone through a lot of messes together and come out unscathed more times than they really should have.

"I promise," Tracker grunted, lugging his saddle onto the horse's back. "Once we reach the end of this journey, it will be nothing but open pastures for you. Maybe your own herd of pretty mares, yes?" They both deserved a gentler ending.

Except hounds didn't just up and retire, they couldn't. There was the duty or their death. For as long as there were spellsters in Demarn, there would always need to be hounds ensuring the safety of regular citizens.

Lullaby turned his head and lipped at Tracker's sleeve before nudging him with enough force to tip over a small child.

Chuckling, Tracker stroked the horse's velvet-soft muzzle. "Impatient brute." Pushing the animal's head to one side, he set about tightening the girth. "I am getting on with it." He didn't typically linger on simple tasks like this, but a piece of him was reluctant to leave.

If he was honest with himself, that same reluctance was likely the reason behind why he had spent the morning in the town's guardhouse. The guards stationed there had few lingering doubts amongst the city guard of spellsters hiding in and around the town, but Tracker had convinced himself that he needed to ensure those in the upper ranks still remembered the signs he had taught. He'd left the place with plenty of assurances of how they knew what to watch out for. Ultimately, he had to let them stand on their own.

Was this what hounds stationed at the bigger cities and towns felt like? He recalled Whisper, a man who'd overseen Oldmarsh for decades, rarely left the city and seemed to consider the place as his home, rather than the dank dungeon of Wintervale's castle.

The footsteps of another entering the stables briefly drew Tracker's ear.

He ignored it. The stables attached to *The Blade and Blanket* were often bustling with people. That he'd any sort of peace was only due to the stable hands vacating the place for a midday meal.

The figure stopped outside his stall and cleared their throat. He knew that sound, had heard it often enough whilst at Commander Rhiannon's side.

He glanced over his shoulder to find her leaning against the stall, her gaze pointedly not on him, but still aware he knew of her presence. "My guards said you were leaving, but I didn't believe it. Guess it's true."

"I was on my way to speak with you." There wasn't much to be said, but a personal farewell was the least he owed the woman.

"Thought you might have mentioned it earlier." The words carried a definite hard edge. "At least said goodbye. Or was that what last night was?"

"My apologies." Clearly, he had made the altogether different mistake of thinking the woman knew what their dalliances were. He should've laid down the terms behind it at the beginning. He'd little experience with longer affairs, most of his more sexual connections involved coin or a single night. "I am not very proficient at goodbyes. If it helps, then consider it a farewell until next time."

Rhiannon sighed. "I'm not some love-struck maiden. I understand that you have a duty to the king and Demarn, that it needs you to move on to where your skills are of use. But I know other towns have a hound permanently stationed there and I had hoped you might choose to stay."

"That is true. But we are also a limited resource and the places with hounds stationed there are strategic." He could've taken up the vacant post in Stonebay, but then, he never would've come across the spellsters he had recently encountered. Nor would he have saved a ravaged village or stopped a bandit leader from ensnaring more innocents.

"And Toptower isn't one of them." It wasn't a question. Many of Toptower's residents had a dreary outlook on precisely how safe they were and their importance to the kingdom. He supposed such cynicism came from centuries of having the army a mere few days' ride. Close enough to spot camp smoke, but far away that he never once sensed a ghost of magic.

Except, he could've sworn he did. Just a flicker, but somewhere to the west.

Impossible. For magic to reach his senses, he would need to be standing amongst the debris of a wrought spell, sharing a moderately sized building with an unleashed spellster, or within a few hours of one actively using their power. To feel it over any distance would require enough power to level a fortress.

He froze in adjusting Lullaby's girth. There it was again. Less a flicker and closer.

And swelling.

Rhiannon straightened. "Is something wrong?"

He shook his head, more to clear it than in answer. "It is difficult to be certain. I must go." He needed to head west. Heading towards the sensation would help him figure it all out.

He leapt into the saddle and tore out into the street, dodging carts with ease and people with less simplicity. He wove around those who hadn't the ability, or time, to dive out of his way, forcing Lullaby to leap over a few as they huddled into whimpering balls.

The closer he got to the western gate, the more people crowded the way. They milled about, confused and frustrated. It forced him to slow down and pick his way through the best he could. Some people drew out of his way, many hadn't the space.

He rounded the corner and hauled on the reins, bringing Lullaby to a halt so abruptly that the horse's rump dropped into a slide.

The gates stood shut.

From his placement atop his horse, Tracker was able to see right over the multitude blocking his path. It didn't answer much.

The guards stationed around the entrance spoke with those at the front of the crowd. From the way they waved their arms, they were clearly giving people instructions to vacate the area.

Those stationed atop the wall paid no heed to the raucous below. Their attention was on something beyond the town walls. Could they see what Tracker felt? Human eyes weren't capable of spying details from a distance and he knew there weren't any elven guards. If it was obvious enough for them to spot, then something had gone terribly wrong.

He needed to get up there, but the crowd was thick. Moving through it would be practically impossible without using force.

Tracker swung his horse around and aimed for the central tower. What had once been a solitary fortress had become a government building years ago, but the parapets were manned by city guards. Both them and the mayor were aware of his presence in the town, they would let him go wherever he deemed it necessary, even if that meant climbing right up to the flagpole sitting on the rooftop.

By the time he reached the base of Toptower's namesake, Commander Rhiannon was also aiming for the main door. The concern on her face at his arrival was no greater than when he had sped off. Tracker took no comfort in the sight. Her lack of unease didn't mean all was well, only that she was just as uninformed.

"Did you find out what was wrong?" she enquired, falling into step with him as he dismounted and trotted up the stairs.

He shook his head. "Your people have sealed the western gate."

The two men standing guard on either side of the entrance opened the doors with barely a twitch from their commander.

Rhiannon inclined her head in acknowledgement of the guards before turning back to him. "I certainly gave no such order." She frowned, her small eyes narrowing further. "Did they say who did?"

Again, he could only answer in the negative. "The crowd was too dense to wade through." He pointed to the parapets high above them, currently obscured by several levels of ceiling. "I need to get to the top. Which is the quickest way?" He'd only met the mayor once during his entire stay here and that had been in their official meeting chambers on the second level.

Rhiannon lengthened her stride, the hesitancy in her gait melting away under the confidence of knowledge. "Follow me."

They wove through the tower's levels, encountering only the occasional soul as the commander led him via back passages, and a few doorways that carried the look of secrecy.

Eventually, they reached the parapet. It faced the opposite side of the city, the peaceful sight of farmland and distant forests. Rhiannon continued to lead the way.

A single young guard stood watch. He trailed after them, jabbering, as they strode by. "Commander, the army encampment? It— There's smoke. Too much. And I—" He visibly steeled himself, straightening his stance. "Your orders?"

"Take it easy, son," Rhiannon said in the surest, most commanding, voice Tracker had heard from the woman. "We'll handle it." Even in that assessment, she sounded a great deal more confident than Tracker could.

She halted before another door, hauling it open to reveal little more than a flight of stairs leading up into darkness. She gestured for Tracker to head in. "Leads to the flagpole. Not enough room up there for two."

Nodding his thanks, Tracker raced up the stairs, taking the steps in twos and threes. A trapdoor sat at the upper end. He pushed on it.

The hinges groaned their objection, refusing to move. A little more fumbling revealed a simple bolt wasn't the only thing that kept it shut. Someone had fastened a heavy lock to the mechanism, as if people had nothing better to do than steal flags.

Magic continued to thrum through the air, great bursts that put to mind the billowing of a ship's sail in the wind. How much power for it to tug at him across such a distance?

Skidding down the stairs, he erupted back onto the parapet. The commander and her young guard had barely turned to acknowledge his re-emergence before Tracker was up the wall, his fingers finding purchase in the gaps weather had eroded between the slabs of stone.

He clambered onto the roof and up to where the flagpole sat. Clinging to the pole, he stared in the direction of the army, an iciness settling into his bones.

Smoke dominated the skyline. Thick and black, it hovered over the trees like a seahawk closing in for the kill. Flares of red and orange bloomed within its core, coinciding with the bursts of magic vibrating through his senses.

Peering at the mass, trying to determine just where the smoke originated, was of no use. He'd never been to the army's main encampment, had never been given a reason to, but he had spoken enough times with Fetcher to know the place was largely tents of canvas and wood. But the encampment sat several days' ride away. From this distance, he couldn't be certain of what was burning or who to blame.

Maybe it was their own troops trying to flush out the enemy by setting the forest on fire. He hoped with all his heart. Deep inside, he knew the truth. The magic he felt was more than he could expect to feel from the leashed ones the Demarn army utilised.

The Udynea Empire had finally turned its forces towards them.

"Sir Hound?" Rhiannon called frantically from the parapet. "What is it?"

Danger. Tracker tore his gaze from the plume of smoke to the commander, trying to imagine her and the people under her command protecting the town from what he had just felt. *A massacre.* The crown had convinced its citizens that ordinary people were a match for trained spellsters.

Maybe they were, but only in the same way a rodent was to a mouser.

"Alert your people," he replied, dropping from the rooftop to land beside her. Of the man stationed here, he saw no sign. "Double the guard on the walls and ready the physicians for any casualties." He didn't hold out much hope for the latter.

Rhiannon nodded. "What did you see?"

"Same as you." He waved his hand at the black plume continuing to expand across the sky. "Your guardsman is right. That's far too much smoke. It can mean only one thing."

The woman's expression stiffened. "The Udynean forces are on the move," she murmured, seemingly dazed. How many years had she lived in Toptower? Had commanded the town's guards? Surely, the idea that the army would fail must've crossed her mind at some point.

Or perhaps she hadn't considered it would ever happen in her lifetime.

"Regretfully, I will need to leave your side. I will return," he swiftly added as helpless panic took her face. She knew as well as he that, if what he feared to have transpired actually had, Toptower was now the final bastion for the kingdom and they were in no way prepared for it. "Send someone to *The Blade and Blanket*. The owner, Carwyn, used to be a sergeant in the army." The man might've been close to eighty, but his mind was still sharp. He could, at the very least, ensure the town was ready to defend itself.

"What are you going to do?"

"Find out precisely what is happening." As the nearest hound, it was on him to investigate and bring back any information he could. *Let me be wrong*, he pleaded to the heavens. He needed to have reached the wrong conclusion. Just this once.

CHAPTER 14

Darkness slowly drained away, leaving Dylan staring up at the grey sky. It took him a moment to realise the sunlight wasn't blotted out by clouds. Thick, black smoke tumbled in the wind, heading westward.

The ambush. The memory of heat invaded his mind. The screams of the dying. The bright light. The faint hum of his magic vibrating through his veins.

Was he dead? He should be.

But his head ached. As did his throat. Surely, such pains didn't follow the dead into the afterlife.

He raised a shaky hand, absently rubbing his neck. Skin greeted his fingers. The patch at his throat seemed different. Smooth like the marks the lightning left on Nestria's shoulder. No sign of—

The collar!

He jerked upright to the sound of another's shocked scream.

A woman crouched just outside the archway of the dwarven ruin, her eyes wide and her hand gripping the dagger sheathed at her hip. She looked so... vibrant. Now his vision wasn't only of the skyline, everything had the same vivid halo. From the woman's light brown skin and hair to the way the dim light from the sky seemed to bleed into the stone walls and blackened trees.

Frowning, the woman shuffled closer. "Are you all right?" Although she spoke his language—each word leaving her lips precise and whole—there was a melodious hint to her accent, a sort of slight breathiness that he had long associated with the dwarves.

Dylan wordlessly took in her attire. The apron-like dress made of buckskin leather atop another linen dress of ashen brown—runic symbols embroidered along the cuffs and neckline of both. She was from the neighbouring country of Dvärghem. And, if he was to judge by the intricate tree sigils stamped into the faces of her apron brooches—gorgeous discs of brass that glittered in the sunlight—she was a hedgewitch. Their land's scholars, sent abroad to learn all they could about the ancient dwarves.

Dylan slowly raised his hand, cupping her jaw. She was so very bright and beautiful, like a spirit from beyond. He had to be dead, then.

Had the Seven Sisters sent this angel to show him the way?

The hedgewitch pressed the inside of her wrist to his forehead. "You don't have a fever." Her frown deepened. "Do you understand me?"

He did. Although she now chose to speak Udynean rather than his native tongue, he understood every word. His gaze slid from her mussed hair to her face. A neat slice, caked in blood and dirt, ran from her forehead to her cheek, bisecting the freckled skin between her large, hazel eyes. Not an angel, then. She was just as mortal as he and...

Alive.

He lived. All that heat, the burning at his throat, the screaming fates of the unfortunate...

He had survived it all.

The woman took hold of his chin. Concern altered the crease in her brow as she tilted his head this way and that. "Can you hear me?" she asked, first in Demarner before repeating the phrase in Udynean. She was gorgeous, alive and breathtakingly gentle.

He grabbed her head, drawing her mouth down onto his. Her lips tasted of soot with a faint hint of sweat and the heavenly addictive glow of life.

She stiffened in his grasp and reality flopped onto his head like a dying bird.

Dylan released her and scurried back across the ground in one movement. "I'm sorry!" Shock and shame mingled in his gut. No one just up and kissed a hedgewitch. They weren't even meant to engage in intimacy. *And I just forced myself on her.* What in the world was wrong with him? Not once had he ever forced a woman to engage with him. Not even for a kiss. "That was wrong of me, I know. I am so very sorry. I've no excuse as to..."

The dwarf gave him a wavering smile and brushed back a wayward lock of her hair. Wisps remained, dancing on the breeze, still shining with that haze of light. "I am admittedly unfamiliar with a great number of Demarn customs." The language she spoke changed again, abandoning the harsher foreign words of the enemy and returning to his native tongue. "Does everyone here kiss before knowing the other's name?" She extended her arm. "I'm Katarina, by the way."

The heat flooding his face grew hotter. He grasped the offered hand and shook it. "Dylan," he mumbled. "And I am completely mortified." A barbarian. That was what he had become. Some savage too vile to even be considered an animal much less a civilised being. "I cannot apologise enough. I know hedgewitches are sacred, that they're not to be touched. I—"

Katarina clasped his hand in both of hers. "Be still." Her gaze drifted to their surroundings, settling on the archway. "You survived all that? I think a kiss is well-earned."

He clambered to his feet and, managing a few wobbling steps, leant in the archway to take in the full view of what lay around them, of what had become of the clearing. *The fire.*

Blackness dominated the land. Some trees standing just on the edge of the aftermath of the attack still smoked. The grass was gone and strange charred clumps dotted the—

His stomach came to the realisation far faster than the rest of him. Dylan collapsed to all fours, heaving despite nothing coming up. The twisted and charred lumps surrounding them were bodies. His mind rang with the memory of their cries. The help they had begged for that he hadn't been able to give.

A sword the lieutenant had called him. He'd been less useful than that. A sword could be wielded by another without permission.

Katarina knelt next to him. "I thought everyone was—"

"—dead," he finished for her. Why wasn't he dead alongside them? Whatever force had enabled him to free himself from the collar had to have been massive. The spellsters attacking would've seen it. Did they think he had died from it?

Nodding, the hedgewitch laid a hand on his shoulder. "I know it's a lot to take in, but we have to move on. Where do we go from here?"

He jerked his head up, incredulous. "You're asking me?" This had been his first time beyond the camp grounds. No one had told him much of anything, certainly not the direction they were heading. "I don't—"

Hadn't the sergeant mentioned a rendezvous point? That could be anywhere.

He dared another look over his shoulder and out the archway, trying to make out anything familiar that would lead him back to the front line. He rubbed at his neck. How strange that, even after only a few weeks of wearing the collar, he almost missed the tepid touch of the metal.

The collar. He recalled struggling to remove the band. Clearly, he'd been successful. Only now, there was nothing to distinguish him from a Udynean spellster beyond his tatty army robes.

Where had the collar gone? He searched frantically about them.

Two twisted lumps of purple metal lay where he had awoken. Unthinking, Dylan grabbed the pieces. Much like the shield back at the tower, they smouldered and sparked. Hissing, he dropped them before they could burn his hands.

"Just leave them," Katarina said.

"I can't," he croaked. Focusing on his power, he coaxed a funnel of cold air over the pieces. His magic responded hesitantly, a flush of warmth that soaked through to his core and was gone just as quick. "I need them." His superiors would kill him if he returned to the army camp unleashed. As it was, he would require some sort of proof that he wasn't a spy. The collar wouldn't be enough on its own and explaining how he had managed to free himself was going to be difficult when he wasn't entirely sure, but it was all he had.

Then, if they believed him, he'd be sent back to the tower. *To be leashed again.*

Convinced that the pieces of *infitialis* were now cold enough to touch, he let his magic fade. Never had he noticed how much his blood sang when he used his power. How tempting it was to let the song continue.

Wetting his lips, he stuffed the urge deep into the darkness of his thoughts. This was why they leashed those outside the tower.

Katarina collected the pieces, gently placing them into one of the many pouches she carried.

Dylan watched her, the brightness of the world slowly returning to normal. "Where did *you* come from?" he asked. There'd been no dwarves amongst their scouts.

"I came with an escort to survey these ruins." She gestured to the surrounding soot-caked stone. "But... I think they either got caught up in this mess or abandoned their posts at the first attack." Her lips twisted. "Whoever gave the order for this did so knowing these ruins were here." The woman thumped her fist into her other hand. "*And* in direct violation of our alliance. I must report the transgression to the Coven, but I won't find my way back to the Udynean border unaided." Those hazel eyes—earthy brown in the centres fading into a thick ring of pine green—settled on him. "*You* have people down here. Scouts, guides. I need you to take me to your camp."

Dylan shook his head. "I don't know what way camp is."

The hedgewitch jerked back. "How could you not know? Did you not take note of markers, any abnormalities that would help you get back if you were separated from your troop?"

Blinking, he scanned the tree line. What sort of markers could he possibly use in a forest? One clump of trees looked pretty much the same as another clump. "No?"

Sighing, Katarina stood. She dug into the large pouch hanging in the front of her belt, rummaging about until her search produced a small wooden hemisphere.

Dylan got to his feet as the hedgewitch unscrewed the top. Inside sat a metal disc and a little arrow that wobbled and swung to point in the same direction no matter which way the woman turned it.

"Is that a compass?" He'd seen drawings of them, far cruder designs than this. It was old dwarven technology, always sought to be improved upon by Dvärghem's greatest. Never did he dare to believe he would actually see one in action.

Katarina laughed, the sound clear and musical. "It is. Not many are able to recognise one at a glance." She swung about and pointed in a seemingly arbitrary direction. "North is that way and your camp is...?"

"To the east." Somewhere. The sergeant's path had meandered so much that anything beyond the man travelling in a vague westerly direction could be a fair bet. "A few hours away, maybe?"

"Then we go east." She strode out of the ruin and across the clearing in what he assumed was the correct way.

Dylan gingerly followed. His boots crunched across the ash-covered space between the dwarven ruins and the trees. He focused on the line of charred trunks and branches ahead, uncertain if his stomach wouldn't try to leap from his mouth if he dared to look anywhere else.

Strange how the charring just stopped when there were still plenty of trees to be consumed. Had the Udyneans also put out the fires they created?

Katarina waited under the canopy of untouched trees. "We've several hours before nightfall, it would be best to get as far from this place as possible." She absently rubbed at her face, hissing as her finger slid over the wound on the bridge of her nose.

"Wait." He slipped his hand into the crook of her elbow, halting and turning her in one gentle movement. "Let me see to that." Cupping her jaw, he focused his magic on the injury. Warmth flowed through him. The more familiar bliss of life poured out his fingertips and into her skin. Beneath the encrusted blood and dirt, the slice down her cheek slowly knitted itself back together. "How did you manage this, anyway?"

A fresh bloom of red adorned her cheeks. "Certainly not through some daring deed. My escorts and I were marching through the forest when one of them caught sight of smoke through a break in the canopy. We rushed this way and—" She flashed him another wobbly smile. "Well, I was so focused on trying to see the smoke and worried over what effect it might have on the ruins that I... didn't see the hole. I must've been knocked out, because the next thing I remember, it was morning."

Dread knotted his stomach. He hadn't realised this was a different day from the ambush. *Knocked out for a whole day.* His disappearance for so long would only make it harder for him to explain the lack of a collar.

The length also meant whoever had attacked the scouting party would have a considerable lead on them should they be part of the Udynea Empire's vanguard. And what of the thick smoke still dominating the sky? How long would it take for the wind to clear such remnants from the air?

Taking a deep breath, he withdrew both his magic and his hand from the hedgewitch. "That should do it."

She felt along her face, running a finger down the scar. "I wouldn't have thought they'd put a healer on scouting duty."

"There aren't any healers in the army. I'm a *weapon*." But, very soon, the army would be in need of both talents. "We should leave. East is this way, yes?" He jerked his chin in the direction the woman had originally set out for.

"It is." She fumbled with her compass, holding it before her. "Depending on how much your company veered from straight west, we should be able to hear your people even if our direction is a little off. Come on." Beckoning him to follow, she resumed her eastward trudge. "I'd prefer to reach your camp before nightfall."

He tramped through the forest, trying to keep up with the hedgewitch. They travelled in silence, vocally at least. The lack of other sounds made it that much easier for him to hear the twigs snapping beneath his boots. Somehow, his feet managed to find every raised tree root in their path.

How Katarina was able to walk the same trail without a single misstep was beyond him.

The brief patches in the undergrowth where he was able to set foot without a sound were more bothersome. When he first walked through here, his every move had been dogged by birds, filling the forest with their ever-cheerful chirps and the whistling songs, and the barely audible scurry of small animals. Without those sounds, the forest seemed empty. That couldn't be a good sign.

He lost track of the time of day. The canopy screened out much of the sunlight, throwing odd shadows, but his aching legs suggested they'd been walking for hours. His stomach grumbled in a seemingly endless complaint and he caught the dwarf pressing her hand to her belly once or twice.

How long ago had there been food? This morning? *No.* If what the hedgewitch had said was correct, he hadn't eaten since *yesterday* morning. Small wonder he felt so wretched.

He rubbed his stomach, trying in vain to shut it up. There would be food once they were back at camp. Nothing else he could do about it before then except walk.

All at once, Katarina came to a halt and, gasping, threw herself to the ground.

Dylan swiftly followed suit, landing next to her. "What is it?" he whispered. He doubted she would act this way for wildlife. That meant people. Scouts. *Us or them?*

Pressing a finger to her lips, she indicated the bush before them with the twitch of her brows.

His stomach knotted. He crawled through the undergrowth, flinching at every rustle, creak and snap of the foliage beneath him.

When he at last reached the bush, he slowly peered between the leaves. There were indeed people. They'd also the small quantity of weapons and light armour of scouts. However...

The hedgewitch settled at his side. "Udyneans," she breathed.

Dylan nodded, although there'd been no question. He may not have seen those who had ambushed his company, but no one in the camps wore such armour. The fabric was in similar mottled shades of green and grey to the Demarn soldiers, yet the similarity ended there. The main body of their attire looked like a tailored, knee-length, button-up tunic with very little metal to protect them and no sign of leather beyond a few belts. Puzzling when they had short swords at their hips and quivers on their backs.

"What are they doing?" he whispered. Although their movements didn't exactly take them in a straight line, they were certainly heading westward. The wrong direction to be scouting ahead. They looked too collected, too clean, to have been in battle.

Katarina shrugged. "Maybe they're returning with information."

He frowned. If that was the case, then it was all the more reason to stop them.

The longer he watched them, the more his gaze was drawn to one of the shorter elves as the woman flit from one side of the group to the other. There was something familiar about her. He tried to ignore the feeling. There had to be hundreds of elven women with her combination of height and black hair. But the more he stared, the more recognisable she became.

Jasilla. She'd worn the uniform of a Demarner scout the last time he had seen her, but he was certain. Katarina was right about the Udyneans using the dwarven ruin as bait, which meant someone had led them to it. If not Jasilla, then one of the other two scouts.

Power and anger sung in his veins, begging to be used, to bring them down like her people had done to the scouting party. He slowly rose from behind the foliage.

A hand gripped his shoulder, bearing him back to the ground. "Stay down!" Katarina hissed. She slowly pulled aside a wispy branch blocking their line of sight. The scouting party didn't appear to have noticed.

"Those are Udynean troops, you said it yourself." And so close to the front line. Why hadn't their own scouts spotted them? His gaze returned to Jasilla. The woman seemed jitterier than before. "*She* was there, the dark-haired elf. She was part of my company. She has to be some sort of spellster spy."

The dwarf pursed her lips. "No. Udynea leashes any elf who shows the slightest sign of magic. They wouldn't unleash one, not even to become a spy."

Magic or not, she was here amongst the enemy now and had been complicit in the ambush. Even if she never loosed a single arrow, she still bore part of the blame. "I have to avenge my—"

The grip Katarina still held on his shoulder tightened. "Not now."

"*Not now?*" he echoed, his voice barely above a whisper. "Have you already forgotten what was left of my people?"

Those hazel eyes turned on him. "I remember."

"You only saw the aftermath, though. I watched them die." *All those bodies*. Bile burned his throat at the memory of the flame-shrouded figure battling to stay alive. And there was the woman who'd given her life to save his, the captain who had died before giving the order that would've allowed Dylan capable of fighting back. "They left me to watch people burn. I need to make them pay."

The hedgewitch shook her head. "You *need* to return to camp, to warn the rest of your people or more are going to meet the same fate."

"I can't just let them go." If anyone found out he let the enemy walk away, they would brand him a traitor.

Sighing, Katarina released the spindly branch and faced him. "Let me tell you a little something about their scouting parties. They never venture far from camp without magic to back them up." She jerked her head at the bush. "The two marching at the rear are most likely spellsters."

He peered through the brush, taking in the arrogant stride of the aforementioned man and woman. Unlike the others, the pair wore not even a short sword at their hips.

"Could you take them on and win?" the hedgewitch whispered into his ear, her warm breath on his skin stirring the small hairs lying at the nape of his neck and sending a chill through his body. "As well as the other scouts? Alone?"

His pride wanted to say he could. He had taken down more than two spellsters at once without breaking a sweat. This would be no different to the brawl.

"And could you guarantee *my* safety whilst doing so?"

He turned his head, unable to look her in the eye. Dwarves, whilst once the sole proprietors of the continent, were no longer as numerous as even elves. To put one in danger, and a hedgewitch at that? "I can't, no." He'd be better off throwing himself before the mercy of the Udynea Empire than to report her injury—or worse, her death—to the Dvärghem Coven.

"Then you know what action you must take." Katarina took up his hand, squeezing it tight. Pity welled in her eyes. "I'm sorry it has to be this way." She slowly tucked herself beneath the bush where the undergrowth was the thickest, motioning for him to do the same.

Dylan burrowed his way into the surrounding ferns, gritting his teeth as twigs and branches caught on his clothes and hair. Hopefully, the dark green of his dirt and soot-stained robe would aid him in remaining unseen should a scout come too close. He prayed the same could be said of the hedgewitch's attire.

They lay still, waiting for the scouting party to move out of sight and hearing distance. The bitter bite of betrayal gnawed at his gut as he listened to their footsteps crunching through the undergrowth. He should be sending these murdering bastards to the foot of whatever gods they believed in, not cowering under leaves.

"I still don't understand why they told us to pull back," one of the men grumbled.

Dylan froze, scarcely daring to breathe. That voice was loud enough for the speaker to be almost on top of them. Slowly twisting his head, he spied the dirty leather of a boot naught but a few feet away. He calmly readied his magic, prepared to unleash everything he had if they were spotted.

"You weren't brought here to understand, *elf*," a woman replied. The way she all but spat the final word, as if speaking it caused her some great distress, was all Dylan needed to be sure it was one of the spellsters. So many of them came from nobility, used to having slaves serve their every need. "You were given an order, you obey it."

"Yes, mistress," the elven man replied. "You are right, of course."

The boot lifted, crunching down on some unseen part of the forest floor.

Dylan released the breath he hadn't been aware he was holding. To his right, he heard the hedgewitch do the same. They remained in place, waiting for the fading sounds of the scouts' footsteps to vanish completely, then lingering in the dead silence that little bit more before, finally, he caught Katarina's signal to move.

He untangled himself from the foliage, brushing bits of dead leaves from his clothes, his mind still churning over what he'd heard. "They're pulling back?" He winced upon trying to free a bit of twig from his hair. All these years, the centuries of fighting to keep the empire at bay, and they just gave up advancing?

That couldn't be true, could it?

The hedgewitch glanced up from her compass. "It would seem that way." She smiled, a wide and warm expression that he hadn't seen since leaving the tower. "I believe congratulations are in order. I would say your kingdom won't need quite so many people in the army if the Udynean forces are pulling back."

Dylan frowned, trailing after her as she resumed their eastward course. "Maybe." It would take more than his word to have anyone believe the Udynean threat was gone. Even then, it would be foolish to leave the border undefended. "Maybe not." A far more likely scenario was the army's vigilance remaining unchanged for several decades to come.

Katarina halted. Her hand flattened against his chest, urging him to do likewise. "Do you smell smoke?"

He cautiously sniffed the air. There was indeed a certain burnt aroma. Faint and not the warm scent of a wood fire, but a cloying, oily and all-too-familiar stench. His stomach churned. He clapped his hand over his mouth, willing himself to swallow the burning liquid pooling in the back of his throat.

No. Just because the smell was sickeningly similar to what had happened in the clearing didn't mean anything. The camp was still a good hour's walk from here. The smoke could be coming from anywhere. The Udynean spellsters could've mistaken a deer or boar for a person and fried the poor creature before realising their folly.

Or I could be too late. With his scouting party gone, the Udyneans would've had a clear path to the front line. There would be no warning beyond the first assault and, with most of the leashed spellsters on similar missions as he'd been, the soldiers would have limited means to counter a magical attack.

"East." He grabbed Katarina's shoulders. "Which way is east?"

With her hazel eyes already wide, the hedgewitch scrabbled anew at her compass. The little metal arrow wobbled north. "That way." She pointed in the direction where the smoky smell seemed to emanate from.

No... It couldn't be.

Could it?

Snatching the compass from her hands, he raced through the undergrowth, constantly checking his heading. The cloying stench grew with every step. All too soon, he could make out low clouds of smoke clinging to the canopy. Too much to be the campfires. Panting, he pressed on, stumbling and tripping on the uneven ground.

Over his lumbering movements, he caught the far nimbler steps of the hedgewitch on his tail. He couldn't stop, couldn't slow to explain, he had to reach the front line.

The hint of a clearing beckoned ahead of him. Dylan exploded out of the undergrowth into the clearing, stopping dead on the tree line.

No.

Katarina came to a halt at his side, glaring up at him as her chest heaved. "I'll take that back, thank you." She claimed the compass from his unresisting fingers. "Of all the foolish—" Frowning, the woman glanced up from her examination of the device. "Oh."

Where there had once been neat lines of canvas and wood was now a smouldering plain. Oddly, the smell wasn't as bad here. Charred lumps dotted the scorched mass. Unidentifiable as bits of wood or bodies.

Dylan stumbled a few steps towards the smoking remains, his legs threatening to give. *I'm too late.* Everything, everyone, was dead. That was why the scouts were turning back. There was no one left to oppose them.

Demarn had lost.

Just thinking of the scouting party he had let walk away fanned the banked embers of anger burning in his soul. Where were the monsters responsible for this? It would've taken more than a pair of spellsters and a few archers to take out the front line. They should've come across dozens of men.

Unless...

His gaze settled on the path he first walked to get here. It was thin, not like the dusty road leading carts to the main encampment, but difficult to lose track of. All the enemy had to do was walk it and they would come across the last defence along the western border.

"I have to go." If whoever attacked this camp were the same people that had taken out his scouting party, then they had no more than a day's head start. If he pushed himself, he might reach them before they'd the chance to attack the main camp. "I need to warn them that the enemy's on its way."

Katarina trotted after him.

Dylan frowned at the woman. "It would be best if you didn't follow. There's going to be a battle." And, being unleashed, he could assist in both the fighting and the healing. "You were right before. I can't protect you and fight at the same time. This isn't your war. Coming with me just puts you in danger. You'd be safer if you headed north now."

"Where my only option is to wander the forest without food or an escort? Never mind the wild animals I might stumble upon, what if the nature of creature I meet is Udynean?"

"You're a hedgewitch." Dvärghem had the same treaty with the Udynea Empire as it did with Demarn. Once it was made known she wasn't the enemy, no harm would come to her.

She wrinkled her nose at him. "And I'm sure they'll be very

remorseful when they pluck the arrows from my corpse, but a neutral stance works best when you aren't in the middle of a battlefield. Until then, I'm better off sticking to a healer's side."

Shrugging, Dylan lengthened his stride. "Then stay close to me." He would do his best to keep her from harm. To shield all of them. Even if it meant his last breath, he would ensure that no one else under his protection died.

CHAPTER 15

They walked through the night. With the canopy of leaves obscuring the scant moonlight, Katarina insisted on taking the lead. Dylan hadn't bothered with arguing. He entrusted the dwarf's far more superior night vision and travelling with the full cover of darkness would make them invisible to all but elven scouts.

Dawn saw them skulking amongst the undergrowth whilst keeping the path in their sights.

It still wasn't fast enough.

It had taken a day or so to travel there from the main encampment to the front line. No matter the speed they travelled, however much his body screamed for food and rest, it felt as though he would need to walk for weeks more before reaching their destination.

That they hadn't come across a hint of Demarner or Udynean troops did nothing to soothe the dread bubbling in his gut. His thoughts continued to dwell on the scenes they'd left behind. The scouting party. The front line camp. All dead.

What could he have done differently? There had to be something. A way he could've warned them that he hadn't been aware of?

Would it have made a difference? What if he had fled into the forest instead of the ruin? He could've reached the front line then, alerted everyone. Found a superior who could've given the order to fight back.

Everyone was dead because of him, because he fled for safety like a coward. His guardian had been right. Even if it had meant life-long imprisonment, or death, he should've thrown the brawl. Who knew what difference one of the other competitors could have made?

"It's not your fault."

He jerked his head towards Katarina, staring at her incredulously. The hedgewitch had been quiet for much of the night, speaking only to warn him of an obstacle his vision couldn't make out in the utter blackness of the forest. She had chosen to adopt full silence with the encroaching light of dawn.

"I know that look," she continued. "You're blaming yourself for what happened, but you're not responsible."

Dylan grunted. How could he still be standing here, breathing, and not be part of the problem? "So the fact I'm alive and they're all dead is just a happy coincidence? When my party was attacked? I *ran*."

The memory flashed before his eyes. Fire and confusion everywhere. The screams of the dying. Heat and death choking him.

He shook his head, desperately trying to banish the images, but the vision remained, dancing in the back of his mind. "I ran in the wrong direction and doomed the entire front line." Only the gods knew what was currently happening at the main encampment. Clearly, they weren't aware of the attack at the front or there would be soldiers seeking answers.

Her gaze dropped to the tattered and singed ends of his robe. "If there were archers, you would've been struck down well before you could reach your people. That you're alive now is likely more due to your healing abilities than their negligence."

He grunted, his thoughts swiftly turning to a far greater concern. "We should've come across someone by now. A scout. Some hint of soldiers heading for the front line..." Anyone.

Katarina delicately sniffed the air. "I don't smell any smoke."

She was right. The breeze blew from the east and yet carried no hint of smoke. His thoughts wandered to the fires he recalled dotting the lines of tents. Through both the main camp and the front line, the air always carried a lingering smoky scent. "Doesn't that strike you as odd?"

"Strategy isn't my strongest point, but perhaps someone managed to escape from the front line before..." She trailed off, shook herself and continued. "They could've gotten word about the attack and those at the main camp might've fallen back without realising the Udyneans have withdrawn."

"Maybe." He might have believed her if she sounded a little more convinced by her own words. It seemed far more likely that everyone was dead, which gave Udynea a higher ground to bargain. Anyone who'd spent enough time learning the empire's history would know that the Udynean Empire hadn't technically fought anyone for centuries. The armies his country fought against were not imperial.

Their emperor—*Mhanek* as they called him—probably didn't even see Demarn as being worthy of invasion. They were a pathetic creature huddled at the foot of a giant. His talks with visiting hedgewitches taught him that what the kingdom had struggled to hold back for so many centuries was a collection of border lords and their personal armies. Their fighting? A protracted attempt to expand their estate. A nudge of the giant's foot. But they had to bite back or suffer being trodden on.

The abrupt tug on his sleeve drew him back from his musing.

Katarina towed him towards the road, almost hauling him off his feet. "Quick!"

He stumbled behind her, uncertain what she had spotted. *Survivors?* His feet fell a little surer. Perhaps her dwarven hearing had caught the pained cry of someone left for dead. Or her sharper eyes had spied the movement of a soldier.

They exploded out of the undergrowth bordering the path.

A deer stood amongst the ferns on the other side, it froze as they stopped, staring at them with those massive brown eyes before scampering deeper into the brush.

Katarina's shoulder's sagged. Shaking her head, she resumed their march towards the main camp, forsaking the cover of bush for the ease of the path. "You'd think I would be able to tell the difference between a person and a—" She halted, her hands flying to her mouth.

Dylan caught her whispered "Oh, no." before spying what the dwarf had found.

People lay amongst the ferns. Demarner and Udynean both. Scouts, judging by the attire, although there were a few more heavily armed Udynean warriors amongst them, their bloated bodies bristling with arrows. Shock troops caught off guard?

It was the bodies of those wearing the armour of Demarn that drew his eye. Scorching marked the ground around them in the spidery vein-like pattern of lightning. A stark contrast to the fallen Udyneans surrounded by the dried pool of blood, their bloated corpses having succumbed to blade and arrow.

The dreadful drone of flies filled the air as they crept closer. A stench he'd never smelt before hit him, a rancid mixture of used chamber pots and spoiled meat.

The hold he had kept on his stomach failed. Dylan doubled over, every muscle in his gut cramping, and heaved. Mucus and bile poured out his mouth and clogged his nose. He continued to retch until there was nothing left to give.

The hedgewitch crouched at his side. She grasped his arm. Concern raised her brows. "Dylan? Are you—?"

He waved her back. "I'm all right," he managed to gasp between heaves. His gaze slid to the corpses, morbid fascination overcoming the initial assault to his senses. Already, the animals had picked at the bodies, birds for the most part and probably a few smaller creatures. Flies dominated the air, but there were no signs of maggots. They couldn't be more than a day or two old. "We should keep going."

Katarina gave a curt nod and, with her fingers firmly pinching her nose shut, led the way along the path. Once past the corpses, Dylan picked up the pace, forcing the hedgewitch to jog every at other step to keep up.

If the scouts were dead, slain by magic, that meant the main encampment was gone or in the midst of being destroyed. Either way, they hadn't come across any other living Udyneans beyond the withdrawing scouting party. Perhaps the main bulk of the attack force was still ahead. He might not be strong enough to take them all out, but he was willing to try.

It was a while before Katarina spoke again. "I meant what I said earlier. You're not to blame and, no matter what we find, that opinion still stands. But hurrying won't bring them back."

He halted, heard her gasp and the grunt of her trying not to stumble into him. "I could've saved them." Tears pricked his eyes, hot as the flames that had scorched his company, had wiped out the front line. Everywhere he trod, he found death wrought by magic. "If I'd been there, they wouldn't be dead." He was a coward, hiding instead of fighting until his last breath.

Not anymore. Dashing his tears, he marched onwards, the hurried footsteps of the hedgewitch following close behind.

They remained in silence, but his thoughts refused to slow down. Like his feet, they plodded an endless path. Scraps of strategy learnt in his youth, suppositions of force strength and placement. He hadn't gotten a decent look at the main encampment before being sent to the front line. It had been big, not perhaps as large as it could be, and exposed.

The war with the Udynea Empire had gone on for too long. Where the tower history books spoke of massive armies in the tens of thousands, there'd been quite a bit less at the main encampment. Perhaps a generous two thousand. Still, it was impossible to presume no one had survived. And...

His pace increased until he was running. The path before him started to climb. Dylan pushed harder, ignoring the wobble and burn in his legs. The only sound was the rasp of his breath. In his wallowing, he had forgotten about the other spellsters. Those back at the front line would've been out scouting. Not so here. They could be holding back the invading force, waiting for that one moment when they would have the upper hand.

He could be that moment. The Udyneans wouldn't expect a Demarner spellster to be running loose in the forest, much less at their flank.

Dylan gathered his magic, letting it charge the air around him. He could attack before anyone realised he was there, vanish into the undergrowth and do it again. Be the distraction that would give others space to regroup and counter.

In a time that seemed far too long to reach, his feet brought him to the top of the incline.

Dylan froze.

There was nothing. No enemy army to attack. No kingsmen to alert. Not even much of a camp left. A few tents remained, but the majority were reduced to charred frames and less. They'd seen no sign of smoke only because the flames had already consumed all there was to burn.

As his gaze slid over the carnage, he slowly came to the realisation that he hadn't heard any fighting.

He fell to his knees, his body drained of strength. Although he couldn't see the corpses, the bitter stench of charred flesh permeated the air. His stomach cramped and Dylan reflexively clamped his hand over his mouth, but he'd nothing left to offer up.

How? His mind screamed over and over. How could this have happened? How had everyone missed the Udyneans' return? How could the Udyneans have managed to get so close without contest?

Katarina came to a gasping halt at his side. She stared out at what was left of the camp, then hung her head. "I'm sorry."

"So am I." He should've slain those bastards in the forest, should've taken his chance in being able to protect the hedgewitch in the attack and torn through them all.

"We need to press on. Is there a fallback position we can reach?"

He shook his head. "I don't know." He rather doubted there had been anyone left to fall back. "But the closest settlement is Toptower." It had taken them several days to ride from there to the camp. How long was it on foot?

"Do you know the way?"

Nodding, Dylan pointed to the other side of the encampment where a gap in the trees suggested the beginning of a road. It would be easy enough to follow and, after that?

They would just have to keep taking the northward roads and hope.

"Then we should see what can be salvaged. Food and water would be a priority." She indicated the left of the camp where a lone tent, one of the large and official-looking ones, still half stood. "Let's start there."

They picked their way through the debris, Dylan taking great pains to keep the tattered ends of his robe and undertunic free of anything that might snag them.

Everywhere he looked, the charred faces of the dead glared back accusingly. Their screams bounced about his mind. Why was *he* alive?

How had *he* managed to come away unscathed? What did the gods deem so special about *him* that he was allowed to freely walk away from all this?

He wished he'd an answer to that last one. Some would no doubt call it luck. He didn't feel lucky.

They had almost reached the tent when a woman, covered in soot and dried blood, emerged from it. Her short hair stood like a halo around her, orange like the fires that had consumed scouting party, and not quite hiding the telltale point of elven ears. Her armour wasn't like most of the Demarn military-issued garb, but at least it wasn't Udynean.

She saw them and started heading the other way. "Stay back!" The sword she carried awkwardly in her left hand came up, the point wobbling as her arm shook. "I'm warning you."

Even with her armour not marking her as one of the army's common soldiers, her accent certainly did. It was faint with a soft, slightly undulating, tone hinting at a childhood in middle Demarn.

Katarina grasped his sleeve as he went to move towards the elf. "Be careful," she whispered. "She's wounded."

He gave the woman a second look and caught what the hedgewitch had spied. The elf favoured her right arm, holding it tight to her stomach, wincing at every movement.

Dylan stepped closer. Whatever ailed her, he could make it better. "Your arm. Let me see it."

Viciously shaking her head, the woman continued her retreat. "I said, stay back!" Fear coloured the words.

He halted near the tent opening and glanced inside. Nothing but a table along with a few other bits and pieces strewn about. "I can help."

"Please," Katarina said. "Listen to him. We mean you no harm."

The woman's eyes narrowed at the hedgewitch. "That's not a Demarn accent."

"No," he agreed. "She's from Dvärghem."

The woman's sea-green eyes returned to him. "And you're a spellster. Don't lie, I know those robes."

"I am." There was very little point in denying it. Even if she hadn't recognised his distinct military attire, she would find out as soon as he was given the chance to mend her arm. And he *would* find a way to do so. If he could be sure of the bone being whole or set right, he would've already tried without touching her, but he wasn't prepared to take that risk. "Let me see to your arm."

She jerked the sword between them. "I'm not letting a *spellster* touch me."

Dylan bit his tongue, choosing to ignore the bitter way she spat the word. He didn't blame her being wary of him. She had already seen what a person with magic at their command could do. "It's all right. I've trained in this sort of thing." Seeing that wasn't enough to sway her mind, he changed tactics. "You normally use that arm for fighting, right? If the bone isn't set properly, you might never be able to hold your sword again."

The elf eyed him, then Katarina. Finally, she lowered the sword point.

Dylan wasted no time. He cradled the woman's forearm and carefully felt along the swollen skin. Broken bones hadn't been all that common in the tower, not for adepts like himself to work on, but he had come across a few before leaving the expert training. What he felt now... both bones seemed to have broken.

She had likely used her arm to ward off a blow, for whilst the thumbward bone seemed more or less where it should be, the other side of her arm bulged where it shouldn't. "This is going to hurt for a bit, but I have to set the bones first, all right?"

"What?" Panic turned the previous rolling tone of her voice shrill. Her heavily freckled face, already quite pale, somehow grew whiter. "Don't you need to gather things like wood and cord for a splint first?"

"This won't take long, I promise." He manipulated the bones back into place to the barely audible sound of the woman's gasp. "Just keep still and I'll be done soon." With his hands holding the bones in place, he drew on his magic.

The woman was weary, hungry, likely hadn't slept since the attack. There were other injuries, a graze on her knee, a stubbed toe, a cut on her left finger... the list continued. Trying to tend to them all divided his attention and slowed the already difficult knitting together of the bones.

He focused a little harder on the spot directly beneath his fingers, putting a little of his strength into the magic to quicken her healing. It tightened his chest and caused the rapid pounding of his heart to fill his ears.

Then it was done.

Dylan withdrew, staggering back a step as his breathing became easier. He'd forgotten how much harder it was to mend other people's bones compared to flesh. If he had ever known it would be required of him, he would've continued training with the tower healers on an expert level.

The woman levelled her sword at him, both of her hands firmly clamped around the hilt.

"Easy now!" He stepped further back but the elf followed, her sword still pointed at his chest. "I just fixed your arm."

"With *unsanctioned* magic," she snarled. "You're an unleashed spellster, just like those bastards who ripped through here."

"I'm on your side." He tugged at his army-issued robe. "See?"

"How am I supposed to know you're not some spy trying to sneak his way into the kingdom?"

Dylan opened his mouth, the retort already on his tongue. His thoughts turned to Jasilla and the others who had led his scouting party straight into an ambush. The woman had a point. It must look particularly suspicious for him to appear well after the attack and seemingly unharmed, doubly so in being a spellster.

"If he is, dear," Katarina said, "then he does a wonderful Demarner accent."

Which one? There were three, possibly four, distinct accents across the land. Even a few that sounded uncomfortably close to the way they spoke in Udynea. The tower carried a rather wide assortment, sampled from everywhere, with the majority sounding very much like the elven woman.

This observation did nothing to placate the elf. "*Our* spellsters are leashed. I gave you no sanction to use your magic on me." Those sea-green eyes narrowed at him and the sword point lifted to his neck. "If you're one of ours, then where's your collar? Show me!"

"It..." Ever since discovering the enemy scouts, he had stopped thinking as to how he would explain the collar's defective nature. He didn't remember what had happened, only that it had. "It came off." Even to his ears, the answer was pathetic.

"Liar!" She thrust the sword closer, forcing him to move or be decapitated. His feet caught on a fallen tent pole. He dropped to the ground and scrambled out of reach, not daring to waste time by getting back up.

"It's true." The hedgewitch hastily opened the pouch containing the remains of his collar to produce one of the pieces. "I saw him wake. This was near where he lay. There wasn't anyone else."

Seeing that piece of twisted, purple metal seemed to mollify the elf. She still eyed him, but with less ire. "Why now?" she whispered. "Why weren't you here when those bastards tore down our defences like a windstorm?" Her head snapped back to him. "Where were you when they were slaughtering your kingsmen?"

"Quite likely discovering what had become of the front line," Katarina replied. "It's been a hard few days for the both of us."

"A hard few days?" the woman laughed. A harsh, forced sound. She clapped a hand to the side of her face. "Oh deary me, look at the terrible thing that happened whilst I wasn't here." The hand fell to her side as if it were a dead weight. "Well, I watched them *die*," she snarled. "I'm a warrior, you hear? Not some simpering maiden. I saw the very elements tear apart those standing at my side."

"They attacked my scouting party," Dylan shot back. "They slew my warden before he could give me sanction. Got him right in the throat. Everyone else, they—" The memory of the woman who had saved his life filled his mind, her face wide-eyed and gaping with the tip of an arrowhead breaking through her forehead. The shrieking of the burning figure still echoed in his ears. "They killed everyone else."

"You should've been here," the elf grated, the words hissing between her teeth. "You may not be some Udynean spy." The sword drew closer. "But I swear, if you had any idea as to what they had planned, I will send you to the same grave."

He held up a hand before realising it could be misconstrued as a threat and hastily lowered it. "You're right. I should've been." If he hadn't pushed the lieutenant on his first day, hadn't given the man any cause to expedite his assignment to the front line, he might very well have still been here. "I could've helped."

"Were there no other spellsters situated at this camp?" Katarina asked.

Others. His thoughts turned to the woman the hound had brought back from the tower with him. What had her name been? *Ava*. If he hadn't been so quick to show the overseers what he was capable of, if there'd been more uncertainty on who to send to the front line, she could still be alive.

The warrior nodded. "Half of them. About ten in all." She waved her hand about the area. "As you can see, they're all dead or taken. There's no one else here. I've checked everywhere. Those miserable magic-wielding bastards." She spat onto the ashen ground. "They attacked and just... up and left."

"Maybe one more spellster would've been enough to turn the tide." It had been drummed into him for years by his tutors that changing one variable could alter what should've been a simple spell into a catastrophe. Being here when the Udynean forces attacked could have changed things.

Katarina crouched at his side. "Or you could've been one more corpse."

"You don't know that," he muttered.

The hedgewitch either hadn't heard him or chose not to. She turned her attention back to the other woman who seemed less inclined to skewer him. "Which way did they go?"

The elf shrugged. "West. It's so strange. They didn't try looting or checking on the fallen. Just gathered up a few of the obviously alive ones and vanished back into the forest." Her eyes grew misty and distant with memory. "I tried to fight them but, what can an ordinary being do against such an attack?" She settled on a pile of rubble, all the anger draining from her. "It feels like cowardice to turn tail and run to the king, but the people in charge have to be warned before they send more soldiers."

"There's no shame in a tactical retreat." Katarina glanced at him as she spoke before asking the woman, "Do you have a map?"

"I think I saw one in there." With a jerk of her head, the woman indicated the tent she had emerged from.

The hedgewitch disappeared into the tent, returning swiftly with a small square of paper. Her lips mumbled soundlessly as she trailed a fingertip along the map. Finally, she glanced up at him. "This Toptower settlement you mentioned, it's not all that far from here. There might be more who have survived."

"If they have," the elf muttered, "they won't want to come back."

"We can gather supplies, maybe even find a way to get word to your king without travelling the full distance."

Dylan slowly got to his feet, mindful that the elf could decide she would rather have him dead. "I need to return to the tower." Sidling to the dwarf's side, he pointed at a dark, unnamed spot on the map. "There." He glanced at the elf. "I'll also require an escort." He might be capable of making it across the kingdom on his own, but there was the added chance that doing so alone would make him a bigger target for the King's Hounds.

Katarina nodded. "I can head that way with you if she cannot, but Toptower is still our first stop. I believe all that remains to be done here is find what we can salvage to barter with once we arrive." She deftly folded the map and tucked it into her front pouch. "And perhaps, some introductions." The dwarf held out her hand to the other woman. "I am Madam Katarina, hedgewitch of Dvärghem."

The elf eyed the hedgewitch's hand as if expecting it to burst forth with all manner of magic. Finally, she shook it. "Authril of Danny's Cutthroats."

Katarina tilted her head and a piece of her bun slithered free of its confines. "That sounds like a mercenary company."

Authril nodded. "Sure is." She frowned. "Or was. About fifty of us signed up to push the bastards back after they took out our captain." Those sea-green eyes slid his way. Rather than look less wary about him, her expression hardened. "I know what you are, spellster. What are you called?"

"Dylan," he replied, not bothering to offer his hand. He rather doubted she would've shaken it anyway.

Her lips flattened. "Such an innocuous name for something so dangerous."

His gaze dropped to her sword arm. Now the bones were healed, the woman grasped the hilt as if the blade was an extension of her hand. He wouldn't be surprised to find she slept with it. "I'm not the only dangerous thing here."

A smirk tugged at her lips. She jabbed the point of her sword in his direction. "Just you remember that, spellster."

Dylan inclined his head. How could he ever forget?

CHAPTER 16

D ylan tipped his head skyward, trying to avoid looking at his surroundings. The three of them had spent the better part of the afternoon rifling through the ashes and amongst the dead in search of anything that could be of use in their journey to Toptower. The remains offered up little beyond what Authril had managed to scrape together in the large tent, the structure being one of the many things they would need to leave behind.

Hopefully, their haul of trinkets and scattered coins would be enough to boost their supplies as well as procure a more suitable canvas shelter in the village. The weather had been agreeable thus far in not dousing them, but he had already had his taste of travelling in the rain on his journey down here. He didn't fancy sleeping in it as well.

Luck gifted them a single water skin, found beneath an overturned pot. Food was the more elusive commodity. What hadn't been consumed in the flames was made inedible by ash and soot.

That lack would quickly become a problem if he wasn't careful. His magic was capable of collecting moisture from the air to refill the water skin, but without food, he would become a hindrance to their group. As it was, his stomach growled its demand to be fed. Between the trek here, the healing and the shortage of food, he had precious little energy left to give. Hopefully, they'd be able to forage something, even if it was a few berries.

"Are we set?" Katarina enquired of them. Already, the woman carried one of the three small crude packs fashioned from bits of canvas and leather. She handed him another. "I would like to put this place a few hours behind us, just in case there are any Udynean stragglers."

"Give me a moment and I will be," Authril replied.

The muffled scrape of metal sliding over metal had Dylan turning as he secured the pack straps over his shoulders.

The warrior was in the process of buckling her breastplate. Smaller pieces of armour lay atop the shield resting at her feet. Apart from the helmet, the bits looked like they belonged on limbs.

"You're bringing all that with you?"

The elf arched a brow at him. "Of course?" She nudged several bits of armour with her boot. "I'm not planning on tramping through the forest in full plate if that's what you're thinking. I won't slow us down. This…" The elf thumped her breastplate. "This'll protect the important stuff if we're attacked." She moved on to donning her greaves. "The rest is all leather and padding. Danny liked us to be protected, but agile. After all, someone's got to keep your innards where they should be." The vambraces were next, followed swiftly by her sword belt and helmet. Those sea-green eyes glared at him from the shadow of the brim. "Or not, if you choose to cross us."

"If that had ever been my intention, I wouldn't have wasted energy healing you." That wasn't true. Leaving people to suffer hadn't ever been his strong suit. He just hoped he'd enough strength left on the off chance the hedgewitch was right about stragglers.

"You've still got enough in you to walk until sundown, though?" Authril asked as she shouldered the last of the packs and hefted her shield. "I'd rather not have to carry your soft arse through the forest because you've fainted." Although she was of average height for an elf, around level with his shoulders, the addition of armour did little to bulk her appearance. Nevertheless, Dylan could well imagine her being capable of lifting him.

"I'm sure that won't be necessary." He was by no means as fit as either woman, but he could handle a few hours of walking before they made camp. From here, the road ran downhill. An easy task. The way would flatten out before long, but would still be better than the forest floor he'd been stumbling over for the past two days. Sleep would see him capable of more come the next day.

"Good," the warrior replied. "Because I'd like to get you back where you belong as quickly as possible."

Katarina halted at his side, shrugging her pack into a more comfortable position. "Then we'd best be on our way if we're to find a suitable place off the road to camp before sunset." She placed a hand on his shoulder. "Don't think you have to push yourself."

"I won't hold us back." The sooner he reached the tower, the sooner he would be able to return and make the Udyneans pay.

Dylan turned from the woman and headed for the gap in the trees. The soft crunch of footsteps caught his ear as his travelling companions followed at a casual, but firm, pace. He forced his gaze to remain steadfast on the road as he strode through the camp. If he didn't, then it wandered, settling on what he didn't want to see.

The burnt remains weren't as numerous here as at the front line. That meant more corpses like the ones back on the path. Only now, the birds had started appearing. He could see the fluttering of piebald wings just on the edge of his vision. Above, the brown and white-speckled body of a falcon circled, its cries scattering the scavengers before it dove.

Ignoring it all was far harder than he had expected. Each new movement tempted his eye and tricked his thoughts into courting the possibility of there being an impending threat.

There's only us. Dylan took a deep breath, trying to calm his nerves. The stench he'd been carefully avoiding the thought of for the last few hours now invaded his nostrils. Swallowing the bile sliding up his throat, he pressed on. If the enemy was around, they wouldn't bother with picking through the bloated bodies of the dead.

Their little trio truly were the only people alive out here.

Besides, Authril had said the Udyneans had headed west whereas the road would take them on an easterly route. And once they reached Toptower, it was on to...

He frowned, not able to recall the place the King's Hound had led him through on his way down here, but he knew their first stop. He could consult Katarina's map once they arrived at the first settlement.

They'd almost cleared the camp remains when a figure far larger than a mere bird emerged from the forest shadows.

Dylan halted, peering up ahead as the figure slowly became the more defined form of a horse and rider. Someone who had been away when the attack happened? One of the army's messengers, perhaps?

On his left, Katarina gasped and dropped behind the shredded remains of a tent. At the same time, he caught the warrior reaching for her sword. Dylan didn't waste time asking what their superior eyesight made out, he flung himself next to the hedgewitch and threw up a fully transparent barrier large enough to encompass them all.

Crouching, Authril motioned them to shift somewhere off to her left. "We need to find proper cover."

"Don't move," Dylan muttered out the corner of his mouth. "I've got us shielded. It'll keep us safe from mundane attacks, but if you take even a single step back, then you risk being outside that protection." It was possible for him to encompass them all whilst on the move, but not adequately enough for his liking. Staying in one spot afforded him the chance to keep the barrier large and strong.

Both women rolled their eyes upward. Did they spot the faint ripple his defence caused in the air? It took some concentration to keep the usual translucent purple sheen from the barrier's surface, but it appeared relatively invisible to his eyes.

Authril shook her head and slunk behind the rubble to lie beside him. "We'll be spotted if we stay here much longer."

He frowned. If they moved, the rider would sight them far sooner. "It's one man." The three of them could handle a single attacker, even if that man turned out to be a spellster. Still, perhaps luck was on their side and it was an ally.

Either way, they could certainly use the horse.

"No, it's not." Even as the hedgewitch spoke, other shapes emerged from the shadows.

Dylan's hopes plummeted as he watched them advance. The group wore the same armour as the scouts they'd evaded between the dwarven ruin and the front line. Even the rider was attired in the same mottled green and grey colours.

Seeing they weren't moving, Authril further flattened herself on the ground. She peered around the rim of her shield to glare at the encroaching group only to duck back, swearing under her breath. "Staying put is a really bad idea. What if they decide to wait us out? How long can you keep this barrier up?"

"Long enough," he replied, unable to tear his gaze from the group. After everything he had seen, everything he'd been through, he wasn't about to let this lot walk away. Dylan examined the people walking in formation around the rider. There were more than the last scouting party. Nine in all. The rider had to be a spellster. He'd be harder to take down but, with Authril's aid, not impossible. "Just be ready."

The elf's orange brows lowered in a definite scowl. "For what?"

Katarina clasped his shoulder before he could answer. "It seems we've been spotted." Already, her dagger was out. He didn't see what use it would be against their enemy.

The group hadn't stopped, but they'd certainly slowed their pace. Those on foot chattered between themselves and the mounted man, one of them pointing in Dylan's direction. Another nocked her bow and loosed an arrow.

The shaft hit Dylan's barrier and shattered. Katarina flinched, pressing close to him. He caught Authril sucking in a hissing breath.

"It's another leashed one!" the woman called over her shoulder.

The rider urged his mount closer. He leant forward in the saddle. "Really? And here his lordship said he caught them all."

Caught? Not slain outright like so many others, but taken to suffer a worse fate at the hands of these monsters. Did they mean all of the leashed spellsters? There'd supposedly been only thirty of them. Hard to believe every single one had succumbed to non-lethal attacks.

Dylan scanned those surrounding the rider, desperately hoping his original assumption was wrong. But no, he'd been right the first time, they were all Udynean. If any of the army's leashed spellsters were still alive, then they were now on their way to the Udynea Empire's slave market.

"If you drop your barrier," the rider said, a little louder as he switched to speaking Demarn in a slow, halting manner, "and surrender without quarrel, I guarantee your life will be spared."

Authril answered him in a string of curses.

The man straightened in his saddle. "I don't know why I bother," the man said, returning to his native tongue. He turned his horse away, waving his hand as if shooing a fly. "Kill the elf. It'll be more trouble than it's worth to capture it."

"*It?*" Authril growled, clearly able to understand Udynean enough to know she'd been slighted. She sprang to her feet, keeping crouched even as she drew her sword, perhaps conscious of Dylan's shield shimmering a few inches above her head. "Can I get through this blasted barrier?"

"I would think so," Katarina replied when Dylan didn't. "And you'd find yourself riddled with arrows the moment you do."

Grunting, the warrior remained in place, waiting like the tower mousers would for their prey to near. "It," she muttered under her breath. "I'll show them *it*. You *are* planning to attack, aren't you?" This question was also directed at him.

Dylan didn't answer. All the pain and fear of the past few days. The sense of helplessness. The anger. It boiled through his veins, charging the very air. It wasn't enough for the enemy to have already taken the lives of all those lying dead at his back. They had to take everyone's. All in the pursuit of another's greed.

No more.

He raised his hands and focused everything he could spare on the advancing men. Bolts of lightning jumped from his fingers to strike them down. Their bodies jerked and flopped much like his opponents back in the tower. Unlike with his sparring partners of old, he didn't stop his assault until smoke began to leak from their bodies.

Arrows bloomed around them, ricocheting off his barrier. A few made their way through the weaker points, albeit, sluggishly. By the time the fletching passed through, they had lost all momentum.

This didn't appear to be enough for Authril. She crouched behind her shield, dragging the hedgewitch down with her. "I thought you said this damn barrier would keep us safe?"

Dylan barely heard her. His focus was shattering, just like the first arrows. He allowed the two lifeless bodies to fall, waiting until his heart stopped hammering quite so hard before turning his attention to their remaining enemies. How many more could he take out before the barrier failed completely? Certainly not the whole seven.

His gaze swung to the rider. That man would be the greater threat to his companions. But taking on a Udynean spellster, one who was no doubt powerful and well rested, wouldn't be easy if Dylan hadn't spent the last few days tramping through the forest and healing people.

"Hold your fire!" the rider bellowed. "I want the leashed one alive! Let's not have a repeat of last week's attack."

Dylan frowned. *Last week?* That had been when he first arrived, when there'd been suspiciously few attacks. He would've recalled any mention of a spellster—

The infirmary. One of the leashed ones had been amongst the scouts. She had died from her injuries before the survivors could return to the front line.

They still think I'm leashed. And why wouldn't they? Even in Udynea, where the *infitialis* collars were for slaves and prisoners, he doubted there were any reports of a leashed one removing their collar. And if they wanted him alive, that meant they would target his companions, the warrior specifically if they were aware of Katarina's hedgewitch status. He could use that knowledge to predict their actions.

Like right now, the remaining six on foot were fanning out, looking to flank them.

He adjusted his shield, seeking to ensure every inch was strong enough to repel all weapons. His magic responded slowly, the barrier flickering with the threat of failing altogether. "We can't let them draw this out," he muttered over his shoulder. "I don't think I've enough energy for much."

"Understood," Authril said as she got to her feet. "I've never fought beside a spellster. Do you have a plan?"

"Leave the rider to me. Concentrate on the others. When they get close, I'm dropping the barrier." It wasn't ideal, but he needed all the energy he could muster to be any match against the Udynean. "Be ready."

"I am," the elf replied.

"Where do I fit into this?" Katarina asked.

"You're a hedgewitch." And their enemies were close enough to make out her attire. "I can't ask you to risk your life. It would be best if you found somewhere safe to wait this out."

The dwarf mumbled something under her breath. Judging by the tone, it wasn't civil. "They used my people's ruins as bait," she snarled. "I'm not hiding this time."

"Then you better stay close to me," Authril said.

Katarina gave the other woman a grim smile and brandished her dagger. "Don't worry about me. This isn't my first fight." She turned her attention to him. "Are you able to do that lightning trick again?

Take out another few?"

He shook his head. If he'd had enough rest, then it'd be no different to the brawl in terms of strain, but now? "One, maybe." Providing they fell swiftly. He would need to conserve much of his energy for the rider and hope it was enough.

"Doesn't matter," Authril said as she bounced from foot to foot. "I'll take them."

The soldiers were close enough for their bows to be cumbersome. They advanced with swords drawn.

"Now?" the warrior asked, the eagerness in her voice sharp enough to bite.

"Now." He let the shield drop and aimed a fireball at the closest enemy, cursing as the woman dove out of the way. *So much for that tactic.* His attention swung to the rider. The man merely sat there, content to watch his lackeys fight.

Authril's advance fared better. She ran at the group, screaming and sending the soldiers in all directions. Her blade sliced through the sword arm of one before her shield bashed in the woman's face. This seemed to give the remaining three grounds to pause as they circled her like wary dogs.

Dylan frowned. He hastily counted the soldiers around the warrior. Four in all.

But hadn't there been six left?

Movement danced on the edge of his vision. He turned his head, searching, when he spied another of Authril's attackers lunging for her, aiming to attack the woman's flank. Before a warning could pass his lips, the warrior had swung about to block her attacker. A few moments later and the man fell back, clutching at the slimy tubes spilling from his belly.

The rider straightened in his saddle and bellowed, "Oh, for—!" He kneed his mount towards them. Lightning shot from his hand in one enormous bolt.

Instinct had Dylan flinging up a shield between Authril and the rider. The barrier shuddered, but held against the onslaught. That was his cue. He prayed he'd enough left in him to defeat the man. Drawing in a deep breath, Dylan threw a fireball at the man, letting it explode ahead of the horse's path.

The horse reared, throwing its rider.

Staggering to his feet, the man glared at his mount thundering off into the forest. "You little shit," he snarled. A cloud of dust kicked up as the man flung his hands forward.

Dylan braced himself, barely having the strength to shield himself from the blast running through the air. It hit low, almost knocking him off his feet. He righted his balance with far more difficulty than it should've taken and altered the barrier from a sphere to a bell-like shape. "Get back!" he ordered Katarina. The last thing he wanted was to have the hedgewitch in the radius of the man's attack should the shield fail.

There was no reply. Dylan could only hope she had heard him and obeyed.

A figure marched through the dust, too tall to be an elf. Dylan flexed his fingers, holding back only because he wasn't certain if it was the dwarf.

The man halted none too far away. Dark eyes glared at him from beneath a pair of thick brows. "Why won't you have the good sense to go down, you backwater-bred cretin?"

How Dylan wished he had the energy to pound the smarmy bastard into the ground. For now, he had to wait and see what else the man would throw at him. Hopefully, the attacks would reveal a weakness he could exploit. "Are dust clouds and talk all you have to offer, Udynean?"

The man's lips twisted smugly.

Dylan barely caught the man's hands twitch before another blast rocked his shield. He swung the full force of his barrier to the fore as a barrage of iridescent specks hit, constructs much like the spear back in the arena. As small as a wasp's sting, they hissed as they struck and fizzled against his barrier.

"You're no match for a properly trained spellster," the man snarled, closing the gap between them with each word until he was but a few paces away.

Dylan peered at the area directly around the man, eventually spotting the faint translucent shimmer of a shield. No telling how strong it was. Likely stronger than he could penetrate in his current state.

"Just come quietly," the man continued, seemingly oblivious to Dylan's scrutiny. "I'd rather not have to report you joined those pathetic fools on the front line in death." He swept his arm wide. "I might even ask my lord to let me keep you, if you cooperate."

Dylan's gaze slid to the corpses at his back. Those near the rear of the main attack had suffered little in the way of burns, but it wasn't them he saw. The memory of the charred masses of the scouting party, the mounds at the front line, overlaid his vision.

Red blazed across his mind, the searing heat of fury reborn. So many left broken and burnt by men like this one. Had those monsters stood with the same smile as they took all those lives? For what? A handful of leashed slaves?

Dylan wordlessly wrapped his own barrier around the man, maintaining the finest of balances in keeping it invisible. "You take pleasure in burning people alive?" he hissed. In a snap of thought, he tightened the shield, forsaking translucency for density. "Let's see how you like roasting."

Focusing on the air trapped between the two shields, Dylan allowed a trickle of magic, a small puff of heat from an unformed fireball, to bloom. It should've been harmless, naught but a mild concentration of warm air. But trapped as it was? That flicker of heat fed on itself, growing hotter with each second.

All he had to do was keep the barrier in place.

Sneering, the man pushed out with his shield, but Dylan was ready for him. His barrier held firm. The man's skin, originally a pale olive tone, turned red. His eyes bulged. He put more force behind his actions.

Dylan gritted his teeth and rammed the remaining scrap of his magic into the heat blazing away inside the shimmering ball of his shield.

The Udynean collapsed to his knees. A scream Dylan couldn't hear tightened the man's throat. The air had become too hot for his lungs, scorching the soft tissue just as it blistered the man's face and hands.

Dylan continued to watch, the sight of the enemy dying by his actions had an almost dreamlike quality. Should taking a life feel so effortless? It wouldn't be long now. A few more minutes and he could be certain that *this* Udynean would never harm anyone ever again. Should he not feel gratified in knowing that?

Behind him, he caught Katarina cry out in pain.

The other two soldiers. They had wounded her. Fatally?

Dylan jerked his head to one side, a part of him pulled by the call. But he couldn't dare shift his full attention from the Udynean spellster lest the man managed to slip free at the last second.

Could he send a pulse through the earth like he had done in the arena? Did he have the strength? After he had finished with this man, perhaps. Without knowing what Katarina faced, any action could work against the hedgewitch far too easily. He just had to hope she could stand her ground for a while longer.

"Watch out!" Katarina screamed.

Something hit the back of his head and the world turned black for a moment. He staggered forward. Lights danced across his vision, dizzying him.

Intense heat blasted at his face. The barrier had fallen.

Pain lanced his side. The searing agony of lightning haphazardly channelled. Instinct lifted his hand and had him throw everything behind the flames that sprang from his fingers.

The brief wail of a victim hit his ears. Dylan sorely hoped it had been the right target. Smoke billowed around him. The stench of cooking flesh and burning hair filled his lungs. He hacked up all he could, the taste of it thick on his tongue.

In too short a time, there was little left for the fire to burn.

Dylan lowered his hand. He stood there, staring at the crater he had made. His body shivered, the once gentle wind now like a caress of icy needles. His chest heaved for each breath, every muscle in his torso aching from the attempts to expel the smoke.

He laid a hand on his side, coming into contact with bare skin. The flesh beneath his fingertips was healing, sluggishly. He needed rest. Needed food.

Katarina. Her warning was the last thing he had heard. Where was she? Safe? He tried to search his surroundings, the world too bleary for him to make out more than shapes. He shook his head, fighting to clear his eyesight.

That proved to be the wrong action. His legs wobbled, then gave. He crumpled to the ground, hitting face-first, and fell into darkness.

The world was shifting shadows of grey and black. A powdery grit blew over Dylan as he stared out into an endless, charred plain. His eyes watered, but he refused to let them close. Ash drifted across the cracked surface, kicked up by the bitter wind.

He covered his mouth with a sleeve. It did nothing to stop the granules trickling through the fabric's tight weave.

Was this the afterlife? He took a few shambling steps. Where was the river of judgement? The Seven Sisters? The priests visiting the tower always said there would be a boat to carry him to paradise.

He spun about, searching. There wasn't even a dribble of water.

What if the boat didn't appear? What if the lieutenant was right and his magic left him tainted? He would be stuck wandering through this lifeless mockery of a land for all eternity.

He peered into the distance. A suggestion of darkness sat amongst the grey hillside. A cave? Perhaps the very one that led souls down into the watery tunnels where judgement and paradise awaited. The distance was difficult to judge, but nothing else looked anywhere near as promising.

Pulling his sleeve tighter around his face, Dylan set out in that direction, picking his way over the larger cracks splitting the scorched earth.

He had barely taken a dozen steps when the ground heaved.

The dirt beneath his feet splintered, flinging clumps of crumbling rock in all directions and tossing him about. He scrambled for solid land, raking at the earth. His fingers found a tree root, thin and strong. He clung to it with one hand, pawing at the ground around him for a second handhold.

Bony fingers clawed through the cracks. They grasped his robe, hauling him deeper into the sinkhole. Their weight on his clothes grew heavier with each second. The stitching groaned, threatening to break. His boots were already gone, swallowed by the churning ground.

The root he clung to so ferociously bent. Dylan dug into the sod surrounding it, seeking to unearth more. His fingers carved out great trenches, but there was nothing to be had.

"Join us," dusty voices echoed from the very air.

Faces broke through the earth. Black and bleeding. Melted. They stared at him with empty, weeping sockets. "You belong here," their fleshless jaws creaked. "Down amongst the dead. Embrace the earth. Join us in the ashes of your failure."

The clammy coldness of the earth greeted his legs. He was torn from the side of the hole. Bony arms wrapped around his chest, chilling his heart.

"He has joined us," a jawless face hissed into his ear.

All around, the walls slowly folded upon themselves. Mud, thick and slimy, covered his torso. Most of the grasping hands had fallen away, only the corpse on his back remained.

Above, the sky stretched out in a sea of grey clouds. Dylan raised a hand in supplication, but the mud continued to pour in. It was at his neck now and climbing. He fought to keep his head above the ever-rising sludge, spluttering as watery gloop filled his mouth.

This couldn't be it. It just couldn't. He wasn't ready to go. Not like this. There was still so much he needed to see, so many things he hadn't experienced.

Muddy water trickled down across his face, clogging his nose and throat. He spluttered and gagged, fighting to keep his airway free to no avail. A wet clump of dirt landed on his face, caking his eyelids and sealing him in blackness as the slurry of earth and water continued to suck him under.

Then there was only the stillness of oblivion and a faint, reed-thin cry.

"Join us."

CHAPTER 17

Tracker urged his horse to go faster, unsurprised when his insistence gained him nothing. He had pushed Lullaby to the animal's limit over the past two days. The fresh presence of magic filled his senses to the brim. Never had he felt such power anywhere but from the spellster tower. Yet, there was no doubt that the burst came from one source.

In the days that followed the outpouring of magic, Tracker had encountered a handful of people along the road leading to the encampment. He had expected far less.

The survivors had greeted him with tearful relief, jabbering of death and magic before he drew level with them. They were things he'd already gathered. No doubt the spearhead of the Udynean army. But this sudden bloom of power was new. Did it mean a Udynean spellster lingered still? He hadn't fought one before, but it wouldn't matter. They could match the power of the sun and a direct hit would still have no impact on a King's Hound.

The intense blast of power abruptly dropped to a mere vibration through the air, difficult to sense with the rest of the magic radiating from the encampment.

The road grew steeper and no less hemmed by the undergrowth. He had to be close. Continuing to whisper encouragement to his horse, Tracker let the animal have its head whilst he focused on that point. He wouldn't lose them, not easily. They seemed to be on the move. Slowly, but with a definite purpose.

He should've paid more attention to Fetcher when she spoke of this place, had even considered asking his fellow hound about the layout. But coming out here hadn't ever crossed his mind. And for the entire encampment to fall when it had already withstood the Udynean onslaught for centuries? That seemed even less likely.

They reached the top of the incline. The road opened out until the full stretch of the encampment lay before him.

Tracker drew his horse to a halt. *By the gods*. He had seen the smoke, understood what must've transpired here. He had even witnessed so many atrocities wrought with magic, had come across plenty of half-cremated remains of the unfortunate burnt to death.

Never this many at once.

Half of the area laid charred, pockets of it still smouldering. The bones of tents and bodies jutted from the ground in equal measure, making it difficult to distinguish just how many had fallen. The remainder of the encampment sat barren or heavy with the dead.

His senses were drawn to a particular section radiating magic like a recently extinguished furnace.

Tracker urged his horse closer. Lullaby snorted his distaste and pawed at the ground, but obeyed the command after a second nudge. They trudged by mounds of dead bodies, untouched by flames.

Amongst it all, a burnt patch carved out of the dirt.

This reeked of magic, more so than what vibrated from the rest of the clearing. It crackled in the air, leaving behind the aroma of a storm. The same scent that trailed off towards the forest.

Dismounting, he crouched by the crater. Sheer heat had warped the earth, hardening it into a massive bowl. That explained the burst of magic. The thing in the centre appeared to be the half-cremated remains of a person. Power also flowed off them, an echo of dry heat, faint in the electrifying glow of what had slain them.

Spellster fighting spellster. Not something he had come across before. The King's Hounds searched for children with signs of magic or hunted those who sought to flee. Few dared to travel with family, spellster or not. None of them had fought amongst themselves.

Had the spellster responsible for this been on Demarn's side? Nothing Tracker had gleaned from the survivors suggested any leashed spellster would've lived through the attack.

He looked around, piecing together the scraps of survivor recollections and what his eyes told him. The attack had come swiftly, that much had been constant. The front had fallen in the blink of an eye, enveloped in fire before the enemy emerged from the forest. The rest? Those that lay around him now? They'd been slaughtered in the confusion like chickens before a rabid dog.

He hadn't heard of the imperial forces forging this deep into Demarn defences, but he wasn't surprised. The kingdom's army might not have been dealt as heavy a blow as this before, but they'd given up plenty of land in the past. *Never enough.* It seemed as though the Udynea Empire wouldn't be satisfied until it had the whole continent under its control.

His gaze drifted further west, to where the army's front line stood. Or not. If this was the outcome for the main encampment, a place that didn't see direct combat, then he'd a sick feeling the front line was in a worst state.

Dusting off his hands, Tracker straightened and returned to his examination of the immediate area. The majority of the fallen here looked to be less soldiers and more the folk needed to attend a camp's needs of food, repair and cleanliness.

A few wore armour vastly different to that of Demarn's warriors, their mottled-green overcoats showing little in the way of protection from physical weapons. They had to be Udyneans. He knelt by one. The corpse looked fresher than those they had collapsed upon, still warm, their wounds still bleeding. *Scavengers.*

Either the enemy had turned on itself or someone had survived this slaughter.

He turned back to the crater's edge, following the radiating magic to where the spellster responsible for it would've stood. The magic was strong here, too. The ground scorched except for an arc.

They hadn't been alone either.

Three distinct footprints sat on the non-charred side of the arc, ones he couldn't attribute to the Udyneans. Of those three, one was wearing armour and likely responsible for the deeper wounds in the fresher bodies.

Were they also perhaps a spellster's warden? Could one of the army's spellsters have survived? Could they both be out there?

No. Not enough added up there. For one, he still sensed that storm-like magic disappearing deeper into the forest. A leashed spellster, no matter how strong, would feel no different than any other non-magical person when they weren't given sanction.

And why would they choose to leave? They could clearly handle themselves, even if there was any danger left amongst the corpses. The choice to head north was just as puzzling. There was nothing that way except for the mountains. Any army recruit who'd spent a day here would know that.

A lot of woodland stood between here and Toptower. Deliberately traipsing into the unknown suggested a desire to skirt the town. The only explanation he could fathom for doing so was to take the kingdom by surprise.

Not on my watch. He would have to be careful. If the spellster amongst them truly was responsible for this destruction, then they were deadly proficient with fire. He couldn't have them burning down the forest. Magic-born flames, once they touched a fuel source, were no different to the normal kind and no King's Hound had protection against that.

He settled back into his saddle and pointed Lullaby in the direction. The forest looked largely untouched, the undergrowth pushing beyond the tree line to encroach on the encampment. It would make slow going, both for himself and those he pursued, but their passage would also leave a nice trail for him to follow. He might even reach them before sundown.

Whilst he would've preferred to cross what was left of the encampment with haste, Tracker let his horse pick the speed they traversed the mounds and hollows dug into the land. Everywhere they trod, the bodies of the fallen weren't more than a few feet away.

They were halfway to the trees, cresting a ridge that once housed a large tent, when his senses tingled. *Magic.* A different source to the one he followed. Fresh, weak…

And coming from his left.

Static and a clean, crispness filled the air. The hum of an angry hive whispered in his ears.

Tracker yanked his horse to one side, silently apologising as the abruptness jerked the animal's feet out from under them.

A bolt of lightning flashed by. Lullaby's scream was almost lost in the rumble of air that followed.

Tracker found himself lifting off the horse's back. He flailed for the saddle, his fingertips grazing the pommel before it was beyond his reach.

He hit the earth hard, the air rushing from his lungs. He tumbled down a mound, fighting to regain his breath all the way, halting only when he reached the ditch carved into the base. He remained still, slowly orientating himself as he waited for his lungs to no longer burn. His view was partially obscured by his braid, but it was one of the sky and the distant tree line where the attack had come from.

Once he could move, he rolled onto his hands and knees, keeping his profile low. There was no telling what else the spellster had at his disposal. If they'd warriors or archers nearby, they'd be the greater threat.

Flipping his braid back over his shoulder, he searched for where Lullaby had gone, finding his horse collapsed atop the mound.

Tracker pursed his lips, preparing to whistle a command that would send the warhorse out of harm's way, when his gaze fell on the jagged wound running along the animal's side.

No… The sight grew blurry. He shook his head, furiously blinking and scrubbing at his face to get the dirt out of his eyes. Even though he had tried to avoid the blast, Lullaby had taken the brunt of it.

There could only be one outcome.

The charge of another bolt lit up his senses. He instinctively ducked moments before the blast struck mere inches from him. It hit a pile of bodies, sending chunks of charred and rotting flesh in all directions. The scent of it choked the air and coated his tongue.

Gagging, Tracker rolled back to face the direction the lightning had come from. His vision darkened the longer he focused. The world grew a red tint along the edges. He didn't need his hound senses to tell him the spellster was still near—hiding like a coward amongst the trees—but it pinpointed their position.

Unsheathing his scimitar, he launched himself from the ditch and raced towards the spellster. Death would be a mercy once he was done with the murderer of his Lullaby.

Again, lightning crackled through the air. Tracker faced it head on, screaming, daring the spellster to give their all.

The bolt reached him and branched off, finding other targets not immune to its power.

A cry rang out; a command pulled reed-thin in terror. The sound was answered by others, all in a language he didn't understand. *Udyneans*. It had to be.

People emerged from the trees. They ran towards him. Some fumbled with their weapons, others already had blades and bludgeons at the ready.

Tracker was faster. With the distance between them steadily closing, he flung throwing knives at everything that moved.

An arrow whipped by Tracker's head, drawing his attention to a figure hidden amongst the branches. Another arrow soared towards him, following the same arc as the first. Tracker cut it out of the air with a swipe of his scimitar and sent a knife back in answer.

The archer's body crashed through the branches, hitting the ground in a crumpled heap. No one else appeared. Nor did any further arrows spring from the trees.

Tracker aimed a final throwing knife at his target. It would end their life far quicker than they deserved, but King's Hounds weren't meant to toy with their targets.

The knife barely reached halfway across the space between them before it turned back.

Snarling, Tracker dodged the blade, then again as the spellster sent the weapon twirling back. He snatched it out of the air on the third pass.

His target chose that moment to disappear beneath the trees. As if it would matter. Tracker would catch up to them soon enough, and see how they fared against something they couldn't bend to their will.

Beneath the tree line, the spellster dashed through the trunks like a startled deer. Tracker chased after them, gaining with every wild swing they took. He caught flashes of them through the brush, the purple sheen of a shield bright in the shadows.

Close enough and Tracker slammed into them, sending the spellster off their feet. They tumbled through the undergrowth, fire and lightning flaring all around. Several of the blows hit him square on to little effect. The bolts of lightning merely avoided him and the fire either petered out or parted like water around a rock.

Tracker strode through it all. He grabbed the spellster by the shirt and slammed them against the trunk of a tree. "Where are your fellow spellsters?" There was no chance this destruction had been the work of one being. Not *this* one, at any rate. He had felt far too much power. The ground was soaked in it.

They mumbled something. Tracker didn't understand the words, but the tone suggested they weren't making pleasant conversation.

He pinned the man to the trunk with a dagger to the shoulder.

The Udynean screamed. He sagged, remaining upright only due to Tracker's hold on his shirt.

Tracker waited only until the spellster caught his breath before asking again. "*Where?*"

The man grimaced. "As though I would tell *you* that." He spoke haltingly, the Demarner language clearly not one his tongue was comfortable speaking. "You will kill me regardless."

Tracker wordlessly twisted the dagger, watching for a hint that the man might pass out from the pain. He didn't typically jump straight into torture during an interrogation, but he found himself lacking the ability for compassion or patience.

"Gone!" the spellster gasped on the edge of a scream. "They're all gone. We were called back by the *vris Mhanek*."

The last two words meant nothing to Tracker. It had to be a Udynean title. Someone high in the ranks. A general? "Yet, you remain. Are you alone?"

The man remained silent for a heartbeat, regarding Tracker with bloodshot eyes. "Yes. I was meant to escort Lord Yaash. Something got to him first. The charred body?" He pointed a bloody hand towards the clearing.

"I noticed." There were so many, but only one reeked of excessive magic used against them. That desiccated being had been a Udynean? Then the fallen soldiers around him must've been the lord's personal guard.

That had to mean the spellster Tracker felt was from the tower.

How was that possible? He could still feel them, their magic a pulse in the distance. Leashed spellsters didn't radiate that amount of power. They couldn't. Not unless a warden instructed them to use it.

"If you're going to kill me," the man grated through his teeth, "then do it quickly. I have made my peace. Jalaane will not find me unworthy."

"You seek death?" A part of him wanted to leave the man there for the wildlife to slowly tear to pieces, but the flash of anger that first drove him had faded into a simmering rage. He couldn't leave a spellster wandering about out here, especially not a Udynean one.

Rather than remove the dagger still in the man's shoulder, Tracker unsheathed the purple blade and drove it into the spellster's heart. "Consider it found, yes?" It wouldn't be enough. Demarn spellsters had the good sense to stay dead. Udyneans were a trickier lot.

He took up his scimitar and decapitated the man. Only with the spellster's head rolling across the forest floor could he be completely sure the death was permanent. He pulled the daggers free, letting the body collapse at his feet, then wiped the blades clean on the man's clothes.

He needed to go after the other spellster. This was a greater chance of them being on Demarn's side, but letting them wander freely was no more of an option than this man.

He backtracked through the forest, finding the other fallen Udyneans and retrieving his weapons. Each time, he paused to ensure his targets stayed dead. None of them, beyond the man, had been spellsters, but it was always prudent to make sure he didn't leave wounded hostiles at his back. If he left and they marched on Toptower whilst he hunted down the rogue spellster, he'd never forgive himself.

His passage across the field took him past his horse. He already carried much of his weaponry, but the saddle still bore supplies. Albeit, a meagre stock designed for the few days it would've taken to get here and back. He didn't have much hope of anything being salvageable, not with the saddle being a charred mess.

Flopping to his knees before Lullaby's body, he laid a hand on the animal's muscled shoulder. The flesh beneath his fingers was still warm. It would be for quite a while longer. The muscles shifted in little tremors that could almost be mistaken for living movement.

He bowed his head. "Forgive me," he breathed. He should never have opted to purchase his own mount, much less spend the time training one. No matter how quick and intelligent an animal Lullaby had been, the horse could never have the same protection as a King's Hound.

Having Lullaby, or anyone he cared for, around had always left him with a liability. He'd been too careless, too soft.

Puckering his lips, he whistled a final song, the very first he had ever taught the animal.

Lullaby's body lurched, legs flailing in an effort to regain footing.

Shock rooted Tracker in place. His horse was alive? How? He'd seen the aftermath of cattle and horses after a thunderstorm. That this strike had magical origins shouldn't have made a difference.

Had it been because Tracker was aboard? The blast would've been aimed at him. His abilities as a King's Hound would've redirected the lightning, hitting Lullaby, but not with enough force to kill. His horse had survived by sheer luck.

That wouldn't mean much if Lullaby kept thrashing about.

He lunged for the horse's head, fighting to keep the animal still. "Easy, boy." He whistled long and low, a tune he'd only ever sung whilst setting up camp.

Lullaby rolled his eyes, showing their whites. His nostrils flared with each breath.

He gently unbuckled the girth, letting his useless saddle tumble onto the ground. The wound in its entirety greeted him in a swathe of raw, bloody flesh and charred skin.

Tracker pawed through his saddlebags, hauling out everything that could possibly help. Much of his equipment was geared towards taking lives, not saving them. He'd a few salves and some bandages, nothing big enough to fully cover the wounds. Right now, he needed to staunch the flow of blood, anything would have to do.

It took the sacrifice of his spare undershirt and smallclothes, but he finally managed to stem the flow to the occasional drip.

Content Lullaby wasn't about to die of blood loss, his gaze slid from his horse to their surroundings. The piles of corpses and twisted lumps of charred bodies didn't give him much hope of finding anything to help him. "We will make do, yes?" he murmured to his horse. They always did. Somehow.

The more pressing question was what to do once he could be certain his horse wouldn't die. The spellster was out there, their power burning like a beacon in the night. *I should go after him.* That was his duty. Enemy or ally, he needed to ensure they caused no more harm.

Lullaby blew out a shuddering breath. His whole body still trembled.

He caressed his horse's head and scratched beneath the animal's forelock. "Easy, old boy, I am not about to leave you here." There was little he could do to aid Lullaby, but he would try. "We will make it back to Toptower, yes? You and me. Together."

Then, once his horse was where he could receive proper care, Tracker would return to the hunt. No spellster escaped a King's Hound. Not for long.

CHAPTER 18

Dylan slowly became aware of being elsewhere. Darkness surrounded him. The realisation set his heart to hammering. Was he still beneath the earth? He struggled to move, only to find his limbs refusing to obey.

Was he dead? *Truly* dead?

No. His senses were sluggish to piece together his surroundings, but they were definite about him reclining on his back. That didn't seem like the act of a dead man. His breath came swiftly and, whilst it shuddered through his chest, the act was unobstructed. There appeared to be the warmth of a body cradling his head rather than the clammy coldness of mud.

Thighs. He was lying down with his head pillowed on someone's thighs.

His eyelids fluttered. They, too, failed to respond as he wished, due more to his body's demand for rest than the weight of mud. There wasn't absolute darkness. Flickering light illuminated the side of one eyelid. Fire? That seemed to stir a memory, the fullness too slippery to keep for long.

Long fingers slid over his scalp, stroking his hair. That didn't seem like the act of an enemy or, rather more importantly, someone intent on his immediate death.

The dull clang of metal reverberated through his skull.

Groaning, Dylan rolled his head to one side. His eyes also chose that moment to heed his command and open. He stared blankly at the scene before him, trying to make sense of the world. Katarina stood near a campfire, stirring a little pot suspended over the embers. His nose caught the scent of heavily overcooked grain, setting his mouth to watering.

Never in his life had anything smelt so divine.

"He's awake."

That voice. So close. The elven warrior, Authril. *Her* lap beneath his head. They had all survived the attack? Or were they now prisoners?

The world spun as he sat up, sending him back to the ground.

"Careful," Katarina cautioned.

When his head stopped messing with his eyesight, he gingerly positioned himself upright to take in their surroundings. It was pitch dark beyond the light of the fire. He didn't need to see much to know they were alone. They appeared to have moved on from the army camp, too. The stark outlines of trees hemmed them on all sides, looming over them and crowding the night sky.

He licked his lips. His tongue had a distinctly papery film coating it. "Where are we?" he croaked. "How long was I out for?" Carrying him couldn't have been difficult. The warrior might've struggled immediately after an attack, but she looked more than capable. How far could the pair of them have lugged him through the forest before night fell?

"We're just a little ways into the forest," Katarina replied. "No more than a few hours. It's good to see you're awake." She laid out the three mismatched and battered bowls he also didn't remember anyone adding to their packs and filled them with some sort of brown gloop.

He eyed the steaming bowls, his stomach growling as if he had swallowed some sort of beast. When had he last eaten? Had it really been several days?

Authril grunted. "I was beginning to think I'd have to carry your arse all the way to Toptower after all." Her gaze kept flicking to the top of his head as she talked. Was there something wrong with it?

Dylan gingerly felt his hair. A section at the back was clumped together by a tepid congealed substance. He didn't want to dwell on what it could be. His gaze dropped to the thickly-woven fabric draped over his lap. He didn't recall either woman packing a blanket. "What happened?"

"You took the pommel of a sword to the skull," Katarina replied.

"And you bled *everywhere*," Authril helpfully added. "Head wounds do that, of course, but I thought we'd lost you for sure. Yet you seemed to knit yourself back together quick enough."

Dylan frowned. He recalled fighting the soldiers before everything went red. He'd vague memories of being struck on the back of the head and then...

The blast of lightning to his side.

His hand slid to where the bolt had struck. Exposed skin greeted his fingers. Unmarked, not even a hint of the attack. The same couldn't be said for his clothing. Both his robe and undertunic were scorched and torn, leaving a gaping hole. He would have to find a way to patch the fabric before the holes got any bigger. "And what of the Udyneans? Where did they go?" Seeing that they were gone for good wouldn't bring anyone back, but it was a start in keeping more Demarn soldiers from joining the dead.

"Away," Authril replied with a shrug. "We didn't stick around to find out more."

They hadn't all died, then. Did that mean he failed in his attempt to take the enemy spellster's life? He licked his parched lips and braced himself for the answer as he asked, "Did their spellster make it?"

The warrior shook her head, the tangled strands of her orange hair almost glowing in the firelight. "He's dead."

"Are you sure?" He thought the man had been beyond any sort of retaliation when the shield fell, yet he'd been struck.

Her lips flattened into a grim smile. "Unless the sod can revive from ashes and grow a new upper half from nothing, then yes. Here." She handed him a water skin. It didn't look like the soot-stained one they'd pulled from the tent remains. "You sound terrible."

He took a swig. The coolness soothed his throat and washed away the sourness in his mouth. It tasted strangely familiar. Cleaner than what he had grown accustomed to on his journey down here and reminiscent of home. He took several more long swallows before handing it back to the elf. "What happened to the rest? Are they likely to return?"

"Well..." Katarina offered one of the full bowls to the other woman. "After you killed the Udynean spellster and Authril dispatched the woman responsible for your head wound, the remaining two fled."

"Like roaches," Authril muttered before shovelling in a spoonful of food. "Cowards wouldn't even offer themselves up for a decent death. I don't think they'll return."

Katarina cleared her throat. "The Udyneans have a rather different outlook on what constitutes as a good death."

"Pity," the warrior sneered. "But at least we saw to it that there's one less blasted spellster in the world."

Uneasiness bubbled in his stomach. He tried to convince himself it was only because he hadn't eaten in several days, but the way she spoke that word. *Spellster.* An echo of the derision of the other soldiers. *One less of* them. As if he hadn't the same power.

The hedgewitch crouched before him and offered up the remaining bowl. "Sorry." Her wide mouth twisted into a grimace. "I'm not much of a cook. If it's any consolation, it tastes better than it looks."

Dylan barely gave a glance to what he'd been given before shovelling heaped spoonfuls into his mouth. His tongue said it was porridge, if a little on the burnt side, his stomach didn't care enough to comment.

He was a third of the way into the bowl when another question surfaced through the mindless slog of his movements. "Where did we get oats?" There'd been nothing in the way of salvageable food when they'd scoured the camp remains.

"The Udyneans," Katarina replied as she turned to her own meal. "They'd other travel rations as well, perhaps enough to get us to Toptower."

"It's a bugger the horse ran off," Authril muttered into her bowl.

The hedgewitch nodded. "We certainly could've carried a great deal more of their gear if it had stayed, the saddlebags might've even held a tent. But we should be able to make do just curling up in blankets, providing the weather holds. And if we supplement the travel rations with a little foraging, we won't have to buy quite as much food for the journey to your spellster tower."

Dylan absently returned to the porridge. The concept of money was a murky one. He wasn't a stranger to exchanging one thing for another—bartering ran rife through the tower's spellsters—but he failed to see how a disc of metal carried any worth beyond the alchemical, especially when it came to provisions.

Food had always been something that was just there. A part of him knew that wasn't how it worked beyond the tower walls, but knowing a meal came only through work or money had long been another man's concern.

Now? He wasn't sure how to hunt, but he knew a little about foraging from his forays into the garden to help out Henrie during harvest season. Perhaps the forest held a few of the non-toxic plants he remembered from his childhood teachings.

Authril watched him eat. She had scraped her own bowl clean swiftly enough, but didn't seem to be looking to procure a portion of his food like many of his elven friends back in the tower. "Have you ever been in a fight before today?"

"Of course," he replied around his spoon. "I've been training for most of my life to be in the army." Against wooden men who stood there whilst he blasted them, people who could shield themselves from his attack and globes of light that had no sense of self-preservation. Not like this. Not even the brawl could've prepared him for this.

She stretched out her hand, offering the empty bowl to the hedgewitch who managed to find a few more spoonfuls to refill it. "But you've never actually fought to the death."

Had it been that obvious? How many battles had she witnessed? More than one, surely.

Dylan shrugged, trying to maintain a nonchalant demeanour. Fighting was why he'd been brought here. Such skirmishes and the death that followed shouldn't trouble him. "I never got the chance. I arrived a little less than a week ago. The day we were ambushed was my first time with the scouts."

The elf grunted. "You were fortunate to be there," she mumbled.

He recalled the screams of those dying. The all-encompassing heat. The cloying stench of burning flesh coming from beneath his collar as he desperately sought for a way to defend the scouting party.

Dylan lowered the bowl. The porridge was starting to sit less easily in his stomach. "No, I wasn't."

Authril had resumed picking at the small pieces left in her bowl. He couldn't see how she could do so and still talk about the death of her comrades. "I meant for you to be away when they attacked the main encampment," she said between chews.

Dylan shook his head.

The Udynean spellster's words stuck sharply in his mind. *They caught them all.* It had to have been by choice, rather than them treating the leashed spellsters as spoils of war.

Was that why he had survived when the scouting party he'd been with hadn't? The ambush should've left him slain or enslaved. Why hadn't they captured him whilst he was unconscious?

He ran his finger along his throat. The too-smooth patch of skin hadn't changed over the last few days. He hadn't scarred since gaining adept status amongst the tower healers. The wound on his side had healed perfectly, why not this?

The collar must've been the cause. How? Recalling what happened when he had removed the metal band eluded him. Every time he thought of it, the only thing that came to mind was heat and pain. *Light.* Great arcs of it stinging his skin. *That* had to be what caused this scarring, forever branding him as once being leashed.

Perhaps the only reason he wasn't with the other spellsters on his way to the Udynean slave market was because his attackers thought he had died.

Where had the Udyneans taken the others? Not along the path he'd trod with Katarina. He might have recognised all their faces, but he would've noticed the difference in attire. Could they track them? Find a way to free the captives and bring them back home? None of the leashed ones would be able to fight back with magic without a warder to give them permission. Maybe Authril could—

A strange rustling sound pulled him from his musing. The hedgewitch had retrieved their found map and was tilting the face towards the firelight in an attempt to read it.

Dylan focused on his hand, coaxing a small ball of pure white light. It sputtered and wobbled in the air, flickering even more uncertainly until it hovered just over the dwarf's shoulder.

On the edge of his vision, he spied Authril inching away from him and the light.

He frowned. She didn't seem all that bothered by his abilities when they were fighting. Had she not witnessed magic beyond the weaponised variety?

Smiling her thanks, Katarina laid the map flat on the ground and removed a slender case from one of her pouches. The burnished bronze of a compass gleamed in the combined light of the globe and campfire as she measured off the distances across the map, mumbling numbers under her breath.

Finally, she sat back. "I originally intended to travel via the roads, but after encountering those Udyneans, I can't be certain how safe of an idea that is. However, if this map is accurate, we could reach Toptower in a similar amount of time if we avoid any unnatural paths and travel through the forest in a more direct line. It should also reduce our chances of encountering further hostile forces."

Authril grunted. She eyed him as he allowed the ball of light to dissipate, but said nothing further.

Katarina also swung her attention to him. Where the warrior was wary, the hedgewitch's face showed only concern. "Will you be able to keep up?"

He nodded. Whilst it had been a trying few days of stumbling through the pathless forest between camps, he felt confident that he could do better with a little rest and food.

Those hazel eyes drifted over his body, forcing him to resist the urge to squirm. The way she examined him was reminiscent of his guardian. "We might be able to find a replacement for your attire once we arrive at Toptower."

His gaze dropped to his robe. Even without the hole in the side, the ambush and their trekking had left the hem ragged, scorched and stained. His undertunic was in no better state. "To be honest, I'm not sure if we should linger in the town for that long." He had been measured for his robe the afternoon of his arrival and donned it the following morning, but the main camp must've had a dozen or so tailors under their employ. It couldn't have taken them more than a few hours, especially if several hands joined in. For a single man and, possibly, an assistant? Perhaps two days from the time of measurements to the very last stitch.

The hedgewitch frowned. "You can't travel for weeks as you are. Healer or not, you'll get sick."

He smiled. The last time any sickness had befallen him, outside of his journey to the main camp, had been during his late teens. "If we've money to spare, I'll buy some cloth to patch them." If they couldn't afford to do that, then he would have to sacrifice a section of his blanket.

"If you're sure," she said, retrieving the bowls from him and the elf.

The small slip of cloth wrapped about her forearm caught his eye. The off-white linen was dark with dried blood. Dylan stared at the bandage, recalling her pained cry during the fight. "You're injured." He extended his hand, inviting her to lay her arm in his grasp. "Let me—"

"No." Katarina clasped her hands over his. "Before the Udyneans attacked, you spoke of having little magic left to give."

"And I've slept since then." He wasn't certain how long, but if the sun had set, then several hours must've passed.

By the way the dwarf's lips pursed and her brows knitted together, his answer wasn't good enough. "Admittedly, I'm a little rusty with how much of a toll fighting can take on a spellster's body. It has been some time since the Coven gave me any cause to study your people's abilities. However, you didn't appear to sleep all that soundly." She picked at the bandage, readjusting its position. "The wound isn't as bad as it could've been. If it still bothers you in the morning, I'll let you see to it then. *After* proper rest."

Dylan's throat tightened at the idea of sleep, his thoughts swiftly dredging up the nightmare. His skin pebbled.

He casually drew his blanket around his shoulders. It had been the wind that chilled him, a wisp of a breeze slipping beneath his clothes via the hole. Nothing more.

"If we're sleeping here," Authril said. "Then we'll have to sort out who's taking the first watch. I don't fancy the idea of being asleep without one of us on guard, not when those bastards are still out there. They could be tracking us, waiting for the time we let our guard down and they can slit our throats."

"I'll do it," he replied, his face steadily growing hot at the hasty way the words fled his mouth. Trying in vain to shrug off the sensation, he continued. "Neither of you could've slept since I've been unconscious. You both should. I'll keep an eye out for anything suspicious." What that would be, he didn't know. His training hadn't exactly touched on surviving in the forest. Best bet would be to wake either of them at the slightest sound of movement.

Authril rubbed behind her ear. Those sea-green eyes narrowed at him. "I'd have to go with the dwarf on you needing sleep. You were thrashing around an awful lot. I don't know how much rest you got. Probably best if I took the first watch."

"If it's all the same, I'd rather not." He really wasn't certain if he'd ever be able to close his eyes without envisioning those bony hands and their creaking voices. *Join us.* Swallowing, he tightened his grip on the blanket. He didn't want to find out so soon.

"Very well," Katarina said, pinning him with a stern look. "But you wake me as soon as the moon reaches its height. Is that understood?"

"Yes, Madam Hedgewitch." Dylan snapped off a mock salute, trying to alleviate the severity in her face. It didn't work. "I'll go check our perimeter whilst you two settle down." He stood, shaking back the feeling in his legs as he wobbled his way towards the trees.

Ducking behind a particularly sturdy trunk, he took the opportunity to relieve himself whilst being certain his companions wouldn't follow. He hadn't been able to do something so simple without company since leaving the tower. Strange how gratifying it was to do so alone.

He circled the rest of their little clearing, weaving through the undergrowth as he kept the campfire in view. The flames put out more light than he would've expected. An easy target for someone to track.

By the time he returned to the fireside, the women had curled up on the ground, making the most of their packs and pilfered blankets. Soon, the soft rumble of a snore came from one of the women.

Dylan settled near the fire, carefully banking the coals before once more wrapping himself in the blanket. Darkness enveloped them. His heart fluttered as he rolled his gaze upwards, but the moon, when it eventually rose above the trees, was a mere sliver of light in the sky.

Stars peeked through the canopy of branches. Normally, those specks of light would invoke wanderlust. Not tonight. Everywhere he looked, the branches jutted across his viewpoint like bony hands.

"Stop it," he muttered under his breath. "It was just a bad dream. You're not trapped underground." Just in the middle of a forest, with who knew how many predators? Whilst his haphazard sleeping couldn't have restored the full extent of his magical ability, he felt capable of shielding them from something as banal as an animal attack.

What if the threat was more than his magic could handle? Authril seemed to think it a possibility of there still being Udynean soldiers nearby. How likely was that? Surely, there could be but a few lost out here. A few wouldn't be any trouble at all.

Thoughts of the attack tumbled through his mind. The first two had fallen so swiftly and yet...

A part of him had enjoyed taking their lives.

Well, they either were slavers or worked for them. They'd also been responsible for the death of hundreds at the encampment. He had merely ensured they would never harm another person.

They *deserved* the death he'd given. Didn't they?

Enemy or not, they were still people. They still had lives and loved ones. But it had been so effortless. Even tired and all but drained of the ability to use his power, they had fallen as easily as it was to crush a bug.

Maybe his tutors back in the tower were right. Maybe spellsters didn't deserve to be amongst normal folk. Maybe he didn't deserve to be anywhere.

Join us. How simple would it be to throw himself at the next threat? To fall rather than go on knowing he hadn't been able to stop the attack? He couldn't keep his magic from healing him, but there were ways to keep him from coming back.

What if his inaction made things worse? The Seven Sisters wouldn't look favourably upon him then. The unworthy spent eternity trapped on their boat, drifting through the darkness.

His gaze swung to where the women lay, just dark lumps on the ground. There was nothing to suggest either woman was actually asleep. He shuffled to where the dwarf slept, intent on waking her as agreed, before deciding against it.

Instead, he stood and, feeling his way through the darkness, halted at the side of a tree to press his forehead to the bark. He wasn't usually the type to ask forgiveness from the gods, but it couldn't hurt.

Dylan closed his eyes and clasped his hands over his chest. His lips moved in the silent prayer he'd spoken at every bimonthly sermon since he could talk. "I don't know if you can hear me," he whispered. "The priests say you don't answer people's prayers and you're all probably busy judging and guiding everyone who died here, but I've got to know… Why me? Why am *I* still here?" He should've been at the main encampment to help. All those lives might never have been wasted if he had just been there. "What did *I* do to merit saving that they didn't?" Nothing. He'd done absolutely nothing. He hadn't been able to.

He waited, both hoping and dreading that, for once, the gods would answer.

How long he stood leaning against the tree, he didn't know. The passage of time came only through his aching limbs. His legs shook, tired from being rooted to the spot. Still, he waited. *Just one sign.* All he needed was one little sign.

Nothing came.

Dylan slid to his knees, his legs unable to hold him anymore. He clung to the tree, his fingers digging into crevices within the bark. Anger bubbled through his veins, making a sour mixture in his gut. "What gives you the right to choose who dies?" he whispered into the darkness.

It wasn't only those soldiers who had lost their lives. There would be families waiting for loved ones to return, not learning that they never would for weeks, months. Children who would never meet their parents. Siblings who would never hold kin. Parents who were left bereft of their children. Spouses, cousins, friends. Every life torn because of one moment.

"Were we meant to fail? Was I...?" He took a deep, quivering breath, a far more insidious thought surfacing. "Was I supposed to die?" The gods hadn't come to his aid in his nightmare. Perhaps that was meant to be a sign that he had somehow missed his destined end.

Warm wetness flowed down his cheeks to drip off his chin. He was nowhere near ready to die. "Please, tell me what I'm supposed to do now."

The king would learn of their defeat. He would send more people to the border. Demarn would always need more people to guard against Udynea. Whilst he...

Dylan sniffed back his tears. He would be amongst them and, this time, he wouldn't fail. He would do everything in his power to ensure this second chance at life counted. "I'll try harder." Every last piece of himself would become dedicated to those he travelled with. No one under his watch would succumb to the same fate as the scouting party. "I promise."

"Dylan?"

The concern in that hushed, musical breath of his name had him rocking back to sit on his heels. *Katarina.* His breath shuddered through his chest. Was he not meant to wake her earlier?

He hurriedly wiped his face dry. "Sorry," he croaked. Had he been blubbering loud enough for the woman to hear? "I didn't mean to disturb anyone." What of the warrior? Elves had far superior hearing than both humans and dwarves. Had he woken her, too?

Dylan dared to glance over his shoulder at where Authril slept on, or so he hoped.

The hedgewitch crouched at his side. In the shadows beneath the trees, she was little more than a suggestion against the gloom. "Are you all right?"

He choked back the welling urge in his chest to continue mewling like a newborn kitten. He must've looked quite the sight for her to ask. "I'm fine."

Silence followed his answer. Didn't she believe him? *Probably not.* He wouldn't have either.

A hand grasped his shoulder.

He flinched, a high-pitched gasp leaving his lips, before realising it was merely Katarina. He didn't cling to the woman's fingers and he most certainly did not squeeze them due to any fear of her not being real.

"Come on," she said, coaxing him to his feet. "Let's get you back by the fire. I think I saw your blanket near Authril." She grunted as his legs, still reluctant to bear his full weight, gave ever so slightly. "You must be exhausted. You should get some rest. Even a few hours will do some good."

Together, they crossed the short distance from the tree to where they'd piled their supplies. She waited until he was settled by the banked fire and wrapped up in his blanket before striding off to circle the camp.

Hunched over, staring blindly at the dim suggestion of a glowing coal, he listened to her footsteps, barely discernible from the surrounding hush of the night. Swift, too. If she hadn't been kept back by his bumbling, she might've been able to reach the main encampment before it was hit and raise the alarm.

But she had stayed with him. Dooming everyone.

Katarina emerged from the shadows to sit next to him. "Are you truly all right?"

Dylan eyed Authril's sleeping form. The warrior slept far heavier than any elf he'd known, but that was a good thing. He wasn't quite ready to bare his reservations to the woman. Katarina should be capable of keeping anything he said in confidence. "Not really," he whispered.

"This might sound harsh, but you need sleep. Whatever thoughts you have going through your head right now won't improve if you deprive your body of a necessary function."

"I know," he murmured. However, sleep came with its own problems. "I'm not sure I can."

She shuffled closer, patting the earth between them. "Lie down and try. I'll be right here if you need me."

Dylan did as instructed, pillowing his head on his pack. It was far bigger and more forgiving than he'd expected, no doubt stuffed with their looted rations. The ground wasn't as cooperative. He wriggled, trying to find a comfortable position without sacrificing the blanket's warmth.

A hand brushed his head, freeing his face of hair, much like his guardian had done when he'd been unwell as a child. "Be still," Katarina murmured.

He lay there, letting her stroke his temple. Humming emanated from the woman. A low, dreamy tune he hadn't heard before. He closed his eyes, letting his thoughts drift on the notes, trying desperately not to think of the bony claws waiting for him in the shadows.

CHAPTER 19

After two days of trudging through the forest, being unmercifully drenched with every step, Dylan was certain the rain fell not in little droplets, but in a single continuous one. He'd had about enough of the weather, enough of stumbling and squelching amongst the dripping undergrowth.

They walked in single file with Authril at the fore. She sheltered beneath her upraised shield, although it did little to keep the water off anything beyond her head. The rain bounced off the metal's curved surface as if the droplets were a hundred raucous fleas, the sound reminding him of a turning drum of seeds.

Dylan had shielded them the best he could during the first day, but the strain of maintaining a barrier that dense had long since sapped him of energy. Not even the trick of securing it in the back of his mind had helped.

The best he could manage now was a little heat and he clung to that ability, waiting for a dry place that would allow him to get warm again. He needed warmth, a decent night's rest and a hearty meal. Things they weren't likely to find amongst the trees.

The lack of shelter had been the most jarring. In the fairytales his guardian used to read to him, the trees would be enough to keep bad weather off the weary travellers building little fires out of miraculously dry logs and sleeping against the trunks all wrapped up in warm blankets.

In reality, nothing seemed to completely halt such a downpour and the ground was sodden even at the foot of the heartiest tree.

Never had he been this soaked outside of bathing. Water trickled down his exposed side, further chilling his already saturated skin. That particular part of his body had stopped aching sometime last night. His legs cried out to stop. His eyelids begged for him to let them close.

He couldn't risk doing either. Not until they'd found somewhere sheltered for the night. A goal that was looking to be less certain with each passing hour.

Authril abruptly halted. She twisted to face him, her mouth moving, all sound drowned out by the hissing rain atop her shield.

"What?" he yelled back, cupping a hand behind his ear.

Pursing her lips, she pointed off to his right. There was something large just beyond the trees, difficult to make out in the increasing gloom and the screen of a thousand raindrops. Perhaps it was a fallen tree or some sort of rock formation. Maybe even a cave. All of those sounded promising.

Nodding, he tugged at the hedgewitch's sleeve and pointed towards their new destination.

The closer they got, the easier it became to make their way through the undergrowth. In some places, there seemed to be a path travelling in the same direction they were headed. As they wove through the trees, he would spy a flickering light coming from within the shadowy hulk of their destination. Survivors? That had to mean shelter.

The slog of his passage picked up, the thought of being warm and dry again reinvigorating him.

The foliage thinned out to a clearing. He halted, stumbling a few steps more when Katarina collided into his back.

The shape they'd veered towards was a hut. An inhabited one if he was to judge by the smoke coming out of the chimney. The flickering light peeking through the shutters sealing off a window had to belong to the fireplace. *Warmth.* The simple thought pushed his feet across the clearing to the door.

Authril was already there, pounding on the weathered planks. "I know you're in there!" she bellowed. "Open up!"

Dylan winced. "Is it wise to antagonise them?" His teeth chattered as he spoke, barely missing biting his tongue. From the outside, there was no indication of how many people lived here. Although, surely the occupants wouldn't be alone. They could easily opt to leave a sodden trio of strangers to the elements. If he could avoid spending another night trying to sleep in the rain by being cordial, it was well worth the effort.

There was the faintest scrape of a bolt being pulled back. The door creaked open a little ways.

Dylan stepped back, unsure what to make of this silent invitation.

Authril pushed the door open further, hesitantly at first, then with more vigour when she came upon no resistance. She crossed the threshold in a few wary steps, her shield held at her side, only to halt just inside the room.

Dylan crowded her, the desire to be out of the rain superseding his caution.

A human woman, clad in a simple linen shirt and trousers, stood in the middle of the room. The warm yellow glow of a fire pit burned merrily at her back, obscuring much of the woman's features. The scent of food cooking nearby tickled his nose.

He had taken a single involuntary step towards the warmth when Authril dropped her shield with a mighty clang and threw up her hands.

Dylan's gaze returned to the hut's owner and settled on the bow she had aimed at them. He didn't know much about archery—had only fleetingly seen a few of the army's archers honing their skills in the main encampment before being sent to the front line—but the woman looked very sure of her ability to hurt them. He mimicked Authril in holding his hands where they could be seen.

"You've exactly one minute to explain yourselves before I skewer the lot of you," the woman snarled. "But if you're looking to rob me, you're shit out of luck there. I've nothing that's worth risking your lives for." Her accent was almost undetectable to his ears, not quite as undulating as Authril's.

Dylan found himself exhaling in relief, despite the arrow she aimed at them. The woman was as Demarner as himself. That meant they'd a chance to reason with her.

"I assure you that we're not here to rob you," Katarina said, pushing past Dylan to stand by the warrior's side. "Please, we've been walking through the rain for two days. All we seek is a chance to be dry and warm for the night."

The woman remained silent. With her expression shadowed, Dylan couldn't begin to guess what she was thinking. She made no move to lower her bow, but she seemed less inclined to use it.

"We don't have anything to pay you," the hedgewitch continued, "but I swear, if you let us just spend the night here, we'll be on our way come dawn."

"To where?" the woman demanded, the words thick with suspicion. "My home doesn't exactly sit in the middle of a main thoroughfare. You can't tell me you were merely having a stroll through the woods and got lost."

"We're on our way to—"

"Toptower," Dylan blurted before the hedgewitch could mention anything else. He didn't know why this woman was out in the forest, seemingly alone, but she clearly hadn't marked him as a spellster. He'd no idea how she would react to the presence of one on her doorstep. "At least, that's our first stop. We came from the army."

"The army?" She snorted. "Look, I told you buggers that I'm a born Demarner, if scouts keep knocking on my door, I'm going to start putting holes in people. And you can take that back to your commander."

"We can't," Authril said, her voice the smallest it had been since they met. "The encampment was overrun. Everyone's dead."

"What?" The woman finally lowered her bow. "No." The bow came up, bending as she drew the arrow back. "That's a lie. I've seen the encampment. There's thousands of people there."

Authril's head slowly bobbed in agreement and Dylan caught himself mimicking the act.

The woman scoffed. "You really expect me to believe there's no army between here and the border?"

Yes. Had she not seen the smoke? The trees made an impressive canopy, but it wasn't absolute. Even if it hadn't drifted above her hut, the plume of it would've filled much of the sky.

"Believe what you want," Authril replied. "It's still the truth. The Udynea Empire tore through our defences like a blade through canvas."

"And where are they now? Think I wouldn't notice something like those arrogant pricks marching by my home?"

"They're gone," Katarina answered before the warrior could open her mouth. "It appears they've orders to retreat. I can make guesses as to why, but I can't be sure of the actual reason—we didn't exactly stop to ask them. However, I do know that they could return at any time, they may very well be headed this way right now. They'll find no resistance."

"Right," the other woman snapped. "Because it's completely logical for them to destroy the entire army and just wander back home. Job done, boys. Let's leave them to set up for another round."

The same thought had gnawed at Dylan ever since stumbling upon the scouting party he let walk away. Perhaps the spellster he had fought was right, that they were after slaves. Spellster ones in particular. He wasn't certain as to the magical nature of slaves born in the empire, but he wouldn't be surprised that, of their number, those trained in magic were rather thin on the ground.

The woman's head swung from side to side, the act freeing a lock of dark, ruddy auburn hair. She stepped back, once more lowering her bow. The firelight illuminated her face and the uncertainty twisting her mouth. "Say I believe you. Toptower's not very far to go. An army could be there in under a week."

"Our goal is much further," Dylan replied.

"The spellster tower, right?" She smiled when he attempted to feign ignorance and jerked her chin at him. "The robes. I've seen them before, standard army issue." The twitch of her head indicated the other women. "You two are taking him back to get more of them?"

"Something like that," he muttered.

The woman leant her bow against the wall. "Well then, I

recommend we leave first thing in the morning."

"*W-we?*" Authril spluttered, her eyes all but bursting from their sockets.

With hands on her hips, the woman looked the elf over. "Well, yes. I know this forest. I know the way to Toptower. Or would you rather spend a few more days bumbling about?"

"We weren't bumbling."

"No?" the woman sweetly replied. She bared her teeth in what he supposed was meant to be a smile. "Then how did you wind up at my little hut, hmm? I'm Marin, by the way."

That was all the invitation Dylan needed. He shuffled past the fuming form of Authril and made for the fire pit. He rubbed his arms, trying to get some heat back into them. The weight of the pack tugged at his shoulders. He let the bundle slip to the floor, sighing as he spied water oozing from the canvas. That meant his blanket would be well and truly saturated and who knew what state the travel rations were in?

"We were attempting a more direct route," Katarina confessed.

Marin shook her head. "If you've come straight from the main encampment, then you're veering too far north to hit the village."

"Not according to this." The hedgewitch fished out their map from her belt pouch. Unlike the contents of Dylan's makeshift bag, the map was completely dry.

Marin took the map over to the fire pit and read it, making a small, disapproving sound every so often. "Cheap workmanship," she muttered. "Fine for the study wall. Terrible if you want to travel. See here?" She pointed to the little spot marked as Toptower. "It should be here." Her finger moved down about half of its width. "A small margin on paper, but follow it and you'd wind up at Oldmarsh."

"We'd have to go through there at some point anyway," Dylan said. "What difference does it make if we take the road to the town or the forests?"

"Without food?" She examined him, especially the gaping hole in the right side of his clothes. No longer backlit by the fire pit, her eyes were a light brown hue a shade or two darker than her tawny skin. "Or shelter?" Returning the map to the dwarf, Marin left the fireside to rummage in a nearby chest. "Of course, you won't be going anywhere if you're all dead from the cold."

Dylan huddled over the fire, rubbing his hands. He had a faster way to get warm and dry, but he wasn't about to test their host's sudden hospitality by blatantly using magic in front of her. The trick would also work best on his clothes if he wasn't wearing them and, whilst he was in no way ashamed of his body and had been naked before others, that didn't mean he was prepared to strip in front of all and sundry.

Marin returned with an armful of thick-looking cloths. She gave several to the others before coming to him. Her gaze aimed pointedly at his right side. "There's an alcove just on the other side of those pelts if you want to strip and get dry," she offered, indicating a section of the room that had pelts draped across it. "I also think I might have something to patch that."

He paused in getting to his feet as she spun about to rifle through another chest tucked beneath the shuttered window.

After a few moments of muffled mutters and grumbles, Marin produced several scraps of cloth and leather along with a small container that he hoped was full of sewing supplies. "Let me know when you've disrobed and I'll get them all patched up once they're dry. The fabric won't match, of course, but it's better than catching your death."

Smiling his thanks, he took the pieces and container from her unresisting grasp. "I think I can manage. Through there, you said?" Barely waiting for her affirmative nod, Dylan shuffled off behind the curtain of pelts, surprised to find a bed on the other side.

An unlit candle sat on a little shelf near the headboard. He ignited it with the click of his fingers and set to work on undressing, taking pains not to get too much of the area wet whilst peeling off his clothes. Rubbing himself dry took a little longer than he would've liked, the task hampered by the fabric being the less absorbent sort, but it worked well enough once he used his magic to apply a little warmth to the threads.

A prickling in his side drew his attention. Examining his skin under the flickering light, he discovered the exposed patch had turned red from the constant cold. His magic had done its best to soothe the area, but without fixing the cause, it would've been a constant draining battle.

Wrapping the length of cloth around his waist, he turned his attention to his sodden clothes. Drawing the moisture from them was a relatively easy task, allowing him to swiftly don his dry smallclothes before turning to the scraps of cloth. A few were instantly discarded as being too small, a couple laid aside due to their coarseness.

The mattress rustled and shifted under his weight as he settled on the bed. Dylan bounced a few times. It wasn't the giving comfort of his bed back in the tower, but nor was it as hard as the ground he'd been forced to sleep on since arriving at the main army encampment. Strange, how much of a luxury a simple bed felt.

Sighing, he flipped open the box to find the required needle and thread along with a few crude pins. It would likely take him an hour or so to repair both robe and undertunic, but that was no reason to leave off starting now and it would give the women time to dry off in relative privacy.

Stitching his chosen patch onto his undertunic was a fiddly task. Much of his skill with a needle had come during his tutorage under the healers, yet even the flesh of an unlucky patient cooperated far more easily than linen. IIe would need to trim thc patch later and do a proper job of the edges so it wouldn't fray.

The hems were a different story. The only thing to be done with them was to fold the shredded fabric and sew, but they were tasks he could deal with once his robe wasn't quite so exposed on one side.

Shrugging back into the undertunic to keep the chill off his skin, he started on his robe. With its thicker fabric, it seemed easier to deal with, even if he had to fight the needle through the brown leather he'd chosen. That the tear had needed two of the patches to be fully covered didn't help matters, but it was eventually done. Until he could neaten it up, at least.

He was part way through hemming his robe when there was a muffled scratch at the pelt blocking the doorway.

"Are you decent?" Marin called. The words carried a slight tremor, as if she was afraid there very well might be a naked man on the other side of the pelt.

A roguish part of him was tempted to strip back to his smallclothes and announce that she enter. He banished the impish thought and laid his half-done robe aside. "I'm never decent, but I am clothed if you wish to come in."

There was a muffled snort and the woman slipped into the room, a steaming bowl-like cup balanced in each hand. "Oh, I didn't expect you to be…" Those light brown eyes swept over him, no doubt noticing the distinct lack of him looking like he'd ever been wet. Her brow creased slightly. "Here." She held out one of the mugs. "This ought to finish warming you up."

He accepted the cup, swirling the dark brown liquid within before taking a sip of what his tongue told him was some sort of watery mushroom-based soup.

"I'm afraid it's not much." She settled on the bed next to him. "I wasn't exactly expecting company."

Dylan smiled. Whilst the rations the women had liberated from the Udyneans were nourishing, they'd a distinct lack of anything resembling flavour. Unless sawdust counted. "Believe me, compared to what I've been eating for the last few days, this is a feast."

She rested her own cup atop her leg, picking at the blankets with her free hand like a nervous child. "They tell me that you're unleashed."

He nodded. With his neck exposed, there was little point in denying it. "I am. Is that going to be a problem?"

"Not unless you plan on being problematic."

"Damn." He clicked his fingers. "There goes my idea of completely warping the fabric of existence to suit my whim. And I was so looking forward to bringing about the end of the world."

Marin raised a brow at him. By her expression, she was considering whether or not to believe him. "You can't actually do that, can you?"

He shook his head. "If I was that powerful, do you think we would've turned up here looking like drowned rats?"

"I suppose not. Unless you were a god trying to hide amongst mortals."

Dylan gasped and clutched at his chest. "You've gone and figured out my secret. Wicked mortal." He leant back on the bed. "You know, when I considered leaving the comfort of my crystal throne, I knew I would definitely have to come to a place where they leash spellsters rather than where they are nobles. And I'd most certainly opt to spend twenty-nine years just existing in a tower." He stretched his legs out in front of him, crossing them at the ankles. "I think I'll choose Obuzan next time. I hear the country has a low tolerance for magic, shouldn't take as long to die there. I could be back in the afterlife by noon."

"Fair enough," she said, giggling. "You know, you're far less serious than I expected a spellster to be."

"I'm getting a lot of that, but no one will tell me why."

Frowning, Marin bit her bottom lip. A freckle, darker than any of the others, sat on the right side of her face just above the right curve of her mouth. "Well, they say that you spend a lot of time studying and training. I guess I sort of equated that to you all being bookish snobs."

Dylan chuckled. "Is that all? To be fair, some of us are." He recalled quite a number in the tower who fitted that description. "And they'd likely be overjoyed you think of them as such."

"But you seem to be a bit of a goof. That's quite the relief. I don't think I could stand travelling with the other kind of spellster." She peered up at him. "But I think we'll do all right together."

He sidled across the bed a little ways. None of their trio had the money to pay the woman for their impromptu arrival, but there were other arrangement they could make. "Is that so?"

"Don't let it go to your head, either of them. I merely meant that it can grate having a travelling companion you don't get on with. If you're after anything else you're not really my type."

"Oh?" He set down his mug. "Perhaps if you told me what your type is, I could try being it for you? At least long enough to show my thanks in letting us stay the night."

Marin grinned. A mischievous glint sparked in her eyes. "You can become a woman?"

Ah. He returned his focus to the cup, his face burning. "That I can't do. Sorry."

There was a long pause, in which he silently cursed himself for even thinking about flirting with the woman when they'd just met.

Marin cleared her throat. "Are my ears mishearing or did you just apologise for not being able to turn into a woman?"

The tension he didn't know that had been in his shoulders fled. He let out a small breath. "You didn't mishear. It's not the first time I've been rejected on such grounds." It *was* one of the softer rejections he had gotten in a long time, which was certainly a nice change of pace. Usually, he'd be due a stream of abuse by now, roars of how dare he think they were attracted to his gender. Apologising for his mistake was often the only way to prevent such a tongue-lashing. "Nor is it the first time I've rejected someone because of it." Amazing how one glance too many could make a man think he was interested in them. "I get it. Truly. I'll just be your goofy and utterly sexually unappealing travelling companion."

Marin laughed. "You're just afraid I'm going to stick you full of arrows, aren't you?"

He remained quiet on the fact that she wouldn't be able to reach her bow before he'd a shield up. Never mind retaliating. Instead, he affected a casual air, picked up his cup and drank deep of its contents before saying, "Whatever would I do to give you cause for that?"

A sneer curled her lip and a contemptuous little snort blew through her nose. "You've either no imagination or are incredibly dense."

He pressed a hand to his chest. "It seems you don't need arrows to wound me, madam."

She stared at him for a while, then smiled and held up her drink. "Here's to goofy travelling companions."

He clinked cups with her and took another swig. "Thank you, though, for letting us stay. And for the offer to escort us to Toptower. I truly wish we'd a way to repay you."

"Ah, you know me. If there's one thing I can't resist, it's a drowned rat of a spellster knocking on my door." She fiddled with the handle of her mug. "So, being able to change your form isn't an actual thing?"

"No." If it had been, he knew of at least one person who would've jumped at the chance to learn it. "At least, not in Demarn." Who knew what magic they were capable of in the lands where spellsters were given leave to do as they pleased? "Nor is the whole turning people into frogs story." He wasn't even sure where that rumour had come from, but the idea had run rife through the soldiers.

"That's a shame. I've met some people who are already halfway there."

His thoughts drifted to the men who'd been in command of him in the army. The priest said it was wrong to think ill of the dead, but he couldn't muster much sympathy for the lieutenant or the captain, no matter their deaths. "As have I."

"Still, I suppose if you could, the country would probably be overrun with them by now. They breed like crazy as it is."

Dylan chuckled. "Causing a frog epidemic wouldn't exactly endear us to the people, no." Finishing the last of the soup, he handed back the cup. "You wouldn't happen to have a pair of shears I could use?"

Her gaze swung to the half-finished sewing he'd done on his robe. She nodded. "Let me go get them." With that, she disappeared back behind the screen of pelts.

He dug around in his belt pouch for his mirror whilst he waited. It had been a few days since he'd been able, or even willing, to attempt shaving. Sure enough, there were a few patchy hints of stubble forming.

A small basin and pitcher sat perched atop a chest near the bed end, the latter of which being completely empty. The lack of water wasn't much of a problem. He focused on the inside of the basin. With this much moisture in the air, convincing it to crystallise into ice was a simple matter of manipulation. A child's game.

"Neat trick," Marin said, jolting him from his task. How long had she been standing there? "But wouldn't ice be the last thing you'd want?"

Dylan placed his hand atop the block of ice and switched his focus. "It's not ice that I'm after," he agreed. Heat poured down his hand, melting the ice in a matter of seconds and steadily raising the temperature of the water.

She offered up the shears, eyeing the steaming basin.

"I'll let you have your bed back as soon as I'm done here." It would likely take him several hours with the leather, but he could do that by the fire pit once he had sorted out his undertunic.

The woman waved her hand. "I tend to sleep in front of the fire on nights like this, anyway. We're going to be sleeping outdoors a lot before we reach your tower, feel free to spend the night in it."

He bowed his head in thanks and, as she left him, fell to the task of shaving before he returned to mending his clothes.

CHAPTER 20

The rain had finally stopped by the time morning arrived, allowing their group to leave the hut as soon as it was light enough to see. Marin led the way with Katarina at her side, their passage winding along trails the animals had worn through the forest. Dylan still wasn't certain why the woman had chosen to live alone in the middle of the forest, but he doubted he was the only one grateful for her presence.

Marin had done more than give them a warm place to stay overnight. Their waterlogged travel rations were replaced with the jerked meat the woman had hunted and prepared for the coming autumn months. She'd also unearthed a few packs, older but more robust than the previous sack he'd been lugging through the rain. Heavier, too. She'd added other things to their packs, such as the mug and bowl wrapped up in his blanket.

Travelling with a guide who definitely knew the way meant they covered a great deal more ground, stopping only when the shadowy fingers of night stretched out across the forest canopy.

They settled in to lay out the tents, another gift from Marin. There were only two—Marin's newer piece and a slightly worn spare—and both were of similar size. Although he'd insisted that he didn't mind sharing the space with another, all three women seemed intent on sleeping crammed into one tent.

He was willing to bet a large chunk of their reluctance was due to his ineffectiveness in the task of getting even half of his tent to stay upright for longer than a few seconds. The women, whilst fumbling in the beginning to harvest enough branches of the same length, managed to set up their shelter in no time.

No matter how Dylan attempted to keep the fiddly pieces from falling, the length of wood at the top end always seemed to tip off the fork at the other end before he'd a chance to finish righting the first.

Although the shape was similar to the triangular tents that'd been numerous in the army camps, these tents were made from several pieces of leather and had rawhide ties in places he didn't recall seeing on the other wedge-shaped tents. Of course, he hadn't seen any of those shelters dismantled.

"You know," Authril said, jolting him from his hushed mantra of senseless muttering. "You're not meant to stake the corners quite as far apart as that."

Dylan glanced over his shoulder at the warrior, then back at the uncooperative mass of leather and wood. He had stretched out the ground section as far as the leather would allow and it did seem to be fighting him. "That actually explains a lot." He bent down and hauled the closest of the stakes from the earth.

"And having the top pole inside the tent might also help you."

He nodded absently as he removed a second stake. That made a lot of sense, too. "Do you think you could lend me a hand?"

Shaking her head, Authril picked up the palm-sized rock he'd been using as a hammer. "Move over, then."

Dylan stood back as she re-secured the corners, taking pains to watch what she did for the next time. During his journey down from the tower, he had either slept in the back of the cart or was ushered into an inn room. He doubted either option would be available during their current travels.

Maintaining his attention on her actions wasn't an easy task. His gaze kept wandering, travelling up the woman's arms to her face. With her skin not quite so dirt-smeared and her hair dry, as well as being rather less explosive than when they first met, he was able to clearly define her features. The sharp angle of her jaw gave her a certain heart-shaped quality that rather complemented her large eyes and the numerous freckles.

It was her lips that distracted him the most. They were already the perfect amount of plumpness, somewhere between full and thin. But the way she bit the bottom one whilst lining up the tent side and the firm press of them against each other as she hammered each stake in...

It was almost enough to make a man want to never stop kissing them.

"There," she said, breaking him from his reverie. Authril stood back, brushing the grass and dirt from her hands. "That should do it, help me with the rest of it."

With the tent sides not pulled out quite as tightly as in his solo attempt, they were able to right the poles with little effort. The supports wobbled as they lashed the top pole to the others, but mercifully, the structure didn't collapse. It actually looked like a tent now.

Convinced he could finally stake down the sides as well, he grabbed his makeshift hammer and set to work.

"I wonder if you could help me figure something out," Authril said whilst lashing the last of the poles together.

He sat back on his heels, glancing up from the stake he'd half hammered in. "That depends on what it is."

Finished with her task, she leant back on the tree he'd chosen to pitch under. "Well, you're human."

He grinned up at her. "I am indeed and I'm fully prepared to prove that should you ever wish to check."

She rolled her eyes. "And Marin is also human."

"Obviously." There were only three options and, whilst she could have elven blood, it clearly wasn't as apparent as on Authril. He crouched at the next staking point and rammed the short length of wood into the ground. "Is this going somewhere?"

"How can Katarina not be human?"

"Ah." He ducked down the other side of the tent before the woman could catch him grinning for an entirely different reason. He had heard of elves being confused by the close resemblance between dwarves and humans. There were no obvious differences between the races like there were with elves, but then, their pointy-eared brethren had come from somewhere else. "Katarina is from Dvärghem. They believe they're all, technically, dwarves." Although there were supposedly non-dwarven hedgewitches, they'd be in the minority and unlikely to be wandering the forest without dwarven company.

Authril shook her head and creaked an abrupt denial. "See I know that. You can tell me that until you pass out, but I see no dwarves here."

He peeked over the top of the tent. "Well, I wouldn't recommend calling Katarina human." Whilst it could be little more than rumour turned folklore, there was a very popular tale about a prince who made such an accusation of a hedgewitch. Dvärghem as a whole might now lean towards more diplomatic resolutions, but the individual had challenged the young prince to a fight and won, proving that the hedgewitch had agility and strength that surpassed a mere human.

"She can't be anything but human, though," Authril insisted. "Everyone knows real dwarves have been extinct for thousands of years."

Did everyone know? "I think the Dvärghem Coven might disagree with you."

She wrinkled her nose. "They were short people. They found burial sites on the border of Heimat. I know that much."

Frowning, Dylan resisted the urge to ask where she had heard that. He'd no knowledge of any such sites being discovered. Perhaps it was a new one. "Katarina *is* short." Shorter than Marin and himself, at least. The top of her head perhaps reached the base of his ears if he was being generous.

Authril huffed in pure exasperation. "That doesn't count. Everyone's shorter than *you*. You're like some weird giant. Scrawny, too. Even for a spellster."

Dylan thrust out his bottom lip. He could let the weird remark slide, but… "Scrawny?" In the last year, he had managed to put on at least a stone and he'd eaten a great deal before that happened.

Again, the woman rolled her eyes, but failed to stifle the little smile that tugged at the corners of her mouth. "Will you stop pouting if I said lanky?"

Standing, he brushed the skirt of his robe clean. "What were you expecting?"

"I'm… not sure. The other spellsters—the ones Udynea took?— they weren't like you. They'd more meat on their bones."

He chuckled. He'd never been the most physically strong amongst his peers. "You should've seen me in my teenage years." Scrawny would've been an apt description back then, with Henrie often comparing him to a walking skeleton. "I haven't exactly been away from the tower long and the only heavy things we have lying around there are each other and some of the bigger tomes. We don't really do much lifting of either." Even then, he would rarely attempt to carry a tome without aid.

She smiled. "My point is that dwarves are meant to be shorter than elves. Shorter than *me*, than the humans that this hedgewitch is actually taller than."

He shrugged and tossed his makeshift hammer into the undergrowth. "If you breed an elf to someone of human descent enough times, you would never guess they'd an elven ancestor unless they told you."

The woman raised a brow at him. Something cold flashed in those sea-green eyes.

Dylan held up his hands. "Not that I'm suggesting anything. I meant it purely as an example. Dwarves used to be everywhere, but there hasn't been any new dwarven stock for centuries and they aren't averse to unions with either human or elf. It's not my place to question if they have the ancestry they claim."

There was evidence of some difference, documented in both dwarven texts and human records. The ancient dwarves never used magic and a spellster who had a child with a native of Dvärghem ended up with one who was irrefutably non-magical. Some of that had to be in modern-day dwarves.

Authril opened her mouth, closing it swiftly as something in the forest caught her attention.

Thoughts of an attack grasped his heart. The flicker of a shield stuttered for a beat before he pushed down the urge. "What—?"

She clamped her hand over his mouth, stifling the rest of his question. With the other hand, she pressed a finger to her lips, demanding silence from him.

Dylan nodded and she let her hand drop.

He tilted his head, straining to hear what she could. Trees creaked in a breeze that didn't reach them quite as strongly. There was the hushed drone of bees drifting from flower to flower in a nearby bush. Something small scurried through fallen leaves.

Authril grasped his arm, wordlessly pushing him towards where the others stood by the unlit fire. It wasn't until he was still again that he caught what she had heard. Or rather, what they couldn't hear.

The birds had stopped singing.

In place of low chirps and whistles, came the faint rustle of something large moving through the undergrowth, the sound punctuated every so often by a deep grunting. The longer he listened, the louder the grunts got. It raised the hair on his neck and sent a shudder down his back.

What sort of animal made such a noise?

Marin abandoned the campfire she was attempting to light. She jumped to her feet, her bow at the ready. "Get behind me!" The woman jerked her head, frowning when Authril merely drew her weapon. "Your sword won't be any good with this, leave it to me."

Dylan threw up a shield to encompass the hedgewitch and himself as Katarina scurried to his side. Was it a bear? Were there bears in this kingdom? He rather wished he knew the answer to that because, whatever it was, it sounded angry. And enormous. "What is it?" he asked.

"With luck," Marin muttered. "It's dinner."

A heavy black beast erupted from the undergrowth. Roaring like a demon, it ploughed through the middle of their camp.

Before Dylan had time to think on how to deal with it, there was the muffled whoosh of an arrow leaving the hunter's bow and the thing veered off into the bush.

"Oh no, you don't!" Marin growled. She rushed after it, her massive hunting knife bared.

Authril followed quick on the woman's heels.

He watched their passage in silence, still unsure what he had seen. Definitely not bear-shaped. Too low to the ground to be a deer.

"You can drop the barrier, now," Katarina said. "It's not coming back."

Uncertain whether he should believe her, Dylan opted to leave the shield in place. "What was it?"

She raised a brow at him. "You've never heard of a boar?"

"A boar?" Dylan echoed. That crazed beast had been a boar? "I've heard of them. Seen one?" He recalled one particular book he used to pour over in his childhood, filled with animals from all over the continent. Porcine of all kinds had featured on one of the pages. The images he remembered looked nothing like that monstrous creature. "Not in the flesh. There aren't more of them, are there?"

"Well, Marin might be a better person to enquire about that, but in my experience, they don't tend to travel alone." She smiled and patted his shoulder. "But I'm sure this one was. I don't hear any others nearby."

He tilted his head, straining to distinguish the grunt and crashes of the other two women, and the boar they'd gone after, from the rest of the wildlife. The occasional birdsong might pipe up for a few notes, but the forest seemed to be holding its breath. Even the creak of the trees sounded muffled.

Further grunts and rustling preceded Marin and Authril's return. The women entered backwards into the clearing, each one with a hind leg of the beast in hand. The boar slithered on the ground in front of them. They didn't stop until the beast was once again in the middle of their camp.

"Well now," Marin huffed, brushing the hair from her face with the back of a hand. "That should feed us for a few days." She looked over the prone animal with a sort of grim satisfaction. "We can roast him up, stuff ourselves and prepare what's left for travelling."

"Look at the size of it," Katarina said. "It'll take hours to cook and we don't yet have a fire going."

Marin frowned. "Bugger," she muttered, nudging the boar with her foot. "I'd hate to just leave him here to rot. I suppose we could cook a leg or two for the morning and carve up a few pieces to cook tomorrow night." The woman looked up at them, suddenly hopeful. "Or we could stay here and let it roast overnight. Dry some for the journey? It's a bit of a pity we're nowhere near my smoking hut, could've chucked half of him in there."

"Except all that would take time," the hedgewitch pointed out. "I was of the opinion that having a spellster unleashed outside of the tower was illegal in Demarn."

"It is," Authril replied, plonking herself near the unlit campfire and taking up the flint. "He needs to be returned to the tower. There are people who hunt down unleashed spellsters. The King's Hounds? If they find us in Dylan's presence and think we're trying to help him escape—"

"But no one's going to be looking out here for him, are they?"

Marin pressed. "And a day or two won't hurt. We can afford to stop if it means more food, can't we?"

The elf glared at the logs, viciously striking the steel across the flint. She muttered under her breath, but made no sign of disagreeing with the other woman.

Dylan eyed the hedgewitch, but Katarina seemed to have opted to remain silent.

"Then it's settled," Marin said, tying a length of rope around the boar's hind legs. Once the legs were trussed, the woman dragged the carcass to the base of a tree. "We're going to need lots of dry wood."

"That shouldn't be too difficult, should it?" Authril waved her hand about to indicate everything around them. "We're surrounded by wood."

"Wood, yes. Dry wood?" Marin shook her head. "Let's just say I really don't fancy our chances there. Everything's soaked. Even the logs we've gathered will take a fair bit of drying to be usable and I don't see that happening quickly in this weather."

Dylan eyed the pile of wood set out for the fire. *Anything burns if it's hot enough.* That had been his first lesson before his instructors would even allow him to learn how to craft his magic into a flame.

He focused on the wood, encasing the pile in heat. At first, little happened. A gentle hiss came from the logs and steam began to unfurl from under the bark. Then, in one mighty *fwoomph*, the wood caught.

Authril jumped back, her eyes bulging.

Laughter, deep and rolling, came from Marin. "By the gods," she wheezed, pointing a forefinger in the warrior's direction. "Look at your face! It's all pale." The woman tilted her head. "Well," she amended, "*paler*. Could you get more wood?" This question was directed to him. "Or are you able to help with cleaning the boar?"

Dylan eyed the hairy carcass in question. He wasn't entirely sure what cleaning it entailed, but he'd a suspicion it wasn't going to be pretty. "I can gather wood." He didn't exactly think the forest put out the precisely cut chunks of wood he remembered from the tower, but he'd a fair idea of what to collect.

"We'll need as much as you can carry and then some." She had picked up a length of wood sometime during their talk and tied it around the other end of the rope. This was chucked over the thick branch above and, with a bit of help from the other women, the boar was lifted into the tree. "As for the rest of us? I don't fancy attracting any predators, so we should set to digging a hole about here." She stomped on the spot just below the boar's snout. "I've a trowel in my pack, but it'll still take us a while, so—"

"I can do that," he said. His first attempt at manipulating the ground via magic had begun with scooping out small holes of dirt. It wasn't as finicky as influencing an object and he was certain he could shift earth on a slightly larger scale. Worse case, he'd reduce the time it took the women to enlarge the hole. "How big do you need it?"

"As big as this fellow should do it." Marin patted the boar's shoulder. "Just make sure it's deep. Last thing we need is more of them snuffling about in the middle of the night looking to root up their friend's entrails."

Dylan focused on the indicated ground. Sliding his influence beneath the surface, he wrapped his magic around a small section and tugged.

Nothing happened.

He tried harder to a similar outcome. *Odd.* It had always worked back in the tower when he practised this very technique.

Maybe the trick only worked on tilled soil. This earth was harder, more compacted and full of roots than the soil of the tower gardens. He might as well be back in his nightmare, fighting the influx of mud, for all the influence he was having.

Switching tactics, Dylan slowly formed an ovoid barrier just beneath the ground. He hardened the shield and tried to lift it. Sweat beaded his brow as it resisted, but there was the tiniest bit of give that let him spin the shield in place. The muffled creak of breaking roots emanated from somewhere beneath his feet. Tiny cracks formed in the earth, growing as he heaved the section upwards.

Like a giant's hand, the shield rose out of the ground with the earth still nestled within. Dylan waited only until the barrier was free of the hole before letting it dissipate, dumping the earth in one conical clump.

"Well now," Marin murmured as she unsheathed her hunting knife. "Aren't you full of surprises."

Panting, he grinned her way. "It was wood you wanted, right?" Before she could answer beyond a nod, Dylan headed out into the forest. Authril was right, they were surrounded by the stuff. It shouldn't take him long to find enough to serve their purpose.

After a lot of searching, he decided the forest had been waiting to prove him wrong. Much of the wood he encountered lying amongst the leaves was rotten. The rest required him to possess an axe or the ability to slice at it with precise swipes of thin constructs, a skill he'd never had the knack for.

By the time he returned with enough to fill his arms, the boar hung a little higher in the tree above where the hole had been. Authril and Katarina were steadily carving chunks from the carcass. The animal was already absent of its forelegs, they were secured on a pole sitting above the campfire and being turned by Marin.

What seemed stranger still was the peculiar framework of wood standing where the smoke curled.

Dylan dumped the armful of wood near the fire and frowned at the array of sticks. The structure looked to be made of saplings, the long horizontal poles at the top forming a grill-like pattern. Strips of meat dangled from this. "What—?"

"Jerky," Marin replied before he could finish asking. "Or it would be if I'd a proper drying stand. Haven't done it this way for some time."

He eyed the stick she was rotating before realising it was actually metal. "And what are you doing?"

"Roasting dinner. Hopefully. It would be a lot faster if I could get the fire to stay hot, but it'll do the trick eventually. We'll cook the rest of the boar tomorrow." She tilted her head. "Haven't you ever seen something roasting?"

"No," he confessed. The tower servants would occasionally serve them cuts of roasted animals, but most meat was typically found in a stew similar to the fare the camp cooks dished out.

"Have you ever seen anything cooking? Or even cooked anything?"

He shook his head. "I wouldn't know where to start with cooking something." He rubbed the side of his neck. "Beyond fire, obviously." He'd done a few stints in the massive kitchen the tower servants used to prepare their meals, but the manual labour had been a punishment from his guardian for…

He could no longer remember why she'd sent him there, only the hours spent peeling and dicing so many things. He never did find out how the cooks turned the things he had a hand in preparing into edible food.

"You don't know how to cook?" Marin threw her free hand up in exasperation. "Did no one think to teach you how to survive out here? Sure, they couldn't have predicted what happened, but they take you on scouting missions, don't they? What if you got lost? What did they expect you to do then?"

"Die," Authril replied as she placed more strips of pork on the drying frame. "If he was foolish enough to get separated from his warden, then he's more likely to die before being found. Supposedly so they're less of a threat to the general populace if they do ever become unleashed."

Dylan grunted. It sounded like something the army would agree on.

Marin snorted. "That's stupid." Her gaze ran over him, those light brown eyes molten in the firelight. She patted the ground next to her. "Sit down," she ordered him. "I'm teaching you how to spit roast boar legs."

The elf frowned at the other woman, her eyes hardening. "He's not meant to be taught anything other than how to kill the enemy."

Marin stuck out her tongue and made a long flatulent sound at the elf's back as Authril returned to carve more strips off the boar carcass. "Tough," Marin yelled. "I'm not part of the army and, except for you, they're not here to stop me." She swung her attention back to him. "Sit, already."

He slowly sank to the ground next to the woman. "I don't—"

"Just listen. It's not really the fire that's cooking it, you see?" She nodded at the rotating chunks of pork. "Sure the flames touch, but it's the heat they put out that's doing most of the work here. Now…"

Dylan remained silent as she continued to explain. It all sounded very familiar to his old teachings of thermal conductivity. Most of the principles didn't seem all that different to what he'd done to the enemy spellster, just over a longer time and on a smaller scale.

"I think I have a rough idea of it," he eventually said, finally cutting her off. Focusing on the fire, he cupped a shield over both it and the meat. It was a fine balance leaving enough space near the ground for fresh air to enter as well as keeping the barrier porous enough for smoke to escape.

Marin jerked back, eyeing the barrier between her and the food. "How is that supposed to help?"

He took up the handle and resumed turning. "Like you said, heat cooks it. My shield can hold most of that heat in."

"You mean it'll work like an oven? Yes!" Flinging her arms around his shoulders, she planted a kiss on his cheek. "You're such a quick learner."

"Wow," Dylan breathed, rubbing his cheek. "What do I get if I actually cook it?"

Laughing, she ruffled his hair and sat back. "Dinner, of course." She motioned him to lift the barrier and threw another bit of wood on the fire. "It's a shame there aren't more spellsters I could teach." Gasping, she grabbed his arm. "Do you think—? I mean, I'm not likely to go back home, not if there's nothing between me and Udynea, but do you think your tower would let me teach spellsters how to survive in the forest?"

"Honestly? I don't think so." It was possible the orders not to teach leashed spellsters how to survive on their own came from the overseers. Or even the king. "We're rather discouraged from thinking about beyond the tower walls."

They sat and waited for the boar legs to cook, taking turns rotating them. Small tendrils of steam escaped the barrier, tweaking his nose. Even when the tower cooks served them meat, pork wasn't usually a staple. It smelt good.

Soon, they were joined by Authril and Katarina. The hedgewitch gave a single appreciative sigh and settled down to watch the forelegs cook. Authril, on the other hand, looked ready to devour the meat half raw.

Night settled and his stomach was growling by the time Marin declared the meat ready. They didn't stand on formality, or use utensils, opting to eat straight from the bone. It was a little gamier than he remembered and a little charred near the feet, but not terribly bad.

Authril didn't appear to mind the flavour as she tore off great chunks of pork with her teeth with much abandon. He wasn't even sure she chewed all that long before swallowing and moving on to the next bite.

Marin watched the elf, her expression one of sick fascination. "You put away a lot of food for someone so small."

Authril glared at her over the boar leg. One side had already been stripped to the bone.

"Elves usually do," Dylan said, earning him a portion of the woman's glare. "Especially meat." He recalled quite fondly the way his elven friends would fall upon their evening meals like ravenous wolves, devouring all on their plates and scrounging off their nearby human companions for more.

Katarina, having eaten her fill, stood and disappeared into their tent with a farewell nod in their direction. Marin made a few more adjustments to the drying rack before joining the hedgewitch, leaving him on watch with strict instructions to keep the fire burning.

The warrior watched him over the leg she still munched, her sea-green eyes narrowing as the other woman left the fireside. "You're staring again."

His gaze swiftly dropped to his own half-eaten meal, almost forgotten in his hands. "My apologies. I didn't mean to." He risked a glance up to check that she was still looking in his direction. "You just rather remind me of the women back in the tower."

Those luminous eyes narrowed further, turning sharper than any blade. "If the word beautiful passes your lips, I'll punch you."

He grinned. "Would you settle for gorgeous, then?"

She stiffened, the leg of pork almost slipping from her hands. A flush of pink darkened the fair skin between her freckles. She turned her face, just as he caught her eyes turning glassy with tears. "Stop that right now."

Frowning, Dylan ran their conversation through his head. Admittedly, he hadn't known the woman long, but he couldn't see anything inherently wrong in anything he had said. Of course, the words didn't always matter. There were far too many variables to try guessing which line he'd inadvertently crossed. "I meant no offence. I just—" There hadn't been any heat behind her voice, the words more a plea than a command. "If you'd prefer I didn't call you that word, would you be offended if I used handsome? Or perhaps imposing? Terrifyingly commanding, even?"

She eyed him as if trying to solve a particularly difficult blacksmith's puzzle. "Exactly what are you expecting to happen with your poor attempts at flattery? I'm not the type of woman to swoon into a man's arms because he flashes his stupidly charming smile at me."

He shuffled across the ground until their legs touched. "I've a charming smile?" He hadn't heard that line for some years. Although the last person to say it had been a man.

"I believe there was a 'stupidly' in there somewhere."

Dylan grinned. She had tried to mask the inflection, but amusement crept through her words. "So there was. My mistake. As to what I expected?" He shrugged. "Nothing really. A smile, perhaps?" It had been a rough few days. For the both of them. Grinning stupidly, he bumped her shoulder with his own and whispered, "Deep down, you and I both know you want this scrawny arse."

A great peal of laughter escaped her lips before she could stop it. "That was terrible." She shoved him, tipping him onto his side. "If you think I would sleep with the likes of you after that, then you're dead wrong."

The likes of him? Was she like Marin, then? Preferring women, just less inclined to let him down gently. Still, being uninterested in men hadn't been the only reason an elven woman would turn him down. He'd weathered several lashings from sharp tongues purely because he was human. And Authril was clearly a little uneasy around his magic, so there was also his spellster status to consider. Maybe it was all three?

Sitting up, Dylan brushed off his sleeve. It was nice to know where he stood on that, even if getting her into his bed hadn't been his intention. "That may be so, but still..." He picked a wayward leaf from his hair. "I made you laugh."

"That you did." She wiped a tear from the corner of her eye and beamed at him. Her crying, even though a source of joy, had turned her face a patchwork of freckled red and white. "And I needed that. Thank you."

He flashed another of his supposedly charming smiles. "Anytime."

They returned to eating in silence. Authril finished first, the bone bare in every place her teeth could reach.

Dylan offered up the rest of his meal, watching as she wordlessly took it and methodically stripped the remaining flesh. The ease in her actions was oddly disconcerting. He didn't expect her to savage his throat in his sleep but, like most elves, he could imagine it wouldn't be difficult.

Clearing his throat, he waited until he had Authril's full attention. "I won't pry—honestly, you can tell me to shove it—but I take it there's a personal reason behind your dislike of... *that* word?"

She nodded. "I'd a friend amongst the mercenary company." She fell into silence, frowning. "I suppose the more appropriate term would be my lover. He used to call me every compliment under the sun."

Used to. Dylan stared into the fire, mentally kicking himself. "I'm sorry," he murmured. "I didn't lose anyone close to me when they attacked." He'd been so caught up in what he hadn't been able to do to stop the enemy that he hadn't even begun to consider what Authril had gone through. "Do you know what happened to him? Did he suffer?"

Authril shook her head. "He clashed against one of their brutes. Bastard took his head clean off."

"That—" The closest relationship he had was that of his friends. He couldn't imagine how well he would've coped if one of them had been in that situation. "It couldn't have been easy to watch that."

A sarcastic grunt of air left her nose. "Well, I certainly wasn't ecstatic." She picked at the boar leg, toying with the hooves. "Danny always said that, in our line of work, death was an occupational hazard. It never really felt like a threat until that day."

Dylan nodded. He understood that feeling all too well. Everything he'd ever been told about the army and the battles against the Udynea Empire had sounded far less severe than the grim reality. "If it upsets you, I won't mention that word again." If they were going to travel together, then the last thing he needed was her mad at him.

But openness was also a requirement and, if he was honest with himself, he wasn't entirely sure what Authril would do once they reached Toptower. If he could get her to be less wary of him, and his magic, he would consider it a win.

CHAPTER 21

Tracker trudged along the road leading to Toptower. The town was no longer obscured by the forest, but that just made the gates seem even further away. They appeared to be shut, even in the middle of the day. Likely at the commander's orders.

Lullaby hobbled beside him, grunting and puffing with every other breath. They had spent several days stuck amongst the remains of the army encampment. Tracker had scrounged for supplies for hours in the fading light whilst Lullaby hovered near death. He had commandeered every scrap of cloth, even tearing it from bodies, justifying his need as greater and that rotting flesh had no need for garments.

It would've been simpler to fetch what he needed from the town, but the journey would've taken days even if he travelled laden with only necessities. He hadn't been able to bear the thought of returning to find the warhorse had succumbed to his injuries, or worse, predators. Demarn hadn't the claim of massive bears like the northern lands, but a wild pig was no less destructive. He had spent the first few nights watching as the beasts cleaned up the bodies, their squeals sharp in the darkness beyond his little fire.

Food and clean water had been harder to come by, their need for the latter answered only when the sky unleashed a torrent upon the land. It had also washed away a great deal of the ash, leaving sludge in its wake.

Blessedly, feeding Lullaby hadn't been as taxing. The army horses had been penned in the far east of the encampment, which included a surplus of grain and hay tucked beneath an awning. He didn't know what he would've done had he found nothing, had shunted the mere thought of it to one side as soon as Lullaby looked well enough to travel.

A warhorse like Lullaby required years of training, of trust. He didn't think himself capable of starting over if the animal didn't pull through, refused to dwell on the possibilities for a second more.

At least the rain had eased, giving them both a chance to dry off.

Shelter hadn't been too bad, not once he'd been able to get Lullaby back onto his feet and under the forest canopy where Tracker had stretched his tent between the trees. But journeying through the downpour would've exacerbated the horse's wound.

Tracker twisted to eye the jagged mark. It meandered down Lullaby's side, from his wither to his flank. The raw flesh had scabbed over, but the sight was no less gruesome. Hair was missing a handspan from the wound's edge, the dark skin beneath swollen, but intact. He hoped that meant recovery was an option, even if he couldn't ever ride the animal again.

Resettling his pack—a pieced-together mix of his saddlebags and strips of leather from his ruined saddle—he returned his focus to the town and its eastern entrance. There appeared to be a lot more figures walking atop the wall. The glint of untested armour suggested new recruits.

A hail sounded out from atop the wall before Tracker reached the gate. The heavy panels of wood and steel swung open enough to grant him entry. Several guards rushed to his side as he walked through, questions about the army and what they had heard tumbling out in a snarl of words.

They all halted as he held up a hand.

"I will speak to your commander at a later time." He needed to get his horse somewhere the animal could rest and as well as be cared for. That meant *The Blade and Blanket*, where Commander Rhiannon would expect to find him, should she truly need the information after the firsthand recollections from surviving soldiers.

He whistled to keep Lullaby moving. The cobblestones would be harder on the horse's legs—not too jarring if they kept up the slow pace—but they couldn't stop now they were so close.

Lullaby trailed behind him, still grunting at every step.

Despite the streets being no less packed, the civilians going about their daily business in the same pace as when he'd left, their presence drew attention. Maybe more than when he first set foot in the town. How much had they heard of the attack? None of them looked frightened.

Or perhaps this was the brave face they showed the world. He had a fair bit of experience when dealing with such masks. They couldn't last forever. All they had was hope that the Udynean army didn't return before the king sent more troops.

He entered the inn stables to the gasp of Carwyn's daughter-in-law. She hastened from the stall door to Lullaby's side, her hand hovering just shy of touching the wound. "The poor dear," she whispered. "What did this?"

"Spellster's lightning."

Her already slim lips pressed together until a thin line was the only remaining evidence of her mouth. "Monsters," she muttered, a hard edge stiffening her face. "Leave him with me, there's an excellent horse doctor about a day's ride from here, practically a miracle worker. Managed to save a mare in foal after the mare was struck in a storm this winter gone. Wasn't this injured, but I reckon if he's lasted this long, he'll only improve. I'll send for her."

"You have my utmost gratitude, my dear."

She finally turned her attention to him, her dark eyes narrowing. No doubt at his dishevelled appearance. Clasping his head within her firm grip, she turned him this way and that. "*You* look more ready to fall down than your horse, Sir Hound. I recommend you pop yourself into a warm bed this instant."

Chuckling, Tracker freed himself enough to give a salute. "As you command."

She shot him an unimpressed look, then flapped her hands to shoo him out of the stables. "Food and rest is the best thing for both of you right now. I will oversee your horse. *You* tend to you."

Having no stance to argue with, he left Lullaby in her care and stumbled his way through the inn doors. The closer he got, the more his feet dragged. Now he had reached his destination, he no longer had to be vigilant. It seemed his refusal to rest was looking to take its toll.

Once inside, he slumped against the bar counter, his backside finding its way onto a stool through sheer luck. "I need a drink," he said to the man tending the room, barely taking in just who he spoke to. "And a place to sleep."

Emyr eyed him as one might a ghost. "Are you all right?" He filled a mug with mead, keeping it just out of Tracker's reach. "The guard commander came in over a week ago demanding my father. He's spent all that time shoring up the westward defences for some attack. Meanwhile, we've survivors coming in claiming the whole encampment was turned to ash."

Tracker nodded, mostly to himself, as he snatched the mug. He had forgotten the last order given to Commander Rhiannon had been to harness Carwyn's army expertise. "The attack was over before I got there." He took a long swallow of mead, trying to wash the taste of ash from his mouth. "Burnt half the encampment, slaughtered the rest like diseased cattle."

"Then, there's no hope."

"Regretfully, I cannot speak of it either way." No Udynean troops had appeared during his time there. The only hint of magic, beyond the fading residue coating the encampment, came not from the east, but the ghostly whispers of whatever spellster still wandered the forest to the north.

"But what if—?" Emyr's head jerked up, his attention diverted to the figure entering the inn.

The commander's familiar footsteps across the floorboards answered the question of who.

"Thank the gods you're back," she breathed, settling on the stool next to him. "You were gone for almost a week. We stopped getting survivors days ago, thought you might've..." Her gaze ran over him, her lips fighting to remain neutral as she clearly marked his appearance. "Are you all right? What happened?"

"Bastards wounded my horse." His grip tightened around the mug. The mead within sloshed about, droplets spilling out. He might've slaughtered the lot, but the desire for revenge still fuelled him.

"If you need to hunt them down, we've several mounts in the guard stables. You're welcome to take your pick."

"Thank you." Travelling through the forest might be easier on foot, but there was no denying he would get back to the start of the trail faster on horseback. "They have already been dealt with, but I will need to leave in the morning. There are other matters I must attend to." He needed to find the rogue spellster that had fled into the forest. They couldn't have gotten far.

Rhiannon frowned. "Surely, any trails will be cold by the time you return."

The downpour that had blanketed the land in the past few days would've washed out physical markers, but he'd more in his arsenal than most hunters.

Tracker tipped back his drink and drained half the mug's contents in one go. "Not cold enough," he said upon coming up for air. A spellster strong enough to leave a trail when the area was drenched in residual magic should be easy to sense once he returned to the spot.

Be they a loose Demarner spellster or a Udynean straggler, he would find them.

Yawning, Dylan flopped onto the blankets that made up his bed. He unbuckled his belt and toed off his boots, kicking the latter towards the tent entrance before moving on to shed his robe. Authril had taken over tonight's watch, leaving him with several blissful hours of sleep before they finally broke camp and continued their journey to Toptower.

Knowing they were set to move on felt strange. They'd only been here for three days, but he'd gotten used to sleeping on the ground, surrounded by the hush of the forest. With much of the elements kept at bay, he could almost see why Marin chose to live so far from any village.

Not that leaving wouldn't give him plenty of opportunities to listen to nature—Marin estimated that it would take roughly a week to reach Toptower—but he had no knowledge of what their next campsite would look like, or even if they would find a suitable place before darkness forced them to stop.

The faint scratch at the entrance was all the warning he had of an intruder entering his tent. Dropping his recently shed robe, Dylan scrambled about on his knees to face the tent flap, ready to attack his intruder if need be.

Had someone, despite Marin's assurance that no one could, managed to track them down? Were they here to kill him? Would intruders request entry before attacking? He'd heard no alarm from the others and Authril was...

Right in front of him.

He took in the half-dressed figure before him. The light came over her back, but it was definitely their staunch warrior. "Aren't you meant to be on watch?" They'd come across no more boars, or much in the way of any big wildlife, but no one was willing to take a chance that this night might be different.

The tent flap fell, throwing them into relative darkness. He blinked hurriedly, willing his eyes to adjust faster. When the elf was still a shadow against the canvas, he coaxed a tiny ball of light into being.

She stood there, her hands on her hips and her legs planted. "We'll be fine, but you said things a few days back that suggested you might have a desire to sleep with me." Her gaze roamed the tent, the ground, everywhere but directly at him. "I'm here to take you up on that offer." Those sea-green eyes fell on him. Hot and wanting.

Dylan stared at her. His mouth moved, but nothing came out. This was the last thing he would've expected from the woman.

"Are you still willing or are you content standing there catching flies?"

"I... Yes." Realising the ambiguity of his answer, he tried to make himself clearer. "That is to say— I mean... *now*?" Was this a trap? Some sort of joke? She didn't actually want to sleep with him, did she?

Rolling her eyes, Authril crept closer. "I wouldn't be here if I wasn't meaning to do it now." Her lips moulded against his. Sweet and delicate. Much like the rest of her face, it was a place where refined bones and soft angles hadn't been overlaid with raw power.

He leant into the kiss. His hands wandered across her shoulders, slipping down her arms. They sought out the hem of her undershirt, lifting the fabric to brush his fingers over the warm, silken skin beneath.

Just when he'd managed to gather up enough of the light linen to remove it, she sat back.

Dylan withdrew his hands. Had he gone too far?

A small smile graced her lips. She slowly peeled off the undershirt before moving on to the rest of her attire.

He sat back on his heels, his heart thundering in his ears as he watched the increasingly-naked beauty before him. He'd spied Authril a few times without all her armour and padding. But now? *By the gods.* Even with just the light undershirt gone, he realised he'd been ill-prepared for what lay beneath.

The slim frame he had long associated with elves had vanished, no doubt moulded by years of training and battle. Like upon her face, freckles speckled her body in a mighty dusting of brown stars across the lightly-tanned sky, collecting at her shoulders and thighs. Scars also decorated her skin, varying between tiny slashes to what must have once been a nasty burn on her right shoulder. Each one silently begging to be kissed.

She knelt before him, seemingly ashamed. "Sorry I'm no great beauty."

"No—?" He shook himself. "Why would you think that? Because of these?" With one wide sweep of his arm, he drew her against him. He kissed along the scars, adoring each one in turn. The muscles beneath his lips were firm, leaving him in no doubt that this was a warrior's body, beautiful and strong in equal measure. "They just show that you've lived. That you fought." His lips reached the puckered skin covering her shoulder. He gently lipped and pecked his way across the area, making for her neck. "And won."

Authril trembled in his hands. The warmth of her breath heated his face only moments before their lips found one another. He sank his fingers into her hair, relishing the taste of her as their tongues twirled around each other. She tugged at his clothes, growling and biting his lip.

Dylan obeyed the request, leaving her grasp long enough to strip his undertunic and smallclothes.

Feeling watched, he glanced up to find her tracking his every movement. The depths of those sea-green eyes burned with such hunger, uncoiling a familiar warmth within his gut.

He tried to be gentle in coaxing her to lie down, misjudging the distance to the ground by an inch or so. She bumped onto his bedding with a shocked squeak, a sound he hadn't expected to ever come from her.

A groan bubbled in his throat and he buried his face into his palms. There went his chance.

Muffled giggling drew his hands down.

Authril lay propped on her elbows, smiling up at him. "Oops," she snickered.

He grinned. That she could face his clumsiness and laugh only fuelled his desire for her. "Sorry," he said, lowering himself on top of her with less incident. He adorned her neck in tiny kisses, relishing the little purrs vibrating her throat as he drank in her scent.

His gaze lifted to her lips, still curved in humour, then to the heavily lidded eyes that watched him from between thick lashes.

Dylan slithered down the bed, worshipping every inch of her body along the way. He cupped her breast, a nice handful and typical for an elf. His mouth closed around the other nipple, eking out a breathy squeak from her lips. Her fingers dug into his hair, trembling but gentle. His other hand drifted down, seeking to tease.

She rose beneath him as his searching fingers brushed over light curls. A sigh ghosted through her lips when his hand slid further still, fast replaced with whimpers as he toyed with her. Authril wriggled and puffed, her hips lifting at every touch.

Usually, he'd let a little spark of magic drift along his fingertips, no more than the slightest buzz of lightning, but Authril had already proven skittish at the sight of his abilities. He doubted she would readily welcome the additional pleasure his power brought.

His finger slowly slipped inside, curling, seeking. Tiny moans escaped her lips. Her thighs squeezed his arm and he groaned against her stomach. The thought of those legs closing around his waist was almost too much. Dylan slid further down her body, settling between her knees, kneading the hard flesh of her thighs.

Her hips rolled at his touch. Moaning, she spread her legs wide. He didn't need to be told twice.

Dylan sank his head between her legs to the sound of her hitched breath. The first brush of his tongue was rewarded with a soft moan. Encouraged, he dove deeper, licking and sucking like a madman. Searching for what she enjoyed the most and using that newfound knowledge to its fullest.

Authril huffed and panted at every stroke, groaned at each suck and gentle nip. Every sound collected in his gut, creating a pool of steadily rising heat. Every sweep had him wanting to please her more, to have her body sing.

Her thighs shifted and squeezed around him. It wasn't enough. He slipped a finger deep inside, crooking it to the sound of her soft, drawn-out gasp. She arched, gifting him easier access.

Her breath quickened, turning into a bevy of groans and hushed pleading that he couldn't quite make out. Still, he kept it up, delving deeper. Determined. His hips ground into the bedding, desperate for his own release even as he sought to give Authril hers.

She grasped his hair, directing his actions. Dylan followed, pausing whenever she wordlessly indicated he'd hit the right spot until that direction indicated she wanted him elsewhere. She trembled, her hold on him continuously adjusting. Her legs closed on his shoulders, pinning him in place.

Dylan slowed, savouring the taste of her as each sweep of his tongue increased the pressure of her thighs. He slid his hands beneath her rump, lifting her, and descended on that little bundle of flesh. She hovered so very close to the edge that it wouldn't take much to push her over. He flattened his tongue, lapping at the spot. *One... Two... Thr—*

Sure enough, her legs tightened around his head, her hips rising, pushing herself against his face. Her long fingers slid over his shoulders, digging into his flesh, entwining themselves in his hair. His name came on the wings of a gasp.

Small though it was, the sound was almost his undoing.

Patience, he reminded himself. Dylan kissed along her inner thigh, giving his heart time to slow down as he listened for her breathing to return to normal. When it did, he surfaced to kiss his way up her body, halting only to lavish her breasts with his attention.

He licked and nibbled across her skin, rolling his tongue around the already taut nipples. His hands stroking and kneading what his mouth couldn't reach with equal abandon.

Once again, her fingers slipped into his hair, this time coaxing his head up. He eagerly complied, continuing to adorn her skin in kisses. His mouth drew level with her neck. Her heart pounded so heavily, he felt the pulse of it against his lips.

Authril stared up at him, her eyes glittering with the desire for more. Such a strong pull he couldn't dare deny. Her knees slid up his thighs, making his limbs shiver at the gentle pressure of his length against her abdomen. She smirked. Her lower leg hooked behind him, rocking his hips.

Dylan gasped. He fumbled between them, seeking entry. Each brush of the tip against her body sent a fresh wave of pleasure through him, turning his limbs to water.

He was trembling with pure need by the time he slipped inside her.

She bit her lip, a moan tumbling out as he moved, and the world around him dimmed to just them. He forgot about being in the forest, about the others not so far away. He even forgot they were in a tent.

Her nails raked down his back, gripping his buttocks, seeking to draw him closer. He tried to comply, but there was no more room to be had. She clung to him, her face buried in his shoulder. He felt her body tense beneath him and—

Dylan found himself flipped onto his back.

Authril straddled him, wicked determination moulding her face. She sat back and rocked, causing little spikes of pleasure.

So that's how you want to play it. Laughter bubbled in his chest. He didn't mind this position as it left his hands free to traverse her body. Dylan cupped handfuls of the elf's rear, then slid his grip to her hips to aid their movement, matching her pace. "You should've said you wanted to do it this way."

Her fingers clumsily brushed across his chin and squished his nose before settling on his lips. Was she trying to silence him? He slowly drew her hand away. If she wanted him to be quiet, there were far better ways to muffle noise.

His mouth returned to her breasts, teasing with both teeth and tongue. Encouraging fingers slid into his hair. The pace of her movements increased in force, bouncing her body, driving his hips into the ground no matter how hard he pushed back.

She shuddered, tightening around him. A soft, hushed moan filled the tent and heated his blood.

The world shrunk further. It was all pure sensation now. His body thrust into hers, moving mostly of its own accord, chasing release before she demanded he stopped. The edge, that bright and warm bliss of completion, lay so close. He lifted her hips, ready to ram himself to the hilt and tumble over the edge.

He'd just enough coherent thought left in him to lift her further and pull out before he did.

She gasped, the gentle whine leaving her lips almost enough to have him drive back into her.

Dylan slid free just as he fell over the edge. He lay there, with her sprawled atop him, waiting for his heart to stop pounding and his breath to return in full.

Slowly, Authril shifted, lifting her weight from his chest. "You stopped," she puffed, settling on his stomach.

"I had to." He always did. He knew how children were made. The tower was very explicit on that. The healers had ways to terminate an unborn child, although the technique was rarely used as it was an uncomfortable experience for everyone. He'd learnt such a procedure for Nestria's sake, but it was something he never wanted to repeat. Ever.

Authril nestled her head on his chest. Her soft humming—close but not quite on the verge of purring—filled the tent.

Dylan gently massaged her hip, content to let her lay there for as long as she wanted. Snuggling after sex was an act he scarcely got to enjoy. At least in the rare moments where a bed was involved. It didn't usually last long owing to them having to part ways before the guardians found out, but here? Maybe, she would stay.

With his lids growing heavy, he groped for the blanket and, once found, draped it over them. His eyes slid shut.

A soft snore ran through his nose, jolting him awake. Should he not see that she returned to her watch? His hand shifted to rub across her back.

A purr emanated from her, vibrating through his chest.

He would wake her shortly. They could afford a moment more. Dylan lay in the dark, counting the seconds as he stared at the tent roof whilst listening to her purring. Each blink was taking longer and longer to make. Outside, the forest seemed quiet.

His head lolled to one side. *Just a little while…*

~ ~ ~

The chill air nipped at Dylan's bare skin, rousing him from a dreamless sleep. Shuddering, he rolled over, seeking warmth in the other body that shared the tent.

The only thing that greeted him was the dry coolness of the tent floor.

Puzzled, Dylan sat up. The grey light of predawn stained the tent sides. Outside, he caught the birds chirping and whistling their morning cries.

No Authril.

Had it been a dream? His memory was certain she had entered his tent last night. His body insisted she'd done more than that.

He scrubbed at his face and glanced down. Well, he was most certainly naked and didn't tend to sleep in such a state, keeping on his smallclothes even through the hottest of nights. That just left the possibility of her fleeing whilst he slept. Not the best option, but he had experienced worst.

Dressing, he stumbled out of the tent to duck behind a tree and relieve himself. Having dealt with nature, he took in the camp's half-dismantled state. They had packed the rations last night, parcelling them out amongst everyone to limit the risk of their entire supply being damaged or lost in one foolhardy move, but he hadn't expected the other tent to already be collapsed and in the process of being folded.

Dylan glanced over his shoulder at what had been his accommodation for the past three nights. Whilst his pack was neatly nestled inside, waiting only for him to put it on, his tent was another matter. He gathered taking the poles out would collapse it, he just wasn't certain how to do the rest.

Authril sat near the remains of their campfire, chewing on a bit of the dried pork that dangled from one corner of her mouth and tending to her sword as she waited for the others to finish packing.

He strolled over to stand at her side and cleared his throat. "I was wondering if I could get your assistance in packing my tent."

Amazing how much she flinched at such an innocent request. With her possessing superior hearing, he doubted he had startled her. Did she feel guilty for leaving him to wake up alone after they'd been intimate? A ridiculous reason, but then he wasn't entirely sure what light casual sex was seen in outside of the tower.

"Can't," she mumbled around a mouthful of jerky. "Eating."

"You can eat whilst we walk. We can't, however, leave until everything is packed."

Shrugging, she carried on with rubbing a stone over her sword, seeming a little too focused on her task.

"Very well." Dylan settled cross-legged on the ground next to her. "Let's talk about last night, then." If there was a problem, a boundary he had overstepped, he needed to know so he wouldn't repeat such a mistake.

Pinkness bloomed in full force across her face. "Yes, well. You caught me in a moment of weakness. It won't happen again." The sword was returned to its sheath. "Besides, you wouldn't want it right now. I'd explain, but I doubt you'd even understand woman problems let alone wish to hear about them."

A small smile curved one side of his mouth. He understood a great deal more of her rambling than the woman credited him with. "Does it hurt much?"

The incredulous look she gave him almost had him laughing.

He contained his mirth as well as he could and idly scratched the underside of his jaw, marking how he would need to shave tomorrow. "Both of my oldest friend's get them." Although, Henrie's affliction, as the man called it, didn't seem nearly as bad as when Nestria's time of the month arrived. "One of them gets the most horrific cramps I've ever witnessed. Sometimes they're so bad that she passes out." Seeing Nestria prone on the floor and surrounded by healers trying to free her from the agony had been a terrifying sight to stumble upon as a teenager. The older his friend got, the worse they were. He hadn't been so useless in easing her pains for some years, but the memory wouldn't fade. "I asked her what it felt like once. I got a swift kick in the groin for my troubles." He grimaced at the memory, but figured the warrior was the type of person who would find it amusing.

Sure enough, laughter shook Authril's shoulders.

"So, every month I used to take the pain away." He leant closer. "I could do it for you. It's quite simple."

Biting her lip, she shuffled out of reach as if expecting him to try without her permission. A reasonable assumption given he had healed her arm under dubious consent, but this was somewhat different than an injury that could've left her crippled if not attended. "That's not necessary."

"Please, you've done so much for me and the others. Helping you is the least I can do." The only thing he could do to repay her, especially when she could've easily ended his life at any time.

She stared at him for a while, those sea-green eyes narrowing. Was she imagining this as some sort of trick? He couldn't see how.

Finally, she nodded.

Dylan laid a hand on the small of her back. Although touch was touted as a requirement for proper, low-risk healing in the tower, it wasn't needed. Nor did that touch necessarily have to be on the affected spot. A shoulder or an arm sufficed, just not as well. He focused, drawing on the natural warmth of their bodies, directing where it flowed, soothing the area from within.

Authril gasped, then a soft purr left her lips. His reward.

Grinning, he removed his hand. Her hips tilted, instinctively following the source of her relief. "The effect will last a few days, that should be long enough. If you need me to do it again, let me know."

"Actually," she blurted, grabbing his sleeve when he went to stand.

The pinkness in her face had returned, spreading down her neck as she released his clothing. "I was wondering if you'd be agreeable to changing the current sleeping arrangement?"

"You want to share my tent?" He was certain that was her meaning, but waited for her to nod before continuing. "Of course. There's more than enough room in there for two." He had thought the three of them must be cramped in the other tent.

"Good." Smiling, Authril bounced to her feet. "Come on, I'll show you how to pack a tent." With that, she strode off in the direction of the shelter, leaving him scrambling to catch up.

CHAPTER 23

Dylan remembered passing through Toptower, although he hadn't seen much of the place. Back then, he had been weary and suffering from the sun-sickness brought on by days of travel with little shelter. Both were improved once his hound escort allowed him to use his magic to heal, but he still hadn't entered the town.

This time, if they had to enter, he was determined to see more than the outer walls.

Toptower sat on a hill, the town's many buildings clustered around the very structure that was responsible for its name. His history lessons told him it was once considered the most heavily fortified village in the kingdom, able to withstand an attack from even the most powerful of spellsters.

Dylan eyed the walls as they trudged closer. He rather doubted the old fortifications would hold up against common siege weapons much less magic. Yet, this was the last defence standing between the Udynea Empire and the vast unprotected lands of Demarn.

Their little group had joined the road some hours back, travelling alongside people and carts with the same goal of entering the northern gates before sundown. With the spellster tower in the opposite direction, their destination seemed counterintuitive, but their supplies were dwindling. Heading for Oldmarsh without replenishing them could put them in a worst state.

Unlike the others, his passage didn't go unnoticed. Being so close to the army camp, he supposed his attire was more than a little conspicuous. He could perhaps pass himself off as a priest to the unknowing, the cut of his robe wasn't that different from their garb, although he knew of no ranking that had them in such a colour. Nor could he be sure how many of those who watched him could identify an *infitialis* collar much less the lack of one.

They neared the gates and Authril dropped back from where she led them to march at his side. "Keep close to me," she whispered. "If anyone asks, I'm your warden."

Dylan tucked up the collar of his robe, ensuring it covered his bare neck. "Understood." The last thing he wanted was to draw even more attention. If they'd been able to get away with it, he would've opted against venturing anywhere near here.

They passed through the gates with only a cursory glance from the guards who seemed to have more on their minds than one more group of people amongst the throng trying to enter. Did they know what had become of the army? Surely, they'd seen the smoke. Maybe even sent someone to investigate.

That could be a problem. Probably for the better if they didn't mention where they'd come from until they knew the full situation, if at all. Night would come in a few hours. Their goal was to gather what food they could, find an affordable place to sleep and be ready to leave at first light.

On the other side of the wall, the town roared with life. The garble of noise hit him first, deafening after a week of travelling through the forest. His shield sputtered to life, there for an instant and gone as he hastened to banish it. The shield hadn't been big, barely an inch or two from his skin.

Dylan glanced around, relaxing only after confirming no one had noticed. He would need to be mindful of his power, keep it suppressed as much as possible. His attire could already be enough to alert people of his abilities, letting his nerves dictate what his magic did would only cause further panic.

Slowly, his ears were able to separate the sounds. The creak and rattle of carts bumping through the streets. The steady clop of hooves and the patter of booted feet. The mumble of dozens speaking at once. The piercing cries of merchants. He didn't recall it being this harsh before.

His gaze ran over the heads of those crowding the streets. The prickling sensation of being watched lingered in the back of his mind. He shrugged his shoulders, hoping to shake the feeling. Either someone was intent on keeping him in their sights or he was getting paranoid. *It's just for tonight.* All he had to do was play the part of still being leashed, limit his magic to nothing and, hopefully, they'd be on their way to Oldmarsh before anyone could alert a hound.

Authril took the lead once they were clear of the bottleneck the gate made of the crowd, taking off in the distinct stride of someone with a clear destination in mind. She marched them by stall owners hawking their wares, down streets where the only sounds were the flap of clothes drying on lines high above, and into a dead-end where grubby children in tattered clothes squealed and tumbled about.

She stopped before one of the many single-storey buildings. A sign reading *The Drunken Pilgrim* hung over the door. An inn. Dylan had vague memories of staying in one at Oldmarsh.

They entered the building to be shrouded in the watery, sputtering candlelight. He blinked hurriedly, trying to adjust his eyesight. There wasn't much to the inside. Even full of tables and a handful of drinking patrons, the place had a distinct hollowed-out look. There was a faint hint of coal smoke in the air, overlaying the more familiar woodsy smell of fire.

"I don't think I've ever been in here," Marin muttered. "Cosy-looking place, isn't it?" She rolled her eyes upward and wrinkled her nose. "If you don't mind the whole entombed feeling anyway."

Dylan was inclined to agree with the hunter. The space would've looked better if it was lighter, but that would've taken some scrubbing and for the candles, set in the big iron wrought wheels hanging from the ceiling, to throw more illumination than wax. The high windows running along one side of the room being blackened by years of smoke didn't help. Much of the room's light came from an open fire near the far wall. Even it burned with a dim, sooty glow.

His eye was drawn to the walls above the hearth where carvings adorned the vaulted stonework. Primitive runes and swirls ran from wall to ceiling and back again. *Wards against evil.* Or, more likely, against the all-too-possible threat of the encroaching Udynean spellsters.

That he stood in the room was proof the markings weren't worth the time taken.

"Hush," Authril said to the hunter. "If you've been to Toptower before, then you know there's only two inns we can afford and, believe me, you don't want me stepping into the other one." She marched up to the bar and banged a fist on the counter.

An elven woman, not much taller than Authril, tottered through the door on the other side of the bar. Her dark, leathery hands gripped her apron, clearly hiding something within its folds. She eyed their group with a distinct lack of trust. "Can I help you?"

Authril leant closer to the woman, lowering her voice as she said, "I was told you're acquainted with the leader of Danny's Cutthroats?"

"Danny?" The woman's face grew even more suspicious. "Jilted you has he? Well, I'm afraid you won't find him here." She patted the warrior's cheek. "Don't take it the wrong way though, love. He's always been a sucker for a pretty face, but you can't tame a rogue like him on looks alone. He's got the wanderlust in his soul. Much like his father, bless him."

Authril shook his head. "I'm not after him, madam. Did Len not get the word to you? He died last month. The Udyneans got him." Her voice dropped. "They got them all."

"Oh." The woman clutched at her chest. "Danny…"

"I'm part of his company. All that's left of it, actually. He always used to say that, if we ever needed a place to sleep in Toptower, you would be the one to give us a fair deal." Authril rifled through her belt pouch, withdrawing a small bag. She tipped the contents onto the bar top to the gentle clink of metal. "I don't have much, but my friends and I need a place to spend the night."

The woman eyed them over Authril's shoulder, her gaze lingering a little longer on him than Dylan would've liked. Did she recognise his robes as being army issue? More importantly, did she know of any hounds in the area? "I can't give you a room for that, love," she replied to the warrior, her attention still on him. "There's a fair deal and there's beggaring an old woman. If Danny's gone, then this business is all I've got, and it's bad enough around here what with all those rumours of young women going missing and—"

"It's a big place," Marin said. "People must go missing all the time."

"That they do," said one of the nearby patrons. A human, rotund and balding, his pasty, pockmarked face reddened from drink. "We get all kinds coming through here. Army deserters are the worst sort, spreading lies about escaping the end of the world, stealing anything that's tied down. They don't usually take off with young women, though. That was the work of some brothel up in the rich quarter. I hear the guards are—"

"Shut your trap, you old sot." Barely batting an eye, the woman withdrew a cork from her apron pockets and threw it at the man, hitting him square on the head. "These good folk don't want to hear your gossip." She turned back to them to pat Authril on the shoulder. "Ignore him, he's had so much to drink that he'll fall asleep soon enough. But to the matter at hand. If you're desperate for a roof over your head, I've a few straw mats near the hearth that aren't seeing any use. In memory of my Danny."

"We'll take them," Authril declared.

"Wonderful." The coin was swiped off the bar and into the woman's apron before the word had finished leaving her lips. "Just be sure to be in before midnight. That's when I lock up." Giving another glare to the man who spoke earlier, she shuffled back through the door.

The man watched her in turn, his head bobbing and a distant look taking his eye.

Army deserters. Dylan supposed that wasn't too uncommon. But ones mentioning the end of the world? "Do you think more than us survived the attack?" he asked Authril.

She shook her head. "Because of what he said?" She jerked a thumb at the man, who now had his face planted on the table. "I wouldn't take the ramblings of a drunk man as serious without other evidence. I was there. I *saw* them rip through that place. No one could've survived."

"*You* did," he reminded her. He hadn't been at the main encampment long, but he recalled the horses being near the road leading to Toptower. And the spellster they'd encountered had clearly been in pursuit of someone.

Authril frowned but said nothing further. Her brows lowered thoughtfully.

Marin cleared her throat. "If we're going to have any hope of boosting our supplies, I better see if my usual traders are in town." She patted her pack, a slightly bigger and fuller version of what they all carried, crammed full of pelts, horns and other assorted bits.

Authril nodded. "I think I'll visit a blacksmith, see if I can't get a few dents hammered out of this." She banged on her somewhat tarnished breastplate. "We should meet back here at sundown. That should give us an hour or two."

"If it's all the same," the hedgewitch said, eyeing the drunk man the innkeeper had hit. "I'll linger here. I want to hear more about these disappearances. We hardly ever have such things happening in Dvärghem."

Marin wrinkled her nose. "I don't think you'll get much out of him, but suit yourself." Smiling up at Dylan, she hooked her hand into the crook of his arm. "Come on. I'm saving you before she sucks all of us into listening to some drunken man's rousing rambles. Besides, I want to see if I can find a cloak that fits that beanpole of a frame."

Eager to have something decent to shield him from the elements, he allowed Marin to tow him out of the inn. Maybe they would also get lucky and find a place to exchange his robe for something nondescript. If Katarina did happen to garner anything important from the man, they'd plenty of time to hear about it after they were settled before the inn's hearth.

Tracker rode through Toptower's western city gates, waving his thanks to the guards for admitting him entry at such an early hour. His search insofar as encountering the spellster he hunted had rendered itself fruitless, but he had a general idea of where they headed. *Oldmarsh.*

Normally, he wouldn't believe a Demarn spellster capable of traversing the forest, not if they were from the tower as he believed, but this one wasn't alone. The footprints he had found suggested someone armoured along with another. His searching had led to other revelations and the certainty of the group settling into an easterly direction.

It would take them a while on foot, even if they had adequate supplies, a possibility he had to factor in after discovering a hunter's hut whilst following the spellster's trail. Forging through the trees after them would've eventually led Tracker to their side, but skirting the forest and catching the group on the other side diminished the risk of breaking his horse's leg. The gelding was definitely not on par with Lullaby's training, but Tracker had witnessed nothing about the spellster that suggested such a risk to his mount was necessary.

He would need to find Commander Rhiannon before he set off tomorrow, see about paying for the horse, or find out where he could purchase one, even if it was from the surrounding farms. As much as he hated leaving Lullaby behind, there was no chance the warhorse had recovered enough to bear a saddle, much less Tracker's weight. He wasn't sure if Lullaby ever could again.

His mount skittered sideways as the gates slammed shut behind them. Tracker corrected the animal's path, urging them onwards. More people crowded the streets than usual. Most went about their business, carrying loads or pushing handcarts.

Every alleyway he passed had a handful of dishevelled people lingering in them. Those who couldn't find such shelter huddled against buildings, tucking themselves into whatever nook granted them refuge. They eyed his passage with the tenseness of a bowstring ready to snap. The closer he got to the familiar section of the upper quarter, the more watched he felt.

Where had they all come from? No town was without its homeless, but Toptower hadn't this many when he'd left a week ago. Were they from the surrounding hamlets, thinking a walled settlement would protect them more than their homes?

How much did the townsfolk know of the army's fate? He should've asked the commander what had become of the survivors before he'd left to hunt down the spellster. Keeping rumours to a minimum should've been one of the guards' major concerns. If the Udyneans attacked, Toptower was little more than a gift.

Tracker halted outside *The Blade and Blanket*. Judging by the noise coming from within, the inn was packed. Not unusual for the place, if a little on the early side for such revelry. With everything else he'd seen, the joyous din put him on edge. He hitched his horse out the front, nodding to the stable hand who watched over the animals already there, and strode inside.

The music and dancing assaulted his ears the very second he opened the door. He paused in the entrance, waiting for his senses to grow accustomed to the bang of drums and the rhythmic pounding of feet upon the floorboards. Only then did he venture further into the building.

Just as the noise had suggested, the tavern taking up much of the inn's lower level was packed. Everywhere he looked, patrons drank or ate, diced or danced. Two women in the far corner were busy sucking each other's faces and a man near the fireplace appeared to be in the middle of a nap his spine wouldn't thank him for later.

If the majority of these people were travellers, here to escape being caught out in their less-protected homes, then they certainly weren't the sort to sit around worrying over it.

Did that also mean there were no spare beds to be had? He was no stranger to sleeping out in the elements, and would likely face such a situation in the coming days, but the comfort of even a simple cot was always welcomed.

Tracker continued his perusal of the room in search of a seat or the inn's owner, whichever came first, spying the town's commander of the guard comfortably settled at one of the tables. He waited until Rhiannon's gaze idly swung from the dancing to his section of the room before getting her attention.

Recognition had the woman launching to her feet. "You're back!" She waved him over, beaming as he settled next to her. "I didn't expect you to return so soon!" she shouted over the noise, eyeing him, then their surroundings, before leaning closer. "Did you find *them?*"

He shook his head. "I took too long."

Rhiannon laid a hand on his shoulder, stilling his tongue. "Let's go somewhere quieter." Gesturing for him to stand, they crossed to the inn stairs, pausing to snag Tracker's usual drink.

The upper level wasn't entirely silent, but the lack of people milling around the hallway and the distance they put between them and the stairs certainly helped to muffle the raucous. Rhiannon continued to lead the way until they'd reached the far side of the building where a balcony jutted above the stables.

"I've heard plenty about what happened to the army," Rhiannon said. She leant on the railing, her drink dangling precariously from her fingertips. "If I hadn't known some of them, hadn't seen the smoke with my own eyes, I'm not sure how much I would believe."

Tracker joined her near the railing. The sight the balcony showed wasn't the most thrilling, tall building crowded either side and the street the inn sat on was empty save for a few drunken civilians weaving their way home.

The commander ducked to peer at him, the act almost putting her onto her knees. "The spellster you hunt? Are they on our side or *theirs?*"

"Ours, I believe." That belief didn't mean they were Demarner. At worst, he was chasing a Udynean spy.

"And if I asked for details, would you tell me?"

Bowing his head, Tracker obliged Rhiannon's curiosity, frowning into his mead the whole time he relayed the past few days.

It should've been easy.

Retracing his steps hadn't been an issue, the way back faster with a fresh horse and little in the way of gear. It had still taken two days to return to the remains of the encampment, the sight no less dreary after the downpour.

Despite the rain washing away most of the signs, Tracker had rediscovered the spellster's trail leading into the forest. The footprints started off as two distinct pairs, the toes of both facing towards the army, yet bearing their weight in the heels.

A few hours of following that trail had led to a crude campsite where the duo of footprints turned into a trio. The residue of magic there had also been stronger, the spellster clearly having recovered from his fight with the Udynean lord. It also led him to the possibility of a defector. The *infitialis* collars shielded the leashed from a hound's senses unless they were given leave to use their magic, but he didn't feel any of that. The being he followed was clearly unleashed.

He'd spent a couple of days on that trail, heading north in what seemed to be their attempt to subvert Toptower. It had brought him to the doorstep of a hunter's hut. A quick survey of the place revealed no one around, with crucial belongings missing from within. Scouring the surrounding land confirmed the spellster had been here, along with the two they travelled alongside. The footprints leading away appeared to have a fourth addition, no doubt the hut's owner.

He couldn't tell if the trio had gotten lost and sought the hunter's expertise or if the hunter was an unwilling guide. But a day of following them into denser forest had led him back here.

"I will require the use of your barracks," he concluded. "Just for the night. Then I am headed for Oldmarsh." He would also like to look into whatever bathing facilities the barracks had. Who knew when he'd have another chance to slough off the travel dust? Certainly not after finding the spellster.

Rhiannon nodded, her face gaining the stiffness of someone who'd heard what they didn't want to hear. "You'll be missed. Not only by my guards." She straightened, her face growing more flushed. "But why resort to the barracks? My chamber is always open for you." She held up her hand, forestalling any protest on his part, before he could do more than part his lips. "You've been of immense help to me, giving you a proper thank you before you trot out of my life is the least I can do."

"Well, when you put it that way." He made a display of thinking it over, even though they both knew he wouldn't refuse the invitation, using that time to take several swallows of his drink. "It would be rude of me to—"

The stutter of magic tweaked his senses.

Tracker all but crushed the mug in his grip. The mead within trembled, threatening to splash over his hand. He'd been so involved with relaying the past that he almost missed what he felt in the now. *Radiant power.*

Beyond that one blip, the spellster didn't hone their abilities to any particular task. The strength, though. Was it the missing spellster the Udynean claimed had killed one of their own?

It couldn't be. If his judge on where that group would pop out was correct, then they would need to double back to wind up here.

A spy, then. One who might be strong, but not very clever.

Putting aside his mug, he silently returned to the inn's lower level, trotting down the stairs, the commander following behind. He kept an eye on the tavern entrance. With such power, the spellster had to be entering any moment.

Several people entered the tavern, none of them his target. Tracker waited for a while longer. The sensation merely continued to grow.

"Track?" Rhiannon whispered, her brows drawn tightly together. "What is it?"

"I am afraid I will be postponing a lovely evening." He turned on one heel, trying to pinpoint the direction, the act harder when it wasn't an active use of power. *From the north.* Had they reached the gates? Simple wood and iron wouldn't stop a determined spellster, but if he could keep them out of Toptower, then it would limit casualties.

That still didn't explain the strength. A passive signature of this magnitude had to mean more than one spellster. Had the Udynean army returned? Or perhaps a small group set on infiltration. *Not on my watch.*

Outside the inn and his senses were no less insistent on magic being in the area. He walked along the cobbles, forsaking his borrowed horse for his own two feet. He didn't think on where to go. He couldn't. The sensation felt everywhere and ahead all at once, like a blood drop hitting water.

The main thoroughfares were no less crowded than any other day. He wove haphazardly through the throng, his attention divided between avoiding bumping into people and the glow of recent magic. It slowed him to a crawl. He eyed the rooftops, wondering how much of a scene it would cause if he used them as his personal walkway. *Too much.* He couldn't risk startling the spellster with news of his presence.

He reached the northern gates with no further signs of magic. With the afternoon steadily approaching, the gates were largely occupied with people leaving. Guards patrolled the battlements above, their presence only noticeable due to the gleam of helmets in the torchlight. Their pacing suggested nothing of note to worry about.

Tracker's senses disagreed and they were never wrong. Magic had been used here. He felt it everywhere, plucking at every nerve in his body.

Racing up the stairway leading to the battlements, he ignored all exclamations and cries for him to explain himself. One daring man tried to bodily block his path and found himself flat on his back before he could speak.

At the top, Tracker took in the northern road.

The sight was awash with carts, some bearing goods, others empty of their wares. A few were on foot, plodding alongside the road to make room for bigger things. He shielded his eyes and peered into the distance, barely making out another cart disappearing beneath the shadow of trees. More likely a neighbouring farmer on his way back from a day selling his wares than a fleeing spellster.

He was too late.

And wrong about where the magic had been. With his thoughts no longer focused on what could wait beyond the gates, the sensation of power clearly sat at his back.

The spellster wasn't seeking to enter Toptower, they were already *in* it.

Tracker slammed his palm onto the parapet wall and spat out several curses. What was he to do now? Run around the town as if playing some warped game of Warmer whilst hoping the spellster remained in place? Toptower mightn't be the kingdom's biggest settlement, but any such search would take time.

"Sir Hound?" Captain Owain strode along the battlements to halt at Tracker's side. "Is something the matter? Can we help in any way?"

Collecting himself, Tracker faced the man. "You were amongst those manning the gates earlier today, yes?" He barely waited for the captain to nod before continuing. "Did they—did *you*—happen to notice anyone who looked like they might have been in the army?"

The captain shook his head. "The last of them arrived over a week ago. If what we've heard is true, the only gateway any others would see is in the afterlife."

Grunting, Tracker stomped his way down the stairs, the man following. "There is a spellster within these walls."

"By the gods," Captain Owain whispered. "We've no reports of suspicious sightings or people. Everyone entering looked perfectly normal."

He paused halfway down the steps to stare incredulously at the man. "I am uncertain what you think spellsters are supposed to look like, but their appearance is no different to ordinary folk." If picking them out was a matter of looks, his job would be far easier. It did explain why he occasionally needed to debunk the idea that those with atypical features were also magical.

This revelation seemed to bother the captain. "Then how do you find them?"

"We hounds have our ways." Few were of use to him if the spellster didn't use their power in this moment. If they were leashed, he would need to be almost upon them to know, but they'd also be less of a threat.

Resuming their descent, Tracker trailed after the presence of residual magic, stopping only once he stood in the middle of the street. He crouched over the spot, ignoring the curses thrown his way by those merely attempting to use the thoroughfare as intended.

The area drawing him was no bigger than the space a single person took up whilst standing. The cobblestone held no lingering heat beyond the usual, yet the radiating power was enough that Tracker expected the spellster to be right beside him.

What had they done that could've gone unnoticed in the middle of a crowded entrance, yet be so powerful?

He breathed deep, focusing on the magic lingering in the air. *The sky after a storm*. The same aroma he had encountered around the charred Udynean spellster at the army encampment.

That could only mean this was the same being he'd been tailing.

Why did you not head for Oldmarsh? The question bounced around his mind, unable to find an answer. Any leashed Demarn spellster would head for their tower, coming here was the opposite direction.

Unless the spellster *was* originally from elsewhere. Did he hunt some Udynean traitor after all?

Beyond this one patch, there was no definite path to follow. Even if the ground hadn't been covered in cobblestones, the sheer number of people and wheels passing through this gate would've already destroyed any footprints.

Standing, he strode up the street to where it forked, trying to find the direction they headed, the silent presence at his back the only indication that the captain continued to follow.

As it had done in the forest, the residue of magic tapered off until it was too weak for even him to trace. Whatever the spellster's goal within the town was, it didn't put them nearby.

A brisk game of Warmer it was.

"Send a signal to the other gates," he ordered Captain Owain.

"They are to shut immediately and remain so until my order. Not another soul is to leave Toptower until I find this spellster." He didn't like the idea of trapping someone this powerful in the same place as innocent folk, especially when he knew nothing about their nature, but it was the only way to secure them.

"It will be done." The man snapped a salute and hurried back to the gates.

The last wisp of magic suggested a south-western direction. There were a few taverns in that quarter. Not especially clean establishments, but hopefully a warm place to sleep was all the spellster wanted. If not...

Tracker unsheathed his purple dagger, examining the edge's sharpness in the afternoon light as he marched down the street. Those from the tower feared the blade. Be his prey born of this kingdom or the empire, that terror had to be universal.

And if the spellster turned out to be hostile after all? He would do what hounds did best.

Kill.

CHAPTER 24

Dylan spent a few hours following Marin through the streets as she flitted from one trader to another, selling her wares. He listened to her haggling down to the last copper, then using that money to restock their supplies. Sadly, none of them involved a cloak.

The time seemed to drag on. Eventually, boredom got the best of him and, as they met up with Authril outside the blacksmith's shop, he parted ways to stroll through the village whilst the last of the day waned.

In the twilight, the tower that gave the village its name was just a dark shape against the sky, much like the spellster tower did over the gardens and its walls.

His stomach knotted at the thought of home. He halted, leaning against the corner of a building. People scurried by, involved in their own business. The streets steadily grew more deserted, the press of evening driving people into homes flooded with light.

A pair of men clad in armour marched out one street. Dylan scrunched closer to the wall, but they marched on, their sights seemingly set on a man hurrying through a doorway on Dylan's left.

He released his breath in one go. If the guards had turned their attention his way, they might've noticed his robe, paid heed to the dark green colour, and realised he was a spellster from the king's army. Then they might've wondered why he wandered about without his warden.

He moved further around the corner, his gaze lingering on the tower in the hopes that if he stared long enough he could convince himself that *this* place housed everyone he'd ever considered as family, that he was only in the gardens and the time outside of those walls were just nightmares.

It didn't work.

The tower wasn't his home. Not anymore. Dylan scrubbed at his face. *What am I going to tell them?* What were the overseers going to think of his return? Would they make an example of him or merely send him on his way? And where would he go if they leashed him again? There was no army camp.

Wintervale. His only hope was in following Authril to the capital and joining whatever defence the crown could muster. Surely, they'd want more spellsters to replenish those they'd lost.

Sighing, Dylan let the tower slip out of view and carried on down the streets. The light began to wane as he walked aimlessly and with it, the people.

He glanced about, panic tightening his chest. He had meandered so much, both in Marin's company and on his own. What path led back to *The Drunken Pilgrim*?

It didn't help that, in the lantern-lit gloom, the streets all looked alike. He could wander for hours before finding the inn.

But sunset meant the others were all back there. They'd come looking for him, wouldn't they?

"Who am I fooling?" he muttered under his breath. If *he* had been stuck with an unleashed spellster, one who barely knew a thing about surviving in the real world, a bastard who then got himself lost in a stupid city…

Well, he probably wouldn't have the heart to leave them behind, but he'd give it some heavy consideration. And everything would be far easier for the others if he wasn't there. They could all head straight for Wintervale, Katarina to the dwarven embassy, Authril to whatever was left of their defences, whilst Marin could find herself another place to build her home.

If he couldn't find his way back on his own, then it was for the best.

Dylan breathed deep, trying to calm his mind. Beating himself up over being lost wasn't going to solve anything. He just had to think. He'd been climbing for the past hour, so that meant the inn was downhill, which didn't mean much as half the town seemed to fit the description.

What landmarks had he passed? Hadn't there been a cart on the last corner? One with a lot of barrels?

It took a little wandering and backtracking before he found an empty cart over by what looked to be a cooper's workshop. He turned the nearby corner. The street was empty save for the odd cat prowling across the rooftops, but familiar in a vague fashion. A dog barked somewhere far away. Another answered. It was a strange sound, one he'd only read about before leaving the tower.

His travels took him by an alley entrance he didn't remember passing earlier. There was the faintest of movements within, dancing on the edge of his vision and swiftly accompanied by a dull thud.

Dylan slowed, focusing on letting a small, invisible shield wrap around him. Should he just defend? Whoever lingered within the shadows, they were either confident or stupid. If he misjudged which one it was, things could turn sour very quickly.

A blast of air should do the trick, just strong enough to knock them off their feet. A relatively harmless move and once that would give him time for a more lethal attack should the need arise.

He took a few shuffling steps into the alley, searching for the source of the noise. *There!* Two little glittering specks in the gloom beyond the lantern's reach. They had to be eyes and their owner had to be aware they'd been spotted. Yet they didn't attack.

Curious, he let a small ball of light drift on the air to illuminate the figure.

A large, black cat blinked back at him. It sat on a barrel, the remains of a rat between its front paws. The creature hissed, its back arching. Before he could think to move, the cat grabbed its meal, vaulted off the barrel and slunk into the alley shadows.

Shaking his head, Dylan let the shield and light dissipate. He turned from the alley entrance. *Getting jumpy over a cat.* What was he thinking? This wasn't the forest. There were no massive boars, no enemy spellsters looking to kill him in the most painful way possible. No enemies of any kind. He was the most dangerous thing in this village. Nothing here could harm him as long as he remained vigilant.

"There you are," someone snarled from the shadows.

A hand grabbed Dylan before he could face them. He hit the alleyway wall, the back of his head thumping against the brickwork. His vision blurred, leaving him disorientated.

"Do not think about taking another step, you will not get far." The figure pinning him to the wall spoke with the vaguely similar smooth accent of Dylan's old roommate, the words tumbling off their tongue much like rocks down a hill, catching occasionally on a soft trill or hiss.

Dylan blinked, trying to refocus. The back of his head tingled as his innate healing hurried to fix whatever damage had been done.

The dagger was the first thing that came into clarity. Curved and sharp. In the lantern light illuminating the alleyway's entrance, the blade bore an insidious purple sheen. *Infitialis.* Wielded by someone who was either an alchemist or who had stolen it from one.

Barely daring to breathe, Dylan followed the blade down to the bronze hand and onwards to the elven man glaring up at him.

Was he being mugged? "If you're after money," he managed, the words warbling out. "I have none."

"Money?" An amused huff warmed Dylan's chin. As well as sharing a similarity in accents to his old roommate, the man was quite tall for an elf. Not as much as Sulin, but the top of the man's head easily reached the base of Dylan's neck. "My dear spellster, do I look like I need your paltry coin?”

“I don’t—” They knew he was a spellster? That could become problematic if the man also knew of a hound in the area. He kept his hands flattened against the wall, careful to ensure his palms faced away from the elf. “Look, I really don’t want to hurt you.”

Laughter hissed out the man’s lips, chill enough to prickle Dylan’s skin. “Hurt *me*? It has not occurred to you that attacking me will do you no good?” He pressed closer, the palm of his hand slapping against the wall. “I will make it clear for you, yes? You try and you will be dead well before myself.”

His gaze dropped to take in the man’s armour. Hard to tell with the man so close, but it looked well-made and leather. Not a common thief, then. A mercenary, perhaps?

Something about the armour’s style nagged at him. He’d seen it before, as far back as the tower. Not on the guardians, but on a single other. The hound, Fetcher, might’ve been human and a woman, but her armour was almost a perfect match.

“You’re a hound,” he breathed, amazed he could say a word when it felt like his heart had abruptly relocated to his throat.

The man’s lips twisted into a humourless smile. “Not entirely without wits, I see. Yes, I am a hound. One who has been following you for days, I may add.” The dagger’s point returned to his neck.

All the stories Dylan had ever heard about the hounds, the tales of what they did to those who fled the tower, flooded his thoughts. Did they *really* drink spellster blood? He closed his eyes, biting his lip to hold back the whimper tightening his throat. *The hounds will hunt you*. His guardian’s words echoed in his ears. He was safe in the tower. Safe with a neck banded in metal. But to venture outside whilst being unleashed? Practically a death sentence. Any spellster rumoured to have fled the tower was never heard from again.

“*What* are you doing?” the hound asked.

“Aren’t you going to kill me?” He dared to open one eye enough to peek out from between his lashes. “That’s what hounds do.” It was also a hound’s job to bring spellsters to the tower, just as they’d done with Sulin, Launtil and countless others who’d been born outside the walls.

He didn’t think this one was about to offer that sort of assistance.

“That is quite the question. But I have a few of my own. Ones you *will* answer.” The elf’s eyes narrowed, throwing them into shadow. “You see, I know you were at the army encampment, I tracked you from there. I saw what you did to that spellster. *And* I know you did not travel all this way alone.”

“No,” he admitted. In all their travelling through the forest, not once had they attempted to conceal their passage.

"You wear the clothes of one who has been in the army, tattered though they may be." The blade at his throat slid down, taking the neck of Dylan's robe with it. "Yet, you are unleashed. Does that make you a spy bad at his job or a foolish runaway?" the man purred. "The crown does not take kindly to either."

"Wait," Dylan pleaded, trying to keep the terror quaking in his bones from his voice. He needed the hound to listen long enough to explain why he was unleashed. Surely, once he showed the man how damaged the collar was.

The collar. Katarina still had it in her possession. He hadn't asked for it back, hadn't wanted to look upon its mangled remains. The very thought of it returned his mind to that day. The smell of smoke. The screams. The heat. "I—"

The dagger flashed up with barely a twitch from the elf, the flat of the blade tapping Dylan on the lips. "Hush," the hound hissed. "You will speak only to answer my questions. If they are not what I want to hear, if I think you are *lying* to me, I will make you regret ever leaving the tower. Are we clear?"

"Yes, but I—" The returning of the blade's point to his throat stilled his tongue.

"Let us start with the simple matter of telling me where the ones you were with are."

"Right here," Marin growled.

Dylan rolled his eyes towards the alleyway entrance. All three women stood across its breadth, Authril with her sword bared and Marin with her bow already nocked.

Never had he been so relieved to see a person as he was to see them.

Katarina straightened. It was hard to make out without turning his head, but something gleamed in her hand. Her dagger? "That man is under the protection of the dwarven Coven. As a hedgewitch, I insist you unhand him."

"Dear woman," the man replied, barely glancing away from Dylan, "this is a matter for the King's Hounds. You might have escorted him here, but he is mine now. Please, kindly go about your business."

Marin drew her bow, the whisper-thin tap of the arrow against wood loud in the relative silence of the alleyway. "I don't think you grasped what my friend here was saying. Get away from him. *Now*. We won't ask nicely again."

The hound's hand dropped from the wall to his side. There was the barest twitch of his body and a knife flew past Marin's head.

She jerked back, swearing and clutching at her ear. Her bow fell from her grasp, but not before she released the arrow. It streaked across the alleyway, headed for him.

A shield enclosed Dylan, flickering with his uncertainty of using magic, even defensively, around a hound.

He needn't have worried. The man snatched the arrow from the air, hurling it to the ground. "Try that again," he snarled at Marin, "and my next throw will be less forgiving."

"Bloody assassins," Authril snarled. She didn't carry her shield, but her left arm was up all the same. "That's a spellster you're tangling with. You're lucky he hasn't tried to burn your face off."

"He's a hound," Dylan replied before the man could. "Trying to burn his face off would only sign my death warrant." If the hound died tonight and others discovered magic had been involved, not even returning to the tower would help him.

"Precisely," the man agreed. "And as you say, he is indeed a spellster. Who are not supposed to be freely wandering the countryside never mind a town. For one to be doing so at night is very suspicious. Especially with everything that has happened with the army."

Dylan swallowed. He had to agree with the man there.

"He came with us," Authril said. "He's only been here since this afternoon. Look at him, surely you can place the uniform."

"I can. And such a ratty thing it is. How simple do you think it might be to put on a dead man's robes and look the part?" He sneered, revealing a rather prominent canine. "Any fool knows that a spellster who joined the army ranks is leashed."

Katarina dug about in her pouches. "I have his collar." She produced the twisted pieces of *infitialis*, the sections glittering in her trembling hands. "See?"

The hound eyed the remains, his brows twitching in uncertainty. "That amount of destruction could only mean it exploded." His gaze snapped back to Dylan. "And, if that were so, then the wearer would be very dead, yes?"

Dylan shrugged. "Or he was a very lucky and scarred one." They'd only the truth and, if the hound wasn't content to believe that, then there was no way to resolve this without violence. Taking pains to move slowly, he further parted the collar of his robe and tipped his head back to give the man an unobstructed view of the scarring at his throat.

The hound peered at his neck, his russet brows knitting closer together in confusion. He lowered his dagger, seemingly content to at least entertain hearing them out. It did much towards loosening the tightness in Dylan's chest.

Cautiously rubbing at his neck revealed no sign of injury. An additional relief. He'd no idea if the man's *infitialis* dagger was the same as those in the tower, but he wasn't willing to find out. "If you've seen what became of the army, then you'll know why we fled it."

"I do. But I am also left wondering how *you* evaded such destruction? Or why you chose not to take the road back?"

"It's a long story."

"And I am a patient man."

Dylan recounted everything that had happened, from the ambush on his scouting party to the far wider assault on the main camp. Every so often, Katarina or Authril would chime in with additional information.

The hound stood there, quietly listening, his gaze flicking between the women and Dylan even when they'd finished. Was he trying to determine if they were lying?

Why not? Dylan didn't think he would believe himself.

Finally, the hound sighed. "Either you are all telling the truth or you are a most exceptional group of liars. I will choose to believe your little story until I can confirm otherwise." He swung back to Dylan. Eyes in the shade of rich honey examined him, the considering glint in that gaze slowly twisting Dylan's insides. "And you wish to return to the tower?" Disbelief coated the question.

Dylan nodded. Even without the hound discovering him, he had no other option but to head back. It wouldn't be a happy reunion, but whatever the overseers planned to do with him had to be preferable to being slain here and now.

"Then duty binds me to the task of escorting you."

"What?" Marin said. "A few minutes ago, you were planning to skewer him. If you expect me to believe that you're not going to do him in the second we turn our backs, you're missing arrows from your quiver."

"You are quite welcome to travel with us or go on your way without him. Even if he is *not* a Udynean spy, he *is* still an unleashed spellster outside of the tower. I must stay at his side until that is rectified one way or the other." He tipped his head, eyeing them all anew. "You are staying at *The Drunken Pilgrim*, yes?"

"Yes," Dylan replied, earning Marin's wordless ire. What point was there in lying about where they were spending the night? The elf already knew. If he had truly been tracking them all this time, then the innkeeper might've even been the one to tell the man.

"Excellent. I shall join you there at first light."

Huffing, Marin folded her arms and fixed the hound with a look that should've dropped him on the spot. "Fine," she conceded. "So you know where we're sleeping. Not difficult to find out. What makes you think we'll still be around when you arrive?"

Dylan shook his head. She didn't understand. There was little point in trying to evade a hound. Their entire existence revolved around hunting down spellsters such as him. And if this one had truly tracked them from the encampment and through the forest, then anywhere else would be child's play.

The elf grinned as if the woman had made a huge joke. "Something as foolhardy as running would not keep me from my duty, my dear archer. Regardless of whatever childish attempts you make, I would find him sooner than you believe." He turned to leave the alleyway, halting at its entrance. The long tail of his braid whipped around as he faced them. "Oh, and since we will be travelling together, you may call me Tracker."

CHAPTER 25

Dawn arrived without further incidence. Dylan had slept surprisingly well before the fireplace, the first decent night's rest he'd achieved since leaving the spellster tower. He wasn't sure why. The pallets the innkeeper had offered as a bed were softer than the ground, but no less lumpy. He put it down to the effects of exhaustion and the aftermath of shock completely draining him.

They had packed their things and vacated *The Drunken Pilgrim* only to find a distinct lack of the hound's presence. Still, they lingered at his insistence. The last thing Dylan wanted was to incur the man's wrath.

"This is bullshit," Marin grumbled for the fifth time. She paced the space between the inn's entrance and the street, her every dragging step kicking up little puffs of dust. "What do we need a hound for, anyway?"

Authril sleepily lifted her head from where she leant against the inn wall. Conversely to the rest of them, she had gotten little sleep, largely thanks to the ruckus from the wealthier customers upstairs. "Hounds are meant to keep spellsters under control," the warrior mumbled. "And kill them if they become a danger. I thought everyone knew that. Haven't you ever heard a spellster-hunting tale?"

Marin grunted and waved a hand in Dylan's direction. "But according to your own word, he hasn't attacked anyone who wasn't trying to harm him. By the gods, he barely uses magic unless we ask. You think someone that full of power would piss it."

Dylan winced at the image the woman's words conjured in his mind.

She whirled on him, curious. "You haven't actually done that, have you?"

"Not to my knowledge." There were a few babies who were capable of more than rudimentary protection magic, but for the most part, their abilities didn't start to manifest themselves at will until they were children. Typically around five years old.

He couldn't imagine how his guardian used to discipline him.

"My dear woman," replied someone in a rich, rolling tone. "It hardly matters whether or not he chooses to use his magic, it is that he *can* use it whenever he so desires, even if it were only to 'piss it' as you so eloquently said."

Dylan spun at the voice to find the hound standing in the open doorway of *The Drunken Pilgrim*. How had the man managed to get there without any of them seeing him?

Tracker's gaze fixed on Dylan, leaving him rooted to the spot and unable to do anything but watch the man trot down the steps. The end of the man's waist-length, russet braid bounced from side to side in a fashion that brought to mind the cup-and-ball toys the children of the tower servants played with. Dylan hadn't ever seen the attraction in the game—spellster children tended to have other activities to occupy their minds—but it was hypnotic to watch.

"The gates have the order to open," the hound said, clapping his hands together. He eyed the rest of the group. "We are all ready to be on our way, yes?"

"It would've been better to leave before the crowds gathered and the roads became choked," Authril said.

Tracker shrugged as he strode passed the woman. "Naturally, but I had business to finish up before we left." He halted in front of Dylan, giving a considering hum as those honey-coloured eyes looked him over. A dozen little silver and gold rings and cuffs adorned the elf's ears. They glittered in the early light as the man tipped his head up.

Straightening his back, Dylan staunchly resisted the urge to shuffle on the spot.

Something familiar lingered in the way the man's lips twisted. "You seemed rather less tall in the dark. No matter. What is it that they say in the army when handing over charge of you to another?" He snapped his fingers. "Ah, yes. I believe it is... your arse is mine."

Dylan jerked back a step, his brows lifting. "I... They— That's not what they said." The mischievous glint in Tracker's eyes told him the man already knew that, but his tongue persisted in its task of correcting the elf. "And in any case, I'm not leashed."

Tracker tipped his head, his mouth twisting just that little bit more as he visibly fought to suppress a smirk. "And that is the very reason we are here today, yes? But as long as you cause no trouble, we will be fine. Come." He clapped his hand on Dylan's back. At least, Dylan was certain the man had been aiming for his back. What those long fingers had connected with was a little lower. "It is a long journey to the tower, but not as long as if we continue to stand here."

The hound led them through the streets. It was a different way from the route they'd taken yesterday and, unlike the previous afternoon, their passage was jammed with people and carts. Stalls lined most of the streets they travelled, turning already narrow streets even more so.

Tracker had no trouble with the crowd. People tended to move out of his way, seemingly without even knowing they did, and closed behind the man as he pressed on.

The rest of them weren't as fortunatc.

Dylan squeezed past a few such clumps of people, desperate to keep the hound in sight lest he was accused of attempting to escape. A dog bounded across his path, forcing him to halt or fall on the poor creature. He stumbled a few steps sideways, his shoulder bumping into a pole. His hand lunged for something to keep him upright.

"Watch where you're going," a woman's shrill voice pierced the crowds as the awning the pole held up shuddered. "And get your paws off my melons!"

He swiftly removed his hand from where he'd grasped a crate of... yes, they were certainly watermelons. The pole at his back wobbled under his full weight. *Please, no.* He didn't need some merchant mad at him for destroying her stall on top of everything else.

Strong, long fingers grabbed him, pulling him away from the awning framework, which remarkably stayed in place. "Come on," Authril said, chuckling. "Let's get you out of here before you bring the whole town down around our ears."

He followed the warrior around a corner where the street widened and the crowd, although still quite numerous, didn't press so heavily around them. He exhaled in relief upon discovering Tracker had slowed, clearly waiting for them to catch up.

The rest of their journey to the gates was mercifully uneventful with much of the crowd at their backs. He ducked his head as they reached the gate, though the guards paid them no more attention than the merchants and common folk around them. They trailed behind a cart until they were able to spread out along the road.

It wasn't until they were through the gate that he realised this was the same entrance they'd used yesterday. Whilst they'd originally popped out of the forest somewhere to the left, taking a straight path to the gates, the road meandered for some time. It slithered down the hill, evening out slightly as it travelled alongside fields of grain, then disappeared into a forest sitting in the distance.

Beyond there, the town of Oldmarsh.

Dylan glanced over his shoulder, scowling at the silhouette of Toptower's namesake peeking over the village walls. If he never entered another crowded street, he'd be grateful. Except, he would have to suffer the town ahead if he was ever going to make it back to the tower.

Home. His gaze slid northward. A part of him hoped to spy the massive building he'd spent all twenty-nine years of his life in. Nothing but trees and the haze of the horizon presented itself. Foolish to think he could see the spellster tower from here when it would take them a little over two weeks to reach on foot.

A fortnight between now and when he'd be leashed again. His stomach twisted at the thought. At least he'd be prepared for the skull-crushing pain this time.

The day grew colder as they trudged down the road. Dylan hunched his shoulders against the wind nipping at his face. Clouds obscured the sun, threatening to dispense more rain. He could practically feel the moisture building in the air. If another downpour occurred, he'd be no less drenched than last time.

It would even take a few days before reaching anywhere with a solid roof. At least they'd Marin's tents to shelter under come nightfall should the sky make good on the threat.

The thought of a dry place to sleep did little to ebb the stiff breeze's cutting chill. Entering the forest provided no shelter, the road merely funnelling the wind. Dylan rubbed at his arms, seeking to work up enough friction to keep warm. He tried to take some solace in that he wouldn't be quite so cold once they settled for the night. That just made him more anxious for the day to wind down.

Feeling watched, he glanced to his left to find the hound staring at him. "What?"

"Do you not have other means of warming yourself? A cloak, perhaps?"

"Not any means I can use." If they were to linger in one spot, he could attempt the air-heating trick Henrie taught him several years back. He already used it indoors, to dry his hair and the like, so applying it to his entire body whilst outside wouldn't be too much of a stretch. With them on the move, it was a pointless waste of his energy. "And, seeing as we barely managed enough money to pay for the tavern last night, what makes you think we could afford clothing?"

Tracker silently undid the clasp at his neck, removing his cloak. "Here. It should help keep the chill off."

Dylan pushed aside the offered length of thickly-spun wool. "I wouldn't dare ask you to suffer for my sake."

The man's brows drew up in the middle, creasing sharply above his nose. "It is clearly not as cold for me as it is to you. I insist you wear it." He draped the cloak over Dylan's shoulders. "We hounds are not all unfeeling terrors out to get you. I promise, I do not bite."

"I know." He pulled the cloak further around him. The elf's warmth lingered within the fabric. Drawing the collar up around his neck, he discovered the man's scent permeating the lining, a strangely pleasant aroma that warmed his cheeks. "The woman who brought me to the army camp wasn't as gruff as I expected."

The hound smiled. "Fetch leaves people with that impression, yes."

Fetch. Dylan frowned at the road ahead, his thoughts lost to the first time someone had spoken the other hound's name. Fetcher and Tracker. Odd enough for one to be called such, but both? The more he thought on it, the less the words sounded like names.

"Shouldn't we look about for a place to set up camp?" Marin asked, breaking Dylan from his musing. The woman had joined Tracker at the front of the group. "It'll get dark soon."

With her frame being only slightly shorter than Dylan's, the hound's height didn't quite reach her eyes, forcing Tracker to look up to speak with her. "We can easily walk for a few more hours before the light fades."

Marin scrunched her nose. "For you, maybe. Not all of us can see as well in the dark as an elf. Besides, I want enough light to lay out some traps. See if I can't snag us a rabbit for breakfast."

Tracker sighed. "If it pleases you, dear woman, we shall find somewhere to stop. We will search..." There was a subtle change to the way the man walked. Where each footfall had been in a casual and confident stride, there was now an odd fluidity to the movements. "...for a place momentarily."

Authril's pace also slowed. She grasped her sword hilt, her head swinging towards the dense bushes to their left. "Bandits," she whispered, the word hissing through her barely moving lips. "Stay behind me."

"Well, well," came a voice from somewhere amongst the underbrush. "Look what we have here."

Marin skittered back from the fore to stand beside the hedgewitch.

There was a rustle amongst the bushes. "That's right, lovely," another said, the deeper voice belonging to someone on their right. "Get nice and close with your friends."

Glaring at where the sound came from, Marin fussed with her bow, swiftly stringing it. "Come here and call me that again, you bastard." She nocked an arrow, aiming in the direction of the voice. "I'll put two in your eye before you could blink."

A woman stepped onto the road, her reveal followed swiftly by half a dozen others. The woman spread her arms wide as if she greeted old friends. "Welcome to my part of the forest, weary travellers."

Out the corner of his eye, Dylan caught Marin aiming her bow.

"Tell your red-haired friend to lower her weapon," ordered that same deep voice from the bushes. "We have you surrounded."

Tracker turned his head enough to look over his shoulder. "Do as he says. There are more of them than it looks."

Sneering, Marin lowered her bow.

The bandit leader nodded. "Now, I'm certain you can surmise the sort of situation you've gone and got yourself in. Since you seem so very keen to cooperate, we'll make this quick. Hand over everything you own."

The hound laughed. "My dear woman, just because I am not eager for bloodshed does not mean I am willing to offer up what is rightfully mine." He planted himself before them, his arms spread. "And it would be unwise to continue that line of thought."

"Just listen to Master Elf, here," one of the bandits chuckled. "Thinks he can get off paying the toll with a little chatter."

As one, the rest of the bandits laughed.

"It doesn't work that way, you pointy-eared bastard," they snarled, bouncing a dagger in their hand, the edge glinting with each fall. "You either cough up your valuables or we slit your throat and take them off your corpse."

A smile stretched the hound's lips. Dylan was certain that, had the man chosen to direct such an expression at himself, he would be quickly evaluating his options. "Allow me to make a counteroffer," Tracker replied, drawing his sword. "I will give you this one chance to leave with your lives."

"What?" one of the stockier bandits laughed. "The five of you against all of us? I don't fancy your chances of leaving here alive, elf."

"Priests always have coin," said another.

A third jerked his chin towards Dylan. "Never seen one in green robes before, but I'm willing to bet that just means he has more than the others."

Tracker opened his mouth in silent comprehension. "I see where you and your friends are mistaken. My dear man, he is no priest. Perhaps you should show these good people what you really are?" the hound said to Dylan over his shoulder.

Frowning at the elf, Dylan let a ball of fire flare to life in his hand.

As one, the bandits jerked back. If Tracker had hoped to scare them off, then it wasn't working. They seemed uncertain, wary like the tower mousers against a large rat, but their faces spoke of desperation, of hunger.

He snuffed the fireball and quietly tried to count just how many they were up against. Not an easy feat when they kept shifting about in the undergrowth. Thirteen, maybe? It rather depended on whether the shadows in the foliage held more than just a bandit or two.

Movement in the bushes preceded an arrow.

Dylan threw his hands up in front of him, lowering them only at the bandit's collective gasp. The arrowhead protruded through his shield, the fletching jutting beyond. His palm stung. He glanced at it to find a bead of blood welling there. *That was too close.*

The hound twitched and the archer went down, a blade glittering in his throat.

"Filthy elf," the leader spat. "Kill them! All of them."

The bandits charged.

The two elves met the front of the group. The hound was a whirlwind of death, those who dared to come within reach fell back screaming or dead. Authril followed close on the man's heels. She drove her sword into one of the bandits, bashing in the face of another with her shield as they attempted to close.

Dylan bounced on the balls of his feet, uncertain what he could do to aid them. A barrier would work only for as long as it took for the bandits to change tactics. A direct attack could scatter them, but it could also run the risk of hindering the others. He couldn't be responsible for a hound's death, not even indirectly.

The flash of movement on his flank drew his attention. He spun around, not willing to be caught out the same as last time. A man was closing in on him, his sword already swinging.

Dylan jerked back from the first swipe, his barrier shimmering as the sword tip grazed the outer curve. He sent a pulse rippling through the air in answer.

The man hit a tree with a sickening crunch and fell.

Dylan didn't have time to check if the bandit was dead. Whilst the two elves fought the bulk at the fore, Marin and Katarina were dealing with those sent to surround them. The way those bandits were spread out left him with far more opportunities to assist. He still couldn't risk fire so close to the trees, but a spray of ice would—

An arrow smashed into his barrier, shattering to splinters.

He lifted his arm, sparks of lightning flowed from his fingers to arc between them. Dylan scanned the bushes for the archer.

Marin found them first and another of the bandits collapsed on the edge of the clearing.

A second bandit lunged at Marin before he could cry out a warning, managing to knock the bow from her hands.

Snarling, she turned on him, her hunting knife bared. They fell to the ground, tumbling through the undergrowth. There was a scream, then Marin stood, wiping the blood from her face.

Katarina was having a harder time, harried by several men at once. Dylan ran towards her, slowing as he caught something move in the trees above her. A woman. The glint of a blade in her hand.

"Duck!" Dylan roared, throwing out a bolt of lightning the second the hedgewitch dove to one side.

The bandit jerked, her back arching and arms spread as the bolt ripped through her. Forks of lightning shot off her body, seeking ground. He fought them, forcing the tendrils to spread until they lanced through the stunned bandits, before letting it stop.

He stood there, staring at the four bodies lying charred and bleeding. Not a one moved. The scent of cooked flesh, not unlike that of the roasting boar, filled his nose.

Cold seeped through to his bones. His stomach twisted. Bitterness hit the back of his throat.

Dylan pushed the bile down. This wasn't the time for weakness. There could still be others. He needed to—

Slowly, he became aware of the silence at his back. The lack of screams, of steel hitting flesh.

He turned to find the two elves standing amidst what had become of the other bandits. Or at least, Authril stood, if only barely. The hound moved from one corpse to the other, examining them. Occasionally, he would pluck something from their bodies. Small pouches, rings and the like.

"Utter bastards." Authril spat on the headless corpse at her feet. "I didn't survive the massacre of my company to be taken down by the likes of you." Her shield lay several feet away, discarded or torn from her grasp at some point in the fight. She took a wobbling step towards it, using her sword as a cane. Her other hand was tucked across her stomach, discretely trying to clutch her side.

Dylan picked his way through the carnage, trying not to focus on the broken, twitching bodies or the blood splattered everywhere like a painter's nightmare. Again, his stomach attempted to rebel. He gritted his teeth.

His foot fell on a slippery patch. A quick glance down revealed it to be the loop of a woman's intestines, the rest of it snaking out of her gut like a coiled mass of greasy sausage. His stomach finally took control, doubling him over and heaving up his midday meal all over the corpse before he could stop himself.

The hound eyed him from where he was crouched by one of the bandits, his russet brows lifting even as he cut a pouch from the dead man's belt. "And they sent *you* into the army?"

"He's new to the whole killing and mutilated corpses business," Authril answered before Dylan could find the breath to.

With his stomach still cramping but mercifully empty, Dylan halted before the warrior. "Let me see your side," he rasped.

She grunted and moved her hand. "Damn needle daggers. Slipped right between the plates." Blood stained her side. A smile quivered its way across her lips. "Guess it's a good thing that the hound found you when he did. You would've been pretty much screwed for protection otherwise."

"Stop talking as though you're going to die." He carefully unbuckled the side of her armour. There was a small puncture hole in the padding beneath. "I can heal this."

"It's a bit more complicated than a broken bone."

"Not for me." Dylan placed a hand on her side and let his magic get to work. The outer wound would be easy to mend, even for a simple physician. Inside would be trickier, depending on what the dagger hit. He was pretty sure the blade had been aiming for her kidney. In any other circumstance, he could see why Authril thought the stab wound was a death sentence. "Hold still, this won't take long." He concentrated his focus into convincing the quickening of the elf's natural healing to not let the organ die and, when it responded, loosened his grasp to allow the flesh to seal itself.

Finished, he stumbled back a few steps to lean against a nearby tree and catch his breath. He really needed to get this queasiness under control if he was going to be of any use to the army or they might decide to leave him in the tower. He couldn't go back to that sort of life, not knowing the Udyneans faced little in the way of opposition.

A groan came from amongst the bushes.

Dylan glanced at the other two women of their little group. Both stood there calmly enough all things considered. They seemed intact, or at least didn't clutch at any obvious wounds, which meant the sound came from another.

Pushing himself upright, Dylan staggered towards the noise. He parted the bushes to find one of the bandits. This had to be the man he'd thrown against a tree. He had come to and was trying to get to his feet.

Tracker straightened from his distasteful task of looting the corpses. "What is this? We have a survivor?" He strode over to the groaning man. With one shove of his boot, he rolled the bandit onto his back. "Well now," he said, crouching at the man's side. "That was quite the misjudgement your group made, yes?"

The bandit laughed. It was a watery, breathless sound that spoke of a punctured lung. "Anna said you'd be easy pickings. Told her you can't sneak up on an elf."

A small smile tweaked the hound's lips. He gently helped the man to sit up against the tree. "Tell me," he all but purred. "Are there any more of you?"

Dylan frowned. He could've sworn Tracker had sheathed his dagger along with his sword, yet there it was dangling between those long fingers, hidden from the man's sight.

The bandit shook his head. "This is all of us, I swear."

"Good." With one deft flick of his wrist, the dagger came up to plunge hilt-deep into the man's side. The hound waited until the bandit stopped twitching before withdrawing the blade to silently clean it on the man's tunic.

Dylan's gaze slid to the bandit, vainly searching for some sign of life. "You didn't have to kill him." These people weren't some slavers from Udynea. The man was defenceless, injured. What threat could he have possibly been to them?

"They're bandits," Authril said. "They likely already had a price on their heads. Even then, their lives were forfeit from the moment they attacked us."

He glanced over his shoulder at the death they'd brought, forcing himself to take in every severed limb and lonesome head. A handful more than the original six he'd first seen had engaged the two elves. Nine in all without including those that'd attacked their flank. *And each one lost their life.*

These people were no different to the countless others who called Demarn home. Their lives were the reason behind why the overseers sent spellsters, sent *him*, to fight Udynea.

Tracker cleared his throat. "Consider it this way, if you must. If we had not been here to take their lives now, then they would've only preyed upon others, perhaps even killed them as they sought to kill us. Think of it as doing those honest people a favour."

Dylan frowned. It made sense. It didn't mean he had to like it. It didn't help that the man was covered in the blood of the slain or that his belt pouches were full of their valuables.

"Such a scowl. My dear spellster, if you had glared at them like that before all this, they might have run away." The hound bounced to his feet. "I would suggest digging a grave, but that would take hours we do not have to spare. We should at least wash off this blood, yes? I heard signs of a stream a little ways back. It could lead to something larger."

Dylan stared down at his hand where Authril's blood still stained his skin. Such a small mark required nothing more than a basin and a little time. "I don't have much blood on me," he murmured, more to himself than the others. He should've been dripping in it, should've killed that bandit outright rather than let the man suffer a worse death.

A hand clapped onto his shoulder, the strength behind it dragging his side down. "That may be," Tracker said, "but some of us are not so fortunate. Come, these people likely had a campsite. If luck is merciful, we may find it before nightfall."

They trailed after the man, leaving the road and corpses behind them for the depths of the forest. *Luck be merciful?* He didn't see any of the gods granting him mercy anytime soon.

CHAPTER 26

They reached the stream without a hint of anyone else sharing this section of the forest. It seemed the bandit had been telling the truth of it being all of them. Not that this revelation stopped anyone from being twitchy. Even the hound would occasionally halt, demanding silence as he listened to the forest, before moving on.

The stream the man had heard was a small thing, barely a few feet wide and about as deep, more than enough for Dylan to wash his hands. He plunged them into the frigid water, scrubbing until his skin was pink and raw, tingling slightly with his healing magic.

The others settled around him, doing the same thing. The water turned murky with blood and dirt.

Moving further upstream from their efforts, Dylan rinsed out his mouth, shuddering as the water hit his teeth.

Authril carefully unbuckled her breastplate and examined the side. The damage hadn't looked bad to him, but she wrinkled her nose at the blood-smeared metal. Mumbling, she removed the padding. That had also been soaked through.

Dylan's gaze swung to Marin. He could've sworn the woman had been limping, although she didn't seem to be in a great deal of pain. Surely if she was seriously injured, she would've told him. Like the hedgewitch, Marin showed little fear of his abilities, seeming more curious towards how they worked than anything.

The hound, having finished sluicing the blood off his face, bounced to his feet. "My dear spellster, we should allow our companions to bathe in private, yes?"

Silently waved off by the women, Dylan shouldered his pack and followed the hound into the brush.

They walked through the forest, looking for a suitable spot big enough for three tents. He stumbled along the uneven ground, reduced to lifting the skirts of his robe in order to keep up with the hound. Some of the leaves in the undergrowth had a certain chill dampness to them that they were more than willing to share with his bare legs.

He wasn't sure how long they'd been walking before coming across a clearing surrounded by trees that his time studying dwarven architecture told him were conifers. A pair of such thick-trunked vegetation stood in the middle of the clearing, bits of branches and small bushes dotting the grass around them.

Dylan wasted no time in clearing a spot nearby to set up the tent he shared with Authril. After many previous attempts, and now knowing what to look for, finding the right branches wasn't a difficult task. His struggles to assemble the required framework had also dwindled to little more than the fumbling of still shaking fingers.

Out the corner of his eye, he spied the hound busy with a similar task. Tracker had brought the tent the other two women slept in and, having already set up his own shelter, was currently pitching theirs. They worked in silence, with Dylan pausing every so often to keep an eye on the man.

His gaze drifted over the hound's attire. Whilst the leather bore signs of scrapes and cuts not quite deep enough to part the armour, its dark colour could easily hide an injury. That Tracker showed no sign of being hurt was hardly reassuring.

Finally, the man straightened from his task of hammering in the last of the pegs and brushed the dirt off his trousers. "Is there a reason you stare at me so intently?"

A faint bloom of heat brushed Dylan's cheeks. He didn't think his casual glances had been so obvious. "Are you hurt?"

The man grinned, a brief chuckle slipping through his teeth. "No. Those bandits were amateurs who have little understanding of how to keep a sword sharp. Not that being hit with a steel club is much better, but your concern is unwarranted. I am uninjured." The man slung his pack into his tent. "You probably want a little time alone to gather your strength or whatever it is you need to do, yes? I am going to collect some firewood. I have a feeling our companions will need to dry off a few items of clothing when they return."

Dylan shuffled from one foot to the other. Being alone was perhaps the last thing he wanted, but he wasn't about to tell the hound that. He drew the man's cloak around himself before the realisation that he still wore it came to mind. "I suppose you'll want this back, then?" he mumbled, unfastening the clasp.

Tracker held up his hand. "It is looking to be a cool night, best if you keep it for now. Just do not wander off."

"I'm not stupid," Dylan muttered under his breath. He wasn't quite sure where they were in relation to the road and, if he left their camp, there was the likelihood of never finding a way out of the forest.

"That is good to hear," the man replied, causing a fresh rush of heat to hit Dylan's face. He could've sworn he'd been too quiet for even elven ears to understand him.

Dylan settled near his tent and waited in silence as the hound disappeared into the undergrowth. The forest had seemed altogether hushed as they walked through it, but now that he was still and alone, small sounds reached him. Birds for the most part, alongside the hum of insects. Low and peaceful.

Gentle rustling through the brush heralded something a great deal bigger than a bird approaching the camp. The wild boar attack swiftly came to mind, quietly pulling Dylan to his feet. He let a barrier form, tucking its focus into the back of his mind, as he prepared to defend himself. Hopefully, it was merely the hound or one of the women. If not, then one quick blast of lightning should be enough to stun whatever was out there and give him time to escape.

Tracker emerged from the bushes carrying an armful of twigs and logs. He paused on the edge of the clearing, one russet brow cocked, before striding into the middle of the triangle the formation of their tents made. "Take it easy, my dear man," he said, dumping his burden on the ground near the other bits of wood they had piled up from the clearing's bounty. "The worst you are likely to find out here is a stag and, seeing that it is not rutting season, they are harmless. Mostly."

He didn't like the way the hound tacked on that last word as if it was nothing to be concerned about. If stags were anything like boars, then they weren't harmless at all. "Tracker," he said as the man knelt by the pile of wood. "Do—"

Chuckling, the elf glanced up from his task of building a fire. "Please, we are travelling together. Track is sufficient."

"Do you think your fellow hound left the camp before the Udyneans attacked?" Bad enough he would return to the tower with news of the others being taken, but to know a King's Hound died amongst them would likely place the suspicion on him, even if Authril and Katarina gave their word that he hadn't been near the attack.

"I cannot say for certain. I met her in Toptower some weeks ago, but it is possible she returned to the encampment. That does not change the fact Fetch is a resourceful woman. If she was there when they attacked, I have no doubts that you would have known about her presence. It is far more likely that she was gone after your first night there, she is not at all fond of lingering."

Sighing, Dylan ran his fingers through his hair. He settled back on the ground, waiting for the others to appear. Such a small thing, knowing one life had been spared the fate of so many. Odd how the knowledge made his chest seem less tight.

His brows scrunched together in thought. If the hound knew

where to find her, then she could vouch for him should the overseers doubt his identity. They would have plenty of questions as it was. Questions he had no answers to. He didn't need more to complicate matters.

"Come now, a pretty face like yours should not be frowning so much."

So certain that the hound had been too preoccupied to notice anything else, Dylan jerked his head up at the sound of Tracker's voice to find the man still busy with building the base for a fire and wholly intent on his task.

Nevertheless, Dylan was sure of what he'd heard. "Don't do that." He had seen the man kill a person in cold blood, Dylan was not about to allow him to make any attempts at flirting.

The hound looked up in a perfect picture of wide-eyed innocence. "And what is so objectionable about lighting a fire?"

"You know exactly what I'm talking about." It wasn't the first time he had heard such words from another man. Whilst he would put a stop to any pushier advances by carefully explaining that he wasn't interested, mere words were usually ignored. "I'm in no mood to hear your empty sweet-talk."

"Ah." Tracker stood, brushing the dirt from his hands. "I did not seek to flatter you, but if that is how you feel, then I will desist. However, if you would permit me to speak on a more serious note?" The man waited until Dylan nodded before he continued. "I feel I have not given you the best impression of myself, that we began on the wrong foot as it were. I would like to start again. Providing you are agreeable to the notion. Then you would not be so nervous around me, yes?"

"That's..." Dylan shook his head. "I'm not nervous."

"Shall we say *careful*, then? I understand completely that you would seek to curb certain parts of your nature in my presence. I cannot imagine how they must speak of hounds in your tower." He smiled warmly, although the slightly sympathetic waver at the edges suggested he knew precisely what spellsters were told about them. "But you need not be so concerned with reining in your talents."

"Spellsters aren't supposed to be unleashed beyond the tower much less do magic without sanction." They tolerated it back home, but only because the logistics of giving every spellster permission for any given task would be a nightmare. That was supposedly why they didn't leash everyone.

The hound nodded. "That is true, but your situation is somewhat... unique, yes? You are no runaway or an untrained youth. As such, I see no reason to hold you under the strict edict placed on them." He fell silent, staring at Dylan. "If it makes you feel any better, I give you permission to use your magic as you see fit."

"Providing I don't use it to harm you or the others."

Tracker tilted his head. The sharpness behind those honey-coloured eyes all but bored their way into Dylan's skull. "I did not think that needed to be said. You do not strike me as the type to indulge in random acts of violence."

"Really? You barely know me."

The man gave a short, gasping laugh. "You are right, of course." A few swift strides was all it took before he settled next to Dylan. "Why, I do not believe you have even told me your name."

"Why would you need to know it?" Fetcher hadn't asked. He supposed she saw him as just another weapon being transported to the army. It probably helped her keep detached from the abuse they suffered at their warden's hands.

"Such suspicion. I would like to know for no reason other than we will be travelling together." A small smile lifted one side of the man's mouth. "But if you wish to keep an air of mystery around you, my dear spellster, I welcome a challenge."

"Wouldn't be much of one for long." Any of the women could speak it in the man's presence and then whatever mystery the hound thought surrounded his name would be gone. "It's Dylan."

"And if I may pry, Dylan?" His name escaped the man's lips in a purr that tingled along his skin and pooled in his gut. "Were you not trained to fight?"

"Of course." His guardian had sent him for testing alongside all the other pre-pubescent children who showed the magical strength required of those strong enough to maybe serve the army. "Although, it has been some time since I've stepped into the training arena before they leashed me." He'd lost count of how many, only that they'd been spent in the tower's library, translating scraps of text for the dwarves.

"Perhaps that is it, then. It is just... Well, you seem proficient enough in handling your magic." He indicated the unlit fire with a jerk of his chin. "I am sure lighting that would serve as no great task for you."

Dylan wordlessly waved his hand and the branches burst into flame.

"See? I cannot begin to comprehend what it is like to force kindling alight with a mere thought, but that looked effortless." He turned his full attention back to Dylan. In the firelight, his eyes took on an orange glint. "Yet you are quite reluctant to actually cause any harm unless provoked."

"I would've thought you'd see that as a good thing."

Tracker laughed. "Do not misunderstand, I appreciate that you have the apparent restraint to not set everything alight. I was certain you would attempt such an attack when we met. Especially given my, apparently undue, roughness in handling you." He bowed his head, abruptly sombre. "I apologise for that."

Dylan nodded his acceptance. "You had no idea who I was or what I would do." The former had been clear from the man's questions. If Dylan had been a Udynean spy, then he could've caused a lot of damage to Toptower. "The whole point of the King's Hounds is to keep spellsters in check, right?"

A small, wry smile tweaked the man's lips. "I must say, your unwillingness to cause harm could become troublesome if we are ambushed again. And, seeing that it is my duty to ensure you arrive at the tower in good health, I need to know whether you will assist me in such a goal."

He folded his arms. "I've no intentions of letting myself get killed, if that's what you're asking."

"I am glad to hear that. Travelling alongside someone with a death wish tends to complicate matters." The way the man spoke, it sounded like he'd some experience with such a scenario.

He supposed not all those who'd lived outside the tower would've entered its walls peacefully.

His gaze dropped to the array of weaponry the man sported as well as his sword. Daggers, three of them, and several throwing knives peeked out from the back of his belt. His guardian had been very explicit about what happened to those who tried to escape a hound's clutches. "Have you ever—?"

"There you two are!" Marin called out.

Dylan twisted where he sat in time to witness all three women entering their campsite. Relief unravelled the knot he didn't realise he'd been harbouring in his stomach until now. A part of him had been anxious about whether the trio would be able to find them, leaving him alone with the hound.

Marin held up a rabbit, the limp carcass swinging in her grip. "Found dinner. Or breakfast, take your pick." She threw it before the fire and jerked a thumb at Katarina. "She damn near tripped over the silly thing."

He eyed both the hunter and the hedgewitch. With them both clean, there still didn't seem to be any obvious injuries. He could've sworn Marin continued to limp, although it was hard to tell now the woman stood still. She didn't look to favour either leg. "Are either of you hurt?"

Katarina brushed a lock of brown hair from her forehead, tucking it back into the braid at her temple. Most of the loops had loosened during the fight, making a mess of both bun and braids. "We've a few scrapes and bruises between us."

"I'd be more than willing to—"

The dwarf held up her hand. "There's no need to use your healing talents. I know it takes more out of spellsters than they care to admit."

"Speak for yourself," Marin said, plonking next to him. One leg of her trousers twisted in a manner he didn't recall it being capable of prior to entering Toptower. She pulled back the soft leather, revealing a long gash down her calf. "It's stopped bleeding, but—"

Dylan wordlessly placed his hand on her bare shin. The cut wasn't too deep, which had helped in the clotting process and aided him in boosting the woman's natural healing.

Marin wrinkled her nose, her lips warping into a grimace as she tried to remain still. "Kind of tingles, doesn't it? Like needles all over your leg." She stretched her leg before the fire once he withdrew his magic, brushing off the congealed blood and examining the peachy-pink scar beneath. "Almost like it never happened, huh?"

Dylan shrugged. "I could heal it further if you want." Typically, once the wound had reached the point of a scar, there wasn't much left to do. Pushing the healing process that little bit more would allow the new skin to darken, but it was a superficial matter by then.

"It's fine, thank you." Crossing her legs beneath her, she crinkled her eyes at him. "It's good to see you're looking less green, too."

"Sword fighting's a little more gruesome than I imagined," he admitted, ducking his head to whisper the words.

"That's why I use a bow. Less bits flying everywhere, especially in the face. Get an arrow through someone's head or a straight shot to the heart and—" She flopped back onto the leaf-ridden ground. "They're not getting up. Kind of like your magic."

"I guess." Although Marin seemed to have quite a bit more skill than the archers he'd witnessed practising in the army, arrows were still less efficient than his magic at killing cleanly. And messy.

"Hey," the hunter sat up and nudged his knee with her elbow. "You can help me solve a little debate us women were having earlier."

His curiosity tweaked, he raised a brow in query at her.

"You can light whatever you want on fire, right?"

Dylan laughed. It was going to be one of those sorts of debates, was it? He'd been wondering how long it would take before someone started enquiring about the extent of his abilities. "That's somewhat true," he drawled. "There are limits. Using your fire example, if it's not something that'll burn under a normal flame, then I can't set it alight."

"How does it all work? Like fire. How do you actually make things burn?"

He grinned. "Well, it..." Chuckling to himself, he ran his fingers through his hair. It had been literal decades since his tutors taught him the finer points of controlling the skill. "It seems I've forgotten the nuances. But it's not so much as conjuring fire as it involves manipulating the temperature in the air around the object you want to burn."

Marin frowned. "And you've forgotten how you're doing that?" She gave an exasperated huff, throwing up her arms. "How could you forget?"

"Do you remember how exactly you learnt to walk? Or speak?" He'd been an early bloomer in regards to his magic, like most of those signalled out for military training. "Spellsters—the ones born in the tower, at least—are able to use their power at a very young age. Our first attempt is often a shield when we're just babies as it hinges on our survival defence."

Her eyes grew wide as her jaw slackened. "You could do magic as a *baby?*"

"Only a shield," he reiterated. "And only for a short time." Pulses generally came next, weak ones that expended more effort than a toddler could give. "I lit my first flame when I was four years old. Fire is often the first conscious use of magic." Dylan flicked his wrist, bringing a small fireball to life in his cupped palm. "It's easy. Brief." He blew on the fireball, extinguishing it. "I can manipulate it like you would do your breath. Concentrating too hard can make things more difficult, so you learn to trust your instincts."

"But if I asked, you could set fire to..." Marin twisted her head every which way, taking in their surroundings. "*That?*" She pointed to the leafless skeleton of a nearby bush hovering just on the edge of the encroaching shadows of night. "Just—" She clicked her fingers and spread her hands wide. "Whoosh!"

"I'd be more inclined to ask you why you wanted me to set the dead bush on fire, but yes, I could do it like *that.*" He mimicked her actions.

"Except you will not," Tracker said. "Stop encouraging the woman."

Marin stuck her tongue out at the hound. "Why don't you use fire when we're fighting? It's always lightning or..." She waved her hands in a pushing motion.

"Safety, mostly." The guardians were always very clear on them remaining mindful of their surroundings, of being sure where an ally was in relation to an enemy. Basic training he'd forgotten in the very first fight where lives were taken. "Lightning goes to ground and stops when I want. And any pulses I send through the air last only as long as there's energy to drive them." He plucked a twig from the pile.

With the snap of his fingers, he conjured a single flame to dance on the tip of his thumb before transferring it to the twig. "Once magical fire meets fuel, then it's merely fire and just as unpredictable."

Marin eyed the burning twig. "But you could put it out whenever you wanted."

Dylan enclosed the flame in a small dense shield, holding it there until smoke filled the bubble. "Yes." He threw the twig into the fire. "But if I was to get knocked out like I did the first time I fought..." Even magically created fire couldn't tell friend from foe. When he'd been blinded by pain at the main encampment, he had just been lucky the person he attacked had been an enemy.

Tracker settled on the opposite side of the campfire. "You allowed an enemy close enough to you to let them knock you out? Are you certain they sent you to the army to fight and not, I do not know, play physician?"

Before Dylan could open his mouth, Authril said, "There are no healers in the army, only weapons."

Dylan rubbed at his cheek, the one the lieutenant had struck on his first day there. It had stopped stinging by the second day and the bruising had vanished once the collar broke, but he could still feel it, still taste the bitter tang of his blood.

You're a weapon. The man's words echoed in his mind. *Nothing but a sword with a big mouth.*

Tracker shook his head. "So you say, my dear warrior, but I distinctly recall him mending your side. Clearly, the lack of healers in the army ranks cannot be true."

"I wasn't brought to the army to heal people," Dylan whispered. "I'm meant to be a sword, not a scalpel." If he'd been a little more invested in playing the former role, then maybe he might've been able to save those people. Instead, he had watched them die, powerless, terrified.

He squeezed his eyes shut, trying to ignore the flickering of the campfire. It was best not to wander down that path again lest he couldn't find his way back a second time.

Feeling watched, he lifted his gaze to find Tracker staring at him, a peculiar expression drawing the man's face tight.

Pity? It was there only for an instant, then the man's attention was diverted by Katarina.

Had he seen right? He couldn't imagine why a hound would pity him.

All at once, the man leapt to his feet and retrieved one of the longer branches from the fire. "Since you are all here. I think I shall finish removing this blood before it permanently adheres to my skin." He eyed Dylan, tilting his head. "Normally, I am not meant to leave a spellster's side once they are found, but I can trust you to not attempt vanishing into the undergrowth once I am out of sight, yes?"

"Unique circumstances, right?" His gaze turned to the darkness encroaching on the forest. Already, much of the area beneath the canopies was in shadow. Even in the daytime, a man could get lost. "I'm not going anywhere, I promise." The safest way to reach the tower was at the hound's side.

He'd be a fool to leave it and invite more trouble.

CHAPTER 27

Dylan slunk through the undergrowth, picking his way carefully as the sun hadn't quite broken through the dense canopy of trees. He was determined to reach the pond they found yesterday. It sat a short distance from last night's camp, their discovery due to them abandoning the road after the attack and following the stream north for several days until it led to what appeared to be the end.

Marin's insistence that they didn't sleep next to the body of water puzzled him, but he supposed the hunter knew how to deal with these matters. Not that he'd been able to sleep. Even after a few days of trekking through the forest, that moment when the bandits chose to attack kept invading his mind. Whenever he closed his eyes, those broken, bleeding bodies sprawled on the roadside haunted him.

He needed calm. Peace. Just for a moment.

He stepped out into the clearing surrounding the pond. Early-morning sunlight, free from treetops and leaves, bathed the area in a hazy glow. Stalks of lavender speckled the grass near the pond's shallow end.

Dylan strolled through the grass, breathing deep as the scent from the bruised flowers drifted on the breeze. He had long since associated the woodsy, floral smell with the wild.

There'd always been lavender around the tower. Patches of the stuff used to spring up in the herb gardens no matter what they did. In his youth, Tricia would sprinkle the underside of his pillow with dried petals to help him sleep. He wasn't sure if fresh flowers worked the same, but if it helped ease the bad dreams, then he was willing to try.

Giving no thought to the motions, he plucked a handful of the sprigs and twined the stalks into a small circle. Weaving flowers was an old elven tradition with courting couples making elaborate garlands for their prospective partner. Nestria had taught him the technique several years ago. She had then spent the rest of their thirteenth summer sulking when he surpassed her crude attempts, much to Sulin's amusement.

Donning the crown of lavender, his gaze slid between the pond and the way back to camp. Unlike the women, who carried spare undergarments—courtesy of Marin—his clothes consisted of what he currently wore. Although no one had said anything, the time for them to be a little more on the cleaner side had passed several days back.

He hadn't washed his own laundry for years. Such activity was reserved for the tower servants and unruly teenaged spellsters. He remembered how well enough, although he hadn't access to one of the massive copper basins or lye to deal with any stains. However, he was more than capable of heating a section of the pond for his use and scrubbing any loose dirt.

Dylan chucked his leather belt to one side and quickly stripped off his robe. If he was to do this, then it was best done before anyone else got the idea to wander this way. He studied the fabric. The patch he'd sewn into the side seemed to be holding up and the stitching on the hem showed no sign of fraying. All things considered, the robe didn't look too dirty. But how long would it be before he found another opportunity like this?

He picked an area of the pond where the incline wasn't too shallow and knelt at the edge. Frigid water met his fingers as he dipped his robe. Shuddering, Dylan poured heat through his hands. He wasn't used to heating anything larger than a bathing barrel, and the pond's sluggish current was still enough to wick away the warmth, but he eventually had a small section of steaming water.

Wavelets lapped at his knees as he set to work on dunking and scrubbing the robe, soaking his undertunic. *Might as well get it all over with*. He shrugged out of the second layer of clothing. He'd see to his smallclothes once they reached Oldmarsh, when he could be certain that no one would happen upon him whilst he was naked.

Dylan continued with his task, the water around his hands growing cloudy. He hummed as he worked, a little tune his guardian used to sing him to sleep with. He used to know all the words. Now they were a haze of knights and—had it been stars?—something else he couldn't quite recall. He had barely listened to much beyond the melody.

Eventually, both his undertunic and robe were clean. Or at least, as much as they could hope to get outside of a proper laundering. Standing, he squeezed the excess water from the robe before shaking it out and setting his magic to work on drying it. Caught in the hot air surrounding him, the scent of lavender thickened.

He breathed deep, growing giddy on the fumes, and stretched. How he had missed the scent. Again, he reminded himself to pick a few of the sprigs later to carry with him.

His ears had grown tired of the old lullaby. He spun about with the drying robe twirling along with him, trying to use the clearing's natural breeze rather than make his own, and switched to the drone of a chant taught in the temple, one that the priests would often call upon him to lead during prayer.

The tale woven by the lyrics spoke of a departed lover drifting on the river, denying the Seven Sisters' judgement and suffering the eternal dark to linger for the one they'd given their heart to.

His voice started off as a mumble, but soon rose to its limits as he belted out the crescendo. Picking up the sleeves of his robe as if it were a partner, he danced in the middle of the lavender patch with the scent of crushed flowers invading his nostrils. His singing drifted on the air, all alone for once in a very long time.

It was a bittersweet tale. Years passed in the mortal realm whilst the fallen lover sat in unending silence. Boats bearing the lovers of other hearts would come and go, but never the desired one.

And yet, the song's melody always carried a sort of wistful delight as if the lover had come to the conclusion that, as long as they lingered in the dark and the quiet, shut off from the rewards of the afterlife, their heart still lived.

The priests back in the spellster tower would end the song there. But Dylan had unearthed a copy of the whole chant in the library. He knew the ending, understood that even the longest life must come to an end and, in the mortal lands, people continued their battles. He'd read the final section of the tale only once, of how the lover's heart finally faltered and the two were reunited on the river to be judged as one.

As he'd gotten older, he had noticed a distinct lack of that particular chant being used during their prayers. He understood the reasoning behind leaving it out, even before finding the ending. Spellsters weren't meant to have spouses or partners, so why have them sing a chant of an eternally devoted lover?

Still, the melody was pleasant and it brought back memories of a time when things were simpler, when his path in life hadn't been fully set by others.

~ ~ ~

Tracker awoke to the soft call of birds heralding the dawn. He lay still for a moment, listening for any sign of distress from outside his tent. Hearing only the subtle motions of a camp starting to wake from its slumber, he followed suit in readying himself for the day, sheathing the *infitialis* dagger he'd kept just within reach during the night and donning his undershirt.

Dressed with everything except his sword belt, he nipped out of his tent and into the forest to relieve himself, pausing on his way back to the camp to focus on the spellster's presence. It wasn't necessary, Dylan appeared eager in returning to the tower, but Tracker had escorted a multitude of less-than-willing spellsters and the habit was deeply ingrained.

The man's tent sat on the opposite end of the campsite and he often wasn't the first one to rise. Yet, when Tracker sought the storm-like tang of the spellster's presence, it appeared to be further away than it should.

Authril had been the last on watch. He had spied her crouching next to the banked campfire, prodding the embers back to life, clearly confident that Marin's traps would once again yield results.

He halted on the edge of the camp, catching a glimpse of the hunter herself as she disappeared into the undergrowth, no doubt to do as he'd done before bringing back whatever prey her traps had captured. Even though she was human and had none of the advantages in eyesight and hearing that the average elf claimed, Marin was quite sharp when it came to hunting.

He felt a little spoilt in having fresh meat whilst on the road. Typically, his supplies consisted of dried meat and nuts, with bread and cheese whenever he could. At a pinch, he could chew away at the bland squares of sailor's tiles cringing in the bottom of his pack.

The tent the warrior shared with Dylan showed the entrance was still slightly askew from a recent exit. Tracker checked to see if the spellster was inside, parting the flap enough to not disturb anyone.

As he had expected, there was a marked lack of the spellster's presence.

He regarded Authril and how she sat comfortably by the fire. Whilst it was possible for the man to have slipped by Marin's notice or that of the hedgewitch, Authril's hearing would be close to his own.

He'd been certain that, if the spellster attempted to run, she would've alerted him. Strange that the man's disappearance now hadn't drawn her to demand Tracker hunt him down. But then, a lot of things about the woman were peculiar, including her attitude towards the spellster.

She clearly didn't trust the man, or his magic, yet willingly shared a tent with him. She had even rebuffed Tracker's offer of altering the sleeping arrangements by moving Dylan into his tent. He thought it made sense, they both had the same equipment, or so he assumed, negating any need to tiptoe around each other when it came to shedding clothes and having the spellster close would be a necessity once they reached Oldmarsh.

Yet, Authril acted as if he'd been trying to con her. What she thought would happen with the pair of them sharing a tent was beyond him. Dylan had already reacted negatively to a casual compliment. Granted, Tracker hadn't meant it as a flirt, but it had been received as one and rejected, placing the man firmly in the not-for-him category.

He cleared his throat, drawing the warrior's attention from the embers. "You saw where our dear spellster went, yes?"

Shrugging, she jerked her head in the direction of the pond where they'd filled their water skins yesterday evening. "He headed that way not too long ago. Figured he was relieving himself."

Tracker conceded her point with a grunt. Maybe that was it. A simple draining of the bladder, or an evacuation of bowels, wouldn't take the man long. He could afford to give the spellster privacy to deal with such matters.

He returned to his tent to fetch a few effects from his pack. If Marin's hunting continued its streak of success, then they would be lingering whilst whatever she'd caught cooked. That gave him plenty of time to bathe.

Magic flared to life somewhere ahead, brief enough to skitter across his senses before fading back into a familiar radiating hum.

Tracker straightened. Even for a spellster, seeing to basic needs didn't require magic. He grabbed his sword belt, buckling it as he headed into the forest. "I will return," he shot over his shoulder. Hopefully, with the spellster in tow.

Away from the immediate perimeter of their camp, there was but a single trail of footprints made by them yesterday as they staked out a clearing. One set was fresher and headed in the opposite direction, the same direction as he felt the spellster. *Dylan.* At least the man hadn't veered off into places unknown.

What was he doing this far from the camp? He hadn't wandered the previous few nights. Was he headed for the pond? Perhaps it was simple curiosity. There were no such bodies of water near the spellster tower. Had the man encountered something sinister along the way? Was he still alive?

The glow of more magic being utilised answered that last thought. Low but sustained. Not at all like the frenzied blasts the man harnessed whilst fighting. *Not bandits, then.* Yet, the power continued to shift, weaving as though the path the spellster took wasn't straight.

Tracker continued following yesterday's trail towards the pond, more inquisitive than concerned. The man's footprint eventually deviated, only slightly, but enough to warrant following it. Was he trying to run away? It didn't feel like the magic was growing fainter.

What then?

The airy notes of someone singing reached him. He peered through the trees, catching a flash of movement. Slinking closer, he spied what looked to be a person—no, two—moving erratically through a clearing.

One of them had to be Dylan; the movement matched the flow of magic too well to be anything else. Who was he with? Katarina? He hadn't seen the hedgewitch. Was *she* singing? Had the man stumbled upon someone else?

The trees became less of a barrier. Tracker halted in their shade, unsure what to make of the scene before him.

In the handful of situations he expected the spellster to be in, coming across Dylan parading through a cluster of lavender hadn't been one of them, doubly so for the man to be in little more than his boots and smallclothes with what appeared to be sprigs of lavender entwined upon his head. But it was indeed the spellster.

Dylan was also the source of the singing, for the clearing held no one else. What Tracker had mistaken for another person was the man's robe and Dylan appeared to be... dancing with it?

He watched for a few steps. It wasn't any dance Tracker was familiar with, but the movements did complement the singing. The man held the robe by the arms, close enough to what one would do with a partner. Utilised magic continued to radiate from the man, although Tracker couldn't pinpoint what that use was.

He also seemed oblivious to Tracker's presence.

Content to let the spellster cavort and sing in peace for a while longer, Tracker leant against a tree trunk.

When he'd first encountered the man, he had anticipated someone far more serious. Spellsters who fled the tower looked only for a way out of Demarn. They had no time to be playful, certainly not with the very hound hunting them. Those new to their power who he had found amongst ordinary folk were often frightened. Many closed themselves off to outside stimulation, their minds too focused on what was to come.

Dylan didn't have to worry about either of those factors. He was no runaway and knew precisely what awaited him back at the spellster tower.

Still, this was unforeseen. Not merely because of the man being solely in his smallclothes or even that he used his clothing as a dance partner. The simple joy of Dylan's actions pulled at him, just as the choral lightness in his voice soothed something within that he hadn't noticed was aching.

Tracker found himself softly humming a few notes, the song vaguely familiar. His foot tapped in time to the man's steps. A part of him longed to join in, to be just as carefree and in the moment, but he'd a feeling Dylan only continued because he believed he was alone.

Pity. Tracker considered himself as a more-than-adequate dancer, definitely better than an empty robe. Whilst most of his attempts at finding even a scrap of heart-thumping pleasure in the world came via dancing of the horizontal sort, he did enjoy the traditionally vertical kind. At least the man was fun to watch, and certainly more nimble than Tracker expected for someone with so much leg.

Although he had considered the man as off limits, he wasn't entirely sure. Finding out if Dylan was game could prove interesting.

He ran a considering eye over the man. In terms of looks, Dylan was pleasing to the eye. His face had the sort of soft classic beauty that would make a sculptor swoon.

A swathe of dark hair covered the man's chest. Tracker could definitely see himself enjoying that. Elves had little to play with, certainly nothing thick enough for him to sink his fingers into, to listen to his nails lightly running across the ivory skin beneath. Maybe he could even go so far as to toy with the man's nipples and see how he reacted to the wetness of a tongue or a teasing pinch.

On the other hand, there was a lack of softness about the rest of him. Wrapping around that beanpole of a frame would definitely be more akin to hugging a lamppost. Whilst Dylan didn't look stick-thin or sickly, there was a marked lack of substance. It put Tracker in the mind of a much-loved stuffed doll that had become stretched over the years. Tracker hadn't met many adult spellsters who were otherwise, even the children tended towards gangly.

Not once would he have ever considered such power could be contained by someone so slight.

Or maybe that immense power was, in part, responsible? He hadn't considered a correlation between a spellster's magic and their physique before now. He knew that using magic tired them, that it required a spellster to be healthy and fed—the same as any person doing manual tasks, be that typical labour or fighting. Whilst Tracker doubted the man could ever be considered beefy, no matter how many clothes he tried to hide that physique under, he did wonder if it also had a hand in how they grew during childhood.

The man also seemed softly spoken—the current belting out of song notwithstanding—and willing to let others guide him. That was a trait Tracker could definitely work with. In the bandit fight, Dylan's attacks were more defensive and methodical, yet he had been swift to offer his healing abilities. A caring nature was never a bad attribute to have, but it was a curious one to find in a spellster the overseers had sent into the army. Whatever their reasoning, Dylan was no fighter. Perhaps that was for the best.

Dylan's voice grew stronger and Tracker realised just what the man sang. *A temple chant.* One of the more romantic ones about a devoted lover waiting in the watery tunnels before the true afterlife.

Tracker knew it well, although he considered it a fantasy for children. Such love didn't exist. Not for long. Experience told him that betrayal was a far more common certainty and people who were as truly loyal to another as the being in the song were nothing but myths.

He would discover the truth eventually, providing his deceased lovers had been as devoted to him as they claimed. Most likely, he would find himself drifting alone in the dark for eternity.

Shaking the thoughts free, he returned to enjoying the man's display. Death came to all, the King's Hounds often faced it sooner than most. One day, it would be his turn. He had made peace with the fact years ago. All he had left was the ability to make the best of whatever came his way. Be it as simple as good food lining his stomach or as unexpected as a certain spellster's singing.

He joined in, relegating himself to only humming the tune. He caught himself singing along, stopping a few times before he got too loud. It was difficult, Dylan's enthusiasm had an infectious strain, encouraging him to get steadily lost in the song and the rhythm of the man's dancing.

CHAPTER 28

Dylan spun, suddenly aware that his voice wasn't the only one shaping the song. He searched the forest, finding the hound leaning against a tree.

Tracker smiled guiltily. "Please, do not stop on my account."

"I..." he squeaked. His gaze dropped to the clean and dry robe he clutched to his chest, his face burning furiously. "I didn't even hear you approach." He'd been so caught up in just being free to do as he pleased with the morning that he hadn't considered anyone might return.

"That is the point of sneaking, yes?" The elf held up his hand, forestalling any reply on Dylan's part. "Startling you was not my intention and I hope you will forgive me for the intrusion. Our dear warrior said you had gone this way, then I heard singing and..." He shrugged. "I was intrigued. It is not every day that one hears such delicate music in the forest. You have quite the high range, yes?"

Of course he heard me. It should've crossed his mind how far a countertenor voice like his would've carried. Everyone knew that elven ears heard better than both dwarven or human, but they were also more sensitive to certain ranges. Authril likely had, or would've, had the camp been closer.

"I thought it was the hedgewitch at first, that she had joined you, which would have been quite strange as I am certain Marin would have mentioned it. Then I considered you had, perchance, encountered another woman to join our little group."

And that makes me feel so much better. Dylan eyed his undertunic. It sat in a wet lump near the water. "I was just—"

"You were in the middle of laundering your clothes," Tracker finished. "I understand." The elf stood right next to him, one russet brow raised. "So, you do your own laundry *and* sing? People must have been lining up to have a piece of you back at the tower, yes?"

"Not really," he mumbled. How much could one of the King's Hounds know about the running of the spellster tower? "Doing laundry was a punishment."

Tracker chuckled. "I thought as much. However, I wonder..." He slowly reached up and removed the crown of lavender sprigs from Dylan's head. "Do you often dance about in your smallclothes?"

The revelation that he was all but naked in the man's presence hit him. Dylan hastened to don his robe. The rest could wait until later.

The man hummed as he examined the woven circlet, his generous mouth flattening. "And you have gone so very silent. You think I mock you, yes?" Those honey-coloured eyes flicked up, seemingly examining him. "If so, then I apologise. Truthfully, I have never heard a man sing so lightly. I was not even aware one could. It was a surprise to discover yourself as the source, but a pleasant one. You sing beautifully."

Heat took Dylan's cheeks. "Thank you," he managed, turning his back to the man and making his way to where his belt and sodden undertunic sat.

"I admit," Tracker continued, clearly following him. "I am amazed that you were so familiar with such a chant more than anything."

Why wouldn't he be? Granted, it wasn't sung often, but that didn't mean he couldn't be familiar with it. "As are you." He hadn't been mistaken in the confidence behind the elf's deep, silken voice.

"Of course." Tracker shrugged. "I remember the bimonthly outings to the temple as a child quite fondly. Our mistress demanded nothing less from us and it was one of the few times our carers were unable to beat us."

Dylan froze in the act of retrieving his belt. "They... beat you?"

"Not for some years now. My training was completed quite a while back."

"And beating you was part of your training?" He peered at the man, trying to determine the truth. The hound didn't look to be holding back any laughter or forcing his expression to remain neutral.

"Naturally. There are a great number of physical strains placed on pups as well as mental hurdles." He spoke very matter-of-factly. "Not everyone makes it through such trials, of course." His brows gained a perplexed twist. "They did not treat you this way back in the tower?"

"Never." Tricia had never even threatened to hit him and he didn't know of anyone who'd been treated in such a fashion. There was always the odd rumour surrounding this or that guardian and how harshly they would treat their charge, but those rumours often died down or the guardian was rarely seen around spellsters again.

"Truly? How bizarre." Tracker offered back the crown. "It is wonderful weaving, by the way."

"Thank you." He fiddled with the circlet, picking at the buds as his face warmed once more. He had learnt from Sulin that not every elf was aware of their people's traditions. Was Tracker one of them? Or had he noticed the little intricacies in the weaving, realised Dylan had learnt it from an elf, and opted to keep his thoughts to himself? "We should probably return to the camp. The others must be awake by now."

"They were indeed stirring as I came here. Marin has likely already emptied her traps by now and preparing breakfast whilst the others no doubt pack up the tents. However, I think…" He circled Dylan, his strides fluid like a cat sizing up his prey. "Well, we have been walking for quite some time and there was the fighting. Have you considered washing more than your clothes?"

"Not really." He'd given himself a brief wash down in a basin just last night and typically did so most mornings, but actual full-body bathing? "There's no bath."

Tracker laughed. "There is indeed such a convenience." He indicated the pond with a jerk of his thumb. "And I think I shall indulge fully whilst the women are occupied." He waved a little pouch, which had a familiar soap bar bulge in one corner. "You are welcome to join me."

He eyed the pond. The water was relatively clear and revealed nothing sinister lurking under the surface. "It'll be cold." Not that it would stay that way for long if he wanted, but if the hound thought Dylan was about to heat an entire pond for his use, then the man was very much mistaken.

Tracker shrugged. "It is an incentive to be quick, yes? Consider it as my gift to your sleeping companion that you return to her smelling sweeter." He sniffed the air. "Not that you would notice any change with the rather thick perfume you have made of these poor flowers." He tipped his head, a playful grin skewing his lips. "Or is it that you are afraid of a little cold water?"

Knowing he was being goaded, Dylan still conceded and let his robe fall alongside his sodden undertunic. He had shared the tower bathing room with a group of naked men before, surely he could handle being in a pond with one. His boots swiftly joined the rest of his clothes before the elf could finish unbuckling his belt.

Dylan slipped into the pond. The coolness bit into his skin. He waded down the gentle incline, shuffling to keep himself from kicking up too much water, stopping only when he reached what seemed to be the deepest part of the pond.

That still meant the water only came to his knees.

Probably for the best. It wasn't as though he could swim.

The hound's laughter, rich and light, drifted across from the shore. "My dear man," he called. "You seem to have forgotten to remove a piece of your attire. Or were you planning on bathing in your smallclothes?"

When there was a chance of being snuck up on by the others? Definitely the latter. Not that it mattered. He could've chosen to bathe fully clothed and the fabric would've dried quick enough once he turned his magic to them. This way, at least his smallclothes got a rinse of sorts.

Shrugging, he knelt. His breath was stolen from him in the brief moment his waist slipped beneath the waterline. Turning his magic to gently heat the water made it bearable. He expanded his focus until a comfortable circle of warmth surrounded him, constantly reheated as the current swirled cooler water into the mix.

There wasn't much he could do to cleanse himself without a cloth or soap, but he rubbed at his damp skin anyway, hoping to sluice off the lavender pollen and whatever might've stuck to him on the short walk from camp.

Perhaps if he asked, the hound would share usage of the soap in that pouch.

A small sigh parted his lips as the water sloshed against his chest. How long had it been since he had encountered a body of water big enough to kneel in like this and still cover so much of him? *Decades.* If it wasn't for the certainty that he'd all the buoyancy of a rock, he would've dared to lay back and stretch upon the pond's surface.

He glanced up to find the hound had shed the top half of his armour. The man still wore a thin undershirt, but it did little to obscure the way the elf's muscles shifted beneath the off-white cloth. Dylan found himself unable to avert his eyes from such a view.

Something deep in his gut stirred as the rest of Tracker's attire—everything from the leather boots and trousers to the man's smallclothes—was swiftly discarded.

Despite trying not to look, Dylan's gaze swept over the man, his breath rasping through his throat. Like other elven men, the hair on Tracker's chest and limbs was sparse. The man was surprisingly well muscled. Not the trained robustness of Authril nor the leanness of Marin, but a definition that spoke both of suppleness and strength.

What he hadn't expected was the myriad of tattoos marking the hound. They accentuated his bronze skin and rather invited the eye to travel downwards.

Dylan swallowed, his mouth left rather dry by the sight.

Tracker strode into the pond, spraying water with every step and seemingly oblivious to any scrutiny. "I see you have found the deepest part of the pond." He settled into the water not that far from where Dylan knelt. His brows lowered. "It is… warmer here? Surprisingly so. I know there are hot pools in the southern lands, but—"

"It's my doing," Dylan blurted. Closing his eyes, he continued, "I used my magic to heat the water."

The gentle slosh of water followed the sucking silence made by his confession. The hound's presence suddenly seemed a lot closer. "And that is also the reason for your sudden ill look, yes?" Tracker chuckled. "My dear man, I am not planning on reprimanding you for not wanting to bathe in cold water. I… simply had no idea that such a thing was possible. Does that also explain the warm air amongst the lavender?"

He nodded, his chest still tight. Albeit for a different reason than fear of being scolded. Even without looking, he knew the hound was close. Enough for the hair on Dylan's arms to brush the hound's skin and send a shiver through his core.

The man's warm hand closed around Dylan's forearm. "And how far can you make it reach?"

"Not very," he mumbled, risking a peek.

Tracker did indeed kneel as close beside him as he had believed. The man's honey-coloured eyes regarded him, bright with curiosity and something else Dylan preferred not to linger on. "If that is so, then would you mind if I stayed close to you? I am not averse to bathing in cold water, but if I can avoid it…" He spread his hands wide, relinquishing his hold on Dylan in the process and giving a good view of his torso.

Dylan opened his mouth, his tongue freezing in place. The spot where the hound had touched him still hummed, the area cooler in the absence of the man's warm grasp. His stomach bubbled, but that could've easily been last night's meal not sitting well with him. Averting his eyes to the opposite side of the pond helped everything but his steadily warming face. "I…"

The man sat back. "I am making you uncomfortable, yes? You are allowed to refuse such a request. I assure you, I will not be upset."

He worried at the inside of his bottom lip. "Have you ever dealt with a spellster before?"

Tracker glanced up from where he had started to scrub a small piece of cloth over his bar of soap. "No small number of times, yes." One russet brow lifted. "Why do you ask? Do I not put out an air of experience?" The final word left Tracker's lips in a breathy tone that tingled across Dylan's shoulders. There was a certain quirk in the twisting of the hound's mouth that told him the reaction had been noticed.

Dylan shuffled across the pond floor a little ways, trying to put some distance between them without being too obvious. He moistened his suddenly dry lips. "It's not that. I—"

The elf laughed. "Ah, you mean your head is swimming with tales of the evil King's Hounds, yes?" The fine lines around the man's eyes deepened. "They use our presence like a mother uses the bogeyman."

The way he spoke suggested he had heard directly from the source at some point.

"And where would you hear such tales? Not from the tower." He was certain word would've gotten about if Tracker had ever stepped foot inside the tower walls. Even without being a hound, the man would've drawn the attention of several tower inhabitants and Dylan was pretty certain he would've remembered that face if they had met before.

"No." The hound scrubbed at his neck as he spoke. "I have been inside many times, but the guardians are, let us say *reluctant*, to let us linger for long." He continued on to his shoulders, heedless to the suds running down his chest in thin pearlescent lines.

Dylan followed their trail to the water's surface, his breath tight. He watched, not quite focused, as the man bathed.

The air quickly gained the aroma of citrus and a pungent spice that seemed familiar, but Dylan couldn't quite put his finger on. He breathed deep until it filled his nose. *Cinnamon.* The taste of it was in the back of his throat, setting his mouth to watering. Bad enough that the man wasn't exactly unpleasant to look at, did he have to smell so accursedly edible as well?

The hound's soft chuckle had Dylan refocusing his attention, surprised to find he'd been staring at the man the whole time. "Do we perhaps see something we like?"

Snapping his gaze back up to the man's face, he shook his head. "Not at all." It wasn't the first time he had seen a naked elf, of more than one gender, and the man had absolutely nothing that could interest him.

And yet, there was something about the hound that made it difficult to look away. It had to be the tattoos.

"Is that a bit of blood in your hair?" Dylan managed, pleased to have found something to divert the man's attention.

Surprised, the hound pulled the long braid over his shoulder. He gave a disgusted grunt and released the thong keeping his hair together. The tight braiding unravelled, his hair springing into small corkscrew-like curls as if it possessed a life of its own.

Dylan covertly watched Tracker wash his hair, unable to keep his gaze from travelling down the man's body. The tattoos kept tempting his eye.

Some of them were simple, like the faded interlacing weave of elven design banding the man's right bicep. Others were clearly merged, such as the tattoo running the length of his left arm—a mixture of an angular, tribal-like snake weaving through a splay of what looked to be a Demarn leaf-like motif—with both the snake's head and the leaf pattern extending across the man's shoulder to encompass the pectoral.

An array of dots and lines scrolled down the man's right side, following the musculature, coaxing his gaze to trail down to the end. Scars criss-crossed a number of the tattoos, marring some of them beyond recognition, whilst others had been inked over. Some of the designs reminded him of fire, like the delicate, almost sketchy, bloom of what looked to be a bird at the man's left hip. Its head pridefully arched up the man's side, framed by its own flaming wings.

Dylan's gaze travelled down to the bird's long tail feathers, splayed wide to curl around the hound's thigh.

"Keep looking at me like that and a man could get ideas."

He jerked his gaze back up to find the hound smirking at him.

Warmth slowly blossomed in his cheeks. "Sorry, I—" His mind worked frantically for an excuse. "I wasn't—" He halted his tongue before the outright lie could finish. "I just haven't seen hair that long before." The words came out in a rush, but they were true. Not on a man, at least. Certainly not of such a texture. "Doesn't it get bothersome?"

"Oddly enough, I find day to day more manageable with it at this length."

"Really? I've a friend back at the tower who would claim otherwise." Sulin's hair had been of a decent length when he first arrived at the tower. Not as long as the hound's and denser, more tightly curled. The first thing the young man had done was chop it back to an inch thick. He'd kept it that way ever since. "But then, he's an alchemist."

"Ah." The elf wrung out his hair. "I suppose growing it to such lengths is impractical when things keep going boom around you."

"What do you know about alchemists?" Few hounds came to the tower without either a leashed one or a young spellster present. How many would've been allowed to venture into the underground rooms where not even other spellsters were permitted?

"I know they are trained to work with *infitialis* and are responsible for the collars."

The mere mention of them set Dylan's neck to itching. He rubbed at it, very much aware that he shouldn't be able to, that his fingers should be touching cool metal rather than scarred skin. "Do you know the word means negative in the Ancient Domian language?"

"I did not," the hound murmured as he resumed bathing. "But then, I also do not speak such an ancient language."

Few in Demarn did, even amongst those in the tower. Dylan had learnt through his dealings with helping the hedgewitches. Most of the older texts involving ancient dwarven sites were written in Domian. The once prosperous empire of Domian was where the usage of using collars to bind each other started. It continued until their land was consumed by the growing Udynea Empire, who kept the metal's name as well as its use.

Dylan had heard several tales from Launtil and the other escaped slaves on how the emperor reputedly had half-a-dozen highly-trained alchemists at his command just in case the nobility needed keeping in check. He wasn't certain how much of it was true, but it sounded like something an emperor would have. "Most alchemists refer to *infitialis* as dog metal." He wasn't sure why, figured it was something the younger ones picked up and carried on until they'd forgotten the origins.

Nevertheless, this titbit of information garnered a chuckle from the hound. "Cute."

Dylan sat there, unable to think of a good reason to leave even though he was essentially done with the water. He supposed he could wash his hair, but that seemed pointless without the soap currently in the man's possession.

"So, tell me..." Tracker said, breaking the silence. "What *is* the tower's current thought on hounds nowadays? Do they still believe we drink your blood to enhance our abilities?"

"Some might believe such tales. I don't."

"Ah, a sharp one, are we?" The man bent to wash his legs and Dylan discovered that the tattoos extended to more than one, with several light-inked shapes curving over his buttocks and down his thighs. "Of course, the tales are somewhat less gory than they used to be. I remember one from when they first sent me out on the hunt. There was this young elven spellster..." He grimaced. "She was terrified I would sacrifice her under a full moon, because that is apparently what we do."

"I..." Dylan tilted his head. There were hints of other designs up the man's spine, obscured by the wet curls draped over his back. "I haven't heard that one."

He just caught the glint of the man's gaze looking his way before it was obscured by an arm. "Oh, yes. And your entrails are supposed to make a decent diviner's aid. Never discovered what we were meant to be divining for that would constitute such a messy business."

Dylan hummed, his thoughts drifting elsewhere as his gaze idly tracked the lines travelling down the man's side. His fingers itched to touch them. He balled his hands. "Ancient Domian used to perform haruspicy." He didn't recall the tower library holding any records of the Domian priests using either human or dwarf for the act. Although, it was possible they didn't class slaves or the leashed as people.

"But some are willing to believe anything, yes?" The elf slid closer.

"Such as how much someone is unlikely to notice them staring."

His heart all but leapt out of his mouth. "I don't know what you're talking about." He couldn't have been staring that much, surely. A few glances here and there.

"Do we not?" Tracker grinned. "Come now, my dear spellster. We have the same equipment. There is no need for you to hide yourself behind these." The man's long fingers slid down Dylan's side, hooking into the waist of his smallclothes and tightening every muscle in his body. "Or to be so modest."

"I'm not being modest." He wasn't quite sure why he'd chosen to keep his smallclothes on in the first place, especially since the appearance of either of the three women was unlikely, but he wasn't about to remove them with the man so close. And insistent.

"Then how about you take them off?" Tracker purred, his breath skittering along Dylan's ear. "We could help each other get clean, yes?"

He swallowed, his mouth having gone completely dry. "Actually, I..." His smallclothes felt that little bit too tight. He was certain it had nothing to do with the water and everything to do with the warm hand creeping up his thigh.

Dylan stood in a rush of water, keeping himself slightly hunched over. "I'm fine!" he blurted, hedging towards the pond's edge. "Done. Clean. I'll just go and wait with the others whilst you finish up."

Tracker raised a brow at him and Dylan could've sworn the man was smirking. "If you feel you must depart so quickly." The hound's gaze returned to his armour. "But camp is the other way."

He stared at the man, then their surroundings. The crop of wild lavender he had previously walked through graced the far side of the pond. *Of course it is.* Skirting the pond, he gathered up his clothes and rushed for the nearest bush.

Confident the elf didn't follow, Dylan flattened himself against a tree trunk. His heart pounded almost hard enough to make him believe he was about to pass out. He clutched his clothes to his chest, uncaring that his sodden undertunic was steadily undoing his work at drying his robe.

Had he really stirred at something as simple as the man's touch? It wasn't as if he hadn't ever had a man show interest in him before and, yes, a part of him enjoyed the attention. But never had he reacted quite like *that*.

He brushed back his hair. *It's not what you think.* It couldn't be. Even the sight of a naked woman wouldn't have garnered this sort of reaction. It had to be the warm water playing tricks with his senses.

Yes, that had to be it.

Even as the thought crossed his mind, he knew that wasn't the answer. That didn't fix the fact he didn't get those sorts of feelings for men. He most certainly didn't respond.

Then what, by the gods, *what* had just happened?

CHAPTER 29

"You're far more lenient than I expected from someone who hunts spellsters," Katarina said. "Especially as he's unleashed."

Tracker glanced up from his task of hammering in a tent peg to where the dwarf did similar with her shelter. It was just him and the hedgewitch in this evening's chosen site. Marin had vanished into the bushes to lay her traps, Authril was out scouting their surroundings for any sign of trouble and Dylan gathered wood far enough away to be out of immediate earshot.

That last point had likely been the cause for Katarina's observation.

"Why would I not grant him some measure of freedom?" he countered. "Dylan has shown himself to be trustworthy." At least, he showed no interest in leaving their side whilst they remained travelling and spending their night in the forest. The man's placid demeanour could easily shift once they reached Oldmarsh and he had other options close at hand. Albeit, he seemed smart enough to know that running wouldn't guarantee an escape. "As for the leashing..." Shrugging, he returned to hammering in the tent pegs. "There is nothing I can do about that." He hadn't the abilities, or the metal, to even make an attempt. He wasn't certain if it would make a difference.

Having finished pitching his tent, he made a start on the one shared by the spellster and the warrior. As always when he needed to deal with the third tent, the addition irked him. Divvying their space in such a manner might've made sense when it had been the four of them, but he slept alone and the shelter the hedgewitch shared with the hunter appeared big enough for three.

Being this spread out meant more time given to setting up, and tearing down, each campsite. It also amounted to less time on the road. Without a horse, everywhere felt as though it sat on the other side of the continent. The distance to Oldmarsh wasn't great, a little over a week on foot. But if they kept dallying like this, it would take twice as long. Even without pushing, and having the spellster ride double, a decent horse would've brought them to the city's walls by now.

A decent horse. He grumbled wordlessly at the thought. He didn't want just any horse. He wanted *his* horse. The one duty had forced his hand into leaving behind.

Tracker bit his cheek, crushing the twinge of not having Lullaby near with a fresher pain. That he didn't know how the animal fared only added to his bitterness. He hadn't been without the stallion's presence for years.

When this was over, he would return to Toptower and retrieve Lullaby to retire somewhere northward.

The hedgewitch assisted him with securing the tent's sides. They completed the task in silence and set about clearing a space for the night's fire. The area held enough kindling to get a decent flame started. Anything sustainable would rely on Dylan's foraging, but he was confident in the man's abilities.

With their tasks done and waiting the only option left, Katarina settled next to the fire. As she often did at the end of the day, she retrieved a little book from her hip pouch and began writing in it. He assumed it was a log of sorts, but couldn't fathom what could be so interesting in their journey that she would have need of daily documentation.

Normally, he would be content to sit in the calm before the rest returned, but his body demanded some manner of action. With Authril checking the perimeter, no sign of trouble and the nearest brothel being still days away, it left only training to occupy him.

After decades of wielding a blade, he hardly needed to remind himself how to use one. Still, he unsheathed his scimitar and moved from the fireside, idly falling into the first set of moves he'd ever been taught. The clearing was only big enough if he wove around their tents, but hounds were supposed to be ready for any obstacle and the tent pegs were merely an incentive for him to be precise with his footing.

He practised in silence, keeping an ear out for the others returning. As it had since its creation, the blade sliced smoothly through the air. His childhood trainers might have selected the sword as his main weapon, but *he* had made it an extension of himself, had perfected this deadly dance to the point where few could best him.

After a while, he spied Katarina glancing his way. She did so several times, briefly pausing in her writing to watch him, before finally setting the book aside. "I know we've only been travelling together for a short time, but since we're currently alone, I wish to ask something."

"Ask away," he replied, not halting his practising.

"Did something happen between you and Dylan a few days ago?"

"Not at all." Encountering the man dancing mostly naked beside the pond had been three mornings ago. He was still marginally surprised how worked up he'd gotten at the thought of the spellster, to the point where he had needed to tend to himself before returning to camp. Since then, Tracker hadn't said or done much beyond the occasional word or gesture.

He'd slept with a handful of spellsters over the years, but they'd been dangerous lapses of judgement. Hounds were allowed to satisfy sexual urges—albeit, few made a habit of it—but those they escorted were meant to be off limits.

He was also aware that those in the spellster tower weren't supposed to engage in sexual activities. Whilst it would be delusional to believe the entirety of the tower followed such a rule—especially as *he* had been born not far from its walls and, as far as he could determine, was a product of what went on within—Dylan being a virgin was no less of a possibility.

Tracker no longer had much to do with those lacking certain experiences, not since his mistress summoned him back from his stint of enforced employment at *The Gilded Lily*.

Regardless of whether Dylan had experience involving more than his hand, the glances he gave Tracker suggested he definitely had some understanding of the act.

"His demeanour has changed," Katarina pointed out.

"I have noticed." Dylan had become far more easily flustered since that morning at the pond, largely when being alone with Tracker was unavoidable. It was as though Tracker's interest had come as a surprise and he had no idea how to respond. Had no one in the tower expressed such an opinion before? That could explain why Dylan uttered no desire for Tracker to stop when he had subtly flirted yesterday. Nor the day before.

The mixed signals baffled him. Never had he encountered so many. There was the chance he hadn't been obvious enough, but he was willing to play along for now. The forest held little else in the way of entertainment and watching the man's ivory cheeks gain a delicate pink hue at simple words was its own reward.

Tracker halted by his tent. Swinging his sword about, even if it was in proper form and with perfect footwork, did nothing to relax the itch for action. What he needed was someone to spar with. Dylan would be the ideal. It would also aid in training the man to battle against people. But any protracted fight with a spellster was meant to end in their death, and quickly lest they discovered that the King's Hounds were immune to magic. No spellster could be allowed near those within the tower with such information.

Grumbling to himself, he collected his cleaning gear and joined the hedgewitch near the fire. He unravelled his kit of vials, plucked one of the many oils from its sleeve and settled into rubbing it over his scimitar. It might not be the action he craved, but the rhythm and familiar motion would eventually calm him.

Katarina threw a thin branch onto the fire. They'd only scrounged a handful from the clearing. If Dylan didn't return soon with more wood, then they would have to let the flames die. The hedgewitch further rifled through her pouches, fishing out what appeared to be leftovers from breakfast. She skewered the already cooked meat, dangling it over the flames.

"Hungry?" she asked, offering a piece once they'd sufficiently warmed. "I know elves require more in the way of meat than others."

Tracker graciously accepted the morsel, savouring the warmth. "Indulge me, if you will, for I am curious. What is the reason you insist on travelling with us?" Parting ways might not have been an option before reaching Toptower, but a good horse would've seen her settled in better accommodations with a proper escort by now. "The spellster tower may reside to the north, and your homeland beyond that, but there are no northern roads leading directly to Dvärghem from there." The closest was at Wintervale and Tracker's task of shepherding the spellster to the tower would be over by then.

"*I* was the one who found Dylan." She prodded at another of the meat chunks, seemingly unsatisfied as she returned it to the flames. "He was lying unconscious just within the entrance to a dwarven ruin, protected by its walls."

"And that ruin was the reason for you being there?" Tracker doubted any dwarf would choose one human realm over another, certainly not those with the intent of using them to spy, but she had already admitted crossing the Udynea border. It was possible the imperial army used her presence as a means to close on the Demarn forces.

She nodded, seemingly oblivious to his suspicions. "I wish we'd been able to linger. There aren't many records of our ancestors burning trees to ashes and salting the ground, but I'm sure that ruin marked such a place."

"Forgive me, I make no claims of being an expert of dwarves or their ancestral traditions." Especially when in comparison to an actual hedgewitch. "But destroying trees would be a strange thing for your people to do, yes?" Everything he'd ever heard about dwarves painted them as a peaceful people who lived with nature.

"It is," she agreed, grinning. "The text we have on the subject comes from even older oral tales and they're vague on why, like it was common knowledge. The most we can deduce was the trees were dangerous in some way." She threw up her hands in defeat. "And once humans enter the records, mention of them grows scarce. There hasn't been a monstrosity like that for hundreds of years."

Having tended to his scimitar, Tracker sheathed the blade and pulled out his daggers. The one made from *infitialis* never needed more care than cleaning the blood from the surface, but the other was made from the same normal steel as the rest of his weapons.

His thoughts buzzed as he worked, snagging on one small point in Katarina's tale. "Did you say you found Dylan in the entrance to your ruin?"

Again, Katarina bobbed her head in agreement. "I thought him dead to begin with."

"If the ruins were to mark a place as dangerous as you say, then why would they leave an opening in the walls?" And how had centuries-old masonry withstood a blast that had knocked Dylan unconscious?

The hedgewitch frowned.

"Is it possible the site was *not* dwarven in nature?" The land near the border had changed hands many times over the centuries, the forest encroaching on abandoned fields. The ruin could've easily been a shrine to a god long forgotten or a hut owned by a hermit from a realm swallowed decades ago by war.

"The runes carved onto the outer wall were dwarven."

Content his dagger was sharp and clean, Tracker sheathed it and moved on to his throwing knives. He hummed as he glided his whetstone across the edges, considering the possibilities that led to either Dylan or Katarina lying. A lot could be answered if he'd seen the place for himself, but doubling back now would be pointless. "What colour was your ruin's stone?"

The hedgewitch shook her head. "Hard to tell after the fire. Grey, I think. And mottled white. Or that could've been the layer of soot. What does it matter?"

"Because there are certain stones that have a reasonable amount of tolerance when it comes to magic. They do not possess the same nullifying effect as *infitialis*, but the strongest can absorb a blast. Most of Demarn's older fortresses were built from them." Right up until they learnt their wooden doors turned any corridor into a handy funnel for the invading party. "Some are still standing." Those that hadn't seen spellsters storming their gates. "Such as the spellster tower's central structure and the royal castle at Wintervale."

Her eyes narrowed. At first, he thought the woman would argue the point, but she flipped open her book and began writing furiously. "I always assumed the resistance came purely from the way they were built. It never occurred to me that there might be other reasons. It absorbs, you say?" She continued on before Tracker could answer. "What do you think those ruins originally were? Some sort of spellster prison?"

Only when she'd been silent for more than a breath did he realise she was waiting for his response.

"I would be more inclined to think it was once a bedchamber." He had stumbled upon enough scenes of children scared of their own power to see the benefit of having a room they could release their magic without fear. "Before the kingdom confined spellsters to a single place, people tried to suppress its appearance in their family line, especially amongst the wealthier inhabitants. Your little ruin could be the remnants of a much larger building."

"How would you explain the runes carved into the archway? Those were dwarven. *Ancient* dwarven. Of that much I am certain."

He shrugged. "Who is to say they were not put there later, yes? By someone familiar enough with such markings? Perhaps with the intention of fooling you into thinking they need your help?" What better way to cross enemy lines than under the pretence of escorting a hedgewitch?

Katarina shook her head. "I would know if they were fake. And if you're insinuating that the people escorting me weren't honest..." She fell silent. Her fingers traced the scar running across her face. "They died protecting me from Udynean forces who weren't even meant to be there."

"And an exploding collar should have killed the one it leashed." He'd heard of such tales, so old they were more fable than reality, but *infitialis* was an unstable metal around magic.

"I was there in the beginning. I saw him wake, witnessed his fear and confusion at just being alive. He wasn't pretending. If your conclusion is that Dylan is some Udynean spy or defector—"

He held up a placating hand. "Your insistence on vouching for him is admirable but unnecessary." For himself, at least. The overseers would never believe Dylan's story. They might hear Authril's recount of events, although her word would carry little weight. Even Tracker's testimony would be barely considered.

But a hedgewitch? *Her* they would listen to. He just hoped she was able to recount matters well enough for the overseers to believe.

She nodded. "I admit, I'm also curious how he managed to free himself. I've examined the collar so many times. I can't imagine how he didn't die."

Tracker stretched out his hand. "May I see?" He'd caught only a glimpse during their encounter in Toptower, the low light combined with the tense air had made any extended scrutiny impossible.

"Of course!" She untied one of the pouches from her belt, upending the contents into Tracker's hands.

The collar hummed, a typical reaction to them being touched by a King's Hound. Strange that the *infitialis* dagger didn't, even though they were both made from the same metal, but he supposed the reason resided in the difference of their crafting.

The collar's damage was far beyond anything he had thought possible for a leashed one to survive. Broken in two, the smaller half was little more than a melted chunk, crumpled as though it was a piece of paper. Such warping would've taken the heat of a forge yet, if he ran his thumb along the inside curve, there were clear indentations. Finger marks.

How? Nothing he'd ever been taught could explain it. The very idea that Dylan had extracted himself from the collar's hold was, as far as he knew, unprecedented throughout Demarn's history. It was deemed impossible.

The evidence spoke otherwise. What it told him was implausible.

The collar had snapped from extreme heat and someone pulling on it, no question. Yet, any leashed spellster would've cooked his hands to the bone long before the metal was pliable enough. Dylan's palms showed no evidence of experiencing that.

And the scarring on the man's throat? Likely caused by the same blast that knocked him out. How had he survived *that*? Wounds took time to mend. After a week, it should've still been raw, but it looked older than some of Tracker's that were months old. He knew the man could heal others, but himself? Whilst knocked unconscious?

There had to have been another. Katarina made no mention of someone else being near the man when she found him, living or dead. He believed her. The spellster's recounting of it was less convincing.

"What are you doing with that?"

Tracker tore his attention from the collar to the man who'd worn it. Dylan stood at the edge of the clearing, his arms laden with wood. Those dark eyes regarded Tracker with a caged wariness.

"I wished to examine it," Tracker replied. "It will be of interest once we reach the tower." As would the nature of his unleashing.

Authril emerged from the forest at the man's back, also carrying a load of wood. She side-eyed Dylan as they both deposited the wood near the fire. "I'm sure they'll have a lot of questions for him to answer. Such as, how did you remove your collar?"

Dylan laid a hand on his throat, running his fingers along the scar. His gaze flicked in their direction, lingering on Tracker for some time. The man's hesitancy in speaking could've been attributed to the collar being out in the open, but Tracker doubted that was the only reason. Whilst he hadn't tried any advances as overt as his attempt at mutual bathing in the pond, Dylan's not-so-subtle glances were no less frequent, and at odds with the man's other body language.

"I wish I knew how," Dylan finally confessed, his gaze darting to the forest. "I don't think the overseers will be satisfied with me telling them I don't remember."

They certainly will not. Tracker had only encountered the overseers, and their charming presence, the once. He had left under suspicious circumstances, returning alongside another one was definitely going to put him under his mistress' eye.

But this was duty. He couldn't abandon it.

"I might not know about how these collars work," Authril confessed. "But I do know that the leashed can't remove them at will."

"That is the general understanding of it," Tracker agreed. "Although, the metal is notoriously unstable, yes?" he asked of Dylan.

The man nodded. "Just touching it with magic in the wrong way could cause an explosive reaction."

"Like maybe melting it with your bare hands?" The way the imprints sat, they could only have come from the wearer. Or perhaps someone standing behind the man, but that would've been a ridiculous way to unleash him.

"Maybe," Dylan mumbled. "I don't remember much. Just heat and... and..."

"Desperation, yes? I understand." He truly did. He might never have faced the same struggle, but the helplessness was no different.

Rustling through the bushes preceded Marin's return. She ducked beneath a tree branch, looking doubtful as she dusted off her hands. "There aren't many good tracks in the area. Might catch enough for a snack. But if—" She halted, taking in the camp. "Did I interrupt something?"

"Not at all," Tracker said. "We were merely discussing our dear spellster's collar, what remains of it, and how he unleashed himself."

Beside him, Katarina hummed. "I've always wondered, how the collars work. I've been told it reacts to one's mind, but how can it know you're getting a command from someone higher in the ranks? Do the alchemists weave spells into the collar?"

"I'm not sure," Dylan admitted. "The process of a leashing digs into your mind, true enough." He rubbed at his neck. "I think it links with my subconscious. *I* know a lowly soldier has no authority over a sergeant, so even if they ordered me to attack, the collar holds. Unless I also know his superiors are dead."

"I know a little more than that," Tracker said. He held up the larger chunk of the collar. This piece still had visible links. "The design is not only to make it pretty and pliable against the skin. There is magic woven through the links, enough to let your power slip between the cracks. It requires an intricate amount of detail. That magic attaches to your psyche, permitting you the usage of your power only on command."

Could that have been what had held the man back during the ambush? If Dylan's warden had been taken out and, in the chaos, he hadn't known who was next in command, then he would've been just another soldier. One with no weapons or the ability to use them.

Dylan narrowed his eyes, the act leaving a gleam of darkness. "How do you know that?"

"It is taught to us," Tracker replied, raising one shoulder. The more interesting question was how a leashed one didn't know, but he kept his mouth silent on that matter. "I also know how to remove one." Not that it was necessary here.

"Why would you remove a spellster's collar?" Authril queried, her expression briefly one of horror.

"Because they are dead?"

She frowned, clearly considering, then nodded as if deeming that reason an acceptable one. A peculiar stance given her shared sleeping arrangement with Dylan.

Katarina shuddered. "I had no idea the process was so horrid. I can't imagine anyone willingly doing that."

Marin wordlessly grunted her agreement with the hedgewitch.

"We don't exactly volunteer," Dylan replied.

"No," Tracker agreed, returning to tending to his throwing knife, giving the edge one solid swipe with his whetstone. "The overseers choose who is acceptable. They pick the fastest, the most creative…" He glanced towards the spellster, surprised to see the man's head drooped as if deep in the past. "And, of course, the strongest."

How had Dylan managed to evade being selected for so long? Had he hidden his strength? He certainly hadn't exerted much effort when the bandits attacked. Or when he heated the pond. Was it something the man did without thinking? Or something the guardians had drummed into him as a child?

"How can you actually want to be leashed again?" Marin asked the man.

"*Want?*" Dylan shook his head. "It doesn't work that way. I *must* be leashed. I can't stay in the tower. No one has ever permanently returned once that metal touches their necks. If I can't stay, then I have to be leashed. If I'm not, then I'm dangerous." The dual timbres of pain and panicked desperation thrummed through his typically light and pleasant voice. His magic crackled and bounced around him, not enough to affect his surroundings, but erratically present. "And if I'm dangerous…"

Then you will not live long. If the overseers deemed Dylan beyond saving, even for the army, he would be killed.

Such realisation seemed to only now occur to the man.

Tracker tightened his fingers around the hilt of his throwing knife. He focused on honing the blade, forcing his every scrap of attention to be on smoothing out the tiniest of nicks. It was the only way to keep himself from bundling Dylan into his arms and squeezing until not a hint of fear remained.

Fortunately, Katarina had no such restraint in comforting Dylan. She drew him close, quietly rubbing his back and shushing him until he fell silent.

Had the spellster not been through enough? He had survived the impossible, chosen to return to his duty rather than flee, and yet he faced a journey with the knowledge that a cruel fate could befall him once he reached his destination no matter what he did.

What was the alternative? *Death*. He didn't believe the man was a threat, but there weren't many within Demarn who would looked kindly upon a spellster wandering free amongst them. He would be hunted. Perhaps even by the unexpected.

His gaze slid to Authril. There was an air of suspicion about the woman. It had taken a few days to realise the source was not himself, but the spellster. Where Katarina showed no fear of Dylan's abilities, and Marin seemed to follow the hedgewitch's lead, Authril gave the distinct impression that she was waiting for the man to slip.

Did she fancy herself as a hound? Few outside the pack knew the truth behind their abilities, with many of them being long-dead spellsters. Based on the woman's swordwork alone, she would've never had a chance at gaining such a mantle.

"There's one thing I don't understand," Authril said. "You were unleashed inside the tower. Everyone is, correct? If the collars stop you from using magic except when you're told you can, then why not leash everyone?"

Tracker rolled his eyes. *Typical*. As though the same question hadn't been asked by would-be hounds throughout the ages. He'd been one of them, insisting it was the right answer until his trainers explained how the collar's worked and why leashing everyone wasn't viable. "*Infitialis* is a rare metal," he replied, echoing those old lectures. "And there are literal hundreds living within the tower. That is without even touching on how leashing everyone would lead to repurposing as children outgrew their collars." They didn't craft them to be tight, but the links he'd seen sat snugly against the skin, a fit that wouldn't be possible on a growing body. "Such tampering would make them highly unstable and—"

Authril wrinkled her nose. "Right, right," she said, waving her hand. "I remember it goes *boom!* really easily." She eyed the broken pieces sitting at Tracker's side as if talking about it might make the twisted remains do just that.

"I am certain an alchemist could explain the process better, but yes." His gaze slid to Katarina. The woman was back to writing in her little book, no doubt recording everything he said. He would have to be careful with what left his mouth.

"We still must be taught how to control our power," Dylan added, the conversation seemingly drawing him from his circular thoughts. "Even forming something as instinctual as a shield isn't easy without a threat. Learning it takes time and focus. Just like you trained how to swing a sword or Marin learnt to use her bow. Leashing a child whilst they're still fumbling with the basics would teach them to rely on that safeguard, which could lead to them endangering a lot of people through sheer ignorance if they ever found themselves unleashed."

Authril nodded, wordlessly agreeing with his every word. It wasn't surprising. Most people had the same outlook on spellsters that Dylan currently expressed.

Was that also the reason why Dylan hadn't once used the full strength of his power? Why he hesitated before fighting? Because he thought himself too dangerous? Tracker had seen enough proof over the past week to be confident in the man's ability to control his power. If Dylan hadn't caused an incident within the tower, he was unlikely to do so outside of its walls.

"I understand the training," Authril said. "But leashing doesn't stop a spellster from using magic. They just can't without someone giving them permission, right? What's to stop your guardians from being the people who sanction the use of magic whenever it's needed?"

"Such permission has to come from a place of authority," Tracker replied. "That is why a common soldier cannot order a spellster to do their bidding."

"So, if you were leashed now," Marin asked of the spellster, "who would you need to obey, Authril or Tracker?"

"Me." The reply fell from Tracker's lips without hesitation. Even if the man were to stumble upon those who'd been in the army, a hound's order overtook all but the highest ranking.

Dylan nodded. His gaze lifted, staring into the forest in the direction of the tower.

"And did you say there are *hundreds* of spellsters?" Marin continued.

"I believe the overseer's last census put them at little over a thousand," Tracker answered. "Although, you understand that a decent percentage of that number would be children and babies. And the guardians must answer to the overseers. Leashing everyone could very well mean the overseers would have to continuously sanction every lesson. Everywhere. That would involve hundreds of orders every day."

"Like a general having to dictate how every arrow is fired in battle."

"Exactly!" Tracker agreed, pleased that she saw the reasoning even if Authril still wore a puzzled frown. "So leashing is only used on those considered worthy of leaving." A few dozen people at most, all with their individual wardens.

"And those that leave for the army are all Dylan's age?"

"Yes," the man mumbled, still paying more heed to the trees. "They were."

Tracker shrugged. "I cannot vouch for all of them. The last time I was at the tower, they had chosen to send a young girl with the ability to create expansive illusions."

Dylan's head snapped back around. "What did you say?" The passive crackle of magic surrounding him abruptly froze, drawing closer to Dylan's core, readying itself for use. Just as it had in the moments before the man joined in attacking the bandits.

Tracker repeated himself slowly and softly. He might not have been under any immediate danger, but their companions were and the hedgewitch currently sat between them.

"That's a lie!" His face contorted into a snarl. "I heard what happened to her. She wasn't chosen for the army, they would *never* send a child."

"I assure you, that was the overseers' intention." They'd been testing the strength of several children when he'd met with the group of elders in charge of the spellster tower. "Her leashing was to be the next morning."

Dylan shook his head. "You're wrong. The overseers said her guardian was sick, delusional. She helped her charge escape and got caught in the process. And the girl?" His mouth twisted sourly. "Well, everyone knows what happens to runaways."

"I don't," Katarina admitted.

"Neither do I," Marin added.

"They kill them," Authril said, looking a little too pleased about the idea.

"The King's Law decrees that no spellster who leaves the tower is allowed to return," Tracker clarified. It was one of the higher laws, something no hound was supposed to break. Returning runaways was deemed too risky. They were too likely to learn what truly made hounds dangerous to spellsters. He'd known it when he had let the girl and her guardian slip through the tower's secret entrance, when he had helped stage the girl's death, when he had led her to the caravan that had ultimately been her doom.

And he knew how it would look now.

"Did you...?" Realisation smoothed the angry creases from Dylan's face. "You were there? You were the one sent after her, weren't you?" Sorrow darkened his eyes as Tracker nodded. "You killed her?" The thunderstorm scent of the man's power thickened in the air. "She was a *child*."

Authril clutched her sword hilt. Uncertainty stiffened her face. She had to know that drawing a weapon, especially a metal one, would be a bad idea in the man's current state.

Tracker held up his hand, stalling not only Dylan's actions, but the warrior's. "I will not deny I was there. I had arrived at the tower for another reason entirely about an hour before they set me on her trail, but I swear, I am not the one who took her life. Bandits are responsible for that and they paid for that act with their lives."

Dylan didn't look convinced, but seemed prepared to listen. Tracker took that silence as a chance to recount the last time he saw the young spellster. He left out most of the details. The last thing the man needed to hear was the grisly description of a charred merchant caravan. Nor could he exactly tell a spellster destined for the tower that he had also assisted in her initial escape.

The very act that had led to her demise.

Dylan remained silent for a long time after Tracker had finished. Those dark eyes fixed on him. The sharp focus of his magic slowly mellowed into a surrounding haze. "You are *sure*? I never saw them, but the illusions she made were supposedly extremely detailed."

And something Tracker's senses completely ignored. Again, not a secret he could reveal. "I buried her remains. Believe me, I am more than certain. I sincerely wish it was not true, that I was wrong, but..." He spread his hands in defeat. He'd been too late, plain and simple.

Dylan bowed his head, a weary breath parting his lips. "I'm sorry. I shouldn't have immediately jumped to accusing you of—"

"There is no need. I am aware of the tales spellsters are fed about us. It is logical that you would assume the worst." Maybe another hound would've played along, lived up to such horrific tales. He couldn't bring himself to. Not knowing everything the man had already been through.

Clearing his throat, Tracker hastened to gather up his gear and bounce to his feet. "I think it best we retired early this evening, yes? Leaving at first light would make better use of our time travelling." The sooner they reached the spellster tower, the quicker he could be on his way and done with this task. That was all he could do.

No matter how he wished otherwise, a King's Hound had no influence when it came to what the overseers did to the spellsters once they were within the tower walls.

CHAPTER 30

Their journey through the forest picked up pace. Dylan expected to come across signs of bandits, even if they wouldn't rejoin the road until tomorrow, but each day remained free of their presence. They were a mere two days from Oldmarsh now. Hopefully, the road beyond the city was just as clear. As much as he enjoyed travelling through the forest at the start, it had lost quite a bit of its romance.

Tracker strode ahead of them, the hound had ever since the attack. He'd made no further mention of finding the missing spellster child or the true extent of her fate. It must've been a grisly end. Whilst Tracker hadn't gone into any details, just the mention of burying her had been enough to disturb the man.

Now, Tracker seemed intent on redressing that lapse of showing emotion by being outwardly chipper. All the jokes and teasing had returned twofold.

It had Dylan re-evaluating all the tales about the King's Hounds he'd heard over the years. The belief of them being emotionless killers always felt off, but he had thought them cold. The woman who escorted him to the army certainly had been. *Distant.* He had thought it because she didn't care what became of them.

Now he wondered if perhaps that was simply her method of stopping herself from caring too much.

Most of the spellsters the hounds brought to the tower were children. He recalled many nights, lying awake in the dorms as a child, unable to sleep due to the bawling of newly-arrived youngsters longing for their parents. He couldn't imagine having to actually wrest those souls from their families, even if it was for everyone's safety.

"She's coming back," Authril declared. The warrior marched at Tracker's heels, her head swivelling from one side of their chosen path to the other in search of trouble.

In this instance, her announcement was of Marin's return. The hunter typically walked at their back or at the hedgewitch's side, occasionally vanishing into the surrounding undergrowth only to reappear ahead of them.

Sure enough, Marin popped out from the undergrowth. The brightly feathered carcass of a plump pheasant dangled from her pack.

Dylan eyed the bird, silently grumbling to himself. He couldn't recall ever dining on much in the way of game quite as frequently in the tower as he did out here. Back home, stews thick with vegetables rather than meat had been the typical evening repast. The midday meal was generally light, if at all, consisting of soups in the winter or sometimes a pie would be brought to those training in the outside arenas.

All this meat was starting to do weird things to his insides. He could've sworn he felt stronger, too. Not only in regards to his magic.

At Dylan's side, Katarina cleared her throat. "Sir Tracker—"

The hound glanced back, flashing a grin. "My dear hedgewitch, please. I have told you, we travel together, we have shared meals, there is no need to be so formal."

"Of course." She lengthened her stride, easily catching up to the elf. Although she wasn't as tall as Marin, her head still looked to top the man by a few inches. "If I may, I was wondering if you'd be able to help me piece together a few things regarding the history of your people."

Tracker twitched a brow at her. "My people? Is it elves or hounds that you wish to speak of?"

"Elves." She twisted to smile over her shoulder. "I've already asked all I can of Authril and I thought that, with the difference in your backgrounds, you might have access to other resources."

The hound tilted his head and gave a considering hum. "I do not see how I can aid you there. Just what is it that you wish to know?"

"Well..." The hedgewitch cleared her throat. "Legend says the elves reached the continent via massive ships. Based on old reports, the vessels were bigger than even those used to navigate the Independent Isles."

Dylan slowly nodded to himself. He recalled his childhood history lessons quite well. Being that those ships had landed on the opposite side of the continent, in lands that now abhorred spellsters, the truth of it would always be contested. That the ships had carried vast quantities of elves was the only accepted fact.

"Indeed?" Tracker murmured. "I have heard the same tale."

"Is there truth to it?"

The hound laughed. "How would one such as I know? I grew up in Wintervale, listening to the same stories as every other child there. I have always thought the idea of a single ship transporting a thousand people sounded rather implausible."

Katarina pursed her lips, not impressed. "Clearly, you haven't seen some of the major ships from the Independent Isles. They can carry close to half a thousand and make regular voyages far from land."

"Do they? I have indeed seen such a ship—they dock in Wintervale all the time—but I had no idea their crews could be so large. I wonder though..." Tracker tilted his head. "If you seek truth, why not ask those of Heimat if they are willing to impart such history?"

The dwarf fell silent, although Dylan believed she knew the answer well enough. "The Heimatian leaders don't trust the Coven," she finally admitted. "They think we are humans."

Tracker gasped. "No." He slapped his hand upon his cheek, his mouth still hanging open. "What could possibly lead them to think you are not dwarves?"

Katarina sniffed. "Yes, that's the same cheek the coven gets from them."

"Hedgewitch or not," Authril piped up from where she had taken up position at the rear. "You look human to me."

Katarina glared over her shoulder, her lips pursed. She swiftly turned her attention to their surroundings before pointing towards the canopy. "You see that bird, the fantailed one on the high branch?"

Dylan peered into the trees. All he saw were more leaves.

Tracker glanced up. "Of course, it is an easy enough target to spot and I know a human could not possibly see such a small creature at this distance. What of it?"

"Obviously, if *I* can," Katarina said, "then I cannot be human."

Marin hummed. She frowned up at the canopy, likely having as much luck in spotting the bird as Dylan did. "Why not do the bird spotting trick in front of a few Heimat locals?"

The hound chuckled. "It is not as simple as that, my dear woman. Half-elves are common enough, after all. Although, I will admit that you lack the ears and are perhaps a little on the tall side."

"And they wouldn't believe us anyway," Katarina added. "They don't trust anything that comes from human mouths. They barely listen to our request."

Dylan didn't blame them. Ever since elves landed on the continent in search of safety, humans had terrorised their every step. The Udyneans had enslaved all they could, and those who escaped were still at the mercy of kingdoms who either didn't look kindly on their wandering or relegated them to a lesser status.

Even the tower wasn't immune to those ideals, it wasn't anywhere near the prejudices he had witnessed during his few days in the army, but it was there. Minor aggressions that he likely would never have noticed had he not friends affected by them.

"What of the nomads?" Authril asked. "They enter Heimat all the time, don't they?"

Dylan nodded. From the first time his tutors mentioned the elven nomads, he had longed for such a lifestyle. The travellers were the first to evade slavers. They wandered the continent from Heimat to where the elven ships first touched land. That spot now resided on Obuzan's shoreline, but the land had originally been in Udynean territory, back before the little country became the empire that pecked at neighbouring lands like an ill-tempered bird.

"They do," Katarina agreed. "And we've gotten a number of reports from them, but their records are inconsistent from one clan to the next. As a people, they carry few written accounts and their legends are verbally passed on by the elders, which the Coven no longer accepts into their archives. We must have solid records."

"Do you not have elves amongst your hedgewitches?" Tracker asked.

"A few," the dwarf admitted. "Very little comes from sending them. They're allowed to mingle at the border, but not enter. I think Heimatian elves just don't want to commune with anyone outside their land. They don't even seem to share much with their nomadic kin beyond trading goods."

"Perhaps it is that they would vastly prefer to forget what others are so intent on remembering," the hound suggested. "What I was taught of the Heimatian people, they occupy the land only because they escaped the original elven enslavement. That *is* true, yes?"

Authril bobbed her head in agreement, the act making her bright orange hair bounce like a bird.

"I would not wish to be reminded of that every time I spoke to a foreigner," Tracker continued.

"Which was why the Coven sent elves in their first attempts to contact them," Katarina said. "The nomads have a similar background—worse when you think of how they've been in constant contact with humans for centuries—yet they willingly speak of that time. There are even records of clans accepting humans into their caravans."

Tracker shrugged. "Then I am unsure what it is you think I can tell you on this matter. You seem to know far more than I."

"Yes, but..."

Their chatter continued for some time. Dylan plodded behind them, content to let his attention drift in and out of the conversation. It was almost like being home, walking the halls in the evening with his close friends. Sulin would natter away at some theological task whilst enduring Henrie's good-natured bickering. Tracker's accent was close enough to Sulin's and, whilst she didn't sound quite the same, Authril's voice carried a similar heat to Nestria's whenever his friends debated. The comparison curved his lips.

At his side, Marin smiled and shook her head. Catching his gaze, she rolled her eyes and mimicked their chatter with the opening and closing of her fingers.

Eventually, their talk turned to other matters, including finding a place to camp. The task was completed easily enough. At least, once a few saplings had been cleared from their chosen site. Dylan gathered wood for a fire as the others pitched the tents. He had the flames burning merrily by the time Marin finished preparing the pheasant— a far more gruesome task than mere words made it seem.

They dined on dried fruit and strips of jerky whilst the pheasant cooked in preparation for tomorrow.

Still full from the food they'd snacked on at midday, Dylan picked at his meal. His gaze swung to where Authril, having already devoured her portion of food, had turned to her usual evening routine with her sword.

First she would check the blade, a task that could take anywhere from a few minutes to half an hour depending on what she used it for. Then she would adjust her armour, hoist her shield and finally go through an array of moves.

Tracker seemed intent on the other elf's motions. So much that his chewing would slow for a moment or two.

Marin stood, wiping her hands on her trousers. "I think I spied a trail a little ways from here. I'm going to set a few traps whilst it's still light. See if we can't add rabbit to our supplies."

This declaration was greeted by an array of nods and grunts. She always returned with something, but the last few days of hunting hadn't brought them anything of substance. Dylan wasn't one to complain, not when it came to food, but he did wish there was more than small animals to hunt down. Maybe even a boar. The idea of being confronted with another one wasn't pleasant, but he would risk it for a chance at all the pork it could give them.

Marin hadn't been gone long when Tracker chucked the remains of his meal into the fire and stood. "My dear woman," he called out to Authril. "It has been of my experience that training works better when there is an opponent. Would you be game for a little sparring?"

She halted and eyed him. One corner of her mouth lifted in a sneer. "*You?* Against me? That's a bit unfair, isn't it?"

The man spread his hands wide. "Quite right. I will even the playing field and go easy on you." He drew his sword and a needle-like dagger, the latter of which he twirled in a flamboyant fashion.

Authril nodded at the other elf's left hand. "Put that away."

Tracker gasped, pressing his hand to his chest. "What is this? You with your shield would put me at a disadvantage by denying me my own defence? If you fear injury, allow me to ease your concerns by saying I have no plans to see you skewered again. A little sparring with an actual partner wielding such a weapon may even help you prevent a similar unfortunate outcome in the future, yes?"

The warrior watched the man as one would a snake. She fingered her side, where the padding beneath her armour had been sewn shut. Then her gaze flicked Dylan's way and, whatever thoughts ran through her mind, it seemed enough to have her nodding. "Very well," she muttered, snapping her attention back to the hound. "But if that blade goes anywhere near my side, I'll feed you that fancy sword of yours rectally."

A smile stretched Tracker's lips. He tipped his head back and laughed. "Such hostility is unwarranted. I swear, you will not feel the bite of my blades."

With her eyes narrowing at the challenge, Authril charged the man.

Dylan watched them spar. Where the warrior used her shield as a sort of personal battering ram, she could never quite reach the hound. Tracker practically danced around the woman, harrying her from all sides. She didn't seem willing to close and, with the way the man held his dagger—low and angled in some ready stance to stab her kidneys—Dylan didn't blame her.

Eventually, Tracker stumbled back, his arms raised in surrender. "One moment. All this sparring has made me quite hot. If you will allow me some time to rectify this?"

Authril inclined her head, her lips twisting in a poorly concealed smirk.

"You are most gracious." The hound dropped his weapons and slowly peeled off the top layers of his clothes, tossing them towards the fireside. They landed by Dylan's feet.

The warrior backed away, clearly uncertain what to make of this strange turn in their sparring. Dylan was inclined to agree with her. He hadn't ever witnessed any of the army soldiers train in anything less than their armour.

Authril waved her sword, indicating Tracker and his discarded attire. "What's this?"

"What better way to cool down than to shed a few clothes?" the man replied, peeling off his undershirt so that he stood naked from the waist up. "Much better." Tracker scooped up his weapons and fell back into a ready stance. "You can begin again."

Authril tipped her head to one side. "And if I hit you? Granted your leather armour was unlikely to stop a blade as well as this—" She tapped her breastplate with the hilt of her sword. "—but it's better than nothing."

Dylan's thoughts slipped back to when they had fought those bandits. The hound had come away covered in blood, but unscathed. Seeing how the man fought now, he was certain that a large part of Tracker's defence came from being too fast and agile to hit.

Tracker rolled his shoulders as he circled Authril. He grinned as if the idea of her actually managing to graze him was an implausible one. "There is a little more to my garments than mere leather, but consider this merely as an extra incentive for me not to get hit."

She shrugged. "It's your funeral." Authril bunched her shoulders and shuffled closer, ensuring her shield remained between them. Using her shield as cover for her strikes, she attempted to lever his weapons aside and bash the hound with the upper curve of her shield.

This tactic failed and their swords fast became weaving blurs of steel. Tracker's moves were rather snake-like. He'd strike like a viper, coiling both weapons and arms around his opponent's body as if they were pythons of metal and flesh, then dart out of reach before she could react.

After enduring the fifth such move, Authril staggered back. Swearing just loud enough for Dylan to make out the words pouring from her clenched teeth, she shook herself and lunged at the hound.

Dylan tracked them as the pair danced about the cleared patch. There were hints of more designs on the hound's back—something very central on his upper spine that the others were situated around—but the way the man kept twisting out of Authril's reach made it difficult to make out what exactly.

"He's very inked, isn't he?" Katarina said, causing Dylan to jump. He had forgotten the hedgewitch sat next to him. She also watched the pair, although clearly not as intently.

"I wasn't looking," he said, the words rushing out before he could stop them. Heat blazed across his face as she arched a brow at him, and he mumbled, "I mean... I hadn't noticed." His attempt to gloss over the outburst only raised the woman's brows further.

"They appear to come from a mix of cultures," Katarina continued as though he hadn't spoken. "The elven and Demarn designs are obvious choices—I've seen similar combinations on elves in other countries. However, there are a few curious additions. Like the firebird on his side. Do you see it poking out from the waist of his trousers?" she asked of him as though the head and wings were easy to miss. "Such creatures stem from Stamekian myths."

Dylan shrugged. "Maybe he read about them and liked the idea." The literate requirements of a hound's training could very well have them studying other cultures lest they mistake an emissary for an escaped spellster. There were several countries that didn't keep those with magic separate from the common folk. Stamekia was one such place.

"Perhaps," the hedgewitch murmured, her frown warping the upper section of the diagonal scar on her face. "It is curious that he would have a sword more suited to the region. Did you notice the curved design? That's also Stamekian, or possibly from the Independent Isles." She twisted in her seated position to face him. "Do you think the king allows his hounds to leave the kingdom?"

"Honestly, I have no idea what the crown does with them." At least, beyond the obvious fighting and tracking techniques needed of a hound. *And the occasional beating.* A handful of the spellsters born outside the tower had stories of receiving such treatment. Some grew up spiteful, others timid.

Dylan wasn't yet sure what to think of Tracker. He doubted the crown would set a timid man on rogue spellsters, but he also didn't appear as cruel as the old tales portrayed them. Single-minded perhaps.

His gaze swung back to the sparring duo. Tracker seemed to be leading Authril on a merry little trip around the clearing. The hound would twist their way every so often, as if checking that their sparring still had an attentive audience. It allowed the warrior to get close, but he was always well beyond her reach whenever she swung her sword.

Katarina also returned to watching the pair. She remained silent for quite some time before a fit of coughing took her. It sounded suspiciously like she was attempting to conceal her laughter. Poorly. "I do believe he's strutting," she managed between wheezes.

"Pardon?"

She waved her hand, signalling him to wait as she swallowed a few mouthfuls from her water skin. "There's a type of bird in southern Udynea where the males are immensely colourful. The nobles like to keep two males in a cage because the birds then engage in mock fights. It displays these marvellous wings and tail feathers, which is how they attract a mate." She ducked her head and murmured, "It probably helps that he's toying with her."

He had come to the same consensus regarding the hound's taunting of Authril, however...

Mock fights? Dylan resumed picking at his meal as his mind wandered. He knew elves had several courtship rituals that weren't generally mimicked in human circles, even within the tower, but this? "You think he's trying to attract her attention by proving he's the better fighter?" He hadn't heard of that one.

Grinning, she nudged him. "I didn't say he was doing it specifically for *her.*"

"So, it's for you? Or…" He looked around the camp, taking in the distinct lack of Marin's presence. It seemed the woman hadn't yet returned from setting her traps. "*Me?*" The word squeaked through his throat. "I don't…"

His thoughts turned to the pond he had shared with the man several days back. Tracker hadn't attempted anything further, flirting or otherwise, after sending Dylan fleeing from the pond. He must've realised persisting was pointless.

That lack hadn't helped Dylan shake the memory from his dreams.

The hot press of the hound against his shoulder. The way the man's voice stirred something within Dylan. The lust smouldering in those rich, honey-coloured eyes. The curve of those lips. Teasing. Welcoming. Kissable…

Shaking himself, Dylan returned to his food, plucking what he hoped was a piece of dried apple from the pile. "You're mistaken." Tracker wouldn't be attempting to draw the attention of someone he knew wasn't interested. The hound was a lot of things, but foolish wasn't one of them.

Authril had abandoned her shield sometime during the sparring duo's circuit of the tents, opting to grasp her sword with both hands. Whilst the swings appeared harder and came at an increased speed, they still didn't pose much of a hindrance to the hound. Tracker merely took this new tactic in stride, dodging each blow before counterattacking with the same steady confidence.

Eventually, the pair's meandering led them back to the campfire and Authril conceded.

With the hound giving her a bow, they separated. "Thank you for indulging me, my dear warrior," Tracker said, puffing. "That was most invigorating."

"You've a strange way of fighting," Authril replied between gasps. "I've never seen anything like it."

"Ah, but you trained with common soldiers, fought against those who have learnt only to counter the same moves they were taught. A hound's training is a little more advanced. However, at the heart of it, we are taught to be very… flexible." His gaze flicked Dylan's way and his lips twitched. The man's focus returned to the warrior so quickly that Dylan wasn't certain if he'd even seen correctly. "Our trainers take great pride in making us adaptable to whatever position we find ourselves in."

By the way she screwed up her nose, Authril was on the fence when it came to believing the man. "And the advantage in being half naked is?"

Cool affront took Tracker's face. He laid a hand on his chest as if he'd been wounded. "That was merely because I was hot. Besides, not every battle gives you the opportunity to gird oneself. You should try it some time. You may be surprised how responsive your body can be when it is stripped of all defence."

Dylan shivered. The soft purr in Tracker's voice added an admittedly pleasing note to the man's already rolling accent.

The hound paused in bending to collect his clothes. "Do you not agree, my dear spellster?" Teasing glee danced once more in those honey-coloured eyes as they met Dylan's.

He swallowed, his breath catching for but a moment. "I... wouldn't know."

Tracker paused in shaking out his undershirt. "No?" He tipped his head to one side, his lips twisting. "That truly is a terrible shame." Still naked from the waist up, he settled next to Dylan, resting his head on an upturned fist. "If you ever feel the urge to try, you will find me quite the willing victim."

A small smile tweaked Dylan's lips. His cheeks felt so hot that there was no chance Tracker didn't notice. The man *was* still talking about fighting, wasn't he? It was probably Dylan's mind playing tricks on him but, ever since their stop at the pond, everything the hound said sounded like an innuendo.

Dylan cleared his throat. "I rather doubt there'd be much you could teach me. I'm not exactly built to handle typical weaponry."

One of the man's brows twitched up. "So I have seen."

Dylan's gaze flicked up to where Authril stood behind the man. Those hard eyes of hers were trained on the back of Tracker's skull. She couldn't possibly know about the pond incident. Unless the man had been foolish enough to tell her and he didn't see that as a possibility.

The hound didn't seem to notice. "I am certain that, given the few weeks we have on the road, I could train you in the basics. Something simple. Sword fighting, perhaps." His gaze ran over Dylan, hot and piercing. "Or unarmed combat. Your slender frame would suit either one."

Slender? Yes, there wasn't much to him in the way of excess flesh, but he was nowhere near as graceful as the word implied. Especially when compared to the two elves.

"Forgive me," Katarina said. "But I thought Demarn spellsters weren't allowed to use alternative means of fighting."

"They aren't," Authril replied.

The hound gave a noncommittal grunt. "There may be some truth in that, but I see no harm in him learning. Of course, you would have to make some adjustments to your attire. I do not recall seeing any splits in either your robe or undertunic."

Dylan drew his legs closer together, just on the off chance that the man decided to attempt such alterations then and there. "That won't be happening," he mumbled. "I've only my smallclothes underneath."

"Truly?" Tracker shuffled closer. "No trousers? I could have sworn…" He trailed off, frowning at the ground. "Are they not a part of the army's uniform?"

Dylan nodded.

"And you refused to wear them?" A low chuckle creased the corners of the man's eyes. "We have a little rebellious streak, yes?"

Authril snorted. "A big idiotic one, more like. The uniform is designed that way for a reason."

Dylan scrunched in on himself. "I don't like the feel." He hadn't refused outright, donning the full attire for all of a few minutes before dumping the trousers amongst a pile of rags. And it wasn't as though the robes didn't cover him. The hem originally fell to his ankles, meaning no one could tell unless he lifted the skirts. He doubted it was entirely evident even with the slightly higher hem. "I find them too constricting."

The teasing spark in Tracker's eyes grew bolder and more mischievous. His gaze dropped to Dylan's waist. "I do believe something else would be just as confining. If not more so."

"Well, I—"

Authril slammed the shield between them, causing Dylan to jump. "So sorry," she said, the sweetness dripping from her voice just as false as the overly toothy grin. "Hold this," she demanded of the hound.

Tracker complied, grasping the shield before it could fall, his brow furrowed in confusion.

Rather than explain herself, she grabbed Dylan's collar and, before he had time to register what was happening, hauled him to his feet. "Tent," Authril growled into his ear. "Now."

"I haven't finished eating," he protested as she towed him towards their tent. A quick glance over his shoulder told him the remainder of his meal was now scattered all over the ground. It hadn't been much to begin with, but it was still a waste.

"If you're that hungry," Authril grumbled. "I'll sneak a piece of pheasant for you later. Now, get in." She gave him a gentle push towards the tent flap.

Dylan obeyed, his face burning hotter as their exit was followed by the hound's rich laughter.

CHAPTER 31

They reached Oldmarsh without complication or even a hint of bandits. Although, the armed men in the uniform of the city guard marching along the road leading to the city might've had something to do with that.

Dylan had only vague memories of the last time he came through here. The sun had gotten to him, leaving him terribly burnt and delirious. He recalled Fetcher grumbling as she gave him the necessary sanction to use his magic and heal the damage, but not much else.

There were obvious differences between this city and Toptower. The latter had been built around an old fortification, the buildings huddling inside the walls like a bunch of timid kittens.

In Oldmarsh, somewhere along the line, the residents had forsaken the town's original walls in favour of expansion, making the town sprawl across the land much like a drunken spider trying to build a web in a storm. Navigating the outer parts of the city was a matter of trailing after Tracker whilst the man wove through endless narrow streets.

The haphazard nature of the new buildings continued not only in the layout, but the structures themselves. Many were built from a hodgepodge of materials with boards nailed across most of the windows. Clothes and sheets of cloth hung wherever there was space, whether that was from lines running between the buildings or from an opening in the wall.

However, after his first misstep into a puddle of what he sincerely hoped was muddied water, Dylan found himself paying more attention to his feet than their surroundings. There was evidence here and there of cobblestones, but if the streets ever were fully paved, then the vast majority was buried beneath a thick layer of muck and mud.

Although the sunny days had hardened much of the road's surface dirt, there seemed to be a perpetual dankness to the dull greyish brown crud they walked upon. Perhaps it was due to the uncaring nature of animals and people alike adding to the street muck.

Unlike Toptower, where the people moved along with purpose, these folk shuffled through their duties as if in a daze. If the residents acknowledged the passage of five newcomers, it was fleeting and lacklustre before continuing with their tasks. Several pushed carts clearly more suited for animals to pull, whilst others carried loads that looked almost as heavy as themselves.

The further into the city they walked, the more rubble crowded the streets. Wooden crates, broken cartwheels and piles of shattered bricks interspersed with rotting straw. A few spots had the look of people attempting to clean up the refuse, but they mostly spilt onto the street and all but blocked off a number of alleyways.

"Spare us a little coin, sirs?" a thin voice piped up from one such pile.

Dylan slowed. That had sounded like a child.

A mud-encrusted plank moved aside to reveal the grubby face of a small human boy. The child tumbled out of his hole and scrambled towards them. "Please, sirs?" He fidgeted with his tunic, a raggedy thing that was more hole than linen and far too big for his scrawny frame. "I haven't eaten in three days."

Snorting, Authril made a shooing motion with her hand. "Get lost, kid. Go back to your gang."

The boy shuffled closer, his huge brown eyes welling with tears. He grabbed Dylan's robe, blinking the tears free. "I've sisters, sir. We're all so very hungry."

Dylan swallowed, trying to convince himself that there was no lump in his throat. "I don't have—" He might not have any coin, but there were a few strips of the jerked pork left in his pack. It had to be better than nothing.

"Come here," Tracker said, crooking his finger and crouching when the boy scampered to his side. "I hope you are good at remembering faces, child, because I am and this is something I will do only the once. You understand this, yes?" Tracker opened his hand as the boy nodded, revealing a silver coin nestled in his palm.

The boy snatched up the coin as if believing the hound would change his mind at any sign of hesitation and scampered off into an alleyway.

Authril watched the boy. She shook her head. "You shouldn't have given him money."

With his mouth twisting into a half smile, Tracker stood. "Ah, consider it as the bandits donating to the unfortunate with me has their middle man. What was that you said about a gang?"

The warrior shrugged. "It's nothing new. I grew up here. Pulled the same tricks as a girl, too. The inner city doesn't care about the slums, so we used to shaft them as often as we could." She sneered at the now-vacant alleyway. "Not that sloppily, though."

Tracker's brows lifted. "You were a slummer?" His gaze ran over the woman as if truly seeing her for the first time. "It would seem fate was far kinder to you than these people."

"Only because I worked for it," she muttered.

"You feel no kinship to your home? Or those still living here?"

"This place stopped being my home the second I could escape. Why should I care about it?" Authril marched past the man. "There's a small gate into the city this way." She indicated a narrow street veering off the main way. "Just don't stop for any more beggars. If word gets around, they'll send the big boys."

Dylan lengthened his stride to catch up with her. "What happens when they send them?"

"If you're lucky, you'll get left for dead and naked as the day you were born." Chuckling, she patted his arm. "Don't worry, they mostly come out at night and we'll be out of here soon."

Sure enough, the passage Authril led them through opened out on a pair of guarded gates. Judging by the thick walls stretching either side, this had once been the town's outer defence.

Tracker retook the lead, speaking to the guards as the rest of them walked through the gates.

The space beyond was completely detached from the mess of the slums. The cobblestones underfoot were uneven in places, but discernible. Carts rumbled by to the slow, rhythmic clop of a cow or draught horse instead of the guttural groans of people. Stalls took the place of rubble. Merchants filled the streets with their calls.

The further from the gates they ventured, the more the buildings loomed over them, most of them two and three storeys high. Wooden bridges connected some like open-air corridors. Lines of sheets ran from rooftop to rooftop just as they'd done in the slums, but these had a little more order and fewer tears in the fabric.

Dylan glanced back the way they'd come. He could no longer make out the walls sealing off the poorer people from the town. The idea of going without wasn't a familiar one even if the tower ensured the spellsters got what was essential, sometimes more. He had experienced the lack of decent shelter and scant supplies, but they were all temporary hardships, nothing like the endless grind those people suffered.

Did anyone here know what kind of life sat beyond their little streets or the walls? Did they know that people just like them lingered on the other side, begging for whatever they could get and stealing when they could not? More importantly, did they care?

Eventually, their group came to a street where the entrance was barred by thick iron gates and guards in burnished armour. Again, Tracker spoke with one of the men, pressing obscenely close. Dylan caught the flash of silver exchanged between their hands and the man waved them through.

His gaze returned to their surroundings with renewed interest. This had to be the richer sector of the city. Where the buildings at his back crowded each other, those they now walked by had small gardens and elaborately carved fronts. Stores with large signs over even larger windows appeared to replace the common stalls.

There were still plenty of people on the streets, carts still carried goods and there seemed to be even more guards patrolling than beyond the iron gates. The one thing that stood out the most was how everyone's attire appeared less ragged. Those people watched them as they trailed the hound, the myriad of faces uniform in curiosity and disdain.

He shrugged his pack higher, very much aware of how worn his robe looked. Perhaps that was what drew everyone's eye. At least the tower would be able to give him new clothes.

The hound aimed for a hulking building. The place sprawled across its allotted section, stables and smaller buildings tucked off to the side. On the opposite side sat a tower, three-storeys high that had an air of exclusivity about it. A large, carved sign running along the front declared it as *The Silver Flagon.*

The lushness of the inn's front continued inside. Where their inn at Toptower had been dark and unkempt, this place was bright and so clean that the wood practically shone. Amber light streamed through the massive windows, washing the interior with a warm haziness.

And it wasn't the only thing filling the room.

Even though the brassy glow of twilight had barely begun to spill across the tables, the tavern already had a fair number of patrons. Some seemed engrossed in the task of stuffing their bellies, a few others were involved in a game of dice and there was a pair in the corner playing chess, but most appeared to be here for the sole purpose of drinking. They were, by and large, the rowdiest of the bunch.

Men and women carrying trays and tankards walked between the tables. One of the patrons tried to get a little friendly with a serving woman and was swiftly dealt with by her dumping the contents of a drink over his head before a hulk of a man hefted him none too gently out the door.

Soft music reached Dylan's ears as they strode deeper into the room. He stretched onto the balls of his feet, peering over people to find the source.

A woman was perched on a stool near the fire, strumming a small harp. Flanking her, stood a man with a flute and another seated near a small drum. Both looked rather bored.

Authril shook her head, her baleful gaze fixed firmly on Tracker. "If you think we can afford to stay in a place like this—"

"Then it is fortunate you travel with someone who has that sort of coin upon their person, yes?" Tracker jingled his belt pouch in emphasis. "Whatever would you have done if I had not found your dear spellster?"

"Slept in the forest?" Marin replied.

"You are welcome to do so if that is your wish. I, however, would vastly prefer to take the opportunity to sleep in a bed whilst I can. The relatively free of unexpected guests sort." He swaggered up to the bar and tapped on the stained bench top with a gold coin.

"Ah, Sir Tracker," the innkeeper said as he waddled to their side. "Brought along your own entertainment, I see." The man stroked his thick black beard. "Although, I'm not sure if our beds have recovered from the last workout you gave them."

A small, slightly wavering, laugh shook the hound's shoulders. "In all fairness, I did not expect it to break so easily. You would think wood that thick could withstand such weight."

Dylan tore his gaze from the tavern interior to stare at the hound. Just what had he been doing to break a bed?

The innkeeper's grin suggested that whatever had happened last time wasn't a first for the hound. "It's not like they were made for that many people."

Tracker smiled. "My mistake. However, I *do* recall paying for the damages."

The man laughed. "That you did."

"And I promise this stay will be a little more sedate."

The innkeeper winked. "Better not let Annalise find that out. Poor girl will be heartbroken."

Tracker grunted. "I am certain she will find herself other amusements."

Dylan eyed the man. After the hound's attempt in removing Dylan's smallclothes and Katarina's observations, he thought for sure that Tracker was interested in men. But if his assumptions on what the innkeeper meant were right, then perhaps the hound had merely been teasing him.

"The usual room it is, then?" the innkeeper asked, returning to business. Wiping his hands on his apron, he went to take the money, stopping when Tracker laid a finger on top of the coin.

"Not quite, my dear man. I require *two* rooms for the night. One for these dear women and another for him and myself." He jerked his thumb, indicating Dylan. "Separate beds, if you please, and whatever you have cooking back there."

The innkeeper's black brows shot up. The man peered at Dylan. He had expected that, just not with the curious glint the man's gaze carried. There was a particular smugness about his face, too. Nodding, he took the gold. "Why don't you all find a seat? I'll fetch one of the girls to serve you."

The suggestion was easier said than done. More people had entered whilst they talked, spreading themselves around most of the tables. Some of the more inebriated patrons had passed out, sprawling across their tables or slumped in chairs.

The harpist was soon replaced by a man with a fiddle and, as a lively tune streamed from the sawing bow, a woman danced on one of the long benches to the cheers and whistles of her adoring viewers. The steady and quick thump of the drummer had Dylan tapping his toes as they sought out a table.

They settled near a group of rowdy dicers who periodically jeered and thumped the table. Dylan peered around the shoulder of one such man as their group waited for food to be brought to them. He'd never been all that interested, or good, at dice, but the game looked familiar.

The dancing woman had drawn others who were also cavorting around the floor in a mess of limbs and laughter. Dylan leant back to watch the crowd. Would the women amongst them object if he asked to join in?

He caught Authril watching them. The woman bounced her leg in time with the beat. Surely, she'd permit him a dance.

Grinning, Dylan quietly slid from his stool to slip his arms beneath those of the warrior. "Care to dance, my lady?" he whispered into her ear.

She stiffened in his grasp. A soft hitch of her breath preceded a hurried, "Yes." The woman sprang to her feet, all but knocking him to the ground. She grabbed his hand and led him into the whirling throng.

Someone in the crowd had started clapping out a beat. The dancers mimicked the claps with the stamp of their feet. Dylan lifted the skirts of his robes higher and followed suit, allowing Authril to take the lead as they twirled and kicked up their legs. He fast lost himself to the beat of the music and the raucous of those watching.

Their dinner had arrived by the time they collapsed back at the table, both puffing and altogether hot.

Authril beamed up at him. Her skin carried a particularly rosy hint around the ears. "I didn't think you'd know how to dance."

"They encouraged such activity at the tower. Helps burn energy."

And the guardians knew that an exhausted spellster child was less likely to sneak off and attempt unsupervised magic.

"Well, dancing with a bean pole certainly has its advantages."

Dylan chuckled, recalling the other women having to duck to go under their partner's arms at certain parts of the dance. He had barely needed to raise his arm level with his shoulder to let Authril pass under.

His gaze dropped to the food laid before them. A whole leg of what his nose told him was mutton and glazed root vegetables graced the middle of the table. Trays of dark bread, cheese and fruit sat to one side, as did several tankards of beer. Compared to the meagre camp side fare of jerked pork and travel biscuits, it was a feast.

Authril wasted no time in grabbing the carving knife and hacking off several chunks of mutton for herself. Dylan carefully piled some of the vegetables onto a plate before grabbing a hunk of bread and biting into it. He groaned around the mouthful. In all his life, he didn't think he would ever miss bread or that it could taste this good. Nutty and slightly sweet.

"Can we afford all this?" Katarina asked whilst the other two women tucked in.

Tracker laughed. "Relax, my dear hedgewitch. You are travelling with a hound. You would be amazed what I can buy. Eat up, now. We will be back to chewy strips of meat and lumps of chalky baking in no time."

"You don't have to tell me twice," Marin mumbled over her mountain of food.

Unlike the campfire, where meals were eaten swiftly and in relative silence before people separated to sleep or patrol, everyone seemed content to linger in the tavern. Dylan stuffed his face with copious amounts of vegetables and bread, leaving the greater portion of meat for the elves to devour, much to the apparent amusement of the hound, who easily packed away twice a human's consumption of food.

Marin skewered a carrot on the end of her knife and held it aloft as if she'd never seen one before. It was only when he caught Authril sticking her tongue out at the other woman that he realised the hunter was comparing the vegetable to the shade of the elf's hair. It wasn't a bad match.

One of the serving women, the plumper one with hair the colour of a midnight sky, bent over to collect Tracker's empty plate. Under the warm light of the candles, their skin shared a very similar bronze hue. She smiled up at the hound. "Will that be—?" She stiffened, jerking upright again. "Oi!" the woman shouted over her shoulder as she rubbed her backside. "Keep your bloody hands to yourself. I'm not part of the service."

"What?" The man sitting behind her laughed. "With what he charges for drink in here?" The drunkard reached out and clumsily snaffled her around the waist.

The woman struggled in his grasp, clearly losing ground. "Let me go right now or I'll have Rhys toss you out."

Beside them, Tracker casually sipped at his tankard. One russet brow rose along with the woman's voice.

"Aw, come on, love." The man jigged her and leered down her cleavage. "Don't be like that."

"Dear man," the hound said into his tankard. "I suggest you let the woman be."

The drunkard turned his bleary brown eyes on Tracker. "Keep your nose out of it, elf. If I want a little fun with the lady, I'll have a little fun. Isn't that right, love?"

"I'm not your love," the woman snarled. "Now let me go, you tosser."

With his cheeks hollowing as if he had consumed something sour, Tracker twisted on his stool enough to face the pair. "She does not appear to be enjoying your attention. And I am sure she would much rather do her job than be pawed at by your putrid waste of flesh."

Sneering, the man shoved the woman to one side. He lurched to his feet, looming over the hound. "You want to say that to my face, *elf?*"

"I believe I just did." Tracker took another swig of his beer. "Or perhaps that unseemly growth on the front of your head has atrophied your brain. Should I perhaps speak directly to the organ in charge?" he asked, nodding at the man's crotch.

The drunkard squared his shoulders. "If you were any real man, elf, you'd—"

"Again with the elf?" the hound taunted. "Is that the best your undersized mind can think of? If *you* were any real man, you would not feel the need to harass these dear women."

The man grabbed Tracker's jerkin and hauled the hound out of his seat. He held Tracker close to his face, leaving the hound barely balanced on his toes. "You're a dead man," the drunkard growled.

"Hold up." Marin leapt to her feet, the stool crashing to the floor behind her. "You unhand our friend right now."

The drunkard leered at her. "This your little mistress, elf? Standing up for your pet, are we, love?" He grinned, his teeth appearing far too big for his mouth. "He won't look so pretty once I'm done with him."

"Touch him and I'll rearrange your face," she bit back.

"My dear hunter," Tracker said, "Your concern is unnecessary. He is welcome to test his luck, but I have survived far worse than a drunken beating." He gave the man a toothy smile. "Although, if I may direct your attention down."

Dylan's gaze dropped to where Tracker held the point of one of his seemingly endless collection of throwing knives to the man's crotch.

The man stiffened, having become aware of the situation he had put himself in. His brows drew together, forming a veranda of wheaten hair over his bulging eyes. "Pointy-eared scum," he growled as he slowly lowered the hound back onto the floor and released his grip. "I'm going to break every bone in your body."

"Not tonight, it would seem. Now run along, my dear man, before I decide to separate you from your little brains." Tracker righted his stool as the man stepped back, casually sheathing his knife before sitting down and returning to his drink.

Snarling, the drunkard lurched at the hound, his hands clasped and raised above his head.

Tracker leant to one side as the man's fists came down on the table where he'd been sitting. "Predictable," he said, shaking his head. "Very well, my dear man. Let us do this the hard way." Before the drunkard could react, the hound slammed his elbow into the man's chest, followed swiftly by a fist to the neck.

The man staggered back, his eyes bulging. He clutched his throat. His mouth moved, but all that came out was a dreadful choking sound.

Tracker followed the drunkard, ramming the heel of his boot into the man's crotch.

Dylan winced as he watched the man go down, certain everything in his smallclothes had just contracted in sympathy.

The screech of wood across wood preceded the rest of the dicers getting to their feet. There were six in all. Each armed with a dagger or a knife, although only a couple had drawn their weapons.

Tracker spun to face them, a throwing knife in each hand.

Dylan slowly got to his feet. It seemed his preference to sleep in a bed tonight wasn't going to be a reality. He examined the men. A simple pulse through the air would be enough to knock them all down without causing too much damage to their surroundings. Of course, it would also knock over Tracker, but that couldn't be helped.

The hound's head twitched. Dylan caught the gleam of the man's eye looking over his shoulder. Had he somehow sensed Dylan readying to attack?

Impossible. No one was capable of predicting magic.

"That's quite enough," someone said, the words sounding as if they had to grind their way out of the owner's throat.

Dylan joined the others in looking to see who had spoken, sinking back onto his stool as he caught sight of a burly man about the same height as himself. He'd a face like tanned leather and shoulders that looked as if he would barely fit through most of the tower doors. A dull thud preceded every second step, drawing Dylan's gaze down to find the man had a wooden leg.

"All right, sunshine," the man said as he clapped his meaty hand on the drunkard's shoulder. The man's forearms looked easily as big as Dylan's thigh. "I think it's time you went off home."

Tracker's grin widened into a far friendlier version. "Evening, Rhys." He sheathed his knives as if this was an everyday occurrence for him. "So sorry to intrude on your quiet like this."

The man glared down at the hound. "Why is it that every time you're here my workload doubles?"

Tracker shrugged. "Come now, this is nowhere near as bad as last time. No one is bleeding and everyone still has all the bits they came here with."

Rhys grunted as he hefted the drunkard over his shoulders. His gaze swung to the other dicers who had returned to their seats upon his arrival. "Let's keep it that way." He strode off, grumbling inaudibly under his load as he made for the exit.

Tracker slowly turned on his heel to face the other dicers as the man vanished outside. He spread his arms wide in a silent challenge.

To a man, none appeared willing to meet the hound's gaze. One player toyed with the dice, another became overly interested in his stack of coins. Several seemed to be admiring various sections of the tavern architecture.

"I thought not," Tracker muttered as he returned to his stool.

The serving woman wasted no time in plonking herself on his lap. "As I recall," she said, running her finger along his shoulder. Her voice was huskier than it had been before the fighting. "Knights tend to wear shiny armour."

Tracker chuckled and Dylan fancied he caught a faint blush touch the man's cheeks. "My dear Annalise," he purred. "There are no knights in Demarn."

"Oh?" Her finger worked its way up to the point of the elf's ear with a deliberateness that spoke of knowing exactly how sensitive they were. "Then I guess I'll have to show my saviour thanks in another way." Annalise tilted the hound's head back and kissed him, quite deeply if Dylan were to judge by the way Tracker clutched the woman.

Feeling his face heating, Dylan engrossed himself in the remains of his food. The meat had gone cold, the gravy beginning to form a film on the top, but it was better than watching the woman try to fish out the hound's tonsils with her tongue.

Marin cleared her throat. "Do you think you could do that elsewhere? I'm trying to eat." Her announcement was enough to draw Annalise's attention away from the hound's face.

"Yes, well." Tracker swiftly deposited the woman back onto her feet. "Your gratitude has been noted." He pushed back his stool and stood, laying a friendly hand on the serving woman's shoulder as he addressed the table. "I am sure Annalise will be available to show you to your rooms when you so desire, but this is where I part ways with you for a time. There is someone I must speak with who can tell us what lies ahead and it is not a place one should loiter near for long." He eyed Dylan, his lips quirking into a faint smile. "I think it would be best if you come with me, dear man, for your own protection. We do not want to risk someone stumbling upon you the way I did."

Dylan nodded as he swallowed his current mouthful. Although he now carried the remains of the collar in the same pouch Katarina had, the likelihood of another hound willing to believe the truth was slim.

Authril peered at the man. "How do we know you're not just going to leave him dying in a ditch somewhere?"

Tracker laughed. "You are such a suspicious woman. If I was going to kill him, why would I bring him all the way into town? Or waste food on him? However, if you think me so untrustworthy, you are more than welcome to come along. I have nothing to hide." With that, the hound turned on his heel and strode towards the door. "Come, my dear friends. The later the night gets, the harder it will be to speak with her."

Dylan followed, not entirely sure where they were headed. If this contact of Tracker's was any good, then perhaps they could send a message ahead of them to warn of his return and the situation surrounding it. The overseers could use the time to prepare another collar rather than leave him in an isolation cell whilst one was made.

Strange to think there was little more than a week's travel separating him from his home. Just the thought had him anxious to keep moving. He had resigned himself to never again setting foot within the tower walls. Now he would, even if only long enough to be leashed once more.

None of his travelling companions had understood what leashing meant. They saw it as restrictive, but it would've given him far more freedom. If he was leashed right now, he'd be free to soak in the tavern's ambience without the hound's presence. He'd be normal. Safe.

CHAPTER 32

Dylan walked at Authril's side through the lantern-lit streets, tailing Tracker as the man made for whatever destination he had in mind. They entered what looked like a market square, vacant now beyond the occasional seller still packing away their goods. The scent of spices hung heavily in the air.

There appeared to be another inn ahead, a massive stone and timber structure, its front illuminated by a lantern hanging across the street. Lights flickered in every window of the multi-levelled building. The entrance opened as they neared and a man staggered out, a grin splitting his face. He wound his way past them, smelling heavily of incense and spiced wine.

Dylan's idle gaze caught a sign declaring the place was *The Gilded Lily* as he followed Tracker up the stairs.

A man, quite broad and muscular, stood by the door. He unfolded his arms as they neared, thrusting a huge hand towards the hound. Tracker silently pressed a small silver coin into the man's palm, patiently waiting as the man bounced it against a piece of wood. Seemingly satisfied, the man grunted and indicated the door with a jerk of his head.

The main entrance opened into a room that encompassed much of the lower level, the ceiling held aloft by a series of carved wooden pillars. That was all he caught before his eyes began to water at the heavy smoke in the air. The burning incense gave the area a hazy touch, as if Dylan peered at the world through a layer of fine gauze.

Blinking, his gaze drifted to the curtains flanking the pillars like huge red wings. Paintings of men and women in various stages of undress and revelry adorned the walls. A trio of musicians sat to one side, playing soft alluring music, whilst a young man sang.

Dylan caught all of two words before he registered the other people in the room. His thoughts of this being a high-class inn of sorts slowly veered elsewhere. Judging by the half-naked people lounging about in cushioned chairs and couches almost big enough to be beds, he'd a rather sneaky suspicion that there was more on offer here than alcohol. "Is this a… brothel?"

Tracker chuckled. "Not quite as innocent as you look, I see."

He only knew that because Trix, one of the spellsters he had studied healing alongside, had come from such a place near the north-eastern border.

"You are correct, of course. Although, *The Gilded Lily* is more than *a* brothel. This is the most expensive establishment in Oldmarsh. Perhaps even in all of Demarn." He indicated the room with a sweep of his hand. "Every man and woman you see here is the finest the town has to offer."

Dylan's gaze drifted across the room. A great deal of the patrons merely drank and lounged about, ready to be pampered via touch, presence or even food. A few of the brothel's employees appeared to be in the process of securing various deals, but the majority seemed content to recline there, silently tempting those who were undecided.

Whilst those who waited were all in various stages of undress, it was especially true of the men. Most of them wore only trousers or smallclothes, a few had forsaken both for lengths of cloth and glittering adornments that drew the eye.

A handful of lean men swayed to the young man's song. Each one wore only a scrap of cloth draped before their crotch, the folds of fabric swinging back and forth. Teasing with glimpses of what lay beneath.

The longer Dylan stared at the hypnotic display, the more tempted he was to get closer.

"I take it," Authril said, still sneering at the hound. "This is your home away from home."

Grinning, Tracker waggled a finger at her. "You have such a sharp tongue, but I am not ashamed to admit I have spent quite some time here in the past. Not only for the reasons you would think. My contact works here."

She eyed the hound, clearly trying to determine if he was lying. "And who would that—?"

"Precious!"

Tracker turned at the cry, waving to the short woman who imitated the gesture with all the enthusiasm of a child.

"I found it," the woman announced, clambering over several of the couches to greet them. "The sword! Alwyn had it stashed in the vault." Her dress was of fabric sheer enough to give the casual watcher a good idea of what lay beneath. The skirt hitched higher with each movement, leading to her pausing at every other step to yank it back down.

Her chosen passage also had her shoving past people, both patrons and prostitutes. The former grumbled whilst the latter seemed used to this behaviour.

Dylan glanced at the two elves. Where Authril watched the display with clear disbelief, Tracker appeared just as indifferent to the chaos the woman caused as her fellow workers.

Finally, she halted before the hound, beaming and giving her clothing a final adjusting tug. "I can't believe you're back so soon. Thought you'd be literal months, but here you are!" She flung herself into his arms, squeezing tight as though welcoming a long departed sibling.

"And a good evening to you also, Petal dear," Tracker said. "I see your grip is still just as strong as your mind."

The woman chuckled and, giving the man one last squeeze, released him. "I'll go get the sword." She turned on her bare heel, making for a set of stairs leading to the upper levels. "Don't go vanishing on me."

The hound laid a stilling hand on Petal's shoulder. "Normally, I would be happy to indulge your request, but I—" He fell silent as the woman's lips shifted into a trembling pout. "Petal, that is an unprofessional look. Your mistress would not approve, yes?"

Frowning, Petal stuck her lip out even further. "You said you'd dance next time you came, remember? *This* is next time."

"My dear, the circumstances have changed. I am here to speak with Treasure on matters only she can help me with."

"That's what you said the last time." She poked his chest with a forefinger, the tip of her nail leaving a half-moon dent in the leather. "You promised."

"That I did." Sighing, Tracker smiled fondly at the woman. "Fetch it, then."

The woman bounced on the spot, causing all manner of interesting movements beneath her dress. "He's going to do it!" she yelled, drawing everyone's attention. "I'll go get the sword." She took a single step before rocking back to thrust an authoritative finger under the man's nose. "You better wait right here."

"As you command, my sweet Petal." He bowed as the woman trotted up the stairs to fetch the sword.

Dylan turned to the hound. What was so important about this particular sword when Tracker had a perfectly decent blade already at his side? Was there some reason why the man couldn't just use the scimitar?

Before he could open his mouth to ask, Authril's harsh voice invaded the brothel's soft atmosphere. "You're not actually going to hang around whilst she grabs some stupid weapon?" she demanded of the hound. "I thought you were here to speak with an informant, not mess around."

Tracker shrugged. "I promised her." He leant against a nearby pillar. "It will not take long and you are free to return to the inn at any time."

The woman's sea-green gaze flicked Dylan's way. Her lips flattened. Rather than further voicing her displeasure she stalked off to wait by the stair railing, lingering only long enough to march back, then repeating the cycle, grumbling under her breath the whole time.

A particularly lean fellow and his giggling client blocked the sight for a moment, snapping Dylan's attention back to his surroundings. He idly tracked the prostitute as the man escorted his client towards the stairs. The man's patron fondled the bulge in the prostitute's smallclothes before the pair began their ascent, leaving rather less to the imagination than there'd been a moment ago.

Dylan reflexively wet his lips, unable to tear his gaze from the pair until they were out of sight. *By the gods.* No wonder the client giggled his head off.

The pair crossed paths with Petal trotting her way back down the steps. The sword she clutched wasn't like one Dylan had ever seen. Whilst the blade bore a slight curve—nowhere near comparable to Tracker's scimitar—the hilt looked to be half as long. The fist-sized ball it ended with also appeared to carry a decent amount of weight.

"Hold these," Tracker commanded, thrusting his sword belt and the upper half of his attire into Dylan's grasp.

Blinking, Dylan wordlessly obeyed. The jerkin was surprisingly stiff in places, as though the leather was covertly reinforced. The aroma of citrus and cinnamon permeated both linen and leather, along with what had to be that of the hound's natural musk. What was the man planning on doing that involved a sword and partial nakedness?

Tracker took the sword from Petal, idly twirling the weapon as he trailed behind her. The woman hastened to clear the dancers from the dais, apologising to the handful of objecting patrons.

People slowly fell silent as the hound stepped onto the dais, his boot heels loud upon the bare wood. Those who knew what was about to happen—far better than Dylan could determine—sat forward with keen interest, a couple almost slipping onto the floor.

With so many gazes remained fixated on the man and his movements as Tracker simply walked into the middle of the dais, the most intent amongst them came from the prostitutes. Petal in particular being the most animated of them all, bouncing on the spot and tapping her fingertips together in a silent clap. A few others whispered and giggled to each other from behind their hands.

The music changed pace. Rather than the dreamy tone the other dancers had swayed to, this song carried a fiery tune, the more sultry strings of an elven lap harp replaced by the sharper notes of a lute that the musician sawed at with a bow.

Tracker rotated slowly on the spot, swinging the sword widely as he turned, the point mere inches from the floor. He then kicked the flat of the blade, launching the sword into the air, only to have the hilt tumble along the back of one arm to the other and be caught in one hand.

The music increased its tempo, the slap of drums weaving their way through the string's notes in a rolling beat.

The hound spun and jumped, his booted footsteps adding their own rhythm. He twirled on the spot, balancing the weapon on his wrist, up over his arm and onto his shoulder. He tipped his head back, allowing the sword's momentum to carry it close to his throat before making its way down the other arm.

If the man's mere appearance on the dais had piqued interest in the brothel's patrons, his dancing had fully captivated them. Even Authril's muttering ceased. She watched with slack-jawed interest.

Dylan had seen the hound spar often enough, both with and without the man having his torso clothed, and some of the moves were even the same. But this act displayed feats of limberness Dylan didn't think possible. His braid waggled from side to side, giving Dylan teasing glimpses of the tattoos running down the man's back.

Through it all, the sword continued to spin. The edge glinted in the lantern light. A reminder of how sharp it was. *A deadly barrier.* How did the man not cut himself with this foolery?

The answer was simple. The sword flowed as though a part of him. It swung one way, then tilted another, heeding Tracker in its every movement to elegantly balance or twirl on his wrist, his shoulder, his neck.

Tracker abruptly somersaulted, the sword tucked between shoulder and neck, dropping onto his knees in the centre of the dais. Leaning back, his throat exposed to the ceiling, he set the blade twirling atop his chest with a series of shimmying movements.

The man continued to move to the music, snaking like his spine and ribs were mere suggestions. His hips twitched to the drum beats sneaking through the softer rolling notes, thrusting his groin into the air as though he made love to the heavens.

Dylan found himself unable to look away from the display. The man's abdomen shifted in ways Dylan wasn't aware the muscles were capable of. His breath quickened, rasping out his mouth. His skin tingled. Warmth pooled in his gut.

No. Not his gut.

He casually adjusted his hold on the man's bundle of clothing, lowering it until they shielded his groin. The cut of his robe wasn't formfitting, but it should deter any curious gazes. Not that anyone appeared to be looking this way.

The flash of a sword hilt broke Dylan's concentration on the man's abdomen. Tracker had taken up the weapon again, twirling it from one hand to the other, the edge barely missing his bare skin.

Tracker threw the sword into the air to the chorus of appreciative gasps. It spun close to the ceiling, the blade glinting amongst the chandeliers.

The music stuttered to a halt, leaving only the drum. That frenzied beat continued to rumble away, each new thump quicker than the last, yet also taking an eternity.

Dylan's heart raced alongside the rhythm. He couldn't tear his gaze from the sword. Why was Tracker calmly lying flat against the floor? *Move.* The blade would impale the man if he didn't get out of the way.

The sword completed its final arc and descended, point-first, towards the hound's exposed chest.

The drums ceased with a single sharp bang, almost taking Dylan's heart with it. He squeezed his eyes shut. The damn man was going to kill himself in front of all these people and not a one of them tried to stop it.

A shriek pierced the silence.

Risking a peek, he found all was well. Tracker still lay in the middle of the dais. The sword hovered above him, its blade caught on the flat by the man's hands, the point a mere inch from his heaving chest.

The crowd exploded into cheering.

Dylan swallowed, mildly surprised to find his heart hadn't relocated to his throat. His body trembled, barely holding him up. Even suppressing his shield was more of a struggle than usual.

Grinning, Tracker flicked the blade away from his body and rolled to his feet. He bowed before the crowd who increased the already cacophonous level of their praise.

Petal bounced forwards to relieve him of the sword. "As breathtaking as always, Precious. I see we still like to up the ante." She drew the sword hilt close, wrapping both arms around it.

Shrugging, the hound wordlessly approached Dylan, his arms half-reaching for his clothing before he was close enough.

Dylan swallowed. After the exertion Tracker had undergone, the aroma that was the man's alone had grown. Not to a disgustingly unbearable level, but enough to set a soft hum in Dylan's gut.

"Afraid the younger boys will upstage you?" Petal continued, her smile bright and clearly meant to take the sting out of the words.

"Never was," the hound replied.

The face Petal gave suggested she didn't believe him.

Dylan held his breath as Tracker collected his gear, trying not to look or think about the half-naked being standing so tantalisingly close. The prospect of witnessing the man's last moments had done more than chill his blood, but his body remained coiled, as though his unexpected erection might spring back to life at any second if he let his mind wander even the slightest.

"I'm more impressed he'd the balls to do a stunt like that," another prostitute piped up. "The mistress would've killed you all over again if you had damaged the dais."

"Then it is fortunate I did not," Tracker curtly responded in the midst of donning his clothes. Only when he had fastened his sword belt did he turn back to Petal, his warm smile wide. "Make sure the sword returns to the vault, my dear."

Nodding earnestly, Petal trotted back up the stairs, past several other prostitutes who had obviously appeared to watch Tracker dance. How did they all know his performance so well? The man had made no secret about visiting the place often. Had he also danced like that every other time?

"That was a foolish move," Authril said, her grumpy demeanour having returned now she wasn't distracted by the very display she belittled. She stood before Tracker, her arms akimbo and her face flushed. "What if you'd been hurt? Or killed? Who would've escorted Dylan, then?"

"I am certain that is a mantle you would have eagerly picked up."

"That's not the point! You—"

"I thought I heard my favourite elven man was nearby," someone said, drawing the hound's attention.

Dylan turned to find a voluptuous woman descending the stairs. Like the other prostitutes, her attire was made of a sheer fabric, the dress a light blue shade and looked to be a single piece of cloth held up by a chain necklace.

The hound grinned. "Treasure."

She sashayed through the crowd as if they weren't even there. "I thought you were moving on from here." Halting before the hound, she captured his lips in an open-mouthed kiss. "Don't tell me you've been around all this time and haven't come to see me. I'd be positively heartbroken." She swatted at his armoured chest with the back of her pale hand before facing Dylan and Authril. "And you brought friends!"

"Not exactly," Tracker replied. "This dear man is under my care and my other companion is merely here to babysit. And, I am afraid to say, my stay this time shall be quite brief. We are merely passing through and I am on the hunt for a little information of what lurks along the northern roads."

Treasure cocked her hip. Her skirt parted at the side, revealing a creamy thigh. "You know information costs you."

The hound acquiesced with a bow. "The usual fare, I imagine."

"Wait." Authril frowned at the man. "*This* is your contact?"

The woman turned her attention from Tracker to run her cool, green gaze over the warrior. Her lips—a deep shade of pink that Dylan doubted was natural—curved into a warm, and altogether practised, smile. "Well, we certainly can't all be impressive creatures of muscle and steel."

A faint pinkness, almost impossible to notice in the smoky light, fast bloomed upon Authril's cheeks.

"It is not so strange, my dear warrior," Tracker said. "*The Gilded Lily's* prowess is renowned all over Demarn and a great many people come through here."

In more ways than one, I'm sure. Dylan's gaze slid to the patrons lounging on the closest couch. They didn't seem to go much further than kisses. He supposed that was what the rooms upstairs were for.

"—and Treasure hears a great deal of gossip," Tracker continued.

"That so?" Authril took another step closer to the woman. "Then tell us, what news have you heard from the north?"

Treasure's smile barely shifted. "I couldn't tell you that, darling," she said in a tone that was overloud. "Anything my clients say is strictly confidential." With her voice dropping to a whisper she continued, "I could, however, tell you in private. For a fee."

"Why you money-grubbing—" Authril stilled as the hound laid a hand on her shoulder.

"Relax, my dear woman," Tracker purred. "I will handle this. Just give me a moment—say... half an hour or so—and I will return with the information we need."

Authril sneered. "I don't think so. I don't trust you, hound. If you're going, I'm coming with you. I want to hear exactly what she has to say."

"Of course, darling," Treasure piped up. "The more the merrier."

Dylan took in the prostitute's smug smile. Had she also noticed Authril's blush? Was the woman interested in other women? Did she think the warrior would be interested? He wasn't certain, but it seemed a possibility.

Treasure circled the other woman, brushing her hand down Authril's arm before linking their fingers. "Come," she breathed. "I've just the place to discuss whatever you like."

With her entire face having gone deep red all the way to the very point of her ears, Authril offered no resistance as Treasure guided the woman towards the same stairs he'd seen the previous client travel up.

Dylan cleared his throat, drawing the hound's attention, if not Authril's. "What am I to do in that time?" If the whole reason Tracker had brought him along was to keep him safe from other hounds, how did the man expect to do that whilst with the prostitute?

"You're welcome to linger down here," Treasure offered. "I'm sure someone would be eager to take care of you." She indicated the room with a broad sweep of her hand.

Authril whirled around, her face horror-stricken. "No!"

"Goodness," the prostitute exclaimed. "Such vehemence. It was a mere suggestion. I had no idea you were also the man's bodyguard."

"More his lover," Tracker replied.

Authril frowned. "He's not my lover."

The man's brows shot up at her denial. His gaze darted between her and Dylan. "My apologies. I was under the impression that you two are intimate."

The warrior folded her arms. "We are. Not that it's any of your business."

"Intimate, but not lovers? I understand." He turned back to the prostitute, his brow still furrowed. "Sadly, I would have to side with my companion on this one, Treas. This dear man has lived a sheltered life. He certainly has not had the pleasure of visiting such a place as this. And, given he is practically an innocent, it is perhaps not the best idea to let him loose where there are so many aphrodisiacs."

"And the last thing I need is to catch some disease off him," Authril added.

Dylan opened his mouth, ready to explain that it wasn't possible for him to become diseased. At least, not for long. His innate healing could fix more than wounds. It could clear his body of poisons and all manner of illnesses.

"Darling," Treasure interjected, one brow arched high. "That might be true for a lesser establishment, and I'm frankly shocked that you'd insinuate we aren't clean when that's simply not true."

"Besides," Tracker said, smoothly putting himself between the two women. "There are many ways to care for a patron and those of *The Gilded Lily* are skilled in them all."

"If we're going somewhere private, he's coming with us."

The hound's gaze slid Dylan's way. The charming smile he had levelled at Authril wavered slightly in the corners. "As you wish, my dear woman." He gestured for the women to ascend the staircase, moving on to silently guide Dylan up with a simple hand not quite touching his back.

Dylan walked beside the hound, less certain of following Treasure than either elf appeared. "We're not actually going to have sex with her, right?" Joining her in a room wouldn't be so bad if it was all just pretence, but he'd a feeling that both Treasure and the hound were quite serious in their meanings.

"It is how things are played here," Tracker replied, his voice oddly sedate. "You buy her time, you use it, then she tells you what she knows."

"And if she doesn't know anything after all that?"

The hound shrugged. "Then at least the sex is good."

Dylan halted at the top of the stairs. He glanced over his shoulder at the floor below. The way the room sprawled before him, it rather put him in mind of a buffet. Others had resumed their place upon the dais, their movements nowhere near as intense or alluring as Tracker's dance.

He grasped the railing, his gaze running blindly over the scene, his mind still lost in the swaying of the hound's hips. No being should be able to move so fluidly.

Tracker leant next to him. "Are you all right, my dear spellster? I ask only because you look rather flustered. It *is* nice to see a little colour in those cheeks, but if you are uncomfortable..."

"I'm fine." If sex was a thing that had to happen, no one said he needed to participate. He could stare out the window with Authril whilst the hound did whatever Treasure wanted.

"There is no need to put on such a brave face. It is no fun if you are ill at ease with the idea. You are free to wait in the common room until we have the information. I am not one to push people into something you would prefer not to do."

"Like you tried to do back at that pond?"

A small, altogether nervous, laugh trickled out of the man's lips. "Thank you for reminding me of that rather embarrassing moment. I do not believe I apologised for it either, for I am truly sorry. I had no idea you and our dear warrior were a couple. If you had told me then and there, I—"

"You mean it would've made a difference?" At the time, he had shared only a handful of intimate moments with the warrior and the last time he'd lain with her before the pond incident had been the previous night. He didn't think that was enough to assume anything, but if sleeping with someone was all it took to be considered as a couple, then he really didn't know how intimacy worked beyond the tower.

"Of course it would have. It still does. I may be a great many things, but a cheat?" Tracker shook his head. "That is one line I have not willingly crossed." The man's gaze ran over him, soft and considering. The candlelight caught in his eyes, deepening their honey-like colour. "It is a shame we did not meet earlier, though."

If he had wanted the hound instead… "It wouldn't have made a difference." He didn't want the man. He didn't want *any* man.

Tracker shrugged. "As you say."

"Are you two boys coming?" Treasure called. "Or were you looking for a little alone time with each other? I'll warn you, Precious, it's not like old times, these rooms are for paying customers. Although, I might consider waiving the standard fee if you let me watch."

Dylan swore his heart truly did leap into his mouth this time. Surely, that wasn't going to be the condition for getting whatever information the woman had. He stared out at the couches far below, fully prepared to vault onto them if that were so.

The hound laughed. "And subject him to all your helpful comments? I would never be so cruel to him. Look, he is like a stunned deer at the mere suggestion. You must rein yourself in, my dear." He gave Dylan's shoulder an amicable pat. "Stay or follow, that is your choice, but mine has been made for me. Just do not leave the building. There are more hounds than myself in this city."

And that little fact essentially made up *his* mind for him. "Let's get this over with," he muttered. Being in the same room as another having sex was a small sacrifice to ensure he remained under the protection of the hound who believed him. The gods knew he'd been fortunate enough there. He wasn't about to test the extent of that luck.

The room Treasure led them to was a decent size, perhaps slightly smaller than the one he used to share with Sulin back in the tower. A massive bed dominated most of the space, a chair and cabinet took up a portion of the remainder, along with what looked to be a leather hammock suspended from the ceiling in the far corner.

"All right," Authril snapped as soon as the door clicked shut behind them. She seemed to have regained some of her previous composure, although her face was still quite flushed. "You've got your privacy, now talk."

Treasure ignored the woman to sit on the side of the bed, leaning back and twisting in a fashion that accentuated her curves. "Did you know that these walls are so very thin?" She toyed with one of the tassels on the corner of a cushion. "Every single moan escapes. The usual, is it, my darling Precious?" she asked the hound.

"If that is all you want," Tracker replied, sounding somewhat distracted. He made for the far corner, shucking his jerkin along the way. "I do not recall you having a swing last time I was here." He curled his long fingers around the ropes, then dropped to stroke the hammock, his bare hand blending almost seamlessly with the leather in the candlelight. "This feels familiar."

"It should." She tipped her head to one side, resting her chin on the back of her hand. "Someone had to take in all your toys once you left."

Left? The hound had owned the hammock? He had *worked* here? Dylan had thought the King's Hounds went through years of training. How could the man have done that and been here?

"Have you used it with anyone?" Tracker enquired further, interest sparking to life in his eyes.

Treasure pouted. Over the man's question or his clear lack of getting down to business, Dylan wasn't sure. "Not as of yet. Not many of my clients are as adventurous as yours were."

"How does it work?" Dylan asked. Given its surroundings, he gathered it was for sex. The hammock's ropes didn't run all the way up to the ceiling, but connected to a webbing of pulleys, allowing it to be raised and lowered. He assumed to allow for ease of entry and varying heights.

Chuckling, Tracker patted the harness as another might do to a favoured pet. "This is a little too advanced for you," he fired over his shoulder.

He glared at the man. "I was born in the tower," he muttered through clenched teeth. "That means the one who birthed me also lives there." Who? He would never know. The overseers made sure of that, separating each tower-born spellster from their parent at birth for the guardians to raise. "There are hundreds of us. Do you think we don't have sex if we want to?"

"Want to, yes." The hound grinned. It rather reminded Dylan of a cat having spotted a mouse. "Yet I distinctly remember that you are not supposed to."

"Clearly, I've had some experience." Even if the man hadn't realised that before the pond, he must've heard Authril having her way during the night, especially when their tents weren't that far apart. He wouldn't be surprised if the other two women could hear them, even if he did try to be quiet.

"Clearly," Tracker echoed, his head tilting to one side. "Did you ever get caught?"

Dylan shook his head. He had come close multiple times, but always managed to escape suspicion. Sometimes, by a whisker.

"Oh?" The man's laughter was small, brief and a little intrigued. "That must spark a whirlwind of inventiveness, yes?"

"It might," he admitted, his face warming slightly as he caught Treasure's hushed chuckle. "But you're not going to find out the truth."

Tracker's mirth returned, silently shaking his shoulders. "Tease."

Authril sharply cleared her throat, waiting until she had everyone's attention before continuing. "Aren't we here for information?" She glanced at the prostitute. "Although, I don't know what you could possibly tell us."

"You are right," Tracker agreed. "We have wasted enough time with me heeding Petal's request, Marin and our dear hedgewitch must believe themselves abandoned." Sighing, the hound turned from the hammock and finished ridding his upper body of clothes.

Dylan shuffled backwards until his rear connected with the door, unable to tear his gaze from the elf's tattooed skin. He wet his lips, struggling to find his voice. "Wh-what are you doing?" His focus dropped to where the man was unbuckling the belt holding up his trousers, his sword belt already propped against the dresser.

"Like I said, you buy her time, you use it. Meanwhile, she will tell you what she knows." The man's trousers hit the ground.

Dylan's gaze remained right where it had started. He focused on the designs inked along the man's abdomen, stringently refusing to follow the flow of them downwards.

His stomach knotted as Tracker's smallclothes joined the rest of the man's attire. He felt along the door. The handle had to be somewhere just behind him. "So you *are* actually going to have sex with her with us right here?"

"You are welcome to watch," Tracker purred. "It would not be the first time I have performed before an audience."

The knots in Dylan's stomach tightened further at the very idea of being in the building and knowing that these two were otherwise occupied, much less sharing the room. There were quite a few spellsters in the tower who didn't mind being intimate in the presence of those not participating. He wasn't one of them.

Maybe it wasn't too late to wait outside. He didn't have to go far, standing on the other side of the door would be enough.

If he could just find the handle.

"You're even more welcome to participate," Treasure added. "I've never had the pleasure of entertaining a spellster before. I won't even charge extra."

His head whipped around to eye the woman. He had completely forgotten her presence whilst mentioning the tower. "I-I'm not a—"

She gave him a wide smile. "Of course you are. Even if my dear Precious hadn't taught me the signs years ago, I've seen enough of your kind being escorted through Oldmarsh to recognise another."

"I'll still pass." He'd never been in a situation with more than one person. It was risky enough being intimate with one. More only increased the chance of discovery and punishment. He couldn't just push that thought from his mind any more than he could consider doing any act that involved the hound.

Treasure shrugged. "As you wish." She unclasped the chain around her neck, letting gravity disrobe her to the waist. "What of you, my strong beauty?" she asked of Authril, the husky tone in her voice turning breathy. She lifted a finger to her lips, the tip of her nail dragging across the bottom one. "Am I allowed to play with *you*?"

It was only then that Dylan realised the fourth member of their group hadn't made the slightest objection to anything. He glanced at Authril, expecting to find her glaring at the pair.

Authril shuffled on the spot, the redness adorning her face slowly slinking down her neck. She lowered her head and managed a very small, "Maybe? But not with him involved." Her expression turned hard as she eyed the hound. "Let me make this clear." One finger rose in warning. "If I get naked and you touch me, I'll rip your balls off."

Tracker held up his hands in surrender. "You wish to be under my dear Treasure's care? I completely understand." He turned to Treasure, kneeling before her to aid in the removal of her dress from where it pooled around her waist.

The woman's mouth descended Tracker's body in a row of wet kisses as he stood. Her hands slid up his thighs, moving higher still to fondle his backside, parting the cheeks to run a finger along the crease.

Groaning, the hound gently pushed Treasure onto the bed until she fully reclined before him. Rather than join her, he remained standing at the side, lifting her legs and hoisting her into position.

Dylan turned his back on them before they went any further. Now that he faced the door, finding the handle was easy. He grasped it, fully prepared to leave.

There are more hounds than myself in this city. Tracker's words echoed through his mind. What were the odds that others like Treasure knew what Dylan was and alerted the other hounds? Maybe not within the brothel, but the inn? The people they'd passed out in the street?

He released the door handle. The other hounds might come regardless of where he was. Staying at Tracker's side would ensure his safety from being treated as a King's Hound might do a runaway. *Or a deserter.* His clothes were patched, torn at the hems and a little scorched in places, but still clearly army-issued attire.

The rhythmic slap of flesh connecting with flesh echoed through the room. That told him all he needed to know about what the hound was doing. *Ploughing into Treasure.* With some measure of force if he were to judge by the way the woman grunted.

You are welcome to watch. The hound's invitation bounced through his thoughts.

Dylan staunchly kept his back on the pair. He had seen quite enough of the man. Tracker nonchalantly bathing in the pond already haunted Dylan's dreams. The dancing would also likely join after tonight. He didn't need to add seeing him being intimate with another to the mix.

He closed his eyes for good measure.

It didn't work. The blackness behind his lids only served as a blank canvas for his mind to conjure all manner of scenarios. Visions he still saw upon the door once he opened his eyes again.

There was a window on his right. He shuffled over to it, staring out into the darkness through warped panes of glass. They'd travelled only one level above the ground floor and were surrounded by equally tall buildings. The looming shapes of rooftops and blank walls crowded the streetlights. Even if he had the light of day, the view wouldn't be any more spectacular.

The prostitute's moans grew louder.

Dylan dug his fingernails into the windowsill and fixed his sights on the distant shape of a chimney. The structure peeked out from behind a neighbouring rooftop, illuminated by the rising moon. Smoke flowed from the tip, barely visible against the skyline.

His ears vaguely noted that the slap of flesh had stopped. It seemed the hound was done. *Already?* They couldn't have been at this for more than a few minutes, surely.

"Come closer, my battle-harden warrior," Treasure purred.

Authril hovered just on the edge of his vision. Dylan risked glancing her way to find she had already removed her armour and was in the process of disrobing further.

Once the warrior was fully naked, she stepped closer to the duo on the bed and out of Dylan's immediate sight. Even though he couldn't see them unless he turned back around, he still felt rather self-conscious being the only clothed person in the room.

He caught Treasure's husky giggle, followed by a faint "Naughty".

His grip on the windowsill tightened. The skin behind his nails paled. His magic buzzed along his fingertips, healing a pain he barely felt, just as it always did.

The noises behind him changed again. Without the slap of bodies meeting to fill the air, the smaller noises were clearer. Hushed gasps and murmurs of pleasure, the brush of skin sliding against cloth. The slick sound of a tongue gliding over something even wetter.

His gaze shifted focus from the outside world to the warped reflection upon the glass. He hadn't seen much within the windowpane when it was Treasure and the hound, but the two women had shuffled in a different spot atop the bed, exploring each other's bodies with their mouths and hands.

He twisted on the spot, searching the room for wherever the hound had gone. Perhaps Tracker, having had his fill of the prostitute, had left the room, leaving the two women to enjoy themselves.

He finally spotted the man sprawled in the armchair by a cabinet of bottles, quietly sipping at a goblet.

Their gazes locked. The way those honey-coloured eyes burned with desire should've been illegal. Right along with that smirk and the subtle roll of his tongue across his bottom lip. The goblet hung by its rim in his fingers, all but abandoned as his full attention switched to Dylan. The man's chest heaved, making his tattoos move in a way that practically dared Dylan not to follow their passage downwards.

He succumbed to the temptation far quicker than he thought possible. *By the gods.* Dylan bit his lip, unable to look away from the sight. It seemed Tracker was nowhere near sated. How could the man wilfully ignore his erection in favour of staring at Dylan?

Tracker's lips twitched into a knowing smirk. His fingers dug deeper into the plush fabric of the chair arm in time to the women's moans. His attention remained locked on Dylan. All whilst the women continued to enjoy each other.

Dylan swallowed. Even though that man did very little, there was something strangely thrilling about watching him. It buzzed through his body. His skin prickled with the sensation. His breath rasped between his lips, quickening as though he had raced up the stairs to get here.

The hound leant back, thrusting his hips upwards. He bit his bottom lip, his left fang pinning the flesh in place.

"I have to go," Dylan blurted, the words almost colliding into each other as one drawn-out whimper.

He fled the room. He didn't care if it meant risking capture by another hound. Just being in Tracker's naked presence, as well as that of two very unclothed women, was obviously confusing his senses.

He stumbled along the corridor, his feet refusing to stop until he reached the stairs leading down. He flopped against the railing, gasping. His heart pounded feverishly. If he didn't know better, he would've sworn he'd been close to the edge.

Gathering himself, he descended the stairs.

A few of the people below turned their heads, disregarding him with the same lack of interest he had witnessed to their patrons. No one seemed to be afraid or even wary of his presence, a definite change from the soldiers back at both the army encampment and the front line.

The cavorting below had returned to the same state as when they'd first arrived. Dancers paraded about on the dais, patrons and prostitutes lounged about the couches and cushions. Servers wound their way through the ever-shifting crowd with pitchers of drink or trays of food.

Dylan traced the passage of the latter, spying what looked to be a bar, the same kind he'd seen in the taverns. He wet his lips, his thoughts turning to procuring a nice mug of whatever they had to moisten his throat whilst he waited for the others.

He would need to pay for that privilege, wouldn't he? He hadn't a single valuable thing on him, not even his personal effects. The latter had been transferred to his pack, which was back at the inn. He doubted his shaving knife, strop and mirror were worth much.

Resigning himself to going without a drink, he scanned the available seating, searching for somewhere that didn't have too many people. A couch tucked in a dark corner of the room appeared completely empty. Dylan made his way through the crowd, pausing every few steps to tug the skirt of his robes from people's grasp.

Sighing, he finally settled into the couch. From here, he'd a clear line of sight of both the dancers and the stairway. How much the others would spot of him was a different matter. He would simply need to keep an eye out. How much longer could they possibly be, anyway?

He hadn't been sitting long when the woman Tracker had identified as Petal approached with a tankard.

Smiling, she set the drink on the table next to him. "I thought you might be thirsty. Don't worry," she blurted, holding up her hands in surrender. "It's not laced with *elfenwurzel* or anything. I figured you could use a rest, Precious and Treasure are a handful on their own, I can't imagine how intense they'd be together." She giggled into her hand. "Actually, I can. I've seen enough of their clients staggering out of his room."

Dylan frowned. "So, Tracker... I mean Precious," he quickly amended as Petal's face scrunched in confusion, "*did* use to work here, then?" He would have to ask the hound about the name.

Petal nodded. "It's been two decades now, but yes. He was popular, too. Like Matz."

Unsure who that was, Dylan remained silent. As long as the woman only talked, he didn't mind the company and it would help keep other prostitutes from wasting their time on him.

"Everybody always wants the elf," she continued, arching her brow at him before her gaze drifted back to the room. "It's the ears, right? Can't be the goods. I've seen them, they're pretty average."

It hadn't been a question, but Dylan still felt compelled to answer. "I wouldn't know." He also had no idea what she was using for comparison as the man was definitely above average. At least, what was average in the spellster tower.

"Oh?" Surprise saw her attention fastened on him. She plonked herself on the couch with enough force to bounce slightly. "I'm sorry, I thought you went upstairs with your orange-haired friend. Or are you her escort? We see priests all the time."

"Priests?" Dylan echoed, sharply reminded of the bandits who had attacked them just outside Toptower. No one in the priesthood wore green robes, but the cut had to be close enough for people to assume. "They come here?"

"Mostly the younger ones. That's not why you're here, is it? To stop them? I've never entertained one myself, so I can't be sure they're not disregarding their vows, but they're all very polite." She sidled closer. "Don't tell anyone, but I've always thought about joining."

"What's to stop you?" He knew little of the full creed, but he couldn't recall there being anything against those in the priesthood needing to be a particular way beyond spiritually willing to serve. The matriarch who oversaw the priests within the tower had allegedly come from a small village to the north. "Can you not leave this place?"

She shook her head. "It's not that. The master and mistress have never held a soul against their will. I just…" She wrapped her arms around her shoulders and whispered, "I can't read. It's not exactly a skill you need here, so no one ever taught me."

"If you wanted to join the priesthood, they would teach you." If not to understand the written word, then to at least know the scripture by heart.

"You don't think I'm too old?"

Dylan couldn't put a precise amount of years to the woman. A couple of decades was the closest he was willing to go. Maybe three. "You're never too old to learn. Or to chase after what you want."

Petal's nose wrinkled, the tip of it twitching, as she grinned. "That's such a priest thing to say. I love it." She threw her arms around his neck, draping herself over him like a grateful child. Maybe she was one. But then, why would a child be in a brothel? "I'll leave first thing in the morning." She bounced to her feet, whirling to give him one last beaming smile before she left.

He watched her move through the crowd, ducking trays like they were mere branches, clambering over couches and people in equal measure. The priesthood would definitely have their work cut out for them, but he'd never known them to turn down a challenge.

As she vanished up the stairs, he spied the hound standing near the top looking straight at him. Their gazes connected and the man started his descent. Alone.

Dylan scanned the landing. No sign of Authril. That meant it would be just him and Tracker. At least the man was fully clothed and they weren't exactly alone.

Still, his stomach knotted. *I can do this.* He grabbed the drink Petal had given him and took a hearty few gulps, not pausing to savour the malty taste washing over his tongue. The vapours tickled his nose, nothing as strong as what he had consumed with his last meal, but enough to soothe his nerves and let him think rationally.

Tracker was coming down here to wait, same as he, not to pounce on him. The man clearly enjoyed women, and any flirting he'd thrown Dylan's way had to be nothing more than good-natured teasing. No different to the jabs his friends used to make with each other.

Besides, he was a hound. They probably had laws against fraternising with spellsters. The only reason he thought of it in another light was due to the atmosphere.

By the time the tankard was empty, Dylan's nerves had fully vanished. If anything, he should be grateful the hound had appeared when he did. It meant Dylan was safe from another coming to claim him and that he must've gotten whatever information he was after. And the man had money to buy more drinks.

Waiting for Authril was simply a matter of killing time.

CHAPTER 34

Tracker closed the door following the spellster's abrupt departure. The two women didn't seem to mind, both being utterly wrapped up in each other. Authril in particular showed no sign of being bothered about Dylan's absence, despite how much she had objected earlier to the man remaining in the common room.

Although, her lack of concern could've been due to the fact she was currently suspended in the air with Treasure straddling her face and keeping her tongue too busy to voice her objections.

Seeing Authril laying like that, her legs splayed and at the mercy of Treasure's infrequent ministrations, he was tempted to at least join in on the teasing. But the woman had been very clear in her boundaries with him. They were not something he overstepped without reason and, even then, he'd found very few of those reasons warranted it.

Besides, he'd a far more interesting person in mind.

He focused on the spellster's residual magic. It had spiked rather suddenly whilst Dylan had stood at the window, infusing the man in a manner Tracker hadn't witnessed before. Something taught in the tower? But he had fought escaped spellsters plenty of times. Perhaps the man had simply been restraining his power.

At least he hadn't gone far. He had come to a stop somewhere below, heeding Tracker's warning of remaining in the building. *Good.* As far as hounds went, Whisper wasn't the most aggressive, but even he would baulk when it came to Dylan's tale.

The main floor was the safest place within *The Gilded Lily.* Nothing further than petting was allowed and the man was unlikely to take anyone up on the offer of a fun time. None of that negated certain parties feeding Dylan all manner of aphrodisiacs. Experience told Tracker that humans reacted slower to them than elves, but he'd no idea what effect they would have on a spellster.

He needed to get whatever information Treasure had and get back to Dylan's side.

Gathering up his clothes, he made a show of donning them in clear sight of the prostitute. "This has been fun, my dear, but I must be on my way. So, if you *do* have any information…"

"Ask away," she said calmly as if the other woman wasn't currently lapping away between her legs.

"What have you heard about the army recently?" With several weeks having passed since its fall and many of the survivors fleeing even Toptower's walls, he didn't expect not a word to be spoken. However, the nature of those words could prove themselves just as troublesome.

Treasure nonchalantly lifted one shoulder. "It's gone. They—" She laid a hand on Authril's chin, guiding the woman back to her previous position. "Don't stop, my sweet. You're doing such a fine job." She tipped back, clutching the swing's ropes and moaning, as Authril resumed.

"Treas," Tracker growled.

Blinking, she shook her head. "Right, yes. Word is that the Udyneans overran the camp. Slaughtered everyone. People around here are taking it as deserter tales."

"I see." A lot of the kingdom didn't understand the odds of ever winning against the Udynea Empire. Most places were far enough that little beyond fables reached them. Only places like Toptower knew the truth, that the king's army had only held its ground this long because of the empire's patience in claiming the land.

For Oldmarsh, the worst thing the city had ever faced was an uprising from the slums. The fighting had seen the city's poorest pushed beyond the outer walls. That had been a century and a half ago. Too far back for many but the affected to care. "What word has come to you from the north?"

"Strange things."

"What kind of things?"

Groaning, Treasure swung her leg over Authril's head. She left the other woman suspended to sashay over to the cabinet and pour herself a drink. Despite its meagre weight, the pitcher shook as she lifted it. "There's an armed host heading west from Wintervale. Merchants who've gotten close say it looks and acts like a mercenary company. The last messenger I entertained claimed it was big enough to be an army."

Tracker paused in buckling his sword belt. "Are they aimed for the border?" Word of the army's downfall would've reached the king by now. He doubted a whole new army could be gathered in a scant few weeks, but they did train soldiers in Wintervale's northern fields. Perhaps enough had joined to aid Toptower in its defence.

Treasure shook her head. "If they were, then their destination can't be for where the army encampment is—was?—or they'd be outside the city by now. My sources say they came from downriver and seem to be following it. Whatever they're after must be further north."

Frowning, Tracker's mind raced to recollect every map of the kingdom he'd ever seen. The spellster tower sat directly north of Oldmarsh. The upper half of Demarn stretched beyond. They shared the northern border with Dvärghem, which was of no threat to them and the king surely wouldn't start a war with a land they'd been allied to for centuries, especially not when the true enemy had broken through to the west.

What could be of interest to a host big enough to rival an army?

Tracker bowed. "Thank you, my dear. Your assistance has been as delightful as ever." He pressed a large black coin of the royal sigil into her hand. One alone granted the bearer a pretty sum in gold if presented to the right places. "For your services. Farewell, my dear woman." He'd only a short journey to the tower ahead of him, then it was back down to collect his warhorse and, finally, freedom from his duties.

Shock parted Treasure's lips. She clutched the coin to her chest, thoroughly aware of its value. "Precious, this is…"

He patted her shoulder. "I know." He glanced Authril's way, noting how the woman was seemingly content to remain suspended. "I will leave you and my companion to your fun. Try not to do anything I would not," he warned the prostitute.

Treasure smirked. "As I recall, there's not much that you won't." Turning her smile on Authril, she sauntered back to the warrior's side. "I do hope you're enjoying yourself."

Tracker was out the door and closing it before he could hear the other woman's reply. Whether Authril was enjoying herself or not wasn't a concern any King's Hound need worry about. Seeing that the spellster in his care remained safe was.

As Dylan expected, after descending the stairs, Tracker's passage had the man heading straight for him. The way he wove through the crowd was almost as if he danced along with them, and far less invasive than the route Petal took.

The hound flopped onto the couch, one arm casually coming to rest on the back section behind Dylan. "Your stay down here has been without issue, yes?"

He nodded. "And you have the information you were after." Stood to reason that was why he appeared now and not immediately after

Dylan left the room.

Tracker grunted what sounded like an agreement. "It is what I thought in regards to information surrounding the army, but there are other whispers of what lies ahead that are of equal interest. I will speak of them when we have more privacy than this." He gestured to the booth.

Dylan followed the man's hand, also noticing a distinct lack of another elf. "Where's Authril?"

"Still having fun." He wriggled closer. "You could be off having fun, too, yes? A certain someone is not here to say otherwise."

"No." It was one thing to let Authril use his body to indulge herself, quite another to choose a woman here and run the risk of impregnating her with a spellster child. Surely a hound would be aware of how more of what he hunted came about.

"We can leave now, if you are uncomfortable. Our dear warrior is capable of finding her own way back to the inn."

Far better than he would've been able to. Authril had likely been paying close attention to their passage, the length of time they'd walked and the corners they had taken. "I'll wait."

Shrugging, Tracker leant back into the couch. He stared out at the room, his expression neutral. Did he not enjoy the entertainment *The Gilded Lily* provided for their patrons?

He swept his gaze over the room, taking in the display of bare skin, flexibility and grace. Most were men, many being half-naked or wearing even less. A few strutted around the room, flaunting themselves like birds during the spring. The majority lounged about the place, some striking a pose similar to Tracker's. Those who weren't in the process of charming their client waited to be admired like prised mousers.

Even Dylan could admit the array before him was pleasing to the eye. Although, he supposed if the hound truly had been working here as both Treasure suggested and Petal outright claimed, then he must've seen this hundreds of times.

"I enjoyed your dance earlier. The one with the sword?" he swiftly added, his cheeks growing warmer. Why had he felt the need to elaborate? That was the only dance he'd ever seen the man perform.

Astonishment took the hound's face. A small laugh escaped him, sounding a little on the embarrassed side. "Thank you. It was not my best routine, but I have not danced like that in many years."

"Not since you worked here?"

Tracker raised a brow in his direction. "Yes, not since then."

"I didn't mean to pry. I—" The heat from his cheeks spread across his whole face. "Treasure mentioned you owning the swing and Petal said you were a favourite for years. So I assumed it wasn't a secret or anything that you might regret or..." Coming to the realisation that he was rambling, he let the sentence drift into silence.

"Regret?" the hound echoed. "There are many things I regret in my life. People I wished to have saved. But this place? I am not ashamed of it. Nor do I blame you for knowing such things. Petal always was a gossip."

"She seemed nice."

Tracker grinned. "She usually is. I hope she was also behaving herself. Those born in *The Gilded Lily* can lack the notion of boundaries in others."

"She mistook me for a priest. Said she wanted to join them."

The other of the man's brows rose to join the first. "Really?" Poorly restrained humour twitched along his lips. "Having Petal amongst the clergy will be quite the education for them. She is a rebellious one. Has been since childhood."

"You knew her as a child?" How far back had it been since the hound worked here? A decade? More? *Less?* Exactly what sort of establishment was *The Gilded Lily*?

The hound chuckled mirthlessly. "By the look on your face, it would appear your mind has conjured an unsavoury circumstance. It is not as you think. Petal is one of the more common outcomes of brothel work for those with the ability to carry life. One that almost took the life of her mother. She would've been in her early teens when I—"

"She was raised here?"

Shocked disbelief flickered across the man's face before the smile returned. "Of course. Where else would she be but at her mother's side? Not when she was working, obviously. *The Gilded Lily* does not accept the sort of patrons that would allow a child into the rooms above."

"And down here, amongst all this—?" Dylan gestured to the room in one sweep of his arm. People were in all states of undress, including a couple that were completely naked. "That is better?"

"When the alternative is the streets? Yes." The hound's expression hardened. "Folk are so quick to blame their misfortune on spellsters that they forget there are monsters out there who are just as dangerous without magic. And far more plentiful."

"I find that hard to believe." Anything that had the same capacity to do harm as a spellster would be confined, if not slain.

A mournful smile curved the man's lips. "Good people often do." His attention drifted to the scene beyond their shadowed corner of the room.

Dylan's gaze followed. Little had changed. People still danced, others still reclined. The selection of patrons to dote over seemed to have dwindled. One trio was in the midst of disappearing upstairs, whilst others had either done the same or vacated the brothel entirely. Remarkably, one had somehow fallen asleep.

With fewer people, the remaining prostitutes fanned out across the room. One came their way, turned back with a disinterested flick of Tracker's hand.

"Authril's going to be a while, isn't she?" Dylan asked. Not one for asking personal questions regarding others' sexual activity, he had no idea how long it took for two women to reach mutual satisfaction. He did know Authril was somewhat of a greedy lover.

The hound shrugged. "It is possible. Treasure is a thorough woman."

"Then how come you're not... you know...?" He gestured vaguely at the room.

"Indulging myself?" Tracker supplied, a hint of the familiar cockiness returning to his smile. "I have already lain with over half of the prostitutes in this room alone."

Dylan glanced at the throng. The ratio of men hadn't changed. At least a dozen of them still mingled with prospective clients. Given the size of the building, there were likely twice that many elsewhere.

By half, did Tracker mean he'd also been intimate with men? *These* men specifically? He didn't dare make any guesses about those wearing a little more clothing than the rest, but many of them had the same equipment as himself. As did some of the women.

Had his first assumption about the hound been correct? That the man was only interested in men? Or was it those who possessed a certain hard member no matter their gender?

What of Treasure? Dylan hadn't imagined hearing the hound with her and she was definitely lacking in a certain department, but the man also hadn't seemed that enthusiastic about finishing with her.

No, he'd been far too interested in teasing Dylan.

The sweeping of his tongue across his lip. The undulation of his stomach. The thrusting of his hips. The bob and sway of his engorged length, still glistening from his time with the prostitute.

Dylan mentally shook the image free, steadfastly ignoring how his body tingled at the memory. His gaze darted to the man's groin. There was no telltale hint of a contained erection. Maybe he'd dealt with it in the time Dylan was gone.

Wasn't there also the woman in *The Silver Flagon*, the one Tracker had saved from that drunkard? She acted as though they'd been intimate in the past and the man seemed to enjoy the attention.

Did that mean Tracker was indecisive?

How did the world outside the tower treat them? The thought hadn't even crossed Dylan's mind before. They wouldn't have people outing them, would they?

No.

That sudden clarity hit like a lash. Unseen pressure tightened around his chest, squeezing the more his mind raced. His heart kept pace with his thoughts, setting his whole body thrumming to its furious beat. Magic sang through his veins, trying to fix whatever ailed him.

Of course they wouldn't be outed, there was no one to out them to. No threat of their guardian endlessly looking over their shoulder. No being shunned. No complete and utter absence of autonomy. Without all that lingering over their heads...

They'd be treated just the same as every other sexuality. No being written off as too greedy to pick a side. No one labelling them as confused or reckless or untrustworthy.

Just ordinary.

Normal.

Tracker slid closer, laying a hand on Dylan's knee. The contact further constricted Dylan's throat. "Are you all right?"

He nodded, hoping he didn't look as wide-eyed as he felt. "Just wondering what of those you haven't been with?" he managed, trying to divert the man's concern in himself.

"I have no interest in them." The hound shuffled his position on the couch, a leg tucking beneath him. One hand reached out, hesitantly hovering over Dylan's chest. "But you...?" He shuffled closer. His thigh brushed Dylan's and all he could think of was the vision of the man reclining naked and erect in the chair.

Tracker caressed the underside of Dylan's jawline. Those long fingers coaxed his head to one side.

A silent keen constricted Dylan's throat as he obeyed, his mind still back in the room he'd left and the way those honey-coloured eyes had beckoned him closer.

"Dylan?" the man purred. The pad of his thumb, calloused from years of sword fighting, swept across Dylan's lips and dropped to his chin. He pressed closer still, his mouth mere inches away, his breath warm and smelling faintly of spiced wine. "I—"

Someone cleared their throat, loudly.

It took all of Dylan's willpower to break eye contact. *Gods.* Bad enough the man had been watching—teasing—him this whole time, but he hadn't just tried to *kiss* him.

Had he?

Authril stood before the couch, her ire locked on the other elf.

Tracker bounced to his feet, seemingly unconcerned with what had almost transpired or the woman's glowering. "We have had our fill, yes?"

Unbidden, Dylan's gaze dropped to the man's groin. What he had felt stirring against his thigh was still in evidence. Clearly, the man's words weren't true for everyone.

"And you got what you wanted," Authril replied, the even tone of her voice at odds with the anger on her face. "We should return to the inn now if we are to leave at first light." She turned on her heel, marching for the exit.

Tracker followed, motioning Dylan to do the same.

He tailed the two elves as they wound through the crowd, studiously ignoring the hound's very presence. Authril continued to shoot poisonous glances at the man, her expression clearly illuminated by the massive chandeliers.

"Such fearsome looks, my dear woman," Tracker said to her. "What have I done to offend you so? If it is a simple matter of not being satisfied, then perhaps you should direct your glares to the woman whose crotch you were face-deep in. I have never known Treasure to leave a client disappointed and I am certain she would be all too happy to finish you off."

"What did you think you were doing with him?" she snarled, indicating Dylan with a jerk of her thumb over her shoulder.

The hound's sudden laughter cut through the sultry music. He halted near the exit. "All this hostility is over seeking a kiss? My dear, what I was doing was as precisely as I pleased. You two have exchanged no commitments of monogamy and you have already admitted you are not lovers. That makes him fair game if he wishes, yes?"

Dylan's gut bubbled at the thought. The warmth of the man's breath still heated his cheeks. *If I wish it.* He didn't wish for anything. Not from Tracker.

The ghost-like brush of the hound's thumb lingered on his skin all the same. The man's every movement had been restrained, but very clear on what he wanted. Never had Dylan been touched that way before. There was no time for such things in the tower, and beyond it, Authril was very direct in her desires. Forceful, just as she currently was in jabbing a finger into the hound's chest.

"Keep your lips off of him," she growled, baring her teeth.

Tracker gave a low, rich chuckle. The smile he replied with was far too toothy and revealed canines far longer than the woman's. "Where I choose to place my lips is no one's business other than the one I place them on." He pulled open the door, re-entering the city's night-shrouded streets.

Confident his actions were concealed in the darkness, Dylan dared to run a finger along his lips. They still tingled from the man's touch, mirrored by a similar fluttering sensation in his gut. He reflexively wet his lips, convinced he could almost taste wine.

He took a great lungful of cool air. The sooner they reached the tower, the better. He needed to be leashed and free of the hound's presence before these gentle touches got the best of him and he agreed to something he would regret.

CHAPTER 35

Tracker lay sideways atop the inn bed, his head partially resting over the edge and his legs idly stretched halfway up the wall. With his face pointed at the ceiling, he closed his eyes and waited in silence for the spellster to fall asleep.

The man was restless.

Tracker didn't blame him. The situation in the brothel had gotten well out of control. Attempting the kiss had been a foolish move. A whim Tracker was well aware he should've ignored. One that complicated things.

Yet, as he lay there, the ghost of Dylan's breath continued to swirl in his lungs, warm with the faint aroma of alcohol. His lips still tingled with how achingly close they'd come to meeting the spellster's.

He wanted more. Craved it as another might long for the necessities of life. If he was alone, he would've already jerked off and been done with the damn fancies flitting through his mind. He couldn't do that with Dylan in the same room, not if he wanted to keep the man close.

If only Treasure had entertained the warrior for a few moments longer, then maybe he might've been able to...

Do nothing. Even if Authril's appearance hadn't been a factor, there was no chance he could've convinced the man to follow him into another room. And if, by some miracle, he had? Dylan was plainly too jittery for him to have done anything to warrant such privacy.

Tracker didn't understand it. The man was clearly interested in men. Those dark eyes had glazed over in *The Gilded Lily*, following practically every male prostitute. He had grown increasingly flustered around Tracker and had definitely enjoyed the sight of his nudity when they were in Treasure's room. The man had looked ready to devour him.

Now he had to oversee a spellster who was likely to misinterpret his every damn move. *Stupid.*

He shouldn't even be thinking that way about the man. Hounds weren't discouraged from sex, and sleeping with a spellster once wouldn't cross the line, but he wanted to do so much more.

Maybe he should've stayed behind, let the warrior escort Dylan back whilst he soothed his base needs. *With who?* Treasure? *No.* She hadn't the equipment his body currently desired. Should he have sought out one of the brothel employees who did?

Pointless. No matter how well they performed, they'd never be good enough purely because Tracker didn't want any of them.

Slowly arching his spine, he tipped his head further back and peered through his lashes to eye the spellster's reclining form. Tracker's braid slithered off his shoulder, the end hitting the floor with a faint thud.

Dylan had burrowed beneath the blankets, leaving only the circle of his face exposed to the night. His violent tossing from one side of the bed to the other appeared to have finally subsided, not fully absent as his head still twitched every so often and his lips mumbled scraps of what sounded like pleas.

Bad dreams or good? Impossible to tell without waking Dylan and Tracker was reluctant to disturb the man now he was settled. And he'd a fair idea of the reception he'd get if he tried, even if he wasn't currently straining the capacity of his smallclothes.

Tracker slowly ran his fingers over his groin. He bit his lip, muffling a moan, the sharpness of his fang coming close to drawing blood. It wasn't as though he hadn't gone without sex before, or had even had his advances rejected, but there was something about Dylan that tweaked a primal urge that he hadn't ever felt.

Straightening his back, he settled more comfortably onto the bed. The new position took Dylan's sleeping form from his sight, but that was fine.

Closing his eyes, Tracker idly stroked himself through the layers of leather and linen as he relived the recent memory of the brothel. Of how the spellster's dark eyes had boldly traced his nakedness, lingering on Tracker's erection. The way those ivory cheeks bloomed such a delicate pink in near-perfect unison. The exquisiteness of his lips parting just enough for the hint of a tongue to moisten them.

Tracker slipped his hand into his smallclothes, trying to imagine the grip that tightened around his length belonged to Dylan. Not an easy thing when, by virtue of being human, the man's fingers were nowhere near as long. Nor as rough.

Nevertheless, he pushed into the touch, his hips rocking slightly. With his other hand, he muffled his panting, digging the point of a canine into his finger in an effort to keep himself grounded in his surroundings.

The idea of getting caught sang through his veins, further heating his desire. It had been decades since the last time he'd been under any such risk. Back when—

Just the wisp of thought towards his youth was akin to a dousing in a winter-cold river. The memories were swirls of darkness and terror filled with bad decisions and even worse heartbreak.

With his desires effectively quashed, if not in the manner he would've preferred, he withdrew his hand from his trousers. The echoes of pleasure still whispered through his blood, tainted with bitterness. Even if he'd wanted more, the effort to free his mind wasn't worth it.

Besides, Dylan was too restless, the man's muffled whimpers and groans speaking at great lengths towards the sorts of dreams he suffered. If he awoke to the sight of Tracker with his dick in his hand, the man was not about to leap up and join him.

Maybe the leaping part. But only to vacate the room. The last thing Tracker needed was to spend the night trailing after a spooked spellster who was actively fleeing him. That sort of activity would draw attention to the hound stationed here.

Except, Whisper should already know of Dylan's presence. Tracker knew he was more sensitive than most other hounds when it came to identifying magic, but Dylan was strong. That Whisper hadn't arrived to investigate the flair of magic in the brothel spoke of trouble. The man was one of the older hounds and had been fine a month ago, but every one of them was always one bad encounter away from death.

Checking on Whisper seemed prudent, especially after what he had heard from Treasure. And armed host in the north. Maybe it was something simple, like fresh troops for the army. Or a mercenary company. The last one he'd spent any time with had been quite large. Certainly big enough to hide a spellster in their ranks.

But leaving would mean waking Dylan and the man had looked exhausted.

He rolled onto his stomach, eyeing the seemingly sleeping bulk in the other bed. Dylan had once again shifted. This time, it was to put his back to the room. A hound would never let his guard down in such a vulnerable position. Did the army not train their spellsters in the finer points of survival?

Of course not. If Fetcher's word was true, and he'd come to believe them all the more the longer he was in Dylan's presence, then the wardens wouldn't want their precious weapons learning how to survive without them. *Tough.* If he'd more time, he would've made abusing at least *this* spellster more effort than it was worth for those bastards.

Maybe he still could, if Dylan was amenable to learning a few defensive techniques. It would be frowned upon, but what could they do once the man had gained the knowledge?

When he could be certain Dylan wasn't about to wake anytime soon, Tracker slipped out of the room. He paused outside the accommodations he'd secured for the women, listening for any sign of stirring within. Nothing beyond the wisps of Marin's snores reached his ears, the sound quiet enough that, if there was trouble, Authril would hear.

He descended the stairs only to be greeted by the innkeeper. Both the man and his night staff looked to be in the midst of cleaning up the remains of an exciting time that had involved several plates and at least one chair. "Someone had a little too much fun, yes?"

The innkeeper chuckled and straightened from picking up another piece of furniture. "If gaining several broken bones and a concussion in a brawl is your idea of fun, then I'm definitely passing on any of your offers for a good time." Wiping his hands clean on his apron, he headed for the bar. "What can I get you?"

He held up a hand. "Nothing, my good man. I am simply headed out."

"Thought you might've found enough fun for yourself, although I didn't know tall and skinny was your type. Thought you were more into—" The innkeeper mimed a crude impression of breasts. "—the curvy sort."

He thought of Rose, the person who had instigated the bed breaking that transpired the last time he was here. Even they didn't really match the man's assumed description of Tracker's taste. "Many things are my type, but his presence is less pleasure and more business."

The man's cordial grin dropped. His bulging eyes flicked towards the stairs in fearful anticipation. "You mean he's a—?"

Tracker wordlessly inclined his head.

The innkeeper's brows drew tighter together. "You know my policy on lodging *them*."

"It is but one night and we will be on our way in the morning." Dylan was a man trained in controlling his magic, not a frightened child or a rogue whose only experience came from haphazard bursts. "If there is any sign of trouble, please inform Madam Katarina." Whilst he was certain that Authril would jump at the chance to once again lead their little group, when it came to Dylan's safety, he trusted the hedgewitch's intentions more than he ever would the warrior's.

With the innkeeper's insistence that he'd alert the Katarina of the slightest hint of an issue, Tracker exited the inn. The sudden brush of a cool breeze caressing his skin did much to soothe the dredges of desire lingering in his blood.

The hound station for Oldmarsh was situated in the warehouse sector. A guarded gate and over half of the city lay between Tracker and his destination. On foot, it was an hour's worth of travel through the winding streets.

He turned his gaze to the night sky where the moon neared its zenith. If what his searching found was simply a lazy hound, then he'd be back well before sunrise. It seemed he wouldn't be getting much in the way of sleep tonight. Not the first time he'd gone without. He'd catch up on it later.

The streets always looked too wide when they weren't brimming with the usual traffic of carts, riders and pedestrians. His footsteps echoed off the buildings, mingling with the softer scurries of animals and people in the alleys. Even with the richer part of the city cordoned off from supposedly unsavoury types, they still found a way over the wall. They watched him with guarded interest. Humans likely wouldn't be able to distinguish his ears even in this light and other elves would notice the outline of his scimitar.

Being so late, the street lanterns had burnt through the little amount of oil they held. It didn't matter. The moon's cycle sat at the point of fullness, even with that thin arc of darkness, the moonlight glittered along the cobblestones and shimmered in puddles. The occasional glow emanated from a window or beneath a closed door, adding a pocket of warmth to the otherwise cool beams from the heavens. Shadows shifted across some of those lit windows, most likely that of servants busy in their routines.

Beyond the rich sector, the rest of the city steadily carried the solitary coldness of the moonlight. There was still the odd person up and about, the glow of their candles illuminating a window, but barely reaching the world beyond their rooms.

He passed several taverns closer to the warehouse sector. Most were about as lively as *The Silver Flagon*. A couple looked to still be plying their trade. Music, laughter and a disjointed mixture of people singing assaulted his ears every time he neared one.

"Watch out!"

The warning came seconds before a person landed in front of Tracker. He skirted the obviously drunken figure, surprised when they picked themselves up, dusted off their shirt and staggered across the street into another well-lit building. More familiar noises came from within the open door. Softer.

Unlike the iron fence that separated the rich sector from the rest of the city, there was no definite line determining when he had entered the warehouse quarter. The buildings were no taller, but they shifted from being ones built for the accommodation of people to the boxy sort that suggested they held only things.

A dog bayed in the distance, its territorial cry challenged by another. Their calls set off a nearer group who continued their snarling even as Tracker passed a corner. Hopefully, they were confined to their owner's property. Being chased down by overly aggressive guard dogs wasn't how he wanted to waste this night.

Eventually, he reached the hound station. The structure was small in comparison to the squat warehouses surrounding it, but had a turret that jutted several stories towards the sky. No lights shone from above. Not surprising at this late hour. Seeing that Whisper rarely left the city confines, he likely also went to bed at dusk.

A jiggle at the front door revealed it to be locked, an unusual sight for a manned post. Hounds were trained to sleep lightly, but allowing the frightened to find refuge within these walls did much to soothe their nerves. Perhaps Whisper was actually out patrolling the city.

He glanced over his shoulder. Should he return to the inn? If his fellow hound was heading that way, Tracker would never reach the place ahead of the man, no matter how many years Whisper had on him.

And if the man was *not* here, then Tracker needed to know where he'd gone and how soon his replacement was to be expected. Things he couldn't learn waiting at the front door.

He brushed aside the flap covering the lock. The mechanism looked to be as old as the building, easy to deal with. Ensuring he was still alone, he retrieved his lock picking pin from where it nestled amongst the tie keeping his braid together. A few twists later and he earned the satisfying click of the door unlocking.

The door opened to a flight of stairs leading up. Not uncommon seeing that each hound post also had messenger pigeons to contend with. He trotted up the stairs to be greeted by the darkness of an enclosed room. If there were windows, no light managed to enter them.

He tucked his shoulder against the wall, firmly gripping his sword hilt in anticipation of trouble, and listened for any sign of habitation. Only the breeze whistling from the door at his back and the soft coos of the birds in a room above answered his questing.

After a little searching, he found the stairway leading to the upper level. The inquisitive cooing of many pigeons greeted him as he reached the top. Moonlight leaked through the westward shutters, illuminating several large bird enclosures along with what looked to be a table sitting in the middle of the room.

This area was more in line with what Tracker expected.

A lantern sat atop the table. With a little fumbling in the gloom, he managed to light it. The ruddy glow revealed the room to be far more expansive than suggested from the outside. Still, he was definitely inside the turret section of the building. A row of shelves dominated one of the eight walls with barely a space to be had between the books, boxes and scrolls for anything more.

Unlike some of the other manned stations, there was no sign of a bed or any other amenities. Had he passed the living quarters on his way up? The darkness had been close to absolute, but he hadn't made out anything beyond walls. He would need to descend and find where Whisper bunked, ensure his fellow hound hadn't passed away in his sleep.

As he turned to head back down, a crate full of curled strips of paper caught his eye. It sat at the foot of a desk near the shelving, clearly being used for old messages. The desk itself was clear bar an empty inkwell and a case of blank missive slips.

Curiosity had Tracker plucking one of the old messages from the top of the pile. He froze as his gaze alighted on a familiar summons. *Come home*. Nothing more. No explanation. No announcement of a replacement. He hadn't expected those additions in the missive sent to Toptower, as there was no official King's Hound for that town.

For Oldmarsh? The hound stationed here had always been Whisper for as long as Tracker could remember, maybe even for Tracker's whole life as a fully-fledged hound. The man might not patrol as regularly as a hound should, but Whisper knew the streets, knew the way the city was meant to feel.

To not send another to take his place, to not even allude to it, didn't feel like something their mistress would allow. The spellster tower was the next settlement of any size. Many of those fleeing that place ran straight through Oldmarsh. To leave the city unattended was a foolish move, yet another mistake their mistress would never make.

Had she died? He hadn't been near Wintervale for far too many years, definitely too long to guess at the current state of her health. She would be in her sixties. Not impossible for her to be just as hale and hearty as her brother, the king.

But what other reason would there be to call all of them to Wintervale? And if she had fallen, then control of the King's Hounds fell to her son. Tracker knew nothing of the man save that he was the king's nephew. Neither his character nor whether his personal feelings towards spellsters aligned with his uncle's.

Getting Dylan to the tower and leaving his side would be the safest option for everyone. Even if Tracker had admittedly grown a little attached.

"Fool," he growled under his breath. Had he learnt nothing from his past? Attachments were weaknesses. Hounds weren't permitted to be weak. And to feel this way over a spellster? Doubly unwise. After all, they were meant to be on opposite sides.

The cry of someone outside drew his attention. The expletive fast followed by the pounding of footsteps coming up the first flight of stairs.

Tracker unsheathed his scimitar. No hound would announce his presence so sloppily.

"Who's in here?" a voice boomed. "If you're a thief, I'm warning you now, you've chosen your target poorly. This is the domain of a King's Hound."

"That is true," Tracker shot back, positioning himself at the top of the stairs. "But your threat would hold more weight if you actually were a hound."

A shadowy figure stepped out of the darkness. They dove for the steps, their sword drawn.

Tracker flung a throwing knife, aiming an inch left of the intruder's head. The blade bit into the wood with a satisfying *thunk*. Before the man could finish reacting, Tracker was already down the stairs and had the length of his scimitar levelled at him. "You have one chance to tell me why I should not kill you."

"You're a hound."

Seeing that the man wasn't intent on an immediate attack, Tracker took his time evaluating him. He was around the same age as Whisper, balding grey hair and all. He even filled out his fellow hound's uniform. Yet his mannerisms were all wrong. "And *you* are not."

"No," he agreed. "I'm Whisper's... uh..." He gave a watery smile. "I guess you could say I'm his assistant and—"

"Hounds do not have assistants." That wasn't completely true. There were times when older hounds trained the newer members in specialised tasks, but they were few and often taught in Wintervale, under the mistress's watchful gaze. "And you have yet to tell me what you are doing in his armour." If the man knew Whisper well enough to work alongside him, he had to know impersonating a hound was illegal. And how the punishment for such was the lethal sort.

The man's smile fell. He rubbed at the back of his head, his nails scraping through what little hair clung to his scalp. "Whisper left. He received a missive about three weeks ago and headed east."

Tracker held up the message calling them home. "This missive?"

The man nodded. "No one's heard a word from him since. The people... the first day they noticed him missing, the mayor was close to panicking and I just..." He gestured to the desk and the pigeon enclosures. "I know how all this works. I've watched Whisper do his job for years. Hell, in my prime, I even helped him wrangle a few spellsters."

"And, naturally, you figured you are more than capable of filling in the position." What had Whisper been thinking, allowing a being with no protection against magic to assist him in the hunt?

"Temporarily," the man agreed. He smoothed the front of his jerkin, the touch almost reverent. "Everyone knows this armour and it fits well enough." His head snapped up. "Are you his replacement? Is he coming back?"

"I am not here to replace him. Nor do I know if and when he will return."

The man nodded, his gaze distant. "When he left, I-I thought they had found out about..." He trailed off into silence.

Tracker waited, wondering if the man would notice if he left. With Whisper having returned to the capital, any risk to Dylan's safety had also disappeared, along with Tracker's need to speak to his fellow hound.

Abruptly shaking himself, the man refocused his attention on Tracker. "You wandering hounds cross paths with each other all the time, right? If you find him, send him back to me. I-I mean, *us*. The... the city is a mess without him."

Peering at that face, wrinkled with age and concern, a stark realisation struck Tracker. "You are his lover."

Panic took the man's features. He flailed his arms, waving them before him in strict denial. "No, no. We? No, I... I told you. I'm his *assistant*."

"As you say." Clearly, Whisper had informed the man of how dangerous such a thing was for a hound. They weren't meant to be romantically involved with anyone, not even their fellow hounds. Tracker had learnt that lesson the hard way. "It would still be wise to stop with your impersonation."

The man frowned, his grey brows forming a bushy veranda. "Where's the harm if it stops the people from panicking?"

"And when a spellster comes knocking?" If the man had truly been around Whisper for years, had helped in some cases, then he'd understand the full extent of a hound's job. It was so much more than securing dangerous spellsters. The vast majority of his tasks involved escorting terrified children and adolescents to the tower.

Those jobs haunted him the most. The screams of children who didn't understand why. Their begging, the promises to behave, to be quiet, good, if only they could remain.

The man scoffed. He leant back against the wall, folding his arms before him. "There hasn't been a spellster in the city for at least a decade."

"Really?" He knew of at least three, had hunted one. Clearly, Whisper hadn't shared everything with his lover. "Then the one currently residing in *The Silver Flagon* must be entirely my imagination."

The man's eyes bulged far enough that Tracker thought they might burst out of his skull. "Here? *Now?*" His complexion paled further as he nervously slathered his tongue across his lips. "I guess I had better—"

"Get out of that uniform and tell the mayor the truth," Tracker finished for him. "You are fortunate that this spellster is not only under my care, but also fully trained in his power and destined for the army."

Relief took the man's face. Colour flushed his cheeks. He nodded, reluctantly, but with the heavy weight of comprehension resting squarely on his shoulders. "The mayor won't like it, but I will."

"Now for the reason I am here instead of guarding my charge. What news have you about the current state of affairs to the north?"

"Let me see." The man strode past Tracker to pull out a scroll from the upper shelf. They ran down the list, none of the information being anything that Tracker hadn't already known. It seemed that, after the order to head for Wintervale, all other communication amongst the posts had stopped.

Tracker left with a promise to inform the man of Whisper's whereabouts should he actually come across his fellow hound. He didn't hold out much hope of that without venturing closer to Wintervale.

His return to the inn was as uneventful as his journey to the hound station. Getting back into the rich sector took a little more finagling. With the guards currently stationed at the gates having regarded him with barely concealed sneers on his way out, he doubted they'd let him return.

A simple scaling of a building close to the walls cordoning the area saw him back within its confines without needing to involve them. He'd an even easier time entering *The Silver Flagon* and creeping back into the room he shared with the spellster.

Checking the space by the light of the moon, he found nothing had changed. His bunkmate for the evening didn't appear to have moved from his bed. *Heavy sleeper.* He had gathered as much during their time on the road.

Having already half undressed in silence, he was in the middle of undoing the ties to his trousers when a soft whimper drew his gaze to the spellster's bed.

The man still slept, although far from soundly. He had resumed his tossing and turning beneath the sheets. Wisps of pure magic danced all around him, several on the cusp of becoming something of dangerous substance.

Tracker settled on the side of the bed. "Easy now, my dear man," he whispered, brushing the back of a forefinger across Dylan's temple, marking how clammy the pale skin was. "It would be bad form to set the room alight in your sleep, yes?" He had seen the outcome of that. A young girl, the village had claimed, her head full of terrors. In the light of morning, the villagers had found the charred remains of the family huddled around the child. Whether they had been attempting to wake or soothe their daughter, he could never be sure.

The only thing he knew was he'd been too late.

Sighing, Tracker shuffled further onto the man's bed. He pillowed Dylan's head in his lap and gently stroked the glossy black hair. "I do not know what horrors you saw amongst the army, but I can guess readily enough." He had seen the aftermath, walked through the field of burnt and mangled bodies, knew the spellster caused the gruesome death of a Udynean.

Dylan's lanky form scrunched in on itself. At first, Tracker thought the man had awoken, but the spellster simply let out a shuddering breath and grew still.

"Whoever trained you spellsters for war has done you a great disservice." Clearly, they didn't prepare them to fight in an actual battle, much less a losing one.

And this fear he had of his power? It was one thing for some villager who had never met a spellster to speak as if they were all dangerous monsters. He could even understand why a soldier who'd fought the Udynean forces would consider them as such. It was quite another to witness someone who clearly thought that of themselves.

Yes, spellsters should be wary of their strength and how misusing it could irreparably harm others. And true, the vast majority of upsets and disasters caused by spellsters were, in turn, triggered by fear, inexperience and a sudden isolation from loved ones.

But no being should ever be taught to fear their own self.

The man wouldn't escape such beliefs in the army, either. Tracker had spoken with Fetcher too many times, had listened to his fellow hound as she lamented her task of escorting spellsters to the army. She was a soft soul and he had always thought her tales of the injustices spellsters sent into the ranks suffered, of how the army treated them as instruments, were pure exaggeration.

Never would he have believed she was right.

Dylan should never have left the tower. Whoever was responsible for placing the man in the army had made the wrong choice. Only luck had seen it not become a fatal one.

And sending him back now would only return the man to the same cycle. Not a thought Tracker wanted to consider. Definitely not one he could shake. He didn't know how Fetcher coped with knowing what became of the leashed ones.

Sure that he could get some rest, Tracker gently slid off the spellster's bed and tiptoed to his own. He climbed beneath the sheets, keeping one ear trained for any sign that Dylan's nightmares might return. It wasn't the best way to sleep, but anything was better than nothing.

Only the man's rhythmic breathing answered him.

Tracker closed his eyes, letting himself drift in the nothingness behind his lids. Impressions of colour darted across his mind's eye, the foggy formations of dreams. He avoided their lure, content to linger in the formless dark.

"No!"

Jolted fully awake, Tracker sat upright in his bed, his dagger at the ready.

There were only the sounds of the night. The wind gently rattling the window latch, the distant murmur of people in a room below, the nearer sounds of snoring, that of a couple enjoying each other's company.

And Dylan.

The respite the man had gained under Tracker's gentle caress appeared to have worn off. Was this what Authril dealt with every night? Nothing he had heard whilst on watch suggested it. Or maybe the whimpers he'd mistaken as coming from intimacy had a less pleasant source.

Dragging his blanket with him, Tracker wrapped himself in the itchy fabric before climbing onto Dylan's bed. "You better not wake up before me." If the man found they shared the space so intimately, it likely wouldn't matter to him that they were both clothed, or that Tracker slept atop the rest of the bedding. Not after the brothel.

His gaze lifted to the man's mouth. Even beyond the brothel's hazy golden light, those lips looked so soft. He hadn't even wanted much, just one sweet brush against them.

If he believed he could've stopped there, then he really was a fool. Doubly so to think he deserved even a taste.

He should've insisted Authril remain at the inn, then Dylan wouldn't have been in Treasure's room and they wouldn't have ended up on that couch together. But she was hardly to blame. That misstep sat squarely on his shoulders. Of all the things that he should've done, the one he should *not* have attempted was that kiss.

Rolling over, he wriggled until his back barely brushed the spellster's side. This last leg of their journey had the potential to turn extremely awkward.

CHAPTER 36

Dylan groaned. His head felt packed with wool. Everything was fuzzy, including his teeth. An aching exhaustion had leached into his bones, so deep that even his innate healing seemed unable to soothe him.

It took him a moment to realise someone was calling his name. He was being shaken, too. The grip on his shoulder was barely enough to rock him, but it was definitely responsible for the movement.

"Go away," he managed, his tongue even less awake than the rest of him. His hand flailed above the blankets as he sought to free his shoulder from whoever tried to wake him. When that didn't work, he rolled over.

And promptly found himself on the floor.

He lay still for a moment, trying to orientate himself. His blankets had slid off the bed with him, draping over his face and tangling his limbs. He fought the fabric in a bid for freedom, just missing cracking heads with Tracker as he finally sat up.

A yelp escaped Dylan's lips. He scurried backwards, stopping only when his shoulders bumped into a wall. Daylight shone through the window above his head, illuminating the room.

He took in their surroundings, a small room with bare, wooden walls. Two simple beds filled much of the area, both only big enough to fit one person. This was their rented room at *The Silver Flagon*. Yes, he recalled numbly stumbling into the space on their return.

Had they actually left the inn? He remembered... being somewhere else. Much of his memory was a tattered mess of what he assumed was reality and fragments of dreams.

"Easy," Tracker said, kneeling at his side. The man was in the middle of buckling one of his vambraces, the leather clinging to his forearm by virtue of a single fastened strap. "Are you all right? You have been tossing in your sleep ever since your head hit the pillow." He pressed the back of his hand to Dylan's temple. "You do not seem feverish."

"No," he agreed, rubbing where the elf had touched him. His head wasn't hot, just jumbled. His dreams had jumped from one nightmare to the next. He recalled running through a maze of charred bodies, their lipless mouths creaking for him to slow. Severed and bleeding limbs had grasped at his robe, tripping him into a sea of bloated corpses that exploded into flies.

And in between?

Winding pathways thick with incense. A woman's laughter chasing him around every turn. The walls alternating between crumbling stone and naked, rotting bodies before turning into dancing men with eyes the shade of rich honey.

Dylan looked up at Tracker's frowning face. How long had the hound been waiting for an answer? "I..." His head worked to clear the fog from his mind. He recalled entering a brothel. There'd been dancing, half-naked people, and a woman with the sultriest voice. Any other details were just as hazy as his nightmares, shrouded by his grogginess. "You..."

Authril had been there, not exactly an unwilling party. And Tracker...

The flash of sharp steel. The hypnotic roll of a naked stomach. The thrusting of hips. Those eyes boring into him. Hot. Wanting. The weight of the hound against him. The heat of his breath...

His gaze dropped to the man's lips. *Had* all that been a dream?

Concern moulded Tracker's brow. "Are you plagued by these nightmares often?"

"I didn't have a—" The lie halted on his tongue as the man's brows rose in a perfect example of disbelief. "They only started since the attack on the army." Sleeping with Authril saw them subside for a short while, but they never truly left.

Nodding slowly, the hound returned to buckling his vambrace. "If you like, we could discuss this in greater detail once we have set camp tonight. Horrific scenes and I have become close friends over the years. I hear talking can help and I am sure I can relate."

Can you? What regrets would a man who'd slain a defenceless bandit have? What horrors could a hound stumble upon? But then, what possibilities couldn't he be faced with? The tower was rife with stories of fleeing spellsters going mad. He hadn't ever believed them, but if what had happened at the main camp was anything to go by, one such person could easily destroy a small village. "I suppose being a hound isn't always pleasant."

"If that is your way of asking if there have been times when my work did not involve an easy stroll to the tower, then…” His lips flattened into a grim line. “No, it is not always pleasant.” The man gathered up Dylan’s robe and tossed it into his lap. “But we are wasting daylight. My offer to speak of it further is always open. Take me up on it if you wish. For now, it would be best if you dressed before the women come barging in.”

Dylan ran his fingers over his jaw, sighing as hints of stubble greeted his fingertips. Ordinarily, he would settle down to shave. But even without the factor of time, he would be better off leaving it in favour of the next morning when his hands weren’t shaking quite so much. Hopefully, it wasn’t enough to be terribly noticeable.

Donning his robe, he hastened to buckle his belt and hop into his boots. He had just managed to shrug his pack into position when someone knocked on the door.

Tracker answered it to find all three women standing outside.

“Finally,” Authril muttered, uncrossing her arms with a huff. “We’ve been waiting for a good half-hour for you to come down. You said you’d be quick.”

“My apologies, dear woman,” Tracker said, giving her a mockingly low bow. “We were held up by technicalities.”

Those sea-green eyes narrowed. Her gaze darted between them. “I hope you weren’t the technicality holding him up.”

Tracker laughed and threw his arm over her shoulder. “What is this? You think I would dare attempt anything? Did the workout my dear Treasure so willingly gave you also addle your mind?”

Hearing the hound speak of Treasure was akin to being doused in cold water. *It wasn’t a dream.* The events of last night flooded his thoughts. The brothel visit, and everything within, *had* happened.

That meant Tracker…

Dylan took a deep breath in an attempt to calm his racing mind. Nothing had happened. Even if it had, it was just a kiss. People kissed all the time without things leading to anything else.

Were such things even permitted amongst the King’s Hounds? Did the man even remember? That he made no mention of it could only mean one of two things. And how possible was it that Tracker had imbibed to the point of not remembering his actions? *Slim.* Clearly, he favoured putting the attempt behind him and acting as though nothing had happened.

Dylan could go along with that idea.

Tracker shook his head, still in conversation with the warrior. “Our dear spellster is merely tired. With the nightmares that take him during the night, is it any wonder he requires more sleep than the rest of us?”

Authril’s gaze shifted to the man’s hand resting casually on her shoulder. "I believe I've told you not to touch me."

The hound merely smiled and removed his arm. "It is nothing to get upset about. I am not trying to get into your smallclothes."

"Just make sure you keep it that way," she muttered over her shoulder as they descended the stairs leading to the tavern.

At Tracker's insistence, they remained in *The Silver Flagon* for breakfast. It was a simple meal, slightly lumpy porridge with bits of bacon sprinkled on top, but comforting and far more nourishing than anything amongst their current supplies.

Dylan couldn't help noticing the waitress was jitterier compared to last night. So was the innkeeper. Their gazes kept sliding his way, even though he did nothing untoward. What was it about him eating a simple meal that made them so uneasy?

Had they realised he was a spellster? The innkeeper clearly knew Tracker, as did the waitress. They had to be aware that the man was a hound.

Yet, they acted as though Dylan was about to burst into flame.

He wolfed down the rest of his food, his skin prickling from all the gazes trying not to stare at him and failing. With every passing second, he expected someone to lunge for a weapon, force him to use his shield to defend, then blame him for using his magic.

Dylan leapt to his feet at the first sign of the others being ready to depart.

"Such eagerness," Tracker remarked. He flashed a smile that Dylan guessed was supposed to put him at ease. It didn't.

"I just think we've wasted enough daylight." He threw on his pack, fiddling with the straps when no one else made a similar move. "We really should be heading out."

"Finally," Authril muttered. She also hoisted her pack onto her shoulders and gave the hound an unimpressed sniff. "At least one of you is making sense. If I didn't know better, I'd say you were stalling in getting him back to the tower."

Tracker tilted his head, his lips still wrapped around the tip of his spoon, cleaning the surface of every last morsel. His gaze flicked between the warrior and Dylan. "Not at all." He dropped the utensil into the bowl and stood, along with the other two women. "But we did need to wait for the market crowds to clear a little and we still must gather some supplies."

"Beyond these?" Katarina lifted the bundle of food given to her by the innkeeper. The man had pressed them into her arms whilst they'd waited for the porridge, insisting she take them.

The hound inclined his head in answer to the hedgewitch. "We require more than food during our travels." He made for the exit, trailing the rest of the group. "Fortunately, much of what I need can be bought on our way to the city gates."

Their path through the rich sector ended quickly, the guards seeming almost glad to see them exit the region. Dylan wished the remainder of their journey through Oldmarsh continued so smoothly, but it became delayed as they reached a market square and Tracker started perusing the stalls.

The man was true to his word. His restocking of their supplies was not only a hardy array of foodstuffs, but several smaller items that Dylan recognised from his days learning the rudimentary medicine folks used outside of the tower. The hound was never long when it came to choosing his purchases, but it could've gone faster if he stopped meandering by stalls he clearly had no intention of buying from.

By the third stall, Dylan couldn't help but observe the increase in a product's value. Where the person before them might buy a similar item at one price, those same merchants would demand almost double from the hound. They wrinkled their noses and pulled faces when they thought the man wasn't looking, smiling only when he handed over the payment.

Tracker didn't seem to notice.

The same couldn't be said of Authril. She frowned at the man's every stop, eventually speaking up as Tracker acquired his fifth purchase—a cloak that actually fitted Dylan. "You know they're overcharging you, right?"

The hound's lips curved, flashing teeth in what should've been a grin. There was a marked lack of warmth to the expression. "You think me unaware of that, my dear warrior? I am in no mood to waste time with haggling."

"So you waste your money? It's only a week until we reach the tower."

"Many things could happen during that time," Tracker countered. "Do you wish to always rely on Dylan's magic?"

Her face darkened. "The cloak is pointless. I'm sure the tower will just take it from him.

"Maybe. Besides, it is not my coin."

Her brows quirked in disbelief. "Do we still thank the wealthy bandits for their donation?"

"No, but the money I carry belongs to the crown. I am merely given leave to use it as I see fit. If they seek to swindle me, they will only be lining the crown's pockets when the taxman appears."

They left the city via the northern gates and stuck to the roads until the sun began its drift below the horizon.

Cultivated land stretched before them as far as Dylan could see, just as it had on the other side of the city. It had been quite a shock the first time he saw them on his way to the army camp. The huge fields of wheat he'd heard about from those who once lived outside were nothing like the oversized garden plots he had imagined.

Fat hedges and low stone walls marked boundaries amongst the fields, some almost encroaching on the road. Marin paused whenever they came upon a tree, hacking off the more promising branches with her hatchet for later use.

They set camp on the roadside, poked into a small area between two walls caused by a fork in the road. There was just enough space for them to pitch a single tent, which the women claimed without argument. Sleeping out under the stars this once promised to be a pleasant night. The sky showed little in the way of clouds and, if he tucked himself into the section between the two walls, he had enough shelter from the wind.

Dinner had been courtesy of *The Silver Flagon's* innkeeper. The bundle given to Katarina turned out to be oval pies built from cold pastry so thick that it could've been used to roof a house. The filling was a pale meat that his tongue couldn't quite agree was chicken or pork. Either way, it left him comfortably full.

With little else to do as the day drew to an end, their group settled on menial tasks. Marin set about checking the contents of her pack, unravelling several lengths of the thin rope she used for traps and testing their strength. One snapped and was sacrificed to the fire.

Katarina had procured a new map—he wasn't quite sure where from, but suspected it might've belonged to the hunter. She scoured over it, measuring out distances and checking her compass. Authril had removed her armour and was busy running a hand over the surface, muttering and tut-tutting to herself. Even the hound seemed occupied with sharpening one of his many throwing knives.

Dylan shuffled off towards the area he'd already pegged for a sleeping spot and huddled beneath his blanket. After the nightmares of the previous night's sleep, he could do with an early night before his turn on watch duty.

~ ~ ~

He sat atop a bed. A luxuriously soft four-poster. Dylan flopped back, the sleek iciness of the sheets welcoming his descent. He wriggled across them, indolent in the way his shoulders slid along the fabric.

Rolling onto his side, he snuggled up to one of the plush cushions. His face grazed across the smooth curve of warm flesh.

Jerking back, Dylan lifted his head to find Tracker's lean chest before him. He swiftly unravelled his arms from around the man's torso and scurried back across the bedding.

"Come now, my dear man," the hound purred. He laid back on the bed, a vision of tattooed skin and wicked smiles. His stomach undulated, exaggerating the thrusting of his hips and the bobbing of his erection. "There is no need to shy away." His eyes glowed in the low candlelight, as luminescent as a cat's. And just as predatory. "I know what you desire."

The world shifted. One moment, Dylan was on his feet before the bed, the next, he reclined upon it, Tracker's naked warmth pressing against his side. At the same time, he drifted above the scene as a spirit, passively watching the elf grind against his thigh.

Their mouths met. Tracker's lips slid over his in the gentlest of caresses, each brush soft and welcoming. Dylan parted his lips, drinking in the man's breath for the few seconds it took for the elf to fill the space with his tongue.

The hound's knee slid between Dylan's legs, slowly making room for him to kneel there. Those long fingers snaked down Dylan's body, massaging through the layers of robe and undertunic.

Through it all, not once did the man relinquish their kiss. It remained innocent and light, a delicious contrast that steadily robbed Dylan of all sense.

Tracker's hand slid over Dylan's groin, leaving him keening as the questing fingers moved on after a brief while. Tracker tugged on Dylan's undertunic, inching it ever higher, the drag of cloth over his legs its own exquisite torture.

His name fell from the man's lips, rich and hot with desire. The hound's fingers slipped beneath the undertunic, teasing as they rubbed Dylan's length through the thin linen of his smallclothes.

A low moan shuddered out Dylan's throat. His hips rose, desperately seeking more contact. "Please," he whispered, the tone just shy of begging. "I want—"

~ ~ ~

"Come now," an exasperated voice grumbled. "You simply must wake up."

Dylan's eyes flicked open to find a person leaning over him, backlit by the gibbous moonlight. Launching himself backwards only served to slam his torso into the uneven face of the wall and wind him. He stared up at the figure, his chest heaving as he fought to regain his breath.

The being straightened, throwing Tracker's grimacing face into the light. "My apologies, I had no intentions of giving you a fright.

You were moaning and thrashing about again. Was it another nightmare?"

"Of a sort," Dylan mumbled, his face growing hotter the longer the man stared. He couldn't very well tell the hound he'd been having an erotic dream about him. He didn't even know why, out of all the things his dreams could've settled on, it had been *that*.

He took a deep breath. It was just a dream. A very vivid dream. No doubt, a culmination of everything he had witnessed in the brothel.

Concern furrowed Tracker's brow. "I know it is meant to be your turn to take the watch." He glanced over his shoulder at the road leading back to Oldmarsh. "But there has been no one so far and I think it will stay that way until the morning."

As Dylan listened to the man, he came to the realisation that he was very much erect. *Wonderful.* He drew his blanket around him, trying to hide his true intentions behind a careful mask of neutrality. The last thing he needed was for the hound to notice.

"If you would prefer," Tracker continued. "We could spend this quiet talking about your nightmare. Air any uncertainties you might have about the path ahead, yes?"

"No!" Dylan leapt to his feet. He sidled away from the man, keeping the blanket tight around him. "I'm fine. You should get some sleep."

"If that is your wish," Tracker replied, settling where Dylan had lain. "Feel free to wake me if you change your mind."

Dylan grunted, hoping the man would take it as acquiescence, before settling next to the banked campfire. The chill night air slunk beneath his robe and nipped at his bare legs. Checking that there was no one else awake, he rearranged the blanket to cover his lower half before bringing the embers back to life with a few pokes of a stick.

He stared into the burgeoning fire, feeding it small branches one at a time. The flames danced along every length of wood, swaying seductively. As his gaze unfocused, they grew more defined, like tiny figures. Twirling. Bobbing. Undulating.

Blinking the images away, Dylan extinguished the fire.

This wasn't the first time his mind had conjured these sorts of visions, he just hadn't been plagued by them since his adolescence. Why were they back? Granted, they were somewhat of an improvement on the nightmares, but not by much. Not if he was going to wake up erect every time.

It had to have been that damn dance. The alternating flashes of steel and skin, the music that had made his blood sing. All of it was designed to scramble his senses. Coupled with their almost kiss...

The heat of the moment. That was what it had been. And

something that almost happened, to boot. He just needed space to collect himself.

How though? It would take them roughly a week to reach the tower. He couldn't outright avoid Tracker whilst also travelling with him.

He would just have to limit his time alone in the hound's presence to very little and forget anything happened. He could do that.

Just like forgetting a bad dream.

CHAPTER 37

Since leaving Oldmarsh, they had spent two days travelling, much of it in silence. Dylan didn't think he would ever become accustomed to how fast the landscape could change. After their first day of wandering by idyllic fields, the road had slipped beneath the lush canopy of a forest. They'd followed its passage without incident, winding up and down a hill, passing the remains of what Tracker claimed had once been a guard post.

They'd camped on the forest edge last night, everyone still solemn from mourning a gravesite Tracker said belonged to the young spellster with great illusionary talents.

Dylan hadn't seen a grave before. Those who died in the tower were cremated, although what they did with the remains was a mystery, but it had to be better than being lowered into the earth. How could the spirit free itself to drift through the tunnels towards judgement and the afterlife if they were entombed?

Surrounded by the cold, uncaring soil. Roots and worms wriggling their way into the body, feasting without compunction until only bones remained. A lifeless, empty structure residing forever in the dark whilst centuries ticked on and the world forgot.

Shuddering, he pulled his blanket tighter around his shoulders and carefully gathered up a few twigs to reignite the fire Marin had cooked their meal on that evening. The heat was meagre, but he was more after something to chase away the darkness. No matter how full the moon remained, it wasn't bright enough to shake free the chill in his gut.

Tonight, their shelter was thanks to a farmer's shed. Tracker had managed to convince the owner to allow them the use of this place for the night, meaning they'd no need to pitch even one of the tents. The rest of the group slept on, the women all huddled together like a pile of kittens between their turns at taking watch.

Dylan leant back, his shoulders brushing the weathered-beaten wall. He stared out into the night. Sheep moved about the fields, clustering here and there. In the moonlight, they were barely discernible from bushes. With the land being so open, any approaching danger could be seen in plenty of time.

He poked the campfire. He supposed the same could be said of the flames, but if someone had planned to ambush them, they surely would've done so by now.

"Are you looking to set a beacon?"

Dylan jerked back, grumbling a few curses as his head hit the wall. His magic dealt with the injury swiftly enough, allowing him to regain some measure of composure with which to face the hound.

He hadn't heard Tracker leave the shed, much less walk the short distance between where Dylan say bundled up by the wall and the building's entrance. Or perhaps the man had been standing nearby this whole time.

The man leant against the doorframe, a soft breath of amusement curving his lips. "I do not recall you being quite this jumpy before. It is the lack of trees, yes? Or do we grow tired of the evenings being uneventful?"

He eyed Tracker. Rather than answer any of the hound's questions, he shot back with one of his own, "Shouldn't you be getting some sleep?"

"Oh, I dozed for a while, but I—" Tracker settled next to him on the ground. "Well, you have been doing your best to avoid me since we left *The Gilded Lily*—a most tricky thing to attempt when we must travel together—and I am certain I can surmise why so..." He fell silent for a breath, his steepled fingers pressed to his lips. "I wanted to apologise. For attempting to kiss you. It was impulsive and entirely my fault. I was rather caught up in the moment and the music. Throwing myself at people like that is not common of me."

"That's good to hear." If a little unsettling. Had he given the man some indication that he'd be receptive to such an act? He was certain he had made his stance on that line of thinking plain.

His gaze dropped to the elf's mouth. His lips tingled at the memory of the man being so close. The rasp of his breath, heavy with desire. The slight sweep of his tongue, wetting the skin in preparation.

Dylan cleared his throat. His heart pounded, most certainly *not* because he wanted to kiss the man. *Maybe once.* Under his own terms. Just to see what it was like. "So..." he drawled. "Since you're content to join me in keeping watch and we're somewhat alone." He twisted his head around, checking to ensure that was still true, he asked, "What's your real name?"

Grinning, the hound leant back against the shed wall. "Been

waiting to ask that one, yes?"

"Tracker's an unusual name for an elf. I mean, it's not very—"

"—elven?" The man scoffed. "First the hedgewitch asks me and now you? In truth, I see little point in continuing this tradition most elves seem to insist on. All the tales say we fled wherever we came from. Why keep honouring the place?"

"I guess for the same reason Katarina's people honour their ancestors. It's your heritage." In the tower, where an elven man or woman was born with no more ties to the outside than a human, the guardians made sure each one was named according to tradition. Even if only a handful were able to be raised by elven guardians.

Tracker scowled at the fire. The flame's light danced across his face, their sharp shadows lending a sinister air to the expression. "My heritage is buried amongst the rest of the hounds."

Dylan frowned. He seemed to have hit a raw spot for the man. But if Tracker was unhappy with being a hound, then why did he remain amongst them? "That's not what your tattoos say. The one on your left arm? If I'm not mistaken, it's a classic Demarn floral motif interspersed with angular elven patterns." If the man wasn't honouring his heritage of being both an elf and a Demarner, then Dylan didn't know what such a design was meant to represent.

The skin-prickling silence coming from the hound had him facing the man. Tracker's full attention lay on Dylan. At this angle, the firelight turned his eyes into twin pools of molten gold. That faint quirk to the man's lips had also returned. Repressed humour.

Dylan shrugged his shoulders and shuffled a little further around the fire. "What's with the look?"

The gentle twitch of Tracker's mouth widened into a definite grin. "Oh, I was merely wondering how long you had to stare at my naked arm to make out the two patterns."

"I-I didn't stare," he managed. He turned his face from the man and ran a hopeful eye over the moonlit fields, searching for anything untoward amongst the sheep. He couldn't see the road from this angle.

"Of course not," Tracker continued. "It was merely an innocent perusal of my skin. For academic purposes, yes? I thought you were a little more preoccupied with staring out *The Gilded Lily's* windows for such a careful examination of my person."

Would it be too much of the gods to send something to distract the man? A traveller seeking shelter? A lone caravan? Even a few outlaws like the group they had come across in the forest would be better than this.

"I was," Dylan finally confessed. "But I noticed the ones on your arms during your sparring sessions with Authril." Whether the hound was aware of what had drawn his attention was a whole other matter he would prefer not to venture into. "It just strikes me as odd that you'd deny your elven heritage when it adorns your skin. It's not as if you can't have more than one."

Grunting in what sounded like reluctant agreement, Tracker poked a twig deeper into the fire. "You say that so easily, but this is my lot in life. We hounds do not choose our duty, we are born to it and we must live for it or—" He shook his head.

Dylan shuffled around to better face the man. "Or what?"

Tracker's gaze remained steadfast on the fire. "Be put down."

"I'm sorry. I had no idea."

The man shrugged. "It is how it has always been. I have long made peace with it." He peered at Dylan from the corner of his eye, seeming to consider his next words. "If you must know, it was given to me because I am exceptionally good at finding those who would prefer to remain hidden. That is my duty. Other hounds have different tasks set before them and are named as such."

Dylan's thoughts flitted back to Fetcher. A title, not a name. "What *is* your name, then? Your actual name, I mean. I'm assuming they didn't call you Tracker as a child. They'd have to have quite a bit of luck to call you something you just so happen to be good at." And why would they call him by a different moniker in the brothel? "Or is it actually Precious?"

"It is *not*." Tracker gave no further explanation, opting to continue his silent stare into the fire for some time. Then he sighed. "*The Gilded Lily*'s mistress gave me that name to use when I worked at the brothel because I had no other. Unless you would consider being called by a series of numbers as a name, of course. Before I became a fully-fledged hound, I was just One-four-eighteen-seventy."

He peered at the man, trying to determine whether Tracker was serious, and found no hint of jesting. "That..." Something else peeked through, an unease that felt equally unnatural to the hound. Had the man not revealed this to anyone else before? "That sounds like a date."

"It is." Tracker's gaze dropped to where his hands were neatly folded in his lap. "The day I was born, to be exact."

Uncertain how to respond to that, Dylan remained silent. His mind quietly churned away at the figures. The first day of the fourth month in the year eighteen seventy. "You're thirty-two?" Elven ages were harder to guess, the years tended to slide off them like water over a rock. Even with the man looking as if he hadn't yet reached his mid-twenties, Dylan had assumed Tracker to be at least a decade older than that. Especially, after hearing he had worked at the brothel before becoming a hound.

A small smile creased the man's eyes. "I am indeed that old, give or take a few months. Since we are prying, what of you?"

"Twenty-nine this summer gone." Just a few months ago now.

Tracker bumped Dylan's arm with his shoulder. "Ah, practically a child. Why are you so quick to return to the tower? You should be out in the world, yes? Having adventures." He smirked. "Meeting handsome elves."

The ghost of a smile curved his lips. "Handsomer than you? I don't think such a person exists." Dylan clapped his hand over his mouth. Had he really just said that out loud? "I..." he squeaked before falling into a bout of coughing. "I meant—"

The hound held up his hand. "No, no. There is little point in denying it. I know I am quite the specimen." He tipped his chin up. "Just look at this profile. It is gorgeous, yes?"

Yes. The combination of his narrow face and those generous lips— which silently promised to roam every inch of skin until he was in ecstasy—were undeniably attractive. The intense, honey shade of his eyes only added to the effect. "Will you hurt me if I answer differently?"

"Such a mouth!" The elf clutched dramatically at his chest and threw his head up, the back of a hand resting daintily on his forehead. One eye cracked open, gleaming in the firelight. "What have I done to deserve such cruel slander?"

Dylan rolled his eyes. An unwanted chuckle huffed through his lips. "You don't need me to stroke your ego."

"You wound me, my dear spellster." The hound pressed both hands to his heart as if in prayer. He pouted and his eyes grew big, the pupils widening in the dim light. "I am but the epitome of humbleness."

Dylan snorted, then a small squeak slipped through his lips that, before he could stop it, turned into a giggle. He muffled the sound with his palm. Turning his deeply-flushed face from the man helped him regain some control, but not by a lot. It felt good. He hadn't genuinely laughed since leaving the tower.

When he finally managed to stop and turn back, the elf was reclining on the ground, his head propped on an upraised arm. A small, slightly bemused, smile lifted one corner of the man's mouth.

A hot thread of embarrassment wove its way across Dylan's cheeks and forced him to focus his gaze elsewhere. That didn't use to happen quite as often as it did of late. If the man would stop staring at him so intently, he might be able to get his blushing under control. "I," he mumbled from behind his fingers. "I—"

"Is it true that you and our dear warrior are intimate?"

Startled by the abrupt change in topic, Dylan whipped his head around to find Tracker staring back with candid curiosity. "We are." Had the man not heard them? Authril wasn't exactly quiet.

"But you are not lovers?"

He shook his head. He'd never allowed anyone close enough to let that happen, had learnt from a young age that it was far safer when both parties agreed to casual intimacy. "You seem a little surprised."

The man's brows rose. "Do I? I suppose that is because I have not come across many willing to lie with a spellster. Especially one who has also been fighting them."

"Clearly, you've never been near the army camp. Apparently, it was quite common." His gaze fell to the fire. "Whether they wanted to or not."

The man's silence had him turning his head.

Tracker's expression was a mural of emotions, concern for the most part. "I am aware that our dear warrior is most protective of her desires. However, since she is unlikely to hear us at this moment." He glanced over his shoulder at the shed entrance.

Dylan mimicked the act, spying nothing that suggested anyone beyond the two of them were awake.

The hound seemed to come to the same conclusion. "I would like to ask a question."

He motioned Tracker to continue with the flex of his fingers.

"Is she forcing you to...?"

"Lie with her?" Dylan finished for the man before shaking his head. She might be direct when it came to what she wanted from him and no-nonsense in the execution, but she never used force.

The hound shuffled closer. "Do you think she would mind if I—?"

"Propositioned her?" Dylan blurted before Tracker could suggest what he believed the man was leading up to. "Quite likely. I don't think she's your type."

One brow rose in brief query. "That was not quite what I was going to ask, but now you have made me curious. Exactly how is an elven woman not my type?" He peered up at Dylan through his lashes. "I like a lot of things."

Dylan wet his suddenly dry lips. The faint gleam of the man's eyes did strange things to his gut. "I meant personality-wise. She can be a little abrasive."

"Bah. What does that matter? Even if I did actually have any wish to sleep with her, I am not looking for marriage. Besides," Tracker purred. "I am well-versed in the art of being anything a person desires."

"Anything?" Dylan rasped.

"Indeed." The word left Tracker's tongue in such a breathy, intimate fashion that Dylan felt the hairs on his arms stand.

Shivering, his gaze flicked to the man's mouth and back up to those intense honey-coloured eyes. They really did glow in the firelight. "I…" He cleared his throat. His face seemed warmer than either the small fire or blanket could account for. "I was wondering."

Grinning, Tracker sat up and sidled closer. "Yes?"

Having the man's mouth within reach all but sealed Dylan's throat shut. He found himself unable to keep his gaze from Tracker's lips. They sat slightly askew, self-confidence tugging one corner upwards.

Warm, his thoughts reminded him. *Inviting*. Dylan hadn't ever been much of a kisser. Not since his teens. It wasted time when there were far more interesting things.

He'd been panicking over what had almost happened, too much to stop and think what the worst thing could've been had Authril not interrupted at that moment. What harm could a kiss have done? It wouldn't change him because he wasn't some indecisive. He couldn't be. Such thoughts would've announced themselves years ago, wouldn't they? *Yes*. And Tracker had to be aware of that.

And yet, he found his desire to kiss the man refused to lessen. It stalked his dreams, fuelled not by lust but a simple curiosity to know what he had been denied.

"Dylan? Are you—?"

Dylan wordlessly tipped forward, his eyes closing. Somehow, even without seeing the man, he still managed to perfectly plant his lips upon Tracker's.

He felt the hound's smirk shift, sliding against Dylan's lips in an almost coy fashion that melted the tension from his body. Even when Dylan reciprocated the act, there was no urging for him to take it further, just a gentle caress reminiscent of a bashful innocence that had long been spent.

Then it was gone.

Dylan's eyes fluttered open to find Tracker sitting back, his head tilted to one side. The man stared back shamelessly and there seemed to be a knowing tilt to his lips, but a wisp of confusion also furrowed his brow.

"Sorry," Dylan mumbled, his cheeks heating. "I didn't mean to—" He froze as Tracker's hand landed on his knee.

"I rather think you did." There was no teasing in the words. Just a simple tone stating a simple fact they both knew.

Dylan nodded. The hound was right. "I was curious," he admitted. "Not that it was bad." The heat in his cheeks slunk further across his face as his ears registered the words currently pouring out his mouth. He hoped the ruddiness of the firelight was enough to mask his blushing. "I mean, it was nice f-for a—"

"Nice?" Tracker's lips twisted into a smirk, one brow lifting along with Dylan's pulse. "My dear spellster, puppies are nice. A warm fire in winter is nice." He leant closer. The firelight threw strange shadows over his face and picked up the gold flecks in his honey-coloured eyes. "*I* am not *nice*."

Dylan's throat constricted. He tried in vain to swallow the lump in his throat. The slight purr as Tracker spoke that last word. The small, and just a little self-satisfied, quirk of the man's lips...

No chance of mistaking it for anything but flirting.

Dylan had ignored the subtler attempts following the transparent suggestion back in the pond, thinking the hound would give up. But this, coupled with the kiss...

He tried to move, to put some distance between them, but found himself rooted to the spot. In truth, he missed this sort of harmless flirting. A part of him even enjoyed the familiarity. It wasn't something he got from Authril. The warrior might sleep with him and dance at his side, but she didn't respond, or even seem to appreciate, his attempts at flirting with her. Marin did, and was good-natured about it, but it was rare for her to linger long at camp. As for Katarina... Being that she rather reminded him of his guardian and was a hedgewitch to boot, he had no desire to try.

"I would like to kiss you again," Tracker confessed, the words barely a whisper against the crackle and pop of the campfire. "Properly. May I?"

"I..." Dylan's gaze dropped to the man's lips, taking in their faint glisten in the firelight. "Yes."

The hound's breath escaped in a gust of amusement. That same emotion sparkled along the golden flecks in his eyes. "Have I truly reduced you to single-word responses with a chaste kiss?" He shuffled across the ground until their thighs touched. "Do you not fear a proper one may render you speechless?"

He hoped it would. At least then he couldn't utter further foolishness.

Tracker's hand slid into Dylan's hair, those long fingers cupping the back of his head, gently guiding him closer. He slanted his mouth across Dylan's, caressing with those warm, pliable lips. Each sweep was less reserved than the previous kiss, but still clearly restrained.

Dylan dug his fingers into the blanket, bunching the ends into his lap. His skin tingled, sensitive to even his own clothing.

The hound adjusted his hold and Dylan had one brief irrational flutter of uncertainty on what the man might do if he noticed, but Tracker's fingers remained tangled with Dylan's hair.

The slow sweep of the man's tongue ran across the seam of Dylan's lips, coaxing them apart and slipping in to play. A breathless moan filled his ears.

Dylan echoed the sound, swallowing Tracker's breath, tasting a hint of honey on the man's tongue. He thought this might be similar to Authril, but the man's lips didn't hold the same cold familiarity as hers. This wasn't like kissing his childhood friend, Nestria, either. Her mouth always dictated what they were doing as well as the intensity.

Tracker was no less sure, but he was also soft. Gentle. Although clearly in control of this act, he guided more than imposed.

The world slowly became a haze.

Just when Dylan thought he might pass out if they didn't separate to breathe, Tracker broke the kiss. Dylan gulped down several breaths, each inhale of the night air setting his head to spinning just as much as the man's lips had.

"So then," the hound purred. He didn't sound out of breath, not even a puff. "Am I still *nice?*"

He nodded slowly, his mind still partially fogged with a strange bliss. Despite them both being fully clothed, the kiss felt a lot more intimate than anything he had shared with another. It carried a warmth that burrowed into his core rather than further heat his already flushed face.

"And I have fully sated your curiosity, yes?"

Nodding again, Dylan paid great attention to keeping the excess of his blanket before him. All the while, his mind scrambled to rearrange the jumble it had become.

He had just needed to get it out of his head, the fulfilment of an incomplete act, the wondering of what it felt like. He hadn't been able to stop thinking about it, as though his mind refused to let it go. Wouldn't. *Couldn't.* Maybe now it could.

The situation in his smallclothes spoke a different story.

And he'd done it with only a kiss! He couldn't blame it on anything else. The man's hands hadn't left Dylan's head until they'd parted. With the faint chill in the breeze, he still felt the heat of the hound's palms against his scalp.

If the hound was only half as good with other acts, then Dylan knew the answer to Petal's question of why Tracker had been so popular in the brothel.

His gaze slid to the man's lips. The desire to let Tracker kiss him again sang through his veins, visceral and strong.

No. Once was enough to put him close to the edge. Again would see him tip over it.

From a *kiss.*

Dylan turned his attention to their campfire. He poured the heat surging through his blood into the wood. New tongues of flames flared to life, briefly lapping at the sky as they flickered then died. Watching it quelled the chaos in his body, but not his thoughts.

People who were only attracted to women didn't go around kissing men because it felt good, did they? It had definitely been that way within the tower. Not even as a joke. Not unless they wanted to be labelled as indecisives and outed.

How different was it out here? Those the tower would've declared as indecisive seemed to be treated on equal footing with everyone else. If it wasn't viewed the same, then maybe…

Don't even consider it. Speculation of any sort was dangerous, especially when he would soon return to the tower. He would already be under enough observation once he re-entered the grounds, he didn't need more hanging over his head.

Their time in *The Gilded Lily* had clearly taken leave of his senses. Or maybe his nightmares had finally wrung him of his last drop of sanity. He would never want a man. Not for sex. Not for kissing. Not now, not later or ever.

The memory of his roommate, Sulin, flashed through his mind, stark against the dying flames of their campfire. He had definitely entertained the idea of kissing the man.

But that was different, less about any attraction he might or mightn't have to Sulin and more a curiosity over the man's split tongue. Not that he would ever actually *do* anything. Sulin would've slapped that thinking down well before—

"Dylan?"

The way the hound spoke his name was like nothing he'd ever heard, a softness that seeped into his ears and trickled along his nerves until it hit his spine in a shiver.

He slowly tore his gaze from the flames.

Tracker knelt next to him, his brows pressed together in concern. "You have been staring into the fire for some time. Are you all right?"

"I'm fine."

Disbelief etched itself into the lines of Tracker's face. "I would apologise again, but—"

"I kissed you first." He'd only done it to sate his curiosity, not out of any attraction to the man. "And I'm the one who agreed to let you kiss me again."

But why did he think it acceptable to do *that*? Because he had learnt the hound frequented brothels? That the man had *worked* in one? What kind of person heard that about another and thought it all right to toy with them, even unthinkingly? *A bad one.* That Tracker didn't seem to mind the teasing or the advances wasn't an excuse.

Not only was he not indecisive, he'd clearly lost any notion of higher reasoning somewhere along the road.

He also needed the hound to leave or to turn their conversation away from what had just happened before he also lost the ability to control himself. "D—" He coughed to clear his throat and managed to rasp, "Does the crown know its hounds get their information by soliciting prostitutes?"

Tracker's grin melted into a wry smile as the man softly chuckled. "It knows *this* hound does. It is thanks to my mistress that I ever set foot in *The Gilded Lily* in the first place."

Years ago. He hadn't forgotten that. "Do you trust the information your contact gave you?" Dylan might not have been in the room to hear the woman's exact words, but Tracker had relayed them well enough. If only she'd been able to tell them why that armed company occupied the lands they were heading into.

"Treasure has never once fed me wrong information. She and I, we…" A small, fond smile creased the hound's eyes. "Well, let us just say we go back quite a way and leave it at that. She has no reason to lie to me. That is not to say others have not lied to her, but she is exceptionally good at getting the truth. Almost worthy of a hound's status." He leant back on his hands. "However, if it eases your mind, I did check on another contact whilst you slept last night. Their absence was curious, but it does corroborate with what Treasure has heard."

"How?" Did the man think those people would've been a part of the group to the north? Or merely that they would be the sort of people to check the facts of the matter if word had reached them? "If they weren't there when they should be…?"

"They would not leave Oldmarsh unless it was a very good reason."

Dylan chewed on his lip. "Do you think we should've bought horses?" The animals could cut their travel time journey in half. Maybe enough to reach the tower and learn first-hand what was going on.

The hound brushed the idea away with the wave of his hand. "Where would we have gotten the coin? Granted, I do have royal sigils on my person, but—"

"What are royal sigils?" Dylan thought he'd a fair grasp on currency, but this was one he hadn't heard of.

Tracker dug about in his coin pouch and produced a black coin. "This." With a flick of his thumb, he twirled the royal sigil into the air, caught it and slipped it back into his pouch. "They're a promise of payment. Each one is worth fifty gold."

Dylan frowned. "They let you walk around with one to give to whomever?"

"Not exactly. The crown does not pay us as one would a soldier. We are given an annual sum of six royal sigils to exchange for actual coin at certain cities. I still have three on me."

"Would that have been enough to buy horses?"

Tracker laughed. "Plenty! But, given how we do not know what we are facing, I would prefer stealth, regardless of the increased time. Riding up on horseback would alert others of our presence. Word of the army's fall would have reached the king by now."

"Do you think he has sent out an order for more spellsters?"

"If the armed company is the new army, I see no reason why the king would not order more spellsters to fill its ranks."

Sighing, Dylan closed his eyes. *More fodder to throw at the empire.* That'd been exactly what he had hoped his leashing could avoid.

Only, it was worse now. The overseers wouldn't call for another brawl, they'd merely leash everyone who'd participated in the last. From Sophie with her all-but-useless fire tricks, to the man with the green eyes, all the way to Fredrick and his strange trick of making people collapse with a tap to the head.

It wouldn't affect just them, either. Whilst he didn't know if Sophie had a lover, Fredrick did. The man had won in the bouts just so his lover could win a bet and now he was about to lose everything.

This was precisely why he never allowed anyone that close. Love was dangerous. It brought nothing but heartache and bitterness.

He stared into the fire. Not for the first time, the insidious toxic wondering snuck up on his thoughts. If he'd been at the main encampment when the Udyneans attacked, would it have been enough? Even if he couldn't have stopped the full destruction of the army, if he had been capable of saving a mere few...

Would it have been enough?

"Of course," Tracker said and Dylan came to the sudden realisation that the man must've been talking this whole time without him listening to a single word. "There is the question of what so large a company is doing in the north. Is it Udynea? I know Treasure said the company was heading west, but... Do you think maybe the reason the empire attacked the camp and left is because they have an alternate route we have no knowledge of?"

Dylan recalled the maps back in the tower and Launtil's tale of how her mistress had risked a perilous journey over the very mountains keeping the Udynea Empire from spreading an army right across their border. The woman had died in the trek over the peaks, leaving her slave to carry on without her, but two people could traverse a far smaller path than an army. "The mountains are impassable to a large force. They have been for centuries."

"I may not be in the army, and there are perhaps some aspects of your magic that I may be unfamiliar with, but I know we have been at war with Udynea for countless generations. Surely, a single spellster has the ability to carve a passage through the mountains in such a time."

Dylan frowned. It was possible. "It would take a lot of energy and you couldn't blast a path through." The deeper they pressed into a mountain, the more chance there would be of an avalanche. "Demarn has nothing worth that risk."

"How about a tower of trained spellsters? Did you and our dear warrior not say that they took the leashed ones?"

He had. It was one man's word, but the Udynean spellster had no reason to lie and he'd been so intent on having Dylan give himself up. "You think they've been after us all this time?"

Tracker shrugged. "If I was going to the trouble of enslaving someone, I would opt for the people who were most likely to make it worth the inconveniences of a war."

Dylan turned his gaze to the silvery blue darkness beyond the firelight. All this time, the thought of his home being in direct danger had never occurred to him. The tower walls were fortified and the gates would be solid enough to repel an ordinary force.

But magic? He hunched his shoulders. Even hazarding a guess at what it would take for a Udynean spellster to bring down the tower walls felt worthy of punishment.

A week. That's how long it would take on foot from Oldmarsh. They hadn't even travelled half that distance. They'd days more of being on the roads, of wondering when their little group might meet this mysterious armed company that traversed the land near his home, of not even knowing if they meant harm.

They should've bought horses.

CHAPTER 38

Dylan peered through the forest canopy, hoping to catch a glimpse of the tower in the distance. The hound insisted they would reach their destination no sooner than midday. That time was almost upon them, the sun growing closer to its zenith with every passing hour.

Yet, he saw no hint of anything ahead of them but more forest.

They had, as far as he could determine, made good time. Over the past few days, they'd stuck to the road, hunkering in whatever space the roadside offered during the night. No bandits leapt from the bushes. Not that there had been much in the way of undergrowth to hide in during the first few days, where farmlands stretched across the hills for miles.

The closer they'd gotten to the tower, the less cultivated the land became. After the first day, the fields full of crops had given way to herds of cattle and flocks of sheep. Now, it was endless trees disguising just how rolling the surrounding terrain truly was.

The road began to climb again. This far from any major settlements, the road travelled nowhere but north. He'd seen it from the tower windows, how carts destined for elsewhere would stick to the edge of the huge clearing beyond the walls.

A fallen tree blocked part of the road, its descent also bashing a ragged hole in the leafy canopy. Beyond that, a thin tendril of grey cloud drifted across an otherwise clear sky. No tower.

There was a marked lack of any armed company, too. Not even a hint of their passage. That absence only twisted his gut further. How far away had this company been when Treasure was told? How fast could it travel? He'd asked Authril about the latter, the non-committal answer she gave doing nothing to ease his concerns.

What if they were replacements for the army? What if they weren't? What if the Udyneans had somehow found a way over the mountain?

The questions continued to gnaw at him even as they reached the top of the hill and the peak of the tower appeared over the treetops.

Home. So close, he could feel it in his soul. The sight of it lengthened his stride, not entirely with joy. There seemed to be smoke lingering near the tower's peak. He tried to rationalise it, convince himself that the sight was a common occurrence and he'd just never bothered to look up. It was possible.

His stomach churned, bubbling with a mixture of emotions. The giddy knowledge that he was to soon set foot back in a familiar setting drove him onwards, but there was also a pit of worry settling in his gut, brought on by not knowing what was to come next.

Would the overseers see him immediately leashed? Would they throw him into one of the isolation cells until a new collar was created?

No matter what, his very presence would have people talking. No spellster had ever been unleashed. Not living ones. Not by themselves. Not in Demarn, at least. He couldn't even remember any tales of it happening to spellsters outside of the kingdom, either.

Yet, here he was. About to make his mark in history for all the wrong reasons.

Would the overseers believe he didn't know how he had freed himself? What of the hedgewitch's retelling of events? Or the hound's?

Dylan's gaze flicked to where Tracker walked well ahead of them. A strange fluttering joined the rest of the commotion in his stomach. The man hadn't attempted a single flirt since they'd kissed.

Satisfying his curiosity hadn't banished the thoughts of Tracker, and those sinful lips, from Dylan's dreams. Not even a few nights in Authril's arms managed to shake it free.

That Tracker seemed to be ignoring it had happened, to the point of acting almost distant, surprisingly stung. He had expected to find himself needing to exert more effort in iterating that he wasn't interested in men.

Maybe the man recognised that the kiss, however nice it had been, would ultimately take him no further. Maybe he'd come to the conclusion of it being for the better if they returned to how things should've been between them. After all, Dylan was a spellster, one the man was supposed to be escorting. That Tracker even flirted to begin with had to be against some hound code.

Soon, it wouldn't matter. Dylan would be in the tower and the hound would venture off, back to his duty of containing other spellsters.

The others would also move on. Authril had been blunt in her intentions of joining whatever semblance of an army the crown could scrap together. Katarina would continue north, perhaps with Marin as her companion. He would be alone. Trapped amongst people who had no idea what really went on once they were leashed.

It was definitely the cells for him. Maybe even after he was leashed.

Alone in the dark. Only the sound of his footsteps and the cries of others for company. The chill seeping into his flesh always burrowing deeper, gnawing at his bones, and him unable to bring to life a single flame due to the metal lining the room.

"Bloody prison, that tower," Marin muttered as they descended what Dylan hoped was the last wooded hill between them and the tower. "I don't know why you all just accept living there."

Dylan slowed his pace enough to shoot the woman an incredulous look. Where else would they go?

"The tower is a haven for those with magic," Authril said, the tone suggesting she repeated another's words. "Quite the cushy place, if you ask me. A warm, dry spot to sleep, regular meals—"

"I didn't ask you, though," Marin snapped. "And does any of that really make up for the constant watching of whether you're doing something wrong and the punishments whenever you're a bad spellster?" She raised her arms until they were shoulder height and wriggled her fingers in the same peculiar imitation of casting a spell that Dylan had witnessed from the soldiers. "Did they beat you often? Or were you a good little boy?"

"Beat? No one's ever beaten." Not that he had heard of. "The worst you get is a week's solitary." Two days was the longest he ever spent in the cells. That'd been due to a foolish dare going wrong. Back then, he hadn't any intention of leaving, but his presence at the foot of the tower's inner gate was enough. The guards had detained him, summoning not only his guardian, but the overseers.

Tracker glanced back at them. "You know solitary confinement is a form of torture, yes? Usually reserved for enemies."

Dylan's thoughts turned to the man the army had made his warden, specifically the crude display he'd given whilst describing how he forced himself on one of the leashed women. The haunted looks in the eyes of those he had first met on his arrival.

Shaking his head to clear the image from the forefront of his mind, he murmured, "There are worse things." Being snatched by the Udyneans might've been seen as a blessing.

And he was to be sent back there.

His gaze lifted to where he knew the tower sat, hidden by the trees now they had descended the upper half of the hill. There was nothing he could do about the fate laid before him. He was a weapon. He belonged to the army. The overseers would see him returned to fight.

The forest thinned as they reached the bottom of the hill. Tracker waited on the tree line. With the noonday sunlight beaming unbroken across the land, the russet sheen of the hound's hair was a beacon amongst the greenery.

Dylan halted next to the man. Free of the confining forest, the road stretched on ahead of him as well as to the east. What held his attention was the sight of his home.

The tower had seemed so small whilst living in its confines. Beyond the training grounds and the garden, they were restricted to a choice of only travelling up or down to another level. Seeing the structure anew, knowing that the walls alone stood taller than even Toptower's namesake, he was suddenly struck by how much of a beast the central building was. Never had he realised the place that had once been his whole world took up the same sprawling area as that of a village.

The longer he stood admiring the sight, the more something prickled the back of his skull. *The wind.* Something about it was familiar. *The smell.* It tweaked the ghost of a memory, then vanished, leaving him with a queasy stomach and an unease he couldn't shake.

"By the gods," Authril breathed. "I know it's just called the tower, but I didn't expect it to be so big. I was thinking more like the fortress at Toptower. This is…"

"…a lot of building," Marin finished for the other woman. Her head turned his way, although her gaze remained rooted to the tower. "How many spellsters did you say there are?"

"Hundreds," he murmured. He'd never been entirely certain how many until the hound mentioned it.

"Indeed," Tracker said.

"And if we factor in the people guarding and serving them…" Marin muttered under her breath, counting as she tapped each finger. She exhaled in one cheek-puffing breath. "There is pretty much a small city behind those walls."

"And *inside,*" the hound corrected her. "The walls are wider than the average house. The servants live within. It keeps contact with the spellsters to a minimum."

They crossed the open road to the tower gates. He scanned the parapets as they reached the halfway point. There was never anyone on the walls. No one he'd been able to see from the inside, at least. Smoke drifted up on the breeze, issuing from somewhere within the walls. The wind sent it drifting in their direction.

That wasn't normal. There shouldn't be any smoke. Maybe the odd puff whilst the training grounds were in use, but not a continuous stream.

Marin tipped her head up, frowning thoughtfully at the tower. "If there are so many of you, why did they only send one spellster to the front line?"

Dylan tore his attention from the walls. "They didn't. I was a replacement for one who'd fallen."

"Sure. But just the one? There must've been others good enough to join you."

He shrugged. Perhaps not in raw power, but strength didn't equate to the finesse in which a spellster like Fredrick could attack, or even the knack behind honing a single skill set such as Sophie and her talent with fire. "Maybe, but—"

"You wouldn't send all your best breeding stock into battle at once," Authril said right over the top of him. "Got to keep some in the stables. Thought you grew up on a farm? You should be able to relate to that."

"But they're *people*, not animals," Marin snipped back.

Dylan slowly stopped hearing the pair of them bickering. His gaze dropped from the parapets to the main gates. The smoke was strange, but didn't necessarily mean something bad. It may not even come from within the tower confines at all, but beyond. They could've been burning all manner of things outside the—

He froze in the middle of the road, the unease in his gut settling like a rock.

The gates stood open like a giant's maw leading to darkness.

His chest tightened. *There should be guards.* The gates were never open without them bridging the gap. Why wasn't there anyone standing watch?

Blind terror had him running for the entrance.

Tracker darted past him. He halted just outside the gates, his back suddenly stiff. "Stay back," he warned. The man whirled on Dylan, pushing him away from the entrance. "Allow me to go in first and…"

Dylan stopped hearing the hound. He saw easily enough over Tracker's shoulder. The twisted shape of a guard lay just outside the main entrance.

Worst still, the gut-cramping scent he had picked up on the wind was stronger. The stench invading his nose reminded him all too well of the army camp. *No.* He slowly sidled by the hound. *It can't be.* His feet moved sluggishly, forcing him to think about each step. Every part of his body screamed to flee.

Still, he couldn't turn away. Maybe it wasn't as bad as his imagination made it seem. He struggled to think of how, but he had to cling to some semblance of hope.

A loud droning filled his ears as he neared. There was a slight shift to the figure, a ripple that ran across their whole body. Unnatural as it was, it drove his legs. Movement had to mean they were alive. He could fix this. He could—

Hundreds of flies launched into the air, zipping around them to resettle on the corpse. The stench of decaying flesh hit him in full force, sending him reeling back, his hand clapping over his mouth.

Now he was standing in the shadow of the gates, he could see what waited just inside the entrance. Six guards littered the archway, four of them in full armour. All of them covered in droning flies.

What had happened? Had a spellster broken through the second gate?

The hound halted beside him, his nose wrinkling. "We should leave." He gently clasped Dylan's arm, turning them.

"No." He jerked free of Tracker's grasp. This was his home, he couldn't just *leave*. "There are still people inside." People who would need help. Needed *him*.

"Dylan." Those honey-coloured eyes brimmed with sympathy. "I am sorry."

He turned from that look, refusing to accept it. The hound thought everyone inside was dead. Tracker wasn't saying it, but the words were there, plastered all over his face. "No." That couldn't be true. "I'm not *leaving*." He dashed through the gates, vaulting over the fly-bloated corpses blocking his path.

Bodies littered the courtyard, more than he had ever imagined actually guarded the area. The majority of them were armoured.

The second gate stood open, corpses clogged the entrance.

"Wait!" Tracker screamed after him.

He flung his pack to the ground and raced across the courtyard, ignoring the man's call. The pounding of his feet on the flagstones echoed through the space. Dylan pushed himself harder, each footstep jarring him to his teeth.

"You have no idea what is in there!" The hound's words chased Dylan through the second gate. The echo of another's hurried footsteps suggested that Tracker followed.

Dylan didn't bother waiting for the man to catch up. He hastened for the tower entrance, hope sparking anew as he saw the stairs leading the way were devoid of people, living or otherwise. He hauled open the door and stepped inside.

The reek of rotting flesh slapped him across the face. He doubled over, clinging to the door as his stomach vacated everything it had.

Still dry-retching, he glanced at his surroundings. The corridor faded into absolute darkness, but the light leaking through the doorway was enough to make out the shadowy figures strewn across the floor.

Fire sputtered to life in the palm of his hand, blinking out as nausea rolled over him again. He shakily focused on forming another globe, this time of pure light. It wobbled in the air, its cool glow throwing harsh shadows, but he could maintain it without much thought. Holding the globe high and blinking furiously to keep his sight clear, he ventured deeper into the tower.

Stench and flies greeted him everywhere he went, every room, every nook he could think of. Men, women, children. Elven and human alike, all cut down.

He headed for the common rooms, his heart hammering and his chest tight from fighting to breathe. There had to be someone still alive. This couldn't be everybody. It just couldn't. The tower held hundreds of spellsters. *Maybe...*

Maybe they'd been attacked and these poor souls were the aggressors.

No. Reaching the main hall, he collapsed in the middle, his legs finally too weak to obey the need to push on. The people around him weren't the invaders. There were children amongst them. The tiny bodies of babies cradled in a guardian's arms. Spellsters and servants littered the corridors where they'd fallen trying to flee, their bloated faces twisted in horror.

These were the victims and *he* was the survivor.

~ ~ ~

Tracker picked his way through the corridors, hampered by the darkness and the need to skirt bodies he barely saw. Lanterns hung at intervals along the walls, their fuel likely consumed. He didn't dare risk stopping to find out.

Not that he could lose where Dylan was in this place. The bright point that was the man's magic shone like a signal fire. His senses told him it was the only source in the place.

Seeing the multitude of bodies, he believed it.

Still, knowing the very purpose of the building he walked through and sensing only a single source of power felt as though someone had flipped the world on its head. What the hell had happened to cause this massacre? He needed answers, needed to understand this.

He needed to reach Dylan first. There was no telling what the man might do once he began to process the truth of his surroundings.

Where was he even going? Did he head for some secret chamber shielded from even a hound's senses? Tracker wasn't at all familiar with the tower's internal layout, he rarely ventured further than the outer courtyard. If it wasn't for Dylan's erratic pattern, the pauses that enabled Tracker to close the distance between them, he might've lost the man amongst the rabbit warren of passages.

He turned a corner to find Dylan kneeling in the middle of what looked to be a major pathway leading to a set of large doors. Magic flared all around the man, much of it confined to the shimmering hemisphere of his shield. He caressed the floor.

Tracker squatted nearby, placing himself in Dylan's direct line of sight. He could've easily passed through the magical barrier, had done it a great many times. But doing so would only inflict further pain on an already injured soul. So long as Dylan caused no harm, Tracker was content to wait until the man was ready to face the world again.

His true concern was that their group might not be the only living things here. Maybe not another spellster, but he'd seen little in the way of those responsible for these deaths. If they were still here, then everyone in their group was in danger.

The spellster's shield dropped, throwing the room into darkness.

Tracker remained still, waiting for his eyes to adjust.

Dylan likewise hadn't moved. He seemed to stare straight ahead. How well could the man see? Not as decently as an elf, obviously, but enough to distinguish Tracker from the shadows?

A pinprick of light popped into existence, growing as large as a man's head and giving off an icy white glow. It illuminated the room better than any lantern, but also drained what warmth was left in their surroundings just as it paled the man's face.

"Are you going to kill me?" Dylan's question came softly, his voice so quiet and distant that it sounded like another spoke.

"Of course not."

The magic drifting around the man flickered, drawing inward, halting as Dylan took a deep, steadying breath. The harsh shadows the globe threw made him look gaunt. "You can't leash me. Wasn't that the point of coming here?"

It had been. But without an alchemist, the best method they had would be to somehow encircle Dylan with raw *infitialis*. Not an option Tracker was keen on. "We will figure something out."

Dylan wordlessly fell back to caressing the floor.

Tracker shuffled closer. The flagstones beneath the man's hand looked stained. *Blood?* He couldn't imagine the tower floors being touched by such in any other time before this slaughter and there were no bodies nearby that could've caused this patch. "What is it?" Could it be a sign that someone was alive?

"I was here when this happened." Each word falling from Dylan's lips was as devoid of emotion as the one before. "When William slit his own throat." He patted the floor, the slap of his palm echoing up multiple corridors. "Right in this spot."

Tracker bit the inside of his lip. That wasn't the tale he had anticipated. Was he meant to remain silent in this telling? The man's expression suggested some sort of reply was required. "That is an unfortunate thing to witness." Definitely not what he expected to find had transpired within these walls.

"It was two days before I left. He was distraught, because—" Whatever else the man had been going to say, he kept himself from uttering it. "He swiped an alchemist's dagger. His guardian..." He swallowed, gulping down a breath. "She begged him to stop, but it was too late." He bent over, propping himself with a hand on the bare stone. "I tried to save him. I knew it was hopeless, but I tried anyway."

Naturally. He had known Dylan for only a short time, but he understood a great deal about the man—except for his strange insistence in denying having an attraction to men. Dylan was a healer first and a fighter only when threatened. That he already knew nothing could heal a cut from an alchemist's dagger would've served to make him try harder.

"But it wouldn't have mattered if I had succeeded, would it?" Dylan finally focused on him, those dark eyes silently beseeching. The whites were red around the edges, but not a single tear streaked his face. "He would've died in this slaughter. No less terrified than everyone else."

Tracker laid a hand on the man's shoulder, squeezing slightly, surprised when Dylan leant into the touch. "I am truly sorry." If he had known this lay ahead of them, he never would've brought the man back.

"This place it—" He hung his head. "It did bad things, I know that. I won't pretend I don't. It let this death happen, let us believe all the lies. *Fed* us those mistruths. And I believed them. I took every damn lie as the truth. I didn't even doubt it. I *trusted* them."

Tracker nodded. Sometimes, the poison was hidden. Other times, they swallowed it knowingly because it held a comforting familiarity.

"But I still... I'd still take all that over this."

"Of course. Through all that was done, this place was still your home." He wrapped an arm around the man's torso, the other securing Dylan's arm over his shoulders. "Come." He stood, effortlessly hoisting the spellster to his feet. There really was nothing to the man. "We will find somewhere less gruesome for you to rest and try to figure this out. Just keep that light of yours glowing. I do not fancy tripping and adding our bodies to this lot."

Dylan complied, holding the globe aloft as he leant on Tracker, wordlessly permitting him to lead the way through the tower. He stared at every corpse they encountered. "How?" he whispered, seemingly still dazed. "What happened here?"

"I wish I could answer that. I truly do." For all that it did to the spellsters under their care, the tower was supposed to be a haven.

Death was meant to come when their years finally ran out. Something like this should never come to pass. "We will find out. I promise."

CHAPTER 39

They rejoined the women waiting outside the tower. Authril and the hedgewitch stood at the bottom of the stairs with their weapons bared and ready for anything that might pose a threat. Dylan searched the courtyard for the fifth member of their group, finding Marin crouched over one of the guards who had fallen in a gateway.

She stood and made her way over as Tracker led the way down the stairs.

The hound gestured for Dylan to sit upon the bottom step. Those long fingers cupped Dylan's cheek as if he were a child. "You will stay here, yes?"

He nodded. Where could he possibly go that wasn't worse off than this? It seemed the lower floor had taken the least bit of damage. He dreaded to think what it looked like further up the tower or within the servant quarters.

He would have to find out eventually. Once he had steeled himself, he'd go back up and search every room.

"This attack is fresh," Marin announced upon rejoining them. "Most likely no more than a day or two ago. That one?" She pointed at the corpse with the tip of an arrow. Dylan thought it one of her own, but the tip and shaft were dark with blood. "Poor soul took this in the back of the head. Looks like a bunch of them did. The rest seem to have fallen to bladed weapons… daggers, swords, knives and the like. Can't find one sign of—"

"My dearest hunter," Tracker growled, baring his teeth in an unpleasant smile. "Do shut up."

Marin turned her attention to the man. Her brows knitted together whilst her gaze flicked between him and Dylan. "You're worried about upsetting him?" she asked incredulously. "We're surrounded by corpses, how is me being quiet going to change that? Any fool can see how these people died."

"Indeed," Tracker replied, still glaring at the woman. "Just as those same fools can note that the fallen consist entirely of tower folk." He trotted up a few steps behind Dylan, no doubt positioning himself in a place where he could defend if need be. "If that observation does not drive you to caution, then I fear nothing will."

"So we leave," Authril said. "Camp out somewhere in the forest and head the gods' knows where in the morning."

"No," Dylan whispered. He couldn't. Not yet. He looked around them, his empty stomach cramping as his gaze settled on a man who'd been gutted like a boar. *So many*. But that made it harder to comprehend.

Thousands of people lived here. They couldn't *all* be dead.

Clearing his raw throat, he continued, "There must be someone alive." Somewhere on the upper floors, perhaps. The lower level was never the most populated. And this place wasn't like the army camps. The tower was overflowing with magic. Any ordinary invader would've met resistance, especially once they encountered those trained to fight. "I'm not leaving until we've searched everywhere."

"Are you serious?" Authril blurted, those sea-green eyes bulging. She threw up her hand, turning to Tracker. "Can you believe what he wants to—?" The woman froze, staring aghast over Dylan's shoulder. "Where did he go?"

Katarina looked about, perplexed. "He was right here."

Dylan mimicked the others in scanning their immediate surroundings. The hound was nowhere to be found. He stood, in the faint hope that the man would appear. "We should look for him." They'd no way of telling if any of the murderers were still around and he would've preferred not finding out via stumbling over the elf's corpse.

"I'm sure he can take care of himself," Authril said.

Dylan had thought the same of the guards at the gates and the guardians who spent their lives raising every single spellster. *Tricia*. He didn't know what the overseers had planned for her once he was gone. She was here. Somewhere amongst the corpses.

Taking a deep breath, he closed his eyes. They burned behind his lids. He forced that feeling down with the rest of the emotion he refused to let take hold. He didn't trust himself not to lose control of his magic. He couldn't. There was no telling the destruction he would wreck if he did.

He gathered himself and faced the tower doors. If Tracker had gone anywhere, it was inside. "I am going to look for him. You three either come with me or stay put." The last thing they needed was to have everyone scattered across the grounds.

The women's answers were unanimous in staying at his side.

They searched the tower's lower level, the light of his globe illuminating their path. Wherever they went, bodies emerged from the darkness, be they inert shapes on the very edge of the light or grotesque blockades they were forced to pick their way through.

Bitter relief washed over him with every unrecognisable face, each spike slathered with a heavy dose of guilt. He shouldn't be relieved to not know these people. He'd grown up in the same place, learnt in the same rooms, ate the same meals. Shared so many things in common.

Bar one.

They reached the corridor leading to the gardens. The cloying stench of singed flesh and hair started as an acrid wisp that grew with every step. Dylan covered his nose. He tried to breathe through his mouth, but the greasy air left a coating on his tongue. His stomach, having made some rather unpleasant connections with that smell, churned like a milkmaid making butter.

"Argh," Marin drew up a section of her cloak to her face. "Smells like someone's charred a pig."

"More like people," Authril muttered, the words fast followed by the frantic hiss of shushing from Katarina.

They turned a corner to where the corridor ran by the side door and out into the gardens. Pale grey light stretched ahead of them.

A shadowy figure stood in the doorway, solidifying into Tracker's silhouette as they drew closer. The man remained still, barely even acknowledging their approach. The splintered fragments of the door lay scattered across the floor, the remainder hanging from a single hinge.

Dylan halted beside the hound, at last able to see what held his attention.

A blackened mound sat in the middle of the trampled flowerbeds. The heap smouldered, fingers of greasy smoke still pouring from it. Sooty flames flickered to life every now and then.

He stepped closer, heeding the morbid call to know exactly what the mound was made of.

"Dylan," Tracker called, his voice strained. "You truly will not wish to see more."

Defiance kept his legs moving. What could be worse than the slaughter they'd already witnessed inside? He could make out individual pieces of—

More bodies. He staggered back, then fell as his legs gave. It shouldn't have surprised him, yet.

The whole mound was made of burning, smouldering corpses. Now his eyes knew what to look for, he easily picked out individual arms and legs. The heads were worse, many devoid of a body.

His gaze fell on a familiar face. *Sophie.* The fire had claimed her blonde hair and melted one side of her head, but it was undeniably her. The longer he stared, the more people he could identify.

Fredrick... Ben... Several guardians that he knew were in charge of training the children.

He turned from the mound, losing the battle with the roiling in his stomach. He retched, mere dribbles of saliva escaping his lips.

Someone consolingly rubbed his back and held his hair away from his face.

Blinking and sniffing, Dylan lifted his head to find Tracker had crouched at his side, his brow furrowed and his eyes dark with quiet sympathy. With one hand, the man tucked Dylan's hair behind his ears whilst, with the other, he produced a small piece of soft cloth.

Dylan cleaned himself with the proffered cloth. He wobbled to his feet, allowing Tracker to guide him across a path leading through the gardens and back towards the front of the tower.

"Try not to look," the hound cautioned. The grip of the man's arm, wrapped about the back of Dylan's waist like a cradle, tightened. It was sound advice.

Heeding it was an altogether different matter.

Like in the army encampment, the ghostly imprints of magic fizzled through the air. Scorched grass and baked earth spoke of a fire-slinger's final stand. A puddle of what he guessed had once been ice flowed into a hollow that looked very much like a blast zone. It was all the evidence of fighting that was missing within the tower's lower level. These people knew there was a threat, had perhaps been warned.

It still hadn't saved them.

They followed the curve of the tower as it headed towards the training arenas. Bodies were piled up against the walls. Children, for the most part, struck down where they huddled once their guardians had fallen in their efforts to protect them. Cracks ran along the slabs of stone, suggesting a few had tried to break through the wall.

What good would it have done them? The walls were thick, packed with a network of corridors and rooms to house people. Breaking through to the other side would've required a massive amount of concentrated force unless they were lucky to hit a storeroom.

Or the secret entrance. None of the spellsters would know what worth the largely abandoned little shed truly held, but if his guardian knew of the hidden door, then so would others.

He tore out of Tracker's grasp, running for the little shed. It felt like a different world since Tricia had led him to the place.

Would the guardians have been able to herd people through? To cross the fields and into the forest? Maybe a handful before they were caught. It was better than no one making it out.

Dylan rounded the tower, caught sight of the first training arena, and skidded to a halt.

The shed had been blown apart, the bits of wood and stone scattered all over the ground. Like at the main gates, piles of bodies lay amongst the debris. Their intact and bloated forms somehow seemed easier to stomach. Had they been fleeing invaders or thrown by the initial destructive blast? It was hard to tell.

Although the storeroom's interior was still in the shadow of the hulking wall, the door stood open, the rectangle of light beckoning him with its promise of freedom.

He doubted a single soul had made it through. Everywhere they went, the sprawl of bodies seemed endless.

A hand brushed his shoulder, another laid upon his back. He blinked to clear his sight and discovered Marin and Katarina stood on either side of him.

"Looks like they had even this entrance covered," Authril said. She stood on his left, dispassionately taking in the scene.

"Indeed," Tracker replied. "Come, we would do well to press on." He gestured for them to continue walking around the tower's circumference before once again wrapping an arm around Dylan.

There were other people amongst the dead that Dylan couldn't place, men and women in a strange uniform of baggy pants, unbleached linen shirts and dark coats. None of it appeared to be of Udynean make.

He would occasionally catch Tracker frowning at them, but if he recognised the armour, he said nothing.

It wasn't until they were resting on the steps outside the tower's main doors that the man released him. With so much death everywhere else, the lack of bodies here suggested the invaders had begun some sort of disposal. *Burning them.* He'd heard it was often touted as the only reliable way to ensure a spellster didn't return from the dead. He hated to agree, but it did the job.

Smoke still lingered in the air. *Charred boar.* Marin was right about the stench. He didn't think he'd be able to stomach pork again.

Sighing, Tracker collapsed next to him on the stairs. "Leaving you here is clearly not a viable option, especially when I have no clue as to who killed these people or if they plan on returning."

Katarina hummed, settling on the opposite side of the hound. "Those men in the strange armour... I've seen it before."

Grunting, the man nodded. "Talfaltaners. They dock in Wintervale often enough. I would not expect them to come within five hundred feet of a single spellster, let alone a thousand."

Dylan frowned at the flagstones at the base of the steps. A pool of blood marred the spot. He tipped his boot to one side, obscuring the sight. "You think Talfaltaners could've attacked the tower?" Their people had no tolerance for magic of any sort. A spellster caught by them would be better off slitting their own throats.

They were also rumoured to kill anyone trying to protect a known spellster as the guardians were trained to do. *And the servants.* It made sense.

Tracker silently gnawed on his bottom lip for what seemed like forever. The man stared so intently at nothing that Dylan could almost see the mental calculations the hound made swirling before them. "You would need a lot of people."

"The sort of armed company that people might just mention to prostitutes?" Authril asked.

The man's brows rose in the middle. "Talfaltaners are a seafaring folk. A long march across land is not exactly routine for them. There is the river, of course, and it does flow into the sea. However..." He shook his head. "It also goes right by Wintervale. The number of vessels to move several thousand armed men past the capital wouldn't be idle talk."

"Maybe the king knew," Dylan suggested. If Tracker was correct in there being over a thousand spellsters, then their lives had to be quite a drain on resources. And there would always be the constant fear of someone escaping.

The hound's expression grew hard. "No." His lips thinned and his eyes became like chips of granite. "I refuse to believe he would suddenly decide to destroy every spellster and certainly not the servants. Something else is afoot here. I just need a little more information to figure out what."

"Then, what do we do?" Marin asked.

Tracker leant forward, resting his elbows on his knees and pressing his lips to his steepled hands. "My main mission is to keep Dylan safe. That should have meant bringing him here but..." He spread his hands wide.

Katarina hummed, thoughtfully tapping her lips with her forefinger. "Where else would you take an unleashed spellster in Demarn?"

A soft, mirthless chuckle shook the hound's shoulders. "That is the question, is it not, my dear hedgewitch?"

Dylan shook his head. There was nowhere else. Spellsters were either leashed, living in the tower or dead. The massacre here left him with two options and he didn't fancy the latter.

Tracker rubbed his temples. "Ordinarily, I would not suggest this, but it will have to be Wintervale. The king has an alchemist working there. I am sure she would be capable of leashing him."

"Then we should leave at once," Authril said. "Make for the capital as quickly as we can and inform the king."

"I want to search the rest of the tower," Dylan declared. Marin was right that this carnage had happened not too long ago. There was still a chance someone had survived.

"*Still?*" Authril blurted. "After everything you've seen, do you honestly think anyone could've lived through *this*?"

"If we walk away now, we could be condemning another life." He couldn't do that.

The warrior scoffed. "This place is huge and you want to waste precious travelling time because of a chance?"

"My dear," Tracker snapped, "If you were the one cowering in some dark corner waiting for a rescue, would you not want people to look for you?"

Silence followed the man's question.

The hound nodded and, in a far milder tone, asked, "Dylan? Where do you suggest we begin searching?"

"I don't know," he admitted.

Marin cleared her throat, garnering everyone's attention. "The tracks suggest the invaders split into two groups even before they attacked through the secret entrance. They both came through the gates, probably at once, but the majority entered the gardens whilst a small group went straight to the tower."

Tracker nodded. "I noticed. The smaller group was likely tasked with flushing out the tower."

"Right, right." Marin bobbed her head. "But if I were trying to hold back an attack, I'd go somewhere I could barricade myself into. Somewhere isolated from the rest of the building with a solid door between me and them."

"This is *your* home," Tracker said to Dylan. "Where would that be?"

Dylan shook his head. "I don't—" He'd never had to think of where someone could go to defend themselves if the tower was attacked. Everywhere within the walls had always felt safe. "There's nowhere." Not even a means of escape. Once an enemy breached the outer walls, anyone within the tower complex was trapped like a mouse in a bucket.

"Let us start with something simple, then." The hound's gaze lifted as he spoke, eyeing the structure over his shoulder. "The tower is a single building. Very few places to leave from once you get inside. People up the top are likely to get trapped." His attention snapped back to Dylan. "Does it have a dungeon?"

Dylan nodded. "They're isolation cells, now."

"Then that is where we will begin. Start from the bottom up. Do you know the way?"

"I do." He might've only been there a scant number of times, but the way down had etched itself into his mind.

"All right," Tracker murmured before turning to the others. "Our dear spellster and I will check the old dungeons then move on to the lower levels and work our way up from there. The rest of you should search the servant quarters. See if we cannot unearth some trace of whoever did this if not survivors."

Marin narrowed her eyes at the hound. "And the reason we're splitting up is…?"

"Yes," Authril said. "We'd be just as capable of searching the tower."

The flat smile the man gave suggested Tracker thought otherwise. "If there are still people alive in the tower, they are likely to be spellsters. Very frightened spellsters. Considering what we have already witnessed, it would not be too great a stretch to assume they would attack before letting you speak. You would not be able to shield yourself from such an assault, yes?"

"You'll be in the same boat."

"Not quite, my dear warrior. My status as a hound gives me certain abilities not accessible to ordinary people. I will be quite safe should we stumble upon anyone able to retaliate in such a fashion." Bouncing to his feet, he offered his hand to Dylan. "Come, my dear man. This will not be a pleasant business, but the quicker we do it, the greater our chances of finding someone still alive."

Dylan stood and went to lead the way back inside the tower doors, when Tracker laid a hand on his arm. The hound had drawn his sword as if expecting an opponent to erupt from the shadows at any moment.

"If I may?" the man said. "It would be best if you allowed me to go first, in case there are some stragglers. Just tell me where to go."

Bowing his head in acquiescence, Dylan trailed behind the hound. There seemed a marked lack of certainty in the elf's voice. Tracker doubted anyone was still alive. But there had to be, even if it was nothing more than a single child huddled in a closet or a baby tucked out of sight. Whoever had attacked, be it Talfaltaners or someone else, they couldn't have gotten everyone.

But they also shouldn't have known about the secret entrance. So, who had told them? And why, after so many centuries, had they chosen to let the Talfaltaners eradicate the sole place that had offered safety for any spellster in Demarn?

CHAPTER 40

Dylan followed the hound's lead as they made their way down to the tower's isolation cells, their path lit only by Dylan's magic. He had forsaken the globe for the softer light of a flame that flickered merrily in his hand. If people who meant harm still lingered down here, the light could be snuffed with barely a thought.

The steps were warped by centuries of wear. Between the smooth dip in the centre and their compact size, he was forced to walk sideways like those weird pinching shellfish he'd heard Sulin reminisce over.

His chest tightened at the thought of his old roommate. If people like Fredrick and Sophie could die, then what hope did an alchemist have? Or Henrie, for that matter? The man was good in offence, but his shield work was appalling. They both would've been cut down in a heartbeat.

A step rocked beneath his foot, throwing him off balance. He fought the sudden, potentially fatal, grip of gravity. He sought to brace himself. His hand slapped against the wall, the fire in his grip extinguishing to envelope them in blackness. In the last flicker of light, he caught Tracker spinning to face him.

This was it. He had crossed half the country and survived several attacks to meet his end via a simple flight of stairs. An embarrassing tale to explain to the Seven Sisters.

His descent was halted by a pair of hands grasping his waist.

"Be careful," Tracker whispered, the man's breath hot in Dylan's ear and pebbling his skin. Wiry arms lifted Dylan off the steps.

He grunted, thankful the darkness hid his burning cheeks. Dylan hadn't thought the man was this strong. Or careful. Those long fingers hugged the far side of Dylan's waist, holding fast to his robe and keeping him upright until he got his feet back under him.

They continued on as soon as Dylan reignited the flame. Tracker grew more guarded with every step. It was subtle, the slight cocking of his head and the way his fingers tightened on his sword hilt, adjusting their grip in preparation to attack. "And stay alert," he mumbled over his shoulder.

Dylan couldn't be any more alert if he tried. The buzz of a not-quite-formed barrier hummed around him. He flexed the fingers of his other hand, ready to attack at the slightest sign of danger. "Do you think—?"

The hound held up a fist, warning him back into silence. The door at the bottom of the stairs was shut. That had to be a good sign, didn't it? Surely, attackers wouldn't bother about shutting doors behind them.

Dylan strained to hear anything above the sound of his breath and the soft pad of the hound's boots on the steps.

The last two times he had been here—the only times he'd ever done anything to warrant isolation—the cells had echoed with the wails of others. Apologies, mostly, alongside pleas to be released and promises to live within the tower laws. The sound had chilled his blood back then.

Never had he thought silence would be worse.

The hound stood before the entrance. There were no openings within the iron-bound planks. Nothing to peer through to assess what lingered on the other side. Tracker tipped his head, turning an ear towards the door. Did the man's superior hearing pick up something he couldn't?

Dylan didn't dare ask.

Motioning for him to stay put, Tracker flung the door wide open. The boom of it hitting the wall echoed into the stillness and had Dylan's heart racing.

No cries followed the sound. Not of anger or fear. Not a single wail.

Tracker stood frozen in the doorway, the hand that had grasped his sword hilt so fiercely now hung limp at his side. Cold shock flickered across his face, there for a heartbeat.

Dylan dared to take another step down. "What—?"

In one mad burst of energy, the hound whirled and slammed Dylan against the wall. "There is no one here. We should check the other levels."

Frowning, Dylan pushed the man aside and carried on down the stairs.

"Dylan, stop." Those long fingers wrapped around his wrist, a steady pull keeping him from the entrance. The man really was stronger than he looked. "There is no one here that we can help. If someone hid down here, we would have heard them by now. You do not need to see what became of the rest."

He jerked free of the man's grip. A scathing glare kept the hound in place whilst Dylan descended the remaining steps in silence. He was well aware of what waited below, but he had to see for himself, had to listen to that kernel of hope wedged in his core.

No, he hadn't caught any sounds from within and he believed Tracker hadn't either. Yet, there clearly wasn't any danger in searching deeper. There were several dozen cells off the main room and the man couldn't have seen into all of them from the doorway, especially not in the pitch blackness. Dylan had to be sure none of them harboured a silent, terrified survivor before they moved on.

With his stomach already quaking, he peered around the edge of the doorway.

The stench of death hit him with enough force to churn his stomach. Bodies littered the floor near the entrance. Guardians for the most part, along with a few hapless servants. Covering his mouth with his sleeve, he lit one of the torches and pressed further into the room.

All the cell doors stood open. The purple sheen of *infitialis* greeted him as he passed each one. This close to so much of the metal, the numbness frosted over his bones, not quite finding a place to burrow within. A number of spellsters lay prone in the doorways. Not a one of them was whole.

Taking a deep breath, he continued searching each cell until he reached the very last door, behind which was the small corpse of a boy.

He stared at that body, trying to determine why the attackers would even seek down here. These spellsters had been surrounded by walls of *infitialis*. They were as harmless as could be made without leashing and yet even they hadn't been spared.

Tracker's hand hooked into the crook of Dylan's arm. "Let us leave here," he murmured. "There is nothing to be done."

Handing Tracker the torch, he entered one of the empty cells to stand in its exact centre. He brought a globe of light to life. It wobbled, growing dim. The only reason it still existed was because the open door broke the full encircling the metal needed to contain him.

"Close the door," he ordered the hound.

Uncertainty, a perhaps a little concern, escaped the man via a hesitant chuckle. "I hardly think it is necessary for me to—"

"Close it!" His magic flared, the air around him growing hotter as lightning sparked from the globe. He took a deep breath, pushing down his anger. "*Please.*"

The door swung shut. The globe puffed out of existence like a snuffed candle, throwing him into darkness. Iciness leached into his bones. It punctured his skull, dug its sharp fingers into his brain.

Dylan accepted the pain, it meant he was safe. Safe to rage. To grieve.

He fell to his knees, screaming into the dark. He slammed his fists against the floor. The tears he'd been holding back—knowing that if he started, he wouldn't be able to stop—finally spilt out. Just a few at a time in the beginning, but more soon followed, soaking his cheeks.

His whole body heaved with each sob as if expelling everything within would help, but he had already emptied his still-quaking stomach to the point that only bitter globules of saliva dribbled out his mouth.

Only when his throat was sore and his eyes felt too dry to produce one more tear, did he stop. He remained on all fours, panting like a dog, waiting for his pulse to drop and his breathing to even out. He ached from one end to the other. His arms were leaden, his hands bloody from the battering.

Further collecting himself, he staggered over to the door and hammered on the metal panel. He wasn't locked in, he'd heard no slide of a bolt, but the inside of the cell had no handle for him to free himself. "Let me out," he croaked.

The door swung inwards, allowing warm firelight to flood the cell. His magic returned, the innate healing rushing to mend the damage and soothe the weariness flooding his muscles.

Tracker stood in the doorway, the torch still in his hand. He eyed Dylan solemnly. No chance the man hadn't heard him and he had to look a mess. "Did that help?"

"A little." It hadn't drained the hopelessness from his thoughts, but he no longer felt as though he would burst. He wiped the back of his hand across his face, drying his cheeks and cleaning his chin. "We should look elsewhere."

When the hound didn't move, Dylan motioned for him to lead the way back. They ascended the stairs in silence, the going slow as he was forced into the same crab-like motion.

At the top, he directed the hound to the alchemist testing and training rooms. Although the rooms were also located beneath the tower, they were in a completely different section.

The walls were thick and covered in dried blood. The air putrid with decaying flesh and the metallic hum of raw *infitialis*. Dylan searched each body, determined to find out if anything had happened to his old roommate. There was no guarantee that the man had been down here at the time of attack, but he examined each likely corpse until there were no more.

He spotted a few familiar faces amongst the dead. Like Mary, the one whose idea of crafting an *infitialis* shield had almost taken her life along with Nestria's. That choice, and his decision to rush in to save them, was the very reason he'd been put on the path of being a weapon in the army. The last thing he'd heard before leaving had been of her being punished for the misjudgement. Clearly, the overseers had thought her still capable enough to work alongside the other alchemists, if not with the metal.

After finding no sign of life, they returned to the parts of the tower above ground.

They split up as they reached the landing. Even though he had raced through much of the lower level, Tracker insisted on checking. Dylan wasn't sure what the man expected, but he didn't wish to wander the same rooms in a fruitless search.

Whilst the man wandered off clutching the torch, Dylan once more summoned a light globe and turned to the stairs leading up.

He held his breath as he climbed. The next level was one of the tower's most-used public areas, holding not only the second dining hall, but the library and the bathing chambers. Depending on when the attack began, this level could be the most populated. That left a chance of someone being overlooked in the chaos.

He hoped that was so.

$$\sim \sim \sim$$

Tracker knelt next to a body lying face up at the base of the stairs. The area looked similar to the isolation cells he had investigated with Dylan, the only change being that this place lacked the *infitialis* lining the cells.

The body's armour was familiar, as was the face. Albeit, the latter was one he hadn't seen in years. Still, he recognised them even with the garish colouration of bloating and decomposition altering his features.

Trapper. A fellow hound.

He could've written the man's death off as falling whilst defending the helpless, if not for the trio of spears jutting through his chest and throat. Or how the angles suggested Trapper had been attacked by those within this block of cells.

What were you doing? The force those people had used suggested desperation. But why would they suspect a hound of doing them harm?

There was a faint hint of magic about the armour. Nothing anywhere near as strong as what Dylan was capable of, but no other spellster he'd ever met had been. The residue of magic from the same spellster lay in a circle on one of the floors.

Had the shield come before or after they'd attacked Trapper? Had the man's death been a case of striking before identifying their target?

Standing, he headed back up the stairs. This was the last of the underground levels. The ground floor held no survivors. He didn't expect there to be. Still, there could be a lone servant or wounded guardian.

Any hope for that lay within the levels above or somewhere within the outer walls. He needed to catch up with Dylan, see if the man had better luck.

Tracker turned his focus to the spellster's magic. He still roamed the level above, his power a steady beacon. And mercifully stable. Being able to release his emotion in the safety of an *infitialis*-lined cell seemed to have helped his control.

It wasn't a permanent solution to his grief, though. Dylan would need time just being still to fully process and accept what had happened here. He would never heal from it, but the sooner they left this place, the better it would be for the man's psyche.

As he strode through the corridors, one question continued to plague him. What sort of force was capable of slaughtering hundreds of spellsters?

Before seeing the massacre outside, his initial reply would've been the King's Hounds. They trained for years on how to hunt out and bring down dangerous spellsters quickly. The mistress didn't allow them to leave Wintervale until they were adept in their tasks.

But even if every spellster within the tower had gone rogue, not even the entirety of their pack could've done this without casualties. An army of them, perhaps, but there weren't that many. They stood a couple hundred strong at a stretch, including the half-grown uninitiated pups.

And it didn't explain the slaughtered servants. Or the people in Talfaltan attire.

A group of other spellsters could clearly get the job done. But the wounds he'd seen weren't in line with a magical attack. And he would definitely sense them. Nor would Talfaltaners be willing to work alongside those with magic. They barely tolerated any interaction with a hound.

Was it really as simple as the neighbouring island folk sailing upriver to slaughter people in cold blood? Around the same time the King's Hounds were called back to Wintervale and the army was massacred?

Something definitely didn't add up. Once he found out who was behind it, there'd be hell to pay.

CHAPTER 41

Dylan halted as he reached the top of the stairs. The smoke in the garden hadn't found its way this far into the tower, but the smell of it still clung to his clothes. A sickening, choking scent overlaid by the stink of rotting bodies.

The globe of light illuminated the corridors and the multitudes of corpses. Having needed to skirt several on his way up, the sight no longer shocked him. How he wished Tracker hadn't chosen to continue searching the level below. He could've done with having the man at his side right now.

Shaking himself, he headed for the bathing chambers. For the first time in memory, silence reigned wherever he stepped. It was unnatural. Abhorrent. Like the miasma that followed him from room to room.

He paused on his way to check the infirmary. It held a handful of the dead, most of them being the healers he'd trained under.

Reaching the first of the bathing chambers, he peeked through the door, expecting more death.

The room was surprisingly clean. The other bathing areas were also empty. That ruled out a morning attack.

How could this have happened? The tower was supposed to be safe, a haven for every spellster within Demarn. All the bad things he'd ever heard about—senseless murder, beatings that left people crippled, desperate folk stealing for whatever reason—happened beyond these walls. Here, a person might be punished, and harshly, but never without cause.

Now, their little group of five was quite possibly the only living thing here.

Left to their own devices, his legs carried him to the upper level of the library. The dead were here, too. Albeit, in fewer numbers than the lower level. They huddled between the shelves, some half out of cabinets that they had attempted to conceal themselves in. He checked behind every closed door and rifled through storage bins, coming away with less hope than before.

He walked the mezzanine, surrounded by the silence, his way lit only by the globe's harsh light. He had spent decades perusing these shelves alongside other like-minded people. Now, there was just him left to recall what lay within each leather-bound tome.

Wasted years. What had he done with the knowledge he collected? Decode a few mouldering scrolls and a tablet they'd unearthed in the mountains that bordered the Udynea Empire. *Not enough.* Nothing his past self had ever done mattered.

Would the crown seek to rebuild the tower? There would always be spellsters, that was why they made a place to keep them... *Safe.*

Self-mocking laughter bubbled up his throat, reed-thin and perilously close to tearful.

But it had been true for so long. These walls hadn't ever seen bloodshed, not since the first slabs were laid centuries ago. And now it was all gone. Spellsters would still be born into the world and Demarn no longer had anywhere to put them.

He leant on the railing and closed his eyes. So many innocent lives were going to suffer. Folk killed just for being born the way they were. Children slaughtered purely because their magic was feared. Marin had called this place a prison, but to those who needed it, this place was a haven.

The muffled echo of footsteps drew his gaze down to the library entrance on the lower level. The flash of light and a darkly dressed figure appeared in the doorway. It was gone before he could react, then reappeared in the less threatening form of the hound.

"*There* you are." The relief in the man's voice was almost thick enough to taste.

"I thought we agreed to meet back at the stairs in an hour?" That time couldn't have passed already. What had Tracker seen that made him so eager to come look for him instead? "What are you doing down there anyway? Are you checking up on me?"

"Of course not." The hound waved a hand as if to brush aside the very notion. "But now that you mention it." Tracker halted before the bookshelves below the railing. "I do hope you are not contemplating jumping from such a height."

"And if I was?" Dylan doubted the fall would kill him, not unless he was extremely unlucky.

"Then you put me in the rather messy business of trying to stop you." Tracker looked about him and stowed the torch in a nearby sconce. "I am coming up."

Before Dylan could object to the company, the hound had scaled the shelves and clambered over the railing. "There are stairs, you know."

The man shrugged. "This was faster. Now, I must ask..." He

pressed closer, his attention suddenly intensely focused on Dylan. "How are you holding up?"

"I'm fine." It wasn't entirely untrue. He wasn't about to boil over and unleash his magic in a destructive blast. But in its place was... *nothing*. He knew how he was *supposed* to feel. Had felt it bubbling away in his core earlier.

Now he was hollow as though the numbness he'd experienced in the cell had burrowed into his heart. He looked upon all these bodies, some he had spent copious amounts of time beside, and not a wisp of sorrow touched him.

Was something wrong with him? He should've been inconsolable, shouldn't he? How did he continue to function?

Tracker silently stared at him. The hound said nothing, but his disbelief was plain.

Dylan didn't blame him.

"We've searched three levels," Dylan continued, "and found no evidence that there might be survivors." He was beginning to believe Authril's doubts that anyone could have. "The tower's empty." His home a husk. Almost thirty years of living within these walls, never had he thought such carnage could touch this place. He indicated the room with a sweep of his arm. "The people I knew, that I've grown up alongside are—" *Dead.* He couldn't say it.

His throat closed at the very thought, choking him with tears he didn't dare shed lest he lost control of both his emotions and his magic.

"I know," the hound breathed. His fingers slid over Dylan's hand, slow and almost as if by chance.

"How would *you* handle returning to wherever it is you hounds come from and finding it like this?"

Tracker bowed his head. He remained silent for a long time.

Then, exhaling noisily, the man spoke, "That is not a fair comparison. Hounds are taught not to get attached. To anyone. Especially fellow hounds. We are trained to obey orders and attachments could mean the difference between being compromised or not." The fingers laying atop Dylan's hand twitched. "It may not seem so obvious—it has been some years since—but I know what it feels like to lose those dear to you."

Was that why the man hadn't said a word about his breakdown in the cell? Those dear to him? *Tricia, Sulin, Nestria, Henrie, Harriet...* The list went on. He hadn't found their corpses. He wasn't sure he wanted that confirmation. His very core quivered at the idea. He would rather no confirmation and believe they had miraculously escaped.

Dylan took a deep breath. He knew what that hollowness was

now. Like an internal shield, his mind refused any further bad news. "When does it stop hurting?"

A small, pitying smile curved Tracker's lips. "I will let you know if it ever truly does. In my experience, you grow accustomed to the ache. I suppose it is like losing a piece of your body. You know it can never come back, but life rather insists you go on."

And if I don't want to? The question whispered through his mind, chilling all thought. Everything he'd been fighting for was gone. The army was the only purpose left to someone with his abilities. *I could run.* And be hunted by other hounds, if not Tracker himself. At least that path promised a swift end.

"Come," Tracker said, taking up Dylan's hand. He entwined their fingers and tucked Dylan's forearm against his leather-encased chest. "There are still more places to check, yes?"

Dylan nodded. "It's where the children spend much of their time." Large dormitories took up the space. Segregating the children in the middle was their guardian's sleeping quarters and the room where children learnt basic academics before moving on to magic.

He wasn't sure he wanted to see what had happened there.

They made their way through the corridors to the stairs in silence. There seemed to be far more bodies here than on the last flight. Guardians, mostly, with a few of the elderly spellsters who aided them in teaching. They sat in a pile around the bottom of the steps.

Tracker gave a considering hum as he gently made a path through the corpses by pushing them aside with his scimitar. "You know what I have not seen?"

"Any sign of life?" He hadn't asked what the man found in his search, but Dylan could guess by the lack of enthusiasm, what he hadn't discovered.

"*That* and the marked lack of aggressors. The garden was littered with those who fell in a counterattack, but up here?" Tracker shook his head. "A small group should not be able to wreak this much destruction. It is as if everyone was taken by surprise. It suggests a stealth not seen in the attacks below. Or..."

"Or what?"

"They did not perceive the group as a threat. Take them for example." The hound pointed the tip of his weapon to the group of guardians he had piled to one side. "The wounds are all in their backs. They were attempting to flee downwards. That suggests the attacks started at the top of the tower."

"Or they were missed on the upward pass," Dylan countered. "Maybe whoever attacked took out all the spellsters first and cleaned up the guardians later."

The man stayed silent as he seemed to consider the idea. "If that is the case, then their invasion was sloppy."

"Sloppy?" Dylan echoed incredulously. "They slaughtered everyone."

"My apologies, that came out wrong." Sighing, Tracker closed his eyes and rubbed at the bridge of his nose. "You are right, they did indeed claim many lives, that is not to be trivialised. What I meant was starting from the bottom would have allowed them to stop anyone slipping through. That they did not means there is a chance some escaped this fate."

He eyed the hound, trying to determine whether he was the sort to feed someone false hope. "How?" Once the lower level was secured, the tower was a trap. "They even broke through the secret entrance."

"I spied something peculiar with the outer walls through one of the windows," the man said as he started up the stairs. "It looked to be the part of the garden we missed seeing. As well as what must have been quite the scuffle there, a section of the wall was collapsed. Not enough to fully compromise the structure, but definitely without a natural cause."

Frowning, Dylan followed the elf. Who would be capable of such a feat? No one he could think of. It would take an immense amount of control to not let all that stone crumble before it was time. "Do you think the Udyneans are responsible for this?"

"I would say not. They do not strike me as the type to leave a building like this standing. Nor have I seen much in the way of magical wounds on any of the victims. In truth?" The man let out a weary sigh. "I wish I had a proper answer to give you. There is little here that makes sense."

They scoured the children's dormitories, finding them mercifully empty. The school was in a similar state, although there were plenty of signs suggesting people had left in a hurry. He supposed most of the children would've been herded up or down the stairs at the first hint of danger.

Scorch marks decorated the walls, a terrified child's retaliation. Dylan stared at the strange outlines each blast had made. Some of them almost looked like impressions of people, but there were no charred corpses or ash to correlate with such an attack. Signs of someone using a shield that conformed tightly to their figure? It was the purest way the instinctual magic reacted, the bubble shape many used forming only after honing the skill.

Their passage around the level led them by a small room tucked under the stairs leading up. The fond memories of his childhood told him the area was a storage room for the school. He'd never been in there, although he had tried many times with some of his methods getting him into trouble.

He halted opposite the door. The room had always been locked when he was a child. Now, the door hung open a mere hand's span. A dark red puddle pooled from beneath.

Tracker crept up to the gap, peeking around the edge of the door. A faint gasp left his lips.

Before Dylan could utter a word, the man lunged backwards. In one swift move, he slammed the door shut with a kick and pushed Dylan further from the room. "You do not need to see that."

Anger whipped through his veins. He could guess what the man had seen and, no, he didn't want to see it, but... "You don't need to protect me from every little thing." He had seen plenty of death, had even been the cause of some. "I'm not fragile."

By the face Tracker pulled, the man didn't agree. "Unleashed spellsters are always under the immediate protection of the nearest hound." He spoke as if reciting an oath, his voice carrying a dry, passionless note.

Dylan made a show of straightening his robes. "I'm a unique circumstance, remember."

Tracker bobbed his head. "That you are. However, you are also under my protection. That means I am responsible for your mental wellbeing as well as your physical." He halted at the base of the stairs leading to the adult dormitories, his head tilting as though listening to something above them.

Dozens of guardian bodies lay strewn across the steps. Swords of all lengths littered the pile. Dylan tried not to see them, to ignore the perverted call to pick out familiar faces amongst the mass. He doubted his guardian had fallen here, but if she had, he didn't want to know.

"What is it?" Dylan whispered. "Did you hear something?"

"Hmm? Sadly no, I..." The hound removed an unlit torch from its sconce and, after a few strikes from his flint, ignited it. The torchlight alleviated the globe's harsh shadows, giving his features a softer touch. "I think it best if you remained here. The next level might be too much for you."

"You said there was a chance someone might've escaped. What if some were missed? What if you find them?" Would a frightened child trust the hound? Would they even trust another spellster?

A grin, seemingly made of a little more bravado than it should, split the man's lips. He rolled his shoulders. "Oh, there is no need to worry about me. I will be fine. I am rather more concerned about what might happen to you if I let you venture any further, especially if we fail to find anyone."

"In other words, you think I won't cope." It was perfectly understandable. Besides today, the only time the man had seen his reaction to any other carnage was the one-sided fight with the bandits outside of Toptower. "I coped when finding the main army encampment was destroyed and the front line before then *and* when my scouting party was ambushed. I won't fall apart here."

Tracker laid his hand on Dylan's chest. "This is different though, yes? Neither the front line nor the encampment was your home. I know you are trying to remain detached from all this, but no one would expect it of you." He glanced over his shoulder at the stairs. "Whilst it would be remiss to search this far and not any farther, I cannot see how anyone above could have survived. I would rather not expose you to that."

"You want to coddle me? I'm supposed to be a weapon. They don't coddle my kind in the army."

"No, they do not," Tracker quietly agreed. "They just forget you are still a person."

Dylan frowned. He didn't recall seeing the man there and the lieutenant acted as if Fetcher had been the only hound in the entire camp. "What would you know about that?"

"You think us hounds do not talk to each other? Fetch is a dear friend. She has never liked the way the army treats her spellsters."

He recalled his arrival at the main encampment, of the man who had knocked him to the ground with one swing of his hand. "You wouldn't have been able to guess it. They struck me on the first day. Enough that I bled." Fetcher must've known, she had looked right at him lying in the dirt. "And she did nothing."

Tracker nodded. "Once you are in the army's command, there is little she could have done."

"I thought hounds were above all but the king?" That was always how the guardians made it seem.

"We used to be, but not for some time now. A few hounds of old had conflicting interests in what a leashed spellster should be used for. Now, we rank lower than the crown's lieutenants."

"That still doesn't explain why, if Fetcher didn't like what was happening, she kept bringing us. Why not apply for another position?"

"The life of a hound does not work that way. I told you we are named for what we are good at, yes? That is our task for life. You do not question it. Not twice."

"Why? What happens the first time that's such a deterrent?"

Those honey-coloured eyes swung Dylan's way. They'd gone brassy in the torchlight and soul-achingly hollow. "It might have changed since I was a boy, but they flogged me."

"Actually…" he spluttered. "With a whip?"

"No, of course not," Tracker scoffed. "They only use the whips on adults. I was… seven? Maybe eight years of age. Children that old are made to cut their own switches and bring them before their trainer."

He stared at the man, aghast. "Then they used it to beat you?" He'd seen the scars. Had assumed they were battle wounds like Authril's. Now he stopped to think of it, not many spellsters would be running around with blades.

The hound nodded. "They did precisely that. Only once the other hounds had gathered. They like to make a big show of it you see. Sometimes they will tie you down. Other times, you are allowed to protect yourself to a point. *I* was suspended from the ceiling by one arm." He rubbed at his left shoulder. "They had to pop it back in once they were done."

"And you continued to train as a hound?"

Tracker shrugged. "Of course. We are born to this duty. There is nothing else I can become."

"You said that before." It had been a week ago, when he learnt the man's true name was a birth date, but he didn't think he had forgotten the one detail that man left out. "Exactly who decides you're born to it?"

The hound fell silent, reluctance and remorse twitching across his face before a near-perfect neutrality took over. "That is not important. What is, is how serious I am about you remaining here." He patted Dylan's chest. "Actually, it would be best if you went back and waited for the others outside."

Dylan's annoyance at the man for trying to coddle him flared back to life. He had thought the hound was opening up to him, but he clearly didn't trust Dylan. "I'm coming with you. Nothing you do can stop me." If anything, he might be able to retrieve some spare clothes from his old room. Providing the servants hadn't gotten around to clearing it of his things.

"There are several things I could do," the man grated, closing the gap between them until they were practically sharing the same breath. "But I have no desire to tie you up or knock you out, just in the off chance it is not safe to leave you so vulnerable."

"I have a right to know what happened."

Sighing, Tracker stepped away from him. "You do. But I am willing to bet it is a slaughterhouse up there. I have no desire to subject you to that if I do not have to. So, I ask you to stay put."

"No."

"Then I regretfully must command it. Whoever attacked the tower herded everyone upwards." He pointed at the stairs. "Those bodies are a mere taste, I promise you that."

Dylan wordlessly snatched the torch from the man's hand, expecting an objection and getting nothing. "I'm going up there." It didn't matter what awaited him, he refused to be barred from his home.

In the space of one step, Dylan found himself flattened face-first against the wall with his arm behind his back. Pain shot through his shoulder, the pressure Tracker kept on it hampering his magic's attempt to heal. The torch clattered to the ground, sputtering and threatening to die before the flame grew again.

"Do not be a fool," Tracker growled, his breath warm on the nape of Dylan's neck. "I am trying to spare you more nightmares."

"This is my home," Dylan snapped. His magic flared around him, swirling half-formed fragments of a shield. He sent sparks of lightning along his arm, hoping to shake the man off. It had no effect.

He squirmed, panic tightening his chest as every story he'd ever been told about hounds surfaced. He forced them down in an effort to keep his magic under control. The man might be restraining him, but if he wanted Dylan dead, he would've done it already.

"I am going to let you go now," the hound murmured, the soothing tone at odds with his previous ire. "But understand I am not prepared to let you go up those stairs."

As soon as the pressure was off his arm, Dylan turned around to press his back to the wall. He rubbed at his shoulder, certain that something popped back into place as he rolled it.

He eyed Tracker as the man bent to retrieve the torch. He had definitely felt his shield appear in the instant between being grabbed and being slammed against the wall. The hound must've gotten inside the perimeter before it could fully form.

Those honey-coloured eyes settled on him. The hound grimaced and rubbed at his own shoulder. "Sorry. I am not used to doing that on someone quite so tall."

Dylan clung to his silence. He could rationalise Tracker being fast enough to get through a shield before it was fully formed, but that didn't explain how his sparks hadn't any effect. Had they not been strong enough? Had his armour shielded him?

"I ask you again to stay here," Tracker commanded, heading for the stairs.

Dylan summoned a shield, slamming it between the hound and the stairs. He focused on the archway, allowing the barrier to spread and become flush with the brickwork, leaving not a single gap to be exploited. *Try and get through that.* If he could hold back an exploding *infitialis* shield, the hound had no chance. "You are not going up there without me."

Tracker stood before the shimmering barrier, his back to Dylan and his arms akimbo. "Take it down," the command came wearily.

He hardened the shield, tucking it into the back of his mind to ensure it didn't fall without him expressly desiring it. "You'll have to knock me out first."

"Acting like a child will not get me to change my mind."

Heat flushed Dylan's cheeks, made worse by the fact he knew Tracker was right. Taking a deep breath, he tamped down his emotions and reached for logic. "How am I supposed to protect you if I'm down here and you're up there?" He couldn't let anyone run off alone whilst the chance of survivors was still a possibility. "If there's someone up there and you—"

Tracker whirled about. "Allow me to make this clear, you are *not* here to protect me, *I* am here to protect *you*." He grimaced, the torch's flicking light throwing odd shadows over his face and turning the expression into a ghastly thing. "That has already occurred to you, yes?"

It hadn't, but he wasn't about to let the man know. Tracker was keeping something from him, beyond what waited upstairs. He just wished he knew what. "Do you know what happened here?"

The hound shook his head. "I know only the pattern of attack. I am as clueless as you on the rest." His gaze once more slid to the stairs. "*This?* It is not what I expected to find. If you are concerned for my wellbeing, then go and wait for the others. If I am not back by the time they are, you can return for me. I would prefer to not have you doing it alone."

Yes, it was a hound's job to keep a spellster safe whilst escorting them, but not like this. "What if someone is alive up there? What if they catch you off guard and you're injured?"

Tracker shrugged. "For a hound, that is practically a given at one time or another. I will manage."

"And what if they have magic?" A spellster, completely scared out of their mind, would attack before identifying if their target was friend or foe. "If they hurt you—"

"They cannot!" Tracker snapped. His hand slapped across his mouth the instant the words were out. Horror widened his eyes.

"What do you mean they can't? Of course they can. You might be a hound, but you're not invincible."

Growling out a stream of curses, the man paced before the stairs. Not all the words were of the Demarner tongue. Despite the man's claim that he didn't know the language, several of the swears were elven.

What else hadn't he been honest about? "You want me to trust your word, then tell me the truth."

Tracker grimaced. "It is not so simple. This is not something you are ever meant to know. No spellster is. The creed insists I kill any who find out."

"Find out what?"

The hound was silent for a long time. He stared at Dylan, too many emotions vying for dominance upon his face.

Then, he sighed, his head drooping. "Do you know why hounds are so good at capturing spellsters?"

"Because you've been trained in it."

"Yes, but also…" He stepped back, climbing up one step.

Dylan's mind reeled. A multitude of tiny shocks rippled through his body, digging into his brain and blurring his sight. He wobbled, his arm outstretched behind him as his legs struggled to hold himself upright.

He let his hold on the shield fall, seeing the man standing on the far side just moments before the barrier dissipated.

The hound had walked through his shield. He hadn't imagined that. And the man had done it with no hesitation beyond clearly not wanting to reveal he could.

Was it in his armour? The jerkin had felt heavy, clearly reinforced with some sort of metal. But he hadn't felt anything that would've suggested *infitialis*. No humming echo from his magic. No suppression like the isolation cells.

That left only one other option.

"You're a spellster?" One with a single talent, perhaps. Able to get by because it was beneficial to have him in the King's Hounds.

A brief bout of laughter left the man. "*That* is your conclusion?" The mirth fell from his face. "Although, I suppose you would if all you have been taught is that spellsters beget spellsters."

"They do."

"Mostly. Every hound is raised with the knowledge that they owe their existence to a spellster parent. We are not like soldiers, choosing or being conscripted to fight. I told you, a hound is *born*."

"How can you be born as…" He waved his hand to indicate all of the man. "*This?*"

Tracker shrugged. "How are spellsters born? There are tests done on spellster babies and hounds are those who fail them. The crown lays claim to us and we are trained as soon as we can hold a weapon.

They teach us to enhance our natural talent and there are many trials to pass before we are allowed to hunt. Not everyone makes it through, but we all have the one commonality of being immune to magic."

Dylan stumbled back until he reached a wall. *Immune.* That wasn't possible.

And yet, the man had most definitely walked through his shield. No tricks. No slipping through at the last moment. The shield had been up and solid before the hound moved and it had posed absolutely no barrier to him. "Why have I never heard of this?" There were plenty of rumours about the King's Hounds. Surely, one of them would've come close.

"Because it is forbidden for you to know. There are spellsters who have discovered our immunity to magic, dangerous ones, and they are harder to put down because of it. The chance of a hound being born is small. Losing even one of the pack to a rogue spellster makes life difficult for those who remain."

"So the tower kept us ignorant." And fed them tales to ensure they remained afraid, unquestioning.

"Yes. A little backhanded considering the majority of us were born in this very tower. This birthplace should have been *my* fate, but my mother wanted to keep me. She died trying—fled the tower a day or so before having me. The hounds who found me told me of her plight once I was old enough to understand. She fled into the surrounding forest and went into labour not long before the hound chasing her caught up. By then, it was too late. I was born and she was dead." A mirthless smile took his lips. "A suitably fitting tale of becoming a hound, yes?"

It did sound like one of the many rumours Dylan would hear circulating from the tower gossips.

Dylan chewed on the inside of his cheek. "The night we met, you agreed with Marin that using magic on you would be pointless. But if I had..."

Tracker bowed his head. "The creed would have left me with no choice but to take your life."

"Except you're now telling me that supposedly secret information?"

"The words of our creed are quite clear. Any spellster who learns must be put to death to stop the tower from knowing." He spread his arms, shrugging. "I do not think that is a concern."

There it was. The truth he knew in the pit of his stomach but didn't want to believe. A secret remained such when there was no danger of it being shared with the wrong people.

"I still need to see," he pleaded. "I need to be certain there's no chance." If he didn't, he would always wonder, always cling to that kernel of hope that he could've done something.

The man's brow furrowed. Dylan thought the hound would argue again but, with a rueful twist to his lips, he nodded and gestured for Dylan to join him on the stairs. "I still reserve the right to haul your arse out of here if I think it is too much."

"Duly noted." He followed the hound up, trying not to think about why the steps were so slippery.

Tracker was right about the adult dormitories being a slaughterhouse. Every room, every possible space, overflowed with the dead. It appeared that most of the children had fled here with their guardians, their bodies covering the floor in a tangled mat, piled in places that made it almost impossible to check some of the rooms.

The man grasped his hand, once again linking their fingers, as they came to the next flight of stairs leading up. "Are you certain you want to continue?"

Dylan nodded. He had to be completely sure.

They searched each level to the last door, finding only more death. He reached the room he had shared with Sulin. Although two beds still filled the space, one side had been stripped of anything that didn't belong to the alchemist.

He turned from the sight before his resolve could falter.

The rooms of his friends were in a similar state, which took him back to his belief that the attacks had happened during the day. Nestria would've been in the training arenas, assisting the older children with learning to make shields and how to attack. He wasn't sure what Henrie did most days, but if Sulin wasn't in the alchemist's quarters below, then he must've been in the gardens.

Perhaps they had escaped. Would any of his friends be capable of breaking through the wall? Enough to leave the damage Tracker had spied? He wasn't certain if any spellster would be able to do such a thing alone. *Maybe together.*

The important thing was he hadn't been able to identify them from the corpses, which meant there was a chance.

By the time they were ready to descend the tower, he rather wished he had heeded Tracker's advice. Seeing cribs cradling tiny broken bodies was an image that would be etched in his mind for some years. The first sight had left him angry. But now?

Now he was just tired. His thoughts ran in a seamless loop, unable to stop picking apart the reasoning behind it all.

Had the king gone mad? Had Udynea really found an alternate route and slain everyone who didn't surrender? Or was there some fanatic group of Talfaltaners roaming the land, slaughtering whomever they saw as unclean?

He wasn't sure which was the worst option.

Tracker reached the tower entrance to find the women already waiting on the steps. By the look on their faces, their search had been just as fruitful.

"Well," Authril said as she stood. "The pigeons are gone."

He grunted. No doubt, the invaders had slaughtered every feathered body to ensure alerting the king was impossible.

"How is Dylan?" Marin asked. She looked over his shoulder, frowning. No doubt noticing that the spellster wasn't with him. He had left the man to wander the tower's library, he seemed the calmest there, despite the bodies. If he moved elsewhere, it would be easy enough for Tracker to find him.

"I would say he is still in shock at seeing all he has ever known become rubble."

The woman nodded slowly, her cheeks darkening with her embarrassment.

"I suggest we gather our things. We want to reach cover before sunset, yes?" Tracker turned his gaze to the sky. The bright, cloud-strewn blue of the heavens was steadily darkening. "We will be hard-pressed in finding a suitable place to camp before nightfall. I do not fancy sleeping in the open when we have no idea who did this."

"No," Authril replied. "The attack can't be more than a few days old. Whatever force did this had to be immense."

"I am aware."

"Then you'll also know they won't be moving quickly. I say we stay put for the night. I'm not keen on crashing into a forest that harbours the might to take out thousands of people."

"Stay *here*?" Marin piped up, alarmed at the prospect. "As in *inside* the tower? Look, I'm in no way inclined to paint a target on my back, but we're surrounded by the dead. You want us to *sleep* amongst them?"

Tracker nodded his agreement. The tower complex had indeed become a tomb for thousands of poor souls.

Authril waved the point aside. "No one will enter this place. I don't see why we shouldn't use that to our advantage."

"*We* entered," Katarina pointed out.

"With a King's Hound." The warrior jerked her thumb his way. "No average traveller would come near here."

Tracker frowned. "Do you have any idea of the damage that will do to Dylan's psyche?" The man was already grieving. Forcing him to linger would be torture.

Authril scoffed. "Why should I concern myself over the mindset of a dead man?"

"Excuse me?" The spellster had been very much alive when Tracker left his side. Still was. The impression of latent magic lingered in the back of Tracker's mind, strong even within the echoes permeating the tower walls.

"The whole point of bringing him here was to leash him," Authril continued, speaking slowly as if he'd been dazed. "We've no way of doing that now. I've heard all the stories about the King's Hounds. If you can't contain spellsters, you kill them. And there is nowhere, no way, to contain him."

Marin clapped her hand over her mouth. The groan she attempted to restrain still leaked out.

"Let me see if I have this right," Tracker said. "You want *me* to take his life, yes? Despite him showing no inclinations towards being dangerous?"

"No inclinations?" Authril echoed. "You don't let a feral dog hang around unless you're looking to get bitten."

"Dylan is neither feral nor an animal incapable of being reasoned with." In his current state, there was a possibility of him lashing out if triggered, but Tracker had handled that sort of grief before. Dylan needed a gentle hand, not the threat of death.

"No," she agreed. "He's worse. A feral dog can only kill one at a time."

"So can *you*. As can Marin and myself. Even our dear hedgewitch cannot escape such a claim. By your logic, we are also destined for execution."

"It's different," Authril grated from between clenched teeth.

It always was. "You are right, of course. You are nowhere near as dangerous as myself." He had seen enough of her fighting techniques to know her weaknesses, the way she exposed herself. That was often the case with those only taught to fight in a unit. Mercenaries were a handful as a group, but a single warrior rarely stood a chance on their own.

Authril frowned at him. "You've heard his whimpering in the night, don't try to tell me you haven't. What do you think will happen if he actually woke up in the middle of his nightmares?"

"Dylan has been through a lot," Katarina said. "That his soul is troubled makes him worthy of our compassion, not of death."

"I agree," Marin said, standing shoulder to shoulder with the hedgewitch. "I wasn't there, but Kat has told me enough of the situation they found each other in. I watched my village burn and—"

"That isn't the same thing," Authril blurted. "Did you see how he was reacting to all this?" She flung her arms wide. "Absolutely no emotion. What sort of person sees the utter destruction of their home and doesn't become an emotional wreck?"

"Someone who knows the extent of their power and has no desire to cause further harm," Tracker interjected before either of the others could. The man had explicitly waited until he was away from them, had then requested he be shut into an area where his magic wouldn't work before allowing himself to grieve.

"All the more reason to be rid of him."

"Dylan hasn't done anything wrong," Katarina said. "There must be another way." The hedgewitch turned to him, her pleading already turning those hazel eyes dark. "What if I claimed him? As a hedgewitch I—"

"You would not be able to invoke that law unless we were all on dwarven lands." Even then, dwarf-claiming required the human or elven person being taken in to also be a child. She had to know that.

But what was the alternative? He'd never been keen on effectively sending Dylan right back under a warden's abuse, that reluctance had only grown with time. Before now, there was nothing he could've done to sway the spellster.

Maybe, with what he was fighting for gone, he could be persuaded to flee the kingdom. As much as he hated to agree with Authril, she was right in there being no place for any spellster without a tower to house them.

Yet, leaving Demarn would require not only himself to be disobedient, but the rest of their group.

Katarina's offer held some kernel of hope. She might not be able to claim even a child whilst on Demarn soil, but her willingness to accept Dylan did suggest the man would be welcomed amongst the dwarves. And there was nothing to physically bar their passage to the northern border. Unlike to the west, no walls or insurmountable mountains stood between them and Dvärghem.

Getting the man there without alerting the other hounds was a different matter.

What Authril might do if they chose to head north was of greater concern. Would she attack Dylan herself? That seemed unlikely. Alert other hounds? *Not from here.* Not with the pigeons slaughtered.

Whitemeadow sat to the east, less than a dozen days away. They would need to travel that way before striking along the northern roads. There was the possibility of a hound still being at that station, but if the same missive that reached Whisper and himself had been sent to everyone, then that chance was a slim one.

Authril could have the local guard send a message directly to Wintervale. If that was her goal, then Oldmarsh was closer. Keeping her from either city would be ideal. The only way to ensure it would be to take her life. He doubted Dylan would find that an acceptable sacrifice, definitely not in his current state.

Ensuring she stayed with them and remained unaware of their true goal was the only other option.

"We take him to Wintervale," Tracker firmly declared. "He can still be leashed there." The pack already had a leashed spellster. The woman was used with those still training to become a hound. A means to have them adapt to the idea of magic being hurled at them.

"Wintervale?" Authril echoed. "That's weeks away. Just admit you want him hanging around for your own personal reasons. You've been practically salivating at the thought of getting him into your bed." The sneer she gave barely showed her fangs. "You think I didn't see back at the brothel? That I wouldn't have noticed you thrusting your dick in his face? Or the way you pandered to his gaze?"

Katarina and Marin exchanged confused glances. Tracker had no idea how much Authril had told the pair of their time in *The Gilded Lily*.

"Because I must only be thinking of my desires, yes? Not once could the thought that we can trust him have possibly crossed my mind." The former reaction was a typical one to finding out he used to work in a brothel. Everyone he had ever told acted as though he thought with one appendage.

Except Dylan. And maybe the hedgewitch.

"If I hadn't been there, you would've gone further," Authril concluded.

"And what if I had?" Tracker snapped. "By your own admission, and his, you are not lovers. And who I chose to pursue is *not* what is under scrutiny here."

"Taking an unleashed spellster so far is madness. No hound would take that risk."

"No hound?" he echoed. "Correct me if I am wrong, because I must be mishearing you. You are actually attempting to tell me—a *hound*—how to go about the very task I am trained to handle?"

"He is dangerous."

He scoffed. "He is *powerful*. There is a difference." Tracker had witnessed magic wrought maliciously many times, more than he wanted to. Those spellsters revelled in their use.

With Dylan? There was enough raw power flowing off the man to level a village at a thought and yet, outside of healing and a few mundane activities such as starting a fire or gathering water, the man tempered his magic as though he was afraid to use his full strength.

Or perhaps, had been conditioned to fear it.

"If you think Dylan is dangerous," Tracker grated. "Then you have never encountered a truly malevolent spellster."

Authril visibly bristled. "I was there when the Udyneans wiped out the main army encampment. If you had seen the destruction they caused—"

"I did." Although he wasn't certain if what he had felt was the army or Dylan's explosive escape from his *infitialis* binds, he had seen enough of the aftermath to know what happened there. "I have also witnessed spellsters controlling others like puppets or clearing the mind of innocent people so thoroughly that they forget how to live once that influence is gone. I have even seen a spellster bring down trees with her voice all because I refuse to let her continue eating the local children. A few fireballs? A little lightning? These are tricks from childhood." Not once had Dylan brought his full power to bear during an attack.

"All that," Authril said, "and you'd trust an unleashed spellster to walk all the way to Wintervale?"

"*You* sleep with him. That requires trust, yes?" He didn't understand that. Did she think refusing Dylan's advances wasn't an option? The man didn't appear to be the type to force himself upon people. "Or is your toy that dissatisfying that you are so ready to toss him aside?"

The woman rolled her eyes. "I slept with him to keep him placid. Everyone knows that's how you tame spellsters."

Incredulous laughter burst from him. Was she attempting some sick joke? She certainly sounded sincere, but she was also so very wrong. "Who told you this?" He swung to the other two. "Have either of you heard of this before?"

Both women were quick to shake their heads.

"See? Even the hedgewitch has never heard of such a thing. Shows how much bullshit that is."

Authril glared at him, her shoulders bunched and her hands balled. "It's what the wardens always said."

Of course. Stood to reason that she had mingled with the wardens. "They would," he growled. "I assure you whatever they did to their spellster charges, it was *not* consensual."

Authril stared back at him, speechless.

"Allow me to make this very clear, my dear warrior. Dylan is under *my* care. You do anything to harm him or cause him to lash out and it will be *your* head I seek." It would be difficult enough getting the man to Wintervale safely, he didn't need additional challenges wrought by someone who thought they knew better.

"It's settled, then," Authril said. "We camp here tonight and make for Whitemeadow in the morning. The king must be informed as quickly as possible." She stalked off inside, leaving the other two women standing at the top of the steps looking immensely uncomfortable.

"That last encounter you mentioned," Katarina finally said. "The one who brought down trees with her voice? Was she elven?"

"Yes. Why?"

"An Oracle," the hedgewitch breathed. "You found—?" She fluttered one hand before her chest, the other seeking out her belt pouch and the writing implements it contained. "No one has been able to confirm their existence. The Coven wrote them off as nomadic myths, stories of demi-gods and the like. But if you *encountered* one..."

"I did more than encounter her, my dear woman."

Katarina waved his words away, as if he spoke mere semantics. Did she not realise what he would've done? "Where was she? Did you bring her here?"

"No." She had already proven herself too dangerous before they had met.

Nodding, the hedgewitch expelled a relieved breath. "Where can I find her?"

"Nowhere," he snapped. "She is *dead*. I beheaded her outside her home. Set fire to her *and* the building." He could still see it. The fable-like hut in the forest filled with furniture upholstered in human skin. The child he'd been unable to save hanging like a gutted deer in her cellar. "Or did you miss the part where she *ate* children?" For centuries, if the villagers were to be believed.

Katarina frowned. "According to nomadic folklore, Oracles were both respected and feared, raised in such a fashion that no one dared to refute their word or stop them from doing as they pleased."

He had noticed.

"But I doubt one would—"

"As pleasant as this conversation has been," Marin interrupted. "Shouldn't we settle the matter of *where* we're sleeping? We'll need time to clear a space because, I don't know about you, but I'm not keen on sharing with a corpse."

Tracker rubbed at his chin. "There is a whole level in the tower where most of the rooms remained untouched. We could sleep in them." There was the added bonus that, should anyone venture beyond the gates tonight, few would search so high.

The duo nodded, both their expressions grim. If the homes within the tower's outer wall were anything like inside the tower itself, they'd a fair idea of what waited inside. They gathered their packs from the same area Tracker tossed his before he had followed Dylan into the tower.

Tracker did the same, shouldering his pack before picking up the remaining other. It didn't appear to be Dylan's. That man had shucked it as he ran for the main gates, but Tracker had assumed the others would collect it on their way in. "None of you grabbed his things?"

"We all chased after you," Marin replied, shrugging. "I guess the pack slipped our minds."

"I will fetch it." He gestured to the tower entrance. "Light a torch before you head inside. It gets dark fast. Inform our dear spellster of the situation on your way. He is in the library, you can follow him the rest of the way up. And do not breathe a word of what our dear warrior said." They couldn't risk the news further fracturing the man's mind. "Mention only our destination and the leashing."

The disapproving rumble coming from the hunter spoke her mind well before she could verbalise it. "I don't like the idea of keeping him in the dark."

Katarina nodded her agreement.

"Nor do I," he confessed. "But this is not the best time. I swear, once he is in a less fragile state, I will make her opinion known." It was possible that Dylan already knew Authril harboured some measure of hostility towards him—the man wasn't stupid, merely naive—but maybe not to the extent of opting for his death.

"*Before* Wintervale?" Marin pressed.

"Well before." Without a way to contain his power, it would be foolish to let Dylan near the capital. The hounds residing there would practically swarm the spellster. Maybe even kill him before he entered the gates. He had to turn the man northward well before then.

Whitemeadow was the best bet. With luck, Tracker could convince the man to take a boat and speed up their journey. Enough to have a decent head start over any hound his mistress sent.

Of course, getting Dylan alone, somewhere he could be sure the others wouldn't overhear them, could be troublesome. Especially if Authril's distrust in him grew. How was he going to keep Dylan out of Authril's clutches without alarming the man? He couldn't tell him, not on top of all this. Who knew what action he might take?

Later. Definitely before Wintervale was in sight.

That just left losing Authril somewhere along the way.

At least the other two seemed inclined to let Dylan be. He had expected it from the hedgewitch, less so of Marin. But it pleased him nevertheless and had him feeling a little justified in his actions.

Seeing the others off inside the tower, Tracker trotted back to the first gate.

Out in the courtyard, the flies were no less prevalent, even with the fading light. The smell was also in full force. The heat of the day had done a decent job of helping with the decay. He wasted little time in grabbing Dylan's pack and heading back into the tower. The smell wasn't as bad inside. *Small mercies.*

He took a lantern from its post. A small amount of oil resided in the bottom. He tore a strip of cloth from the hem of a spellster's robe and soaked it in the oil. It wouldn't burn for long, but he didn't need it to.

Ascending the first flight of stairs was slow going to avoid stepping on anyone or the puddles. A lot of the injuries dealt to these poor souls had been with sharp weapons, axes, swords and the like. *At least their deaths were swift.* A strange thing to find and clashing with the dead Talfaltaners outside. Had it been two groups?

He tucked that possibility into the back of his mind to mull over later. Right now, he had a far more urgent problem to address.

Dylan.

What was he going to do with the man? Tracker had experience with spellsters who were still processing the losses in their lives. Children leaving behind their parents, adults leaving spouses. All of them still absorbing the idea of never returning home.

But never a loss this great.

How much use would his usual methods of comfort be? Would Dylan be open to an offer of diverting his mind from the world? Despite the hot looks Tracker had spied thrown his way, the man's response to any suggestion given, subtle or overt, was definitely muddled.

Still, he had proven himself susceptible to distraction and had definitely enjoyed kissing. Maybe that was all Dylan liked. He certainly couldn't judge based on what he'd heard coming from the tent the man shared with Authril.

Would he acquiesce if Tracker softened his approach? Not as far as sex, but what of a night snuggled in a warm, compassionate embrace?

There was only one way to know for sure.

CHAPTER 44

The measly glow of a single torch illuminated just enough of the children's dormitory for Dylan to see. He recalled this place from his youth, where he'd been packed in with the other young boys.

At least there were no bodies here. No blood. Not even a hint of a fight. If he didn't know better, he would've thought nothing untoward had happened.

Rows of beds filled the vast room, their mattresses naught but straw. Dylan sat on one and couldn't help but smile. *Just as hard as I remember.* He bounced a little, trying to convince himself that he was merely testing the firmness and *not* attempting to block out all thoughts of the children who had last roamed these rooms.

It was harder than he thought. For the first time ever, there was silence. No laughter. No chatter. *What a senseless waste.* A small part of him hoped the lack meant some of the children had escaped. But where would they go? Were they still out there being hunted?

He was alone for now, the women having chosen a similar room further down the hall. Where the hound had vanished to, he didn't know. *One night.* That was what Katarina had said. He could do that. It wasn't as if the corpses were going to harm them. And it would give him a chance to say goodbye.

The soft creak of the door, followed by the almost nonexistent tread of another's footsteps, drew him back from his thoughts. Someone had joined him. One of the women? They'd probably come to ensure he didn't do something foolish.

He ran his fingers across his face, surprised when they came away damp. When had he started crying? "There's no need to check up on me."

The footsteps continued and his unwanted companion halted before him. Judging by the black leather boots, it was Tracker. His footwear was well-made, the stitching the finest Dylan had ever seen, and looked far more comfortable than his own battered pair. The man's choice or part of the uniform the king chose for his hounds?

"I'm perfectly fine," he insisted before Tracker could utter a word.

He wasn't about to do anything crazy.

"That you are," the man murmured.

His head jerked up, uncertain he had heard correctly.

Tracker smiled wryly at him and, with the shake of his head, clicked his tongue. "At least, that is the lie we choose to tell ourselves, yes?" He set down the two packs he carried and began to unbuckle his sword belt. "I never considered asking you before making the decision, but what *are* your thoughts on striking out for the capital?"

"I have to go." He was one of the last spellsters in the kingdom, if not *the* last one. "The army will need me." And he was prepared to do anything they required of him, especially if it got him closer to avenging the lives taken here.

The man's sword belt was tossed aside, as were the sheathed daggers. "I thought as much. I have an associate at Whitemeadow. If Treasure's information is correct, then the armed company would have passed through there."

"Associate," Dylan mumbled, his gaze drawn to the purple gleam of the *infitialis* dagger. He hadn't paid much attention to the hound's arsenal, but he'd gotten a good look at that one when they'd met. Did all of the King's Hounds carry such a weapon? "Is this person like Treasure? We're not going to find ourselves in another brothel, are we?"

"*Reji?*" Tracker chuckled. "Granted there would be a great deal of people interested in such a man, but no. He is a blacksmith, a well-respected and highly sought-after one at that. If some word has passed through the town of what transpired here, then he would know." Another belt, filled with what Dylan suspected were an array of poisons, was lowered to the floor. "Or of anything else strange in the area."

Dylan nodded, his gaze returning to the dagger. Its curve was definitely akin to the alchemist types. Did they make them for the King's Hounds as well as for their own use? "Have the others decided if they're joining us?" He drew his head up to find the man removing his vambraces, tossing them atop his weapons.

The hound scoffed. "The women are still bickering." He unbuckled the front of his jerkin, sliding it over his shoulders at a leisurely pace. "Mostly on whether it would be safer for us to travel as a group or part ways here. I am rather in favour of the former." The jerkin slithered to the floor. "Regardless, Authril is likely to leave without the others if they are still undecided by morning."

Dylan didn't doubt it, given the woman's eagerness to inform her superiors of what had transpired here. "Maybe your fellow hounds will have answers." Whatever had attacked the tower had to be large and powerful enough to contend not just with the spellsters, but also the guardians.

A force like that couldn't just up and vanish.

Tracker's lips flattened. "Perhaps." The word was further muffled as the quilted shirt came over his head to swiftly join the jerkin, leaving his top half clothed in a light shirt. "Only way we will know for certain is in reaching Wintervale."

Dylan shuffled back, his insides knotting at the spectre of the man undressing right in front of him. If he reached out, he was certain his fingers would connect with that barely clothed torso.

The thought only tightened the knots.

There was a strange glint in that honey-coloured gaze as it ran over him, the soft gleam of the torchlight only aiding the comparison.

"Until then..." He leant forward, pressing obscenely close.

Before Dylan could react, their mouths were sealed together.

He pushed the man away, spluttering. "What are you doing?" After the kiss, he had thought Tracker was done with him. Especially as he had attempted little more than a few teasing remarks since then. "We are surrounded by the dead." Surely the hound wasn't attempting to flirt with him after everything they'd seen.

"Technically, we are not. This level has one room of bodies."

As if that made it better. "That's not the point." Dylan wiped the back of his hand across his lips. They tingled. "You can't just kiss me whenever you want."

Tracker tilted his head to one side. "You did with me. Or have you forgotten that little moment we shared by the campfire?"

He hadn't. His cheeks blazed at the memory. "Even so, how can you think kissing me is a good idea?"

Tracker grinned, his shoulders bouncing in a silent chuckle. "I confess, I have thought of going a little further than that." His gaze slid down Dylan, so intense that he practically felt the man's hands upon him.

He swallowed, trying not to think of how deftly the man had handled himself back in the brothel, or of how flexible he'd been.

"Think of it this way," Tracker continued. "We are alone." One of the man's knees settled on the bedding beside Dylan. "Completely. There is really no need for you to continue with this game of being coy." The other knee joined the first on the bed, on the opposite side of Dylan's thighs. "And do not try to pretend you have no interest. Or think I have not noticed you watching me. You do not have to admire from a distance. You will find me very willing for whatever you desire."

"I..." It was hard—*difficult*, absolutely nothing was hard—to think with the man straddling his lap. "I don't know what you're talking about, but I think you've gotten the wrong impression here." And it was partly his fault for not putting a halt to the man's flirting sooner, for giving into his curiosity enough to kiss him. He would just have to explain like he'd done in the past and that was that. Sure, it would make travelling together a little awkward, but what alternative did he have? "I'm flattered you find me desirable, but—"

Their chests pressed together. "I do," Tracker whispered, his breath heating Dylan's ear. He smelt of warm skin, oiled leather and the slight hint of smoke. "Very much so. And I suspect that, for all your attempts at deflection, the feeling is mutual."

Dylan shivered, every muscle in his body tightening at the hoarse note in the man's voice. A small groan crept through his teeth. "N-no," he stammered. "I—" He swallowed in some vain effort to moisten his suddenly dry throat and, in a rush, said, "I'm definitely not—"

Tracker pressed close enough for their noses to touch. "So when you kissed me, that was you not being interested?"

Dylan blushed. People didn't just go around randomly kissing others, did they? *No.* There had to be interest or affection involved.

But that had been *then*, and then had just been curiosity, right? *Yes.* Curiosity fuelled by memories of the brothel and his erotic nightmares.

He had enjoyed it, though. A lot. The memory of the hound's lips had settled into his dreams, leaving him waking hard some mornings. That didn't happen without some measure of interest.

With them being so close, the disappointed exhale that whistled out the hound's nose warmed Dylan's face. Tracker's weight shifted, lessening as he moved to get off Dylan's lap.

Dylan grabbed the man's shirt collar, dragging him back and crushing their lips together.

Tracker went rigid against him for all of a breath before slipping his tongue into Dylan's mouth.

He closed his eyes, melting into the kiss. Warm, soft, and hardly unfamiliar considering he'd let the hound do this several days back. Granted, he could claim the first time had been accidental on his part, but the second? When Tracker had explicitly asked him? Not a chance.

Nor could he deny Tracker was damn good at it. As at the fireside, it stirred his blood. His hips shifted, seeking contact with the being currently in his lap.

The hound's hand slunk down Dylan's chest, changing angles as it steadily slid lower. The palm massaged Dylan's length through his robes and, unsurprisingly, he felt his body responding.

He couldn't help the moan that escaped his throat. It trembled along his tongue and directly into Tracker's mouth, the sound answered in kind as the hand withdrew.

Tracker pressed them tighter together. His hips, once still, now rubbed what was definitely an erection against Dylan's groin, the act only exacerbating what was going on in his smallclothes. The heat of the man's barely-clothed chest burrowed through the layers of Dylan's clothes, adding to the fire growing in his veins.

He thrust up into the sensation, his thoughts slowly sinking into a swirl of heat and pleasure. His lungs strained, barely able to gulp down a breath between messy, panting kisses. His heart thundered in his ears, close to exploding.

He barely registered Tracker grasping the skirt of his robes until cool air slunk beneath Dylan's undertunic, forcing his mind to think of something other than the man's warmth and the oddly gentle firmness to his actions.

Dylan tipped the hound back. "Tracker, I…" He bit his lip. Clearly, the usual talk wasn't going to work, not with what he'd just let the man do to him. Bluntness would have to suffice. "It's not just the fact of where we are. I simply *don't* want to have sex with you." He winced, the words seeming a little harsh in his ears. "Not that I'm at all against the idea of two men enjoying each other's company, believe me. If that's what you like, then who am I to say otherwise? But I am most definitely not one—" His rambling was cut off as the hound clapped a hand over Dylan's mouth.

Tracker chuckled. The smug sound shivered through Dylan's body, further stoking fires in his gut he hadn't realised were happily blazing away. "Your tower did a poor job of teaching you to lie." He grinned. "And I do not recall mentioning anything about sex. We are *kissing*. Which, we are in agreement to having done so before and *you* just did. *Again*." A thin reed of frustration vibrated through the final word.

"That—" He took a breath, willing the tightness in his chest to subside. Kissing didn't mean anything. "I could kiss my greatest enemy once, it wouldn't mean I'd want to do it again with them. Or anything more."

Tracker hummed, his lips pressing together. "I would believe you more if you had not just ground yourself against me and were not currently at attention." He rolled his hips, once again rubbing the pair of them together, entirely aware as to the nature of what he was moving against.

Dylan bit the inside of his bottom lip, using the pain to keep himself from making a sound. That wasn't as easy a feat as he hoped. "It lies," he mumbled, the words slipping out before he realised what he had said.

The hound's laughter shook the both of them. "I very much doubt that. See, I thought I understood what you were about, that you enjoyed the flirting but not the physical, yes?" The curve of the man's lips took on a hungry edge. "But since *The Gilded Lily*? I am less inclined to believe that is so."

You're wrong. He stared at the elf, his heart thudding uncontrollably as he willed his mouth to move. "I'm not in—" His tongue froze, the word balancing on the tip. No matter how he tried, nothing would come out.

For the first time in his life, he couldn't speak the lie. No matter how he tried to convince himself otherwise, he was definitely interested in the man.

"All these little flirting games and coquettish looks have been pleasant enough and I have not minded playing, but this?" Tracker shook his head, a perplexed smile flattening his mouth. "I admit my confusion. You allow much, then freeze. You kiss me, then claim you would do the same with an enemy. I have entrusted you with knowledge that you should never have learnt because you asked me to be truthful. All I ask is for you to do the same."

Dylan remained silent. There wasn't much he could do but agree. He could see where that would be confusing.

Sighing, Tracker once more slid off Dylan's lap, the absence of the man's weight leaving their surroundings surprisingly colder. "You want me to stop? I will stop." He took a step back, spreading his arms wide. "This is me stopping, yes? Is that truly what you want?"

"I don't know," he admitted. His own mind was such a jumble that he... he...

He had just wanted to feel something solid. Something safe. Being the centre of the hound's attention had offered all that comfort.

The breath that gusted out the hound's mouth carried a heavy load of relief. "Finally, some honesty. I was beginning to think..." The rest of the sentence fell away as he rubbed at his face. "Well, I thought we were of one mind." He paced back and forth, tugging at a little dagger-shaped earring dangling at his lobe. Given the sensitive nature of elven ears, the act had to hurt. "Understand I will go no further than you desire, you have my word on that, but you need to *tell me* where that boundary truthfully lies. Even if—*especially* if—it is not in my favour."

Dylan licked his lips, uncertain where he should begin.

The hound abruptly halted before him, those honey-coloured eyes narrowing as he tapped his lips with the side of a forefinger. "Will you remain honest with me if I ask you another question?"

Bowing his head, Dylan nodded.

"I can see the desire in your eyes." Tracker leant forward, tipping Dylan's head back with the gentle press of his fingertips under the chin. "Burning just the same as when we were in *The Gilded Lily*.

And then, it was not just for me, yes?"

Heat softly bloomed in his cheeks. His perusal of the men in the brothel hadn't been that overt, had it? And looking at beings who had obviously honed their craft wasn't an admittance of interest in other things.

"Yet, you still persist on playing at being so stubbornly hard to get. You are not beholden to anyone, nor are you untried in these matters. Why do you continue to deny your interest in men?"

Dylan shook his head. Even if he did entertain the thought of doing anything with the hound, there were a great many things he had no experience with. Even kissing, to an extent. And playing at anything, especially being hard to get, was perhaps the furthest thought he had. Nor had he been denying anything.

As for the other part? "I…"

The puzzled quirk of the man's brows smoothed as he gave a hushed puff of comprehension. Those long fingers brushed under Dylan's jaw, tilting his head further. "This," he whispered. "It *is* all new to you, yes? You have never been intimate with—?"

"A man?" Dylan blurted. Warmth bathed his face. By the gods, he hadn't blushed at the topic of sexual intimacy since he was sixteen. "No." He knew the mechanics, and had stumbled upon several such scenes in the past, but actually going so far as to *do* it?

He hadn't ever dared that. The risk of being branded as indecisive, of being outed, had never been worth a moment of curiosity.

"Never with *anyone* bearing matching equipment? At all? Man, woman, fluid, null…?" Tracker trailed off as Dylan shook his head. He toyed with his lip, clearly lost in thought. "That sounds… limiting."

Dylan shrugged. He hadn't exactly gone searching for them, but he'd known of five such women. He'd had a boyhood crush on one. She'd been a soft-spoken woman who was always quick with a smile when it came to teaching him healing. She'd also been roughly twenty years his senior and outed well before he was old enough to think about sex.

Of the others… Ida hated men, plain and simple, he hadn't even tried after witnessing her tirade at another man. Sioned had been exclusive with Tomas long before she began referring to herself as a woman. Leah had lost interest after a run-in with Nestria. He didn't know what was said as she refused to be anywhere near him, but he could guess well enough. His friend had done that to a number of people.

Then there was Sapphire, born between the sexes, according to her. She'd only been interested in snuggling. Dylan hadn't complained, her cuddles being their own unique form of soothing magic, although ultimately they weren't worth getting caught over.

He wished she was here now. He could've done with her comforting embrace and gentle voice. He doubted the hound could've compared. The man's body was all muscle, no softness to burrow into.

Tracker knelt on the floor before Dylan. "Then how about this." He caressed Dylan's thigh, lifting the robe hem slightly and allowing another wisp of cool air to slink across the skin. "If you are inclined, we could try taking this as far as you desire. And, should you wish to stop anywhere along the way, you just have to say the word, yes?"

"And you'll obey? Just like that?" Yes, the man had just displayed restraint after feeling him up and grinding against him, but it was different to do so now versus backing off whilst in the moment. Could Dylan trust the hound to keep his word? There wasn't really any way he could force the man to end it if Tracker chose to be rough with him. Dylan clearly didn't weigh much to the elf. "What if I just want to kiss and cuddle?"

Tracker shrugged. "If that is the extent of your wish, then that is all we shall do tonight. Truthfully, my intention *was* only to snuggle."

"Snuggle?" he echoed. "Is that what you call grinding on top of me?"

A soft, wheezing laugh escaped between the hound's teeth. His head drooped, admitting defeat. "You moaned and I..." He wet his lips, visibly centring himself. "I got lost in it."

"And that's all it takes to arouse you?"

He looked up, holding Dylan's gaze. A cocky little smile tweaked his lips. "I believe we have covered my attraction to you, yes?"

They had. Dylan didn't quite understand what the man saw, but he wasn't going to question it.

"You still have not answered me. Are you amenable to..." His lips twitched, fighting a smile. "...snuggling? Although, I believe your desires are rather more advanced than that."

Dylan licked his parched lips, his stomach bubbling. "I don't—" Tracker was right, curse him. He wanted more than the hound's mouth on his, but... *Am I really considering having sex with a man?* Sure, he had toyed with the idle thought from time to time— everybody did, didn't they?—but he'd never given it any decent contemplation. *I am.*

Yet the only thing that worried him was whether he trusted Tracker?

I do. That chilling certainty gripped his gut and wouldn't let go. It wasn't as though the idea of having sex involving two penises hadn't *ever* crossed his mind, fleeting though those thoughts usually were.

But to attempt it *here*?

"If it helps calm your nerves in me being your first man," Tracker said, clearly struggling to remove the humour from his voice. "The only extent I would even consider going to would feel no different to what any other person could do for you. Unless, of course, you have never experienced oral sex?"

A bubble of laughter crept up Dylan's throat. "I have." Not often. The speed of most intimate encounters rarely left anything but the main event. "You want to...?"

Tracker slowly inclined his head. "If you would allow me to go that far. I am quite skilled at it."

Who would know? *Just us.*

His chest tightened at the realisation. The women slept far from this room. They wouldn't hear, would they? Never walk in on them. Even if he was to have an orgy, who could catch them at it? Who could punish them if they did? There was nobody to run to with the news. No guardians to out him to.

No one.

Not a single living soul.

"All right," he heard himself saying, the words leaving in a breathless rush. *So much for not doing anything crazy.* But Tracker was right in that oral sex wasn't new to him. And it required little experience on his part. "Until I say stop."

One of the man's brows twitched upwards. "Until?" he echoed. "My dear spellster, I have no intention of doing anything that would make you want to."

CHAPTER 45

Dylan gripped the bedding as Tracker inched the robe and undertunic ever higher. Both items of clothing were only secured to his body by a belt, giving the man plenty of leeway to slide his hand beneath the linen. Long, warm fingers worked their way up his bare leg, their touch sitting just on the border of tickling.

A pleased smile skewed Tracker's lips. "You know? I forgot you have a dislike of wearing trousers."

Not knowing quite what to say to that, Dylan shrugged. His stomach still churned, but with a definite note of anticipation. Those fingers were getting higher.

Eventually, his robes were pushed all the way to his waist, fully exposing his legs to the chamber's chill air. As well as the erection that was woefully apparent through his smallclothes.

Tracker abandoned caressing Dylan's thigh. He ran his palm across the bulge, massaging through the fabric.

Dylan bit back a moan that threatened to take flight. His grip on the bedding tightened, balling the coarsely-knitted blanket in his fingers. *I can't do this.* The thought flashed through his mind, not quite leaving his lips. Because it wasn't a *can't.* It wasn't even a *shouldn't.*

If the hound didn't hurry it up, then Dylan was going to explode before anything could happen.

It was possible that Tracker had come to the same conclusion as, now the majority of Dylan's clothing was out of the way, he moved on from caressing skin to untying Dylan's smallclothes and curling his fingers around the waistband.

Unbidden, Dylan assisted the man's actions, lifting off the bed whilst the hound tugged. His length was released in one rough pull and the night air welcomed him into its grip.

He went to shuffle himself further onto the bed, halting as Tracker's fingers wrapped around his length, moving up and down in an unhurried fashion.

"Still good?" The hound's hot breath bathed Dylan's skin. "I know you have played *this* part before, but we can stop at this."

He shook his head. "More," he demanded on the wings of a gasp.

"As you like." His free hand gently coaxed Dylan's legs further apart, giving him more room between them. "I promise, I will go slowly." His lips brushed Dylan's inner thigh, working ever higher. "I also swear that my teeth will not get involved, unless you enjoy that sort of thing."

Teeth? Of course, as an elf, Tracker had the customary fangs. An impressive pair. Dylan had forgotten about them, but now the hound brought it up, he wondered how much of a good idea it was to trust the man even this far.

But the hound seemed to be doing precisely as he had promised. His tongue, warm and wet, meandered across Dylan's skin. Those long fingers drew back Dylan's foreskin to let his lips ghost along the tip.

By the gods... Dylan tipped his head back, his mouth silently moving. Yes, he had experienced this plenty of times, but—

A low whine reached his ears. It took a moment for Dylan to realise *he* had been the source. He'd never made such a sound in all his life.

Dylan swallowed, gasping for air, his legs trembling. He clutched the edge of the bed and squeezed his eyes shut, uncertain whether he wanted to discover if this was real or not. Never mind sorting out which was the more terrifying thought.

He had gone into it knowing that *this* act likely wouldn't feel any different. And, judging by the noises Treasure had made back in the brothel, he gathered the hound must've had some skill with his tongue.

But he hadn't expected it to feel this good.

His hips gently rocked to the rhythm the man set, deepening each movement. A soft moan slid up his throat at each sweep of Tracker's tongue, his body content to settle on action whilst his mind was frozen by conflicting emotions. He had agreed to this, so how could he be stunned that he had let it go even this far and also not care within the same moment?

With his breath quickening at the exquisite delight the hound so readily offered, Dylan found himself unable to remain indecisive for long. He *needed* to see, to confirm this wasn't some hallucination.

He leant back, resting his weight on one arm, and struggled to focus on the scene unfolding at his waist. The leisurely bobbing of Tracker's head, the tip of the man's tongue snaking from those sensual lips and up Dylan's length.

His other hand slipped from the edge of the bed. His fingertips brushed the man's shoulder, then the back of his neck, before gliding over Tracker's ear and into his hair.

Those honey-coloured eyes lifted, holding Dylan's gaze. It only served to make the growing fire in his gut burn hotter. Tracker smirked, then opened his mouth wide. The full length of his canines gleamed briefly in the torchlight an instant before he enveloped Dylan's length in a blast of moist heat.

Dylan groaned through clenched teeth. The room blurred, his eyelids fluttering in their effort to keep watching the glorious being at his waist as the man continued to pleasure him.

Unperturbed, Tracker moved on to swallow as much of Dylan as he could. Inch by inch he went, his fingers stroking the little that remained. Then, with his lips tightening around Dylan's girth, Tracker began to suck.

Despite himself, Dylan bucked, thrusting against the man's face.

Giving a soft grunt, Tracker pinned Dylan's hips to the bed with barely a pause to his rhythmic glide. The man's actions seemed fuelled by a hungering need, each movement precise as if rehearsed and damn those who tried to stop him from completing whatever little ritual played in his mind.

Never had Dylan come across such fervour. His gut tightened. He was near the edge. Could see it rushing ever closer. He grabbed another fistful of blanket. His head tipped back. He bit his lip, trying to muffle the rather lewd sounds that constricted his throat in an attempt to speak.

"Tr-ack..." he finally managed, the strangled warning fighting to escape through his teeth.

The angle of Tracker's head shifted. Dylan slid deeper into the man's mouth. The pressure of his tongue along the underside of Dylan's length increased.

That was all he needed to tumble off the edge. The heat coiling in his gut unravelled and a coarse yell threaded through his throat. *Too loud!* He flopped back, struggling to muffle the sound with both hands.

Dylan laid there, his heart racing and his chest heaving. His body gloriously satisfied. *By the gods.* He stared up at the rafters, watching the torchlight flicker over the exposed beams as his personal world slowly returned to normal.

On the edge of his vision, he spied Tracker getting to his feet. "That was not as bad as you imagined, yes?"

He grinned. Bad was definitely *not* the word he'd use. "You don't think—?" he rasped. Swallowing, he tried again. "They... they wouldn't have heard that, right?" The last thing he wanted was to have the women rushing in here thinking something was wrong.

Tracker hummed, pausing in removing his thin undershirt. "I

suppose it *is* altogether possible. It is not as if they all could have grown deaf in the last hour since I saw them."

Dylan propped himself up on shaking arms to glare at the man. How dare he be so utterly *smug* after just having another man empty themselves down his throat only moments before.

It was his fifteenth nameday all over again.

The undershirt slid over Tracker's shoulders to reveal that gorgeous canvas of tattooed skin. "Truly," he continued, his hands falling to the belt of his trousers. "I doubt much sound can actually pass through these walls. They look rather solid."

Dylan took in the chasm of gloom surrounding them. He'd never known the lower levels to be this quiet. Even at night, there was always some small group making a little noise. It had been oddly peaceful hearing those signs of life. This silence was anything but.

"So..." Tracker leant over him. Stripped to the waist, the elf cut quite the intimidating figure, the torchlight giving his bronze skin a warm glow.

Dylan had tried not to look the last times they were naked together—he'd failed spectacularly, but he felt that trying had to count for something. And, even though Tracker wasn't yet in such an extreme state of undress, Dylan still couldn't stop his gaze from running over the man, or admiring every inch of the elf's bare torso. A part of him longed to reach out, to touch that warm skin, to follow the curving lines of the tattoos down to what still lay hidden beneath linen and leather.

He dug his fingers into the blankets. His heart fluttered into his mouth. It stuck in his throat, forcing him to swallow or choke on his own doubts.

"Can we talk about taking this further?" Tracker purred.

"Track," he warned, tilting away from the man. Had the hound forgotten their deal?

The hound's lips curved. He peered at Dylan through lowered eyelashes. "I do like the way that sounds." Tracker settled between Dylan's thighs, the edges of the man's leather pants chill against his bare skin. "I usually abhor bragging, but I feel it would be remiss of me if I did not reiterate how good I am at this. I learnt a great deal in *The Gilded Lily*. Give me a chance and I guarantee you will be screaming my name before the night is done."

Sudden, terrified uncertainty took hold of his limbs. Dylan scurried backwards, realising his folly in the move only when his hand slipped off the opposite edge of the bed. He slid gracelessly to the floor, his legs tangling with the bedding.

The hurried rustle of cloth preceded Tracker's head popping over the edge. The hound eyed him, concern stamped across his handsome face. Then he grinned, seeming to come to the conclusion that Dylan was unharmed, his head tipping to rest on Dylan's upright boot. "You moved a lot faster than I anticipated."

Heat flooded Dylan's face. What a sight he must look, stripped to the waist and lying on his back with his legs in the air. Thank the gods the women hadn't decided to investigate. He probably would've died from sheer embarrassment.

Tracker settled on the edge of the bed as Dylan righted himself. "Do you wish to stop?"

Even with the man's assurance that he only had to say the word, he hadn't expected to be given a way out unless he sought it. Never mind this was a relatively easy one given that he could agree with the man's assessment and leave it at that.

Still...

Taking a deep breath, Dylan summoned all his courage. "It'd be rude of me to leave you in your current state." He gestured to the man's groin. He should at the very least return the favour of giving the man some measure of relief. Perhaps not in the same way, he really wasn't sure he would ever be ready to attempt that particular act. But there had to be other things he could do.

Tracker's gaze dropped. His hand hovered over his belt. Unbuckled, the ends neatly framed the leather-encased bulge. "I *am* capable of creating my own fun, you need not concern yourself about that." Hooking one foot behind the other, he hauled off his boots. "Although, you are more than welcome to watch."

Dylan paused in getting to his feet. "Watch?" he echoed. Hadn't the man suggested something similar back in the brothel? Did he get off on performing acts in front of an audience?

"That is what I said." Tracker stood, undid the laces holding his trousers up and let them slide to the ground. The linen of his smallclothes was more revealing than Dylan had imagined. "It can be a rather arousing experience. For both parties."

Dylan licked his lips, his throat tightening on a whimper. He didn't need to *see* the man pleasure himself to envision it. His mind was already creating a clear enough picture.

He leant on the bed end, trying to sort through the emotions fizzing away in his gut. He couldn't go through with any more. This was his limit, he was certain of it.

Hushed muttering had his gaze sliding back to the elf only to find Tracker battling with the laces of his smallclothes. A grin tweaked Dylan's lips, the ridiculousness of such a sight distilling the fuzzy, bubbling sensation. "Are we stuck?"

"No, I have this." Tracker struggled a little longer, desperately plucking at the knot, before sighing his admission of defeat.

"Apparently I am."

Still on his knees, Dylan shuffled closer. From his rather unique vantage point, he could see where the laces had tangled and was able to effortlessly work them through.

The man's smallclothes fell at an alarming rate, leaving Dylan with a decent view of Tracker's erection. He swallowed. He'd never been close to another's length. Not like this at any rate. The appearance wasn't terribly different to his own, the tip having more of a point and less of a mushroom look than that of a human's.

His fingers twitched. The desire to wrap them around the shaft was powerfully strong. Supposedly, the true difference was in the feel.

Long fingers slid into Dylan's hair. Gentle, but firm. "When you have finished admiring..."

His gaze jerked up. He hadn't been admir— *Yes, I was.* Fortunate, too, that he was still dressed or the stirring effect of such appreciation would've been all too apparent. "Sorry, I just..." He absently traced one of the many designs adorning the man's hip to the sound of the hound's soft groan. "I've never met anyone so heavily tattooed." A truth, of sorts.

Tracker settled on the side of the bed, propping himself on his outstretched arms with all the grace and lethality of a giant mouser. With his lips twisting lewdly, his gaze followed Dylan's fingers as they wove back and forth through the faint hair on the man's abdomen. "You would be more comfortable if you undressed, yes?"

Right. He'd already been stripped below the waist and there wasn't anything the elf hadn't already seen. No reason to *not* remove everything. Dylan swiftly dispensed with his belt and boots, tossing them to one side.

Uncertainty gripped him as he pulled his robe and the long undertunic over his head. He tried to shake the feeling free. The man had seen him naked before, he'd had Dylan in his mouth only moments ago. Yet the insecure tightening of his gut only increased as he shed the last bit of clothing. Whatever was the man thinking?

Tracker stopped him as he went to resume kneeling. "Look at you." His hand slid down to caress Dylan's semi-erect length. "Such doubt. One would think you expect me to attempt killing you during sex."

The thought hadn't crossed his mind, but now the hound mentioned it...

This seemed less of a good idea than it had before.

He stepped back, beyond Tracker's reach, and scanned the bed. There didn't appear to be any weapons hiding amongst the blankets or any place the man could've concealed one.

Tracker chuckled, one corner of his mouth lifting. "My apologies, that was a poor joke. I swear, if taking your life was my goal, I could have done so a hundred times between Toptower and here. No deception required."

"You could have?" That was rather disconcerting. He took a few more steps back, bumping into another bed, and sat heavily onto the mattress.

The man nodded, getting to his feet. "If you still fear it, then allow me to put your mind at ease."

Dylan swallowed. The way the hound stalked the space between them, the hint of deadliness mingled with the husky way his words poured from those lips...

If this was to be his final vision, it was a good one.

"The king keeps his hounds well supplied with whatever weaponry we work best with," Tracker continued. "This includes poisons and there are a number to which I am immune. Of those, there are a few that I could easily coat my tongue in that would have even the most powerful spellster writhing in agony by now."

Poison. Did that mean the pounding of his heart had a far more sinister origin? "That's not exactly conducive to having me continue." And he longed to. That startling certainty hit him in a rush. By the gods, he wanted to trust the man enough to let... whatever was to happen just... happen.

Tracker's lips thinned into a wry smile. "My point..." The man climbed onto Dylan's lap, straddling him once again. With one thrust of his hips, he tipped Dylan onto his elbows. "Is that if I wanted you dead, you would not have made it this far." He bent over Dylan, unabashed amusement dancing in his eyes. "I am not one to toy with my targets," he breathed. Their lips brushed against each other's as he spoke.

Dylan froze, recalling just where that mouth had last been. And, yes, he could taste himself on the man's lips. He reflexively swallowed and sharply reminded himself that this wasn't the first time that taste had touched his tongue.

"Have you ever lain with a spellster before?" Beyond Authril, he hadn't been with someone who hadn't access to magic on some level. How possible was it that the opposite was true of the hound?

"A few were willing," Tracker confessed, sounding more than a little puzzled.

"I see." Had that been before or after they'd known what the man was? Would it have made a difference to them? *He* knew what Tracker was, knew what he must have done and *still* found the man attractive. He even considered allowing him to go further than they had.

He choked down any further questions, the bitterness in his thoughts making him want to retch.

But he knew the source, knew it was all for himself. He'd harboured a vague hope that, by being a first in some sense of the word for the hound, it would help his nerves. But that had turned out to be a baseless wish. Nothing he did would be new for the man.

And *that* notion stung. Why? It wasn't as if he didn't already know Tracker had been a prostitute, had experiences Dylan couldn't even imagine.

No matter how he tried applying logic, it didn't soothe the ache. The only first he'd ever been for anyone was Nestria, back when they were clumsy teenagers. And he felt just as woefully inept now as he had then.

"Dylan." The name purred out of the man's lips, stoking the hot yearning growing in Dylan's gut. The twitching of the man's hard length against his bare stomach was rather insistent. "If you wish to stop, you must say so. That was the rule we agreed on."

"I know." However unskilled he was, he owed Tracker some measure of release. Even if part of him deemed it unwise to entrust such closeness to a man who admitted to using poisons to take down his prey.

Yet, Tracker was also right in that there'd been plenty of times the man could've killed him. Dylan doubted he would try now when there was the prospect of...

Of what? Dylan didn't quite know. Other things? Certainly more than he had planned, but jerking off another couldn't be beyond him. Elves might not be outwardly different to humans, but they were supposedly a little slipperier when aroused to the point the hound was at. Surely, that just meant Dylan could use the man's natural lubrication for this act.

He leant forward, tipping the man back. His hand slid up the man's thigh and to the hound's groin. He knew nothing of pleasing any member beyond his own. Would Tracker care how bad Dylan was at it? He had worked at a brothel, after all. He had to have encountered some clients who were simply terrible.

Dylan wrapped his fingers around the man's length. Warm, eager flesh greeted him, a lot slicker than he had expected despite everything he'd heard about elven penises. He moved his hand in the same movements he had done to himself a thousand times since puberty. *Easy enough.* That Tracker didn't flinch had to be a good thing.

He was a few strokes in before the hound's soft gasp of amusement warmed his face.

Tracker guided him, rotating his hand to a new angle. "Like this," he whispered, closing his fingers over Dylan's so both of them were effectively jerking him off.

Dylan tightened his grip to the sound of the man's encouraging moan. He maintained the pressure, halting when the hound removed his own hand.

"Keep going," Tracker gently insisted.

"You sure? I-I've never—"

"I noticed." Giving a lopsided grin, he caressed Dylan's cheek. "And you are doing so well."

The unexpected praise shivered through his body. Feeling a little bolder, he twisted his head, drawing the man's thumb from his cheek to his mouth, and enveloped the length of it in a wet kiss. The slightly salty taste had him snaking his tongue along the skin.

Tracker trembled in his grasp. The warning growl sending a whole new flavour of excitement sparking through Dylan.

The hound extracted his thumb, using it to seal Dylan's lips shut. "I would not persist with that," he said, his voice deliciously hoarse. His thumb dropped, coaxing Dylan's mouth open. "Not unless you plan on letting something else inside."

The mild flush of shock gave way to the rising bloom of pure embarrassment. He hadn't meant to insinuate that he'd be open to performing the same oral acts in return. But his hand alone clearly wasn't getting the man anywhere fast. How else could he reciprocate?

There was one little trick he knew that the man might enjoy.

He cleared his throat. "If you'll let me," he said, hoping he sounded vastly bolder than he felt. "There is something I could do that I doubt you've had before." Would it be wise to use such on a hound? If what Tracker said was true about his immunity to magic, then he didn't need to worry.

Tracker said nothing, but one brow did twitch upwards in query.

Dylan raised his free hand between them. "This." He let a tiny flash of lightning weave between his thumb and forefinger.

The hound reached out and, before Dylan could move or warn him away, ran a finger through the bolt. The lightning parted as his digit brushed the line, forking around the finger to meet on the other side.

Dylan gasped, unable to pull his gaze away from the sight. Magic truly couldn't affect the hound.

When the display garnered only silence, his attention slowly drifted to the man's face. Tracker appeared fixated on little else except running his fingers through the lightning. Not once had Dylan ever witnessed such a pure expression of wonder. He couldn't bring himself to sully the moment with a single word.

That honey-coloured gaze flicked from the magic to Dylan. His head tilted, the innocent wonder vanishing like mist. The sudden cockiness that took its place almost escaped through a low chuckle as he ran the tip of his tongue over his teeth. "And what would you do with this little trick?"

Smirking, Dylan switched his focus of the spark, letting the energy surge through the hand currently wrapped around the man's member.

"I see," Tracker breathed, his voice thick. His gaze dropped to watch the lightning flare around him. "That is an interesting use of your magic."

A little thrill shivered up his spine. Maybe he could be a first in some way after all. "You can feel it?" Obviously not the full force. If Tracker had, he would've been screaming in agony rather than groaning. Dylan, having had a similar dose from Nestria, could barely stand a fraction of what he gave the hound. Or perhaps the man liked a little pain.

"I can. But not as you are likely thinking. The charge in the air? It—" His breath hitched for a few beats. His hips softly shifted, rocking into Dylan's hand. "It tingles. Like waking a dead arm, but good." His head lolled forward, enough for his forehead to rest on Dylan's shoulder. "Dare I even ask how you learnt you could do this?"

Dylan chuckled. He gently nuzzled along the man's neck before lightly playing with the dagger-shaped earring hanging from his earlobe. Elven ears were sensitive to the slightest of touches and, judging by the soft hitch in Tracker's breath, the man was not an exception. "A spellster never reveals his secrets," he whispered.

The hound let out a shuddering breath. When he spoke again, his voice had gained a gravelly note. "And this is a thing you do often to yourself?"

"No." He had considered it a few times, but hadn't dared to try lest he lost control and burnt himself. "Not that you're the first," he hastily added as Tracker's head and brows rose in surprise. "I've done it for others plenty of times." Mostly Nestria. "Just not on myself."

"Then allow me to show you."

Before Dylan could understand what the man meant, he found his back pressed hard into the bed. The hound certainly could move fast when he wanted to.

Tracker hovered above him, straddling his thighs. He'd slipped out of Dylan's grasp, leaving the lightning to crackle uninhibited against Dylan's palm. It didn't hurt. There was pressure, awareness, much like digging his own nails into his skin.

Wordlessly, the hound guided Dylan's hand, laying it flat on the far side of the man's length so that it was sandwiched between that and Tracker's body. Arcs of lightning flared along the bronze skin, seeking a way around.

Those honey-coloured eyes fluttered. Tracker bit his lip, a groan creaking out. His eyes closed for one brief moment before snapping open as his expression settled into one of determination. He pressed closer, his length brushing against Dylan's in a slow dance, both of them twitching ever so slightly whenever they made contact.

A soft whimper involuntarily tightened Dylan's throat. He'd already begun to soften when the man had started his pursuit, but the contact was steadily rectifying that. And, whilst he might've had his fingers around the man's shaft only moments ago, he hadn't expected how warm or silky the length would feel against his own. His hips jerked upwards each time the contact was lost, seeking to make each encounter last that little bit longer.

The heat of Tracker's bare skin against him blazed hotter than any fire. The faint hint of cinnamon from the man's soap intermingled with his natural scent. Heavy and intoxicating, it filled Dylan's nose.

Then, Tracker seemed to take pity on him. Those long fingers cupped Dylan's length, pressing them together. The pad of his thumb ran over the tips of their members, growing slicker the more he massaged.

Nestled in the palm of the hound's hand, Dylan was shielded from the lightning's full effect. A charge he'd only ever faintly registered on his forearm now thrummed around his most intimate of places. *Tingles*, Tracker had said. Dylan would've described it more as a harmless crackling, like the kind he used to experiment harnessing from rubbing blankets together.

Dylan's free hand slid up the man's arm to curl around the muscular shoulder. Bracing himself, he flexed his fingers, giving the lightning a little more room to buzz.

Groaning, Tracker thrust against him, each sweep sending maddening pulses of heat through Dylan's gut.

Faced with such an enthusiastic response, Dylan kept up the slow pulse of the lightning. He relished in the rich moan escaping the man's lips almost as much as the silken glide of Tracker's length. He increased the pace to the sound of the hound's appreciative whimper.

Tracker sagged slightly, his shoulders trembling as his thrusts gradually increased in speed. His forehead pressed to Dylan's shoulder. It put the full sweep of his ear within reach.

Dylan couldn't resist sliding his tongue along the upper slope to gently nibble the tip. The action was rewarded with another gasp and a second full-body shudder.

The man's moans grew louder. He pressed their hips closer together, trapping Dylan's hand between the hound's length and his abdomen. His thrusts grew more insistent, deepening each stroke.

With few places to go, the subtle spark Dylan had conjured flared and crackled, seeking to escape the hound's presence. A few tiny forks reached the bedding, forcing Dylan to abandon it before he lost control altogether and set the bed ablaze.

The lack of magic didn't seem to bother the hound. Tracker continued without a halt in his rhythm, clearly chasing his end. Each exhale and inhale turned short and heavy. Urgent with need.

Dylan watched, enrapt, in Tracker's every breath and increasingly erratic movement as his magicless-assisted strokes continued to drive the hound ever closer to completion.

A deep intake of air was all the warning he had of Tracker reaching the edge. He arched, thrusting Dylan deeper into the mattress. A hoarse yell vibrated through the man's throat.

Dylan hastened to clamp his free palm over the hound's mouth. Liquid, warm and thick, ran down the fingers of his other hand, dripping onto his stomach. He kept going, working Tracker dry.

Only once the hound had grown quiet did Dylan dare to remove his hand from the man's mouth. They both remained still atop the bed. Their bodies pressed closer with every breath, each gentle movement far more intimate than the very sexual act they'd just completed.

Then, Tracker let forth with one last lingering groan. "Well then," he said, sitting up until he was once more balanced on Dylan's lap. "That was *not* how I expected this night to go."

Dylan was definitely in agreement on that front.

Grinning, the hound brushed back the coils of hair that had escaped their bindings. The heat in his eyes returned as he ran an almost possessive eye over Dylan. "I guess you can no longer say you have not had sex with a man."

He frowned, unsure how the hound had reached that conclusion. "But we never— I mean, there was no..." He gestured vaguely.

The growing confusion on Tracker's face cleared in one blink. "Penetration?" He gave a breathy chuckle. "It is not required. Unless..." One brow arched. "That is what you desire, yes?" He ran the back of his forefinger up the underside of Dylan's length, eliciting a shuddering breath from Dylan's lips. He might've grown harder under Tracker's ministrations, but was nowhere near the edge. "I would not ask it of you during your first time. But I am willing to finish you off the same way as before."

He looked up at the hound, still slightly dazed. His chest rose and fell rapidly, aching with the need to inhale all the air in the world at once. *I can stop at any time.* Yet, he'd gone this far. He might as well continue. Who could stop him?

He grinned, hoping it looked far more confident than he felt. "Well, I haven't told you to stop."

The hound smirked and he could've sworn the man's touch was a little firmer, a little rougher. "No, that you have not. Was there something else you were after?"

"That depends entirely on what you've got on offer," he managed, his voice rasping.

Tracker chuckled. "*Anything* you desire."

Dylan tipped his head back. It wasn't his imagination. Those long fingers were doing all the right things, steadily turning the fire in his gut into an inferno. It moved his body, thrusting him hard and fast into the man's grip. If they kept this up, he wasn't going to last long enough to make a decision.

Anything? He stared at the ceiling as his mind sluggishly caught up with the man's words.

Grasping the hound's wrist, he halted the frantic pace he also desperately yearned to continue.

Relief, along with a slight twinge of disappointment, washed over Dylan when the hound withdrew his touch. That wasn't the reaction he'd wanted.

What did he want?

"I want..." *What?* "In," Dylan mumbled. "You." His cheeks burned as his ears caught up with the drivel coming out his mouth. He could do words. "I want to be inside you." If he was having sex with a man, he was going all the damn way.

CHAPTER 46

The request was met with silence and the briefest of twitches from the hound. Dylan winced. Had that been surprise? Reluctance? Maybe letting Dylan in him hadn't been what the man had meant. "Only if you don't mind, of course." The warmth flooding his face increased, but then everything felt hotter with the man near. Tracker put out far more heat than he expected. It burrowed through to his core.

Tracker bent over him, his movements fluid as though he'd no bones. Those honey-coloured eyes all but glowed with lust. "If I do not mind?" he echoed. "If you are trying to figure out if I have a preference, then it is true that I prefer to… take the lead as it were."

"That's a no, then?"

Laughing softly and shaking his head, Tracker pressed a forefinger to Dylan's lips. "*However*, my dear spellster," he purred. "I am no stranger to others having control and, seeing that this is your first night with a man, I am willing to play the submissive."

Play. As though it was a part, a role, that didn't reflect his true self. *For my sake*. Did people do that? He'd met a handful inside the tower who offered sex without some sort of recompense for the risk but few, outside pairings, would bow to the whims of another, even for a night. Most wanted something in return, yet Tracker made no requests of his own.

The memories of the tower had his thoughts refocusing on the room. Whilst in the warmth of Tracker's embrace, he had forgotten all about their surroundings, of the dark and the silence.

A jagged coldness settled into the pit of his stomach. What was he doing? "You don't have to if you'd prefer otherwise. I won't force you."

Humour gusted out the man's mouth, briefly bouncing him atop Dylan's lap. "I doubt you would ever be the type, even if you were physically able to overpower me, but the point is moot." He cupped Dylan's jaw, turning him back until only the hound's face filled his view. Backlit by the torchlight, the sight was haloed in a warm orange glow. "This is an experience I would be delighted to share with you, I promise."

Their lips met before Dylan could formulate a response. With their tongues entwined, Dylan's quickening breath puffed desperately through his nose. He gulped down air between kisses, inhaling the man's hot breath.

It set his head spinning.

Without words, they fumbled their way up the bed in a tangle of limbs, pressing against each other, thrusting and grinding, seeking whatever release could be found.

Tracker slipped his hand between them. Long, teasing fingers stroked Dylan's length, guiding it to the hound's desired destination.

Groaning, Dylan grasped the man's hips, holding Tracker back. He might not have done this before, but it felt like they'd missed a rather important step. "Track..."

The hound grunted, seeming to be aware of the same thing and rather less concerned about it. "It is fine."

Was it? Practically everything he had ever heard about pleasure between two men involved other things to make it easier. Dylan propped himself on his arms. "I don't want to hurt you." Unlike some of the people he'd been with, he derived no pleasure from harming his partners. And with Tracker, it wasn't as if magic could fix things later.

Tracker's mouth curved into a wide, and extremely toothy, grin. "He thinks he can hurt me. How sweet." He ran a finger along Dylan's jaw. "That is unlikely to happen, I assure you. In any case, I do not mind a little pain."

One of those types was he? Well, that made no difference. Dylan lifted a leg, tipping the man forward until their noses touched. "Has anyone told you that you're a rather depraved man?"

Somehow, the hound's grin widened further. "Why yes, I have heard that before. A great many times."

"So long as you know." He nuzzled Tracker's neck, his teeth grazing across the throat and heavy pulse found there until he sank them into the curve where the neck met shoulder. He was rewarded with a soft, drawn-out moan. Low and guttural, the sound buzzed through to his core.

His hands slid up Tracker's thighs to clench the man's firm backside. With some subtle guidance, Dylan eased himself in. Slowly, desperate to slam to the hilt in one blow. He closed his eyes as, inch by torturous inch, he was devoured.

When he almost couldn't go any further, Tracker chuckled. "Do you take everyone like they are some delicate flower?" he breathed into Dylan's ear. "I will not break if you are a little rough."

Dylan opened his eyes to find that honey-coloured gaze focused on his face, gauging his reaction. His lips twisted, a dozen wicked thoughts darting through his mind.

His final thrust wasn't so gentle.

A soft grunt escaped the man's throat and his eyelids fluttered briefly, but no protests followed.

Dylan grasped Tracker's waist, holding them still as his mind tried to catch up with the rest of him. He was inside the man. Biting his lip, he gave his hips an experimental wriggle to the sound of Tracker's hushed moan. There was some truth to what he'd heard around the tower, it didn't feel all that different.

He withdrew a little ways before driving in again. Over and over, he slammed them together with short, hard strokes. It didn't take long for Tracker to match his pace, pushing down as he thrust up. Still, it wasn't enough. He needed…

More.

Without warning, he flipped them. Tracker grunted as his back hit the mattress. Dylan wordlessly dragged the hound to the edge of the bed by the legs, leaving the man sprawled before him. There, he found the purchase he wanted.

Keeping one of the hound's legs hooked over his arm, Dylan trailed a trembling hand down the smooth chest, marking how Tracker's body flexed, rising off the bed to meet his touch. His fingertips danced down the man's abdomen, toying with the sparse hair to be found there.

Tracker propped himself on his elbows, his gaze focused on their waists. He sucked on his bottom lip, the occasional soft groan slipping out as Dylan kept the pace slow and deep.

At last, Dylan wrapped his fingers around the man's length and squeezed, eliciting a moan from the hound. With his grip firm, he pumped his hand up and down the twitching flesh, chuckling at the rich moan it eked from the man.

In his other hand, he coaxed a spark of lightning to life, holding it just far enough away from the hound to get Tracker's attention. Even though he claimed to enjoy the previous instance, Dylan didn't want to startle the man. "May I?"

Those honey-coloured eyes, the pupils blown wide with raw need, stared at the flickering light like a mouser tracking its prey. His tongue snaked out and he bit his bottom lip, but gave no indication either way.

Then, just as Dylan considered letting the spark die, Tracker nodded.

He switched the flow to the other hand and the flesh in his grip twitched. Tracker's head fell back, a deep groan escaping his lips. Tendrils of lightning buzzed across Dylan's lower torso, raising the hairs along his stomach. Although he suspected it was more than the effects of his own magic that made his body tingle this time.

Their skin quickly grew slick with sweat, forcing him to abandon the lightning in favour of more mundane methods. Tracker, seemingly unaware of the change, continued to thrust into the hand that worked him. Dylan leant forward, bracing himself with his free hand, the leg that'd been hooked around his arm having long since fallen to mirror its twin. He matched the pace the hound had set, driving himself deep with every jerk.

Tracker stiffened, his whole body arching beneath Dylan in one glorious shout. Once again, the elf emptied into Dylan's hand.

Dylan kept going, massaging every last drop from the man, his hips never losing momentum. Tipping his head, he closed his eyes and let himself become lost to the slick sound of their movements and the frenzied, and loud, puff of Tracker's breathing.

The world shrunk to the small, pulsating knot in his gut. He was close to the edge, felt it hovering just beyond his reach.

The world exploded.

He re-entered reality, screaming all the way. He grasped the hound's waist, holding Tracker fast as each jerking movement had him spilling into the man.

Dylan collapsed onto the bedding next to the hound, gasping and thoroughly spent. *Well... that most definitely happened.* Even as he had encouraged Tracker, there'd been the idle thought that some piece of him *would* stop things from going this far.

He silently chuckled to himself. How wrong he was there.

Beside him, Tracker gave a low whistle. "Seeing how you have not attempted to scurry off, muttering how we should not have done this, shall I assume that tonight has met with your approval?"

Wrong? It'd felt no different than it had with past partners. "So far." Dylan replied unthinkingly, groaning to himself as he became conscious of his words. By the gods, he sounded like some sex-crazed monster. If Tracker didn't laugh in his face, it would be a miracle.

The man *did* laugh. A rich, and slightly intrigued, sound. He shuffled about the mattress until he once again lay lengthwise along it. One brow twitched up. "Are you always this insatiable?"

Dylan grunted, the warmth in his cheeks a mixture of residual pleasure and embarrassment. He joined the man in lying properly on the bed, propping himself up on one arm. "Can I ask you about something?"

Tracker's hand lifted from the bed to play with the mess that was Dylan's hair, which had crept over his shoulders at some point. "Certainly."

"Your dagger, the purple one, how'd you get it?" It was an

alchemist's dagger, he was certain of it. They were unique, an alchemist's masterpiece, crafted to prove they could safely work *infitialis* and never easily relinquished.

The man's hand fell. "Not quite the question I was expecting." He rolled his head to one side, sighing into the darkness. "And I think you already know the answer."

His assumption had been right after all. "You killed an alchemist." Hot anger flared in his chest. When an alchemist died in the tower, their daggers were destroyed. A sign of respect. He thought that was true of those slain beyond the tower walls. Clearly not. "Why?"

"You must understand that a hound's duty is to send spellsters to the tower. Death is only a recourse when all else fails."

"And yet you chose death." There was no need to take an alchemist's life. As far as dangerous spellsters went, they were barely capable of being a threat. People like Sulin could only work one or two simple spells beyond their specialised magic. A few alchemists had tried leaving the tower, to return to their old lives, he didn't know of any who actually succeeded.

Tracker sighed again. "Simply put, he went to stab me and I retaliated." He shrugged. "Unlike him, I did not miss. I had no idea he was even armed until he attacked me, only knew he was a runaway."

A piece of Dylan's anger drained away at the admittance. He could hardly fault the hound for defending himself. "You were fortunate that he did." He'd handled one such dagger in his lifetime, back when Sulin mastered the art of crafting the *infitialis* metal. They were as deadly as they were beautiful. Nothing healed a wound made by their edge. The smallest cut was all it took to bleed a man to death.

"Yes," Tracker grunted. "Well, I learnt not long after that he had a wife and two small children. Now that I think about it, he likely escaped through that secret entrance."

The alchemist had been an older man, then. Possibly came into his magic later in life. Probably never gave much thought to what small miracles happened in the years before a hound came across him and dragged him to the tower. That was how Sulin had described his life in Stonebay; tiny coincidences building up until the right people took note.

But none of that answered the one question Dylan wanted to know. "Why keep the dagger?" Obviously, the alchemist had stayed long enough to craft the weapon, maybe even used it during his escape.

"In truth, I thought it was pretty. Plus, it is rare to see a spellster use a blade, your kind is fond of using magic as a primary defence."

The way he spoke...

Everyone in the tower knew they killed runaways and escorted those who were born outside the tower complex. Tracker would've been no different. "Killed many of *my* kind, then, have you?"

Tracker rolled to one side, soft comprehension moulding his brow. "If this is upsetting you, we do not have to speak of it any further."

Fresh heat bloomed across Dylan's face, fuelled entirely by anger. He didn't need shielding from such realities. "No, you will answer me."

"A few, yes. But do not envision them as innocent beings, many could lay claim to a number of deaths themselves, as well as other such atrocities. The rest I sent to the tower."

"Of course," he murmured. *Sent here.* A place that should've been safe, where they could train to control their magic, only to die because of it.

Tracker laid a hand on Dylan's chest. "You have lived here your whole life, yes? Hemmed in by walls? Told you are safe as long as you remain? Well, many of those who run are considered dangerous."

"*I* am dangerous."

A grim expression flattened his lips as he nodded. "That you are," he murmured. "I saw what you did to the Udynean who attacked you. You are an utter terror to behold to any who threaten you and yours. But to innocents?" He shook his head. "Even with an *infitialis* dagger held to your throat, you tried using words before magic. Yet, had I not chosen to believe you and your companions, I have no doubt that one of us would not be here now."

Dylan frowned. Considering the man's skills and the presence of the alchemist's dagger, he very much doubted that person would've been him. "When we met, you said you'd been searching for me." Trailing them for days.

"I was, yes." The hand on his chest slowly trailed down, tickling, and Dylan struggled to focus on the man's words. "But only in the end was for *you*. Before then..." Tracker sat up, his back slightly more rigid than it should've been. His hand crept back up Dylan's chest, sliding into the curls of Dylan's chest hair, the press of his fingers a little firmer.

Dylan bit his lip at the touch, a small whimper dying in his throat.

The hound continued his gentle assault on Dylan's senses, seemingly unaware as to how his actions were affecting Dylan. "I arrived at Toptower because young women were disappearing. The townsfolk blamed spellsters, so they summoned a King's Hound."

"Some women go missing and they blame a spellster? Is it so common for them to kidnap people?"

"Common? No. Memorable, perhaps. The desperate do many things. Sometimes, even reaching for certain sticky myths."

He wrinkled his nose. "You mean sacrifices." His guardian had taught him of such folly. Before the creation of the tower, spellsters used to do such rites. With animals. "They don't work."

"I somehow doubt that is much comfort to those who are used for it."

No, probably not. "So who was responsible for the kidnapping?"

"It turned out to be the work of a brothel mistress. That was some weeks before I encountered you. I should not have been near Toptower by the time the army fell. Once it is determined that a spellster cannot possibly be involved, we are meant to give all related information to the local authority and be on our way."

"But that's so... cold."

Tracker shrugged. "Those are our orders. To disobey them would be..." The hand slid off Dylan's chest to pluck at the bedding. "...unwise."

Dylan propped himself up on his elbows, trying to decipher the man's expression with it being in shadows. Surely Tracker didn't expect him to believe he would be punished for bringing a criminal to justice. "Why?"

The man's nose wrinkled, further warping the unflattering vexed expression already plastered across his face. "Our mistress prides conformity. *Bad dogs must be put down*, as she would say. She believes a disobedient hound is just as dangerous as an unleashed spellster."

Dylan couldn't see how. They hadn't the power to decimate an entire village in a fit of rage. *Mistress*? He thought the hounds belonged to the king. "So, if a spellster *had* been responsible, would you have killed them?"

"That would depend. If the women were dead, then certainly. If a crime has been committed, then justice must be served. If not... then things would have gotten a little more complicated."

"Would you have killed me, if you didn't believe me?"

Tracker shook his head. "Maybe if you had been a spy. When I felt you enter the city, saw you slinking about at night, I thought—"

"That I was Udynean."

He nodded. "Once I found that not to be so, bringing you back here was always my preferred solution. Besides..." His gaze lifted. The hot gleam in his eyes had returned and, surprisingly enough, it fanned the glowing ember of need in Dylan's gut. "I can think of far better things to do with you than take your life."

"I'm sure you can."

A soft, slightly trembling, chuckle shook the man's shoulders. "Well, you have given no order to stop, so I assumed..." He shrugged. "If our talk has not soured you to the notion of lying with a hound, I am willing to let you go again."

"I—" He rubbed at the back of his neck, his face heating like some maiden from those accursed books Sulin used to read aloud as a joke. But then, didn't he have a fair bit in common with them right now? "I do," he admitted. He held Tracker in place as the man tried to shuffle closer. "*But* I want you to... take me."

Tracker jerked back, his lips curving in the smallest of smiles. "Now that is one proposal I was not quite expecting to hear tonight. Or at all, really." He propped his head on the heel of his hand. "I hope you do not think we must do such a thing right away. It is a great many weeks to Wintervale, there will be other times and I am more than happy to pleasure you in another way now should you truly desire more."

Dylan wasn't wholly certain about ever repeating tonight's act. He might've lost his nerve—or regained full control over his senses, whichever one it was that allowed him to be this reckless—before this happened again. Besides, all this talk of spellsters and death had brought back the very memories he wanted to bury. "I want this."

The hound crept along the bed, each movement lithe and graceful. *And deadly*. The once indolent mouser now intent on its prey. He hovered over Dylan, placing his arms on either side of Dylan's shoulders, holding him in place without touching him.

The sight had Dylan's heart pounding all the harder.

"And if I said it will be uncomfortable?" Tracker purred. "Maybe even a little painful?"

Dylan grinned manically, recalling the man's earlier words. "I'd say, I don't mind a little pain." He probably even deserved it for not reaching the tower in time, for not being here, for not having the strength to stop people from dying. Or the ability to bring them back.

It wouldn't be enough, but he was sure that the hound would baulk if asked to actually hurt him until he could think of nothing beyond the pain.

Tracker sat back. His hand cupped one side of Dylan's face, his thumb running along Dylan's cheek, smearing tears he hadn't realised he was crying. "Dylan," he whispered. "We need not go any further."

"I want you to." Dylan groped along the bedding, seeking the man's body. "Make me forget anything else in the world exists." His fingers brushed a well-toned leg, swept up it to the hip. "Just *this*." He grabbed hold of the man's member, stroked and felt it twitch in his grip.

Shock took Tracker's face. It was small, the slight hitch in his breath, the subtle widening of those honey-coloured eyes. His gaze dropped to his lap. "You are far bolder than I expected."

"And you're softer than I thought you'd be."

The hound's gaze snapped back up. "*Soft?*" The trill of an objection vibrated through the word.

"*Gentle,*" Dylan amended.

Tracker stared at him for a long time, utterly speechless, before a small smile took his lips. "If you insist, then one moment." The mattress bounced slightly as the man clambered off the bed and made his way across the room.

CHAPTER 47

Dylan lay still, not certain he could move if he tried. Was he really going to go through with this? *Yes? No? Maybe?* The thought of *actually* doing this thrummed through his body at both a nerve-racking and exhilarating pace. *Definitely maybe.* He stared at the rafters, trying very hard to rein in everything he felt before his chest exploded. *Yes.* He could scarcely believe this was happening, but he had chosen this and...

It *was* going to happen.

He caught the hushed pad of bare feet upon the stone and the rustle of cloth. On the edge of his vision, he spied Tracker rifling through something on the floor. The man's own clothing? What did he need amongst that?

Just as he shifted to see what the hound was up to, Tracker returned clutching a small vial filled with the amber-coloured liquid he'd seen the man use on his many weapons. "This will be easier if you roll over."

Dylan obeyed, rolling onto his stomach. The straw within the mattress rustled as Tracker settled behind him. Dylan moved further, barely registering he followed another's subtle, unspoken directions. Slender fingers guided his legs, manoeuvring him into place until he was on his knees in the middle of the bed.

Tracker's hands, the palms oddly cool and slightly damp, caressed the small of Dylan's back. His breath hitched as the man massaged the muscles up either side of his spine before gliding downwards in a similar motion.

"Relax," Tracker purred. "We will go slowly. Just... try not to be so tense or it *will* hurt."

Tense? He was *beyond* tense. Already, his heart thumped so hard that he wouldn't be surprised if it burst through his chest. Each pulse thudded in his temple like a dwarven war drum.

The squeak of a cork against glass seemed awfully loud in the silence. Cool liquid dribbled along his skin. He took a deep breath, his limbs trembling. Every muscle in his body tightened as uncertainty took hold along with the man's hands upon his backside.

Maybe this wasn't such a good idea...

Tracker's fingers, now slick with oil, brushed his buttocks. Slowly, they slid between his cheeks, seeming to be testing his limits. He squeezed his eyes shut. A fingertip pressed harder against him. That was actually familiar. Although, for the life of him, he couldn't recall where from.

Dylan leant into the touch, encouraging the man further, a soundless complaint droning through his chest when Tracker opted instead to run lazy circles around the area. Teasing him further.

Desire, savage and raw, buzzed through his skin. He kept his eyes closed, trying with all his might to maintain some control. Despite himself, a whimper constricted his throat. Never had he wanted anything as badly as he craved this.

The very tip of Tracker's finger slipped in.

He grasped the bedding and buried his face in the sheets, waiting for the pain. None came. Quite the opposite, in fact. He groaned against the blankets. Why hadn't anyone told him this simple thing felt good?

"Dylan?"

The call pulled him back into himself. He lifted his head, sharply realising that Tracker had stopped.

"Are you all right?"

"*Yes!*" The admittance burst forth far louder than he had intended. Warmth flooded his cheeks. "I'm fine," he heard himself babbling uncontrollably. The heat finished engulfing his face and began making its way down his neck. "Really. Just *please*, keep going." Gasping and eager for more, he rocked against the man's hand, letting the finger slide deeper.

Softly chuckling, Tracker gave a few cautious strokes, still testing Dylan's limit, before a second finger joined the other in pumping in and out of him. Slow at first, then harder and faster, each inward thrust of his long fingers hitting just the right spot.

Dylan clutched the sheets, his breath escaping in pants and moans. The fire in his gut burned hotter. Its cry for more never quite satisfied. This feeling... it...

It was torture, the sweet, unforgiving kind that threatened and promised to go on forever.

After what seemed like an age, Tracker's fingers slowly withdrew. A hand slid up Dylan's back. He caught the murmur of words, too quiet to make out yet oddly reassuring. The mattress moved beneath them. There was another pop of the cork.

Dylan shifted his weight from knee to knee. Restless. Unashamedly needy.

Tracker's hands fell upon Dylan's hip, stilling him. "Ready?" The word came out thick and heavy, full of desire. He was shaking. Or Dylan was. Perhaps both of them were.

He grunted his assent, no longer certain whether he was capable of speaking, much less the words that would give him it. He wasn't entirely sure what words were.

There was pressure. More than before. He held his breath, bracing himself, and waited.

All at once, the press of the hound faded away. The mattress shifted and Dylan slowly came to the realisation that Tracker had stopped.

Soft laughter came from somewhere over his back. "I cannot believe I almost forgot you have never done this. For gods' sake, my dear man, breathe."

The air left his lungs in a rush. He drew another breath, small and shallow. Then another. Little tremors ran across his back. He willed them to still to no avail. He had asked for this. The knot in his stomach shouldn't be there.

Tracker bent over him. The man's length, slick and twitching, slid to nestle between his buttocks. "Dylan," he purred, sending a fresh shiver down Dylan's back. "Try to calm down. I will not go any further unless you truly want it, I swear." His hands wandered up Dylan's side. "If you need me to, I can make you relax. Although, I would much prefer you did it yourself. Unless..."

Dylan inhaled deeply, his head spinning from the sudden influx. "Unless what?" he whispered.

"You wish to stop here." Those long fingers brushed over Dylan's buttocks, grasping them, moulding them. He rubbed himself along the crease in a slow, rocking motion. "There are other ways I can pleasure you, it does not have to be this. Not now. Or ever, if that is your wish."

Dylan shook his head. Stopping wasn't what he wanted.

He tried to do as the man instructed. He gulped down a great mouthful of air, letting it out in one long and slow exhale. Over and over, he drew in another lungful, held it for the count of four and breathed out.

At last, he was finally able to relax. "Do it."

Tracker repositioned himself. The pressure increased, greater than previously. Subtle pain and pleasure wove themselves into one glorious, tangled bundle.

Dylan's mouth dropped open, a strangled gasp passing his lips. His jaw moved silently, the cry that roared through his lungs dying as it reached his throat. Just when he thought this wasn't going to work, when the call to stop almost touched his tongue, he felt the hound slip into him.

On reflex, every muscle in his body stiffened. *By the gods*. Dylan knelt there, his legs shaking. It felt...

Well, that was a bit of a muddle. Different, certainly. A little uncomfortable, but more stretched than painful, like a limb that'd been overworked the previous day. Already, the initial ache was beginning to fade. Overall it wasn't *bad*, just... odd.

He swallowed dryly, straining to hear every sound escaping the hound.

"Try not to move." Tracker's voice was strained, tight. His trembling fingers shifted from Dylan's hips. "Give yourself some time to adjust." Those sure hands caressed Dylan's lower back and the tops of his thighs. One slipped beneath them to stroke Dylan's still hard length.

He remained still, unsure if his immobility was due to Tracker's words or some unheard desire to stop. He resumed the slow breathing, trying to relax and, eventually, the last of his tensed muscles turned pliant under the hound's ministrations.

"There we go." Tracker's hands resumed grasping his hips. "Would you like the rest of it now?"

He dared to glance over his shoulder. His legs almost gave at the sight of Tracker kneeling behind him, the backlit head tipped to one side in question. The torchlight illuminated the points of the man's ears, turning them ruddy.

"You mean it's not all in?" Already, Dylan felt like he was going to burst. Surely the hound jested.

Tracker shrugged. He held up a thumb and forefinger, squeezing them together until they were roughly an inch apart. "You are new at this, I thought you would prefer slow. I can stop this deep if you wish, but I have yet to reach the good part."

Now his body had become accustomed to the hound's presence, there was a certain gentle comfort that fluttered in his gut at every breath. Not exactly mind-blowing, but... nice. How could this not be the good bit? "There's more?"

Tracker gave a small, gasping laugh. "There is indeed, although it would be easier to show you." His grip on Dylan's hips tightened. "I promise, I will be gentle."

"All right," he mumbled. "Show me."

The pressure increased. Not as sharp as the initial push. There didn't seem to be much hindrance as there'd been at the beginning, the hound had either oiled himself to dripping or done a fine job preparing him.

Nevertheless, Tracker was true to his word. It was slow going, he paused with each breath, taking his time to work himself deeper.

Until he finally stopped.

As Dylan readjusted to the incredibly full sensation of having the man in him, he became aware that the cessation of forward movement was only because Tracker couldn't go any further.

The warming brush of lips danced up his spine, lingering on each vertebra. "Are we still all right?"

Dylan nodded and hummed. 'All right' didn't quite define what he was feeling, but it would do until his mind could remember enough words. If this wasn't the part the hound meant, then he was almost hesitant to discover what was.

"Would you like me to continue?" His hips rocked against Dylan. Shallow. Tentative.

Glittering spots danced across Dylan's vision. A moan escaped his lips as heat flooded his body. Not quite sure his tongue could be entrusted to utter a coherent word, he grunted another affirmation and nodded violently.

Tracker drew back until he was all but free, pulling a deep groan from Dylan's throat. The hound drove in again in one smooth movement and, despite himself, a dreadfully high-pitched gasp escaped Dylan's lips. No, not a gasp. A squeak. He had *squeaked*.

Their bodies shook with Tracker's rich laughter. "Shall we try for a manlier sound?"

He glared over his shoulder at the man, but it only made Tracker laugh harder. Fresh heat surged across his face, giving him the strength to speak. "You ought to talk what with the way you've yelled." The cooling thread of healing tugged at his power, soothing him as much as the elf's hands travelling up and down his back.

"I feel... You are doing... something." Concern, poorly veiled by amusement, slipped out as he spoke. "Magic?"

Dylan's face grew hotter still. He hadn't thought the hound would notice this. "It feels a little... strange," he mumbled, hoping that was explanation enough. He lingered just slightly on the edge of unpleasant, the hound's re-entry a little rougher than the first. Not pain, at least not now. Still, his innate ability continued to search for the cause of the initial burn.

"Strange?" Tracker echoed, outright humour tinting the word. "Well, that is one way to put it. Not painful, though?" All traces of mirth faded from his voice at the question.

Dylan shook his head. Any lingering tenderness, no matter how small, had been banished by his magic almost as soon as it appeared. He was very much aware that Tracker was in him, but that was it.

"Good." Those soothing fingers were back, running up his spine, their tips gently raking over his shoulder blades. "The *strangeness* does not tend to last long, but if it is too much for you..."

"No." If he gave the order to stop before they took this to its ultimate conclusion, he'd be kicking himself in the morning. "I can handle it. Continue."

Tracker resumed grasping his hips. "As you like." The hound gave a few shallow thrusts, as if he wasn't quite certain whether to believe Dylan.

When Dylan didn't object, the man began moving in earnest, driving in and out. The thrusts were slow at first and shallow before becoming longer and deeper, the pace gradually increasing as Tracker seemed to settle into a rhythm that suited both of them.

Dylan buried his face into the bedding, his teeth clenched as he struggled to contain the sounds that fought for release. *This* was what the man had meant earlier. The flushes of heat, the molten fire where their skin touched, the spikes of pure pleasure that set his head to spinning, each one building on the next...

Over his muffled moans, he caught other noises. The slap of their bodies meeting, the ragged huff of Tracker's breath, their steadily combining moans and grunts... All of it filled his ears, feeding his hunger. Desire for more burned through his core, overpowering any other thought.

Dylan kept his face in the blankets, biting the rough weave and panting through his nose. His whole body pulsed to the beat of his frantic heart. White rimmed his vision. He was so close to the edge that it hurt. And it still wasn't enough to tip him over.

He leant on one arm and pushed against Tracker, helping to maintain the pace the elf had set. With the other hand, he searched to relieve the building pressure.

Dylan barely felt his fingertip upon himself when the man swatted his hand away and took up his twitching length. A whimper tightened his throat. The touch he had craved so much bordered on painful.

"Track..." he gasped, the word cracking as it escaped his lips.

The hound's fingers squeezed in response and, for a heartbeat or two, blackness filled his vision. He faltered, left temporarily dazed and panting. Blindly, Dylan thrust into the hand as the elf worked him with a skill that made his previous efforts seem pathetic.

Tracker hooked his free hand around a hip. The man's fingers dug into Dylan's flesh, holding him fast. He felt the hound shift beneath him, repositioning. Heat from the elf's chest burrowed into Dylan's back like magma, eating its way to his core.

Before Dylan could object, the hound set a faster pace. Tracker's hoarse pants filled the room, each movement accompanied by a grunt. Dylan's or the hound's, he wasn't certain anymore.

Faced with such an onslaught, Dylan could barely keep himself in place. Each thrust had them inching up the bed. He stretched out his arms, uncaring that the act left him fully at the man's mercy, and searched for something to anchor them.

His palms slapped the headboard, eliciting a hiss. It was far closer than he had anticipated. The wood creaked alarmingly as he pressed against the panel, but keeping his arms braced stopped them from moving any further. His legs shook, threatening to dump him on his stomach. If he wasn't already half straddling the elf, they very well might have.

Still, Tracker persisted. *By the gods, what does the king feed his hounds?* The man had to be as close as he was and had just as clearly been holding back earlier on.

Then, as this whole act started to grow uncomfortable, Tracker went rigid, arriving with a shout. He leant against Dylan's back, panting. Only his hand continued to move.

He needn't have bothered. Dylan's body was already buzzing at the sound of the elf's completion, the molten fire burning in his gut digging deeper. He teetered on that glittering edge. All he needed was a... little... bit... mor—

White flashed across his vision. Tracker's name left his lips in a cry, repeated over and over amongst a stream of expletives and blasphemies, control lost as he rode out the orgasm.

Eventually, reality swung back around and he caught the edge of Tracker's chuckle.

The man's weight shifted, lifting, clearly having come down from the peak of his own height. "Did I not say I would have you screaming my name?" he mumbled, collapsing on the bedding, his chest still heaving.

Dylan rolled onto his side. The dregs of euphoria left him drunk and happily delirious. It tugged at the corners of his mouth, drawing his lips into a grin. *I could get used to this.* He brushed the hair from his face and snickered. That was one thought he didn't think he would ever have.

They lay there, the hound's head resting on Dylan's outstretched arm, both silent as they slowly regained their breaths. Dylan ran a finger over the man's skin, idly tracing the snake tattoo encompassing Tracker's shoulder and running part way down the man's upper arm.

Humming softly, Tracker shuffled closer, his leg hooking around one of Dylan's, until their bodies were flush. He nuzzled into Dylan's shoulder, his warm breath gently skittering across Dylan's neck.

A small smile curved Dylan's lips. He enjoyed snuggling after sex, and would whenever he had the chance. Yet, this felt different. Almost... *Peaceful.* His eyes slid shut. Lulled by the warmth emanating from the hound, he slowly began to nod off.

With his mind no longer addled by pleasure, his thoughts sleepily turned to those he had lost. Images floated before his eyes. His friends, his guardian… *Ness.*

Guilt flooded his veins, jolting him awake. He stared at the ceiling, tears blurring his vision of the wooden beams. Throughout all of their fooling around, he'd barely given a thought towards the people who had died here.

His past lay in tatters, the bird-pecked bones of it all around him. And what did he do with that knowledge? *The Seven Sisters are going to put me in limbo for this.* Eternally floating along the river without judgement was all he could hope for now. Endless stretches of darkness all because instead of honouring the dead by respecting the place they had fallen…

He rutted in its very ashes.

What's wrong with me? Sniffing back his tears, Dylan cleared his throat in some attempt to banish the sobs welling in his chest.

And what of Authril? She claimed she'd no interest in him beyond the physical, yet had clearly been upset over the hound kissing him. He'd given no thought to her at all. Was he really so eager to offer up himself that he couldn't remain with one person for any longer than a few weeks?

I am. No point trying to sugar-coat it.

He was too used to the way things were in the tower. Everyone here understood that sex was a game, that it couldn't be permanent without heartache. But he had been leashed, would be again once they reached Wintervale. He couldn't have been a part of the tower again, even if the tower still stood.

At his side, the hound stirred. "Dylan?" The word came softly, almost tender. "Are you all right?" Tracker propped himself up, the edges of concern moulding his face. He brushed the pad of his thumb across Dylan's cheek. "Does it still hurt? It is perfectly normal to be a little uncomfortable for the first time, but if you are in pain—"

"No," he mumbled, shaking his head in the off chance the man hadn't heard. "It's not that."

Tracker gave an oddly relieved little sigh. "What then?"

"It's not exactly pillow talk." And what comfort could the hound possibly offer except for more sex?

A soft chuckle, absent of mirth, left the man's lips. "I am sure I can cope with a serious topic."

"I—" His chin wobbled as he went to speak. He bit his lip and remained silent. If he uttered a single word now, he was likely to wind up bawling like a newborn.

"Oh." Long fingers caressed Dylan's temple, brushing back the hair that had fallen across his face. "I was beginning to wonder how long it would take for your grief to overwhelm you again. It seems I am too perfect a distraction from your thoughts. Come here." The hound wrapped his arms around Dylan, pulling them close.

He pushed the man back. Or, at least, he tried to. "I can't. Not here. I'll lose control and hurt—"

"Hush," Tracker breathed. "There is only us here and your magic cannot hurt me."

His vision blurred. "B-but the building," he managed, his wobbling chin almost causing him to bite his tongue. He was sure it would take a concentrated blast to blow a hole in them, but he was still capable of upsetting the structural integrity.

"Do not concern yourself with that. These stones look to be the kind that can absorb a hefty amount of magic. If a little ruin can handle your unleashing, I am certain this room will withstand your power." Tracker's arms tightened, tucking Dylan's head beneath his chin. "So there is no reason to fight it," he murmured as his cheek pressed against Dylan's crown. "To grieve is not a weakness, nor can it be abolished with a single bout of wailing."

"I don't need to mourn." Crying wouldn't bring anyone back. What he needed was a target.

"My foolish man. Of course you do."

Dylan tried to protest further, that he wasn't some babe in need of coddling. But having the soothing press of another being against him was the final chink in the barrier he'd been so desperately trying to keep everything bottled into.

Tears poured down his cheeks as Tracker tucked his head against him. Dylan buried his face into the elf's warm chest and sobbed.

The air thrummed and crackled. Wisps of colour danced on the edge of his vision. Purples and blues. Reds and yellows. The air whipped up into a mini whirlwind, lashing at him. The bed frame groaned, threatening to splinter beneath them.

Still, Tracker held him tight. If he noticed anything untoward, he said nothing.

Dylan didn't know how long he cried. He lost himself in his grief, aware only of the hound's warmth, of his gentle touches—the soft circles on his back, the caresses down his hair, the minute rocking—and the barely audible whispers of assurance.

By the time he'd no tears left to cry, the hound's skin was saturated.

Dylan tried to shrink out of Tracker's arms, surprised when the man's grip held fast. "I'm sorry," he croaked. His throat felt far too tight. He coughed, hoping to clear it, to no avail. "I didn't mean to blubber all over you."

Tracker made no move to disentangle them. The hound continued to stroke Dylan's hair and the wet press of lips brushed his crown. "My dear spellster," he breathed. "There is no need to apologise. Besides, this chest has seen many fluids over the years. What is one more?" His long fingers caressed Dylan's jaw, tilting it. "But I swear to you, I will find the one responsible for what happened here and I will make them pay."

Dylan wiped his face dry on the back of his hand. "You don't have to do that." He knew empty promises when he heard them.

"On the contrary, this is something that cannot go unpunished. The king will have questions as to how this came to be. I do not believe for a moment that they did this to themselves, so that leaves only outside forces."

"Like the one your prostitute friend mentioned."

"Yes. Where did they go? A force large enough to do this cannot just up and vanish. There has to be a trace, somewhere. I intend to find it and see that they are dealt with." The man slowly untangled himself from Dylan's limbs and slid to the side of the bed. "But for now…"

Dylan watched in silence as the hound slipped off the bed, too cowardly to speak further. The removal of the hound's warm presence left him far colder than he should've been.

Rather than leave, Tracker carefully removed the soiled blanket bunched beneath Dylan, using bits of it to clean the night's exertion from their skin.

Dylan froze. Usually, this part of sex was something he did to himself, in private. Warmth washed over his face. He turned his head, heeding the strange thought that he could somehow regain control over his blushing if he didn't look at the hound. It certainly didn't help that Tracker continued in silence.

Done at last, the man sought out another bed, stripping the frame of its bedding before returning to dump his pilfered hoard on top of Dylan.

Tracker clambered beneath the blankets, drawing Dylan back into his arms without protest and pressing Dylan's head against his hairless chest. The elf's heartbeat hammered in Dylan's ears, strong and so very real. "Try and get some rest. Authril is likely to push for our departure as soon as the sun has risen."

Quite likely. Fresh guilt bubbled to the surface at the woman's name, clashing with his newer feelings and making a sour mixture in his empty stomach. *I'm a monster.* A damned, sex-crazed beast. Fresh tears threatened to spill down his cheeks. He hastily sniffed them back.

Over the thump of the man's heart, he caught the gentle buzz of the hound humming. The tune seemed familiar. An old lullaby, he was certain of it. Was the man actually trying to sing him to sleep?

He closed his eyes. Hemmed in by warmth and the song, sleep should've been an easy goal. He'd attained it earlier, before remembering what waited outside this room. The death. The loss. How he could've been here to help if he hadn't been so selfish.

Eventually, the humming petered out.

He lifted his head, his gaze sliding to the elf. Judging by the low breathing, Tracker was asleep. Dylan stretched out a hand, seeking to wake the man, wanting to feel the reassuring press of his arms, to hear the strong thud of his heart. To taste the hot brush of his breath.

His fingers halted a hairsbreadth from that tattooed shoulder.

What was he doing? Was he really seeking more intimacy with the hound? *I am.* The way the man touched him, how he coaxed the fire in his gut to blazing at the simplest of movements, left very little room for other thoughts. Under the hound's ministrations, he had forgotten about everything. And, if he asked, Tracker might do it again.

No. Although it might've been fun whilst in the middle of it, there was nothing different about it from any other time he'd had sex. *Well,* he conceded, *a little different.* Still, it wouldn't make him forget forever, nor would it change what'd happened here. He most definitely shouldn't be getting hung up on it.

And yet, what he had felt in the space with the man on his lap as they kissed, the warm wanting welling in his chest right now...

Stop. He was confusing the residue of pleasure and the weakness of wanting to be comforted with deeper feelings. He had to be. The hound had no interest in him beyond the physical. He couldn't have. Spellsters were weapons. No one had such feelings for a weapon.

And yet...

Dylan rolled onto his back. Tracker was just someone to have a quick tumble with. It wouldn't even have gone this far if the tower hadn't been struck down. He should've been leashed by now. All set to travel to Wintervale without his magic to rely on. Instead, he spent half the night fooling around.

And he wasn't even sure if that point was a high or a low.

Fun. That's all he had ever wanted. Never had he needed a lover who was there for him, who cared about more than just pleasure, who he could rely on for support and comfort, in whatever form it took, and the hound—

Dylan rolled his head to one side and stared at the man. Tracker slept on, seemingly oblivious for the moment. But he hadn't been before. Not since they'd arrived here.

It had always been the hound who checked on him. The women

may have expressed concern, but Tracker?

Looking back over the day, the man always seemed to be there, keeping him company, casually veering him away from certain sections of the tower and, now he thought about it with a clinical mind, obviously judging if he was coping. Sex had been a distraction, he knew that, but he hadn't expected to be... comforted whilst he sobbed into the man's chest.

Could it be that the man actually cared about his wellbeing beyond what was necessary to do his job?

Dylan shuffled onto his side, seriously considering wriggling across the small space between them to snuggle against the elf's warm body. Something kept his limbs from obeying. Cowardice. The hound lay so close and he couldn't bring himself to move those few inches.

Instead, he curled into a ball. The smell of Tracker's hot skin lingered in the sheet beneath him. A scent he could happily drown in. He breathed deep and, as the torchlight grew dim, watched the hound sleep on.

CHAPTER 48

Tracker lay flat on his back atop the bed, gingerly rubbing his temples as he stared at the ceiling. The torch had burnt itself out sometime during the night, leaving the grey light of dawn to envelope the room. Even that was slightly on the harsh side for his current state.

Yet, closing his eyes didn't stop his head from pounding as though he had spent the night drinking heavily. It had been a long time since sex left him feeling this hung over.

Not your best moment. He should *not* have let last night go that far. What the hell had he been thinking?

He hadn't been was the obvious answer. Once Dylan had mentioned sex, his mind had refused to focus on anything else. By the time he'd gotten the man naked, had the taste of him in the back of his throat, had succumbed to the gentle buzzing effect of his magic...

Common sense just plummeted off the rooftop.

When he had sought to distract Dylan for the night, to make him forget where they currently bunked, the man's enthusiasm wasn't something Tracker had factored in. Nor how quickly Dylan recovered.

Maybe there was something to that old adage of spellsters being eternally horny. He hadn't noticed it in the other spellsters he'd lain with, but the sample size was small and their power weak.

He lifted his head, squinting as fresh pain invaded his senses. He finally took in their surroundings, finding nothing had changed. A good sign. After Authril's tirade, he wouldn't have put it past the woman to sneak in and do the grim work herself.

Or perhaps she bided her time, waiting until they were back on the road and Dylan close at hand, vulnerable in his dreaming.

How could that be changed? He could request the spellster share his tent, providing this new day didn't see the man rejecting the whole notion of being near Tracker. Would Authril see anything suspicious in the alteration of their sleeping arrangements? Could he count on the others to talk away objections she might make? He hoped so.

The one piece he hadn't been able to place in his plan was Lullaby. He didn't even know how the animal fared. If the stallion had recovered enough to travel. If he ever would.

Every step he'd taken so far had only led him further from the warhorse and helping Dylan would only increase that distance.

If he managed to persuade Dylan to leave Demarn and the other hounds caught wind? They'd brand him as a traitor, demand the dwarves give him up for punishment. And the dwarves would. It was part of the treaty and the reason why he hadn't tried leaving the kingdom years ago.

He could send a missive to Toptower. Not from here, but he could use the hound station once they reached Whitemeadow. He knew where the key to a stash of money was kept in Toptower's unmanned station. He could ask Commander Rhiannon to see that his warhorse was returned to his side.

But where and when? *Hopefully north*. Whoever brought Lullaby to him would never catch up in time. And even if they did, the animal's scarring would make them an easily noticeable target.

Everything depended on Dylan's reaction to the plan. If he refused, then he'd be sending himself to his death.

Tracker rocked his head to one side, his gaze settling on his bed partner's oblivious form. The man seemed to have slept soundly. No nightmares that tweaked Tracker's senses, at least. It'd been more than he had hoped for given the circumstances.

He watched that serene face continue slumbering. The memory of Dylan's body beneath him lingered in the early morning haze. The stirring reaction Tracker had caused with a simple kiss. The man's boldness. The thrum of magic tingling across his skin.

Tracker flung off the blankets, glancing down at his fresh erection. Clearly, the memory was still doing it for him. "Did you not get enough last night?" he grumbled under his breath.

His penis merely stood there, swaying slightly and looking utterly dejected that no one was playing with it.

Harrumphing, he scrubbed at his face. *That* was definitely not happening. Not before a decent night's rest and several pints of water.

The thought of drinking had him licking his lips. Unsurprisingly, they were dry. In spite of Dylan's lack of familiarity with any length other than his own, the damned spellster had done a good job working every drop of excess fluid from Tracker. *Beginner's fortune*. Still, it reminded him that they should've filled the water skins. At the very least, it would save him an additional trip.

Nothing for it than to head down and hunt out a potable water source. There had to be one within the tower itself. Maybe even on this floor.

Tracker got to his feet and padded across the room. The chill air nipped at his skin, working to dispel all thoughts of fun from his nether region as well as help take the edge off his headache. A splash in some equally cold water would see his ardour completely quelled.

A quick rummage around the room brought up no sign of any place to bathe. There was a well out in the gardens, but getting there would require descending several levels. He eyed his clothes. After last night, he wasn't keen on the idea of donning them without even a quick scrub. The scent of sex was easy enough to remove from his skin, less so from cloth that'd had the aroma ground into it over hours of walking.

Dare he risk the journey naked? Would the women have awoken by now? Enough to have left their chosen quarters?

Gathering the necessities, he relit the torch and slipped out the door.

He skulked through the corridors, his ears straining for any sound that might mean another was nearby, his fingers absently twirling a throwing knife in anticipation. They'd been thorough in searching the tower for any survivors, but that didn't negate the possibility of a being tucking themselves away in some dark corner.

Reaching the ground level, his passage took him along the same corridors leading to the back entrance. He hadn't spent much time looking for more than signs of life. Now, his gaze was drawn to the patterns. The clumps of spellsters. The ghostly sweeps of their final magical blow. Shields marked the floor in chaotic whorls. Judging by the many unnatural puddles amongst the dead, diluting the blood, there'd been a few water-based attacks.

But the most prevalent signs were of fire. It scorched the walls, left traces of smoke on the ceiling and ignited a few bodies that had definitely been dead prior to being accidentally cremated.

He paused before what was obviously the sooty outline of a person upon a wall. Due to the lack of a corresponding charred corpse, they had survived the fiery onslaught. He knew of only two ways that was possible and it didn't make much sense for the target of a spellster attack to be one of their own.

That left it being a King's Hound.

Trapper? Perhaps this was the reason he'd entered the dungeon that'd become his tomb. Or had there been another? One who'd gone rogue. Someone Trapper could be mistaken for.

The idea that a hound could be responsible made him sick to his stomach. It couldn't be that. There was no need for them to attack a spellster within the tower. This was where the king wanted hounds to put them. This was the safe place.

Perhaps he was thinking about it all wrong. One outline told him little. Maybe it was as simple as a couple of hounds being here when the attack occurred and getting mistaken for the enemy in the heat of the moment.

He moved on, leaving the torch in a sconce by the doorway as he stepped outside. The scene hadn't changed much. The pile of bodies still smouldered—albeit, with less vigour. The stench of decay had grown, no doubt aided by the warmth of yesterday's afternoon, as had the bevy of flies.

He had walked through worse.

Finding a source of water was a simple matter. Like much of the tower's internal structures, the winch for the garden well remained untouched, including the length of rope descending deep into the hole.

Leaning against the well's edge, he peered into the darkness far below. The hole looked big enough for the desperate to jump in. Had someone? "Hello?" he called, his voice echoing on through the blackness. "Is anyone down there?"

Silence answered him.

"I know trusting me is a gamble, but I mean no harm."

Still, nothing. Not even the splash of someone treading water.

"I need to bring up the bucket. If you are able, grab hold." He cranked the lever, the minimal effort he needed to move it draining what little hope he had left of anyone being attached to the other end.

Sure enough, when the bucket surfaced, it was unaccompanied. He tested the water. It had a vague earthiness about the smell and a familiar metallic taste that suggested someone had indeed jumped in. That ruled out the water being clean enough to fill their water skins, but it would do for a quick wash.

Lathering his soap, he scrubbed himself as swiftly as he was able. Drying without an adequate cloth was a trickier task, one he managed efficiently enough to pull on his undergarments and be confident of not chafing later.

He threw the bucket back down, hauling up another load to cart upstairs for Dylan's use. But before he left the area, there was one thing he wished to examine—the clearly broken section in the tower's outer wall.

Turning on his heel, he marched in the opposite direction they'd taken during their initial venture into the outer yards. Much of the landscape was the same grisly scene, pieces of people scattered like debris, bodies crumpled where they'd been slain, disturbed earth and scorched patches of grass.

And a partially collapsed section devastating the outer wall.

Tracker slowed his approach. The destruction of the brickwork wasn't the only thing to change. He hadn't been able to get a fully clear view of the ground from the window. Only a few feet, enough to know there'd be no casualties directly against the wall.

Concentric arcs of bodies littered the area surrounding the collapse, the majority of them garbed in Talfaltaner attire. The rows their corpses formed coincided with what looked to be the reluctant decreasing of a spellster's shield.

He halted before the wall, standing right in the centre of the arc, craning his neck to eye every inch of the masonry. The usage of the wall seemed deliberate in their defence rather than a section they'd been backed into. That suggested at least one of the spellsters had been trained for battle.

The tower complex's outer defence was made of huge stone slabs cut to fix with precision. Unlike the tower, it wasn't built from stone that fully absorbed magic, but of strong granite. Yet, not one slab before him was whole. The shattering looked to dig deep into the wall, possibly all the way through to the other side.

It would've taken a lot of force. Magic soaked the area, more than anywhere in the tower beyond Dylan's current position. He tried to distinguish just what they'd done, but the impressions were all jumbled. The echo of multiple shields overlaying each other scored the stone, each one a different note on the wind.

He pressed a hand to the shattered brickwork, sensing the vibrations still bouncing around each fragment. Yet, nothing above ground was the source. The initial blast used to doom the wall's integrity had come from somewhere beneath the foundation. Rather than blast through the rock, they'd undermined it and—

Had they really *tunnelled* their way out?

Gods. He looked over the wall anew, his heart thumping. *All that weight.* It would've hovered over them, groaning, cracking, waiting for a sliver of weakness for the chance to crush them. Like the encroaching Talfaltaners, the wall would've stayed in place thanks only to a spellster's strength.

He absently wiped his hand on his shirt, his palm sweaty at the mere thought. Had they managed to escape? Difficult to tell without seeing the other side. If they'd made it, then they would be far from here. If they had perished beneath the rubble, it would have been a far more merciful death than what the Talfaltaners would've given.

Unable to find anything else that would change his verdict, Tracker returned to the well and collected the bucket of water.

He paused before heading back into the tower, absently turning his head in the direction of the not-so-secret entrance. The tower blocked his view, but he didn't need to see it to remember the carnage. The way the bodies were piled around it suggested they'd been caught even more by surprise than the rest of the people.

How would the Talfaltaners have known where to go? He had learnt of the door's existence through a captured spellster and, even after searching, had found it difficult to distinguish from the surrounding wall. That it needed to be opened from the inside also meant a squadron had waited outside for their chance to ambush terrified children.

Monsters. He'd been called such a number of times throughout his service as a King's Hound. His creed had forced him to take children from their families, to bring them here. In all those years, never had he brought his blade down on a child, not even when they raged.

If he ever caught the swine responsible for giving the Talfaltaners such information, they would be pleading for death by the time he was done with them.

He turned from the well, heading for the tower, halting as he reached the side entrance and what remained of the door. The fractured piece that had been hanging on to the hinge now sat in the middle of the archway. Hadn't they left the section where it had been forced open? *Yes.*

Tracker hefted the piece out of his path. Strange how it had fallen neatly across the doorway. He hadn't heard it either nor did the wind seem strong enough to move the heavy, weathered planks.

He froze in reclaiming the bucket, his gaze alighting on the floor. When he had exited the tower, he'd been barefoot, but there currently sat a set of footprints leading up the corridor.

Someone else was here.

Abandoning the bucket, he ran alongside the footprints. The straightforwardness of their passage had them heading for the first flight of stairs leading up.

Dylan. The man's position hadn't changed, he was likely still asleep. *Idiot,* Tracker berated himself. He had considered allowing the man to doze as the thoughtful option, not the one that would lead to his demise.

He could only pray that he wouldn't be too late.

CHAPTER 49

Dylan stirred at the creak of an opening door. Had he slept in? Were the others ready to head out to—?

Wintervale.

All at once, the memories of yesterday flooded his mind, dousing the haze of sleep. Everything about last night seemed surreal. The comfort he had found in the man's arms. The way Tracker had set his body abuzz with pleasure, making him forget all else. He even foggily recalled last night's unvoiced desire to ask the man for more as Tracker had fallen asleep.

A figure stood over him. He sensed their weight shifting the bed. They said nothing. Were they seeking not to disturb him? Perhaps it wasn't yet morning and the hound had merely awoken to relieve himself.

Dylan rolled over, lifting his face from where he had smushed it into the pillow. "Track?" he slurred with a tongue that felt too long for his mouth. He rubbed at his eyes, blearily focusing on the figure. "What—?"

"No!" Tracker's bellow of denial hit him an instant before pain lanced through his side.

Screaming, Dylan arched off the bed, barely registering the figure above him had also stiffened.

A being that suddenly slumped over, pinning his legs to the bed.

Dylan grabbed his side. His magic flared, struggling to heal the damage to his lung whilst something continued to hinder its progress. His fingers closed on the hilt of a weapon, a—

Dagger. The blade shifted inside him, its tip perilously close to his heart. His magic could heal a lot of things, even if he was unconscious, but not that. He struggled to haul the blade out. With his hand slipping on the grip, the twisted angle he lay at and the blade being between two ribs, all he managed to do was make the wound worse.

"Stop thrashing," Tracker said, suddenly a lot closer. "Taking it out is not the wisest." The man's hands fell upon him, removing

Dylan's weakening hold and applying pressure to the wound. "It is far better to leave it in for the moment."

Dylan shook his head. Maybe that was the best recourse in a normal situation. This wasn't that. If the blade was out, he could heal. He tried to explain such, but couldn't muster the strength.

"I know it hurts." The hound's voice remained soft as he repositioned Dylan's head. He drew back Dylan's eyelids before peering into his mouth. "At least it is not poisoned." He pressed an ear to Dylan's chest. "Try to take steady breaths for me."

Following the instruction wasn't easy. Even the minutest shift sent literal stabbing pains through his torso, leaving him barely daring to breathe. Still, he tried.

The hound sat there for a while before slowly lifting his head, his expression grim. "You have a punctured lung."

He had gathered as much. Collecting what breath he had, he fought to speak. "Out," he managed on an inhale, tears blurring his vision. "Take it out."

He couldn't see Tracker's face clearly, but the man's hesitance vibrated through the air. "I do that and you will only die faster. I am sorry. I should not have left you alone. I honestly thought we were the only ones here."

Dylan swallowed, tasting blood. That couldn't be a good sign. If he kept his breathing shallow, he could limit the pain enough to think. "The blade, is it purple?" If he had been cut open by an *infitialis* weapon, then there was no hope.

"No."

"Then I'll heal." His magic might never have mended anything this grievous on himself before—being largely relegated to passively healing nicks and scraps—but it was all the same in the end.

"You can heal yourself? I thought— Hold on." The blade shifted slightly as Tracker grabbed it, once more widening the cut. "This will hurt."

Dylan gritted his teeth as the dagger slipped free. Blood and magic flowed into the space, the latter struggling to keep the former from going where it shouldn't. His lung burned, filling faster than his power could keep up with.

He fought to direct his healing where it was needed the most. His magic would fix him without his guidance, as it had when during his unleashing, but that didn't mean it would do it well. The strain sucked at his energy, leaving him further gasping for breath.

The world grew dim, then slowly faded into blackness.

"Dylan?" Long, slightly tacky, fingers patted his cheek. "Stay awake."

Wheezing, he opened his eyes, spying only a flash of red as

Tracker withdrew his hand. His side no longer hurt, but the screaming through his body hauled him out of his air-deprived haze.

My lung. The wound was gone, yet the sludge within remained. His magic pooled into the area, aimless but incessant. It drained what little strength he had left. If he didn't get it out of him, his magic would finish the blade's job.

He rolled onto his stomach, letting his upper half flop over the edge of the bed, gagging as his body worked to expel the congealing blood. The clotted mess slid up his throat, hitting his uvula on the way out and setting him to dry-retching, his body trembling after every heave.

When he was finally able to stop, he was left dizzy, drained and bone-chillingly cold. He stayed draped over the bed frame, shakily regaining his breath whilst his magic settled.

The sudden burst of light from a flame flaring to life caught his eye. He lifted his head, coming face-to-face with the gaping maw of a corpse.

Panic drove his movements, ripping him from the bed to fumble across the floor. "Wh-who the hell is *that?*" he demanded between pants. "Where did they come from?" Their group had searched everywhere. There'd been no one hiding in the tower.

"*That,*" Tracker replied, pointing to the corpse with the bloody dagger, "is a Talfaltaner assassin. As for where they came from." He jabbed the blade into the corpse's back. "I believe they were already here. Most likely hiding in the outer wall. And they knew where we were. Or rather, where you were. Their trail of footprints led directly here."

Dylan pressed a hand to his side, his palm coming back bloody. He stared at it, shaking from more than the cold that wracked his body. If the hound had been a few seconds later... "Thank you," he whispered. "For saving me."

Tracker shook his head. "That was pure luck. My carelessness put you in danger. I was bringing up water for you to wash off the residue of last night."

"Last night?" he echoed. "You mean when we...?" His thoughts drifted off, tangling in webs of the night's pleasure and the memory of Tracker's hot skin. "Gods, do you think he found us then?" The thought someone could sneak up on them, could *kill* them, in the middle of the act had never crossed his mind before now.

"It is possible. We were both very distracted."

Dylan gawked at the man, still struggling to make sense of everything, from what he had felt during the night—the echoes of which *still* bounced around in the depths of his mind—to the violent way he had awoken.

He lifted his head, spying the growing light of dawn peeking through the high window at the far end of the room. To think, this might've been the last morning he saw due to a lurking, creeping…

"The others!" he blurted, abruptly realising the trio slept in a room on the other side of this level. Too far for them to hear any sort of scuffle. "Do you think—?"

"No," Tracker interrupted before Dylan could finish the sentence. "You would have been his priority. That he clearly waited until you were alone suggests he was, too. Whereas the others are together and Authril would have heard his approach." He gathered up one of the sheets, handing it to Dylan. "Wipe off what you can with this. We will need to head for the garden to wash off the rest. I would *not* recommend filling our water skins from it, though."

Dylan got to his feet, his legs still a little jellified. Now that his focus was no longer on just trying to breathe, the chill air had a certain familiar funk to it, overlaid by the tang of blood. *His* blood.

His stomach quivered as though unsure if it should return to cramping. It was already empty. He would need to eat—if nothing else, to replenish the lost blood—but any appetite he might've had was shattered.

His gaze slid to the clothing. His robe and undertunic still lay where he foggily recalled shedding them last night.

The garden. Why would they need to descend so far to bathe? "We've a whole room devoted to getting clean, you know." Technically, more than one, but he had never been in the others before yesterday's search. All of them had been mercifully vacant. He didn't think he could bring himself to go near them otherwise.

The hound sat on the side of the bed with a grunt. "I did *not*. And I sadly wish I had about an hour ago. We could have avoided this entire sticky encounter." He eyed Dylan, his brows apologetically knotting together. "Is it far? Do you feel well enough to walk?"

A small smile twitched one corner of Dylan's mouth. Odd how the man's concern left him warm inside. "I can manage a few stairs." His legs still wobbled a little, but the shock was fading. "It's only the next level down." If he'd been more conscious, the Talfaltaner wouldn't have gotten close enough to land a blow.

Nodding, Tracker gestured to the door. "Lead the way when you feel able."

Dylan waited only until he was steady enough to haul on his smallclothes and boots. He couldn't dress further without smearing blood all over his undertunic, but he wasn't about to walk through the tower completely naked.

Tracker spent that time carefully bundling the rest of their clothing into a makeshift sack crafted from one of the sheets. He also shouldered both of their packs, leaving Dylan with only himself to worry about.

Wordlessly taking the lit torch from its sconce, Dylan headed out the door, ignoring Tracker's objections or the fact the torch shook in his hands. He needed the warmth.

He led the way through the corridors, steadfastly refusing to take notice of the bodies littering their path. His attention darted everywhere, imagining another assassin around every corner they took. His shield flickered around him, not quite strong enough to stay put for more than a moment.

Dylan did his best to suppress the urge, to cling to what he knew was true rather than let his anxiety get the best of him. If someone was to leap out at him now, he wouldn't have the strength to properly counter a gentle pat on the cheek never mind an actual attack. True? *Yes.* But not helpful.

Having Tracker at his side was, though. Not only could the hound defend Dylan, but his elven hearing would also allow him to catch anyone approaching well before they became a threat. Maybe even before they knew Dylan and Tracker were near.

Never had he needed to rely on anyone that strongly, but if he couldn't entrust the man who had literally saved his life to protect him, then who could he trust?

CHAPTER 50

Dylan halted as they reached the entrance to the bathing chamber. Standing in the single light of the torch, he could almost convince himself that everything he experienced since the last time he had bathed here was naught but a vivid nightmare.

Tracker gave a low whistle, snapping the hazy thought back into the dark. The man wouldn't be here if everything else wasn't real. No chance his imagination could've conjured up someone like the hound.

Dumping their gear by the doorway, the man strode amongst the already full tubs, his attire jingling and steadily growing loose as he shed his trousers. "I can see why a person would be reluctant to leave."

"*I* never was." Maybe if he had been less willing to race to Nestria's aid, then he would've been here when the tower was attacked. He could've helped.

"Yes? Well, some people cannot be satisfied with paradise." Tracker bent to scrub his hands in a nearby tub, flinching during the initial submerging before persisting. "Then again, freezing the extremities is not my idea of a relaxing time."

Dylan wordlessly thrust his hand into the frigid water. He focused, letting the heat of an unformed fireball warm the water until steam rose from the barrel. It didn't take much of his recovered strength and the familiarity helped to calm his nerves. He moved on to heating another tub before the man suggested they share. Although, the tubs weren't even big enough for him to comfortably settle in.

"I had actually forgotten you could do that," Tracker said, all but tearing off the rest of his clothes. "You tend to limit your magic, even during our scuffle with those bandits." An appreciative groan escaped his lips as he sank into the water. "Just right. You have my thanks." He sat cross-legged in the tub, his head tipped back to rest on the tin-bound rim.

Dylan eyed the pose enviously. It had been decades since he could fit in the small wooden barrels without barking his legs or back. Kneeling was the best it got.

With the water in the second tub at the temperature he liked, he quickly peeled off his smallclothes and stepped into the barrel. Several bars of soap lay scattered about the floor, a common sight after the morning's horde had been through. He scooped up the closest and set to scrubbing himself.

The gentle slosh of water alerted him to the hound vacating his tub.

His heart skipped, only to return at double speed. What was Tracker doing? Visions of the man trying to restart last night flooded his mind and knotted his gut. No, he wouldn't do that, not after what had just happened.

Still, he wasn't entirely sure he'd be able to refuse the advance.

Tracker halted beside him, water still dripping down his body. "You are doing a poor job of this." He gently relieved Dylan of the damp cloth he'd been using. "We shall see how good a job your healing has done."

He stayed silent as the man washed Dylan's side. Each sweep of the cloth came gingerly at first, the hound's confidence growing as he seemed to reach the revelation that Dylan already knew.

"Incredible," Tracker murmured. He shuffled closer, his hands hovering just above Dylan's skin. "Will it hurt if I touch you there?"

Dylan hesitated. Just having the hound's hand so close was already starting to do strange things to his insides. He tried to shrug off the feeling. The man had touched far more intimate places. "I don't think so." With the healing complete, the area was no different to the rest of his torso.

Those long fingers ran over the once injured spot. Dylan's skin tingled, the hairs along his forearm lifting. "Not a hint of scarring," Tracker murmured, the awe in his voice warming Dylan's face. "As though it never happened."

Dylan grunted. He wished the memory would leave his mind as easily.

"I have heard of such skills," the hound continued. "But I never considered the ability would naturally extend to yourself." He paused, even his hand stilling. "Is that what I sensed last night? When you said it felt strange?"

"Maybe?" The only one who knew precisely what Tracker had been aware of was the hound himself. "Last night... happened the way I think it did, didn't it?" His body was certain and his memories seemed crystal. "We—" Dylan's tongue froze as the hound laid the entire warm length of his hand atop Dylan's chest.

"All nights happen," the man murmured. "But if you mean to ask if we were intimate, then allow me to put your mind at ease on that count. We were. Prolifically so."

Yes. His recollection told him as much. Never had he been so voracious with his desires. There was something about the man—the tenderness, the sincerity—that tied his mind into also sorts of knots.

Like now.

Tracker had confirmed that the wound was closed, yet he continued to run his hand along Dylan's side in that same infuriatingly *intimate* manner that had him flushing all the way from his neck to the roots of his hair.

"I wish I had known you were capable of this healing sooner," Tracker confessed.

"Then you wouldn't have needed to fuss with me so much, right?" He grinned, trying to put some levity into the words, when he realised the hound couldn't see his face from this angle. "I'm joking, by the way. And I'm sorry I didn't tell you. I wasn't keeping it a secret, I—"

"There is no need to apologise. Encountering spellsters who can heal is rare, but we do know of the talent. It simply never occurred to me that the magic also worked on yourself. It does explain why a few of my targets did not go down as easily as they should have."

"To be fair, it's the first time I've been injured in your presence."

"Injured? I thought you were *dying*." Tracker paused in running his finger across the spot the Talfaltaner's blade had entered. "And I have gotten sick of losing people I—" He fell silent, his hand leaving Dylan's skin entirely.

Trying to keep his actions casual, and with the thudding in his chest quickening, Dylan twisted to peer at the hound. All he managed was gaining a view of the top of the man's head. "People that you... what?"

Tracker stepped back, his expression returning to the same hard mask he'd worn when they met. "That I am meant to be protecting." His mouth twisted sourly for an instant. "Although, I guess your healing makes you pretty much invincible."

"No." As much as he wished to say otherwise, the truth was far less impressive. He could mend bones and flesh easily enough. Drawing those who were near death back from the brink was harder, but doable. Yet it was said that a master could bring the recently dead back to life. "I studied healing in my teenage years, I thought it might give me an edge in being chosen for the army." He shook his head, chuckling at how foolish he'd been to think he was anything but a weapon to them. "It's not an easy skill to master—very few ever have, myself included—but the process leaves us with a... residual healing effect."

"And this ability is always accessible to you?"

He went to nod, then recalled his time travelling to the main army encampment with the other hound and the spellster he had bested in the brawl. "As long as I'm not leashed."

"Then why do you have a scar here?" Those long fingers trailed up Dylan's chest to caress his throat, their silken touch leaving a tingling path.

"I don't know." Had the scar come from the same immense heat that melted the collar, or from the explosion? He wasn't an alchemist. All he had were speculations and scraps of remembered conversations with Sulin. "I think my body was trying to heal when I was still technically leashed and the collar interfered." He shrugged. "You know how volatile the metal is." The man seemed to know more about the collars than himself.

"Still, do you think your healing abilities are what saved your life when the collar broke?"

Dylan felt along his neck, his fingertips quickly finding the too-smooth patch at his throat. The sympathetic healing magic had never left any scarring before. At least, not on himself. "I don't know," he repeated. By rights, the collar should've blown his head clean off.

The hound settled beside the tub, drumming his fingers on the edge.

Dylan relaxed into the water, steadfastly ignoring how red it was. He relieved the man of the wash cloth and continued scrubbing the rest of his body. After so many days of just a quick morning wash in a basin, it felt good to get properly clean.

Tracker leant his elbows on the edge, his fingers dangling just above the water's surface. "Exactly how far does this healing of yours go? Can you say… regrow a severed limb?"

He shook his head. "We're people, not lizards."

"Oh?" The man chuckled. "I do not know about that. I once met this rather lithe young woman who had the marvellous ability to climb walls with only the scantest of footholds. Rather exuberant, too." He tapped thoughtfully at his lips. "Although, I seem to recall her wife was less pleased about that."

Dylan wordlessly shuffled from one knee to the other. The last thing he wanted to hear was of the man's sexual exploits.

"Your healing is clearly not limited to humans, though. What of animals?"

He shrugged. "It's theoretically possible, I suppose, but we aren't trained to heal them." Without that training, any attempt had the potential to do more harm than good. Technically, they weren't trained to heal dwarves either, but their physiology was close enough to a human's that it made little difference. Unlike elves, who needed their own medical texts.

Disappointment coloured the hound's face for a moment, then he shook it off. "If you are clean, we should hurry with dressing. The women will be looking to leave soon and if they find the Talfaltaner's body, they will panic. I have no desire to play hide-and-seek amongst corpses to regroup."

Dylan nodded his agreement. He might've lived here for the entirety of his twenty-nine years, but he didn't know every inch of the place. There were areas he'd never been, rooms he hadn't stepped into since childhood, other spaces that had been barred to spellsters completely.

The hound stood, padding across the room to the stacks of drying cloths occupying the shelves. He took several, tossing a couple Dylan's way. "Not that I suggest lingering in this place any more than is necessary." He briskly rubbed his skin dry, the movement causing all sorts of interesting twirls and wobbles that Dylan found his gaze inexplicably drawn to as though he hadn't seen the same dance numerous times in this very room. "It will do you no good."

"I'm fairly certain I've seen the worst of it." He wasn't entirely sure what the women had found within the outer wall, but he could guess there'd been a similar level of carnage.

The hound glanced up from donning his trousers to give Dylan a grim smile. "I understand your magic has taken care of any physical issues, but you must be tired."

He grunted his agreement. *I am.* As much as he could have denied it, sleep hadn't come easily. Bouts of it, perhaps, his dreams a mess of dead bodies and the man's warm skin. Coupled with the strain of healing, whatever rest he had managed last night had been snatched from him before he was fully awake. "I'll be fine."

Tracker gave a considering hum. "I do not wish to pry into your personal grooming, but human men shave every day, yes?"

Wondering what that had to do with anything, Dylan ran a hand over his chin. He still sensed where Tracker's blood-stained hand had left its mark even though his face was the first thing he had washed. Faint stubble pricked his fingertips in places. "Not always." Not for him, at least. When it was this short, he could easily see to it tomorrow. "I thought you wanted me to be quick?"

"And preferably not with a blade at your neck." He took up Dylan's hand, lifting it flat between them, before letting go.

Without the man's support, Dylan's fingers trembled.

"You honestly think I'd attempt something that could lead to me slitting my throat?" He'd seen how quickly such an act could take a person. However, he wasn't entirely certain if his magic would heal the wound before he could bleed to death. If it did, he'd be left weak— well, *weaker*—for some time.

"Not deliberately, no. You lost a lot of blood and I know how much of a toll magic takes on a body. You have not had time to regain your strength and, once we leave, we are likely to travel until sundown."

"I'm just a little tired."

Tracker straightened. He crossed to their gear and rummaged around inside his pack, returning with several strips of dried meat. "It is not much, I know, but eat."

Dylan chewed on a strip, grimacing at the dryness and the force he needed to break off bite-sized pieces. When was the last time they had bought any kind of meat? Toptower? No, they'd dried their own from the boar. "How long have you had these?"

Rather than answering, Tracker pressed a finger to his lips. He tilted his head to one side, his gaze becoming unfocused as though he listened to some sound Dylan's ears couldn't hear. "You might want to hurry with getting dressed. It sounds like the women have found our Talfaltaner assassin. We should not worry them with an extended absence."

Dylan scrunched himself further into the barrel. The faint reluctance to leave nibbled at his limbs. They'd depart once everyone was ready, taking away any chance of another ambush, but also any remaining nuggets of chance that someone from the tower had survived. "You go on ahead. I'll be out in a bit."

Tracker's brows twitched together ever so slightly. "Leaving you on your own is a far greater concern to me."

Dipping his fingers into the water, he idly swirled his hand around. "You left me alone yesterday." For a longer period of time than it would take Dylan to dry off and dress. "I'm conscious, alert and my magic—"

"Is currently still too weak. I left your side when you were vulnerable once already, I will not make that mistake twice."

He shook his head and straightened in the tub, trying to look stronger than he felt. "No, I'm well enough to—"

"*Dylan*," Tracker growled. "Do not lie to me."

He fell silent. The firmness in which the hound spoke his name fluttered through his gut. *That's new.*

A small, almost rueful, smile tweaked the hound's mouth. "I can sense how weakened you are right now. And maybe that would be enough, but putting your life in danger to test that is not a risk I am willing to take." He crouched beside the tub. "Especially when I cannot be certain the Talfaltaner who attacked you was the only one."

Dylan wet his lips, the thought of encountering more of them drying his mouth more than the meat had. A shield attempted to form around him, the curve fracturing as it encroached on the hound's position. He dispelled the barrier before it failed. "You said they were acting alone."

"They were. I found only one set of footprints leading to you. But if one hung back, I see no reason to ignore the idea that others did the same. This place is too big to eliminate *any* possibility."

"We swept the tower. It was clear."

Disquiet thinned the hound's lips and furrowed his brow. "He came from outside, entered through the side entrance. We have no idea how many could have been missed in the outer wall."

"I understand." He didn't know how the outer wall was laid out to support all of the people living within, but it was enough to house the same number of people living in the tower. That many rooms spread across the entirety of the wall's length would be impossible to fully clear with just a handful of people, especially if anyone inside didn't want to be found.

He slipped out of the tub and hastened to dry himself. His magic hummed around him. Typically, he would reach for it, use heat to aid him, but he didn't dare waste his energy.

Tracker idly tapped his booted foot on the floor, watching the entrance in silence as Dylan continued to dress. His attention kept diverting in Dylan's direction.

At first, Dylan thought the man was trying to hurry him along, until he caught the heated sweep of one such look. The way the man's gaze—sharper now, he was certain of it—settled on him did strange things to his stomach.

"Before we set up camp tonight," Tracker said, breaking the silence. "We will need to discuss your sleeping arrangements. If there are Talfaltaners still in the tower complex, then there will be more on the road to Whitemeadow. You will need protection."

Dylan frowned, that hadn't been what he'd expected. "I think you're forgetting I already share my tent." Only the gods would know what parts Tracker would be left with if the hound attempted entering the space when Authril was there. He wasn't sure what grief she'd had with the man before their time in *The Gilded Lily*, but her animosity towards Tracker had only grown since then.

Tracker wrinkled his nose. "I have not forgotten. I am suggesting a change of security. My tent can accommodate two and I can defend you better if you are closer to me. And our dear warrior does not seem the type to offer consoling words."

No. A lot of the intimacy he shared with the woman was on her terms. Her choice of when, of how and, it seemed, of who else shared him. "But the others..." He fell silent, chewing on his cheek. The right words to explain how he felt about them knowing eluded him. Why did it bother him? They weren't tower folk, they didn't know how indecisives were treated.

Yet, the thought of someone else being aware of him sleeping with a man, with a *hound*, twisted his stomach into a dozen knots.

"They would know something has changed," he finally said.

The man eyed Dylan, seeming to come to some sort of conclusion. "And that you regret that change, yes?"

No. He thought he would've, but with the assumption in the air, he realised that wasn't the truth. He still wasn't certain what last night had been, but pretending nothing had transpired beyond them sharing a room would help.

Unable to voice an agreement of the man's lie or correct him, Dylan focused on tying his belt.

The curve of the man's lips was absent of their jovial tilt. "There is no need to feel guilty over it. This is not the first time someone has wished to forget such a thing happened. I understand." He sounded so convincing that Dylan almost believed the man.

That only made him feel worse. He wasn't in the habit of using people.

"But you need not think of it as us having sex," Tracker continued. "You were in need of comfort, I merely offered my services, nothing more, and then..." A small huff of what almost sounded like a mirthless chuckle escaped his lips. "Well, then you managed to cry all over me."

He had, hadn't he? Heat bloomed across his face as he realised what the man meant. Dylan prayed the hound would mistake it as a product of the warm water. By the gods, how could he *still* be blushing after last night? How did he have enough blood to waste?

But the warmth he'd felt in Tracker's arms, the completeness, how it clashed with the senseless death that had happened here. Even now, the memory was still a comfort. He'd gotten drunk on it, wanting every last drop.

Tracker was right, they hadn't had sex. Not the way Dylan had experienced it in the past. The hound had practically worshipped him.

"What happens now? With us?" he added for clarification.

His question was greeted with gentle laughter, the sound a touch on the nervous side. "*Us?*" Tracker coughed, rather dramatically. "Well if it makes you feel better, you can blame me for everything. Or we could pretend last night never happened. I do not know how these things are handled in the tower, but hounds are generally discouraged from... closeness. I am quite used to meaningless fun."

Dylan blinked, trying to take in what Tracker had said. *Meaningless.* Just like every single relationship he'd ever had. And why wouldn't it be? His whole life had been nothing but one-night stands. This was all just something to distract him from what they'd found here so he didn't do anything stupid during the night. It was that simple.

It should not sting as much as it did.

He opened his mouth, surprised to find "Ah." was all that would come out.

"Still, should you ever wish to repeat it…" Tracker shrugged. "Well, it is not like I will be far. Even if you merely need a chest to cry into."

Not far? Last night, he'd been too cowardly to cross a few inches. Any distance greater than that might as well be on the other side of the continent.

"If you have concerns on my ability to share a space platonically with another, they are unfounded." He bowed his head. "I know last night was not a good example of it, but I am capable of restraint."

"I'm not worried about that." He trusted the man.

Tracker nodded. "You are worried what they will think about your choice last night, yes? A spellster and a King's Hound? My mistress would throw me into the Pit if she knew."

That the man might have his own consequences to face hadn't been at the forefront of Dylan's mind. Were there really repercussions for such an act? "What's the Pit?"

If Tracker heard the question, he chose to ignore it. Instead, the hound cocked an ear towards the entrance. "Judging by our dear companions' calls—a foolish thing to do after stumbling upon the bloody scene we left—they have descended the stairs."

"They're probably after answers." They'd left a confusing mess behind and had seemingly vanished with no trace. "They might think we've been kidnapped."

The hound frowned. "Perhaps," he conceded. "I am sure the only thing currently on their minds is ensuring your safety." Taking a deep breath, he said in a rush, "Which I doubt will continue if we go to Wintervale."

"*If?*" Dylan bent over the man, holding that honey-coloured gaze. "Wintervale was *your* idea." Tracker had to know there was no other way. "I'm a spellster. The only place I belong is in the tower or the army, and seeing that *this*—" He waved his hand around the room. "—is all that's left of option number one, I don't really have a choice but to take the one way I can be leashed again."

Tracker's gaze dropped. The tip of his tongue brushed his top lip. "You could head for the border? That is where most runaways aim, if not for their families. Other kingdoms have rather different rules on what they do with their spellsters, yes?"

He knew that. The Udynea Empire let her spellsters run roughshod over the common people. At least, those of noble birth. He had thought it wishful thinking of others until learning the truth from Launtil.

There was the smaller kingdom of Tirglas, who cloistered their spellsters in a similar manner to Demarn. He'd heard rumours from some of the port-born spellsters that the only acceptable magic there was of the healing sort. Whilst a life of being confined was familiar, he didn't think he could return to it.

Heimat wouldn't admit him on the basis that he was human. Obuzan hunted down and burnt any spellster they found. Talfaltan was no better. A few of the other kingdoms had the same outlook as Udynea, including slavery. None of them seemed like a good option to face alone. And alone was exactly what he'd be if he ran.

Dylan peered at the man. Was Tracker suggesting what he thought? "You're a hound. Aren't you meant to dissuade me from running?"

"What I am supposed to do is bring you back to the tower, but..." Tracker spread his hands wide. "If the alchemist at Wintervale is able to leash you, the general will insist you be put back on the front line. You could be the only spellster—"

"I know!" The words erupted out of him, broken and tearful. The terrified cries bounced off the walls like mocking ghosts.

He turned from the hound, his vision blurring. He didn't want to be the only one left, didn't want to think about it. *Others have survived*. He had to believe it, no matter how impossible everyone claimed it to be.

"Then you must also know that it will make you the only one against however many Udynea sends once the empire turns her attention back to us. You will be overrun in a heartbeat."

Dylan pulled on his boots and stamped his feet deep into them. "Then I will endeavour to make my time there count," he muttered, striding out of the bathing chamber. Did Tracker think it hadn't occurred to him? That he was blindly walking off in some random direction not knowing the path he had chosen ended at a cliff?

What other choice did he have? Running, even at the man's suggestion, would only court death that much sooner. *Better dead in a year than a few months*. Why else would he follow the others anywhere near the capital?

CHAPTER 51

Dylan hesitated as he left the bathing chamber. The absolute blackness of windowless corridors stretched endlessly before him, threatening to draw him into the darkness and never let go. Rarely had he ever needed to carry his own light source whilst walking around the tower. And he had left the torch back with Tracker.

Gritting his teeth, he illuminated his path with a small ball of light, keeping it hovering above his palm so that it showed only the way ahead and no more.

He could probably have trod the corridors blindfolded and make it out faster than the others, if it wasn't for the bodies littering the floor. He picked his way around the majority, gingerly stepping over others, expecting the corpses to come to life the second he straddled one.

It wasn't long before he caught the hurried steps of the hound echoing down the corridor after him. Tracker caught up swiftly after, wordlessly keeping pace as they trailed through the hallways.

He glanced at the man, expecting him to say something, but Tracker remained silent. The tension in his wiry form spoke plainly enough of his disagreement even if he didn't wish to argue further.

Dylan's gaze slid beyond the hound to settle on a young man slumped against the wall. Scorch marks adorned the stonework of the wall opposite him. A strange imprint of what appeared to be a torso. He glanced at the floor, already knowing there would be no body. Just like the wall in the children's school.

Frowning, he slowed to look closer at the impression. How hadn't he noticed that yesterday? This hadn't been the section the hound searched. "Track?"

The man held up a silencing finger. He tilted his head, clearly listening.

Dylan mirrored the act, catching the faint edge of voices. It had to be the others. Yet, it didn't sound like them. Was Tracker right? Were there more invaders? Had some returned to ensure no one had survived? Were they looking for their fallen brethren?

Snuffing his light globe, Dylan followed the hound in creeping along the corridor to peer around the entrance.

The rest of their group stood spread out at the bottom of the stairs. Their heads swung from side to side, stretching to see around corners. They looked flustered, but whole. How long had they been searching?

Relief flooded his limbs. Dylan went to take a step into the light of their torches, when another thought had him rooted to the spot. Would the women be able to tell that Tracker and himself had spent a large chunk of the night being intimate? Was it possibly true that Tracker and Dylan being intimate wouldn't occur to them?

He lingered in the darkness, considering the possible reactions. Despite Tracker's revelation that the man had slept with more spellsters than Dylan, he was uncertain just how common such actions were or even how they were looked upon in the outside world. He was sure that, had anyone within the tower known, they would've been disgusted at the man. After all, Dylan was under the hound's command, even if Tracker used that authority only to suggest a course of action.

Tracker stepped closer to the group and cleared his throat.

Marin's head snapped around much like an owl's. "Where have you two been?" she blurted. "Authril went to check on you and—"

"Bathing," Tracker said, smoothly interrupting her. "The tower has a large chamber for such an activity. We merely made use of it whilst it was available to us."

"*What?*" Authril snapped. The warrior marched across the space between them, her hand raised. Before Dylan could twitch, she swung at Tracker.

The hound was faster. Her wrist hit the man's palm with a muffled thwack. Where his expression had been openly jovial a moment beforehand, it was now very much impassive. "I assume you have a good reason for trying to strike me?" The man's words came softly, each syllable carrying a sliver of ice in its core.

Authril glared at him over their upraised arms. If she had gone to check on them as Marin claimed, then she would've seen the Talfaltaner who had attacked them. But the warrior looked more angry than concerned.

Did *she* somehow know they'd been intimate? How? Had she smelt it in the room? On Tracker, despite the soap? Had she crept in on them and not said a word?

"Here we are wasting daylight searching this hellhole for you two," Authril said through her teeth. "We find bloody footprints leading to the room, a corpse where you've been sleeping."

"And blood all over the bed," Katarina added.

"That too," the warrior acknowledged. "You have these two

worried that some other blade-swinging maniac has stayed behind, and you decided to go *bathe*?"

"Dylan was attacked," Tracker calmly replied, his hand still wrapped around the woman's wrist. "The blood you saw was partly his. He was covered in it, so we went and washed it off."

"Attacked? One man got past the lauded defence of a King's Hound?" Authril eyed him. "And was he also sleeping naked? Because I don't see any blood on his clothes."

Panic and rage squeezed Dylan's chest. Did she think they were lying? What did she think had happened? That they'd killed a man and gone for a stroll?

"Not naked," the hound stressed. "You are aware that smallclothes are a thing, yes? I would assume so as I have seen you shed yours."

The already flushed skin between Authril's freckles deepened a shade. "If he was that injured, why didn't you come to alert us?"

"My apologies, dear woman," the hound replied, bowing ever so slightly. "I assumed you could defend yourself and the others, I shall not make that mistake again. But leaving Dylan's side to alert you would have made him vulnerable to another attack. Or would you have preferred I left him at the mercy of anyone else who might be wandering these halls?"

Her gaze slid Dylan's way, her expression guarded. "Of course not."

Tracker leant to one side, looking past Authril to focus on Marin. "We have decided that we *are* travelling together, yes?"

The woman nodded. "Until we've reached Whitemeadow, at least. I'll decide then if we'll part ways."

"So soon?" Tracker straightened. He released Authril's wrist and placed a hand on his chest. "I shall be sorely wounded by the absence of your presence, my dear hunter."

Marin rolled her eyes. "You're not going to need me all the way to the capital."

"And I need to return to Dvärghem," Katarina added. "Sooner would be better, just—"

"Not alone," the hound finished for the woman. He nodded, seemingly to himself. "But we are wasting daylight standing around, yes?" In one swift move, he spun about to stride off down the stairs, leaving them to follow.

Dylan tried to ignore the corpses as they descended. Shock had numbed him yesterday. He had mourned through most of last night. Now, the sight of his deceased brethren infuriated him.

The king would want to know who did this, if only due to the threat they posed on others within the kingdom. Whoever did this was going to pay. And, as possibly the last spellster at the crown's command, Dylan would be there. He would rend them apart, with his bare hands if need be.

"Wait," Katarina said as they reached the tower entrance. "We can't just leave them like this. Maybe if we dug a big enough pit, we could—"

"A *pit?*" Marin interjected. "There are several thousand people here," She spread her arms wide as if trying to conceive encircling the whole structure. "It would take days to make a hole that big, even with Dylan working his magic."

"Say nothing of carting each one down," Tracker added. "More than a few are in quite the grisly state."

The hedgewitch seemed to consider, and perhaps agree with, the other's points. Still, she didn't move. "A pyre then. Isn't giving to the flame a worthy burial in Demarn?"

It was. When it came to spellsters, the guardians spoke as though it was a necessity. Dylan had always assumed cremation was a deterrent for the master healers, to keep them from attempting to bring back the dead.

"A pyre would indeed be acceptable," Tracker agreed. "But the same problem in moving the bodies would occur. We would require something big enough to encompass the tower."

"So burn it down," Authril said.

The rest of them swung to face her.

She stared back, her face equally as incredulous as theirs. "What? Look at this place. If anyone managed to escape, they're not going to return. And it can't be any different to bringing down some lord's mansion." She pointed to the ceiling. "Those beams will be drier than any kindling. A few torches in the right places and the tower will collapse under its own weight. Same with the wall."

"We are speaking from experience, yes?" Tracker asked. "Set a few mansions on fire in our time, my dear?"

"Enough," Authril curtly replied.

Dylan's mind readily recalled the sight of the smoke from the garden curling around the tower's peak. Only now it was thick and greasy, the stones soot-stained and crumbling under their own weight.

"Dylan?"

He turned at the hound's voice, blinking back the film of tears.

Tracker stood before him. The man's hand alighted on Dylan's shoulder, squeezing just enough to be felt. "This was your home, your people. How do you wish to honour them?"

His gaze lifted to the beams, then down to his hands. His magic could make a fire hotter than any torch and have this place burnt out before midday. He even knew the place to start. *The library.* The scholarly part of him ached at the thought of setting so much knowledge alight, but the books and shelves would fuel the flames for a long time.

There was something he had to do first, something he couldn't let burn with everything else. "Katarina, follow me, please."

The hedgewitch trotted after him as he strode through the corridors, quietly curious. The others trailed behind.

Dylan slowed as they entered the library, his breath catching anew at the thought of all these books alight. He took a deep breath, fighting the screaming voice deep inside. All these books. The pages that were tinder-dry, the shelves that were as flammable as any branch. The beams and railings high above. The many tables and chairs scattered about the room...

Just the place to begin his unstoppable inferno.

Would that he could save it all. A few books would have to suffice.

He halted in a familiar corner of the room to pull a pair of books from the shelf. "These are the records of everything dwarven we've ever unearthed. Placements, descriptions, drawings. You likely have your own records, but I want you to have these, too." He handed over the books.

Katarina hugged the volumes as if they were priceless. Dylan doubted it, but the dwarf wouldn't be a hedgewitch if she treated his gift as anything less.

Tracker cleared his throat. Wrapping an arm over Katarina's shoulders, he gently turned the woman until she faced the entrance, taking the torch from her in the process. "You three go on ahead. I will keep our dear spellster company."

Dylan watched them go, none of them the least bit hesitant to depart from this shell of a place. "I don't need you shadowing me," he mumbled, plucking the rest of the books from the shelf to hurl them into the middle of the room. "I'm not going to run." It would be pointless. Where would he go? Everything he'd hoped to make a difference for was right here.

"No," the man agreed. "But that is what worries me." He frowned at the pile of books and scrolls Dylan had made in the middle of the library. "Are you sure you have the energy for this?"

Dylan nodded. Fire was the easiest magic, often the first a spellster managed outside of shields. The heat from the torch would give him the start he required, then it was a simple matter of whipping up enough hot air to feed the flames.

He halted before the pile. His vision blurred as his gaze latched onto the splayed pages of a book he recognised from his advanced history lessons. So many years he had spent in this room. It had to be done. *Best to make it quick.* Unable to look, he threw the torch onto the pile.

Single pages curled and crumbled into ash. Scrolls burned, book bindings smouldered. Not enough, but he hadn't expected it to be.

Dylan drew heat from every source he could, pooling it around the flame. All his anger, his helplessness, his frustrations, it hung in the air as one great sphere of smokeless haze. He continued to suck all the warmth from the room until the whole pile was alight.

A short blast of air directed to the mezzanine toppled a bookcase. It fell against the railing, dispensing more books into the flames.

Spreading his arms wide, he directed the scorching blast on the surrounding furniture. The flames licked at the wood, charring shelves and dancing their way along each row of benches.

The pings and snap of ropes spoke of a chair's binding giving. The flames stretched into the air. A gentle whirl of wind was enough to let the fire blaze higher. Smoke, thick and grey, fast blanketed the rafters.

Still, he continued with the fiery assault.

Dylan watched the flames devour everything in their path. Heat akin to an oven bathed his face. The tips of his fingers tried to blister from the continued outpouring of flames, his innate healing magic repairing the damage before his skin had a chance to. His chest tightened at the strain.

Just a little longer. Then the fire would be unstoppable. Already pops and groans of burning wood echoed from above. They would have to leave or... *Die*. Oddly tempting, that notion. It whispered of remaining in place, of allowing the fire to consume him and be one with the tower again.

"Dylan?" Tracker tugged at his sleeve, reminding him that the man was still at his side. Sweat slicked his face, running in rivulets down his forehead. "That is enough. We must go, before it is too late."

He lowered his hands. What reason had he to leave? Run and be hunted or follow the hound to Wintervale and be leashed. "Go on without me." It didn't matter what path he followed, it all led to death.

Staying just promised to be quicker.

The tugging at his sleeve became more insistent, then the man's hand wrapped around Dylan's forearm. Tracker heaved and Dylan stumbled to one side moments before the bookcase from the mezzanine smashed into the pile of books, throwing bits of burning debris in all directions.

"By the gods," Tracker growled. "If I have to carry you out of here, I will. Do not think I cannot."

After managing similar feats yesterday, he believed the man fully capable. "I belong here."

A blade flashed in the flickering light. Close enough to his face that Dylan jerked back on instinct.

"If your wish is to die, then so be it." The calm, even tone in the man's voice was enough to make Dylan's skin prickle even with the heat at his back. "I can grant you a far swifter end than that assassin, but do not think I will walk away and leave you to burn to death."

Closing his watering eyes, Dylan tipped his head up. The dusty aroma of burning vellum tickled his nose. The fire had breached the glass concealing the older scrolls. "Do it then." He had seen how quickly an *infitialis* blade could take a life. He'd be gone before the flames had a chance.

A low, hissing growl snaked into his ears. The blade's coolness vanished from Dylan's neck. He peered through his lashes to find Tracker had sheathed the dagger.

"There is no way you can avenge your people if you are dead."

Of course he couldn't. Dying here would be taking the coward's way out. It would absolve him of any responsibility. But he would face the Seven Sisters knowing he could have avenged the dead.

Dylan couldn't rejoin the tower without ensuring the murdering bastards who did this had paid.

In one smooth move, Dylan hooked his hand into the crook of the hound's elbow and pulled him close. The hum of his shield tingled around them. He hardened the filmy barrier until it blocked out most of the smoke. It left them with precious little air to breathe, but better than choking to death.

Tracker jumped as a beam fell not far from where they stood. A table leg flipped into the air, smacking against Dylan's shield with enough force to make him wince.

Those honey-coloured eyes, molten with concern, turned on him. "Will that hold up to the ceiling falling on us?" The hound pointed towards the shield. Beyond the shimmering surface, flames crackled along the bookcases, curling spines and warping the shelves. The sooty light turned the man's face brassy.

Squaring his jaw, Dylan shook his head. A single beam, maybe. Nothing heavier. Not from that height.

A small, tight-lipped smile took the man's mouth. "Best we leave then, yes?"

He entwined his fingers with the hound's and, keeping a strong grip on the barrier, ran for the doorway.

All around them, the roar of the fire grew stronger. Groans and cracks followed in their wake. Visions of the ceiling caving in at their backs only served to make his legs wobble.

Tracker must've noticed, for he wrapped an arm around Dylan's waist to keep them steady.

They exited the library to the horrid groan of masonry. That sound was all he needed to find the last scrap of strength in his legs.

Outside of the library, the smoke clung only to the rafters. Dylan abandoned the barrier to conserve what energy he had left. They raced through the corridors, hurdling everything in their path, Dylan's longer stride leaving the hound panting at his heel.

His legs finally gave as they crossed the tower threshold. He collapsed at the top of the stairs, doubled over and light-headed. He gulped in all the clean air his lungs could manage, the tang of blood hitting the back of his throat with every swallow.

Tracker hauled him to his feet. "Come now," he rasped. "You can rest later."

Clinging to the man, he staggered down the steps. His gaze lifted to the gates. There was no sign of the others. *They're gone.* Was it just Tracker and himself now?

No, there was a flash of a figure in the shadows beyond the outer gate. *Three.* Waiting. "I have to find a place to ignite the wall," he mumbled, uncertain if he had enough in him to light a candle.

Tracker patted his shoulder. "We will see to that, my dear man. *You* just focus on regaining your strength. We have a long journey ahead of us."

He nodded as, slowly, the figures became recognisable. The path to Wintervale wasn't any longer than the one they'd taken to here, but that only meant they were likely to face similar dangers. More so once they neared the bigger towns.

Faced with that prospect, rest sounded divine.

He settled near the outer gate, unable to muster the strength to care how close the corpses were or that flies buzzed around his head. He looked up at Tracker, waiting for the hound to say something more. The man practically vibrated with the intent to speak.

Tracker merely gave him a grim smile before giving his shoulder another pat, then heading off in the same direction as Marin.

That didn't stop Dylan's mind from echoing with the hound's words. *Run.* Could he run? Who knew he was alive? Three women and one hound? No, there were others. Even if Tracker said nothing, word of his passing would eventually escape someone's lips. But after all this?

He couldn't run. Couldn't stay here. Only one path left to tread. *Wintervale.*

He would make it count.

~ ~ ~

Tracker glanced back at the tower. Smoke had begun to drift out the upper windows by the time they'd set fires within the outer wall. Now, thick smoke poured out every available gap, obscuring everything in blackness.

He hadn't been in favour of burning what they could in the hope that it was enough. He had kept his mouth shut, silencing his reservations, once Dylan had agreed.

Now, those reservations returned in full force. There weren't settlements for a few days on any direction, but the fire had turned the tower into a beacon of destruction.

The smoke alone would be noticeable from several farms. There would be talk, the kind that drew hounds to investigate. They'd pick through the charred husk, discover where the fire had spread from and how powerful the spellster who'd started was.

Then, they'd be on the hunt.

"Track?"

He turned at the sound of Dylan's voice. The man waited beneath the canopy of trees, his gaze steadfastly locked on the ground. He didn't blame the spellster for not wanting to see his home burn.

The rest of their group stood further back, perhaps only now realising not everyone followed. Marin and Katarina looked prepared to wait, but Authril stood with her arms crossed and one foot tapping away. He would need to deal with her. *In time.* They had plenty of it at the moment.

Summoning a smile, he caught up to Dylan and wrapped an arm around the man. "Let us be on our way, yes?" Whitemeadow was over a week from here, the space between dotted with fields that'd fed the tower. He didn't hold out much hope that the farmlands were untouched, not if the armed force of Talfaltaners had swarmed by.

It didn't matter. Reaching Whitemeadow and getting Dylan on a boat was the goal. He would explain everything then and, once they reached the fork at Riverton, he'd take them north and be a week ahead of anyone who followed.

It was a lot of variables, a lot of land between here and the city for unsavoury types to hide, but he would find some way to keep them all in their favour. The last spellster in Demarn or not, he refused to sacrifice Dylan to an unwinnable cause.

AND THE WORLD THE CRUMBLED

SPELLSTER AND THE HOUND - BOOK 1.5 -

ALDREA ALIEN

Thardrandian Publications

The air was thick with screams and the scent of blood. Henrie hadn't even known it had a smell. Certainly not this bitter metallic odour. He only ever dealt with blood once a month and it never smelt this bad.

Or perhaps it was the things mingled within that stink. The glistening tubes spilling from bellies or the jellified red-streaked-grey masses leaking from their heads.

He tried not to think about any of it as he stepped over the dead, but the smell clogged his throat and squeezed his chest tighter than his last binder. It didn't help that he was covered in their blood, an unfortunate side-effect of hiding beneath the dying to avoid joining their fate.

A few of the bodies took their final breaths as he passed by. He tried to block out the sounds. The gurgles of those drowning in their own blood. The rattle of crushed airways struggling to carry on. The drawn-out sigh from those who had finally crossed over.

The same sounds as those he had hidden under when this slaughter began.

He hadn't been able to help the dying then and he didn't stop to give aid now. There was nothing he *could* do. He lacked the knowledge or the skill to attempt healing anyone, and he couldn't risk being caught by those responsible for their deaths just to ease another's passing.

If Dylan was here…

Biting back a sob, Henrie quashed the thought before it choked him with its slew of unattainable possibilities. There was so much his friend could've done. He could've healed the fatally wounded, could've fought these monsters with all the ferocity he had shown in the brawl.

But Dylan was long gone. *Dead.* Along with the rest of the army. No more able to help than the bodies currently surrounding Henrie. He wasn't even sure if his friend could've done it. No one else, guardian or spellster, seemed capable of laying a hand on their assailants as they moved from room to room, leaving only death in their wake.

Why? The question once again bubbled to the forefront of his thoughts. Why was this happening? Why them? Why now? Was it somehow linked to the army falling at the border?

No reason would be good enough. But if it could've given him an edge, something he could plan against rather than some erratic attack with no strategic pattern, then he could follow.

Whatever the answers were, they were no clearer to him now than they'd been hours earlier.

He knew only that the people responsible for all this death were garbed identically to the King's Hound who had taken Dylan all those weeks ago. But hounds hunted spellsters *outside* the tower, not within. The tower had always been the one place where spellsters were safe from them.

Yet, for anyone to reach the central tower, they would've needed to enter the outer courtyard and pass through two guarded gates without giving any cause for alarm.

And they had struck swiftly as he'd always imagined hounds might. A single one had taken out an entire room of adult spellsters with very little effort, paying no heed to the panicked bursts of magic flung their way either, as though they were used to fighting against it. Who else but a hound would have that experience?

His gaze settled on the blood-splattered face of an elven child. Blank eyes stared back, the mouth parted slightly in disbelief, the very same emotion that continued to torment Henrie's thoughts.

He had to get out before he joined the dead.

How? Getting beyond the tower walls might've been his goal, but how did he reach the entrance undetected? Every direction held the same potential.

He peeked out into a hallway, straining to hear anything above the pounding in his chest. The screams from above prickled his skin no matter how hard he tried to block them out.

His immediate surroundings seemed empty. At least, as far as the living were concerned. Guardians and servants lay sprawled across the stone, the latter clearly cut down as they fled. He would've thought servants would be safer than anyone, but it seemed these hounds were intent on slaughtering everything within the tower walls.

The central tower had two entrances, one leading into the courtyard and a smaller door that opened to the gardens. The latter was closer. Yet reaching it quickly meant passing the stairs leading to the upper levels with no guarantee of avoiding detection, especially if a hound chose to descend at the wrong moment.

Could he risk the long route?

He turned left, taking pains to tread around the puddles oozing across the floor. This path would eventually lead to the central tower's main entrance. It meant a greater distance to travel, but it took him further from where the hounds were more likely to be.

Unless...

Did anyone currently guard the entrances? What about outside? What few windows the tower's ground level had were also too high to see through. Were the gardens safe? Was... was Harriet safe?

His legs wobbled at the thought of her being amongst the dead, forcing him to brace himself against a closed door. Not his beloved Harry. Never again would he see the sparkle in her hazel eyes, feel the warmth of her smile, hear the grunting hiccup of her unabashed laughter. All of it stolen for some senseless reason that he couldn't even begin to fathom. It—

No. Clutching the doorframe, he straightened. He couldn't let the idea of her death consume him, couldn't even believe it. Until he confirmed her passing with his own eyes, he would continue to believe she still lived. He would reach her and escape this death trap of a place.

Footsteps echoed from the way he had come, faint compared to the rest of the sounds echoing down the hall, but strong and purposeful.

Henrie dove through the door, slowly closing it behind him until the latch gave a barely audible click. He took in the room, searching for a place to hide. The options were few. Five solid tables with chairs left abandoned around them, some merely askew, the rest knocked onto their backs. A row of freestanding cupboards lined the far wall, too obvious to hide in and too heavy to squeeze behind.

He leant against the wall, listening for the footsteps to fade, hearing only the opposite. Be the person friend or foe, each stride continued with no hesitation. Were they looking for stragglers? Did that mean everyone was dead? They couldn't be. He had heard them directly above only a moment ago and there were multiple levels beyond for them to climb.

Perhaps they'd been taken down and the person outside was a guardian searching for anyone who might live.

Henrie reached for the door handle, halting a hairsbreadth from the old brass lever upon hearing the steady pace faltering directly outside the door.

The latch clicked.

He pressed his hands to his face, trying to muffle his breath lest the figure was also elven. Only now did he realise his fingertips were sticky, coated in the blood of others. He fought to keep his breathing steady, but the scent of death coated his nostrils and tightened his throat.

The door swung inwards.

He flattened himself against the wall, praying the door would be enough to hide him. His body trembled uncontrollably, shaking each slow breath.

The flicker of his shield sputtered around him, its purple glow faintly lighting the door's wood grain. He stared at those whorls and lines, focusing on drawing the shield into himself, relief almost taking his legs when the glow faded. He hadn't used the technique for years, not since his childhood when he had longed for his transitioning to be over with. With luck, the magic still worked the same, rendering him invisible to everyone.

The footsteps carried on into the room, halting at every other stride as if trying to pinpoint a sound.

Henrie risked a peek around the door, spying a human man marching deeper into the room. He would stoop at each table, checking with sword and hand as though he wasn't certain someone couldn't be hiding beneath. Was it really that dark in here for human eyes? He knew their vision was inferior to elven sight, but it surely wasn't *that* bad.

Confident in his appraisal of the tables, the man moved on to the far end of the room. He opened one cupboard door with a jerk, jabbing his sword into the space before the door had finished swinging.

Henrie inched out from his hiding spot, keeping his focus on remaining invisible. A part of him screamed to stay put, but he had only a few cupboards worth of time to sneak out into the hall before the man thought to search behind the door with the same finesse he'd given the rest of the room.

The final cupboard door banged shut.

"There you are."

Stiffening, Henrie slowly turned to face the man. He hadn't made a sound, not one a human would hear, and he was still invisible, could feel the faint inward tug of his power.

Yet the man was definitely looking right at him.

Swiftly redirecting the inward pull of his magic, Henrie refocused it into a blast of pure energy turned upon the man.

The books and papers scattered atop the tables flew to the back of the room, scorched along the edges. The chairs that hadn't already fallen now tumbled across the floor. The cupboard doors banged as though caught in a storm. One of the tables even started rattling, threatening to lift at the slightest shift in Henrie's aim.

The man stood in place as if nothing was happening. The most he moved was in calmly redirecting a leaf of paper from thwacking him in the face. His hair didn't stir, even his clothes—too similar to that of a hound's attire for him to be anything but—barely acknowledged the blast.

Henrie let the blast die down in favour of conserving his energy.

"Are you done?" the hound asked, the bored note prickling Henrie's skin.

"Almost." He launched another blast, aiming at the wobbly table.

The furniture flipped into the air, slamming its whole length into the hound. The weight bore the man to the ground, pinning him in place. His sword skittered across the floor, too far out of reach for the man to grab without first levering the table off, but too close to the hound for Henrie to consider retrieving it without confirmation that the man was dead.

Rather than wait to see if the hound would get back up, Henrie gathered the skirts of his robe and fled the room.

CHAPTER 2

He ran through the halls, not stopping to think of his direction. He skirted every dark puddle he could, leapt over bodies and scrambled to keep upright. His lungs burned, straining against his ribs. Both his thoughts and his heart raced frantically. He didn't dare slow down to let either one settle.

In the spaces between his gasps for air, he caught the limping gait of another following him. *The hound.* How the man had managed to free himself from beneath the table, Henrie didn't waste thought on.

"You cannot outrun me!" the hound bellowed, his voice echoing from somewhere far behind. "Sooner or later, I will catch you." The words clawed their way through the halls to rake at Henrie's back.

He dared to push for more speed from his legs, getting only a slight wobble in his gait in return. He couldn't run forever. He needed to find a place to hide. Where? Anywhere. Nowhere. The hound knew he was here, had done the impossible in seeing him when he'd been invisible. How? No one, not even his closest friends, could find him when he didn't want to be seen.

He darted around a cluster of bodies. His ankle caught on an outraised arm. The soft soles of his shoes slipped on something, sending him skidding around the corner and into the wall before his shield could cushion the collision. His breath rushed out of his lungs.

Gasping frantically for air, he pushed off from the bare stone. His chest ached from the impact and his chin stung, but he mercifully hadn't hit hard enough to break his nose. His legs trembled as he went to take another step, unable to resume the momentum he had lost.

He took in his surroundings, making the most of his reluctantly self-enforced rest. Like in much of the tower, a few closed doors lined the halls. He hadn't dared to slow enough to check what sat on the other side of them earlier, but now he'd no other option.

Forcing his legs to move, he hobbled over to the closest door. The handle refused all attempts to turn. He could've broken through with a well-placed blast of air, but the echo of such destruction would only alert the hound chasing him. He moved on to the next door. This one opened out into the lower seating for the tower's main training arena. The vast space beyond was definitely not a place to hide.

The third and fourth doors were no more willing to open than the first. The fifth had a hopeful amount of play in the latch, but it still refused to budge. Perhaps the sixth door would—

"I know you are close," his pursuer said in a sing-song tone that squeezed Henrie's throat.

He put his shoulder against the door and shoved with all his might. The latch gave, issuing an ear-grinding grate as it slid along the stone.

Henrie leant against the doorframe. A set of stairs led the way down into a darkness a shade lighter than shadow.

He slipped into the space, taking pains to push the door back as far as the latch would allow. The slip of metal ground its way back along the stone, reverberating through his arms and screeching in his ears. How much noise did it make in the emptiness of the hallways? He didn't want to think about it.

With the door shut, he turned to where the stairs lay. Absolute darkness swallowed the room, leaving no distinction between the maw of the steps, the walls hemming two sides, or the door on his right.

Not waiting for his eyes to adjust, he groped his way down, sensing each step with a questing toe. The smell of damp permeated the space the further he descended. Was this one of the tower's old storage spaces or a dungeon? He knew of the isolation cells where troublesome spellsters went, and sometimes didn't return, but he was also far from there. Wasn't he? The area didn't seem to match Dylan's recounting of his stint in the cells during their adolescence. His magic was also very much intact, with not even the faintest of pulls from the magic-nullifying metal.

He caught sounds beyond his frantic breathing and erratic steps; the sibilation of another speaking—hushed words too quiet even for his elven hearing to make sense of—followed by an abrupt answering shush, then the hesitant pad of bare feet treading carefully upon stone.

Henrie paused upon reaching where the stairs evened out. His hands remained on the wall to his right, the brickwork seeming to continue in a straight line. Peering into the darkness directly ahead did nothing.

Dare he go further? More than one person waited in the darkness, that much was clear. But the uncertainty of their feelings towards him paled in comparison to what the hound definitely had planned.

Steeling himself, he took a few purposeful strides towards the wall, finding the way ended abruptly, and carried on to his left to where another set of stairs continued down. The second flight was a handful of steps leading into what was definitely the final space. It loomed on his left, the cool unforgiving darkness sucking at his senses and prickling his skin.

He took a step into that abyss, abandoning the wall on his right.

The door at the top of the stairs slammed open. Amber light poured in from the hall, silhouetting a figure and gleaming off the length of their sword.

"You chose wrong."

Henrie scuttled deeper into the darkness, hoping it cloaked him as well as it did the others residing here. Whatever this room was, dungeon or disused storage, there had to be a place he could hide. Some nook he could tuck into until the hound either gave up his pursuit or gave him an opening to flee back up the stairs.

The shadows shifted in his periphery. After the noises, he had expected one or two figures, maybe even a small group of five. The movements coming from all sides, coupled with their hushed footsteps, suggested double that. He whipped his head from one side to the other, trying to track them, to determine what threat they might be to himself.

He inched further back from the stairs, one arm seeking what sat behind him lest he collided with a pillar or a wall. All the while, he kept an eye on the man slowly descending the stairs.

Just how much damage had the table done? The hound's limp didn't appear to hinder him drastically nor did Henrie spy any obvious injury that would hinder the usage of his weapon, but the man also took each step at such a leisurely pace that there was no way to be certain.

Was fleeing still an option? Even if granted the opportunity, did he have the stamina left to outrun the hound any further? The pounding of his heart screamed yes. The growing ache in his legs and chest spoke otherwise.

The tread of someone directly at his back reached his senses a moment before an arm wrapped around his shoulders. He stiffened in their grip as a hand clamped down on his face, covering his mouth before a single scream could escape.

"Hush," whispered the figure.

On the edge of his vision, he caught others slipping through the dark, their forms only faintly illuminated by the light creeping through the distant doorway.

A few of the figures carried themselves as though they bore weapons. Were they tower guards? He heard only the softest slap of bare feet in their passage, too quiet for a human to make out until it was too late.

Could the hound see them? The man couldn't have had time to adjust to the darkness and humans often complained about needing more light than their elven counterparts.

The hound reached the base of the stairs. He turned, the heel of his boot grinding dully against the floor. Even though there was no chance he could see a thing in the dark, he was definitely focused on where Henrie stood.

A shield sputtered around him, despite his best efforts to stop it. The purple glow illuminated flashes of the space, too brief and blinding to make out any details. The afterimages burned his eyes, throwing garish blotches across his vision.

His ears caught the confident stride of the hound heading for him. Then the hurried slap of another's footsteps.

He cleared his vision in time to spy one of the shadowy figures rushing at the hound, a length of something long and thin in their hands. Two others, bearing similar arms, swiftly followed. The first one slammed into the hound, thrusting their weapon before them.

The hound jerked back, his whole body stiffening. The sword fell from his hands, the echo of its collision with the stone floor not quite enough to mask the gurgles as he struggled to breathe.

Henrie's throat constricted at the sound. He had heard far too much of it from the fallen. It set his stomach to bubbling and left an acidic taste in the back of his throat. He tried to swallow. He should've felt vindicated that the hound got precisely what he deserved, but he just felt sick.

At least he was safe, for now. He might not be able to see the people responsible for saving him, but they obviously had clear animosity towards the King's Hounds if they were so ready to kill one.

"I wouldn't struggle, if I were you," said a voice reedy with age. At first, Henrie thought they spoke to him, but they appeared to be addressing the hound.

"Let's put him out of his misery, then." The two figures at the first one's flank rushed forward, finally toppling the hound. They slammed their weapons into the man only to drive them in again and again.

Henrie cringed from the sound. He tried to cover his ears, to block out the shattering of bone and the squelch of flesh, but found himself unable to whilst the person holding him clung tight. Why weren't they releasing him? With the hound dead, he had thought himself safe.

He thrashed within those binding arms, his shield sputtering in and out of existence.

"Let him go, Hans," snapped the same reedy voice. "And stop

hammering at that corpse, you two. The deed is done. He's not getting any less dead."

The hands keeping Henrie in place suddenly released him.

He rushed forward, swinging to confront the person who had kept him from making a sound. It was another elf, a man old enough to have white streaking their hair. He didn't recognise the face, but the central tower alone housed hundreds of people.

The name was a different matter. *Hans.* In a kingdom where most elves bore names that merely sounded exotic or, like himself, were more in line with local trends, a proper elven name stood out. The only Hans he'd ever heard of had been a guardian. One who had disappeared the same day his spellster charge was rumoured to have fled the tower. That'd been five years ago.

What were they doing down here? What was this place?

And why were they the only ones to have survived the slaughter?

The final squelch of force being applied to flesh drew Henrie's attention back to the fallen hound. The people who'd been attacking the corpse had finally heeded the reedy voice. Were they also guardians?

The spark of a flint caught his eye. He glanced over at the same moment a torch flared to life.

Yellow brightness blazed across his vision. Holding up a hand and turning away, Henrie squinted through a wash of tears and burning eyes to finally take in the room. The cold brickwork, the row of alcoves blocked off by bars. The latter had to make this a dungeon. For who? Clearly not spellsters. The tower servants? The guardians?

With his eyes adjusting to the light, he returned to its source. Other torches dotted the space between the barred alcoves, yet the people remained content in lighting the one. They held it aloft over the dead hound, flooding the scene in a sallow glow.

The hound was definitely dead. Even if the man could've survived losing the amount of blood currently pooling beneath him, the trio of spears jutting from his body would be enough to keep him in place. They remained upright, propped against the very one that had taken the hound's life.

Henrie took a second look at the spear shafts. They looked to be made of rusty metal and roughly the same thickness as the bars. A few of the alcove barriers even bore gaps that might've matched their length.

Two humans circled the hound. One of them held up his bare foot to the hound's boot. "Think he might be my size?" he enquired of his red-haired companion in a gravelly tone.

The woman wrinkled her nose and wobbled her splayed hand. "Maybe? But if you're looting his body, then make it quick." Neither of them were dressed the way Henrie typically saw guardians, no dark grey tunics and trousers, but they definitely had the same mannerisms.

Examining the other people crowding around him, he discovered that, elven and human alike, they were all garbed in ragged underclothes held in place with lengths of rope or strips of cloth. Some looked as though they hadn't bathed or been able to groom themselves for months, if not years. "Why are you—?"

"Quietly," a familiar voice softly urged. "We can't be sure more haven't followed this one."

Henrie flinched from the sudden pressure on his shoulder, belatedly realising it was an attempt to soothe. He faced the person, stepping back as recognition hit him. "Guardian Tricia?" He had heard rumours. Some said she was dead, others claimed she'd been retired now Dylan was gone. A few swore they had seen her helping the newer guardians tend to their newborn charges. "What are *you* doing down here? I thought—"

Tricia shushed him as one might a child after a nightmare. "You're one of Dylan's friends. Henrie, right? Edwyn's boy?"

His chin wobbled at the mention of his guardian. The final image of the man flashed across his vision. His guardian had given his life to bide Henrie, and the other spellsters, time.

His guardian strode towards the hounds, even as they continued to eliminate every living thing in their path. He faced down those monsters, screaming his rage. Battle cry or challenge, the words were lost to the surrounding sounds of terror and death.

Edwyn had wielded little more than a belt knife, the same as every other guardian. He stood in the doorway nevertheless, gesturing for everyone to run, to hide, even as the hounds turned their focus to him.

Sniffing, Henrie attempted to dry his eyes with his sleeve, giving up when the undyed linen came back streaked with blood that wasn't his. He had struggled to keep his emotions at bay. He couldn't give in to them now.

"Sweet one." Tricia cupped his face. She deftly wiped his cheeks, seemingly unconcerned that the blood also stained her thumbs. "I didn't mean to upset you." She drew him close, enveloping his shoulders in an embrace that, at any other time, would've evoked safety.

But he wasn't safe. These guardians, despite managing to kill a hound, wouldn't be able to protect him outside the confines of this dungeon. No more than Edwyn had.

"We have to leave." He levered himself out of Tricia's grasp and made for the stairs. And he couldn't stay here. He needed to find Harriet, find his friends or anyone else who still lived, and get out.

He would see that his guardian's sacrifice meant *something*.

Tricia's hand pulling back on his was the only move she made to halt him. It was enough.

"Leave, my boy?" that reedy voice piped up. Now Henrie had light, he discovered it belonged to a human man. With him near bald and withered, he looked to be the oldest of the bunch. "Now, I'm not saying I wouldn't love to see the sky again, but look at us. We can't just go bursting through the halls all willy-nilly. We need a plan, and that means knowing what you're up against. So let's start with you telling us what's happening out there, shall we?"

"Nothing good," one of the other guardians remarked. She looked younger than the rest by several decades and, where a great deal of the others appeared to have been down here for some time, she still had a bit of sun-blanching to her otherwise brown hair. The fire in her eyes suggested she would fight just as viciously as the guardians who'd fallen in the halls. "He looks like he's been wading with my uncle's pigs during the blight slaughter."

As truthful as the words were, it still earned the woman a stern glare from Tricia and a hearty clip across the back of her head from Hans.

"What's happening?" Henrie echoed. He shook his head. How could he begin to describe such madness? "They... they just attacked us." He clapped a hand over his mouth, stifling a whimper.

No warning. No demands. Just screams and the smell of blood. It was everywhere, drifting along the edges of his senses, waiting to swallow him whole.

His chest tightened. The flickering torchlight dimmed, blurring the faces around him. What had they done to deserve this? The tower was meant to be safe. The one place a spellster didn't need to fear the hounds. It had been that way for generations, for *centuries*.

Had the king decided otherwise?

Tricia drew him close again. She gently prised his hand away from his mouth and smoothed back his hair, tucking the strands behind his ears just as his own guardian had done during Henrie's childhood. "Steady," she murmured. "Listen to my voice." Her hands cupped either side of his face, shielding his vision until only she filled his view. "Deep breaths. In and out. That's it."

He followed her direction, focusing only on the measured beat and the lick of bittersweet in her praise. With each exhale, the crushing pressure binding his ribs retreated that little bit more.

"Now," Tricia said, finally releasing her hold. "*Who* is attacking?"

"The King's Hounds."

She exchanged confused looks with the other guardians.

"Impossible," mumbled one of them.

"Explain that," the brown-haired guardian remarked, jerking a thumb towards the body sprawled at the foot of the stairs.

Tricia's lips flattened into a grim line. "I came down here when the alarm was sounded, looking to free this lot and get them out whilst the guards dealt with a threat that should've been minimal."

Henrie kept his expression neutral. How had she planned to get this group out when the only entrance would've been surrounded by the very guards she claimed should've been able to handle a force at their gates?

And, for that matter, how was he going to escape now?

"The plank I had bracing the door got knocked out during the fighting," Tricia continued. "We got locked in here until you came along. I thought that after the army fell…" Her eyes grew distant as her voice drifted off. No doubt remembering Dylan, her charge, had also been in the army. "I never would've thought hounds were the culprits."

"I still can't believe it," the first guardian said, sounding no less willing to bend to the truth. "Why would the hounds, of all people, attack the tower? It goes against their creed."

"The why doesn't matter," Brown-hair declared. "We are meant to guide and protect our charges from all dangers, and protect them we shall." She picked up the hound's fallen sword. "Search him for more weapons. Any length of blade is better than none."

"What about our makeshift spears?" asked one of the others, his gravelly voice rumbling through the murmurs. He had stripped the hound of his boots, although the red-haired woman now wore them.

"Leave them," said the withered guardian, his reedy tone no less authoritative. "They're too cumbersome to be of any use in close quarters."

"Close quarters?" echoed one of the much younger men. "You expect to win fighting close? Against the King's Hounds? That's suicide."

"We took out this one, didn't we?" another woman countered, this one also an elf.

"Technically, *I* did," stressed the old, reedy-voiced guardian. "In the dark, with him focused only on his spellster target. If he had known we were here, if he'd any elven blood, none of us would still be standing. We will not get the opportunity of surprise again."

She shook her head but didn't voice any further thoughts.

"No different to expecting a spellster to survive meeting one," Hans said, shrugging. "Eirian's right, I spent my life raising that babe they gave me. Teaching them how to walk, to talk, to use her magic for good took the best years of my life and, by the gods!" He slapped his hand down onto the red-haired woman's shoulder, gaining him a firm nod. "You best believe I'd give what's left to keep another spellster alive."

Fresh tears pricked Henrie's eyes. Had his own guardian felt the same way when he stood between them and the King's Hounds?

Hans' speech seemed to empower the elven woman. Nodding, she squared her shoulders. "If the gods will it, we'll be enough to make a difference."

"We won't do a thing standing around down here," Tricia declared, having already ascended half of the stairway. "Let's head out. Keep quiet and together." She frowned thoughtfully for a moment. "We should head for the alchemist's quarters. The daggers they craft aren't much, but even a hound isn't immune to a sharp edge. And *you...*" She levelled a finger at Henrie. "No matter what, you will stay centre position."

He bobbed his head in agreement.

"We should head for an exit," Hans argued, earning a scowl from Tricia. "I'm not saying we should avoid arming ourselves, but one sharp edge is as good as another and I'm damn sure hounds are immune to the full damage an *infitialis* dagger inflicts. It's still magic, after all."

"What?" Henrie breathed. He knew the daggers were solely crafted by the alchemists. Knew they were lauded as masterpieces to prove they'd the full training to work with the unstable metal. He had guessed magic was involved in making them so deadly, but the rest? *Hounds are immune to magic?* He hadn't ever heard such a detail.

If any guardian heard him, they chose to ignore his confusion, opting instead to bicker amongst themselves. Some advocated for charging the hounds and taking them from behind, as if it would make a difference. That idea was swiftly suppressed, much to Henrie's relief. But even amongst the majority who advocated leaving, they couldn't agree on the best way to escape. Not a one suggested the possibility of more survivors.

It looked as though he alone held that hope.

Henrie left the guardians to their arguing, climbing the stairs in silence. There had to be others. His beloved. His friends. He would find them. On his own, if need be.

He halted as Tricia laid a hand on his shoulder on his way past her. "Give them a moment. Some of them haven't left this place in years."

Did they have another moment to waste? "If we're getting out of here at all," he snapped. "Then we need to leave before more hounds come." How many others hunted for survivors amongst the dead on the ground level? *More than one.* The tower wasn't tiny, it would demand at least a half-dozen for a proper search.

Henrie turned to the guardians, ready to speak further only to realise they had already fallen silent. In the gloom, their faces weren't clear, but several nodded and hastened to collect what they could and exit the dungeon.

He glanced at the fallen hound before following the last guardian out the door. *Immune.* The way the man had looked right at him whilst he was invisible, how blasé he'd been in the centre of a magical blast. *Unaffected by magic.* If he had known nothing he did would've halted the hound, would he have dared risk moving at all?

No, that wasn't quite true. One thing *had* worked. The hound had collapsed after being hit by a table. An object Henrie had moved with magic. And the man had died via a simple rusty cell bar to the throat.

If they could be killed, then they could be overcome with sheer numbers.

But how many spellsters would think to use anything beyond magic? *Few.* He doubted many even lived long enough to process what was happening much less figure out a plan of attack.

Without a way to halt the hounds for good, they were doomed.

It didn't take long for the guardians' resoluteness to turn into quiet disbelief. They gingerly made their way through the halls, huddled together like children and stepping as though the floor might give at any moment. All whilst brandishing the meagre weapons they had stolen from the hound. *Daggers and knives.* Some of the guardians had nothing beyond their fists.

Henrie had assumed the suggestion to head for the alchemist's quarters was because it would've been the only place to find more weapons, but they had come across several bloody, bent or broken blades along the way. The guardians barely paused to regard them with any interest.

Would being armed matter? The hounds had torn through greater barriers. For the attack to have reached the central tower, the invaders would've clashed with the gate guards who wielded better weapons and stood in greater numbers than the seven surrounding him like a contingent of personal bodyguards.

The guardian's chosen passage took them down different sections than the path Henrie had fled through. He hadn't questioned the decision. Perhaps they thought going in the opposite direction the hound had come from would lessen the chance of stumbling upon another.

For the moment, he believed it to be true. His ears caught no footsteps beyond their own; the pad of bare feet, the lighter step of his own soft-soled shoes, and the firm tread coming from both Tricia's boots and those stripped off the hound.

Henrie was under no illusions that it made them safe. Did it even matter if they were heard? The old, reedy-voiced guardian was right in how the death of the King's Hound being pure luck. Only a surprise attack had stopped the enemy from advancing. Those out in the halls had no such good fortune with blade or barrier.

The shields. It hadn't occurred to him at the time, but the woman who had slaughtered a room of spellsters and guardians had treated every shield in her path as though they didn't exist, striding through each shimmering purple barrier without a hint of hesitation.

Stumbling, Henrie drew his attention back to the hallway they currently trod. He didn't dare to glance down, but the object he had tripped on held a soft quality.

Every turn they took revealed only more death. *So many.* Servants, spellsters and guardians alike lay in piles, some huddled together, others in pieces across a doorway. Everywhere he looked, the only commonality to be found was how the fallen were all those who had called the tower home.

Not a single sign that the enemy had fallen.

He tried to focus on other parts of the hall, to *not* think about the nature of what they stepped over and trod past. It worked, to an extent. His tears flowed less freely. Or perhaps that had more to do with having nothing left to cry rather than gaining control over his emotions. Either way, they no longer blurred his vision. But convincing himself that the bodies weren't really there meant his gaze drifted to what else had been left behind.

And what was missing.

The walls showed scorches from where the stonework had been blasted by fire, whilst other sections bore impact stresses caused from a blast of air. Both instinctive lashings of panicked minds. Only those who showed a certain aptitude for battle were trained to use their magic against an opponent. A lot of the tower's inhabitants would never have fought in their entire life. Including himself.

Icicles, belonging to those more adept in their attacks, filled corners and doorways or stretched across the halls like giant claws. They dripped, slowly melting in the humid air. The remains of similar defences pooled elsewhere.

What drew Henrie's eye were the gaps in those icy forms, the places where a person should've been standing, still encapsulated.

Immune to magic. No matter how many times he repeated this newly discovered truth, a chill still ghosted through his flesh. He pulled the neck of his robe tight as if it would make a difference.

Of all the theories he'd ever heard about the King's Hounds, not a one had dared to suggest they could negate the very forces spellsters had at their command. *Why didn't they tell us?* Had the overseers thought no one would believe it? Several rumours already suggested the hounds gained unnatural abilities by drinking spellster blood.

The guardians would pause at each unopened door. One or two would check the room beyond, occasionally coming back with something that could pass as a weapon. A broom, a leg broken off an old stool and what appeared to be one of the servant's stockings with a piece of the stonework from the dungeon shoved inside. These items armed those who had left the dungeon with only their fists.

The arsenal of the desperate. Knowing what the guardians knew of the enemy and their abilities, he understood why his own had thrown himself at the approaching threat rather than seek a way out. There wasn't much hope in fighting back, but a slim chance was still better than none.

Henrie never tried following the guardians into any of the rooms. He needed only to look at their grim faces to know they'd found the same death that littered their path. Twisted mockeries of people collapsed against walls or sprawled across the floor, some with bloodied hands still clutching at the very wounds that had claimed their lives.

None of them wore the standard spellster garb. Many appeared to be the servants responsible for the tower's upkeep. Their deaths puzzled him. If the King's Hounds were wholly responsible for this slaughter, then why attack the servants?

Were they wrong about who was behind this? Were they assassins pretending to be hounds? *Not all of them.* The man the guardians killed in the dungeon had definitely been immune to the blasts of pure magic Henrie unleashed upon him.

The next door they came across was closed, the first one they had encountered since taking this route. They halted beside it, waiting in silence as Hans tested the handle. The man shook his head.

Locked. Just like the ones Henrie abandoned whilst fleeing the hound. He hadn't wondered why those doors weren't kicked in like the rest, not at first. Could they have harboured people?

The guardians briefly debated amongst themselves in hushed tones as to whether forcing their way into the room was worth the risk of being heard. They hadn't encountered any resistance, hound or otherwise, but that was no guarantee that one wasn't around the next corner. He didn't know just how many there were, but they couldn't all be roaming the level above.

If there was even one other still down here, where would they be? The guardians must have some idea of the strategic points an enemy might claim. Why else would they choose the more involved route towards the alchemist's quarter?

Hans gestured for silence. The man stood still with his ear pressed to the door. When quiet fell over the others, he remained there for all of a few moments before issuing a gasp and summoning the guardian, Eirian. Together, they wedged the stolen sword into the crack between door and jamb, prising it open.

The dry wood gave with a mournful creak that echoed down the hall.

Henrie hunched his shoulders. His gaze flicked from the distant corner ahead to the one at their backs as he waited for something to come barrelling into sight. His heart thundered in his ears.

Along with the whisper of a whimper.

At first, he thought the sound came from one of the guardians, then he noticed Hans had vanished into the room whilst Eirian stood guard outside. The man re-emerged from the room almost as swiftly as he had entered. He clutched a small figure to his chest. Blood soaked their clothes, no patch dark enough to be their own.

Issuing a squeak of surprise, the red-haired guardian scurried to Hans' side. She took the child from his arms, murmuring softly into the small, round ear. "I've got you, little one." She tucked the child's head against her shoulder. "I have you."

If the child heard her, they didn't react. Those huge brown eyes peered at them over the woman's shoulder, but the hollowness in their gaze was much like the lifeless stare of a doll.

Henrie's breath caught in his throat. Never had he seen a child's face look so empty.

Feeling fresh wetness on his cheeks, he wiped them for what had to be the hundredth time. His sleeves were soaked in a mixture of tears and blood, useless at mopping up any further moisture. Somehow, he'd been able to hold it together better when he was alone, unable to see his emotions, his disbelief and horror, mirrored in another's face.

The other guardians surged forward. Tricia checked the child over, announcing that they were uninjured, whilst others further investigated the room despite Hans' claims that there was no one else to save.

"She looks to be one of the servant children," said the red-haired guardian.

Tricia nodded. "That's likely why she survived. They couldn't sense her."

"Sense?" Henrie echoed, the word catching in his throat. Surely, she wasn't implying that the hounds could sense magic as well as being immune to its effects. That would make it impossible for any person, any *spellster*, to escape unnoticed.

If either woman heard him, they chose to ignore him.

"Why was she here?" Red's brow furrowed even as she continued to rock the child. "I thought servant children were kept away from the central tower."

"She probably followed a parent or older sibling. It happens." Tricia stroked the girl's head. "Poor thing chose the wrong moment to be disobedient."

"Did she?" the countered sole elven woman of their group. Since leaving the dungeon, she hadn't faltered in keeping watch over the many ways they could be ambushed. Even now, she kept her distance from the others, bouncing on the balls of her bare feet, the knife she'd taken from the hound at the ready. "They've done all this." She gestured to the bodies slumped against the walls. All of them wore the practical garb of cleaners. "Who's to say for certain that the outer wall hasn't been stormed?"

The other two women fell silent. They exchanged uncertain looks, neither one seemingly willing to admit they had no idea what was actually happening even within the tower, much less elsewhere.

Henrie wet his lips, tasting blood and salt in equal measure. He hadn't thought about the servant housing. He hadn't been there, no spellster was allowed even that, but everyone knew they were built into the outer walls, rumoured to be accessible only through the front courtyard. If that were true, then the people within were just as trapped as everyone else.

"Forget the outer walls," growled one of the other guardians, the low tone coupled with his gravelly voice grounding each word to paste. They were the first words Henrie had heard the man utter since leaving the dungeon. "We'll need to get through both courtyards if we've any chance of escaping as is."

"No," Eirian replied. "The courtyards are too risky. They're too open and there will be guards. If we can get to the gardens and cross the training arenas unnoticed, we can use the secret entrance."

Gravel-voice wrinkled his nose. "That entrance is a myth."

"It's not," Tricia said. She'd been nodding along with Eirian's plan as though in full agreement. "I've seen it. I used it. Why else do you think they threw Eirian and myself in the dungeon with you lot?"

Henrie kept his features carefully neutral. There was another way out? More importantly, she had tried to get Dylan out through it? Had she known the fateful attack on the army was coming?

Did she know more about what was happening now than she let on? Where had she been when the attack started that had given her a chance to free the imprisoned guardians?

"Whatever we're doing," the unnamed elven guardian cut in, "we should keep moving."

"Agreed," echoed Hans. "Having a spellster with us endangers us enough without making it easier for them."

Henrie faced the man, confused. The hounds were clearly slaughtering everyone they found. How did his presence put them in more danger?

"We're not leaving him behind," Eirian declared. She grabbed Henrie's arm, dragging him closer as though he was a child to be snatched away. Was that what had happened to her spellster charge? She had been forced to leave them behind? At this secret entrance? "He is under our care and I refuse to—"

"Peace," Hans said, holding up his hands in surrender. "I'm not suggesting any such thing. Only that, if we are sneaking out, then masking his magic would make it vastly less complicated."

Mask? Even if Henrie accepted the idea that hounds could sense magic—an ability that sounded more myth than truth—it couldn't possibly be strong enough to pick out one spellster in an entire building of them. Could it?

He recalled how persistent the hound had been in tracking him through the hallways. All this time, he had thought his inability to flee quietly had given him away, but it hadn't mattered. He could avoid making a single sound and they'd still find him.

What of when he'd been hiding under the dead, too terrified of being discovered to think of breathing, let alone something to defend himself?

The icy grip upon his skin burrowed through to his core, leaving it quaking. How close had they come to sensing him then? Had they mistaken his latent power for one of the dying?

A sliver of cold whispered along his skin, lifting all the fine hairs and setting the tips of his ears to tingling.

It took all of his strength to slowly turn and eye the way they'd come, catching movement on his periphery before he could fully focus. Were those footsteps he heard rushing towards them?

There was nothing different about the passage. Just flickering shadows caused by the sputter of a dying torch. The measured beat in his ears was merely the rapid pulse of his heart. No figure in the distance. No approaching death.

Relief slowly loosened the tightness in his chest and jellified his limbs. He braced himself against the wall, focusing inwards to steady the quaking.

His focus returned to the guardians and their hushed bickering.

"We head for the alchemist's quarters," Red said, shuffling the child to balance on her hip. "It's on the way to the back entrance, grabbing an *infitialis* collar, even an unfinished one, won't be too much of a diversion. There might even still be survivors down there."

Henrie swallowed in an effort to moisten his throat. Sulin had always claimed that raw pieces of the magic nullifying metal were kept in the alchemist's quarters for a damn good reason, that they would react violently if subjected to the untethered magic most spellsters emitted.

"Dog metal is dangerous in any form," Gravel-voice said. "But using a half-worked chunk is asking for a painful death."

"And where does that risk lie in comparison to having a hound sneak up on us?"

The man's frown deepened. He stared Red down in silence for

several breaths before giving a grunt of begrudging acceptance and a curt upward thrust of his chin.

The alchemist's quarters. A destination they had previously dismissed as being not worth the risk. The place was situated underground, a warren of alcoves and rooms with their heavy doors and dim, sooty lanterns. *Dark and dungeon-like.* At least, if his alchemist friend could be believed to be doing anything other than attempting to scare him.

But all the precautions to keep the tower and the alchemists safe from the metal they worked also meant there was no way out beyond the stairs leading in. *If we're discovered...*

His gaze slid to a figure who had propped themselves against the wall, their hand still clutching the dark patch in their gut. The way these people had fallen looked almost as though they'd been struck in passing, left in agony to slowly bleed out.

If a hound did discover them, he prayed his end came quickly.

CHAPTER 5

Henrie froze as they rounded the corner. Before them stood the stairway leading to the levels above.

They'd taken a fair number of turns throughout their quest to the alchemist's quarters, even backtracking when they found one way blocked by the splintered remains of furniture.

He hadn't realised their path would take them right by here.

The air seemed darker, choked with the stench of blood and spilled guts. Shadows and corpses shrouded the stairs. There were few of the latter compared to the rest of the tower. A handful of guardians lay sprawled across the steps, their crimson life-force pooling in the hollows that so many feet had worn into the stone over the centuries. One figure near the bottom sat in such a bloody state that Henrie guessed the man had tumbled down.

Brandishing her stolen sword, Eirian tiptoed up the stairs with Hans at her side. They halted at the top, their heads tilted.

Henrie held his breath, straining to hear any sign of movement from above. The faintest of screams, the brashness of weapons meeting, even the pleas of the desperate and the dying.

All those sounds, the cries he'd heard earlier whilst hiding beneath the dead, were now absent. The same stillness they'd walked through to get here wadded his ears with pain and the rapid beat of his heart. *Are they really all dead?*

Swallowing through the tightness in his throat, Henrie turned from the stairway. He didn't want to think what that quiet meant, didn't want to give the panic squeezing his heart any further cause to tighten its grip.

It wasn't long before the two guardians crept back down. They motioned the rest into one of the hallways.

"Sounds like they've moved upstairs," Hans whispered.

Eirian nodded grimly. Henrie didn't know exactly what her human hearing picked up, but the elven guardian looked to have heard far more than he had wanted.

Gasping, Red clutched the girl tighter. She turned from the group, putting herself between the girl and the maw of the stairs. "What possible reason could there be for going higher, except for…" She fell silent, staring off down the hall littered with the dead.

The classrooms. A nauseous wave rolled over Henrie at the thought. He closed his eyes, trying to keep himself from vomiting even as liquid continued to pool in his mouth.

The levels directly above were the most used of all the tower's public areas. It held only communal rooms; dining halls, the library, the healer's quarters. All places he had walked through hundreds— thousands—of times without a thought. During daylight hours, that level was the most populated beyond those used for teaching children.

Above those levels were several more catering to adult accommodation along with the bathing chambers. Then the classrooms and the children's dorms. The nursery…

They're trapped. There was no way to leave the upper levels without descending the very stairs the King's Hounds currently climbed. Dozens of lives would be just sitting there with no inkling of what was coming for them. Of the monsters that could sense their magic, that were immune to their every defence.

Losing the battle with his nausea, Henrie doubled over as the first heave gripped his body. With having expelled his last meal hours ago, little came out. Nevertheless, he dry-retched until his trembling brought him to his knees. The world grew hazy as his lungs gasped for air in the mercilessly short spaces between each upheaval, fading until even the sputtering torchlight felt far too dim.

Someone touched his back, the light sensation barely noticeable through his binder. Those bony fingers continued to rub his back as a buzz of speech reached his ears, the words muffled by the pounding in his skull but the tone gently reassuring.

He clung to that sound, using it to orientate himself.

When he finally managed to get his stomach's heaving under control, he looked over his shoulder to find the oldest guardian of the bunch crouched at his side.

"Steady," the man said as Henrie went to sit back on his heels, the reedy note in his voice had grown a softer edge. "Deep breaths now."

Wiping his mouth on his sleeve, Henrie tried to focus on steadying his breathing, on slowing the frantic beating of his heart. He needed to rein in his emotions and keep a tight grip on his reactions. Otherwise, the smallest scare was going to make him a beacon for the hounds.

His gaze slid to the other guardians, settling on Red and the child. She had carried the girl the whole way through the halls, refusing to let her go for anything. Even now, she kept the child's head tucked under her own, shielding her from the bodies as much as she could.

Henrie doubted it made much of a difference. The girl barely blinked.

Slowly, he became aware of two guardians arguing, the hushed tone of the elven woman in their group the harshest as it hissed into his ears.

"We can't just walk away and let them slaughter everyone." She faced down Gravel-voice, barely coming up to mid-chest on the man, her teeth bared as she bounced on in place, clearly eager to seek retribution. "There are children up there. If we attack from behind, we—"

"We will be killed," Gravel-voice interrupted. "Even if we could catch up to them unannounced, we'd need better weapons than these." He brandished what looked to be a stool leg. "We have the girl." He jabbed the end of his weapon in Red's direction. "And we have him." He moved the stool leg to point at Henrie. "*Us* going after the King's Hounds puts *their* lives at risk. As much as I want to go charging up there, how much of a match would we realistically be?"

"More than our fellow guardians are now." She turned on her heel, trotting back towards the stairs. Not a soul tried to stop her. Henrie wasn't sure anyone could have.

He watched the woman vanish from sight, then listened until even her footsteps were gone. "She's going to die." The words slipped out before he could regulate the thought. They had to already know she was running to her death. *She* had to know.

And she went anyway.

The other guardians either nodded or silently bowed their heads, already mourning. Gravel-voice looked ready to follow her, but held his ground at the smallest of head shakes from Hans.

The bony hand returned to offer Henrie reassurance, this time, its firm grip landing on his shoulder. "I know you've been through a lot," said Reedy-voice. "You need to keep staying strong for a little longer. Can you do that for me, son?"

Nodding, Henrie wobbled to his feet. The longer they stayed in one place, especially so near the only way down, the greater their chance of being hunted became. They couldn't stop for anything, couldn't go back for anyone. Not whilst they were still within the tower.

And who knew, maybe one guardian's sacrifice *would* make a difference upstairs. *A life for a life.* Just as Edwyn had chosen to give his to ensure Henrie had a chance at keeping his. It still didn't seem like an equal trade-off.

He'd make it count nevertheless.

CHAPTER 6

They made their way through the halls to much of the same destruction and death. Something in his core wound itself tighter the closer they got to their destination. Henrie found himself holding his breath as they approached each corner, unable to will exhalation until they discovered the way was clear.

To his relief, they reached the stairs leading down to the alchemist's quarters without a hint of being followed. The way down looked no different to the dozen or so other times Henrie had walked by the entrance. No blood stained the steps, no bodies lay anywhere in sight and, no matter how much he strained to hear a thing, not a scream or groan to be heard.

A part of him hoped that, by virtue of having little magic to begin with, those in the alchemist's quarters had been overlooked. He tried to temper that hope with realism. People would have fled down here in search of places to hide, just as they'd done in going upstairs. It would've drawn the hounds' attention.

For everyone to be dead was a far more likely scenario than finding a pocket of survivors.

Sulin. Henrie sunk to the floor, perching himself on the top step. He had tried not to think about his friends or beloved and what they might be facing, tried to remain strong, but it was difficult when faced with the place one of them would've been.

Or had he? Sulin mentioned a few days back about seeking favour from the overseers to help out in the gardens sometime this week, supposedly to work on a project involving *infitialis* and plants, but really to help Launtil. Had he gained that favour? His beloved Harriet often tended the gardens alongside Sulin's current infatuation and she hadn't mentioned anything. But if Sulin had, then it meant there was a chance his alchemist friend hadn't been here when the attack started.

That hope squeezed his chest tighter than any pressure he had ever experienced. He clung to that bittersweet pain, knowing full well it could mean greater anguish to follow. But he had already lost one dear friend along with his guardian and that was too many. He didn't know what he'd do if he had lost everyone.

Tricia, Hans and Red waited near the entrance—the latter to spare the servant girl from further visions of death, whilst the other two remained to protect them—as the rest descended into whatever fresh horror awaited those who dared. Henrie opted to remain alongside the three guardians. If Sulin was down there, he didn't want to see.

Hans paced the width of the stairway. The man's gaze never stayed still for long, nor did his hand loosen its grip on the sword he had procured from Eirian. He occasionally swung the blade as though testing its usefulness. His lips constantly twitched, pressing together just as they'd done whenever they reached a section where spellsters had fought back.

Henrie wished he knew more about the man, if only to understand what he was thinking. Was this grimness a natural reaction? Or did he think they were doomed?

The man halted to eye Henrie, the solid blackness of his irises reflecting the flickering light like twin mirrors. "What can you remember about their pattern of attack?"

"I don't—" He shook his head. Everything about this attack was senseless. Malevolent. How could there be any pattern to it? And what else could he tell them that they couldn't surmise? The hounds had burst through the doors and slaughtered everyone inside. *Except for me.* Because he had chosen to flee instead of fight. Evading the bite of death all thanks to tripping over a body, then having the presence of mind to haul another on top of him. "Not much."

This answer seemed to deepen the grim lines around Hans' mouth. He swiftly returned to his pacing.

Tricia patted Henrie's shoulder. "It's all right, dear. You've told us so much already, no one can expect you to remember every detail." A sharpness took her gaze as it shifted, slipping past him to spear the other guardian.

Hans grunted something that sounded like an agreement. "Knowing their movements would help us—help *him*—get to safety." He closed the distance between them, a sharp, and slightly fanatic, gleam in his eyes. "Did you happen to see who they targeted first amongst the spellsters and guardians?"

"Us," he managed, his throat tight. The man must've already realised that. What was he seeking confirmation for? To save himself over the spellsters he had sworn to protect? Was that downfall the reason why Hans had been in the dungeon with the other guardians?

"It follows what I heard in the beginning," Tricia added. "I'd say they were only focused on spellsters at first, then started attacking everything in their path once blood-lust took hold."

"Then is there any point in grabbing *infitialis* chains?" Red asked. She glanced over her shoulder at the stairway's open maw. "Lingering here leaves us vulnerable."

"It'll be enough to hide any survivors from the hounds once we get beyond the walls," Hans said. "Even if we get out, we can't risk the hounds following some magic trail."

Henrie could wrap his mind around the idea of a hound having the ability to pinpoint a spellster whilst magic was being used. There were times, typically at night, he swore he felt a distant charge in the air. But to hunt down a spellster who actively suppressed their magic? "They can sense us *that* well?"

Hans glanced at the other guardians before nodding. "Like a mouse sniffing out the winter harvest."

"You must understand," Tricia said, her voice almost a whisper, as though she feared retribution. She kept her gaze trained on the hallway opposite the one they'd come down. "The overseers controlled what information we could give our charges."

"Some of us didn't even know certain truths until we were thrown behind bars," Red added.

Henrie bobbed his head. He *did* understand. Spellsters might've feared their guardians finding out certain matters, but everyone knew the overseers' word was law. They sent spellsters to isolation for minor infractions, reprimanded guardians for a simple mistake— were even rumoured to chastise hounds if the mood took them—and caused guardian and spellster alike to just vanish.

"I doubt the overseers are in a position to punish us for sharing everything now," Tricia continued. "And the one who controls the King's Hounds deemed spellsters knowing the truth as unnecessary, claiming it was an advantage for the pack. How much of it is true, I don't know. They don't share specifics, but I doubt it's the same as the rumours the overseers allowed to circulate. It's possible that just having you standing here doing nothing is enough."

A prickling unease squeezed his throat. Suppressing his magic wasn't the easiest, the best he could do was try. He hoped that would be enough. There wasn't much else he could do without the aid of *infitialis*.

Red gave a frustrated sigh. "What's taking them so long?"

"It's a big space," Hans replied just as softly as she. "Lots of little rooms. Have you never…?"

Henrie's attention drifted as the guardian continued explaining the alchemist's quarters. He'd never been, only alchemists and the leashed were allowed, but Sulin spoke much about the place, what it looked like, what they worked on down there. How dangerous *infitialis* truly was to the slightest upset.

Maybe a few had managed to cause the raw dog metal to explode, blocking off any ability for the hounds to attack. Maybe unearthing those lucky enough to survive a blast was the reason the guardians below were taking so long.

Or, far more likely, they were struggling to find any *infitialis* that was safe enough to bring with them. There couldn't be many finished collars lying around and anything not fully worked ran the risk of killing a spellster as easily as a hound's blade.

The faint tap of booted feet echoed down the hall, the steady stride of someone confident they were the most dangerous thing nearby.

At first, Henrie thought it was his imagination, then Hans hushed them into silence. The man's dark gaze remained fixed on the direction they had come from. He clutched the sword hilt, his already pale knuckles turning whiter.

The others had yet to return from the alchemist's quarters. Was it a hound?

Even though Henrie knew it served no purpose other than to bring attention to them, the urge to draw his magic into himself and fade from visibility dug deep into his mind. He struggled to squash the instinct.

Hans wordlessly jerked his head to one side, indicating that they follow him. They trotted down the hallway, slipping into the nearest room and securing the door.

It was only then that Henrie spied the second doorway into the space. The room was more of a short corridor connecting the two parallel arcs of the main hallways. There were a bunch of them throughout the tower's design, especially in the lower levels, radiating from one hall to the other like spokes in a wheel. Only the couple nearer the alchemist's quarters had these doors, a blockade should an *infitialis* experiment go badly.

He raced to fully close the other door. It stood open only by a foot or so, with hinges that were greased enough to not make a sound as he slowly pushed the door shut.

The hurried pad of someone wearing soft-soled shoes reached him a split second before the familiar outline of a woman darted past the steadily closing gap.

Harry? His beloved was here? *Inside* the tower? And alive? Henrie left the guardians behind, heading for the hall beyond.

He reached the door in time to spy a figure vanishing around the corner.

Cocking his head, he listened for those footsteps only to hear nothing above his own rasping breath. Had he been mistaken? *Must be.* Harriet spent her days in the gardens. Safe. At least, he hoped.

What force would possess her to enter a place of obvious destruction?

Still, whoever it had been, even if it couldn't be Harriet, it wasn't a hound. And if there was another spellster still alive down here...

"Who's there?" he hissed down the hallway, not willing to raise his voice any further. "Anyone?"

Silence greeted his call. Not even the tap of boots or the pad of softer shoes. Had he not been loud enough? Maybe the person was human, with all the disadvantages of diminished senses.

He glanced the opposite way down the hall, then back into the room. The corner wasn't far. If anything, a quick peek would clear up the chance of danger coming from that direction.

He tiptoed his way to the corner, taking care to skirt the bodies and pools of blood. The last thing they needed was for the hounds to come upon a definite trail.

Flattening himself against the brickwork, he peered around the corner.

There was indeed someone in the hall. They stood before a pile of bodies blocking the corridor, clearly seeking a way over without disturbing them. Even though their back was to him, he knew that silhouette.

"Harry!" The name blurted out in a mixture of relief and fear before he could think to be quiet.

She whirled about, stiff with shock and terror that quickly melted as her gaze settled on him. Silently flailing her arm, she beckoned him to come closer.

Henrie shook his head and mirrored her movements, hoping his desperation was plain and enough to convince her. Whatever her reason for being in the tower, there was no getting out the way she had chosen.

She wasted no time in arguing, merely stopping her plea for him to join her and raced for him instead, one arm outstretched. Her other hand held tight to the skirts of her robe, giving her the freedom to leap puddles and bodies alike.

He winced at the slap of her feet, gesturing her to favour quiet over speed. But she was almost upon him, clearly too eager to be at his side to pay any heed to his warning.

The faintest hint of movement came from the mound of bodies at her back. They shifted, not as if they were alive, but as though someone shoved them from the other side.

Henrie took a step towards the mound. If someone was still holding on beneath all of that—

Harriet collided into him in a tangle of arms. "You're alive," she whispered into his ear, crushing his chest against hers.

The fear he had been clinging to, the thought of finding her dead, slowly rattled itself up from the depths. "I thought..." His throat squeezed off the rest of the words. He wrapped his arms around her waist, revelled in her softness and warmth. Her realness.

At some point during their embrace, he had laid his head on her shoulder and allowed his eyes to close.

He opened them to the sight of a man emerging from atop the mound of bodies, the curve of their sword glinting in the torchlight. Wet patches pockmarked the dark leather of their clothes. A streak of red clung to the matted, light brown hair and the upper point of a coppery ear dangled by a strip of skin.

The hound smiled at them, the expression twisted further by a bleeding wound scored along one cheek.

Terror squeezed Henrie's throat, sealing off the scream brewing in his chest. He struggled to get free of his beloved's grasp even as she clung to him, her relieved murmurs a noose of hot breath tightening around his neck.

Finally, he slipped free of her hold.

"Wha—?"

"Run." He shoved her ahead of him, aiming for the open door he had left. "Now!"

They bolted for the entrance, skirting what they could, leaping over everything else in their path. No matter how many steps he took, the door seemed to always be that little bit further away, taunting him.

The pounding of booted feet filled his ears. It squeezed his heart and clawed at his lungs, leaving him gasping for the next breath. *Don't look back.* It didn't matter how close the hound was, they were already too close.

His legs trembled. He stumbled, his foot slipping into a puddle of blood as he scrambled to find his balance.

The doorway suddenly loomed before him.

Harriet dove through with Henrie close on her heels. He barely cleared the entrance before throwing himself against the door, knowing his weight wouldn't be enough to keep the hound at bay. They needed a barricade. Of what?

Casting a frantic eye over the small stretch of hall, he saw little of use beyond a few torches. Nor was there a lock or bar to wedge them into.

"Ice the door!" he commanded Harriet.

Even though her brow scrunched in confusion, his beloved did as asked, freezing first the hinges and the point where the door's rolling latch clicked into an indent, before steadily sealing the remaining gaps between the iron-bound wood and the stone archway.

"What are you doing?" Hans growled, his voice low. He remained against the other door, peering through a crack in the wood. "You'll alert them to our presence."

"It's a bit late for that," Henrie shot back. "We've been spotted." Had the hound been following him the whole time? He doubted any of them would've held back for so long. They looked elven. Had they been lured here by Harriet's footsteps?

Something heavy slammed into the door, causing Henrie to jump back. Harriet's hastily cobbled seal seemed to hold for now. It wasn't perfect—it never could be, ice was tricky that way—but the thick build-up around the outer edge of the door fused it to the stone securely enough.

How likely it was to withstand someone thumping on the door in earnest, Henrie didn't know, but even a short pause would be enough. It had to be.

Hans hauled open the second door. "Through," he barked. "Now."

With her expression drifting between bewildered and dazed, Harriet trailed after the other two guardians.

Henrie followed them, pausing only long enough to search for the rest of the guardians and finding no one in sight beyond the trio.

"Now isn't the time for thinking," Hans snapped.

"The others," he replied, not taking his eyes off the stairway. The banging on the door blocked out all chance of hearing their approaching steps. "The *infitialis*..." How much time had passed since the four of them had descended into the alchemist's quarters? There wasn't any more to spare.

Hans followed his gaze and frowned. "You want to wait?" He shook his head. "We stay here and that hound catches us. The best we can hope for the others is that they're not caught trying to find us."

"We're running *from* the King's Hounds?" Harriet blurted, her hazel eyes bulging as she sought confirmation from the other two guardians. "I thought they were helping us."

"I'll explain everything later." Grabbing Harriet's hand, he followed the guardians down the hall. Somewhere ahead lay the path to the tower's side entrance.

Only the gods knew what awaited them out there.

Screaming reached Henrie's ears long before the side entrance was in sight. The sound funnelled down the hall, bouncing off the walls until it was a garbled mess. It didn't matter. The original sounds still rang through his head. The pleas to live, the denials of what was happening, the fading whimpers of the dying all snarled in a cacophony of pure terror.

The growing similarity of those cries told him all he needed to know of what lay ahead. He kept running towards the exit. Whatever lay ahead, it was their only chance at freedom.

Glancing back over his shoulder—and that of Hans who had taken up the rear—he saw nothing but corridors devoid of life. No hint of the hound they had fled from.

That didn't mean they were safe. The door they'd iced wasn't the sole entrance to these corridors, or even a main thoroughfare. Nor did he think the man would just abandon the chase.

So where had the hound gone? Were there others wandering down here in search of survivors? Did they go to alert the rest of the pack?

His magic flickered around him, first as a sputtering shield, then drawing inwards. He tamped it down. Suppression now wouldn't make any difference, not with a hound knowing about them, but he needed to conserve his energy. Who knew when or how he would need it.

His beloved ran a half-step in front of him, her stride hampered by his shorter legs. He had tried to let go of her hand, to give her a chance to outdistance him, but she clung hard to his fingers, all but crushing them. He didn't waste breath arguing with her.

They entered the final stretch of the corridor leading to the side entrance. Natural light already streamed through the opening, illuminating the shattered remains of the door strewn across the floor. *They entered here, too.* They must have to keep everyone in the tower contained. Likely breaching the doors at the same time. *Trapping us like vermin.*

Gritting his teeth, Henrie kept pushing on. He tried to ignore the cracks and scorching on the walls, or the dripping shards of ice that bore strange impressions.

The screams of terror and death had grown with every step until he could make out individual sounds. None of the voices were recognisable. The tightness in his throat couldn't make up its mind on whether or not he should be relieved.

Harriet squeezed his hand. She had to have entered the tower through here. What had she been thinking? Entering a clear corridor of death when she couldn't be certain the people behind it weren't also gone?

A shadow briefly obscured the light, then was gone with a yell.

The two guardians leading the way slowed. Red flattened herself against the outer wall as much as possible. She hesitated in going any closer to the doorway, repositioning the child she had carried all this way, before forging ahead.

Tricia seemed less certain than her companion, slowing further with every step until she had completely stopped. She peered back the way they had come and seemed more satisfied than he that no one followed. "Sounds like outside is no safer than in here."

"Understatement," Hans murmured. He eyed the open door with a great deal more intensity than the two human guardians, yet even human hearing wasn't weak enough to ignore the chaos awaiting them.

"Stay close and follow my lead," Tricia ordered. "We don't stop until we've reached the old shed north of the training grounds, understood?"

Henrie nodded. He didn't understand her thinking of heading there of all places, but she seemed confident and, if he was entirely honest with himself, what other option did they have besides death?

"The old shed?" Harriet echoed, casting a worried glance Henrie's way. "That's just a storage overflow for the garden. What are we supposed to do? Hide and hope no one finds us?"

"No," Tricia replied. "We leave." She waved both Harriet and himself forward. "I need both of you to keep us shielded."

Harriet gave one jerking nod, her lips pressing together. Shield work wasn't her strongest skill, but only the alchemists were unable to manage more than a personal bubble.

Still, something felt off about the guardian's order.

"You said the hounds were immune to magic, that they could feel us using it." Was Tricia planning on trying to draw them out, to lure them into a place where they hadn't the ability to herd terrified children into tight spaces? What use would that do?

"It's a bit late to worry about them finding us," Hans said.

"Will a shield stop them?" Even as the question left his tongue, he knew the answer. Others within the tower would've used their shields to keep the hounds at bay either by personally protecting themselves or by stopping up doorways with a magical barrier. If a shield was enough, they would've found more survivors.

Hans hesitated before sombrely shaking his head. "It just means they'll need to be close." Even so, he gestured for Henrie to exit ahead of him.

Henrie picked a path over the debris of the fallen door, trying hard not to think of the force needed to shatter the old thick wood. Or how an inward blast likely meant the hounds had also invaded the tower through this entrance.

He had barely stuck his head out through the doorway when he spied a figure clothed in black running in their direction. He ducked back into the relative safety of the corridor, his shield flaring to life around him and Harriet.

"What is it?" his beloved asked.

The same time he heard the distinctive wet sound of flesh meeting flesh.

When nothing came barrelling through the entrance after them, Henrie inched forward, peering out the doorway.

A guard stood not far from them. She was a big woman, almost as broad as the doorway and tall enough to easily tower over the average human. A club dangled in her hand, made from what looked to be a sturdy branch. She wore the chainmail and tabard of a tower guard, both heavily splattered with blood. An empty scabbard hung from her hip.

She paid him no mind, her attention on another dark-clothed figure heading for her with their sword held high. She swung her club and her opponent fell, their face caved in.

All around, people fought off more figures in black. Unlike the scenes within the tower, magic seemed to do its job. Seeing that, spying how his fellow spellsters were *winning*, an optimistic ache squeezed his heart. Maybe they could make it out alive after all.

The woman bent to collect the dead man's sword. She glanced over her shoulder at him as he crept further out of the doorway's shadow, seemingly dismissive of his presence at first, then twisting back with a yell of surprise. Relief stretched her mouth wide. "I didn't think anyone else was going to make it out of there."

"What's going on?" Tricia demanded of the guard. "Why are hounds attacking the tower?"

The woman shook her head. "Don't know the why, but it's not just hounds." She dealt the fallen man a kick to the ribs.

She was right. Whilst both the human who had chased down Henrie and the elf that was somewhere at their backs wore the leather armour of the King's Hounds, the dead man at the guard's feet did not. Nor did any of the others seeking entry into the various bubbles of magical barriers scattered around the gardens.

"The one we killed was," Hans clarified.

This new information was met with a grunt from the woman. Where had she been during the initial attack? Henrie had never known ordinary guards to be stationed anywhere beyond the wall and the main gates.

"We need to get beyond the outer wall," Tricia said.

The woman shook her head. "Not possible." She pointed the bloody end of her club in the direction of the main gates before tossing the weapon aside in favour of the claimed sword. "Bastards are pouring in like ants."

"How many are we talking?" Red asked. She had resumed her tight hold on her bundle, ensuring the girl saw nothing. Henrie wasn't sure why Red tried, the screams alone would be enough.

The guard's face somehow became grimmer. "Too many. This is more than some mercenary company. We're being besieged."

"The back way's our only hope, then," Tricia said. She jerked her head, motioning them to follow as she inched alongside the central tower wall. "Quickly."

Despite the guard's brow furrowing slightly, she joined them, walking backwards as she took up position at the other end of their line.

They kept close to the tower. There were no low windows on the ground floor, just solid wall at their backs. The added protection enabled Henrie to focus all his strength on shielding one side. Whilst the shimmering purple film of any magical barrier looked flimsy, it would be strong enough to protect them from any attack, be it projectile or the solid mass of a person—he didn't know how a hound could pass through, but he wasn't going to question Hans.

It didn't, however, block out the sounds of fighting. The screams, the rumble and crack of magic, or the smell of—

Fire. His gaze slid from the shield to the world beyond, searching and seeing no sign of the source. His nose told him the smell wasn't some magic-fuelled flame, but one made of wood and another acrid stench he couldn't place.

Bodies lay everywhere, some were clothed in the tell-tale robes of a spellster, but the majority were of those figures in black. *Not hounds.* Not mercenaries. Then who? The Udynean army? *No.* None of the figures attacked with magic. And why would the hounds help the enemy?

But who else would dare this assault?

Something landed on the ground with a wet splat. His shield

stuttered, failing for one brief instance before he regained his focus.

Another splat quickly followed the first, then another and another, until there was a continuous hail. A few wails preceded their descent, the cries stopping just as abruptly. He caught the flash of a small figure before there was nothing but paste left.

Don't look. He focused on the path ahead, even as a burning liquid rose in his throat.

"By the gods," Harriet moaned. She had slowed, her head craning upward. "Are they really throwing—?"

Henrie tightened his grip on her hand, forcing her to hurry along with him. He didn't want to think about what they could be throwing from the tower, didn't want to remember the nursery sat at the top. Nor did he want to think about all the levels standing between them and how fast the hounds had managed to reach the tower's most vulnerable.

If others noticed, their cries were lost in those reedy wails.

An older child—a small thing no more than five years of age—dropped directly in before them in hiccupping bursts. Dark red streaked the otherwise undyed linen of their robe. Their descent slowed as they got closer to the ground, lowered either by another's magic or through the child having an impeccable talent of balancing on the breeze.

Tricia motioned Henrie to briefly drop the shield, snaffling up the child with barely a pause in her stride. "Hurry now." She abandoned the tower wall, picking up pace until Henrie had to jog to keep her from running into his shield. "We can't be here when they—"

The crush of the people seeking freedom came into view well before the training grounds or the entrance to the small shed. By the time the latter did, it was clear that more guardians than Tricia knew of this hidden exit.

Tricia slowed. She eyed the heaving mass of bodies clamouring for freedom with suspicion. "Something's wrong. They should've found the latch to open the wall by now."

Henrie nodded his agreement. The overseers didn't like groups of spellsters to get too big within the tower's confines, but he'd seen enough scuffles in the dining halls to know there was something off about the crowd's movement. It might heave as a single mass, but the people within were stuck in place. Wherever the secret entrance led, it clearly wasn't accessible.

A rolling rumble struck the earth. Like a sorting drum full of rocks, the sound built upon itself with every cycle. The vibration burrowed into his chest, thumping away at his heart, pushing the air from his lungs.

The wall surrounding the shed entrance bulged. The outer wall was made from massive stone slabs, with most standing taller than a person. Yet, they shifted. Slowly but steadily.

"What the—?" The rest of Red's exclamation was lost as the rumbling increased.

Every hair on Henrie's body tingled. Without thinking, he backed away from the shed entrance. He had watched Dylan spar enough times to know what followed that sensation.

"Back!" Hans roared, not only at them, but at the crowd still struggling towards the shed. "Get out of here before it—!"

The wall exploded in a barrage of stone.

Henrie barely had time to harden his shield before a sizable chunk smacked into them. He staggered back, his shield absorbing the impact and failing within the same moment.

A thundering blast further rocked his body, shoving him hard against the wall. A deep, rumbling roar filled his ears, the intensity muffling all other sounds and blurring his vision. His shield sputtered around him, his magic instinctually seeking to protect him.

Then there was silence.

He struggled to collect himself, hurriedly wiping the tears from his eyes. His vision remained soft around the edges. His ears rang with a terrible high pitch. Holding back the stone had been like a fist to the temple, protecting himself from the blast had sapped much of what was left of his strength. That he remained upright was only thanks to Harriet's support.

He caught the sight of Hans on his knees, his hands clamped over his ears and his face scrunched in pain. Without a shield to muffle the blast like Henrie, the elven guardian had collected the full effect.

The humans seemed less affected. They'd fallen to the ground, likely after the stone hit, but were picking themselves up and helping others do the same. All the while, casting anxious glances at the massive hole the explosion had put in the wall.

Stones and bodies lay scattered over the training grounds, much of it difficult to make out with the cloud of dust and smoke drifting on the breeze. He supposed that was a mercy. Some of the pieces of stone were larger than a horse. Several of those bits had rolled a fair distance through the crowd that had been pushing so eagerly for escape, their jagged surfaces covered in dark blotches.

That same crowd now surged the other way, their movements frantic and their faces frozen in terror. They clambered over each other, causing flashes of magic as people fought the crush.

Watching everything unfold absent of sound, it all seemed surreal.

Henrie took a fumbling step towards the hole. There was something moving within, the cloud not quite obscuring several figures. He peered at them, willing his eyesight to clear to no avail.

A spear flew out of the cloud, trailing a chain. The point clipped one of the fleeing many before embedding into another, who was subsequently dragged back, their flailing form knocking over others in their path.

They hadn't quite fully vanished into the cloud before a rain of arrows spewed from the hole, preceding increased movement within the settling dust.

Harriet's grip tightened around his fingers. Her mouth moved. If she had a voice, he heard not a whisper.

Still, he squeezed back and, keeping her hand tucked inside his, followed her in running from what remained of the shed along the only route open to them. Back the way they'd come.

Back into the path of the hounds.

A choir of death slowly invaded Henrie's silent world as they ran. Screams of terror and agony. Aborted pleads and cries for help. Roars of anger or pain. The insidious crack of lightning or the snap and whoosh of a fireball.

There were other booms and rumbles that he felt more than heard. They shook the ground, making every step a treacherous one. He stumbled throughout his attempts to stay upright, forced to rely on the strength of Harriet's shield to protect him. She wasn't the strongest, nor did she wield the barrier with any finesse, but it did a decent enough job of keeping others from bumping into them.

They lost sight of the others, unable to keep up with the crowd and the quakes. Even with them both burdened, Red and Tricia outpaced him, fast disappearing from sight. Harriet would, too, if she stopped clutching his hand so tightly in her efforts to stay at his side.

Where Hans and the tall gate guard had gone? He had no idea.

Henrie dared a glance behind him, only to witness the brutal severing of limbs of a guardian daring to face this fresh wave of death. She fell, clutching what remained of her arm, a moment before a second swipe took her head.

He swivelled to eye the tower's side entrance as they dashed by, feeling no relief when nothing immediately erupted from within, be it the guardians they'd left behind or the hound who had chased them. No one else seemed to show any hesitation about being near it. Did they not consider an attack from that direction a possibility?

In the chaos, he found the crowd had herded everyone towards the garden. A lot of fighting had transpired here, too. Unlike within the tower, most of the bodies littering the grass appeared to be that of the enemy. The few that survived were being hunted down by the very people they sought to kill.

The surge of fresh invaders at their backs would change that soon enough.

He recognised a few as those who had recently participated in the brawl to join the now-fallen army. Like Sophie. She stood before an array of black-clothed figures, her whole body outlined in flames whilst she hurled balls of liquid fire at the fleeing throng. Being so close, there was no chance of missing. The fire flared across their ranks, sending some fleeing, flailing to extinguish themselves, whilst others fell down, already dead or dying.

She turned as the crowd enveloped her, her eyes widening. The flames kept both friend and foe back far enough to deal with the latter at her leisure. Several figures fell immediately, whilst others ran off into the crowd screaming and flailing at the flames.

But the sheer numbers pouring in forced even her to abandon her position.

A flicker of lightning caught Henrie's eye the second before the thunder growled through the crowd. *Dylan?* His friend had returned? The man had survived the army's fall and come to help them?

Another flash lanced through the throng, its origin near the greenhouse.

Tugging on his beloved's arm, he pulled Harriet along with him. They fought the flow of the crowd, pushing towards what he hoped was one of his friends, their every step forward hampered by others pressing against Harriet's shield. People scrambled all around, some shielded like themselves, others racing unprotected.

Soon, the figures closing on them consisted largely of the enemy. Blades hacked at the shield, causing Harriet to flinch at every blow. The twisted expressions of glee on the faces of their attackers had them looking barely human. The figures snarled in a tongue Henrie didn't understand, but were clearly meant to be taunts.

"Keep going," he urged. They just needed to reach the others, then they could coordinate an attack and maybe even drive these people back before the hounds returned.

Harriet followed a few steps before falling to her knees. She clutched her head, whimpering.

He knelt next to her. "You can do it." If his shield was anywhere near as durable, he would've shouldered at least some of the burden, but they both knew his strength resided in other areas. Sadly, being invisible wouldn't save him here. "Just a bit longer."

"It hurts. I'm sorry, I... I *can't*. It—"

The shield sputtered, reforming with the very weapons that hammered it now stuck in it. The surface wavered and warped as the figures fought to pull their weapons free, the strain only causing his beloved further pain.

One of the men yelled something at his comrades. The way he pointed at Harriet made it clear they knew she would falter soon.

Henrie pulled his beloved into his arms, tenderly kissing her forehead, before getting back on his feet. "Drop your shield on my signal." At this rate, it would fall regardless. "Do you hear me?"

Silence was her only answer. He had to hope that meant something.

"Now!"

The shield dissipated, methodically and clearly under Harriet's control, but slowly. The figures beyond pressed in, pushing through the weak spots.

"Get back!" he roared. His blast rippled through the gaps in the barrier. It flung the attackers off their feet, leaving them floundering or temporarily dazed. "Let's go!" He grabbed Harriet, hauling her upright, and forged ahead.

He caught a glimpse of another's shield as they breached the crowd. A figure stood beyond, lightning sparking from their outstretched arms. *Dylan.*

Then there was only a white light of another's magic hurtling their way.

"No!" On reflex, Henrie held up his hand, his shield sputtering around him. He didn't know a soul who could withstand the full blast of Dylan's magic, and any spellster fighting back would be using their full might.

Harriet's shield enclosed them. She grunted as the lightning hit, but held her ground. That shouldn't have been possible, the last person who tried facing his friend almost died after Dylan's magic smashed right through the defender's barrier. His beloved was nowhere near that strong.

Did that mean it wasn't who he had thought?

He peered through the glare, trying to make out the person on the other end before Harriet's shield failed.

"Hen!" a familiar shrill voice pierced the chaos around them. The assault abruptly halted, leaving its halo emblazoned on his vision. "Harry!"

Ness? Reality slapped him across the face. Not Dylan.

But Nestria was still a friend, still more powerful than Harriet and himself combined. He stumbled in the direction he had heard his friend before his sight was fully restored.

She wasn't the only one there. Another familiar voice reached his ears, although the words were entirely foreign. *Launtil.* She was often out here, tending to the garden. Whatever she shouted, it had to be Udynean. Henrie hadn't learnt the woman's native language. It had always been that of the enemy.

The afterimage cleared in time for him to witness red tendrils erupting from Launtil's fingers. They snaked past Harriet's shield, ensnaring several of the closest attackers. Smoke drifted off their clothes for a moment, eliciting a high-pitched whistle from the men before they grew still. She whirled on another pair, impaling them with a blast of ice before dispatching the dead still in her clutches.

Sulin stood behind the pair. As an alchemist, his inability to use much magic made even shields impossible. He took a step forward, then seemed to think better of it and gestured frantically for them to come closer.

They halted outside the shield sheltering the trio. They'd no way of merging with the group without dropping the very barriers keeping them alive.

Henrie glanced over his shoulder. The enemy wasn't able to close as they'd done earlier, their every attempt to do so kept at bay by the two women. They'd have to be quick, but it was possible.

"Now!" Launtil screamed at Nestria. Those red constructs lashed out like vipers, slicing everything that dared to get too close to ribbons.

The huge barrier separating them fell, reforming even further out to encompass Harriet's far smaller shield.

Sulin collided into them, flinging his arms around their shoulders, before they had fully braced themselves. "You got out!" Tears flowed freely down his face, further wetting Henrie's cheek as his friend's embrace tightened.

He pushed Sulin back far enough to see more than his friend's chin. "I—" He clung to the man's arms. Real. *Alive.* "I thought..."

Grinning and hiccupping, Sulin stepped back. "I was helping Tillie."

Henrie glanced at the other two. Both women were a mess, but appeared intact. The same couldn't be said for the wire frames adorning Launtil's face. The sections of glass looked to be barely holding on, with one of them cracked down the centre.

He couldn't help his attention sliding to the red strands she used. They continued to lash through the air, driving back the other invaders or cooking them where they stood. He'd never seen anything like it in his life. It had to be some Udynean teaching.

"Now isn't the time to get mushy," Nestria snapped over her shoulder. She continued to face their enemies, blasting lightning into the approaching throng. "Tillie and I can't hold this lot back forever. We need to move and it needs to be together. Harriet?" She pointed a finger upwards. "Can you add your strength?"

Harriet bobbed her head the once before reforming her shield to encompass all of them. The shimmer of Nestria's barrier altered, growing more pronounced as the other second shield formed inside. It was thinner than before but, being nestled against the outer barrier Nestria had created, it served as adequate extra protection.

Keeping within arm's reach of each other, they edged away from the approaching throng, never straying far from the centre of the two shields or the wall at their backs. They would have to eventually, but having solid stone in one direction lessened the strain on keeping the shields strong.

Henrie spied other pockets flaring to life amongst the remaining spellsters and guardians. Few seemed to fair well, their shields sputtering and dying as untrained skills were put to the ultimate test.

One by one, they drew more survivors beneath their protective bubble; numerous spellsters, a handful of guardians and servants, and a single gate guard. Those with greater magical strength to bear either aided in counterattacks or added their shield to the whole until they were protected by at least a dozen layers.

As a clump, they rounded the tower, aiming for the only exit left to them.

The main gate.

Other pockets of resistance still fought here, their attacks wiping out the enemy in great swathes. Amongst them, he caught a bunch from the last brawl, the flame-wreathed figure of Sophie standing out like a beacon. Her lips moved, her words lost amongst the roars and screams, but her gestures were clearly taunting.

Kaprina also stood alongside the group. He'd never seen the elven woman get riled up over anything, beyond an amorous human suitor or two, much less use the training grounds. Even now, she patiently regarded the advancing enemy like death awaiting the doomed.

She opened her mouth and screamed, her voice rippling the very air.

Like a flag in a storm, those closest were snatched into the sky. Several further back fell to their knees, clutching at their heads, trails of bright red leaking from their ears.

A sudden surge of movement near the tower drew Henrie's attention. More survivors? He balanced on his toes, trying to see over the heads of others closer to the edge of the shields, dropping back down as he caught sight of a familiar figure.

The hound they had fled the tower from.

He moved through the throng with the same casual predatory stance Henrie had always imagined sharks to have. The crowd parted like ripples in water. If the hound noticed them, he gave no sign, merely swinging his head from side to side, clearly hunting.

Then, just before their entire figure could vanish from view, the man's whole body swivelled in Henrie's direction.

Henrie took a reflexive step back, colliding with others who weren't as quick. As if them merely sensing magic wasn't bad enough, they could apparently pick out one individual amongst a group of dozens. And all whilst he wasn't using magic.

They needed to get out before the rest of the hounds arrived. How long did it take for a person to descend the tower in its entirety? A few hours at best?

The hound's casual stride increased, leaving the man not quite running to follow them. Others jogged alongside him, peeling off as he gave them orders.

Sophie stood before the hound, a ball of molten fire forming in her hand.

No. Henrie raced to the edge of the shields. Her magic had no chance against a hound. "Stop!" he screamed at her. "Don't fight, you won't win! Just run!"

If Sophie heard him at all, she didn't heed his warning. She lobbed her fireball. It flew beautifully, dripping flames all the way. By all rights, it would hit the hound square in the chest.

Henrie held his breath. Maybe the heat alone was enough to do some damage.

The man didn't even flinch as the fireball reached him and parted like water around a rock.

Sophie jerked back, the fire outlining her spluttering with her uncertainty before flaring in full. She whirled her arm, a fresh ball of molten fire forming in her hand. Taking a few steps closer to the hound, she twisted to lob the second fireball.

The hound reached her first, his blade effortlessly slicing through her neck.

Her head tumbled to one side, her expression frozen in shock. Her body crumpled to the ground. Whilst the flames that had harmlessly outlined her had extinguished in the moment of her death, the fireball she still held was a different story. It tumbled down her robe, licking at its surroundings and finding fuel in the very form that had given it life.

The hound barely paused to sidestep her before moving on to cut down others in his path.

"We need to move," Henrie declared, trying to keep the panic bubbling in his chest from taking over. He strode towards the far arc of the combined shields. If he pushed, the layers would let him through, but there were no guarantees he'd be able to defend himself as strongly and there were more dangers beyond the barrier than the hound.

"Did you see that?" Sulin shrieked. "He walked straight through her shield. Straight. Through!"

Henrie glanced over his shoulder in time to spy Kaprina's body sliding off the hound's sword, having been stabbed in the gut. The hound swung his dripping blade, also severing her head.

With two strong spellsters in their group dead, the others that had been standing alongside them chose to flee. A few guardians dared attack the hound, but not a single one reached the man before they were cut down.

Movement near the tower's base drew Henrie's eye. A fresh wave of enemies rounded the corner, their weapons dark with blood. Ice gripped his heart as he made out smaller details. The cut of their clothes. The slow sureness of their combined gait. The way they approached the defending spellsters without a care.

The rest of the King's Hounds had descended.

They fled the approaching hounds. Those who couldn't run fast enough to remain within the shield's circumference were thrown onto the backs of others or half-dragged between whoever was strong enough.

A handful of others beyond the barrier rushed their way to desperately hammer at the outer shield. They let in whoever they could, but dropping their shields, even for the briefest moment caused more and more ripples along the surfaces. It was only a matter of time before the strain eventually got to everyone and their only defence failed.

"Jace!"

Henrie's head snapped around in time to spy a human spellster slipping through the shields, having stumbled on one of the many bits of debris littering the gardens. *Jason.* The man wasn't an alchemist, with minimal power or abilities, but he also wasn't terribly capable in battle, certainly not enough to manage on his own. That he had lasted this long meant Fredrick was nearby.

Sure enough, Henrie spotted a tall figure flagging amongst the rest. "Hold on!" Fredrick called out. His shield wobbled, then vanished completely as he doubled back to help his lover. "I've got you!"

"No!" Jason screamed, gesturing for Fredrick to stay put even as he got to his feet. "Get back! I'll—" He dropped to the ground once more. This time, with a dagger embedded in the back of his skull.

Fredrick's scream of denial reverberated beneath the barriers. He rushed for his fallen lover, barely stepping outside of the shields before he also fell.

Having no other choice, Henrie turned his back on the sight. He didn't need to be a healer to know they were already dead.

All around them, flashes of light streaked the air as people desperately fought to keep the hounds back, the sounds muffled by their combined barriers. The purple domes of other shields shivered, then faded. A few smaller bubbles briefly flared into existence before they, too, were killed.

A chorus of shrieks at the front of their group alerted him to more trouble. They had circled the tower enough for the wall's main gates to be in sight. They stood open and unguarded. An easy escape for anyone who dared.

Except, the King's Hounds also poured out the tower's front entrance.

Their group slowed. There was a chance to get past the hounds. A slim one that a fast runner might risk.

But many in their group carried children, either in their arms or upon their backs. Others supported people injured from the prior blast or the panicked crowd that had formed afterwards. There were also guardians who wouldn't leave their charges, a servant who looked ready to die of fright and so many who were, like himself, already panting with their exhaustion.

No one was willing to try for freedom alone.

Going back wasn't an option, either. Even without the hounds, the blaze caused by Sophia's fireball continued to spread, helped by the monsters piling more dead bodies on top.

We're screwed. Fighting back was pointless and they obviously couldn't hide. Running was their only option, but with every exit blocked, that didn't mean much. *If we could make another way out.* How? The walls protecting them from the outside world weren't just massive in height, they were also thick. The outer slabs were the size of carts, and the space inside was enough to house hundreds of families.

His gaze fell on the archway of a drain, one of many dotted around the wall to keep the grounds from becoming a swamp during winter. It was a small thing, big enough to allow a cat to slither through on their belly. If they could somehow tear out the bars and widen the hole, then they could escape what had become a kill zone. Maybe even seal up the passage behind them to keep the hounds from following. "We need to back up."

"What? Why?" Harriet eyed both him, then the wall. "No. We'd never make it big enough in time."

She was right. The hounds weren't in a hurry at the moment, being methodical in eliminating those with little defence, but they'd surely rush to stop any attempts to escape this killing ground as soon as they realised what was happening.

They needed a distraction, something that the hounds would see as a greater threat. But what. Their magic was useless. Weapons clearly hurt them, even unconventional ones. There were plenty of them scattered nearby—swords, spears and daggers discarded by people in their moment of death—all within easy reach if they dropped their combined barriers. *If we do that, we're dead.*

He doubted anyone beyond the handful of guardians was proficient enough to use a single weapon. What good would wielding them be against those in battle? In the tower, the hounds had cut down everything in their path like a scythe amongst wheat. They didn't look to be slowing down here. Their group had nothing to match that sort of lethality without risking closeness.

Unless…

"Ness!" He grabbed his friend, dragging her to the front of the crowd. "You can throw those, right?" He pointed at the knife still being held in the clutches of a corpse. Levitating objects was forbidden magic—he had never understood why, until now—but he'd seen Nestria flouting that rule often enough to know she'd some skill.

She stared at him as though he had lost his mind.

"The hounds." He grasped her shoulders. She didn't know. She might suspect if given time, but no one *knew*. "They're immune to direct magic, that's why—" He took a deep breath, pushing back the images of the dead crowding his thoughts. "One came at me in the tower. I knocked him down with a table." Temporarily and more through luck. However, if his clumsy attempt could bowl a hound off his feet, then surely a more practised aim could do greater damage. "I'm no good at lifting objects, but you…" He fell silent as realisation lit up her eyes.

Nestria lifted her hand. The knife rose, slipping free of the grasp that once held it. The weapon spun in the air, hurtling towards a hound.

It struck the woman's shoulder, eliciting a beastly snarl. The hound grasped the handle, pulling it free. She glared at them, clearly ready to race forward and embed the blade in Nestria's skull.

"Again," Henrie ordered.

He needn't have bothered. Nestria already had several weapons in the air, aimed at more than one hound.

The woman slashed the second blade from the air, clearly surprised when it merely swivelled back for another swoop.

Other hounds opted to use their allies as shields, forcing them to take the brunt of the blow, then discarding their corpses or dragging the wounded people with them.

"I assume you've another plan," Nestria said, her face flushed. Sweat already dripped from her chin and left patches of damp on her pale robe. The weapons hanging in the air wavered, allowing the hounds to advance and neutralise the threat. "I'm not sure how long I can keep this up."

He patted her shoulder. "Just keep them distracted." He turned to the rest of the group. "Everyone listen up!" He squeezed through the crowd, searching not only for his friends, but also for other familiar faces. People he could trust, people he knew the abilities of. They were few. "We need to get back against that wall. There is a drain. I can—"

"What's the point?" someone screamed back. "We're all just going to die anyway."

"If you are waiting for death," Sulin snarled from somewhere within the throng. "Then I recommend you step outside the shield. I am certain the hounds will make it quick."

"Enough," another voice snapped, the authority behind the deep tone marking them as one of the guardians. Who? Henrie couldn't place. "You've all survived this far, don't choose to lay down now."

The guardian's words seemed to reinvigorate those flagging. One by one, the shields shifted, taking pains to keep everyone within the circumference as they stretched to take back the space behind them until the shimmering barriers nestled against the wall once more.

"Su. Tillie." Henrie gestured for the pair to come closer, waiting only until they were squatting at his side. "I want you to get everyone who can maintain a strong shield to do so," he ordered Launtil. "Keep them coordinated and, for gods' sake, ensure the top stays dense." He had no idea what trying to blast a hole through the wall would do to the surrounding structure, but he didn't want to find himself beneath one of these slabs.

Giving him a curt nod, Launtil pushed the wire frames further up her nose. They seemed to be less together than they'd been earlier, with a section of the broken lens missing completely. She immediately stood to do as requested, taking Harriet with her. Henrie didn't know how much strength his beloved had left to give, but he knew that wouldn't stop her.

"I suppose you are seeking to have me hold your hand, yes?" Sulin asked.

"You can work metal without forge or fire." It was what had enabled his friend to craft a flawless alchemist dagger years before most others his age. Henrie pointed at the bars blocking the drain. "Get rid of them."

Sulin grabbed the first bar and, hissing, released it in a hurry. "Dog metal," he growled.

"Can't you mould it?" He'd always been told that learning how to craft *infitialis* from its raw state into collars and daggers was the entirety of an alchemist's job, that they spent their whole lives doing little else.

"Dangerous to try altering already worked *infitialis*. The slightest touch..." He fell silent, frowning. He caressed the bar as though it was a spooked mouser. "But maybe if I..." The metal warped and shifted beneath his hand.

Henrie did his best to swallow the fear clogging his throat. Everyone who had ever spoken to an alchemist knew how dangerous the magic nullifying metal was. Only one mistake was needed for them to do the hound's job.

But if there was any alchemist he trusted to flawlessly work *infitialis*, it was Sulin.

Sulin stared at the bars for what seemed like an age. Henrie wanted to hurry his friend along, but he didn't dare break the man's concentration. Then, one by one, the bars melted like ice, pooling into one big ball in Sulin's hands. It seethed, fighting to return to its original form.

"Do not look so terrified," Sulin said, his tone impossibly calm. "This metal has not known an alchemist's touch before."

"So it's safe?" He didn't know what Sulin was doing to keep the metal in this liquid state, but he wished his friend would stop.

"I did not say that." Sulin stood, slowly, his eyes not straying from the ball seething in his grasp.

Henrie scrambled to his feet as the ball got closer to him. *Infitialis* couldn't take away his magic without encircling a piece of him, but the faint numbing feeling it gave the air made his skin itch. How could his friend, or any alchemist, be near the stuff and not want to wriggle right out of their flesh?

"Ness!" Sulin raised the ball above his head. "Take it and launch!"

Nestria twisted to focus on them. The *infitialis* started to hum like a shaken hive. Sparks crackled off the surface as it fought the magic wrapping around it. The air warped from the heat.

Then it was gone, whisked through the air to pass effortlessly through the shields and into the crowd.

The explosion that followed was far greater than Henrie had expected. The blast hit the enemy with the force of a natural lightning bolt. Bodies were lifted off the ground, sending many of them flying into others.

"Now what?" Sulin asked.

"We blast our way out of here." He knew what to do, had witnessed Dylan take down the leashed one during the brawl with this move. The principles behind it hadn't looked too complicated to replicate. A concentrated burst of the right vibration should easily put a crack through the earth, then it would just be a matter of widening that space enough for a person.

He breathed deep, drawing all his focus into one hit and slammed the ground, putting everything he had into splitting the earth directly below the mouth of the drain.

The soil cracked. The ground heaved beneath their feet, fighting him. People both inside and outside the shields fell to their knees or were knocked over. At least that helped slow the hounds.

Through it all, the wall stood resolute.

"I don't understand. It should've worked." Sure, he wasn't as strong as Dylan, or even in comparison to some of his other friends, but he had made the ground move. There were cracks behind him to prove that. Why not in front?

Sulin slapped the wall, his brow furrowed in confusion. "Maybe there is more dog metal than we can see?"

"Then we go under." Henrie strode away from the wall, halting at where the cracks began. Having to dig would be slower. He didn't know what the foundation was made of or how far it stretched below the wall. Whatever waited, there was no other choice but to power through.

He blasted at the cracked soil, clearing away everything that stood between him and the drain. The grass peeled away like paper, soil flying up in clumps. The ground below was harder than he anticipated. Rocks and stones made hulking barriers in a mixture of clay and compressed earth.

He bore through the sediment, nevertheless, grinding his teeth as the intensity compounded with every blast. He was no good at constructs—he lacked the finesse for it—but he could twirl his blasts in a manner that mimicked an auger. Dirt churned up from within the hole. That only drove him on, even as sustaining each blast long enough to do more than a few turns put an immense strain on his remaining energy.

It didn't help that he had to physically keep his arms circling before him to ensure his magic followed the same pattern. Every rotation had his binder feeling like the laces were tightening bit by bit. *Impossible.* It didn't stop the burning in his lungs or the cry for release from his ribs. He didn't usually exert himself to this extent. He especially didn't do anywhere near as much physical activity with the binder on. How long could he keep this up before his strength was spent?

His efforts drew even with the wall.

He held his breath, shoving down the screaming from within. Instead of the resistance he had expected, drilling directly beneath the drain was no more difficult than the path he had carved towards it.

It's working. All he needed to do was speed up and—

The wall groaned. Slabs that had stayed in place, even whilst under assault from his magic, now sagged. Further up, pieces bigger than his head tumbled to the ground. Several of them slammed into the shields, sending ripples across the outer surface.

Henrie winced at that. Whoever was keeping the outer barrier up would've taken the full force of the blow. He halted his digging, shifting his attention to shoring up the roof of the divot he'd made. "I need a strong shield over here!" He had no chance of digging out a tunnel *and* keeping it from collapsing. "And someone to brace whilst I dig."

A purple glow filled the entrance as two men took up position on either side of him.

"Let's get some constructs in here," a familiar voice rang out. One Henrie knew better than most. Tricia.

He glanced over his shoulder, spotting the guardian marching his way, the child she had plucked from the air balanced on her hip. He had thought himself mistaken in glimpsing her joining them as they had started collecting others. Never had he been so glad to be wrong.

Others came to aid the men shoring up the wall, either taking over the excavation by way of twin constructs or keeping the tunnel stable.

Tricia clapped a reassuring hand onto his shoulder. "You've done great. Not sure why Edwyn kept you from competing in the brawls, but he'd be proud."

Tears pricked the corners of his eyes at the mention of his guardian. He dashed them away and focused on keeping his breathing steady. The last thing he needed was any emotion making his chest tighter.

"Recoup your strength. It's not over yet." Her gaze kept flicking to what was happening at his back. Henrie had blocked it out whilst digging, sacrificing knowing how close they were to the end to give his full focus to the task.

Now that mantle was shouldered by others, the surrounding panic hit his ears at force. They'd become enclosed on all sides. The enemy hammered on the left and right, the hounds remained at the front, hesitant to come closer thanks to Nestria's skill.

They were going to escape. The twin constructs were churning through the earth faster than he could manage. All they needed was to—

A chorus of pained wails pierced the clamour. The barriers shuddered, some failing completely whilst others dissipated in patches.

The enemy pressed closer, their twisted grins widening. Could they feel the shields weakening?

"Hold!" The order boomed across the group, reverberating off the flickering shields. Their voice was deep, authoritative and belonging to someone Henrie didn't know. "If these shields fall, we're dead!"

Henrie caught the familiar figure of Hans racing through the group as the other guardian spoke. He hadn't seen the man since the explosion of the secret entrance, never mind noticing him joining their group.

Hans reached the right side of the barrier to land a punch on a hound who had slipped inside the shield. Henrie spied the guardian dealing a second blow—an uppercut to the hound's jaw that sent them staggering back through the shield—before the view was blocked out by those far taller than he.

His ears were still free to pick up the panic, the fresh wails of children, the broken sobs of those accepting the inevitable.

"Into the tunnel!" someone bellowed. "Now!"

People surged towards the entrance, crowding together as the shields continued to ripple. The enclosed space slowly shrunk, barriers stuttering before dissipating completely. Others hastened to take their place.

Henrie tried to add his strength, his shield failing the instant something struck the outer curve. Other flash of something dark darted across his vision and a figure to his left soundlessly crumpled to the ground. *They're inside our defences.* Or had at least breached them enough to use projectiles.

The crush of crowd grew more frantic, forcing Henrie to follow. He had long since lost sight of Tricia, of Sulin. He spied Nestria at the rear, still engaged with the majority of the hounds. He'd no idea where Launtil or his beloved had gone. He could only hope they remained safe within the barriers' confines.

With every foot they withdrew, the enemy rushed to fill the gap, harrying them. Henrie once again pushed his own shield out to aid the others. The effort squeezed his heart and had him stumbling as he descended into the tunnel, but he put everything he had left into his final defence.

Their shields flowed beneath the wall, pressing against the roof and sides like a bubble trapped in an upturned bottle. It doused the tunnel in a soft purple glow, not letting a single soul forget just how much rock sat above them, pushing down on their shields, threatening to make them pop at the slightest sign of weakness. Any one of the slabs making up the wall would be enough to crush a person.

Henrie gritted his teeth, trying with all his might to blow out the air-crushing thought of being buried alive. He dared to glance at the others. Many wore similar grimaces.

The rear of the shields slipped beneath the wall edge, bringing the front line of hounds with it.

"Keep going," Tricia commanded as she aided in ushering the stumbling few falling behind. "We'll be safe soon."

Henrie frowned. How could she sound so certain? Although the tunnel's width gave the hounds little room to spread out, they were no less on their tail. If it wasn't for the handful of guardians and Nestria keeping them from fully engaging, the hounds would've already done their gruesome task. As it was, they looked more than willing to wait.

The ground shuddered, throwing everyone off balance. A groan, so deep that he felt it in his bones, rumbled through the tunnel.

A few of the elven hounds froze, their attention squarely on the tunnel ceiling. One barely paused in turning tail and running for the entrance. Two others looked equally uncertain, edging back a few steps, but held their ground.

It took Henrie a moment to realise what had caught their attention. With the entrance no longer supported by the combined effort of their shields, the tunnel was starting to collapse.

A chunk of earth slipped from the ceiling to smack on top of one hound, splitting their head wide open.

The rest scrambled for the entrance. They wove through the falling debris, shoving each other and dodging new obstacles as more and more of the ceiling caved in.

Giant slabs of stone collapsed into place, further shaking the earth. One fell right in front of the entrance, throwing the tunnel into a twilight-like gloom. By the glow of over a dozen layered shields, Henrie caught the impression of a shadowy figure a heartbeat before the last of the tunnel buried them.

The reed-thin wail of a terrified child pierced Henrie's concentration. He clapped his hands over his ears, trying to muffle the noise.

"Easy," murmured someone else, the voice sounding like Red's. "We'll be all right."

Henrie fought his way through the crowd to Nestria's side. She had looked exhausted earlier, now she appeared close to death. He silently offered his support, keeping her upright and moving with the group. It wasn't easy. Although she was shorter by a mere inch, Nestria had always been heavier set than him. With her being almost dead weight and him close to exhaustion, he might as well be trying to carry the whole tower.

He'd taken no more than a handful of shuffling steps before a guardian hoisted Nestria over her broad shoulder as though his friend weighed nothing.

He watched the woman trot off towards the front of the group, content that he at least didn't need to worry about one friend. However he tried, he couldn't find the others. The way everyone pressed together, jostling each other in their haste made it difficult to distinguish one head from another in the gloom.

Nevertheless, he was certain they had made it. Sulin, being near the entrance, would've been swept up just as Henrie had. The fact the shields remained strong had to mean Launtil was still with them and Harriet wouldn't be far.

Hopeful murmurs drew his attention to the way ahead. Light shone from a crack above, the beam pure and warm. It could only mean one thing.

They had passed beneath the tower wall.

The angle of the constructs shifted, aimed to assist in their climbing. More light cut through the darkness with every turn. People crowded forward, eager to reach safety. Shields flickered, weakening as people dropped their guards in the face of freedom.

The wall above groaned, reminding them how easily they could be gifted the same end as the hounds who had followed them.

"Steady," ordered that authoritative voice. "Do not waver now."

The press of the crowd lessened, albeit, not by much.

Earth that had been churned to the tunnel sides now rose in an ever-widening hole. Light flooded the tunnel, unobstructed by building or being.

His feet spoke of climbing. His legs wobbled, objecting to the gentle incline as though being asked to scale a mountain. He bit back the growing ache in his thighs and, focusing only on the few feet before him, continued to trudge. Pressing on wasn't a matter of if he could. He either marched with the rest or suffered the same fate as the hounds.

He wasn't sure how far he had travelled before registering he shuffled through undisturbed grass. He flopped to his hands and knees. The ground beneath his palms wasn't as well kept, the earth dry from a week of summer sun and no rain, the grass shedding its taller stalks to weather the nearing autumn days.

All at once, the shields dissipated. Fresh air caressed his skin.

Henrie inhaled deeply. For the first time since this nightmare began, he was able to breathe freely. A broken cackle that sounded perilously close to sobbing, shook his body. Tears welled in his eyes, dripping directly onto the parched earth.

Behind them, the last piece of the tunnel collapsed. Fresh shields flickered around individuals, Henrie amongst them. Others merely froze in place, either too exhausted or too frightened to do anything else. A few screamed, their wails swiftly followed by a series of shushing.

The wall groaned, crumpling on itself as it sank deeper into the ground to fill the space they'd walked only a few moments prior. Henrie waited until the last sign of movement stopped before letting his shield go.

We're safe. No matter how skilled or immune to magic the King's Hounds were, there would be no chasing them through that path. The wall's collapse might have left the area shorter in this section, but it still stood several stories high. And definitely too unstable to scale.

He caught the impression of a window further along where the wall was still in one piece. Such a feature was absent on the inner side. The servants who helped run the tower lived within that wall. Had they gotten out before the collapse? Would it matter either way? The men who'd spoken a strange language had seemed bent on killing everyone.

"Hen!" Harriet appeared amongst the crowd. She threw her arms around him, squeezing tight enough to remind him of the aching in his ribs. "You're crying. Are you all right?"

"Yes," he whispered, nodding as his tears continued to flow down his cheeks. He was weary down to his bones. And cold. The strength of his magic had become a suggestion. He wasn't sure if he could defend himself if required.

But he was uninjured. Whole. Alive.

Harriet either didn't hear or didn't believe him. She examined him, checking for cuts or broken bones.

He couldn't stop himself from staring back at her. She was the most dishevelled he'd ever seen. The typical tidy bun of her hair was a mess, the wind only further tangling the strands. Soot, dirt and worse smudged her face and stained her torn robe. Exhaustion lined her face, likely just as much as it etched his.

Beloved. He cupped her head, stilling her long enough to pull her back into his arms. They had made it. Escaped the slaughter. Together.

But where did they go from here?

They might be outside the tower walls, but they were no less defenceless than they'd been within. Their surroundings held little beyond grassland with the only sign of shelter being the front line of trees far in the distance. He didn't know what else he had expected to find, it was the same view he saw from his chambers.

However, the trees appeared to sit a lot farther away than they had from above. Could they reach it before the hounds circled the wall?

"Now's not the time to rest," snapped that authoritative voice. The man who it belonged to strode through the group, dragging people to their feet, pausing only to hoist a young boy onto his back. "Don't fool yourself into thinking you're out of danger." He pointed into the distance. "Get to the forest. Now!"

Henrie needed no further explanation. He wobbled back to his feet and, hitching up the skirts of his robe, raced for the trees.

Wild grass, heavy with seed heads, whipped at his bare legs. The air burned in his throat, thick with the scent of blood. His chest ached, his binder adding to the tightness, all but robbing him of the ability to breathe.

They reached the shadow of the trees and Henrie fell to his knees, his fingers clawing into the dark earth in an effort to keep from fully collapsing. His ribs were crushing his lungs, he was sure of it. Each inhalation came only if he fought for it.

He slipped a hand beneath his robe, searching for the binder laces which lay just beneath the undertunic. If he could undo the ties, then maybe he would be able to breathe a little easier without needing to fully strip.

"Hen!" Harriet almost knocked him off his feet in her haste. She breathed heavily, but sounded nowhere near as winded. "Love, it's all right, I'm here. What do you need?" She knelt at his side, following his arm into his clothing. "Are you bound? Let me help." Her fingers tugged at his undertunic. The linen ripped. There was more tugging as she worked to unlace the binder's side and—

The first easy lungful had his head spinning. His chest was still too tight, but it no longer felt as though he was being crushed.

Henrie lifted his head, meeting Harriet's concerned gaze. He had thought her gorgeous out on the grassland. But standing in the dappled sunlight? She might as well have been a goddess.

He threw himself at his beloved, pulling her into his embrace to smother her face in kisses. Like himself, her cheeks were salty and clammy. He didn't care, he continued until she had no choice but to giggle. That sound clutched at his heart, squeezing out tears he didn't know he had left to cry.

Harriet stilled him, pressing their foreheads together. "I know," she whispered.

"We should keep moving," the authoritative-voice man declared.

Henrie slowly unwound himself from his beloved to take in the rest of the people. There were fewer than he had thought. In the press of escape, it had felt like a hundred bodies. He doubted even half that much stood amongst the trees.

A pair of guardians faced off not too far from where he had fallen. One was Red, the other clearly the man who had been commanding them since the tunnel. Unlike the guardians Henrie had discovered in the dungeon, the man wore the proper attire. The dark grey tunic and trousers did much to make him look imposing.

Yet, Henrie couldn't help noticing how the man's belt knife was still firmly sheathed, of how his clothes were barely soiled beyond one rip along his side. How had the guardian gotten through everything so untouched?

Red seemed less daunted. "We can't travel in one group. They're bound to sense this much magic in one place."

"Then we split up," the man declared, thrusting his chest out even though the movement had to hurt the scrapes running down his side. "Take different paths."

"What paths?" another guardian queried. The woman bent to attend a profusely bleeding cut upon a child's forehead. "There are no different paths to take."

Henrie stared at the woman for a while before realisation hit him. *Eirian.* He'd last seen her descending the stairs into the alchemist's quarters. How had she gotten out? When had she managed to join their side?

He looked around, taking in each guardian's face. If Eirian had made it, then maybe so had the others who helped him escape. Few were familiar. *Red, Hans, Tricia.* No sign of the rest of the guardians who'd been imprisoned or even of the hulking gate guard. None of the others they'd left behind in the alchemist's quarters had made it.

Of all the people who had called the tower home, this was all that was left? *Barely forty people.* Not even a handful compared to the hundreds they had lost.

They weren't all adults, either. Easily half their number consisted of children. Some sat on the cusp of adolescence, whilst others were too small to walk on their own, much less flee. Their presence just brought up more questions. How had the young ones survived the tower? Had those secretly capable of levitating objects, like Nestria, snatched them from the very air as they fell?

And where was his friend? Any of them.

He twisted on the spot, searching for familiar faces. Harriet had left his side to help tend to wounds. Sulin crouched protectively over Launtil, who looked close to passing out. Of Nestria, he found no sign. She'd been with them in the tunnel, exhausted but clearly alive. Had they lost the woman who'd been carrying her? Was she flagging somewhere out in the open?

Gathering his strength, Henrie got to his feet. He'd taken a single step towards the foliage blocking sight of the field when the thud of a person collapsing had him turning back. One of the spellsters, a solid-built woman, had flopped to the ground. She lay there, convulsing and foaming at the mouth.

Sulin was at her side, desperately trying to hold her still. "We need to get the poison out. Can anyone heal?"

Silence answered his plea. The healers spent their days, and often nights, busy tending to the unwell within the tower. None of them would have survived.

With one gasping shudder, the woman grew still.

Henrie averted his eyes, closing them in an effort to keep himself from crying. After all the deaths he had witnessed today, another one shouldn't have bothered him. But this wasn't fair. *We had made it.* Freedom. Safety. A momentary respite before they needed to move on, whatever their direction, but still...

Escaping the tower should've meant the end to senseless dying.

Opening his eyes, he found his gaze settling on Hans. Henrie might not have known the guardian for longer than today, but the man was oddly silent. He stared into the void, his face paler than when he'd first seen the carnage in the tower.

Had the explosion of the secret entrance rocked the guardian's mind that much? Henrie thought it might've rendered the man deaf, even if only temporarily, but Hans had seemed well enough to attack a hound.

He took a step towards the man, seeking to express his gratitude for his role in keeping both himself and Harriet alive within the tower, and faltered upon seeing how the man cradled what was left of his arm. Half of his forearm was missing. Cloth covered the rest, the end already dark with blood. A matching dark patch stained his ragged clothes. Henrie hoped that'd been caused by the same wound. Would the gods truly be so cruel to have the man die after securing his freedom?

"Dvärghem is months away on foot," Red said. She had returned to arguing with the guardian who had clearly deemed himself their leader. "We lack the necessary resources for survival out here. Most of these adults have never been outside the walls, never mind the children. They've never travelled so far."

"Anywhere safe is going to require a lot of travelling. We'll make do."

"There are no roads heading north from here. We need to head for where there'll be *food*," Red said. "Some of the young ones require milk. None of us—" She gestured towards the guardians with obvious breasts. "—have produced such for many years. Unless *you* can lactate, we need a cow or a goat. Neither of which we'll find heading into the wilderness."

Henrie's stomach grumbled at the mention of food. He hadn't eaten since that morning. None of them would have. They'd need sustenance not only to keep up their physical strength, but that of their magic.

But where would they get it? And how? Everything else Red had uttered was just as true. He hadn't been trained for hardships and doubted many here could claim otherwise. Not of battle like Sophia. Never a day without a meal like the imprisoned guardians looked to have suffered. As for walking anywhere... All that had ever been accessible to them were the flights of stairs inside the tower.

"We could make do with herbs," Launtil offered. She remained propped against a tree trunk, but had seemingly recovered enough to be aware of her surroundings. "I know what blend we'll need to stimulate lactation, but I'm not sure of the odds in finding it growing wild this far south."

"Slim," Red answered grimly.

Henrie turned his back on the conversation, his gaze lifting to the canopy of trees. They'd only just managed to catch their breath, he didn't want to hear how hopeless survival outside the tower was.

Above them, little fan-tailed birds flit from one tree branch to another, unconcerned with the presence of bigger creatures below. Perhaps they were the same ones that visited the tower gardens, or maybe they were merely kin to those who made nests on window ledges and in cracks dotting the walls.

Watching them had always been a bittersweet experience, but now he felt nothing.

The bird he'd been tracking through the trees darted out of sight, leaving him staring at the top of the tower. He had always known the central structure to be massive, but even from this distance, it dominated the view.

To think it was now no more than a tomb.

A bloom of smoke drifted into the clouds, its beginnings from somewhere over the wall. That had to be Sophia's fireball still merrily burning away. He lowered his gaze, not wanting to think what could possibly be fuelling it.

Movement from out in the field drew his attention, swiftly turning into figures running towards them. More survivors? Hounds? Some other unknown enemy? He pushed through the bushes on the edge of the tree line to get a better look, squaring himself in preparation to face this new threat.

Others came, several bearing more children, either with the precious bundles in their arms or clinging to their backs. Every adult looked ready to fall at the next step, the one exception being the guardian who carried Nestria across her shoulders.

Their arrival was met with much joy. Friends, and those who were likely more, fell into each other's arms. People cried upon learning who hadn't made it. Others collapsed onto the ground, either lost in their own minds or cackling much as he had done.

Henrie hastened towards the woman carrying Nestria, missing arriving first as Tricia got there even before the rest of his friends.

The guardian knelt beneath a tree to gently lower her unconscious bundle to the ground. "She'll be all right," she said before Tricia could do more than open her mouth. "Just exhausted, I'd wager."

Henrie bent to brush the wisps of hair from his friend's face. Nestria had always been one of the palest amongst his friends, but her cheeks lacked their usual colour. Her skin, no longer clammy, remained cool to the touch.

She didn't stir as he continued to neaten her appearance. If it wasn't for the shallow rise and fall of her chest, he would've thought the exertion had killed her.

"We should leave her behind," declared that voice Henrie was becoming to detest.

"*Leave?*" he echoed, anger boiling away some of the weariness in his bones. He had already lost his guardian and his home, he wasn't about to leave a single friend behind. He whirled on the man, stalking towards him and, only realising just how tall the guardian was once he stood directly under the man's nose. "If it wasn't for her holding the hounds back, we'd all be dead!"

Several of the children— those old enough to understand his words and the implications behind them—burst into tears. He winced inwardly, but didn't dare tear his gaze away from the guardian's.

To his credit, the man remained stoic. "She's dead weight as she is and a threat once she recovers."

Henrie balled his hands, fighting back the urge to lash out at the man. So what if she required extra care for the moment? That was only because she had pushed herself to the limit. And what threat could she possibly present?

"Honestly, Caden," said the guardian who had carried Nestria. "Listen to yourself. I almost expect you to suggest we leave the children behind."

Caden's jaw twitched. He continued to loom over Henrie, not uttering anything that might be agreement or denial towards the other guardian's statement. His gaze flicked towards Red, who clutched the girl they'd found in the tower like a mother cat prepared to defend her last kitten. "Regardless of her abilities, if you considered her strength, then you'd see the logic behind why we should leave her here."

"Then leave," Henrie spat between clenched teeth. Maybe there was a chance that the hounds could track them down using Nestria's strength, but she wasn't the only strong one here. And if the hounds came, they knew how to defeat them. "I don't need a guardian like *you* watching my back." He glanced over his shoulder at the familiar faces he had come to trust during this nightmare.

Tricia, Eirian, Red, and Hans. Three who had gotten him out of the tower unharmed. And one who had managed to regroup with them despite the odds.

"I have *them*."

Caden glowered at him. His lips twisted distastefully as he noisily sucked at his teeth. "Then let them lead you to your demise." He turned to the rest of the group. "Anyone who'd rather not suffer a drawn-out death after the hounds hunt you down is welcome to follow me to Dvärghem." With that declaration, he matched off into the forest.

Henrie wordlessly watched the man go. He was pretty sure he knew how this particular guardian had gotten through the chaos relatively unscathed.

A handful of spellsters trailed after him, as well as all five of the servants and two guardians. Henrie didn't blame them. He might've also been tempted to try his luck in the wilderness had there not been people who needed him. Even with their absence, it put those who remained at forty-seven, with over half being children.

He exhaled his relief when the last one vanished from sight. It did nothing to rid him of the fresh tightness slowly coiling his chest. If there was one thing Caden had been right about, the hounds would come searching. They'd follow the lines their fleeing had cut through the grass to the forest.

None of them could be here by then.

"We should move on," Tricia said, seeking confirmation from her fellow guardians and garnering nods from Eirian, Red and the other woman.

If Hans was able to take in anything beyond his own pain, he gave no indication. He didn't even move. He barely blinked.

"I know everyone is tired," Tricia continued. "I know you need food and rest, but we must press on whilst we've still got light. We'll head west." She pointed in what Henrie assumed was the relevant direction. "There are farms, which will mean food and shelter, but they are not close. Keep together and carry the little ones as much as you can." She picked up the child she had plucked from the air during their escape. "Hurry now."

People moved to obey, sluggishly at first, then with some manner of urgency if not speed.

Henrie found himself handed a child barely strong enough to hold up their own head. He'd never held a baby before, had never been around them since he was one.

"Careful," a familiar voice said. He glanced up from the child to see Launtil instructing Harriet how to hold the bundle she'd been given. "They'll make shields if they're hurt, but be mindful of their head nonetheless."

Harriet nodded sagely, adjusting her grip and checking over the baby.

He examined his own given child, marking the light scrape adorning the olive-brown skin of their forehead. It didn't look deep enough to be more than superficial. Without a healer at hand, he would have to ensure it stayed clean.

Steely-grey eyes looked back at him as though etching Henrie's face into their mind.

You'd always had this look like I was the centre of your world. The old story his guardian used to tell him about when Henrie was just a baby echoed through his head. *But* you *were the centre of mine.*

He swallowed hard, blinking away his tears as he trudged through the forest alongside his beloved. He thought he had understood what his guardian had meant back then. It was their role to raise a spellster, after all.

But to be handed something so fragile, knowing that any harm could be fatal, that the hounds could snuff out this light without a thought…

He tightened his grip on the bundle, pulling the baby closer. "I won't let them catch us," he whispered. Like how this child's guardian would've died to see them live, his own had fought like a hawk protecting its nest. He knew of no man to better emulate.

Harriet gently bumped his shoulder. "We'll be all right." She flashed him a confident smile, the expression marred by how red her eyes were. "As long as we're together, we'll get through anything they throw at us."

"Together," he echoed. The tower might've fallen, but it didn't mean the end. It wouldn't, not when they had gotten this far. They would live on. Somewhere safe. Somewhere the hounds couldn't follow. Somewhere they could be free.

About the Author

Aldrea Alien is a bisexual, New Zealand author of romantic speculative fiction of varying heat levels.

She grew up on a small farm out the back blocks of a place known as Wainuiomata alongside a menagerie of animals, who are all convinced they're just as human as the next person (especially the cats). She spent a great deal of her childhood riding horses, whilst the rest of her time was consumed with reading every fantasy book she could get her hands on and concocting ideas about a little planet known as Thardrandia. This would prove to be the start of The Rogue King Saga as, come her twelfth year, she discovered there was a book inside her.

Aldrea now lives in Upper Hutt, on yet another small farm with a less hectic, but still egotistical, group of animals (cats will be cats), and published the first of The Rogue King Saga in 2014. One thing she hasn't yet found is an off switch to give her an ounce of peace from the characters plaguing her mind, a list that grows bigger every year with all of them clamouring for her to tell their story first. It's a lot of people for one head.

aldreaalien.com

www.ingramcontent.com/pod-product-compliance
Lightning Source LLC
Chambersburg PA
CBHW050841210726

48290CB00004B/1031